D0886636

DISCARDED

SOCIETY AND THE VICTORIANS
DEMOS, A STORY OF ENGLISH SOCIALISM

SOCIETY & THE VICTORIANS
General Editor: John Spiers

The Harvester Press series 'Society & The Victorians' makes available again important works by and about the Victorians. Each of the titles chosen has been either out of print and difficult to find, or exceedingly rare for many years. A few titles, although available in the secondhand market, are needed in modern critical editions and the series attempts to meet this demand.

Scholars of established reputation provide substantial new introductions, and the majority of titles have textual notes and a full bibliography. Texts are reprinted from the best editions.

DEMOS, A Story
of English Socialism

George Gissing

**Edited with an introduction by
PIERRE COUSTILLAS**
Director, Centre for Victorian Studies,
University of Lille

THE HARVESTER PRESS 1972

THE HARVESTER PRESS LIMITED
Publishers
50 Grand Parade
Brighton Sussex
BN2 2QA
England

'Demos, A Story of English Socialism'

First published in three-volumes, 1886 by
Smith, Elder, London

First one-volume edition published in 1886 by Smith, Elder,
London

This edition, reproducing the text of the reprint of 1897, first
published in 1972 by The Harvester Press, Brighton

Introduction, notes etc © Pierre Coustillas 1972

'Society & The Victorians' No. 10
LC Card No. 70–183643
ISBN 0 901759 20 1 (cloth)
ISBN 0 901759 33 3 (paper)

Typesetting by Campbell Graphics Ltd., Newcastle upon Tyne

Printed in England by Redwood Press Limited,
Trowbridge, Wiltshire.

Bound by Cedric Chivers Limited, Portway, Bath, Somerset

Contents

vii

Acknowledgements

I wish to express my thanks for help and encouragement given by Mr. Alfred Gissing and Mrs. Lola L. Szladits, Curator of the Berg Collection of the New York Public Library, and I am grateful to Mr. P. F. Kropholler for his generous assistance in clarifying some elusive literary allusions recorded in the Notes to the text. The quotations from the manuscript of *Demos* are made with the kind permission of the New York Public Library.

P.C.

Acknowledgements

Introduction

Gissing was never a party man and we know of no earnest attempt on the part of political leaders, national or local, to enlist him in their ranks. Yet throughout his life he maintained an interest in politics and never swerved from his Liberal allegiance; at least, to the anti-imperialist fraction of the party. In this, as in many other things, he was faithful to the ideas of his father, the acknowledged leader of the Liberals in Wakefield until his premature death in 1870 at the age of forty-two. The elder Gissing had a deep-rooted hatred of the Tories which George imbibed and displayed on a number of occasions. In 1884, in his *Reminiscences of My Father*, the novelist noted a few significant anecdotes testifying to his father's strong political commitment, recalling, for instance, that on his congratulating him one evening when the Liberals had won a local election, Thomas Gissing waved his arm confidently, exclaiming that they could always beat the Tories when they tried. The male friends of the family at Wakefield were all on the Liberal side, and it is likewise noticeable that the writer's own friends and acquaintances also had markedly Liberal sympathies—the Frederic Harrisons, H. G. Wells, Morley Roberts, James Wood, Edward Clodd, Robertson Nicoll, to quote almost at random, were all Liberals. The few MP's with whom he was personally acquainted—William Summers, his schoolmate at Owens College, Justin McCarthy, the Irish historian and novelist, and Henry Norman, literary editor of the *Daily Chronicle*—belonged to the same party. On several occasions he saluted their election or re-election with a telegram of congratulations.

His behaviour and writings as opposed to his general stand as a man and as a voter followed a more flexible line. The young man who returned with a chastening record from America in 1877 declared himself to be a mouthpiece of the advanced Radical party. He associated with his working-class relatives of Paddington, who had strong Radical leanings; he lectured in Radical clubs like his own Will Noble in *Workers in the Dawn*; embraced Positivism for a couple of years, then withdrew disenchantedly from active political-philosophical movements after subscribing for a while to Schopenhauer's pessimistic credo. His essay 'The Hope of Pessimism' marked the turning-point. In *The Unclassed*, he had his protagonist Waymark speak for himself and repudiate his latter-day Radicalism, based on a fallacious equation of his own aspirations with those of workingmen, but he was at the time only half way down the slope of political and social *désengagement*. This second published novel drew to himself a little attention and contributed to extend the narrow circle in which he had moved so far. The stays he was invited to make in the country with the Harrisons and with the Gaussens of Broughton Hall, Lechlade, opened his eyes to a type of leisurely life which of course he had known of all along, but which he had never been able to observe at close quarters and even less, however briefly, to enjoy. *Isabel Clarendon* and the middle-class portions of *A Life's Morning* were the by-products of this short-lived vision of the spacious world of leisure between his garret-and-cellar days (graphically recalled in *The Private Papers of Henry Ryecroft*) and of the period of ignoble decency from which he emerged only after his second marriage.

Demos, written in the wake of *A Life's Morning*, showed him to be further than ever from the radicalism of the early eighties. In it he invested the contemporary rise of socialism with those potential dangers that were keenly apprehended by his fellow-writer W. H. Mallock. But, even *Demos*, as I shall try to show, was not the work of a hide-bound reactionary; it contained the same seeds of humanitarianism as *Workers in the Dawn* and *The Unclassed*. Gissing therefore did not feel there was a solution of continuity between his first two published novels and his 'story of English Socialism.' The same deep sympathy for human suffering, later to develop into an aching, nightmarish sensibility, can be found in *Demos* and it need not be demonstrated that it is amplified in *Thyrza* and *The Nether*

World. Political matters overflowed from *Demos* into the former book through the presence of James Dalmaine, the Liberal MP, whose social work is presented reluctantly as that of the real reformer as opposed to the idealistic, impractical scheme of Walter Egremont—a fact which struck Gladstone pleasurably when he read the novel.[1] After *Thyrza* Gissing returned to political themes occasionally, but his approach, whether in *Denzil Quarrier* or in *Our Friend the Charlatan*, became less and less emotional, more and more satirical and intellectual. Also, while these two novels concentrate on local politics, on the rivalries between Conservatives and Liberals in the parochial atmosphere of the country town, his outlook extended beyond the shores of Britain. *The Whirlpool* and *The Crown of Life* tackled brilliantly and thoughtfully the question of imperialism and international peace at a time when Western powers were eyeing each other menacingly and coveting one another's conquests in Africa. His letters to one Allhusen show that he was not opposed to the idea of a peaceful, English-speaking commonwealth of nations based on human and economic interests, yet when a monthly requested his contribution to a symposium on the future of the British Empire, he flatly refused to give his opinion.[2] The only cause on behalf of which he ultimately consented to raise his voice in public was that of peace: on the outbreak of the Boer War he wrote his article 'Tyrtaeus' and, because of it and his anti-jingoistic novel *The Crown of Life*, was stigmatized as a Little Englander by those newspapers that were blowing the trumpets of patriotism. Militarism he abhorred. He observed it in Italy and Greece in the eighties, in Germany in the nineties, and it distressed him to see it in his own country, fanned by the greater part of the press and directed against a small African state which was in theory no match for England. The general public, however, doubtless on account of the limited audience of his novels and of his dislike of vulgar self-advertisement, hardly knew where he stood politically. The Conservatives respected his novels in which they could find much to please them. (He advocated no violent remedy to contemporary social evils and, though a supporter of progress, he had serious doubts about the capacity of the working classes to help themselves). The Liberals could also find in his stories many things that appealed to them, in particular a criticism of the commercial interests of the conservative party, of its aggressive foreign policy. Even the Socialists appear to have had reasons to believe that he was not averse to them. But this was at the turn of the century, when he was asked to subscribe for the support of Keir Hardie. Had this been fifteen years earlier, at the time *Demos* was published, they would in all likelihood have thought differently.

II

The idea of a working-class story staging labour troubles and socialist agitation first occurred to Gissing in the summer of 1885.[3] While completing the revision of *Isabel Clarendon,* he wrote to his sister Ellen on 2 August that he was working hard at the first chapters of his new book *Demos.* Apparently the project matured so quickly that for fear of losing his grasp of it he interrupted for a few days the less exacting task of reducing the manuscript of *Isabel Clarendon* to the two-volume pattern suggested by Meredith in his capacity as reader for Chapman & Hall. What happened in the next few days was typical—*Demos* was temporarily ousted by a new project. On 9 August, he told his brother Algernon that he was getting on with the planning of *a* new book, no longer *Demos* by name, to be a two-decker. Clearly this was already *Emily*, later re-titled *A Life's Morning*, which remained in that form until Smith, Elder decided on their own initiative to issue it as a three-volume novel. He only turned to *Demos* for good at the beginning of November and by that time two important things had happened. In September the atmosphere of social trouble due to unemployment had degenerated when the police had arrested a banner-bearer in the midst of a Socialist procession and William Morris had been hauled into the jury-box and fined for interference. Gissing commented on the part Morris played in these East End demonstrations in an oft-quoted letter to his brother: 'Alas, what the devil is such a man doing in that galley? It is painful to me beyond expression. Why cannot he write poetry in the shade? He will inevitably coarsen himself in the company of ruffians'.[4] At the time he was reading Dante, *Evan Harrington* and, with his pupil Walter

Grahame, Vergil, Livy and Xenophon. The second event which precipitated his decision to write *Demos* was his interview with Meredith on 31 October. Meredith had admired *The Unclassed* and he thought that his young *confrère* was making a mistake in turning away from lower-class characters and setting. The same evening Gissing confirmed that his new story would be *Demos*, 'rather a savage satire on working-class aims and capacities.' 'A new and good name', perfectly consonant with his classical tastes and his mood of the moment.

Actual work on the story began on 5 November, but the task was a hard one and the opening chapters involved a good deal of rewriting. Progress was also slowed down by the fact that, writing obliquely of contemporary political events, he wanted to witness them, attending the meetings that were announced in the press. The Conservatives, with Lord Salisbury as Prime Minister, had been in power since the fall of the Gladstone Cabinet on 8 June, but a dissolution of Parliament was impossible until both the new franchise (voted the year before) and the new re-distribution of seats were in operation. Salisbury's cabinet, in office without a majority in the House of Commons, was for some months in an uncomfortable position but precisely when Gissing engaged on his novel, the electoral campaign was in full swing. On 22 November, 1885, a Sunday, he attended a meeting of the Hammersmith branch of the Socialist League held at Kelmscott House, the home of William Morris. The Secretary of the Branch, the poet's daughter, was there talking with workingmen. In his description of Stella Westlake in the book, he used practically the same words as those describing Miss Morris to his brother in a letter written two days after the meeting. He thought her very handsome, the very likeness of her mother as known by Rossetti's picture. She wore a long dark fur-trimmed cloak and a tam o'shanter cap of velvet. Doubtless Gissing took many notes on the spot but unlike those he jotted down when he was gathering material for *The Nether World* they do not seem to have survived. On the same Sunday, he went up to Hampstead, where he heard a Socialist candidate, Jack Williams, of the Social Democratic Federation, harangue a meeting of fellow-workingmen in the street. Gissing, the lover of pure English, was not a little amused, albeit shocked, to

hear that the House of Commons was a 'decrippled
institootion!' Williams eventually polled twenty-seven votes—a
ludicrous score. But—worse than that—it became known that
the Hampstead contest, together with that of Kennington,
where another unfortunate SDF candidate had polled thirty-
two votes, had been paid for by 'Tory gold' with a view to
splitting the anti-Conservative vote. In the eyes of the general
public such candidates and practices could only expose
Socialism to ridicule. The revelation of the affair triggered off
wholesale protest. The Fabian Society and the Socialist League
(Morris had asked Socialists not to vote) passed resolutions in
strong condemnation of the SDF executive. Radicals of all
tendencies were no less indignant. Secessions followed,
notably those of James Macdonald (a Trade Union leader who
was also a member of the SDF), of a group which under C. L.
Fitzgerald, a member of the SDF Executive Council, and
James Ramsay MacDonald founded the Socialist Union.

Gissing was closely watching all these developments mainly
through the *Daily News*, which he read regularly at the time.
At first his novel made only slow progress. On 6 December,
half a volume, that is about sixty manuscript pages, lay
completed, and he did not reach the end of the first volume
until early January. From then on, however, he made quicker
headway, writing the second volume in less than a month. 'It is
good, that I know perfectly well', he commented as the
completion of the two-thirds was near at hand, 'and if I am
not mistaken it will bring me a little more bread and cheese'.
During that time crucial political events were taking place. The
Liberals had won the General Election in November but
Gladstone's victory was almost immediately compromised by
the unauthorized news that he intended introducing a Home
Rule bill for Ireland, the Irish Question looming large in
English politics. Lord Salisbury was still in office though his
party had no majority in the Commons, but there were un-
mistakeable signs that the Liberals were going to split over the
Home Rule affair. However, the Conservative Cabinet fell on
27 January when an amendment to a Coercion Bill was moved
by a friend of Joseph Chamberlain. Gladstone formed his third
cabinet on 3 February. Confusion and ambiguity created by
the Irish Question were great and only to grow in the next few

weeks. Meanwhile the Socialists took advantage of the situation; labour agitation started afresh and culminated in rioting as Gissing was beginning his third volume. The remaining leaders of the SDF, John Burns, H. H. Champion (a friend of Morley Roberts' and later, through Roberts, of Gissing's) had recaptured the leadership of the unemployed agitation, and on 8 February, when the Fair Traders, who ascribed the economic depression to Free Trade, organised a demonstration on Trafalgar Square, the Socialists and Radicals joined them and took control of the demonstration. After the speeches, the crowd moved through the West End to Hyde Park. When insults were flung at the demonstrators from the windows of some clubs in Pall Mall, the crowd counter-attacked with paving-stones, and window-smashing extended from Pall Mall to Mayfair, Oxford Street and Regent Street. The police had been taken by surprise and no arrests were made. Yet, as demonstrations went on (a mass meeting of 50,000 in Hyde Park on 21 February was broken up by the police), newspaper pressure brought the authorities to take steps and four Socialist leaders, Hyndman, Burns, Champion and Jack Williams were prosecuted for sedition. In April they were acquitted by an Old Bailey jury.[6]

Making hay while the sun shone, Gissing offered *Demos* to Smith, Elder at the end of February before completing the manuscript. James Payn, who had recently accepted *Emily* for publication, read in hot haste what was ready. By the 26th his agreement was given. Five days later, the first volume was in print and Gissing had finished writing the third. Payn was enthusiastic; astutely he decided to publish the book anonymously. Considering the tense political atmosphere and the precarious life of the Liberal Cabinet now that Gladstone was known to be converted to Home Rule, any story dealing openly with the masses and socialism stood a good chance of being a success. The publishers made earnest efforts to promote the book which was widely advertised. £69.16.9 was spent on advertisements (as against £58.5.10 for *The Nether World*, for instance) and fifty-nine copies were sent to editors and friends (thirty-nine only for *The Nether World*). Gissing, too, did his best to arouse interest in the book. From Paris, where he took a short holiday in anticipation of his success, he arranged to have two of his author's copies sent to his influential friends Frederic Harrison and Mrs. Gaussen. The sale of rights brought him £100, and the book appeared at the end of March 1886.

III

Demos was widely reviewed, and on the whole, warmly praised. There is no doubt that the story, even in its three-volume form, found a respectable number of readers. The title, with its classical and political connotations, intrigued the middle-class reading public. Mudie bought 200 copies which were in great demand, and the other London libraries another 200. The story was discussed in drawing-rooms, its authorship leading to guesses that were wide of the mark. Some people pronounced Gladstone's name; *Vanity Fair*, a weekly which had a reputation for being knowledgeable in current society, political and literary news, attributed the story to Mrs. Oliphant, and indeed there were reviewers to wonder until the late eighties, when Gissing's name had been printed hundreds of times, whether George was not once more of the feminine gender. John Morley, who had once tried to persuade Gissing to write for the *Pall Mall Gazette* and the *Fortnightly Review* without much result, praised the description of Manor Park Cemetery, and found genius throughout.[7] Morley Roberts wrote an interminable letter, from California full of keen critical appreciation. Frederic Harrison taunted Gissing in a friendly way for his so-called aristocratic temper and rejoiced at his success. Only the writer's sisters, whose literary taste was hardly that of competent readers, found fault with the subject or the manner.

Professional critics examined all the aspects of the book: the characters, the dramatic interest and construction, the style, and of course the social and political aspects. The characterization was frequently eulogized; no one denied that the author had a first-hand knowledge of the working-classes and in several cases—*The Spectator, The St. Stephen's Review, John Bull, The Weekly Dispatch* and *The Westminster Review*—special mention was made of the female characters, old Mrs. Mutimer above all.[8] However, Julia Wedgwood, in the *Contemporary Review*, referred to Eldon as 'mere flat wash.' The *Guardian*, for one, would have liked to see more of Eldon and Wyvern; it also complained mildly that Stella Westlake was 'the least intelligible character in the book', but more strongly about the ambiguous final statement that with Eldon Adela 'had achieved her womanhood.' But there were some facets of the novel to reassure the Church of England organ: the two great commandments of Christianity were kept in their proper order and the deterioration of Mutimer's character was, in the reviewer's eyes, a divine visitation. The *Spectator* found fault with the middle-class characters except Alfred Waltham: 'It is a mistake to describe a poetess in whose kiss the heroine finds the bliss of an intoxicating rapture, when the author cannot show you even vaguely the nature of the enchantment intended. Again, Mrs. Eldon and her son, the clergyman, Mr. Wyvern, and even Mrs. Waltham, are by no means powerful sketches.' But the reviewer commended unreservedly the working-class figures, pronouncing Richard 'a very striking and original creation.'

The comments passed on the artistic value of the work were highly favourable. If the *Daily News*, for instance, thought the author rather slow in getting under way, it declared his story 'clever', and 'carefully written.' For *Public Opinion* it was 'a novel of remarkable power and finish', one of the best books of the season, an opinion to which the *Bookseller* subscribed cordially. The *Graphic* responded to the 'considerable amount of pathos and power' in a book implying 'a great deal of insight and experience in exceedingly difficult lines of observation.' It also praised the consistency and construction of the tragedy, as did the *Westminster Review* which followed up a eulogy of the characters with one of the plot; 'the incidents [are] naturally produced, the denouement likely, and at the same time powerful and dramatic.' The discovery of the will, on which hinges the decline and fall of Mutimer, caused no misgiving: the device used by Gissing belonged to the stock-in-trade of Victorian novelists but was not felt as such.[9] In an age of stable currency when the middle classes could live on the yield of their investments, wills assumed a social and financial significance which they have largely lost.

Not even the manner in which old Mutimer's will is recovered—something of a joke between George and his younger sister—caused a critic's eyebrow to rise.

The most striking though less durable characteristic of the book was its opportuneness on the political plane but, going through the thirty reviews on which this survey of the critical reception is based, one cannot help marvelling, close on a century after the novel's publication, how few critics were tempted to judge it exclusively from a political standpoint. In the spring of 1886, *Demos* was somewhat of a political challenge to left-wing readers, from the Socialists of the SDF to the most advanced followers of Gladstone. Yet many reviewers were content to leave this aspect of the story unmentioned or to refer dispassionately to the relevance of the subject in those times of labour troubles: thus, the *Echo*, the *Queen* and the *Literary World*. The most interesting reactions from the political angle were the most biassed ones. Naturally some Conservative journals, like the *Whitehall Review*, the *St. Stephen's Review* or the *Scottish Review* exulted. The first of these wrote: 'There is nothing but the soundest and most conscientious work offered to the public in this story of English Socialism. The author ... has most carefully studied Socialism in all its varied phases, and in the portrait of Richard Mutimer he has created a very fair portrait of the Socialist whose be-all and end-all is not so much advancement of his fellow-men as self-glorification and self-advancement.' The reviewer prolonged his agreement with the author's political opinion with a few good words about the literary merits of the tale, noting that '"Demos" is distinctly a work of observation and analysis, which reveals a profound insight into the springs of human action.' The *St. Stephen's Review*, which devoted much of its energy in 1886 to pillorying Gladstone, acclaimed the novel as an unprecedented success for a story of Socialism or Radicalism: 'Three writers of the past half century have chosen a socialist as hero, and in each case the novel proved unpopular. Charles Kingsley and George Eliot wrote of democracy as democrats and the incongruous became fused in the fire of their sympathy. The author of "Demos" has no sympathy with the democracy, and that he should have succeeded is little short of marvellous.' As for the *Scotish*

Review, it considered that Demos 'is a book not only to read, but to mark, learn and inwardly digest; a most thorough exposure of that most transparent of shams, so called "Socialism", pitiless in its completeness, and total absence of any animus, or trace of personal feeling.' And the reviewer went on to equate the claims of the working class with egotism and the action of its leaders with vulgar personal ambition. That, on the whole, Conservative newspapers saw the teachings in the novel with satisfaction is undeniable; yet satisfaction was not incompatible with discretion in the less blatant dailies like the *Morning Post* or the *Daily Telegraph*, or such a Society weekly as *The Court Journal*.

Naturally enough, the Liberal press reacted far less favourably to Gissing's picture of Socialism and Socialists, though here again reactions ranged from scarcely perceptible reservations to scornful rejection. At one end of the scale the *Daily News* concluded a very favourable notice with the remark that if 'the contrast between the refined dilettante in Socialism and the other comrades who mean business is amusing enough . . . one doubts whether the whole affair is a matter in which it is legitimate to find amusement.' The *Westminster Review*, appreciative in all respects, deliberately played down the political connotations of the story: 'What the author's opinion may be on the "social question" is not perhaps of great importance from the purely literary point of view from which we regard works of fiction; but he is certainly not a socialist, nor even an ardent democrat.' The *Weekly Dispatch*, whose editor afterwards sought to wheedle Gissing into writing a serial story for him, denied the writer any real knowledge of Socialism: 'the hero is an almost impossible creature, and what the author calls his Socialism an even vaguer kind than Mr. Hyndman or Mr. Morris imagines . . . [Mutimer's] crusading is preposterous throughout, and the author's efforts to do justice to Socialism are abortive.' The *Daily Chronicle* called the hero commonplace and unrepresentative and objected implicitly to politics as a suitable subject for fiction: 'Even Charles Reade failed to invest labour questions with sufficient interest for purposes of fiction; and the author of *Demos*, though successful enough with personal incidents, has not grasped either the reality or romance of

Socialism.' Of all English Liberal dailies the *Manchester Guardian* was the most annoyed, uncritical and spiteful; 'The book is well written, but as a pamphlet in fiction it ought to be much more than this. A political novel must be first rate or nothing, as champagne must either sparkle or be thrown away.'

It was, after all, from a few non-political journals that some of the most circumstantial comments came. The *World* refused to accept the book as 'a story of English socialism . . . The Socialism it deals with, and would demolish, is the Socialism of our fathers, not of their sons; the Socialism of Parson Lot, not of Mr. Hyndman and his lively bands of iconoclasts. And as the author's subject is old-fashioned, so is his method. His method is of kin with that of the old dramatists who labelled their characters with names in concatenation accordingly: Roger Formal, Lady Frugal, George Downright, Justice Greedy, and so forth.' An unwarranted simplification doubtless, but a clear perception of one of the pitfalls of the political novel in general—excess of sympathy or antipathy. Much the same lines were followed by the *Athenaeum*, which argued that the story made no advance on the industrial novels of the forties and fifties, reproaching besides the author with choosing as the exponents of socialist ideas 'weak and vicious people' who could easily be confuted and defeated.

Such were the responses to an ambiguous piece of fiction written by a young man of twenty-eight at a time when Socialism in the popular mind meant a jumble of more or less fair, of more or less accurate recollections and expectations: better working and living conditions for factory workers as achieved by Robert Owen; a mass of treatises and doctrines based on a criticism of capitalism and aiming at the reconstruction of society on more equitable foundations; a number of Continental and English names suggestive of much doctrinal squabbling; various practical isolated attempts at creating genuine socialist communities which had all petered out for motives human and economic; recently in England some rioting and inability to conquer the body of voters; and a good many other things. Therefore, a multiplicity of impressions evocative of a scattered longing for change, for progress, possibly gathering force and speed, but—so far—

unsuccessful. The modern critic of *Demos* may perhaps avoid serious misinterpretations if he bears all this in mind.

IV

Despite certain suggestions to the contrary, *Demos* was not a *roman à clé*. Subtitled 'a Story of English Socialism', it must not be regarded either as history. Gissing used the word 'Story' in the sense of 'piece of narrative, novel, tale of fictitious events', not in the sense of 'history.' This is what some recent English and Czech commentators, with heavy ideological bias, have failed to recognize. Gissing drew his inspiration concerning some characters, facts and situations from contemporary events, but he did not in the least attempt to transcribe historical facts. This is so obvious that it would gladly be left unsaid had not *Demos* been condemned for its failure to reproduce accurately some events contemporaneous with the novel as well as the opinions of certain Socialist leaders in the eighties. All we can say, in agreement with Jacob Korg[10] is that various recognizable shades of socialism appear in the novel. The New Wanley works remind one of Robert Owen's experiment at New Lanark: it is a socialist venture under paternalistic rule in a capitalist society. Mutimer, like Owen, thinks that social conditions are bad and he sets out to change them. Workers must be treated humanely, they must be better paid, better housed, work shorter hours, and their children must be sent to school. The influence of Owen is clearly suggested by the presence of his works on Mutimer's shelves: it is from him that he has derived the idea of cooperation, possibly also from Fourier, the initiator of phalansteries, and Saint-Simon, who sought to reorganize society on a socialistic basis and by a better organization of industry and labour. Mutimer's oratory and ideas are a partial transcript of the speeches delivered by the members of the Social Democratic Federation founded in 1881 by H. M. Hyndman, and called at first the Democratic Federation, but it must be recalled that Gissing had had a solid experience of radical clubs and working-class lecturing in his early London days. The secessionist movement headed by Roodhouse is an

echo of the dissensions among the Socialists, especially of
William Morris's secession from the SDF at the end of 1884 to
found the Socialist League with the support of Friedrich
Engels. Westlake, an idealist, a writer and a socialist is intended
as a freely sketched counterpart of Morris but his unaggressive,
urbane Socialism may also be seen as a reflection of the policy
of the intellectual Fabian Society, founded in 1884 whose
socialism was evolutionary and utilitarian in essence.[11]
Marxism is represented by Mr. Keene, a journalist who
commits a number of dastardly actions and embodies the
tendentious propensities of the press. In all these cases Gissing
took good care to differentiate clearly the people, situations
and events in his novel from those in real life. He was writing a
novel, not a text-book of history under the thin disguise of
fiction. Besides he did not wish to incur the risk of being
prosecuted for libel—the usual provision in the publishers'
memorandum of agreement stipulated that, should this
happen, responsibility would rest with him solely. Therefore,
to accuse Gissing of having misrepresented William Morris and
distorted his ideas, as did John Goode in his article on 'Gissing,
Morris and English Socialism' is hardly fair dealing.[12] It is, of
course, interesting to compare the Victorian Socialist poet
with the fictional Mr. Westlake, but to take Morris as the
standard of truth and belittle Gissing's achievement because
Westlake fails to conform with historic truth reveals a sad
misunderstanding of the process of literary creation (as Alan
Lelchuk remarked in his rebuttal of Goode's arguments) as
well as a flagrant intrusion of ideology into the field of
literature. William Morris is a magnificent figure in his own
right, and Gissing's sharply critical attitude to Socialism
cannot be used fairly as an argument either for demonstrating
that he was distorting historic truth (which, I repeat, he was
not trying to represent) nor for establishing that his story is a
poor literary creation. In fact, by making the New Wanley
works an admittedly Owenite community, Gissing forestalled
any excessive *rapprochement* with the socialisms of the hour.

   Demos has many claims to remain a document on the life of
the working classes at the end of the Victorian age. Charles
Booth's well-known tribute to it has lost nothing of its value
with the passing of time. The picture of the Mutimers before

their accession to wealth is as valuable as that of Sillitoe's
Arthur Seaton for the 1950's. The living conditions, and
mental attitudes of Mrs. Mutimer and her three children, of
Daniel Dabbs and the Vine sisters are admirably depicted. The
degradation of Richard, Alice and 'Arry under the influence of
money testifies to Gissing's fine understanding of human
character. Nor does his lack of sympathy for the lower classes
in general lead him to unbalanced characterization of his hero:
insensitive and weak though he is, Mutimer is hardworking, he
behaves creditably towards his brother and sister, as well as
towards his mother, and when the catastrophe is at hand, he
once again appears at his best, displaying truly heroic qualities.
It is indeed characteristic of Gissing that from the moment
Richard's fortune is on the wane we are made to compassionate him. Wherever there was honest failure Gissing
himself was sure to sympathize. He did so more noticeably in
all his other working-class stories, because of his use of
exponent characters, and most conspicuously perhaps when
some person of the other sex like Emily Hood or Thyrza Trent
was concerned. With Emma Vine, more certainly than with
these two heroines, he avoided the danger of sentimentality.

Like all Gissing's books, *Demos* derives its vitality from the
tensions which inform it. He hates poverty, yet shows that
money may lead to ruin and perdition. He is impatient with
the vulgarity, ignorance and insensibility of the poor, yet the
injustice of society and human suffering bring him to take
sides with the underprivileged. He acknowledges the vanity of
revolt, yet the predominance of the cash-nexus makes him a
permanent protester. The leisurely life of the middle classes
appeals to his poverty-warped soul, yet the dull conventional
existence of the bourgeois rouses his satire. Or again, many of
the aims of Socialism are part of his privately formulated
credo, but the average socialist leader, not to speak of the
average militant, causes him to retreat within himself, hence
his temporary refuge in aestheticism, the aestheticism of
Hubert Eldon. To-day it is clear enough that Gissing's response
to socialism was mistaken because he tended to equate it with
mob-rule, debasement of educational standards and rampant
industrialism, but his hatred of capitalist oppression, his pity
for his long-suffering fellow-creatures, his longing for man's

liberation from his mental shackles are sure evidence that he would not have rejected late twentieth-century socialism of the better kind as easily as he did the bourgeois-scaring socialism of the mid-eighteen-eighties.

NOTES

[1] In Vol. I, ch. XI, pp. 242—43, John Tyrrell, a financier, whose daughter Paula will marry Dalmaine, remarks of the latter: 'There's your real social reformer. Egremont's an amateur, a dilettante. In many ways he's worth a hundred of Dalmaine, but Dalmaine will benefit the world, and it's well if Egremont doesn't do harm.' Gissing comments: 'In all which it is not impossible that Mr. John Tyrrell hit the nail on the head.' Gladstone made a note of this point. See *Gladstone Papers*, MS 44792 f, p. 127, British Museum.

[2] 'The Immediate Future of the British Empire.—A Symposium of Opinions and Aspirations,' *The Minster*, III, January 1896, pp. 52—68. Gissing's curt answer to the editor reads: 'The only reply I could possibly make to your question would be—that literary men, pure and simple, best serve the interests of their country by doing their best at literature.' p. 67.

[3] A project entitled 'Demos' was in fact mentioned in a letter to Algernon Gissing dated 29 June, 1884 (Berg Coll.), but the subject was different. The book was to depict the religious, political and social movements of the time among the lower classes.

[4] *Letters of George Gissing to His Family*, 22 September, 1885, p. 169.

[5] Letter to his sister Ellen, 31 January, 1886, *Ibid.*, p. 175.

[6] See Henry Pelling, *The Origins of the Labour Party, 1880—1900* (revised edition, 1965), esp. Ch.III, 'The Socialist Debate on Strategy'; also, Helen M. Lynd, *England in the Eighteen-Eighties, Toward a Social Basis for Freedom* (1945), Bentley B. Gilbert, *The Evolution of National Insurance in Great Britain, The Origins of the Welfare State* (1966), esp. Ch.I, 'The Eighties and the Nineties: The Two Nations', and Gareth Stedman Jones, *Outcast London*, A Study in the Relationship between Classes in Victorian Society (1971), esp. Ch.16 'From "Demoralization" to "Degeneration": The Threat of Outcast London'.

[7] Quoted in a letter to Ellen, 20 August, 1886, *Ibid.*, p. 185.

[8] All references to contemporary reviews and notices are given in the bibliography.

[9] The *St. Stephen's Review* was possibly the only exception: 'The plot is as old as the hills—the girl who loves one and marries another, the lost will, the designing villain with two wives and six names, all have been before us from time immemorial.'

[10]*George Gissing, a critical Biography*, p. 87.
[11]To see Sidney and Beatrice Webb as the figures behind Westlake and his wife would be anachronistic. They married in 1892 and were not even acquainted in 1886.
[12]For the articles by Goode and Lelchuk, see Bibliography, 3.

A STORY

OF

ENGLISH SOCIALISM

DEMOS

A STORY OF ENGLISH SOCIALISM

BY

GEORGE GISSING

AUTHOR OF 'THYRZA' 'THE NETHER WORLD' ETC.

'Jene machen Partei : welch' unerlaubtes Beginnen!
Aber unsre Partei, freilich, versteht sich von selbst'

GOETHE

A NEW EDITION

LONDON
SMITH, ELDER, & CO., 15 WATERLOO PLACE
1897

DEMOS.

CHAPTER I.

STANBURY HILL, remote but two hours' walk from a region blasted with mine and factory and furnace, shelters with its western slope a fair green valley, a land of meadows and orchard, untouched by poisonous breath. At its foot lies the village of Wanley. The opposite side of the hollow is clad with native wood, skirting for more than a mile the bank of a shallow stream, a tributary of the Severn. Wanley consists in the main of one long street; the houses are stone-built, with mullioned windows, here and there showing a picturesque gable or a quaint old chimney. The oldest buildings are four cottages which stand at the end of the street; once upon a time they formed the country residence of the abbots of Belwick. The abbey of that name still claims for its ruined self a portion of earth's surface; but, as it had the misfortune to be erected above the thickest coal-seam in England, its walls are blackened with the fume of collieries and shaken by the strain of mighty engines. Climb Stanbury Hill at nightfall, and, looking eastward, you behold far off a dusky ruddiness in the sky, like the last of an angry sunset; with a glass you can catch glimpses of little tongues of flame, leaping and quivering on the horizon. That is Belwick. The good abbots, who were wont to come out in the summer time to Wanley, would be at a loss to recognise their consecrated home in those sooty relics. Belwick, with its hundred and fifty fire-vomiting blast-furnaces, would to their eyes more nearly resemble a certain igneous realm of which they thought much in their sojourn upon earth, and which, we may assure ourselves, they dream not of in the quietness of their last long sleep.

A large house, which stands aloof from the village and a little above it, is Wanley Manor. The county history tells us that Wanley was given in the fifteenth century to that same religious foundation, and that at the dissolution of monasteries the Manor passed into the hands of Queen Catherine. The house is half-timbered; from the height above it looks old and peaceful amid its immemorial trees. Towards the end of the eighteenth century it became the home of a family named Eldon, the estate including the greater part of the valley below. But an Eldon who came into possession when William IV. was King brought the fortunes of his house to a low ebb, and his son, seeking to improve matters by abandoning his prejudices and entering upon commercial speculation, in the end left a widow and two boys with little more to live upon than the income which arose from Mrs. Eldon's settlements. The Manor was shortly after this purchased by a Mr. Mutimer, a Belwick ironmaster; but Mrs. Eldon and her boys still inhabited the house, in consequence of certain events which will shortly be narrated. Wanley would have mourned their departure; they were the aristocracy of the neighbourhood, and to have them ousted by a name which no one knew, a name connected only with blast-furnaces, would have made a distinct fall in the tone of Wanley society. Fortunately no changes were made in the structure by its new owner. Not far from it you see the church and the vicarage, these also unmolested in their quiet age. Wanley, it is to be feared, lags far behind the times—painfully so, when one knows for a certainty that the valley upon which it looks conceals treasures of coal, of ironstone—blackband, to be technical—and of fireclay. Some ten years ago it seemed as if better things were in store; there was a chance that the vale might for ever cast off its foolish greenery, and begin vomiting smoke and flames in humble imitation of its metropolis beyond the hills. There are men in Belwick who have an angry feeling whenever Wanley is mentioned to them.

After the inhabitants of the Manor, the most respected of those who dwelt in Wanley were the Walthams. At the time of which I speak, this family consisted of a middle-aged lady; her son, of one-and twenty; and her daughter, just eighteen. They had resided here for little more than two years, but a gentility which marked their speech and demeanour, and the fact that they were well acquainted with the Eldons, from the first caused them to be looked up to. It was conjectured, and soon confirmed by Mrs. Waltham's own admissions, that they had known a larger way of living than that to which they adapted themselves in the little house on the side of Stanbury Hill, whence they looked over the village street. Mr. Waltham had, in fact, been a junior partner in a Belwick firm, which came to grief. He saved enough out of the wreck to make a modest competency for his family, and would doubtless in time have retrieved his fortune, but death was beforehand with him. His wife, in the second year of her widowhood, came with her daughter Adela to Wanley; her son Alfred had gone to commercial work in Belwick. Mrs. Waltham was a prudent woman, and tenacious of ideas which recommended themselves to her practical instincts; such an idea had much to do with her settlement in the remote village, which she would not have chosen for her abode out of love of its old-world quietness. But at the Manor was Hubert Eldon. Hubert was four years older than Adela. He had no fortune of his own, but it was tolerably certain that some day he would be enormously rich, and there was small likelihood that he would marry till that expected change in his position came about.

On the afternoon of a certain Good Friday, Mrs. Waltham sat at her open window, enjoying the air and busy with many thoughts, among other things wondering who was likely to drop in for a cup of tea. It was a late Easter, and warm spring weather had already clothed the valley with greenness; to-day the sun was almost hot, and the west wind brought many a sweet odour from gardens near and far. From her sitting-room Mrs. Waltham had the best view to be obtained from any house in Wanley; she looked, as I have said, right over the village street, and on either hand the valley spread before her a charming prospect. Opposite was the wooded slope, freshening now with exquisite shades of new-born leafage; looking north, she saw fruit-gardens, making tender harmonies; southwards spread verdure and tillage. Yet something there was which disturbed the otherwise perfect unity of the scene, an unaccustomed trouble to the eye. In the very midst of the vale, perhaps a quarter of a mile to the south of the village, one saw what looked like the beginning of some engineering enterprise —a great throwing-up of earth, and the commencement of a roadway on which metal rails were laid. What was being done? The work seemed too extensive for a mere scheme of drainage. Whatever the undertaking might be, it was now at a standstill, seeing that old Mr. Mutimer, the owner of the land, had been in his grave just three days, and no one as yet could say whether his heir would or would not pursue this novel project. Mrs. Waltham herself felt that the view was spoilt, though her appreciation of nature was not of the keenest, and she would never have thought of objecting to a scheme which would produce money at the cost of the merely beautiful.

'I scarcely think Hubert will continue it,' she was musing to herself. 'He has enough without that, and his tastes don't lie in that direction.'

She had on her lap a local paper, at which she glanced every now and then; but her state of mind was evidently restless. The road on either side of which stood the houses of the village led on to the Manor, and in that direction Mrs. Waltham gazed frequently. The church clock chimed half-past four, and shortly after a rosy-cheeked young girl came at a quick step up the gravelled pathway which made the approach to the Walthams' cottage. She saw Mrs. Waltham at the window, and, when she was near, spoke.

'Is Adela at home?'

'No, Letty; she's gone for a walk with her brother.'

'I'm so sorry!' said the girl, whose voice was as sweet as her face was pretty. 'We wanted her to come for croquet. Yet I was half afraid to come and ask her whilst Mr. Alfred was at home.'

She laughed, and at the same time blushed a little.

'Why should you be afraid of Alfred?' asked Mrs. Waltham graciously.

'Oh, I don't know.'

She turned it off and spoke quickly of another subject

'How did you like Mr. Wyvern this morning?'

It was a new vicar, who had been in Wanley but a couple of days, and had this morning officiated for the first time at the church.

'What a voice he has!' was the lady's reply.

'Hasn't he? And such a hairy man! They say he's very learned; but his sermon was very simple—didn't you think so?'

'Yes, I liked it. Only he pronounces certain words strangely.'

'Oh, has Mr. Eldon come yet?' was the young lady's next question.

'He hadn't arrived this morning. Isn't it extraordinary? He must be out of England.'

'But surely Mrs. Eldon knows his address, and he can't be so very far away.'

As she spoke she looked down the pathway by which she had come, and of a sudden her face exhibited alarm.

'Oh, Mrs. Waltham!' she whispered hurriedly. 'If Mr. Wyvern isn't coming to see you! I'm afraid to meet him. Do let me pop in and hide till I can get away without being seen.'

The front door stood ajar, and the girl at once ran into the house. Mrs. Waltham came into the passage laughing.

'May I go to the top of the stairs?' asked the other nervously. 'You know how absurdly shy I am. No, I'll run out into the garden behind; then I can steal round as soon as he comes in.'

She escaped, and in a minute or two the new vicar presented himself at the door. A little maid might well have some apprehension in facing him, for Mr. Wyvern was of vast proportions and leonine in aspect. With the exception of one ungloved hand and the scant proportions of his face which were not hidden by hair, he was wholly black in hue; an enormous beard, the colour of jet, concealed the linen about his throat, and a veritable mane, dark as night, fell upon his shoulders. His features were not ill-matched with this sable garniture; their expression was a fixed severity; his eye regarded you with stern scrutiny, and passed from the examination to a melancholy reflectiveness. Yet his appearance was suggestive of anything but ill-nature; contradictory though it may seem, the face was a pleasant one, inviting to confidence, to respect; if he could only have smiled, the tender humanity which lurked in the lines of his countenance would have become evident. His age was probably a little short of fifty.

A servant replied to his knock, and, after falling back in a momentary alarm, introduced him to the sitting-room. He took Mrs. Waltham's hand silently, fixed upon her the full orbs of his dark eyes, and then, whilst still retaining her fingers, looked thoughtfully about the room. It was a pleasant little parlour, with many an evidence of refinement in those who occupied it. Mr. Wyvern showed something like a look of satisfaction. He seated himself, and the chair creaked ominously beneath him. Then he again scrutinised Mrs. Waltham.

She was a lady of fair complexion, with a double chin. Her dress suggested elegant tastes, and her hand was as smooth and delicate as a lady's should be. A long gold chain descended from her neck to the watch-pocket at her waist, and her fingers exhibited several rings. She bore the reverend gentleman's scrutiny with modest grace, almost as if it flattered her. And

indeed there was nothing whatever of ill-breeding in Mr. Wyvern's mode of instituting acquaintance with his parishioner;
one felt that he was a man of pronounced originality, and that
he might be trusted in his variance from the wonted modes.

The view from the windows gave him a subject for his first
remarks. Mrs. Waltham had been in some fear of a question
which would go to the roots of her soul's history; it would have
been in keeping with his visage. But, with native acuteness,
she soon discovered that Mr. Wyvern's gaze had very little to
do with the immediate subject of his thought, or, what was
much the same thing, that he seldom gave the whole of his
attention to the matter outwardly calling for it. He was a
man of profound mental absences; he could make replies, even
put queries, and all the while be brooding intensely upon a
wholly different subject. Mrs. Waltham did not altogether
relish it; she was in the habit of being heard with deference;
but, to be sure, a clergyman only talked of worldly things by
way of concession. It certainly seemed so in this clergyman's
case.

'Your prospect,' Mr. Wyvern remarked presently, 'will not
be improved by the works below.'

His voice was very deep, and all his words were weighed
in the utterance. This deliberation at times led to peculiarities
of emphasis in single words. Probably he was a man of philo-
logical crotchets; he said, for instance, 'pro-spect.'

'I scarcely think Mr. Eldon will go on with the mining,'
replied Mrs. Waltham.

'Ah! you think not?'

'I am quite sure he said that unconsciously,' the lady remarked to herself. 'He's thinking of some quite different affair.'

'Mr. Eldon,' the clergyman resumed, fixing upon her an
absent eye, 'is Mr. Mutimer's son-in-law, I understand?'

'His brother, Mr. Godfrey Eldon, was,' Mrs. Waltham corrected.

'Ah! the one that died?'

He said it questioningly; then added—

'I have a difficulty in mastering details of this kind. You
would do me a great kindness in explaining to me briefly of
whom the family at the Manor at present consists?'

Mrs. Waltham was delighted to talk on such a subject.

'Only of Mrs. Eldon and her son, Mr. Hubert Eldon. The
elder son, Godfrey, was lost in a shipwreck, on a voyage to
New Zealand.'

'He was a sailor?'

'Oh, no!' said the lady, with a smile. 'He was in business at Belwick. It was shortly after his marriage with Miss Mutimer that he took the voyage—partly for his health, partly to examine some property his father had had an interest in. Old Mr. Eldon engaged in speculations—I believe it was flax-growing. The results, unfortunately, were anything but satisfactory. It was that which led to his son entering business—quite a new thing in their family. Wasn't it very sad? Poor Godfrey and his young wife both drowned! The marriage was, as you may imagine, not altogether a welcome one to Mrs. Eldon; Mr. Mutimer was quite a self-made man, quite. I understand he has relations in London of the very poorest class—labouring people.'

'They probably benefit by his will?'

'I can't say. In any case, to a very small extent. It has for a long time been understood that Hubert Eldon inherits.'

'Singular!' murmured the clergyman, still in the same absent way.

'Is it not? He took so to the young fellows; no doubt he was flattered to be allied to them. And then he was passionately devoted to his daughter; if only for her sake, he would have done his utmost for the family.'

'I understand that Mr. Mutimer purchased the Manor from them?'

'That was before the marriage. Godfrey Eldon sold it; he had his father's taste for speculation, I fancy, and wanted capital. Then Mr. Mutimer begged them to remain in the house. He certainly was a wonderfully kind old—old gentleman; his behaviour to Mrs. Eldon was always the perfection of courtesy. A stranger would find it difficult to understand how she could get on so well with him, but their sorrows brought them together, and Mr. Mutimer's generosity was really noble. If I had not known his origin, I should certainly have taken him for a county gentleman.'

'Yet he proposed to mine in the valley,' observed Mr. Wyvern, half to himself, casting a glance at the windows.

Mrs. Waltham did not at first see the connection between this and what she had been saying. Then it occurred to her that Mr. Wyvern was aristocratic in his views.

'To be sure,' she said, 'one expects to find a little of the original—of the money-making spirit. Of course such a thing would never have suggested itself to the Eldons. And in fact

very little of the lands remained to them. Mr. Mutimer bought
a great deal from other people.'

As Mr. Wyvern sat brooding, Mrs. Waltham asked—

'You have seen Mrs. Eldon?'

'Not yet. She is too unwell to receive visits.'

'Yes, poor thing, she is a great invalid. I thought, perhaps,
you——. But I know she likes to be very quiet. What a
strange thing about Mr. Eldon, is it not? You know that he
has never come yet; not even to the funeral.'

'Singular!'

'An inexplicable thing! There has never been a shadow of
disagreement between them.'

'Mr. Eldon is abroad, I believe?' said the clergyman
musingly.

'Abroad? Oh dear, no! At least, I——. Is there news
of his being abroad?'

Mr. Wyvern merely shook his head.

'As far as we know,' Mrs. Waltham continued, rather disturbed by the suggestion, 'he is at Oxford.'

'A student?'

'Yes. He is quite a youth—only two-and-twenty.'

There was a knock at the door, and a maid-servant entered
to ask if she should lay the table for tea. Mrs. Waltham assented; then, to her visitor—

'You will do us the pleasure of drinking a cup of tea, Mr.
Wyvern? we make a meal of it, in the country way. My boy
and girl are sure to be in directly.'

'I should like to make their acquaintance,' was the grave
response.

'Alfred, my son,' the lady proceeded, 'is with us for his
Easter holiday. Belwick is so short a distance away, and yet
too far to allow of his living here, unfortunately.'

'His age?'

'Just one-and-twenty.'

'The same age as my own boy.'

'Oh, you have a son?'

'A youngster, studying music in Germany. I have just
been spending a fortnight with him.'

'How delightful! If only poor Alfred could have pursued
some more—more liberal occupation! Unhappily, we had small
choice. Friends were good enough to offer him exceptional advantages not long after his father's death, and I was only too
glad to accept the opening. I believe he is a clever boy; only

such a dreadful Radical.' She laughed, with a deprecatory motion of the hands. 'Poor Adela and he are at daggers drawn; no doubt it is some terrible argument that detains them now on the road. I can't think how he got his views; certainly his father never inculcated them.'

'The air, Mrs. Waltham, the air,' murmured the clergyman.

The lady was not quite sure that she understood the remark, but the necessity of reply was obviated by the entrance of the young man in question. Alfred was somewhat undergrown, but of solid build. He walked in a sturdy and rather aggressive way, and his plump face seemed to indicate an intelligence, bright, indeed, but of the less refined order. His head was held stiffly, and his whole bearing betrayed a desire to make the most of his defective stature. His shake of the hand was an abrupt downward jerk, like a pull at a bell-rope. In the smile with which he met Mr. Wyvern a supercilious frame of mind was not altogether concealed; he seemed anxious to have it understood that in *him* the clerical attire inspired nothing whatever of superstitious reverence. Reverence, in truth, was not Mr. Waltham's failing.

Mr. Wyvern, as his habit was at introductions, spoke no words, but held the youth's hand for a few moments and looked him in the eyes. Alfred turned his head aside uneasily, and was a trifle ruddy in the cheeks when at length he regained his liberty.

'By-the-by,' he remarked to his mother when he had seated himself, with crossed legs, 'Eldon has turned up at last. He passed us in a cab, or so Adela said. I didn't catch a glimpse of the individual.'

'Really!' exclaimed Mrs. Waltham. 'He was coming from Agworth station?'

'I suppose so. There was a trunk on the four-wheeler. Adela says he looked ill, though I don't see how she discovered so much.'

'I have no doubt she is right. He must have been ill.'

Mr. Wyvern, in contrast with his habit, was paying marked attention; he leaned forward, with a hand on each knee. In the meanwhile the preparations for tea had progressed, and as Mrs. Waltham rose at the sight of the teapot being brought in, her daughter entered the room. Adela was taller by half a head than her brother; she was slim and graceful. The air had made her face bloom, and the smile which was added as she drew near to the vicar enhanced the charm of a countenance at

all times charming. She was not less than ladylike in self-possession, but Mr. Wyvern's towering sableness clearly awed her
a little. For an instant her eyes drooped, but at once she
raised them and met the severe gaze with unflinching orbs.
Releasing her hand, Mr. Wyvern performed a singular little
ceremony : he laid his right palm very gently on her nutbrown
hair, and his lips moved. At the same time he all but smiled.

Alfred's face was a delightful study the while; it said so
clearly, 'Confound the parson's impudence!' Mrs. Waltham,
on the other hand, looked pleased as she rustled to her place at
the tea-tray.

'So Mr. Eldon has come?' she said, glancing at Adela
'Alfred says he looks ill.'

'Mother,' interposed the young man, 'pray be accurate. I
distinctly stated that I did not even see him, and should not
have known that it was he at all. Adela is responsible for that
assertion.'

'I just saw his face,' the girl said naturally. 'I thought he
looked ill.'

Mr. Wyvern addressed to her a question about her walk,
and for a few minutes they conversed together. There was a
fresh simplicity in Adela's way of speaking which harmonised
well with her appearance and with the scene in which she
moved. A gentle English girl, this dainty home, set in so fair
and peaceful a corner of the world, was just the abode one
would have chosen for her. Her beauty seemed a part of the
burgeoning springtime. She was not lavish of her smiles; a
timid seriousness marked her manner to the clergyman, and
she replied to his deliberately posed questions with a gravity
respectful alike of herself and of him.

In front of Mr. Wyvern stood a large cake, of which a portion was already sliced. The vicar, at Adela's invitation, accepted a piece of the cake ; having eaten this, he accepted
another; then yet another. His absence had come back upon
him, and as he talked he continued to eat portions of the cake,
till but a small fraction of the original structure remained on
the dish. Alfred, keenly observant of what was going on,
pursed his lips from time to time and looked at his mother with
exaggerated gravity, leading her eyes to the vanishing cake.
Even Adela could not but remark the reverend gentleman's
abnormal appetite, but she steadily discouraged her brother's
attempts to draw her into the joke. At length it came to pass
that Mr. Wyvern himself, stretching his hand mechanically to

the dish, became aware that he had exhibited his appreciation of the sweet food in a degree not altogether sanctioned by usage. He fixed his eyes on the tablecloth, and was silent for a while.

As soon as the vicar had taken his departure Alfred threw himself into a chair, thrust out his legs, and exploded in laughter.

'By Jove!' he shouted. 'If that man doesn't experience symptoms of disorder! Why, I should be prostrate for a week if I consumed a quarter of what he has put out of sight.'

'Alfred, you are shockingly rude,' reproved his mother, though herself laughing. 'Mr. Wyvern is absorbed in thought.'

'Well, he has taken the best means, I should say, to remind himself of actualities,' rejoined the youth. 'But what a man he is! How did he behave in church this morning?'

'You should have come to see,' said Mrs. Waltham, mildly censuring her son's disregard of the means of grace.

'I like Mr. Wyvern,' observed Adela, who was standing at the window looking out upon the dusking valley.

'Oh, you would like any man in parsonical livery,' scoffed her brother.

Alfred shortly betook himself to the garden, where, in spite of a decided freshness in the atmosphere, he walked for half-an-hour smoking a pipe. When he entered the house again, he met Adela at the foot of the stairs.

'Mrs. Mewling has just come in,' she whispered.

'All right, I'll come up with you,' was the reply. 'Heaven defend me from her small talk!'

They ascended to a very little room, which made a kind of boudoir for Adela. Alfred struck a match and lit a lamp, disclosing a nest of wonderful purity and neatness. On the table a drawing-board was slanted; it showed a text of Scripture in process of 'illumination.'

'Still at that kind of thing!' exclaimed Alfred. 'My good child, if you want to paint, why don't you paint in earnest? Really, Adela, I must enter a protest! Remember that you are eighteen years of age.'

'I don't forget it, Alfred.'

'At eight-and-twenty, at eight-and-thirty, you propose still to be at the same stage of development?'

'I don't think we'll talk of it,' said the girl quietly. 'We don't understand each other.'

'Of course not, but we might, if only you'd read sensible books that I could give you.'

Adela shook her head. The philosophical youth sank into his favourite attitude—legs extended, hands in pockets, nose in air.

'So, I suppose,' he said presently, 'that fellow really has been ill?'

Adela was sitting in thought; she looked up with a shadow of annoyance on her face.

'That fellow?'

'Eldon, you know.'

'I want to ask you a question,' said his sister, interlocking her fingers and pressing them against her throat. 'Why do you always speak in a contemptuous way of Mr. Eldon?'

'You know I don't like the individual.'

'What cause has "the individual" given you?'

'He's a snob.'

'I'm not sure that I know what that means,' replied Adela, after thinking for a moment with downcast eyes.

'Because you never read anything. He's a fellow who raises a great edifice of pretence on rotten foundations.'

'What can you mean? Mr. Eldon is a gentleman. What pretence is he guilty of?'

'Gentleman!' uttered her brother with much scorn. 'Upon my word, that *is* the vulgarest of denominations! Who doesn't call himself so nowadays! A man's a man, I take it, and what need is there to lengthen the name? Thank the powers, we don't live in feudal ages. Besides, he doesn't seem to me to be what you imply.'

Adela had taken a book; in turning over the pages, she said—

'No doubt you mean, Alfred, that, for some reason, you are determined to view him with prejudice.'

'The reason is obvious enough. The fellow's behaviour is detestable; he looks at you from head to foot as if you were applying for a place in his stable. Whenever I want an exam ple of a contemptible aristocrat, there's Eldon ready-made. Contemptible, because he's such a sham ; as if everybody didn't know his history and his circumstances!'

'Everybody doesn't regard them as you do. There is nothing whatever dishonourable in his position.'

'Not in sponging on a rich old plebeian, a man he despises, and living in idleness at his expense?'

'I don't believe Mr. Eldon does anything of the kind,

Since his brother's death he has had a sufficient income of his own, so mother says.'

'Sufficient income of his own! Bah! Five or six hundred a year; likely he lives on that! Besides, haven't they soaped old Mutimer into leaving them all his property? The whole affair is the best illustration one could possibly have of what aristocrats are brought to in a democratic age. First of all, Godfrey Eldon marries Mutimer's daughter; you are at liberty to believe, if you like, that he would have married her just the same if she hadn't had a penny. The old fellow is flattered. They see the hold they have, and stick to him like leeches. All for want of money, of course. Our aristocrats begin to see that they can't get on without money nowadays; they can't live on family records, and they find that people won't toady to them in the old way just on account of their name. Why, it began with Eldon's father—didn't he put his pride in his pocket, and try to make cash by speculation? Now I can respect *him* : he at all events faced the facts of the case honestly. The despicable thing in this Hubert Eldon is that, having got money once more, and in the dirtiest way, he puts on the top-sawyer just as if there was nothing to be ashamed of. If he and his mother were living in a small way on their few hundreds a year, he might haw-haw as much as he liked, and I should only laugh at him; he'd be a fool, but an honest one. But catch them doing that! Family pride's too insubstantial a thing, you see. Well, as I said, they illustrate the natural course of things, the transition from the old age to the new. If Eldon has sons, they'll go in for commerce, and make themselves, if they can, millionaires; but by that time they'll dispense with airs and insolence—see if they don't.'

Adela kept her eyes on the pages before her, but she was listening intently. A sort of verisimilitude in the picture drawn by her Radical-minded brother could not escape her; her thought was troubled. When she spoke it was without resentment, but gravely.

'I don't like this spirit in judging of people. You know quite well, Alfred, how easy it is to see the whole story in quite another way. You begin by a harsh and worldly judgment, and it leads you to misrepresent all that follows. I refuse to believe that Godfrey Eldon married Mrs. Mutimer's daughter for her money.'

Alfred laughed aloud.

'Of course you do, sister Adela! Women won't admit such things; that's *their* aristocratic feeling!'

'And that is, too, worthless and a sham? Will that, too, be done away with in the new age?'

'Oh, depend upon it! When women are educated, they will take the world as it is, and decline to live on illusions.'

'Then how glad I am to have been left without education!'

In the meantime a conversation of a very lively kind was in progress between Mrs. Waltham and her visitor, Mrs. Mewling. The latter was a lady whose position much resembled Mrs. Waltham's : she inhabited a small house in the village street, and spent most of her time in going about to hear or to tell some new thing. She came in this evening with a look presageful of news indeed.

'I've been to Belwick to-day,' she began, sitting very close to Mrs. Waltham, whose lap she kept touching as she spoke with excited fluency. 'I've seen Mrs. Yottle. My dear, what *do* you think she has told me?'

Mrs. Yottle was the wife of a legal gentleman who had been in Mr. Mutimer's confidence. Mrs. Waltham at once divined intelligence affecting the Eldons.

'What?' she asked eagerly.

'You'd never dream such a thing! what *will* come to pass! An unthought-of possibility!' She went on *crescendo*. 'My dear Mrs. Waltham, Mr. Mutimer has left no will!'

It was as if an electric shock had passed from the tips of her fingers into her hearer's frame. Mrs. Waltham paled.

'That cannot be true!' she whispered, incapable of utterance above breath.

'Oh, but there's not a doubt of it!' Knowing that the news would be particularly unpalatable to Mrs. Waltham, she proceeded to dwell upon it with dancing eyes. 'Search has been going on since the day of the death : not a corner that hasn't been rummaged, not a drawer that hasn't been turned out, not a book in the library that hasn't been shaken, not a wall that hasn't been examined for secret doors! Mr. Mutimer has died intestate!'

The other lady was mute.

'And shall I tell you how it came about? Two days before his death, he had his will from Mr. Yottle, saying he wanted to make changes—probably to execute a new will altogether. My dear, he destroyed it, and death surprised him before he could make another.'

'He wishéd to make changes?'

'Ah!' Mrs. Mowling drew out the exclamation, shaking her raised finger, pursing her lips. 'And of that, too, I can tell you the reason. Mr. Mutimer was anything but pleased with young Eldon. That young man, let me tell you, has been conducting himself—oh, shockingly! Now you wouldn't dream of repeating this?'

'Certainly not.'

'It seems that news came not so very long ago of a certain actress, singer,—something of the kind, you understand? Friends thought it their duty—rightly, of course,—to inform Mr. Mutimer. I can't say exactly who did it; but we know that Hubert Eldon is not regarded affectionately by a good many people. My dear, he has been out of England for more than a month, living—oh, such extravagance! And the moral question, too? You know—those women! Someone, they say, of European reputation; of course no names are breathed. For my part, I can't say I am surprised. Young men, you know; and particularly young men of that kind! Well, it has cost him a pretty penny; he'll remember it as long as he lives.'

'Then the property will go——'

'Yes, to the working people in London; the roughest of the rough, they say! What *will* happen? It will be impossible for us to live here if they come and settle at the Manor. The neighbourhood will be intolerable. Think of the rag-tag-and-bobtail they will bring with them!'

'But Hubert!' ejaculated Mrs. Waltham, whom this vision of barbaric onset affected little in the crashing together of a great airy castle.

'Well, my dear, after all he still has more to depend upon than many we could instance. Probably he will take to the law,—that is, if he ever returns to England.'

'He is at the Manor,' said Mrs. Waltham, with none of the pleasure it would ordinarily have given her to be first with an item of news. 'He came this afternoon.'

'He did! Who has seen him?'

'Alfred and Adela passed him on the road. He was in a cab.'

'I feel for his poor mother. What a meeting it will be! But then we must remember that they had no actual claim on the inheritance. Of course it will be a most grievous disappointment, but what is life made of? I'm afraid some people will be anything but grieved. We must confess that Hubert has not been exactly popular; and I rather wonder at it; I'm sure he might have been if he had liked. Just a little too—too self-conscious, don't you think? Of course it was quite a mistake, but people had an idea that he presumed on wealth which was not his own. Well, well, we quiet folk look on, don't we? It's rather like a play.'

Presently Mrs. Mewling leaned forward yet more confidentially.

'My dear, you won't be offended? You don't mind a question? There wasn't anything definite?—Adela, I mean.'

'Nothing, nothing whatever!' Mrs. Waltham asserted with vigour.

'Ha!' Mrs. Mewling sighed deeply. 'How relieved I am I did so fear!'

'Nothing whatever,' the other lady repeated.

'Thank goodness! Then there is no need to breathe a word of those shocking matters. But they do get abroad so!'

A reflection Mrs. Mewling was justified in making.

CHAPTER II.

THE cab which had passed Adela and her brother at a short distance from Wanley brought faces to the windows or door of almost every house as it rolled through the village street. The direction in which it was going, the trunk on the roof, the certainty that it had come from Agworth station, suggested to everyone that young Eldon sat within. The occupant had, however, put up both windows just before entering the village, and sight of him was not obtained. Wanley had abundant matter for gossip that evening. Hubert's return, giving a keener edge to the mystery of his so long delay, would alone have sufficed to wagging tongues; but, in addition, Mrs. Mewling was on the warpath, and the intelligence she spread was of a kind to run like wildfire.

The approach to the Manor was a carriage-road, obliquely ascending the hill from a point some quarter of a mile beyond the cottages which once housed Belwick's abbots. Of the house scarcely a glimpse could be caught till you were well within the gates, so thickly was it embosomed in trees. This afternoon it wore a cheerless face; most of the blinds were still down, and the dwelling might have been unoccupied, for any sign of human activity that the eye could catch. There was no porch at the main entrance, and the heavy nail-studded door greeted a visitor somewhat sombrely. On the front of a gable stood the words 'Nisi Dominus.'

The vehicle drew up, and there descended a young man of pale countenance, his attire indicating long and hasty travel. He pulled vigorously at the end of a hanging bell-chain, and the door was immediately opened by a man-servant in black. Hubert, for he it was, pointed to his trunk, and, whilst it was being carried into the house, took some loose coin from his pocket. He handed the driver a sovereign.

'I have no change, sir,' said the man, after examining the coin.

But Hubert had already turned away; he merely waved his hand, and entered the house. For a drive of two miles, the cabman held himself tolerably paid.

The hall was dusky, and seemed in need of fresh air. Hubert threw off his hat, gloves, and overcoat; then for the first time spoke to the servant, who stood in an attitude of expectancy.

'Mrs. Eldon is at home?'

'At home, sir, but very unwell. She desires me to say that she fears she may not be able to see you this evening.'

'Is there a fire anywhere?'

'Only in the library, sir.'

'I will dine there. And let a fire be lit in my bedroom.'

'Yes, sir. Will you dine at once, sir?'

'In an hour. Something light; I don't care what it is.'

'Shall the fire be lit in your bedroom at once, sir?'

'At once, and a hot bath prepared. Come to the library and tell me when it is ready.'

The servant silently departed. Hubert walked across the hall, giving a glance here and there, and entered the library. Nothing had been altered here since his father's, nay, since his grandfather's, time. That grandfather—his name Hubert—had combined strong intellectual tendencies with the extravagant tastes which gave his already tottering house the decisive push. The large collection of superbly-bound books which this room contained were nearly all of his purchasing, for prior to his time the Eldons had not been wont to concern themselves with things of the mind. Hubert, after walking to the window and looking out for a moment on the side lawn, pushed a small couch near to the fireplace, and threw himself down at full length, his hands beneath his head. In a moment his position seemed to have become uneasy; he turned upon his side, uttering an exclamation as if of pain. A minute or two and again he moved, this time with more evident impatience. The next thing he did was to rise, step to the bell, and ring it violently.

The same servant appeared.

'Isn't the bath ready?' Hubert asked. His former mode of speaking had been brief and decided; he was now almost imperious.

'I believe it will be in a moment, sir,' was the reply, marked, perhaps, by just a little failure in the complete subservience expected.

Hubert looked at the man for an instant with contracted brows, but merely said—'Tell them to be quick.'

The man returned in less than three minutes with a satisfactory announcement, and Eldon went upstairs to refresh himself.

Two hours later he had dined, with obvious lack of appetite, and was deriving but slight satisfaction from a cigar, when the servant entered with a message from Mrs. Eldon: she desired to see her son.

Hubert threw his cigar aside, and made a gesture expressing his wish to be led to his mother's room. The man conducted him to the landing at the head of the first flight of stairs; there a female servant was waiting, who, after a respectful movement, led the way to a door at a few yards' distance. She opened it and drew back. Hubert passed into the room.

It was furnished in a very old-fashioned style—heavily, richly, and with ornaments seemingly procured rather as evidences of wealth than of taste; successive Mrs. Eldons had used it as a boudoir. The present lady of that name sat in a great chair near the fire. Though not yet fifty, she looked at least ten years older; her hair had streaks of white, and her thin delicate features were much lined and wasted. It would not be enough to say that she had evidently once been beautiful, for in truth she was so still, with a spiritual beauty of a very rare type. Just now her face was set in a sternness which did not seem an expression natural to it; the fine lips were much more akin to smiling sweetness, and the brows accepted with repugnance anything but the stamp of thoughtful charity.

After the first glance at Hubert she dropped her eyes. He, stepping quickly across the floor, put his lips to her cheek; she did not move her head, nor raise her hand to take his.

'Will you sit there, Hubert?' she said, pointing to a chair which was placed opposite hers. The resemblance between her present mode of indicating a wish and her son's way of speaking to the servant below was very striking; even the quality of their voices had much in common, for Hubert's was rather high-pitched. In face, however, the young man did not strongly evidence their relation to each other: he was not handsome, and had straight low brows, which made his aspect at first forbidding.

'Why have you not come to me before this?' Mrs. Eldon asked when her son had seated himself, with his eyes turned upon the fire.

'I was unable to, mother. I have been ill.'

She cast a glance at him. There was no doubting the truth of what he said; at this moment he looked feeble and pain-worn.

'Where did your illness come upon you?' she asked, her tone unsoftened.

'In Germany. I started only a few hours after receiving the letter in which you told me of the death.'

'My other letters you paid no heed to?'

'I could not reply to them.'

He spoke after hesitation, but firmly, as one does who has something to brave out.

'It would have been better for you if you had been able, Hubert. Your refusal has cost you dear.'

He looked up inquiringly.

'Mr. Mutimer,' his mother continued, a tremor in her voice, 'destroyed his will a day or two before he died.'

Hubert said nothing. His fingers, locked together before him, twitched a little; his face gave no sign.

'Had you come to me at once,' Mrs. Eldon pursued, 'had you listened to my entreaties, to my commands'—her voice rang right queenly—'this would not have happened. Mr. Mutimer behaved as generously as he always has. As soon as there came to him certain news of you, he told me everything. I refused to believe what people were saying, and he too wished to do so. He would not write to you himself; there was one all-sufficient test, he held, and that was a summons from your mother. It was a test of your honour, Hubert—and you failed under it.'

He made no answer.

'You received my letters?' she went on to ask. 'I heard

you had gone from England, and could only hope your letters
would be forwarded. Did you get them?'

'With the delay of only a day or two.'

'And deliberately you put me aside?'

'I did.'

She looked at him now for several moments. Her eyes
grew moist. Then she resumed, in a lower voice—

'I said nothing of what was at stake, though I knew. Mr.
Mutimer was perfectly open with me. "I have trusted him
implicitly," he said, "because I believe him as staunch and
true as his brother. I make no allowances for what are called
young man's follies: he must be above anything of that kind.
If he is not—well, I have been mistaken in him, and I can't
deal with him as I wish to do." You know what he was,
Hubert, and you can imagine him speaking those words. We
waited. The bad news was confirmed, and from you there
came nothing. I would not hint at the loss you were in-
curring; of my own purpose I should have refrained from
doing so, and Mr. Mutimer forbade me to appeal to anything
but your better self. If you would not come to me because I
wished it, I could not involve you and myself in shame by seeing you yield to sordid motives.'

Hubert raised his head. A choking voice kept him silent
for a moment only.

'Mother, the loss is nothing to you; you are above regrets
of that kind; and for myself, I am almost glad to have lost it.'

'In very truth,' answered the mother, 'I care little about
the wealth you might have possessed. What I do care for is
the loss of all the hopes I had built upon you. I thought you
honour itself; I thought you high-minded. Young as you are,
I let you go from me without a fear. Hubert, I would have
staked my life that no shadow of disgrace would ever fall
upon your head! You have taken from me the last comfort
of my age.'

He uttered words she could not catch.

'The purity of your soul was precious to me,' she continued,
her accents struggling against weakness; 'I thought I had
seen in you a love of that chastity without which a man is nothing; and I ever did my best to keep your eyes upon a noble
ideal of womanhood. You have fallen. The simpler duty, the
point of every-day honour, I could not suppose that you would
fail in. From the day when you came of age, when Mr. Mutimer spoke to you, saying that in every respect you would be

as his son, and you, for your part, accepted what he offered, you owed it to him to respect the lightest of his reasonable wishes. The wish which was supreme in him you have utterly disregarded. Is it that you failed to understand him? I have thought of late of a way you had now and then when you spoke to me about him; it has occurred to me that perhaps you did him less than justice. Regard his position and mine, and tell me whether you think he could have become so much to us if he had not been a gentleman in the highest sense of the word. When Godfrey first of all brought me that proposal from him that we should still remain in this house, it seemed to me the most impossible thing. You know what it was that induced me to assent, and what led to his becoming so intimate with us. Since then it has been hard for me to remember that he was not one of our family. His weak points it was not difficult to discover ; but I fear you did not understand what was noblest in his character. Uprightness, clean-heartedness, good faith—these things he prized before everything. In you, in one of your birth, he looked to find them in perfection. Hubert, I stood shamed before him.'

The young man breathed hard, as if in physical pain. His eyes were fixed in a wide absent gaze. Mrs. Eldon had lost all the severity of her face; the profound sorrow of a pure and noble nature was alone to be read there now.

' What,' she continued—' what is this class distinction upon which we pride ourselves ? What does it mean, if not that our opportunities lead us to see truths to which the eyes of the poor and ignorant are blind ? Is there nothing in it, after all —in our pride of birth and station ? That is what people are saying nowadays: you yourself have jested to me about our privileges. You almost make me dread that you were right. Look back at that man, whom I came to honour as my own father. He began life as a toiler with his hands. Only a fortnight ago he was telling me stories of his boyhood, of seventy years since. He was without education; his ideas of truth and goodness he had to find within his own heart. Could anything exceed the noble simplicity of his respect for me, for you boys. We were poor, but it seemed to him that we had from nature what no money could buy. He was wrong; his faith misled him. No, not wrong with regard to all of us; my boy Godfrey was indeed all that he believed. But think of himself; what advantage have we over him ? I know no longer what to believe. Oh, Hubert!'

He left his chair and walked to a more distant part of the room, where he was beyond the range of lamp and firelight. Standing here, he pressed his hand against his side, still breathing hard, and with difficulty suppressing a groan.

He came a step or two nearer.

'Mother,' he said, hurriedly, 'I am still far from well. Let me leave you; speak to me again to-morrow.'

Mrs. Eldon made an effort to rise, looking anxiously into the gloom where he stood. She was all but standing upright—a thing she had not done for a long time—when Hubert sprang towards her, seizing her hands, then supporting her in his arms. Her self-command gave way at length, and she wept.

Hubert placed her gently in the chair and knelt beside her. He could find no words, but once or twice raised his face and kissed her.

'What caused your illness?' she asked, speaking as one wearied with suffering. She lay back, and her eyes were closed.

'I cannot say,' he answered. 'Do not speak of me. In your last letter there was no account of how he died.'

'It was in church, at the morning service. The pew-opener found him sitting there dead, when all had gone away.'

'But the vicar could see into the pew from the pulpit? The death must have been very peaceful.'

'No, he could not see; the front curtains were drawn.'

'Why was that, I wonder?'

Mrs. Eldon shook her head.

'Are you in pain?' she asked suddenly. 'Why do you breathe so strangely?'

'A little pain. Oh, nothing; I will see Manns to-morrow.'

His mother gazed long and steadily into his eyes, and this time he bore her look.

'Mother, you have not kissed me,' he whispered.

'And cannot, dear. There is too much between us.'

His head fell upon her lap.

'Hubert!'

He pressed her hand.

'How shall I live when you have gone from me again? When you say good-bye, it will be as if I parted from you for ever.'

Hubert was silent.

'Unless,' she continued—'unless I have your promise that you will no longer dishonour yourself.'

He rose from her side and stood in front of the fire; his mother looked and saw that he trembled.

'No promise, Hubert,' she said, 'that you cannot keep. Rather than that, we will accept our fate, and be nothing to each other.'

'You know very well, mother, that that is impossible. I cannot speak to you of what drove me to disregard your letters. I love and honour you, and shall have to change my nature before I cease to do so.'

'To me, Hubert, you seem already to have changed. I scarcely know you.'

'I can't defend myself to you,' he said sadly. 'We think so differently on subjects which allow of no compromise, that, even if I could speak openly, you would only condemn me the more.'

His mother turned upon him a grief-stricken and wondering face.

'Since when have we differed so?' she asked. 'What has made us strangers to each other's thoughts? Surely, surely you are at one with me in condemning all that has led to this? If your character has been too weak to resist temptation, you cannot have learnt to make evil your good?'

He kept silence.

'You refuse me that last hope?'

Hubert moved impatiently.

'Mother, I can't see beyond to-day! I know nothing of what is before me. It is the idlest trifling with words to say one will do this or that, when action in no way depends on one's own calmer thought. In this moment I could promise anything you ask; if I had my choice, I would be a child again and have no desire but to do your will, to be worthy in your eyes. I hate my life and the years that have parted me from you. Let us talk no more of it.'

Neither spoke again for some moments; then Hubert asked coldly—

'What has been done?'

'Nothing,' replied Mrs. Eldon, in the same tone. 'Mr. Yottle has waited for your return before communicating with the relatives in London.'

'I will go to Belwick in the morning,' he said. Then, after reflection, 'Mr. Mutimer told you that he had destroyed his will?'

'No. He had it from Mr. Yottle two days before his death,

and on the day after—the Monday—Mr. Yottle was to have come to receive instructions for a new one. It is nowhere to be found : of course it was destroyed.'

'I suppose there is no doubt of that ?' Hubert asked, with a show of indifference.

'There can be none. Mr. Yottle tells me that a will which existed before Godfrey's marriage was destroyed in the same way.'

'Who is the heir ?'

'A great-nephew bearing the same name. The will contained provision for him and certain of his family. Wanley is his ; the personal property will be divided among several.'

'The people have not come forward ?'

'We presume they do not even know of Mr. Mutimer's death. There has been no direct communication between him and them for many years.'

Hubert's next question was, 'What shall you do, mother ?'

'Does it interest you, Hubert ? I am too feeble to move very far. I must find a home either here in the village or at Agworth.'

He looked at her with compassion, with remorse.

'And you, my boy ?' asked his mother, raising her eyes gently.

'I ? Oh, the selfish never come to harm, be sure ! Only the gentle and helpless have to suffer ; that is the plan of the world's ruling.'

'The world is not ruled by one who thinks our thoughts, Hubert.'

He had it on his lips to make a rejoinder, but checked the impulse.

'Say good-night to me,' his mother continued. 'You must go and rest. If you still feel unwell in the morning, a messenger shall go to Belwick. You are very, very pale.'

Hubert held his hand to her and bent his head. Mrs. Eldon offered her cheek ; he kissed it and went from the room.

At seven o'clock on the following morning a bell summoned a servant to Hubert's bedroom. Though it was daylight, a lamp burned near the bed ; Hubert lay against pillows heaped high.

'Let someone go at once for Dr. Manns,' he said, appearing to speak with difficulty. 'I wish to see him as soon as possible. Mrs. Eldon is to know nothing of his visit—you understand me !'

The servant withdrew. In rather less than an hour the doctor made his appearance, with every sign of having been interrupted in his repose. He was a spare man, full bearded and spectacled.

'Something wrong?' was his greeting as he looked keenly at his summoner. 'I didn't know you were here.'

'Yes,' Hubert replied, 'something is confoundedly wrong. I have been playing strange tricks in the night, I fancy.'

'Fever?'

'As a consequence of something else. I shall have to tell you what must be repeated to no one, as of course you will see. Let me see, when was it?—Saturday to-day? Ten days ago, I had a pistol-bullet just here,'—he touched his right side. 'It was extracted, and I seemed to be not much the worse. I have just come from Germany.'

Dr. Manns screwed his face into an expression of sceptical amazement.

'At present,' Hubert continued, trying to laugh, 'I feel considerably the worse. I don't think I could move if I tried. In a few minutes, ten to one, I shall begin talking foolery. You must keep people away; get what help is needed. I may depend upon you?'

The doctor nodded, and, whistling low, began an examination.

CHAPTER III.

On the dun borderland of Islington and Hoxton, in a corner made by the intersection of the New North Road and the Regent's Canal, is discoverable an irregular triangle of small dwelling-houses, bearing the name of Wilton Square. In the midst stands an amorphous structure, which on examination proves to be a very ugly house and a still uglier Baptist chapel built back to back. The pair are enclosed within iron railings, and, more strangely, a circle of trees, which in due season do veritably put forth green leaves. One side of the square shows a second place of worship, the resort, as an inscription declares, of 'Welsh Calvinistic Methodists.' The houses are of one storey, with kitchen windows looking upon small areas; the front door is reached by an ascent of five steps.

The canal—*maladetta e sventurata fossa*—stagnating in utter foulness between coal-wharfs and builders' yards, at this point divides two neighbourhoods of different aspects. On the south

is Hoxton, a region of malodorous market streets, of factories,
timber yards, grimy warehouses, of alleys swarming with small
trades and crafts, of filthy courts and passages leading into
pestilential gloom; everywhere toil in its most degrading forms;
the thoroughfares thundering with high-laden waggons, the
pavements trodden by working folk of the coarsest type, the
corners and lurking-holes showing destitution at its ugliest.
Walking northwards, the explorer finds himself in freer air,
amid broader ways, in a district of dwelling-houses only; the
roads seem abandoned to milkmen, cat's-meat vendors, and
costermongers.   Here will be found streets in which every
window has its card advertising lodgings; others claim a higher
respectability, the houses retreating behind patches of garden-
ground, and occasionally showing plastered pillars and a balcony.
The change is from undisguised struggle for subsistence to
mean and spirit-broken leisure; hither retreat the better-paid
of the great slave-army when they are free to eat and sleep.
To walk about a neighbourhood such as this is the dreariest
exercise to which man can betake himself; the heart is crushed
by uniformity of decent squalor; one remembers that each of
these dead-faced houses, often each separate blind window,
represents a 'home,' and the associations of the word whisper
blank despair.

Wilton Square is on the north side of the foss, on the edge
of the quieter district, and in one of its houses dwelt at the
time of which I write the family on whose behalf Fate was at
work in a valley of mid-England.   Joseph Mutimer, nephew
to the old man who had just died at Wanley Manor, had himself been at rest for some five years; his widow and three
children still lived together in the home they had long occupied.
Joseph came of a family of mechanics; his existence was that
of the harmless necessary artisan.   He earned a living by dint
of incessant labour, brought up his family in an orderly way,
and departed with a certain sense of satisfaction at having fulfilled obvious duties—the only result of life for which he could
reasonably look.   With his children we shall have to make
closer acquaintance; but before doing so, in order to understand
their position and follow with intelligence their several stories.
it will be necessary to enter a little upon the subject of ancestry.

Joseph Mutimer's father, Henry by name, was a somewhat
remarkable personage.   He grew to manhood in the first decade
of our century, and wrought as a craftsman in a Midland town.
He had a brother, Richard, some ten years his junior, and the

two were of such different types of character, each so pronounced in his kind, that, after vain attempts to get along together, they parted for good, heedless of each other henceforth, pursuing their sundered destinies. Henry was by nature a political enthusiast, of insufficient ballast, careless of the main chance, of hot and ready tongue ; the Chartist movement gave him opportunities of action which he used to the utmost, and he became a member of the so-called National Convention, established in Birmingham in 1839. Already he had achieved prominence by being imprisoned as the leader of a torch-light procession, and this taste of martyrdom naturally sharpened his zeal. He had married young, but only visited his family from time to time. His wife for the most part earned her own living, and ultimately betook herself to London with her son Joseph, the single survivor of seven children. Henry pursued his career of popular agitation, supporting himself in miscellaneous ways, writing his wife an affectionate letter once in six months, and making himself widely known as an uncompromising Radical of formidable powers. Newspapers of that time mention his name frequently ; he was always in hot water, and once or twice narrowly escaped transportation. In 1842 he took active part in the riots of the Midland Counties, and at length was unfortunate enough to get his head broken. He died in hospital before any relative could reach him.

Richard Mutimer regarded with detestation the principles to which Henry had sacrificed his life. From childhood he was staid, earnest, and iron-willed ; to whatsoever he put his hand, he did it thoroughly, and it was his pride to receive aid from no man. Intensely practical, he early discerned the truth that a man's first object must be to secure himself a competency, seeing that to one who lacks money the world is but a great debtors' prison. To make money, therefore, was his aim, and anything that interfered with the interests of commerce and industry from the capitalist's point of view he deemed unmitigated evil. When his brother Henry was leading processions and preaching the People's Charter, Richard enrolled himself as a special constable, cursing the tumults which drew him from business, but determined, if he got the opportunity, to strike a good hard blow in defence of law and order. Already he was well on the way to possess a solid stake in the country, and the native conservatism of his temperament grew stronger as circumstances bent themselves to his will ; a proletarian conquering wealth and influence naturally prizes these things in proportion

to the effort their acquisition has cost him. When he heard of
his brother's death, he could in conscience say nothing more
than 'Serve him right!' For all that, he paid the funeral
expenses of the Chartist—angrily declining an offer from
Henry's co-zealots, who would have buried the martyr at their
common charges—and proceeded to inquire after the widow and
son. Joseph Mutimer, already one- or two-and-twenty, was in
no need of help; he and his mother, naturally prejudiced against
the thriving uncle, declared themselves satisfied with their lot,
and desired no further connection with a relative who was
practically a stranger to them.

So Richard went on his way and heaped up riches. When
already middle-aged he took to himself a wife, his choice being
marked with characteristic prudence. The woman he wedded
was turned thirty, had no money, and few personal charms, but
was a lady. Richard was fully able to appreciate education and
refinement; to judge from the course of his later life, one would
have said that he had sought money only as a means, the end
he really aimed at being the satisfaction of instincts which could
only have full play in a higher social sphere. No doubt the
truth was that success sweetened his character, and developed,
as is so often the case, those possibilities of his better nature
which a fruitless struggle would have kept in the germ or altogether crushed. His excellent wife influenced him profoundly;
at her death the work was continued by the daughter she left
him. The defects of his early education could not of course be
repaired, but it is never too late for a man to go to school to
the virtues which civilise. Remaining the sturdiest of Conservatives, he bowed in sincere humility to those very claims which
the Radical most angrily disallows: birth, hereditary station,
recognised gentility—these things made the strongest demand
upon his reverence. Such an attitude was a testimony to his
own capacity for culture, since he knew not the meaning of
vulgar adulation, and did in truth perceive the beauty of those
qualities to which the uneducated Iconoclast is wholly blind.
It was a joyous day for him when he saw his daughter the wife
of Godfrey Eldon. The loss which so soon followed was corre-
spondingly hard to bear, and but for Mrs. Eldon's gentle sympathy
he would scarcely have survived the blow. We know already
how his character had impressed that lady; such respect was
not lightly to be won, and he came to regard it as the most
precious thing that life had left him.

But the man was not perfect, and his latest practical undertaking curiously enough illustrated the failing which he seemed most completely to have outgrown. It was of course a deplorable error to think of mining in the beautiful valley which had once been the Eldons' estate. Richard Mutimer could not perceive that. He was a very old man, and possibly the instincts of his youth revived as his mind grew feebler; he imagined it the greatest kindness to Mrs. Eldon and her son to 'ncrease as much as possible the value of the property he would leave at his death. They, of course, could not even hint to him the pain with which they viewed so barbarous a scheme; he did not as much as suspect a possible objection. Intensely happy in his discovery and the activity to which it led, he would have gone to his grave rich in all manner of content but for that fatal news which reached him from London, where Hubert Eldon was supposed to be engaged in sober study in an interval of University work. Doubtless it was this disappointment that caused his sudden death, and so brought about a state of things which, could he have foreseen it, would have occasioned him the bitterest grief.

He had never lost sight of his relatives in London, and had made for them such modest provision as suited his view of the fitness of things. To leave wealth to young men of the working class would have seemed to him the most inexcusable of follies; if such were to rise at all, it must be by their own efforts and in consequence of their native merits; otherwise, let them toil on and support themselves honestly. From secret sources he received information of the capabilities and prospects of Joseph Mutimer's children, and the items of his will were regulated accordingly.

So we return to the family in Wilton Square. Let us, before proceeding with the story, enumerate the younger Mutimers. The first-born, now aged five-and-twenty, had his great-uncle's name; Joseph Mutimer, married, and no better off in worldly possessions than when he had only himself to support, came to regret the coldness with which he had received the advances of his uncle the capitalist, and christened his son Richard, with half a hope that some day the name might stand the boy in stead. Richard was a mechanical engineer, employed in certain ironworks where hydraulic machinery was made. The second child was a girl, upon whom had been bestowed the names Alice Maud, after one of the Queen's daughters; on which account, and partly with reference to certain personal characteristics, she was often called 'the Princess.' Her age was nineteen, and she had now for two years been employed in the show-rooms of a City warehouse. Last comes Henry, a lad of seventeen; he had been suffered to aim at higher things than the rest of the family. In the industrial code of precedence the rank of clerk is a step above that of mechanic, and Henry—known to relatives and friends as 'Arry—occupied the proud position of clerk in a drain-pipe manufactory.

CHAPTER IV.

AT ten o'clock on the evening of Easter Sunday, Mrs. Mutimer was busy preparing supper. She had laid the table for six, had placed at one end of it a large joint of cold meat, at the other a vast rice-pudding, already diminished by attack, and she was now slicing a conglomerate mass of cold potatoes and cabbage prior to heating it in the frying-pan, which hissed with melted dripping just on the edge of the fire. The kitchen was small, and everywhere reflected from some bright surface either the glow of the open grate or the yellow lustre of the gas-jet; red curtains drawn across the window added warmth and homely comfort to the room. It was not the kitchen of pinched or slovenly working folk; the air had a scent of cleanliness, of freshly scrubbed boards and polished metal, and the furniture was super-abundant. On the capacious dresser stood or hung utensils innumerable; cupboards and chairs had a struggle for wall space; every smallest object was in the place assigned to it by use and wont.

The housewife was an active woman of something less than sixty; stout, fresh-featured, with a small keen eye, a firm mouth, and the look of one who, conscious of responsibilities, yet feels equal to them; on the whole a kindly and contented face, if lacking the suggestiveness which comes of thought. At present she seemed on the verge of impatience; it was supper time, but her children lingered.

'There they are, and there they must wait, I s'pose,' she murmured to herself as she finished slicing the vegetables and went to remove the pan a little from the fire.

A knock at the house door called her upstairs. She came down again, followed by a young girl of pleasant countenance, though pale and anxious-looking. The visitor's dress was very plain, and indicated poverty; she wore a long black jacket, untrimmed, a boa of cheap fur, tied at the throat with black ribbon, a hat of grey felt, black cotton gloves.

'No one here?' she asked, seeing the empty kitchen.

'Goodness knows where they all are. I s'pose Dick's at his meeting; but Alice and 'Arry had ought to be back by now. Sit you down to the table, and I'll put on the vegetables; there's no call to wait for them. Only I ain't got the beer.'

'Oh, but I didn't mean to come for supper,' said the girl, whose name was Emma Vine. 'I only ran in to tell you poor Jane's down again with rheumatic fever.'

Mrs. Mutimer was holding the frying-pan over the fire, turning the contents over and over with a knife.

'You don't mean that!' she exclaimed, looking over her shoulder. 'Why, it's the fifth time, ain't it?'

'It is indeed, and worse to get through every time. We didn't expect she'd ever be able to walk again last autumn.'

'Dear, dear! what a thing them rheumatics is, to be sure! And you've heard about Dick, haven't you?'

'Heard what?'

'Oh, I thought maybe it had got to you. He's lost his work, that's all.'

'Lost his work?' the girl repeated, with dismay. 'Why?'

'Why? What else had he to expect? 'Tain't likely they'll keep a man as goes about making all his mates discontented and calling his employers names at every street corner. I've been looking for it every week. Yesterday one of the guvnors calls him up and tells him—just in a few civil words—as perhaps it'ud be better for all parties if he'd find a place where he was more satisfied. "Well an' good," says Dick—you know his way—and there he is.'

The girl had seated herself, and listened to this story with downcast eyes. Courage seemed to fail her; she drew a long, quiet sigh. Her face was of the kind that expresses much sweetness in irregular features. Her look was very honest and gentle, with pathetic meanings for whoso had the eye to catch them; a peculiar mobility of the lips somehow made one think that she had often to exert herself to keep down tears. She spoke in a subdued voice, always briefly, and with a certain natural refinement in the use of uncultured language. When Mrs. Mutimer ceased, Emma kept silence, and smoothed the front of her jacket with an unconscious movement of the hand.

Mrs. Mutimer glanced at her and showed commiseration.

'Well, well, don't you worrit about it, Emma,' she said; 'you've quite enough on your hands. Dick don't care—not he; he couldn't look more high-flyin' if someone had left him a fortune. He says it's the best thing as could happen. Nay, I can't explain; he'll tell you plenty soon as he gets in. Cut yourself some meat, child, do, and don't wait for me to help you. See, I'll turn you out some potatoes; you don't care for the greens, I know.'

The fry had hissed vigorously whilst this conversation went on; the results were brown and unctuous.

'Now, if it ain't too bad!' cried the old woman, losing self-control. 'That 'Arry gets later every Sunday, and he knows very well as I have to wait for the beer till he comes.'

'I'll fetch it,' said Emma, rising.

'You indeed! I'd like to see Dick if he caught me a-sending you to the public-house.'

'He won't mind it for once.'

'You get on with your supper, do. It's only my fidgetiness; I can do very well a bit longer. And Alice, where's she off to, I wonder? What it is to have a girl that age! I wish they was all like you, Emma. Get on with your supper, I tell you, or you'll make me angry. Now, it ain't no use taking it to 'eart in that way. I see what you're worritin' over. Dick ain't the man to be out o' work long.'

'But won't it be the same at his next place?' Emma inquired. She was trying to eat, but it was a sad pretence.

'Nay, there's no telling. It's no good my talkin' to him. Why don't you see what you can do, Emma? 'Tain't as if he'd no one but his own self to think about. Don't you think you could make him see that? If anyone has a right to speak, it's you. Tell him as he'd ought to have a bit more thought. It's wait, wait, wait, and likely to be if things go on like this. Speak up and tell him as——'

'Oh, I couldn't do that!' murmured Emma. 'Dick knows best.'

She stopped to listen; there was a noise above as of people entering the house.

'Here they come at last,' said Mrs. Mutimer. 'Hear him laughin'? Now, don't you be so ready to laugh with him. Let him see as it ain't such good fun to everybody.'

Heavy feet tramped down the stone stairs, amid a sound of loud laughter and excited talk. The next moment the kitchen door was thrown open, and two young men appeared. The one in advance was Richard Mutimer; behind him came a friend of the family, Daniel Dabbs.

'Well, what do you think of this?' Richard exclaimed as he shook Emma's hands rather carelessly. 'Mother been putting you out of spirits, I suppose? Why, it's grand; the best thing that could have happened! What a meeting we've had to-night! What do *you* say, Dan?'

Richard represented—too favourably to make him anything but an exception—the best qualities his class can show. He was the English artisan as we find him on rare occasions, the issue of a good strain which has managed to procure a sufficiency of food for two or three generations. His physique was admirable; little short of six feet in stature, he had shapely shoulders, an erect well-formed head, clean strong limbs, and a bearing which in natural ease and dignity matched that of the picked men of the upper class—those fine creatures whose career, from public school to regimental quarters, is one exclusive course of bodily training. But the comparison, on the whole, was to Richard's advantage. By no possibility could he have assumed that aristocratic vacuity of visage which comes of carefully induced cerebral atrophy. The air of the workshop suffered little colour to dwell upon his cheeks; but to features of so pronounced and intelligent a type this pallor added a distinction. He had dark brown hair, thick and long, and a cropped beard of hue somewhat lighter. His eyes were his mother's—keen and direct; but they had small variety of expression; you could not imagine them softening to tenderness, or even to thoughtful dreaming. Terribly wide awake, they seemed to be always looking for the weak points of whatever they regarded, and their brightness was not seldom suggestive of malice. His voice was strong and clear; it would ring out well in public places, which is equivalent to saying that it hardly invited too intimate conference. You will take for granted that Richard displayed, alike in attitude and tone, a distinct consciousness of his points of superiority to the men among whom he lived; probably he more than suspected that he could have held his own in spheres to which there seemed small chance of his being summoned.

Just now he showed at once the best and the weakest of his points. Coming in a state of exaltation from a meeting of which he had been the eloquent hero, such light as was within him flashed from his face freely; all the capacity and the vigour which impelled him to strain against the strait bonds of his lot

D

set his body quivering and made music of his utterance. At
the same time, his free movements passed easily into swagger,
and as he talked on, the false notes were not few. A working
man gifted with brains and comeliness must, be sure of it, pay
penalties for his prominence.

Quite another man was Daniel Dabbs: in him you saw
the proletarian pure and simple. He was thick-set, square-
shouldered, rolling in gait; he walked with head bent forward
and eyes glancing uneasily, as if from lack of self-confidence.
His wiry black hair shone with grease, and no accuracy of
razor-play would make his chin white. A man of immense
strength, but bull-necked and altogether ungainly—his heavy
fist, with its black veins and terrific knuckles, suggested primitive methods of settling dispute; the stumpy fingers, engrimed
hopelessly, and the filthy broken nails, showed how he wrought
for a living. His face, if you examined it without prejudice,
was not ill to look upon; there was much good humour about
the mouth, and the eyes, shrewd enough, could glimmer a
kindly light. His laughter was roof-shaking—always a good
sign in a man.

'And what have *you* got to say of these fine doings, Mr.
Dabbs?' Mrs. Mutimer asked him.

'Why, it's like this 'ere, Mrs. Mutimer,' Daniel began,
having seated himself, with hands on widely-parted knees.
'As far as the theory goes, I'm all for Dick; any man must be
as knows his two times two. But about the Longwoods; well,
I tell Dick they've a perfect right to get rid of him, finding
him a dangerous enemy, you see. It was all fair and above
board. Young Stephen Longwood ups an' says—leastways not
in these words, but them as means the same—says he, "Look
'ere, Mutimer," he says, " we've no fault to find with you as a
workman, but from what we hear of you, it seems you don't
care much for us as employers. Hadn't you better find a shop
as is run on Socialist principles?" That's all about it, you see;
it's a case of incompatible temperaments; there's no ill-feelin',
not as between man and man. And that's what I say, too.'

'Now, Dick,' said Mrs. Mutimer, 'before you begin your
sermon, who's a-goin' to fetch my beer?'

'Right, Mrs. Mutimer!' cried Daniel, slapping his leg.
'That's what I call coming from theory to practice. Beer
squares all—leastways for the time being—only for the time
being, Dick. Where's the jug? Better give me two jugs;
we've had a thirsty night of it.'

'We'll make capital of this!' said Richard, walking about the room in Daniel's absence. 'The great point gained is, they've shown they're afraid of me. We'll write it up in the paper next week, see if we don't! It'll do us a sight of good.'

'And where's your weekly wages to come from?' inquired his mother.

'Oh, I'll look after that. I only wish they'd refuse me all round; the more of that kind of thing the better for us. I'm not afraid but I can earn my living.'

Through all this Emma Vine had sat with her thoughtful eyes constantly turned on Richard. It was plain how pride struggled with anxiety in her mind. When Richard had kept silence for a moment, she ventured to speak, having tried in vain to meet his look.

'Jane's ill again, Richard,' she said.

Mutimer had to summon his thoughts from a great distance; his endeavour to look sympathetic was not very successful.

'Not the fever again?'

'Yes, it is,' she replied sadly.

'Going to work in the wet, I suppose?'

He shrugged his shoulders; in his present mood the fact was not so much personally interesting to him as in the light of another case against capitalism. Emma's sister had to go a long way to her daily employment, and could not afford to ride; the fifth attack of rheumatic fever was the price she paid for being permitted to earn ten shillings a week.

Daniel returned with both jugs foaming, his face on a broad grin of anticipation. There was a general move to the table. Richard began to carve roast beef like a freeman, not by any means like the serf he had repeatedly declared himself in the course of the evening's oratory.

'Her Royal 'Ighness out?' asked Daniel, with constraint not solely due to the fact that his mouth was full.

'She's round at Mrs. Took's, I should think,' was Mrs. Mutimer's reply. 'Staying supper, per'aps.'

Richard, after five minutes of surprising trencher-work recommenced conversation. The proceedings of the evening at the hall, which was the centre for Socialist gatherings in this neighbourhood, were discussed by him and Daniel with much liveliness. Dan was disposed to take the meeting on its festive and humorous side; for him, economic agitation was a mode of passing a few hours amid congenial uproar. Whenever stamping and shouting were called for, Daniel was your man. Abuse of employers, it was true, gave a zest to the occasion, and to applaud the martyrdom of others was as cheery an occupation as could be asked; Daniel had no idea of sacrificing his own weekly wages, and therein resembled most of those who had been loud in uncompromising rhetoric. Richard, on the other hand, was unmistakably zealous. His sense of humour was not strong, and in any case he would have upheld the serious dignity of his own position. One saw from his way of speaking, that he believed himself about to become a popular hero; already in imagination he stood forth on platforms before vast assemblies, and heard his own voice denouncing capitalism with force which nothing could resist. The first taste of applause had given extraordinary impulse to his convictions, and the personal ambition with which they were interwoven. His grandfather's blood was hot in him to-night. Henry Mutimer, dying in hospital of his broken skull, would have found euthanasia, could he in vision have seen this worthy descendant entering upon a career in comparison with which his own was unimportant.

The high-pitched voices and the clatter of knives and forks allowed a new-comer to enter the kitchen without being immediately observed. It was a tall girl of interesting and vivacious appearance; she wore a dress of tartan, a very small hat trimmed also with tartan and with a red feather, a tippet of brown fur about her shoulders, and a muff of the same material on one of her hands. Her figure was admirable; from the crest of her gracefully poised head to the tip of her well-chosen boot she was, in line and structure, the type of mature woman. Her face, if it did not indicate a mind to match her frame, was at the least sweet-featured and provoking; characterless somewhat, but void of danger-signals; doubtless too good to be merely played with; in any case, very capable of sending a ray, in one moment or another, to the shadowy dreaming-place of graver thoughts. Alice Maud Mutimer was nineteen. For two years she had been thus tall, but the grace of her proportions had only of late fully determined itself. Her work in the City warehouse was unexacting; she had even a faint impress of rose-petal on each cheek, and her eye was excellently clear. Her lips, unfortunately never quite closed, betrayed faultless teeth. Her likeness to Richard was noteworthy; beyond question she understood the charm of her presence, and one felt that the consciousness might, in her case, constitute rather a safeguard than otherwise.

She stood with one hand on the door, surveying the table. When the direction of Mrs. Mutimer's eyes at length caused Richard and Daniel to turn their heads, Alice nodded to each.

'What noisy people! I heard you out in the square.'

She was moving past the table, but Daniel, suddenly backing his chair, intercepted her. The girl gave him her hand, and, by way of being jocose, he squeezed it so vehemently that she uttered a shrill 'Oh!'

'Leave go, Mr. Dabbs! Leave go, I tell you! How dare you? I'll hit you as hard as I can!'

Daniel laughed obstreperously.

'Do! do!' he cried. 'What a mighty blow that 'ud be! Only the left hand, though. I shall get over it.'

She wrenched herself away, gave Daniel a smart slap on the back, and ran round to the other side of the table, where she kissed Emma affectionately.

'How thirsty I am!' she exclaimed. 'You haven't drunk all the beer, I hope.'

'I'm not so sure of that,' Dan replied. 'Why, there ain't more than 'arf a pint; that's not much use for a Royal 'Ighness.'

She poured it into a glass. Alice reached across the table, raised the glass to her lips, and—emptied it. Then she threw off hat, tippet, and gloves, and seated herself. But in a moment she was up and at the cupboard.

'Now, mother, you don't—you *don't* say as there's not a pickle!'

Her tone was deeply reproachful.

'Why, there now,' replied her mother, laughing; 'I knew what it 'ud be! I meant to a' got them last night. You'll have to make shift for once.'

The Princess took her seat with an air of much dejection. Her pretty lips grew mutinous; she pushed her plate away.

'No supper for me! The idea of cold meat without a pickle.'

'What's the time?' cried Daniel. 'Not closing time yet. I can get a pickle at the "Duke's Arms." Give me a glass, Mrs. Mutimer.'

Alice looked up slily, half smiling, half doubtful.

'You may go,' she said. 'I like to see strong men make themselves useful.'

Dan rose, and was off at once. He returned with the tumbler full of pickled walnuts. Alice emptied half a dozen into

her plate, and put one of them whole into her mouth. She
would not have been a girl of her class if she had not relished
this pungent dainty. Fish of any kind, green vegetables, eggs
and bacon, with all these a drench of vinegar was indispensable to her. And she proceeded to eat a supper scarcely less
substantial than that which had appeased her brother's appetite. Start not, dear reader; the Princess is only a subordinate heroine, and happens, moreover, to be a living creature.

'Won't you take a walnut, Miss Vine?' Daniel asked,
pushing the tumbler to the quiet girl, who had scarcely spoken
through the meal.

She declined the offered dainty, and at the same time rose
from the table, saying aside to Mrs. Mutimer that she must be
going.

'Yes, I suppose you must,' was the reply. 'Shall you have
to sit up with Jane?'

'Not all night, I don't expect.'

Richard likewise left his place, and, when she offered to bid
him good-night, said that he would walk a little way with her.
In the passage above, which was gas-lighted, he found his hat
on a nail, and the two left the house together.

'Don't you really mind?' Emma asked, looking up into his
face as they took their way out of the square.

'Not I! I can get a job at Baldwin's any day. But I
dare say I shan't want one long.'

'Not want work?'

He laughed.

'Work? Oh, plenty of work; but perhaps not the same
kind. We want men who can give their whole time to the
struggle—to go about lecturing and the like. Of course, it isn't
everybody can do it.'

The remark indicated his belief that he knew one man not
incapable of leading functions.

'And would they pay you?' Emma inquired, simply.

'Expenses of that kind are inevitable,' he replied.

Issuing into the New North Road, where there were still
many people hastening one way and the other, they turned to
the left, crossed the canal—black and silent—and were soon
among narrow streets. Every corner brought a whiff of some
rank odour, which stole from closed shops and warehouses, and
hung heavily on the still air. The public-houses had just extinguished their lights, and in the neighbourhood of each was
a cluster of lingering men and women, merry or disputatious.

Mid-Easter was inviting repose and festivity; to-morrow would see culmination of riot, and after that it would only depend upon pecuniary resources how long the muddled interval between holiday and renewed labour should drag itself out.

The end of their walk was the entrance to a narrow passage, which, at a few yards' distance, widened itself and became a street of four-storeyed houses. At present this could not be discerned; the passage was a mere opening into massive darkness. Richard had just been making inquiries about Emma's sister.

'Yo-'ve had the doctor?'

'Yes, we're obliged; she does so dread going to the hospital again. Each time she's longer in getting well.'

Richard's hand was in his pocket; he drew it out and pressed something against the girl's palm.

'Oh, how can I?' she said, dropping her eyes. 'No—don't —I'm ashamed.'

'That's all right,' he urged, not unkindly. 'You'll have to get her what the doctor orders, and it isn't likely you and Kate can afford it.'

'You're always so kind, Richard. But I am—I am ashamed!'

'I say, Emma, why don't you call me Dick? I've meant to ask you that many a time.'

She turned her face away, moving as if abashed.

'I don't know. It sounds—perhaps I want to make a difference from what the others call you.'

He laughed with a sound of satisfaction.

'Well, you mustn't stand here; it's a cold night. Try and come Tuesday or Wednesday.'

'Yes, I will.'

'Good night!' he said, and, as he held her hand, bent to the lips which were ready.

Emma walked along the passage, and for some distance up the middle of the street. Then she stopped and looked up at one of the black houses. There were lights, more or less curtain-dimmed, in nearly all the windows. Emma regarded a faint gleam in the topmost storey. To that she ascended.

Mutimer walked homewards at a quick step, whistling to himself. A latch-key gave him admission. As he went down the kitchen stairs, he heard his mother's voice raised in anger, and on opening the door he found that Daniel had departed, and that the supper table was already cleared. Alice, her feet on the fender and her dress raised a little, was engaged in warming herself before going to bed. The object of Mrs. Mutimer's chastisement was the youngest member of the family, known as 'Arry; even Richard, who had learnt to be somewhat careful in his pronunciation, could not bestow the aspirate upon his brother's name. Henry, aged seventeen, promised to do credit to the Mutimers in physical completeness; already he was nearly as tall as his eldest brother; and, even in his lankness, showed the beginnings of well-proportioned vigour. But the shape of his head, which was covered with hair of the lightest hue, did not encourage hope of mental or moral qualities. It was not quite fair to judge his face as seen at present; the vacant grin of half timid, half insolent, resentment made him considerably more simian of visage than was the case under ordinary circumstances. But the features were unpleasant to look upon; it was Richard's face, distorted and enfeebled with impress of sensual instincts.

'As long as you live in this house, it shan't go on,' his mother was saying. 'Sunday or Monday, it's no matter; you'll be home before eleven o'clock, and you'll come home sober. You're no better than a pig!'

'Arry was seated in a far corner of the room, where he had dropped his body on entering. His attire was such as the cheap tailors turn out in imitation of extreme fashions: trousers closely moulded upon the leg, a buff waistcoat, a short coat with pockets everywhere. A very high collar kept his head up against his will; his necktie was crimson, and passed through a brass ring; he wore a silver watch-chain, or what seemed to be such. One hand was gloved, and a cane lay across his knees. His attitude was one of relaxed muscles, his legs very far apart, his body not quite straight.

' What d' you call sober, I'd like to know?' he replied, with looseness of utterance. 'I'm as sober 's anybody in this room. If a chap can't go out with 's friends 't Easter an' all—— ?'

' Easter, indeed! It's getting to be a regular thing, Saturday and Sunday. Get up and go to bed! I'll have my say out with you in the morning, young man.'

'Go to bed!' repeated the lad with scorn. ' Tell you I ain't had no supper.'

Richard had walked to the neighbourhood of the fireplace, and was regarding his brother with anger and contempt. At this point of the dialogue he interfered.

'And you won't have any, either, that I'll see to! What's

more, you'll do as your mother bids you, or I'll know the reason
why. Go upstairs at once!'

It was not a command to be disregarded. 'Arry rose, but
half-defiantly.

'What have you to do with it? You're not my master.'

'Do you hear what I say?' Richard observed, yet more
autocratically. 'Take yourself off, and at once!'

The lad growled, hesitated, but approached the door. His
motion was slinking; he could not face Richard's eye. They
heard him stumble up the stairs.

CHAPTER V.

On ordinary days Richard of necessity rose early; a holiday
did not lead him to break the rule, for free hours were precious. He had his body well under control; six hours of sleep
he found sufficient to keep him in health, and temptations to
personal ease, in whatever form, he resisted as a matter of
principle.

Easter Monday found him down-stairs at half past six.
His mother would to-day allow herself another hour. 'Arry
would be down just in time for breakfast, not daring to be late.
The Princess might be looked for —— some time in the course
of the morning; she was licensed.

Richard, for purposes of study, used the front parlour. In
drawing up the blind, he disclosed a room precisely resembling
in essential features hundreds of front parlours in that neighbourhood, or, indeed, in any working-class district of London.
Everything was clean; most things were bright-hued or
glistening of surface. There was the gilt-framed mirror over
the mantelpiece, with a yellow clock—which did not go—and
glass ornaments in front. There was a small round table before
the window, supporting wax fruit under a glass case. There
was a hearthrug with a dazzling pattern of imaginary flowers.
On the blue cloth of the middle table were four showily-bound
volumes, arranged symmetrically. On the head of the sofa lay
a covering worked of blue and yellow Berlin wools. Two arm-
chairs were draped with long white antimacassars, ready to
slip off at a touch. As in the kitchen, there was a smell of
cleanliness—of furniture polish, hearthstone, and black-lead.

I should mention the ornaments of the walls. The pictures were: a striking landscape of the Swiss type, an engraved portrait of Garibaldi, an unframed view of a certain insurance office, a British baby on a large scale from the Christmas number of an illustrated paper.

The one singular feature of the room was a small, glass-doored bookcase, full of volumes. They were all of Richard's purchasing; to survey them was to understand the man, at all events on his intellectual side. Without exception they belonged to that order of literature which, if studied exclusively and for its own sake,—as here it was,—brands a man indelibly, declaring at once the incompleteness of his education and the deficiency of his instincts. Social, political, religious,—under these three heads the volumes classed themselves, and each class was represented by productions of the 'extreme' school. The books which a bright youth of fair opportunities reads as a matter of course, rejoices in for a year or two, then throws aside for ever, were here treasured to be the guides of a life-time. Certain writers of the last century, long ago become only historically interesting, were for Richard an armoury whence he girded himself for the battles of the day; cheap re-prints or translations of Malthus, of Robert Owen, of Volney's 'Ruins,' of Thomas Paine, of sundry works of Voltaire, ranked upon his shelves. Moreover, there was a large collection of pamphlets, titled wonderfully and of yet more remarkable contents, the authoritative utterances of contemporary gentlemen —and ladies—who made it the end of their existence to prove: that there cannot by any possibility be such a person as Satan; that the story of creation contained in the Book of Genesis is on no account to be received; that the begetting of children is a most deplorable oversight; that to eat flesh is wholly unworthy of a civilised being; that if every man and woman performed their quota of the world's labour it would be necessary to work for one hour and thirty-seven minutes daily, no jot longer, and that the author, in each case, is the one person capable of restoring dignity to a down-trodden race and happiness to a blasted universe. Alas, alas! On this food had Richard Mutimer pastured his soul since he grew to manhood, on this and this only. English literature was to him a sealed volume; poetry he scarcely knew by name; of history he was worse than ignorant, having looked at this period and that through distorting media, and congratulating himself on his clear vision because he saw men as trees walking; the bent of his mind would have led him to natural science, but opportunities of instruction were lacking, and the chosen directors of his prejudice taught him to regard every fact, every discovery, as *for* or *against* something.

A library of pathetic significance, the individual alone considered. Viewed as representative, not without alarming suggestiveness to those who can any longer trouble themselves about the world's future. One dreams of the age when free thought—in the popular sense—will have become universal, when art shall have lost its meaning, worship its holiness, when the Bible will only exist in 'comic' editions, and Shakespeare be downcried by 'most sweet voices' as a mountebank of reactionary tendencies.

Richard was to lecture on the ensuing Sunday at one of the branch meeting-places of his society; he engaged himself this morning in collecting certain data of a statistical kind. He was still at his work when the sound of the postman's knock began to be heard in the square, coming from house to house, drawing nearer at each repetition. Richard paid no heed to it; he expected no letter. Yet it seemed there was one for some member of the family; the letter-carrier's regular tread ascended the five steps to the door, and then two small thunderclaps echoed through the house. There was no letter-box; Richard went to answer the knock. An envelope addressed to himself in a small, formal hand.

His thoughts still busy with other things, he opened the letter mechanically as he re-entered the room. He had never in his life been calmer; the early hour of study had kept his mind pleasantly active whilst his breakfast appetite sharpened itself. Never was man less prepared to receive startling intelligence.

He read, then raised his eyes and let them stray from the papers on the table to the wax-fruit before the window, thence to the young leafage of the trees around the Baptist Chapel. He was like a man whose face had been overflashed by lightning. He read again, then, holding the letter behind him, closed his right hand upon his beard with thoughtful tension. He read a third time, then returned the letter to its envelope, put it in his pocket, and sat down again to his book.

He was summoned to breakfast in ten minutes. His mother was alone in the kitchen; she gave him his bloater and his cup of coffee, and he cut himself a solid slice of bread and butter.

'Was the letter for you?' she asked.

He replied with a nod, and fell patiently to work on the dissection of his bony delicacy. In five minutes Henry approached the table with a furtive glance at his elder brother. But Richard had no remark to make. The meal proceeded in silence.

When Richard had finished, he rose and said to his mother—

'Have you that railway-guide I brought home a week ago?'

'I believe I have somewhere. Just look in the cupboard.'

The guide was found. Richard consulted it for a few moments.

'I have to go out of London,' he then observed. 'It's just possible I shan't get back to-night.'

A little talk followed about the arrangements of the day, and whether anyone was likely to be at home for dinner. Richard did not show much interest in the matter; he went upstairs whistling, and changed the clothing he wore for his best suit. In a quarter of an hour he had left the house.

He did not return till the evening of the following day. It was presumed that he had gone 'after a job.'

When he reached home his mother and Alice were at tea. He walked to the kitchen fireplace, turned his back to it, and gazed with a peculiar expression at the two who sat at table.

'Dick's got work,' observed Alice, after a glance at him. 'I can see that in his face.'

'Have you, Dick?' asked Mrs. Mutimer.

'I have. Work likely to last.'

'So we'll hope,' commented his mother. 'Where is it?'

'A good way out of London. Pour me a cup, mother. Where's 'Arry?'

'Gone out, as usual.'

'And why are you having tea with your hat on, Princess?'

'Because I'm in a hurry, if you must know everything.'

Richard did not seek further information. He drank his tea standing. In five minutes Alice had bustled away for an evening with friends. Mrs. Mutimer cleared the table without speaking.

'Now get your sewing, mother, and sit down,' began Richard. 'I want to have a talk with you.'

The mother cast a rather suspicious glance. There was an impressiveness in the young man's look and tone which disposed her to obey without remark.

'How long is it,' Richard asked, when attention waited upon him, 'since you heard anything of father's uncle, my namesake?'

Mrs. Mutimer's face exhibited the dawning of intelligence, an unwrinkling here and there, a slight rounding of the lips.

'Why, what of him?' she asked in an undertone, leaving a needle unthreaded.

'The old man's just dead.'

Agitation seized the listener, agitation of a kind most unusual in her. Her hands trembled, her eyes grew wide.

'You haven't heard anything of him lately?' pursued Richard.

'Heard? Not I. No more did your father ever since two years afore we was married. I'd always thought he was dead long ago. What of him, Dick?'

'From what I'm told I thought you'd perhaps been keeping things to yourself. 'Twouldn't have been unlike you, mother. He knew all about us, so the lawyer tells me.'

'The lawyer?'

'Well, I'd better out with it. He's died without a will. His real property—that means his houses and land—belongs to me; his personal property—that's his money—'ll have to be divided between me, and Alice, and 'Arry. You're out of the sharing, mother.'

He said it jokingly, but Mrs. Mutimer did not join in his laugh. Her palms were closely pressed together; still trembling, she gazed straight before her, with a far-off look.

'His houses—his land?' she murmured, as if she had not quite heard. 'What did he want with more than one house?'

The absurd question was all that could find utterance. She seemed to be reflecting on that point.

'Would you like to hear what it all comes to?' Richard resumed. His voice was unnatural, forcibly suppressed, quivering at pauses. His eyes gleamed, and there was a centre of warm colour on each of his cheeks. He had taken a note-book from his pocket, and the leaves rustled under his tremulous fingers.

'The lawyer, a man called Yottle, just gave me an idea of the different investments and so on. The real property consists of a couple of houses in Belwick, both let, and an estate at a place called Wanley. The old man had begun mining there; there's iron. I've got my ideas about that. I didn't go into the house; people are there still. Now the income.'

He read his notes : So much in railways, so much averaged yearly from iron-works in Belwick, so much in foreign securities, so much disposable at home. Total——'

'Stop, Dick, stop !' uttered his mother, under her breath. 'Them figures frighten me; I don't know what they mean. It's a mistake; they're leading you astray. Now, mind what I say—there's a mistake ! No man with all that money 'ud die without a will. You won't get me to believe it, Dick.'

Richard laughed excitedly. 'Believe it or not, mother; I've got my ears and eyes, I hope. And there's a particular reason why he left no will. There was one, but something—I don't know what—happened just before his death, and he was going to make a new one. The will was burnt. He died in church on a Sunday morning; if he'd lived another day, he'd have made a new will. It's no more a mistake than the Baptist Chapel is in the square !' A comparison which hardly conveyed all Richard's meaning; but he was speaking in agitation, more and more quickly, at last almost angrily.

Mrs. Mutimer raised her hand. 'Be quiet a bit, Dick. It's took me too sudden. I feel queer like.'

There was silence. The mother rose as if with difficulty, and drew water in a tea-cup from the filter. When she resumed her place, her hands prepared to resume sewing. She looked up, solemnly, sternly.

'Dick, it's bad, bad news ! I'm an old woman, and I must say what I think. It upsets me; it frightens me. I thought he might a' left you a hundred pounds.'

'Mother, don't talk about it till you've had time to think,' said Richard, stubbornly. 'If this is bad news, what the deuce would you call good ? Just because I've been born and bred a mechanic, does that say I've got no common sense or self-respect ? Are you afraid I shall go and drink myself to death ? You talk like the people who make it their business to sneer at us—the improvidence of the working classes, and such d——d slander. It's good news for me, and it'll be good news for many another man. Wait and see.'

The mother became silent, keeping her lips tight, and struggling to regain her calmness. She was not convinced, but in argument with her eldest son she always gave way, affection and the pride she had in him aiding her instincts of discretion. In practice she still maintained something of maternal authority, often gaining her point by merely seeming offended. To the two who had not yet reached the year of emancipation she allowed, in essentials, no appeal from her decision. Between her and Richard there had been many a sharp conflict in former days, invariably ending with the lad's submission; the respect which his mother exacted he in truth felt to be her due, and it was now long since they had openly been at issue on any point. Mrs. Mutimer's views were distinctly Conservative, and hitherto she had never taken Richard's Radicalism seriously; on the whole she had regarded it as a fairly harmless recreation for his leisure hours—decidedly preferable to a haunting of public-houses ar 1 music-halls. The loss of his employment caused her a good deal of uneasiness, but she had not ventured to do more than throw out hints of her disapproval; and now, as it seemed, the matter was of no moment. Henceforth she had far other apprehensions, but this first conflict of their views made her reticent.

'Just let me tell you how things stand,' Richard pursued, when his excitement had somewhat subsided; and he went on to explain the relations between old Mr. Mutimer and the Eldons, which in outline had been described to him by Mr. Yottle. And then—

'The will he had made left all the property to this young Eldon, who was to be trustee for a little money to be doled out to me yearly, just to save me from ruining myself, of course.' Richard's lips curled in scorn. 'I don't know whether the lawyer thought we ought to offer to give everything up; he seemed precious anxious to make me understand that the old man had never intended us to have it, and that he *did* want these other people to have it. Of course, we've nothing to do with that. Luck's luck, and I think I know who'll make best use of it.'

'Why didn't you tell all this when Alice was here?' inquired his mother, seeming herself again, though very grave.

'I'll tell you. I thought it over, and it seems to me it'll be better if Alice and 'Arry wait a while before they know what'll come to them. They can't take anything till they're twenty-one. Alice is a good girl, but——'

He hesitated, having caught his mother's eye. He felt that this prudential course justified in a measure her anxiety.

'She's a girl,' he pursued, 'and we know that a girl with a lot o' money gets run after by men who care nothing about her and a good deal about the money. Then it's quite certain 'Arry won't be any the better for fancying himself rich. He's going to give us trouble as it is, I can see that. We shall have to take another house, of course, and we can't keep them from knowing that there's money fallen to me. But there's no need to talk about the figures, and if we can make them think it's only me that's better off, so much the better. Alice needn't go to work, and I'm glad of it; a girl's proper place is at home. You can tell her you want her to help in the new house. 'Arry had better keep his place awhile. I shouldn't wonder if I find work for him myself before long. I've got plans, but I shan't talk about them just yet.'

He spoke then of the legal duties which fell upon him as next-of-kin, explaining the necessity of finding two sureties on taking out letters of administration. Mr. Yottle had offered himself for one; the other Richard hoped to find in Mr. Westlake, a leader of the Socialist movement.

'You want us to go into a big house?' asked Mrs. Mutimer. She seemed to pay little attention to the wider aspects of the change, but to fix on the details she could best understand, those which put her fears in palpable shape.

'I didn't say a big one, but a larger than this. We're not going to play the do-nothing gentlefolk; but all the same our life won't and can't be what it has been. There's no choice. You've worked hard all your life, mother, and it's only fair you should come in for a bit of rest. We'll find a house somewhere out Green Lanes way, or in Highbury or Holloway.'

He laughed again.

'So there's the best of it—the worst of it, as you say. Just take a night to turn it over. Most likely I shall go to Belwick again to-morrow afternoon.'

He paused, and his mother, after bending her head to bite off an end of cotton, asked—

'You'll tell Emma?'

'I shall go round to-night.'

A little later Richard left the house for this purpose. His step was firmer than ever, his head more upright. Walking along the crowded streets, he saw nothing; there was a fixed smile on his lips, the smile of a man to whom the world pays tribute. Never having suffered actual want, and blessed with sanguine temperament, he knew nothing of that fierce exultation, that wrathful triumph over fate, which comes to men of passionate mood smitten by the lightning-flash of unhoped prosperity. At present he was well-disposed to all men; even against capitalists and 'profitmongers' he could not have railed heartily. Capitalists? Was he not one himself? Aye, but he would prove himself such a one as you do not meet with every day ; and the foresight of deeds which should draw the eyes of men upon him, which should shout his name abroad, softened his judgments with the charity of satisfied ambition. He would be the glorified representative of his class. He would show the world how a self-taught working man conceived the duties and privileges of wealth. He would shame those dunder-headed, callous-hearted aristocrats, those ravening bourgeois. Opportunity—what else had he wanted? No longer would his voice be lost in petty lecture-halls, answered only by the applause of a handful of mechanics. Ere many months had passed, crowds should throng to hear him ; his gospel would be trumpeted over the land. To what might he not attain? The educated, the refined, men and women——

He was at the entrance of a dark passage, where his feet stayed themselves by force of habit. He turned out of the street, and walked more slowly towards the house in which Emma Vine and her sisters lived. Having reached the door, he paused, but again took a few paces forward. Then he came back and rang the uppermost of five bells. In waiting, he looked vaguely up and down the street.

It was Emma herself who opened to him. The dim light showed a smile of pleasure and surprise.

' You've come to ask about Jane?' she said. ' She hasn't been quite so bad since last night.'

' I'm glad to hear it. Can I come up?'

' Will you?'

He entered, and Emma closed the door. It was pitch dark.

' I wish I'd brought a candle down,' Emma said, moving back along the passage. ' Mind, there's a pram at the foot of the stairs.'

The perambulator was avoided successfully by both, and they ascended the bare boards of the staircase. On each landing prevailed a distinct odour ; first came the damp smell of newly-washed clothes, then the scent of fried onions, then the work-room of some small craftsman exhaled varnish. The topmost floor seemed the purest ; it was only stuffy.

Richard entered an uncarpeted room which had to serve too many distinct purposes to allow of its being orderly in appearance. In one corner was a bed, where two little children lay asleep ; before the window stood a sewing-machine, about which was heaped a quantity of linen ; a table in the midst was half covered with a cloth, on which was placed a loaf and

E

butter, the other half being piled with several dresses requiring the needle. Two black patches on the low ceiling showed in what positions the lamp stood by turns.

Emma's eldest sister was moving about the room. Hers were the children; her husband had been dead a year or more. She was about thirty years of age, and had a slatternly appearance; her face was peevish, and seemed to grudge the half-smile with which it received the visitor.

'You've no need to look round you,' she said. 'We're in a regular pig-stye, and likely to be. Where's there a chair?'

She shook some miscellaneous articles on to the floor to provide a seat.

'For mercy's sake don't speak too loud, and wake them children. Bertie's had the earache; he's been crying all day. What with him and Jane, we've had a blessing, I can tell you. Can I put these supper things away, Emma?'

'I'll do it,' was the other's reply. 'Won't you have a bit more, Kate?'

'I've got no mind for eating. Well, you may cut a slice and put it on the mantelpiece. I'll go and sit with Jane.'

Richard sat and looked about the room absently. The circumstances of his own family had never fallen below the point at which it is possible to have regard for decency; the growing up of himself and of his brothers and sister had brought additional resources to meet extended needs, and the Mutimer characteristics had formed a safeguard against improvidence. He was never quite at his ease in this poverty-cumbered room, which he seldom visited.

'You ought to have a fire,' he said.

'There's one in the other room,' replied Kate. 'One has to serve us.'

'But you can't cook there.'

'Cook? We can boil a potato, and that's about all the cooking we can do now-a-days.'

She moved to the door as she spoke, and, before leaving the room, took advantage of Richard's back being turned to make certain exhortatory signs to her sister. Emma averted her head.

Kate closed the door behind her. Emma, having removed the eatables to the cupboard, came near to Richard and placed her arm gently upon his shoulders. He looked at her kindly.

'Kate's been so put about with Bertie,' she said, in a tone of excuse. 'And she was up nearly all last night.'

'She never takes things like you do,' Richard remarked.

'She's got more to bear. There's the children always making her anxious. She took Alf to the hospital this afternoon, and the doctor says he must have—I forget the name, somebody's food. But it's two-and-ninepence for ever such a little tin. They don't think as his teeth 'll ever come.'

'Oh, I daresay they will,' said Richard encouragingly.

He had put his arm about her. Emma knelt down by him, and rested her head against his shoulder.

'I'm tired,' she whispered. 'I've had to go twice to the Minories to-day. I'm so afraid I shan't be able to hold my eyes open with Jane, and Kate's tireder still.'

She did not speak as if seeking for sympathy; it was only the natural utterance of her thoughts in a moment of restful confidence. Uttermost weariness was a condition too familiar to the girl to be spoken of in any but a patient, matter-of-fact tone. But it was priceless soothing to let her forehead repose against the heart whose love was the one and sufficient blessing of her life. Her brown hair was very soft and fine; a lover of another kind would have pressed his lips upon it. Richard was thinking of matters more practical. At another time his indignation—in such a case right good and manful—would have boiled over at the thought of these poor women crushed in slavery to feed the world's dastard selfishness; this evening his mood was more complaisant, and he smiled as one at ease.

'Hadn't you better give up your work?' he said.

Emma raised her head. In the few moments of repose her eyelids had drooped with growing heaviness; she looked at him as if she had just been awakened to some great surprise.

'Give up work? How can I?'

'I think I would. You'd have more time to give to Jane, and you could sleep in the day. And Jane had better not begin again after this. Don't you think it would be better if you left these lodgings and took a house, where there'd be plenty of room and fresh air?'

'Richard, what are you talking about?'

He laughed, quietly, on account of the sleeping children.

'How would you like,' he continued, 'to go and live in the country? Kate and Jane could have a house of their own, you know—in London, I mean, a house like ours; they could let a room or two if they chose. Then you and I could go where we liked. I was down in the Midland Counties yesterday; had to go on business; and I saw a house that

E 2

would just suit us. It's a bit large; I daresay there's sixteen
or twenty rooms. And there's trees growing all about it;
a big garden——'

Emma dropped her head again and laughed, happy that
Richard should jest with her so good-humouredly; for he did
not often talk in the lighter way. She had read of such houses
in the weekly story-papers. It must be nice to live in them;
it must be nice to be a denizen of Paradise.

'I'm in earnest, Emma.'

His voice caused her to gaze at him again.

'Bring a chair,' he said, 'and I'll tell you something that'll
—keep you awake.'

The insensible fellow! Her sweet, pale, wondering face
was so close to his, the warmth of her drooping frame was
against his heart—and he bade her sit apart to listen.

She placed herself as he desired, sitting with her hands
together in her lap, her countenance troubled a little, wishing
to smile, yet not quite venturing. And he told his story, told
it in all details, with figures that filled the mouth, that rolled
forth like gold upon the bank-scales.

'This is mine,' he said, 'mine and yours.'

Have you seen a child listening to a long fairy tale, every
page a new adventure of wizardry, a story of elf, or mermaid,
or gnome, of treasures underground guarded by enchanted
monsters, of bells heard silverly in the depth of old forests,
of castles against the sunset, of lakes beneath the quiet moon?
Know you how light gathers in the eyes dreaming on vision
after vision, ever more intensely realised, yet ever of an
unknown world? How, when at length the reader's voice is
silent, the eyes still see, the ears still hear, until a movement
breaks the spell, and with a deep, involuntary sigh the little
one gazes here and there, wondering?

So Emma listened, and so she came back to consciousness,
looking about the room, incredulous. Had she been overcome
with weariness? Had she slept and dreamt?

One of the children stirred and uttered a little wailing
sound. She stepped lightly to the bedside, bent for a moment,
saw that all was well again, and came back on tip-toe. The
simple duty had quieted her throbbing heart. She seated
herself as before.

'What about the country house now?' said Richard.

'I don't know what to say. It's more than I can take into
my head.'

' You're not going to say, like mother did, that it was the worst piece of news she'd ever heard ? '

' Your mother said that ? '

Emma was startled. Had her thought passed lightly over some danger ? She examined her mind rapidly.

' I suppose she said it,' Richard explained, ' just because she didn't know what else to say, that's about the truth. But there certainly is one thing I'm a little anxious about, myself. I don't care for either Alice or 'Arry to know the details of this windfall. They won't come in for their share till they're of age, and it's just as well they should think it's only a moderate little sum. So don't talk about it, Emma.'

The girl was still musing on Mrs. Mutimer's remark; she merely shook her head.

' You didn't think you were going to marry a man with his thousands and be a lady ? Well, I shall have more to say in a day or two. But at present my idea is that mother and the rest of them shall go into a larger house, and that you and Kate and Jane shall take our place. I don't know how long it'll be before those Eldon people can get out of Wanley Manor, but as soon as they do, why then there's nothing to prevent you and me going into it. Will that suit you, Em ? '

' We shall really live in that big house ? '

' Certainly we shall. I've got a life's work before me there, as far as I can see at present. The furniture belongs to Mrs. Eldon, I believe ; we'll furnish the place to suit ourselves.'

' May I tell my sisters, Richard ? '

' Just tell them that I've come in for some money and a house, perhaps that's enough. And look here, I'll leave you this five-pound note to go on with. You must get Jane whatever the doctor says. And throw all that sewing out of the windows ; we'll have no more convict labour. Tell Jane to get well just as soon as it suits her.'

' But—all this money ? '

' I've plenty. The lawyer advanced me some for present needs. Now it's getting late, I must go. I'll write and tell you when I shall be home again.'

He held out his hand, but the girl embraced him with the restrained tenderness which in her spoke so eloquently.

' Are you glad, Emma ? ' he asked.

' Very glad, for your sake.'

'And just a bit for your own, eh?'

'I never thought about money,' she answered. 'It was
quite enough to be your wife'

It was the simple truth.

CHAPTER VI.

At eleven o'clock the next morning Richard presented himself
at the door of a house in Avenue Road, St. John's Wood, and
expressed a desire to see Mr. Westlake. That gentleman was
at home ; he received the visitor in his study—a spacious room
luxuriously furnished, with a large window looking upon a
lawn. The day was sunny and warm, but a clear fire equalised
the temperature of the room. There was an odour of good
tobacco, always most delightful when it blends with the scent of
rich bindings.

It was Richard's first visit to this house. A few days ago
he would, in spite of himself, have been somewhat awed by the
man-servant at the door, the furniture of the hall, the air of
refinement in the room he entered. At present he smiled on
everything. Could he not command the same as soon as he
chose?

Mr. Westlake rose from his writing-table and greeted his
visitor with a hearty grip of the hand. He was a man pleasant
to look upon ; his face, full of intellect, shone with the light of
good-will, and the easy carelessness of his attire prepared one for
the genial sincerity which marked his way of speaking. He
wore a velvet jacket, a grey waistcoat buttoning up to the
throat, grey trousers, fur-bordered slippers; his collar was very
deep, and instead of the ordinary shirt-cuffs, his wrists were enclosed in frills. Long-haired, full-bearded, he had the forehead of an idealist and eyes whose natural expression was an
indulgent smile.

A man of letters, he had struggled from obscure poverty to
success and ample means ; at three-and-thirty he was still hard
pressed to make both ends meet, but the ten subsequent years
had built for him this pleasant home and banished his long
familiar anxieties to the land of nightmare. 'It came just in
time,' he was in the habit of saying to those who had his confidence. 'I was at the point where a man begins to turn sour,

and I should have soured in earnest.' The process had been most effectually arrested. People were occasionally found to say that his books had a tang of acerbity; possibly this was the safety-valve at work, a hint of what might have come had the old hunger-demons kept up their goading. In the man himself you discovered an extreme simplicity of feeling, a frank tenderness, a noble indignation. For one who knew him it was not difficult to understand that he should have taken up extreme social views, still less that he should act upon his convictions. All his writing foretold such a possibility, though on the other hand it exhibited devotion to forms of culture which do not as a rule predispose to democratic agitation. The explanation was perhaps too simple to be readily hit upon; the man was himself so supremely happy that with his disposition the thought of tyrannous injustice grew intolerable to him. Some incidents happened to set his wrath blazing, and henceforth, in spite of not a little popular ridicule and much shaking of the head among his friends, Mr. Westlake had his mission.

' I have come to ask your advice and help,' began Mutimer with directness. He was conscious of the necessity of subduing his voice, and had a certain pleasure in the ease with which he achieved this feat. It would not have been so easy a day or two ago.

' Ah, about this awkward affair of yours,' observed Mr. Westlake with reference to Richard's loss of his employment, of which, as editor of the Union's weekly paper, he had of course at once been apprised.

' No, not about that. Since then a very unexpected thing has happened to me.'

The story was once more related, vastly to Mr. Westlake's satisfaction. Cheerful news concerning his friends always put him in the best of spirits.

He shook his head, laughing.

' Come, come, Mutimer, this'll never do! I'm not sure that we shall not have to consider your expulsion from the Union.'

Richard went on to mention the matters of legal routine in which he hoped Mr. Westlake would serve him. These having been settled—

' I wish to speak of something more important,' he said. ' You take it for granted, I hope, that I'm not going to make the ordinary use of this fortune. As yet I've only been able to hit on a few general ideas. I'm clear as to the objects I

shall keep before me, but how best to serve them wants more
reflection.   I thought if I talked it over with you in the first
place——'

The door opened, and a lady half entered the room.

' Oh, I thought you were alone,' she remarked to Mr. Westlake.   ' Forgive me!'

' Come in!   Here's our friend Mutimer.   You know Mrs.
Westlake?'

A few words had passed between this lady and Richard in
the lecture-room a few weeks before.   She was not frequently
present at such meetings, but had chanced, on the occasion referred to, to hear Mutimer deliver an harangue.

' You have no objection to talk of your plans?   Join our
council, will you?' he added to his wife.   ' Our friend brings
interesting news.'

Mrs. Westlake walked across the room to the curved
window-seat.   Her age could scarcely be more than three or
four-and-twenty; she was very dark, and her face grave almost
to melancholy.   Black hair, cut short at its thickest behind her
neck, gave exquisite relief to features of the purest Greek type.
In listening to anything that held her attention her eyes grew
large, and their dark orbs seemed to dream passionately.   The
white swan's down at her throat—she was perfectly attired—
made the skin above resemble rich-hued marble, and indeed to
gaze at her long was to be impressed as by the sad loveliness of
a supreme work of art.   As Mutimer talked she leaned forward, her elbow on her knee, the back of her hand supporting
her chin.

Her husband recounted what Richard had told him, and
the latter proceeded to sketch the projects he had in view.

' My idea is,' he said, ' to make the mines at Wanley the
basis of great industrial undertakings, just as any capitalist
might, but to conduct these undertakings in a way consistent
with our views.   I would begin by building furnaces, and in
time add engineering works on a large scale.   I would build
houses for the men, and in fact make that valley an industrial
settlement conducted on Socialist principles.   Practically I can
devote the whole of my income ; my personal expenses will not
be worth taking into account.   The men must be paid on a just
scheme, and the margin of profit that remains, all that we can
spare from the extension of the works, shall be devoted to the
Socialist propaganda.   In fact, I should like to make the executive committee of the Union a sort of board of directors—and

in a very different sense from the usual—for the Wanley estate. My personal expenditure deducted, I should like such a committee to have the practical control of funds. All this wealth was made by plunder of the labouring class, and I shall hold it as trustee for them. Do these ideas seem to you of a practical colour?'

Mr. Westlake nodded slowly twice. His wife kept her listening attitude unchanged ; her eyes 'dreamed against a distant goal.'

'As I see the scheme,' pursued Richard, who spoke all along somewhat in the lecture-room tone, the result of a certain embarrassment, 'it will differ considerably from the Socialist experiments we know of. We shall be working not only to support ourselves, but every bit as much set on profit as any capitalist in Belwick. The difference is, that the profit will benefit no individual, but the Cause. There'll be no attempt to carry out the idea of every man receiving the just outcome of his labour ; not because I shouldn't be willing to share in that way, but simply because we have a greater end in view than to enrich ourselves. Our men must all be members of the Union, and their prime interest must be the advancement of the principles of the Union. We shall be able to establish new papers, to hire halls, and to spread ourselves over the country. It'll be fighting the capitalist manufacturers with their own weapons. I can see plenty of difficulties, of course. All England 'll be against us. Never mind, we'll defy them all, and we'll win. It'll be the work of my life, and we'll see if an honest purpose can't go as far as a thievish one.'

The climax would have brought crashing cheers at Commonwealth Hall; in Mr. Westlake's study it was received with well-bred expressions of approval.

' Well, Mutimer,' exclaimed the idealist, ' all this is intensely interesting, and right glorious for us. One sees at last a possibility of action. I ask nothing better than to be allowed to work with you. It happens very luckily that you are a practical engineer. I suppose the mechanical details of the undertaking are entirely within your province.'

'Not quite, at present,' Mutimer admitted, 'but I shall have valuable help. Yesterday I had a meeting with a man named Rodman, a mining engineer, who has been working on the estate. He seems just the man I shall want; a Socialist already, and delighted to join in the plans I just hinted to him.'

' Capital ! Do you propose, then, that we shall call a special meeting of the Committee? Or would you prefer to suggest a committee of your own?'

'No, I think our own committee will do very well, at all events for the present. The first thing, of course, is to get the financial details of our scheme put into shape. I go to Belwick again this afternoon; my solicitor must get his business through as soon as possible.'

'You will reside for the most part at Wanley?

'At the Manor, yes. It is occupied just now, but I suppose will soon be free.'

'Do you know that part of the country, Stella?' Mr. Westlake asked of his wife.

She roused herself, drawing in her breath, and uttered a short negative.

'As soon as I get into the house,' Richard resumed to Mr. Westlake, 'I hope you'll come and examine the place. It's unfortunate that the railway misses it by about three miles, but Rodman tells me we can easily run a private line to Agworth station. However, the first thing is to get our committee at work on the scheme.' Richard repeated this phrase with gusto. 'Perhaps you could bring it up at the Saturday meeting?'

'You'll be in town on Saturday?'

'Yes; I have a lecture in Islington on Sunday.'

'Saturday will do, then. Is this confidential?'

'Not at all. We may as well get as much encouragement out of it as we can. Don't you think so?'

'Certainly.'

Richard did not give expression to his thought that a paragraph on the subject in the Union's weekly organ, the 'Fiery Cross,' might be the best way of promoting such encouragement; but he delayed his departure for a few minutes with talk round about the question of the prudence which must necessarily be observed in publishing a project so undigested. Mr. Westlake, who was responsible for the paper, was not likely to transgress the limits of good taste, and when Richard, on Saturday morning, searched eagerly the columns of the 'Cross,' he was not altogether satisfied with the extreme discretion which marked a brief paragraph among those headed: 'From Day to Day.' However, many of the readers were probably by that time able to supply the missing proper-name.

It was not the fault of Daniel Dabbs if members of the Hoxton and Islington branch of the Union read the paragraph without understanding to whom it referred. Daniel was among the first to hear of what had befallen the Mutimer family, and from the circle of his fellow-workmen the news spread quickly. Talk was rife on the subject of Mutimer's dismissal from Longwood Brothers', and the sensational rumour which followed so quickly found an atmosphere well prepared for its transmission. Hence the unusual concourse at the meeting-place in Islington next Sunday evening, where, as it became known to others besides Socialists, Mutimer was engaged to lecture. Richard experienced some vexation that his lecture was not to be at Commonwealth Hall, where the gathering would doubtless have been much larger.

The Union was not wealthy. The central hall was rented at Mr. Westlake's expense; two or three branches were managing with difficulty to support regular places of assembly, such as could not being obliged as yet to content themselves with open-air lecturing. In Islington the leaguers met in a room behind a coffee-shop, ordinarily used for festive purposes; benches were laid across the floor, and an estrade at the upper end exalted chairman and lecturer. The walls were adorned with more or less striking advertisements of non-alcoholic beverages, and with a few prints from the illustrated papers. The atmosphere was tobaccoey, and the coffee-shop itself, through which the visitors had to make their way, suggested to the nostrils that bloaters are the working man's chosen delicacy at Sunday tea. A table just within the door of the lecture-room exposed for sale sundry Socialist publications, the latest issue of the ' Fiery Cross ' in particular.

Richard was wont to be among the earliest arrivals: to-night he was full ten minutes behind the hour for which the lecture was advertised. A group of friends were standing about the table near the door; they received him with a bustle which turned all eyes thitherwards. He walked up the middle of the room to the platform. As soon as he was well in the eye of the meeting, a single pair of hands—Daniel Dabbs owned them—gave the signal for uproar; feet made play on the boarding, and one or two of the more enthusiastic revolutionists fairly gave tongue. Richard seated himself with grave countenance, and surveyed the assembly; from fifty to sixty people were present, among them three or four women, and the number continued to grow. The chairman and one or two leading spirits had followed Mutimer to the place of distinction, where they talked with him,

Punctuality was not much regarded at these meetings; the lecture was announced for eight, but rarely began before half-past. The present being an occasion of exceptional interest, twenty minutes past the hour saw the chairman rise for his prefatory remarks. He was a lank man of jovial countenance and jerky enunciation. There was no need, he observed, to introduce a friend and comrade so well known to them as the lecturer of the evening. 'We're always glad to hear him, and to-night, if I may be allowed to 'int as much, we're *particularly* glad to hear him. Our friend and comrade is going to talk to us about the Land. It's a question we can't talk or think too much about, and Comrade Mutimer has thought about it as much and more than any of us, I think I may say. I don't know,' the chairman added, with a sly look across the room, 'whether our friend's got any new views on this subject of late. I shouldn't wonder if he had.' Here sounded a roar of laughter, led off by Daniel Dabbs. 'Hows'ever, be that as it may, we can answer for it as any views he may hold is the right views, and the honest views, and the views of a man as means to do a good deal more than talk about his convictions!'

Again did the stentor-note of Daniel ring forth, and it was amid thunderous cheering that Richard left his chair and moved to the front of the platform. His Sunday suit of black was still that with which his friends were familiar, but his manner, though the audience probably did not perceive the detail, was unmistakably changed. He had been wont to begin his address with short, stinging periods, with sneers and such bitterness of irony as came within his compass. To-night he struck quite another key, mellow, confident, hinting at personal satisfaction; a smile was on his lips, and not a smile of scorn. He rested one hand against his side, holding in the other a scrap of paper with jotted items of reasoning. His head was thrown a little back; he viewed the benches from beneath his eyelids. True, the pose maintained itself but for a moment. I mention it because it was something new in Richard.

He spoke of the land; he attacked the old monopoly, and visioned a time when a claim to individual ownerships of the earth's surface would be as ludicrous as were now the assertion of title to a fee-simple somewhere in the moon. He mustered statistics; he adduced historic and contemporary example of the just and the unjust in land-holding; he gripped the throat of a certain English duke, and held him up for flagellation; he drifted into oceans of economic theory; he sat down by the waters of Babylon; he climbed Pisgah. Had he but spoken of backslidings in the wilderness! But for that fatal omission, the lecture was, of its kind, good. By degrees Richard forgot his pose and the carefully struck note of mellowness; he began to believe what he was saying, and to say it with the right vigour of popular oratory. Forget his struggles with the h-fiend; forget his syntactical lapses; you saw that after all the man had within him a clear flame of conscience; that he had felt before speaking that speech was one of the uses for which Nature had expressly framed him. His invective seldom degenerated into vulgar abuse; one discerned in him at least the elements of what we call good taste; of simple manliness he disclosed not a little; he had some command of pathos. In conclusion, he finished without reference to his personal concerns.

The chairman invited questions, preliminary to debate.

He rose half-way down the room,—the man who invariably rises on these occasions. He was oldish, with bent shoulders, and wore spectacles—probably a clerk of forty years' standing. In his hand was a small note-book, which he consulted. He began with measured utterance, emphatic, loud.

'I wish to propose to the lecturer seven questions. I will read them in order; I have taken some pains to word them clearly.'

Richard has his scrap of paper on his knee. He jots a word or two after each deliberate interrogation, smiling.

Other questioners succeeded. Richard replies to them. He fails to satisfy the man of seven queries, who, after repeating this and the other of the seven, professes himself still unsatisfied, shakes his head indulgently, walks from the room.

The debate is opened. Behold a second inevitable man; he is not well-washed, his shirt-front shows a beer-stain; he is angry before he begins.

'I don't know whether a man as doesn't 'old with these kind o' theories 'll be allowed a fair 'earin——'

Indignant interruption. Cries of 'Of course he will!'— 'Who ever refused to hear you?'—and the like.

He is that singular phenomenon, that self-contradiction, that expression insoluble into factors of common-sense—the Conservative working man. What do they want to be at? he demands. Do they suppose as this kind of talk 'll make wages higher, or enable the poor man to get his beef and beer at a lower rate? What's the d——d good of it all? Figures, eh?

He never heered yet as figures made a meal for a man as hadn't got one; nor yet as they provided shoes and stockings for his young 'uns at 'ome. It made him mad to listen, that it did! Do they suppose as the rich man 'll give up the land, if they talk till all's blue? Wasn't it human natur to get all you can and stick to it?

'Pig's nature!' cries someone from the front benches.

'There!' comes the rejoinder. 'Didn't I say as there was no fair 'earing for a man as didn't say just what suits you?'

The voice of Daniel Dabbs is loud in good-tempered mockery. Mockery comes from every side, an angry note here and there, for the most part tolerant, jovial.

'Let him speak! 'Ear him! Hoy! Hoy!'

The chairman interposes, but by the time that order is restored the Conservative working man has thrust his hat upon his head and is off to the nearest public-house, muttering oaths.

Mr. Cullen rises, at the same time rises Mr. Cowes. These two gentlemen are fated to rise simultaneously. They scowl at each other. Mr. Cullen begins to speak, and Mr. Cowes, after a circular glance of protest, resumes his seat. The echoes tell that we are in for oratory with a vengeance. Mr. Cullen is a short, stout man, very seedily habited, with a great rough head of hair, an aquiline nose, lungs of vast power. His vein is King Cambyses'; he tears passion to tatters; he roars leonine; he is your man to have at the pamper'd jades of Asia! He has got hold of a new word, and that the verb to 'exploit.' I am exploited, thou art exploited,—*he* exploits! Who? Why, such men as that English duke whom the lecturer gripped and flagellated. The English duke is Mr. Cullen's bugbear; never a speech from Mr. Cullen but that duke is most horribly mauled. His ground-rents,—yah! Another word of which Mr. Cullen is fond is 'strattum,'—usually spelt and pronounced with but one t midway. You and I have the misfortune to belong to a social 'strattum' which is trampled flat and hard beneath the feet of the landowners. Mr. Cullen rises to such a point of fury that one dreads the consequences—to himself. Already the chairman is on his feet, intimating in dumb show that the allowed ten minutes have elapsed; there is no making the orator hear. At length his friend who sits by him fairly grips his coat-tails and brings him to a sitting posture, amid mirthful tumult. Mr. Cullen joins in the mirth, looks as though he had never been angry in his life. And till next Sunday comes round he will neither speak nor think of the social question.

Mr. Cowes is unopposed. After the preceding enthusiast, the voice of Mr. Cowes falls soothingly as a stream among the heather. He is tall, meagre, bald; he wears a very broad black necktie, his hand saws up and down. Mr. Cowes' tone is the quietly venomous; in a few minutes you believe in his indignation far more than in that of Mr. Cullen. He makes a point and pauses to observe the effect upon his hearers. He prides himself upon his grammar, goes back to correct a concord, emphasises eccentricities of pronunciation; for instance, he accents 'capitalist' on the second syllable, and repeats the words with grave challenge to all and sundry. Speaking of something which he wishes to stigmatise as a misnomer, he exclaims : 'It's what I call a misnomy !' And he follows the assertion with an awful suspense of utterance. He brings his speech to a close exactly with the end of the tenth minute, and, on sitting down, eyes his unknown neighbour with wrathful intensity for several moments.

Who will follow ? A sound comes from the very back of the room, such a sound that every head turns in astonished search for the source of it. Such voice has the wind in garret-chimneys on a winter night. It is a thin wail, a prelude of lamentation; it troubles the blood. The speaker no one seems to know; he is a man of yellow visage, with head sunk between pointed shoulders, on his crown a mere scalp-lock. He seems to be afflicted with a disease of the muscles; his malformed body quivers, the hand he raises shakes paralytic. His clothes are of the meanest; what his age may be it is impossible to judge. As his voice gathers strength, the hearers begin to feel the influence of a terrible earnestness. He does not rant, he does not weigh his phrases; the stream of bitter prophecy flows on smooth and dark. He is supplying the omission in Mutimer's harangue, is bidding his class know itself and chasten itself, as an indispensable preliminary to any great change in the order of things. He cries vanity upon all these detailed schemes of social reconstruction. Are we ready for it ? he wails. Could we bear it, if they granted it to us ? It is all good and right, but hadn't we better first make ourselves worthy of such freedom ? He begins a terrible arraignment of the People,—then, of a sudden, his voice has ceased. You could hear a pin drop. It is seen that the man has fallen to the ground; there arises a low moaning; people press about him.

They carry him into the coffee-shop. It was a fit. In five

minutes he is restored, but does not come back to finish his speech.

There is an interval of disorder. But surely we are not going to let the meeting end in this way. The chairman calls for the next speaker, and he stands forth in the person of a rather smug little shopkeeper, who declares that he knows of no single particular in which the working class needs correction. The speech undeniably falls flat. Will no one restore the tone of the meeting?

Mr. Kitshaw is the man! Now we shall have broad grins. Mr. Kitshaw enjoys a reputation for mimicry; he takes off music-hall singers in the bar-parlour of a Saturday night. Observe, he rises, hems, pulls down his waistcoat; there is bubbling laughter. Mr. Kitshaw brings back the debate to its original subject; he talks of the Land. He is a little haphazard at first, but presently hits the mark in a fancy picture of a country still in the hands of aborigines, as yet unannexed by the capitalist nations, knowing not the meaning of the verb 'exploit.'

'Imagine such a happy land, my friends; a land, I say, which nobody hasn't ever thought of "developing the resources" of,—that's the proper phrase, I believe. There are the people, with clothing enough for comfort and—ahem!—good manners, but, mark you, no more. No manufacture of luxurious skirts and hulsters and togs o' that kind by the exploited classes. No, for no exploited classes don't exist! All are equal, my friends. Up an' down the fields they goes, all day long, arm-in-arm, Jack and Jerry, aye, and Liza an' Sairey Ann; for they have equality of the sexes, mind you! Up an' down the fields, I say, in a devil-may-care sort of way, with their sweethearts and their wives. No factory smoke, O dear no! There's the rivers, with tropical plants a-shading the banks, O my! There they goes up an' down in their boats, devil-may-care, a-strumming on the banjo,'—he imitated such action,—'and a-singing their nigger minstrelsy with light 'earts. Why? 'Cause they ain't got no work to get up to at 'arf-past five next morning. Their time's their own! *That's* the condition of an unexploited country, my friends!'

Mr. Kitshaw had put everyone in vast good humour. You might wonder that his sweetly idyllic picture did not stir bitterness by contrast; it were to credit the English workman with too much imagination. Resonance of applause rewarded the sparkling rhetorician. A few of the audience availed themselves of the noise to withdraw, for the clock showed that it was close upon ten, and public-houses shut their doors early on Sunday.

But Richard Mutimer was on his feet again, and this time without regard to effect; there was a word in him strongly demanding utterance. It was to the speech of the unfortunate prophet that he desired to reply. He began with sorrowful admissions. No one speaking honestly could deny that—that the working class had its faults; they came out plainly enough now and then. Drink, for instance (Mr. Cullen gave a resounding 'Hear, hear!' and a stamp on the boards). What sort of a spectacle would be exhibited by the public-houses in Hoxton and Islington at closing time to-night? ('True!' from Mr. Cowes, who also stamped on the boards.) Yes, but —— Richard used the device of aposiopesis; Daniel Dabbs took it for a humorous effect and began a roar, which was summarily interdicted. 'But,' pursued Richard with emphasis, 'what is the meaning of these vices? What do they come of? Who's to blame for them? Not the working class—never tell me! What drives a man to drink in his spare hours? What about the poisonous air of garrets and cellars? What about excessive toil and inability to procure healthy recreation? What about defects of education, due to poverty? What about diseased bodies inherited from over-slaved parents?' Messrs. Cowes and Cullen had accompanied these queries with a climax of vociferous approval; when Richard paused, they led the tumult of hands and heels. 'Look at that poor man who spoke to us!' cried Mutimer. 'He's gone, so I shan't hurt him by speaking plainly. He spoke well, mind you, and he spoke from his heart; but what sort of a life has his been, do you think? A wretched cripple, a miserable weakling no doubt from the day of his birth, cursed in having ever seen the daylight, and, such as he is, called upon to fight for his bread. Much of it he gets! Who would blame that man if he drank himself into unconsciousness every time he picked up a sixpence?' Cowes and Cullen bellowed their delight. 'Well, he doesn't do it; so much you can be sure of. In some vile hole here in this great city of ours he drags on a life worse—aye, a thousand times worse!—than that of the horses in the West-end mews. Don't clap your hands so much, fellow-workers. Just think about it on your way home; talk about it to your wives and your children. It's the sight of objects like that that makes my blood boil, and that's set me in earnest at this work of ours.

F

I feel for that man and all like him as if they were my brothers.
And I take you all to witness, all you present and all you
repeat my words to, that I'll work on as long as I have life in
me, that I'll use every opportunity that's given me to uphold
the cause of the poor and down-trodden against the rich and
selfish and luxurious, that if I live another fifty years I shall
still be of the people and with the people, that no man shall
ever have it in his power to say that Richard Mutimer misused
his chances and was only a new burden to them whose load
he might have lightened!'

There was nothing for it but to leap on to the very benches
and yell as long as your voice would hold out.

After that the meeting was mere exuberance of mutual
congratulations.   Mr. Cullen was understood to be moving the
usual vote of thanks, but even his vocal organs strove hard for
little purpose.   Daniel Dabbs had never made a speech in his
life, but excitement drove him on the honourable post of
seconder.   The chairman endeavoured to make certain an-
nouncements; then the assembly broke up.   The estrade was
invaded; everybody wished to shake hands with Mutimer.
Mr. Cullen tried to obtain Richard's attention to certain remarks of value; failing, he went off with a scowl.   Mr. Cowes
attempted to button-hole the popular hero; finding Richard
conversing with someone else at the same time, he turned away
with a covert sneer.   The former of the two worthies had
desired to insist upon every member of the Union becoming a
teetotaller; the latter wished to say that he thought it would
be well if a badge of temperance were henceforth worn by
Unionists.   On turning away, each glanced at the clock and
hurried his step.

In a certain dark street not very far from the lecture-room
Mr. Cullen rose on tip-toe at the windows of a dull little public-
house.   A Unionist was standing at the bar; Mr. Cullen
hurried on, into a street yet darker.   Again he tip-toed at a
window.   The glimpse reassured him; he passed quickly
through the doorway, stepped to the bar, gave an order.   Then
he turned, and behold, on a seat just under the window sat
Mr. Cowes, a short pipe in his mouth, a smoking tumbler held
on his knee.   The supporters of total abstinence nodded to each
other, with a slight lack of spontaneity.   Mr. Cullen, having
secured his own tumbler, came by his comrade's side.

'Deal o' fire talk to wind up with,' he remarked tenta-
tively.

'He means what he says,' returned the other gravely.

'Oh yes,' Mr. Cullen hastened to admit. 'Mutimer means what he says! Only the way of saying it, I meant—I've got a bit of a sore throat.'

'So have I. After that there hot room.'

They nodded at each other sympathetically. Mr. Cullen filled a little black pipe.

'Got a light?'

Mr. Cowes offered the glowing bowl of his own clay; they put their noses together and blew a cloud.

'Of course there's no saying what time 'll do,' observed tall Mr. Cowes, sententiously, after a gulp of warm liquor.

'No more there is,' assented short Mr. Cullen with half a wink.

'It's easy to promise.'

'As easy as tellin' lies.'

Another silence.

'Don't suppose you and me 'll get much of it,' Mr. Cowes ventured to observe.

'About as much as you can put in your eye without winkin',' was the other's picturesque agreement.

They talked till closing time.

CHAPTER VII.

ONE morning late in June, Hubert Eldon passed through the gates of Wanley Manor and walked towards the village. It was the first time since his illness that he had left the grounds on foot. He was very thin, and had an absent, troubled look; the natural cheerfulness of youth's convalescence seemed altogether lacking in him.

From a rising point of the road, winding between the Manor and Wanley, a good view of the valley offered itself; here Hubert paused, leaning a little on his stick, and let his eyes dwell upon the prospect. A year ago he had stood here and enjoyed the sweep of meadows between Stanbury Hill and the wooded slope opposite, the orchard-patches, the flocks along the margin of the little river. To-day he viewed a very different scene. Building of various kinds was in progress in the heart of the vale; a great massive chimney was rising to completion, and about it stood a number of sheds. Beyond was to be seen the commencement of a street of small houses, promising infinite ugliness in a little space; the soil over a considerable area was torn up and trodden into mud. A number of men were at work; carts and waggons and trucks were moving about. In truth, the benighted valley was waking up and donning the true nineteenth-century livery.

The young man's face, hitherto thoughtfully sad, changed to an expression of bitterness; he muttered what seemed to be angry and contemptuous words, then averted his eyes and walked on. He entered the village street and passed along it for some distance, his fixed gaze appearing studiously to avoid the people who stood about or walked by him. There was a spot of warm colour on his cheeks; he held himself very upright and had a painfully self-conscious air.

He stopped before a dwelling-house, rang the bell, and made inquiry whether Mr. Mutimer was at home. The reply being affirmative, he followed the servant up to the first floor. His name was announced at the door of a sitting-room, and he entered.

Two men were conversing in the room. One sat at the table with a sheet of paper before him, sketching a rough diagram and scribbling notes; this was Richard Mutimer. He was dressed in a light tweed suit; his fair moustache and beard were trimmed, and the hand which rested on the table was no longer that of a daily-grimed mechanic. His linen was admirably starched; altogether he had a very fresh and cool appearance. His companion was astride on a chair, his arms resting on the back, a pipe in his mouth. This man was somewhat older than Mutimer; his countenance indicated shrewdness and knowledge of the world. He was dark and well-featured, his glossy black hair was parted in the middle, his moustache of the cut called imperial, his beard short and peaked. He wore a canvas jacket, a white waistcoat and knickerbockers; at his throat a blue necktie fluttered loose. When Hubert's name was announced by the servant, this gentleman stopped midway in a sentence, took his pipe from his lips, and looked to the door with curiosity.

Mutimer rose and addressed his visitor easily indeed, but not discourteously.

'How do you do, Mr. Eldon? I'm glad to see that you are so much better. Will you sit down? I think you know Mr. Rodman, at all events by name?'

Hubert assented by gesture. He had come prepared for disagreeable things in this his first meeting with Mutimer, but the honour of an introduction to the latter's friends had not been included in his anticipations. Mr. Rodman had risen and bowed slightly. His smile carried a disagreeable suggestion from which Mutimer's behaviour was altogether free; he rather seemed to enjoy the situation.

For a moment there was silence and embarrassment. Richard overcame the difficulty.

'Come and dine with me to-night, will you?' he said to Rodman. 'Here, take this plan with you, and think it over.'

'Pray don't let me interfere with your business,' interposed Hubert, with scrupulous politeness. 'I could see you later, Mr. Mutimer.'

'No, no; Rodman and I have done for the present,' said Mutimer, cheerfully. 'By-the-by,' he added, as his right-hand man moved to the door, 'don't forget to drop a line to Slater and Smith. And, I say, if Hogg turns up before two o'clock, send him here; I'll be down with you by half-past.'

Mr. Rodman gave an 'All right,' nodded to Hubert, who paid no attention, and took his departure.

'You've had a long pull of it,' Richard began, as he took his chair again, and threw his legs into an easy position. 'Shall I close the windows? Maybe you don't like the draught.'

'Thank you; I feel no draught.'

The working man had the advantage as yet. Hubert in vain tried to be at ease, whilst Mutimer was quite himself, and not ungraceful in his assumption of equality. For one thing, Hubert could not avoid a comparison between his own wasted frame and the other's splendid physique; it heightened the feeling of antagonism which possessed him in advance, and provoked the haughtiness he had resolved to guard against. The very lineaments of the men foretold mutual antipathy. Hubert's extreme delicacy of feature was the outward expression of a character so compact of subtleties and refinements, of high prejudice and jealous sensibility, of spiritual egoism and all-pervading fastidiousness, that it was impossible for him not to regard with repugnance a man who represented the combative principle, even the triumph, of the uncultured classes. He was no hidebound aristocrat; the liberal tendencies of his intellect led him to scorn the pageantry of long-descended fools as strongly as he did the blind image-breaking of the mob; but in a case of personal relations temperament carried it over judgment in a very high-handed way. Youth and disappointment weighed in the scale of unreason. Mutimer, on the other hand, though fortune helped him to forbearance, saw, or believed he saw, the very essence of all he most hated in this proud-eyed representative of a county family. His own rough-sculptured comeliness corresponded to the vigour and practicality and zeal of a nature which cared nothing for form and all for substance; the essentials of life were to him the only things in life, instead of, as to Hubert Eldon, the mere brute foundation of an artistic superstructure. Richard read clearly enough the sentiments with which his visitor approached him; who that is the object of contempt does not readily perceive it? His way of revenging himself was to emphasise a tone of good fellowship, to make it evident how well he could afford to neglect privileged insolence. In his heart he triumphed over the disinherited aristocrat; outwardly he was civil, even friendly.

Hubert had made this call with a special purpose.

'I am charged by Mrs. Eldon,' he began, 'to thank you for the courtesy you have shown her during my illness. My own thanks likewise I hope you will accept. We have caused you, I fear, much inconvenience.'

Richard found himself envying the form and tone of this deliverance; he gathered his beard in his hands and gave it a tug.

'Not a bit of it,' he replied. 'I am very comfortable here. A bedroom and a place for work, that's about all I want.'

Hubert barely smiled. He wondered whether the mention of work was meant to suggest comparisons. He hastened to add—

'On Monday we hope to leave the Manor.'

'No need whatever for hurry,' observed Mutimer, good-humouredly. 'Please tell Mrs. Eldon that I hope she will take her own time.' On reflection this seemed rather an ill-chosen phrase; he bettered it. 'I should be very sorry if she inconvenienced herself on my account.'

'Confound the fellow's impudence!' was Hubert's mental comment. 'He plays the forbearing landlord.'

His spoken reply was: 'It is very kind of you. I foresee no difficulty in completing the removal on Monday.'

In view of Mutimer's self-command, Hubert began to be aware that his own constraint might carry the air of petty resentment. Fear of that drove him upon a topic he would rather have left alone.

'You are changing the appearance of the valley,' he said, veiling by his tone the irony which was evident in his choice of words.

Richard glanced at him, then walked to the window, with his hands in his pockets, and gave himself the pleasure of a glimpse of the furnace-chimney above the opposite houses. He laughed.

'I hope to change it a good deal more. In a year or two you won't know the place.'

'I fear not.'

Mutimer glanced again at his visitor.

'Why do you fear?' he asked, with less command of his voice.

'I of course understand your point of view. Personally, I prefer nature.'

Hubert endeavoured to smile, that his personal preferences might lose something of their edge.

'You prefer nature,' Mutimer repeated, coming back to his chair, on the seat of which he rested a foot. 'Well, I can't say that I do. The Wanley Iron Works will soon mean bread to several hundred families; how many would the grass support?'

'To be sure,' assented Hubert, still smiling.

'You are aware,' Mutimer proceeded to ask, 'that this is not a speculation for my own profit?'

'I have heard something of your scheme. I trust it will be appreciated.'

'I dare say it will be—by those who care anything about the welfare of the people.'

Eldon rose; he could not trust himself to continue the dialogue. He had expected to meet a man of coarser grain, Mutimer's intelligence made impossible the civil condescension which would have served with a boor, and Hubert found the temptation to pointed utterance all the stronger for the dangers it involved.

'I will drop you a note,' he said, 'to let you know as soon as the house is empty.'

'Thank you.'

They had not shaken hands at meeting, nor did they now. Each felt relieved when out of the other's sight.

Hubert turned out of the street into a road which would lead him to the church, whence there was a field-path back to the Manor. Walking with his eyes on the ground he did not

perceive the tall, dark figure that approached him as he drew
near to the churchyard gate. Mr. Wyvern had been conducting
a burial; he had just left the vestry and was on his way to the
vicarage, which stood five minutes' walk from the church.
Himself unperceived, he scrutinised the young man until he
stood face to face with him; his deep-voiced greeting caused
Hubert to look up with a start.

'I'm very glad to see you walking,' said the clergyman.

He took Hubert's hand and held it paternally in both his
own. Eldon seemed affected with a sudden surprise; as he met
the large gaze his look showed embarrassment.

'You remember me?' Mr. Wyvern remarked, his wonted
solemnity lightened by the gleam of a brief smile. Looking
closely into his face was like examining a map in relief; you
saw heights and plains, the intersection of multitudinous valleys,
river-courses with their tributaries. It was the visage of a man
of thought and character. His eyes spoke of late hours and
the lamp; beneath each was a heavy pocket of skin, wrinkling
at its juncture with the cheek. His teeth were those of an incessant smoker, and, in truth, you could seldom come near him
without detecting the odour of tobacco. Despite the amplitude
of his proportions, there was nothing ponderous about him;
the great head was finely formed, and his limbs must at one
time have been as graceful as they were muscular.

'Is this accident,' Hubert asked; 'or did you know me at
the time?'

'Accident, pure accident. Will you walk to the vicarage
with me?'

They paced side by side.

'Mrs. Eldon profits by the pleasant weather, I trust?' the
vicar observed, with grave courtesy.

'Thank you, I think she does. I shall be glad when she is
settled in her new home.'

They approached the door of the vicarage in silence. Entering, Mr. Wyvern led the way to his study. When he had
taken a seat, he appeared to forget himself for a moment, and
played with the end of his beard.

Hubert showed impatient curiosity.

'You found me there by chance that morning?' he began.

The clergyman returned to the present. His elbows on
either arm of his round chair, he sat leaning forward, thoughtfully gazing at his companion.

'By chance,' he replied, 'I sleep badly; so it happened

that I was abroad shortly after daybreak. I was near the edge of the wood when I heard a pistol-shot. I waited for the second.'

'We fired together,' Hubert remarked.

'Ah! It seemed to me one report. Well, as I stood listening, there came out from among the trees a man who seemed in a hurry. He was startled at finding himself face to face with me, but didn't stop; he said something rapidly in French that I failed to catch, pointed back into the wood, and hastened off.'

'We had no witnesses,' put in Hubert; 'and both aimed our best. I wonder he sent you to look for me.'

'A momentary weakness, no doubt,' rejoined the vicar drily. 'I made my way among the trees and found you lying there, unconscious. I made some attempt to stop the blood-flow, then picked you up; it seemed better, on the whole, than leaving you on the wet grass an indefinite time. Your overcoat was on the ground; as I took hold of it, two letters fell from the pocket. I made no scruple about reading the addresses, and was astonished to find that one was to Mrs. Eldon, at Wanley Manor, Wanley being the place where I was about to live on my return to England. I took it for granted that you were Mrs. Eldon's son. The other letter, as you know, was to a lady at a hotel in the town.'

Hubert nodded.

'And you went to her as soon as you left me?'

'After hearing from the doctor that there was no immediate danger.—The letters, I suppose, would have announced your death?'

Hubert again inclined his head. The imperturbable gravity of the speaker had the effect of imposing self-command on the young man, whose sensitive cheeks showed what was going on within.

'Will you tell me of your interview with her?' he asked.

'It was of the briefest; my French is not fluent.'

'But she speaks English well.'

'Probably her distress led her to give preference to her native tongue. She was anxious to go to you immediately, and I told her where you lay. I made inquiries next day, and found that she was still giving you her care. As you were doing well, and I had to be moving homewards, I thought it better to leave without seeing you again. The innkeeper had directions to telegraph to me if there was a change for the worse.'

'My pocket-book saved me,' remarked Hubert, touching his side.

Mr. Wyvern drew in his lips.

'Came between that ready-stamped letter and Wanley Manor,' was his comment.

There was a brief silence.

'You allow me a question?' the vicar resumed. 'It is with reference to the French lady.'

'I think you have every right to question me.'

'Oh no! It does not concern the events prior to your—accident.' Mr. Wyvern savoured the word. 'How long did she remain in attendance upon you?'

'A short time—two days—I did not need——'

Mr. Wyvern motioned with his hand, kindly.

'Then I was not mistaken,' he said, averting his eyes for the first time, 'in thinking that I saw her in Paris.'

'In Paris?' Hubert repeated, with a poor affectation of indifference.

'I made a short stay before crossing. I had business at a bank one day; as I stood before the counter a gentleman entered and took a place beside me. A second look assured me that he was the man who met me at the edge of the wood that morning. I suppose he remembered me, for he looked away and moved from me. I left the bank, and found an open carriage waiting at the door. In it sat the lady of whom we speak. I took a turn along the pavement and back again. The Frenchman entered the carriage; they drove away.'

Hubert's eyes were veiled; he breathed through his nostrils. Again there was silence.

'Mr. Eldon,' resumed the vicar, 'I was a man of the world before I became a Churchman; you will notice that I affect no professional tone in speaking with you, and it is because I know that anything of the kind would only alienate you. It appeared to me that chance had made me aware of something it might concern you to hear. I know nothing of the circumstances of the case, merely offer you the facts.'

'I thank you,' was Hubert's reply in an undertone.

'It impressed me, that letter ready stamped for Wanley Manor. I thought of it again after the meeting in Paris.'

'I understand you. Of course I could explain the necessity. It would be useless.'

'Quite. But experience is not, or should not be, useless,

especially when commented on by one who has very much of it
behind him.'

Hubert stood up. His mind was in a feverishly active
state, seeming to follow several lines of thought simultaneously.
Among other things, he was wondering how it was that
throughout this conversation he had been so entirely passive.
He had never found himself under the influence of so strong a
personality, exerted too in such a strangely quiet way.

'What are your plans—your own plans?' Mr. Wyvern
inquired.

'I have none.'

'Forgive me;—there will be no material difficulties?'

'None; I have four hundred a year.'

'You have not graduated yet, I believe?'

'No. But I hardly think I can go back to school.'

'Perhaps not. Well, turn things over. I should like to
hear from you.'

'You shall.'

Hubert continued his walk to the Manor. Before the entrance stood two large furniture-vans; the doorway was littered
with materials of packing, and the hall was full of objects in
disorder. Footsteps made a hollow resonance in all parts of
the house, for everywhere the long wonted conditions of sound
were disturbed. The library was already dismantled; here he
could close the door and walk about without fear of intrusion.
He would have preferred to remain in the open air, but a
summer shower had just begun as he reached the house. He
could not sit still; the bare floor of the large room met his needs.

His mind's eye pictured a face which a few months ago had
power to lead him whither it willed, which had in fact led him
through strange scenes, as far from the beaten road of a college
curriculum as well could be. It was a face of foreign type,
Jewish possibly, most unlike that ideal of womanly charm kept
in view by one who seeks peace and the heart's home. Hubert
had entertained no thought of either. The romance which
most young men are content to enjoy in printed pages he had
acted out in his life. He had lived through a glorious madness,
as unlike the vulgar oat-sowing of the average young man of
wealth as the latest valse on a street-organ is unlike a passionate
dream of Chopin. However unworthy the object of his frenzy
—and perhaps one were as worthy as another—the pursuit had
borne him through an atmosphere of fire, tempering him for
life, marking him for ever from plodders of the dusty highway.

A reckless passion is a patent of nobility. Whatever existence had in store for him henceforth, Hubert could feel that he had lived.

An hour's communing with memory was brought to an end by the ringing of the luncheon-bell. Since his illness Hubert had taken meals with his mother in her own sitting-room. Thither he now repaired.

Mrs. Eldon had grown older in appearance since that evening of her son's return. Of course she had discovered the cause of his illness, and the incessant torment of a great fear had been added to what she suffered from the estrangement between the boy and herself. Her own bodily weakness had not permitted her to nurse him; she had passed days and nights in anguish of expectancy. At one time it had been life or death. If he died, what life would be hers through the brief delay to which she could look forward ?

Once more she had him by her side, but the moral distance between them was nothing lessened : Mrs. Eldon's pride would not allow her to resume the conversation which had ended so hopelessly for her, and she interpreted Hubert's silence in the saddest sense. Now they were about to be parted again. A house had been taken for her at Agworth, three miles away ; in her state of health she could not quit the neighbourhood of the few old friends whom she still saw. But Hubert would necessarily go into the world to seek some kind of career. No hope shone for her in the prospect.

Whilst the servant waited on them at luncheon, mother and son exchanged few words. Afterwards, Mrs. Eldon had her chair moved to the window, where she could see the garden greenery.

' I called on Mr. Mutimer,' Hubert said, standing near her. Through the meal he had cast frequent glances at her pale, nobly-lined countenance, as if something had led him to occupy his thoughts with her. He looked at her in the same way now.

' Did you ? How did he impress you ? '

' He is not quite the man I had expected; more civilised. I should suppose he is the better kind of artisan. He talks with a good deal of the working-class accent, of course, but not like a wholly uneducated man.'

' His letter, you remember, was anything but illiterate. I feel I ought to ask him to come and see me before we leave.'

' The correspondence surely suffices.'

'You expressed my thanks?'

'Conscientiously.'

'I see you found the interview rather difficult, Hubert.'

'How could it be otherwise? The man is well enough, of his kind, but the kind is detestable.'

'Did he try to convert you to Socialism?' asked his mother, smiling in her sad way.

'I imagine he discerned the hopelessness of such an undertaking. We had a little passage of arms,—quite within the bounds of civility. Shall I tell you how I felt in talking with him? I seemed to be holding a dialogue with the twentieth century, and you may think what that means.'

'Ah, it's a long way off, Hubert.'

'I wish it were farther. The man was openly exultant; he stood for Demos grasping the sceptre. I am glad, mother, that you leave Wanley before the air is poisoned.'

'Mr. Mutimer does not see that side of the question?'

'Not he! Do you imagine the twentieth century will leave one green spot on the earth's surface?'

'My dear, it will always be necessary to grow grass and corn.'

'By no means; depend upon it. Such things will be cultivated by chemical processes. There will not be one inch left to nature; the very oceans will somehow be tamed, the snow-mountains will be levelled. And with nature will perish art. What has a hungry Demos to do with the beautiful?'

Mrs. Eldon sighed gently.

'I shall not see it.'

Her eyes dreamed upon the soft-swaying boughs of a young chestnut. Hubert was watching her face; its look and the meaning implied in her words touched him profoundly.

'Mother!' he said under his breath.

'My dear?'

He drew nearer to her and just stroked with his fingers the silver lines which marked the hair on either side of her brows. He could see that she trembled and that her lips set themselves in hard self-conquest.

'What do you wish me to do when we have left the Manor?'

His own voice was hurried between two quiverings of the throat; his mother's only whispered in reply.

'That is for your own consideration, Hubert.'

'With your counsel, mother.'

' My counsel ? '

' I ask it. I will follow it. I wish to be guided by you.'

He knelt by her, and his mother pressed his head against her bosom.

Later, she asked—

' Did you call also on the Walthams ? '

He shook his head.

' Should you not do so, dear ? '

' I think that must be later.'

The subject was not pursued.

The next day was Saturday. In the afternoon Hubert took a walk which had been his favourite one ever since he could remember, every step of the way associated with recollections of childhood, boyhood, or youth. It was along the lane which began in a farmyard close by the Manor and climbed with many turnings to the top of Stanbury Hill. This was ever the first route re-examined by his brother Godfrey and himself on their return from school at holiday-time. It was a rare region for bird-nesting, so seldom was it trodden save by a few farm-labourers at early morning or when the day's work was over. Hubert passed with a glance of recognition the bramble in which he had found his first spink's nest, the shadowed mossy bank whence had fluttered the hapless wren just when the approach of two prowling youngsters should have bidden her keep close. Boys on the egg-trail are not wont to pay much attention to the features of the country; but Hubert remembered that at a certain meadow-gate he had always rested for a moment to view the valley, some mute presage of things un-imagined stirring at his heart. Was it even then nineteenth century ? Not for him, seeing that the life of each of us repro-duces the successive ages of the world. Belwick, roaring a few miles away, was but an isolated black patch on the earth's beauty, not, as he now understood it, a malignant cancer-spot, spreading day by day, corrupting, an augury of death. In those days it had seemed fast in the order of things that Wanley Manor should be his home through life; how otherwise ? Was it not the abiding-place of the Eldons from of old ? Who had ever hinted at revolution ? He knew now that revolution had been at work from an earlier time than that; whilst he played and rambled with his brother the framework of their life was crumbling about them. Belwick was already throwing a shadow upon Wanley. And now behold ! he stood at the old gate, rested his hands where they had been wont to rest, turned his eyes in the familiar direction; no longer a mere shadow, there was Belwick itself.

His heart was hot with outraged affection, with injured pride. On the scarcely closed grave of that passion which had flamed through so brief a life sprang up the flower of natural tenderness, infinitely sweet and precious. For the first time he was fully conscious of what it meant to quit Wanley for ever; the past revealed itself to him, lovelier and more loved because parted from him by so hopeless a gulf. Hubert was not old enough to rate experience at its true value, to acquiesce in the law which wills that the day must perish before we can enjoy to the full its light and odour. He could only feel his loss, and rebel against the fate which had ordained it.

He had climbed but half-way up the hill; from this point onwards there was no view till the summit was reached, for the lane proceeded between high banks and hedges. To gain the very highest point he had presently to quit the road by a stile and skirt the edge of a small rising meadow, at the top of which was an old cow-house with a few trees growing about it. Thence one had the finest prospect in the county.

He reached the stone shed, looked back for a moment over Wanley, then walked round to the other side. As he turned the corner of the building his eye was startled by the unexpected gleam of a white dress. A girl stood there; she was viewing the landscape through a field-glass, and thus remained unaware of his approach on the grass. He stayed his step and observed her with eyes of recognition. Her attitude, both hands raised to hold the glass, displayed to perfection the virginal outline of her white-robed form. She wore a straw hat of the plain masculine fashion; her brown hair was plaited in a great circle behind her head, not one tendril loosed from the mass; a white collar closely circled her neck; her waist was bound with a red girdle. All was grace and purity; the very folds towards the bottom of her dress hung in sculpturesque smoothness; the form of her half-seen foot bowed the herbage with lightest pressure. From the boughs above there fell upon her a dancing network of shadow.

Hubert only half smiled; he stood with his hands joined behind him, his eyes fixed upon her face, waiting for her to turn. But several moments passed and she was still intent on the landscape. He spoke.

'Will you let me look?'

Her hands fell, all but dropping the glass; still, she did not
start with unbecoming shrug as most people do, the instinctive
movement of guarding against a stroke; the falling of her arms
was the only abrupt motion, her head turning in the direction
of the speaker with a grace as spontaneous as that we see in a
fawn that glances back before flight.

'Oh, Mr. Eldon! How silently you have come!'

The wild rose of her cheeks made rivalry for an instant
with the richer garden blooms, and the subsiding warmth left a
pearly translucency as of a lily petal against the light.

She held her hand to him, delicately gloved, warm; the
whole of it was hidden within Hubert's clasp.

'What were you looking at so attentively?' he asked.

'At Agworth station,' replied Adela, turning her eyes again
in that quarter. 'My brother's train ought to be in by now, I
think. He comes home every Saturday.'

'Does he?'

Hubert spoke without thought, his look resting upon the
maiden's red girdle.

'I am glad that you are well again,' Adela said with natural
kindness. 'You have had a long illness.'

'Yes; it has been a tiresome affair. Is Mrs. Waltham well?'

'Quite, thank you.'

'And your brother?'

'Alfred never had anything the matter with him in his
life, I believe,' she answered, with a laugh.

'Fortunate fellow! Will you lend me the glass?'

She held it to him, and at the same moment her straying
eye caught a glimpse of white smoke, far off.

'There comes the train!' she exclaimed. 'You will be
able to see it between these two hills.'

Hubert looked and returned the glass to her, but she did
not make use of it.

'Does he walk over from Agworth?' was Hubert's next
question.

'Yes. It does him good after a week of Belwick.'

'There will soon be little difference between Belwick and
Wanley,' rejoined Hubert, drily.

Adela glanced at him; there was sympathy and sorrow in
the look.

'I knew it would grieve you,' she said.

'And what is your own feeling? Do you rejoice in the
change as a sign of progress?'

'Indeed, no. I am very, very sorry to have our beautiful valley so spoilt. It is only——'

Hubert eyed her with sudden sharpness of scrutiny; the look seemed to check her words.

'Only what?' he asked. 'You find compensations?'

'My brother won't hear of such regrets,' she continued with a little embarrassment. 'He insists on the good that will be done by the change.'

'From such a proprietor as I should have been to a man of Mr. Mutimer's activity. To be sure, that is one point of view.'

Adela blushed.

'That is not my meaning, Mr. Eldon, as you know. I was speaking of the change without regard to who brings it about. And I was not giving my own opinion; Alfred's is always on the side of the working people; he seems to forget everybody else in his zeal for their interests. And then, the works are going to be quite a new kind of undertaking. You have heard of Mr. Mutimer's plans, of course?'

'I have an idea of them.'

'You think them mistaken?'

'No. I would rather say they don't interest me. That seems to disappoint you, Miss Waltham. Probably you are interested in them?'

At the sound of her own name thus formally interjected, Adela just raised her eyes from their reflective gaze on the near landscape; then she became yet more thoughtful.

'Yes, I think I am,' she replied, with deliberation. 'The principle seems a just one. Devotion to a really unselfish cause is rare, I am afraid.'

'You have met Mr. Mutimer?'

'Once. My brother made his acquaintance, and he called on us.'

'Did he explain his scheme to you in detail?'

'Not himself. Alfred has told me all about it. He, of course, is delighted with it; he has joined what he calls the Union.'

'Are you going to join?' Hubert asked, smiling.

'I? I doubt whether they would have me.'

She laughed silverly, her throat tremulous, like that of a bird that sings. How significant the laugh was! the music of how pure a freshet of life!

'All the members, I presume,' said Hubert, 'are to be speedily enriched from the Wanley Mines and Iron Works?'

G

It was jokingly uttered, but Adela replied with some
earnestness, as if to remove a false impression.

'Oh, that is quite a mistake, Mr. Eldon. There is no
question of anyone being enriched, least of all Mr. Mutimer
himself. The workmen will receive just payment, not mere
starvation wages, but whatever profit there is will be devoted
to the propaganda.'

'Propaganda! Starvation wages! Ah, I see you have
gone deeply into these matters. How strangely that word
sounds on your lips—propaganda!'

Adela reddened.

'Why strangely, Mr. Eldon?'

'One associates it with such very different speakers; it has
such a terrible canting sound. I hope you will not get into
the habit of using it—for your own sake.'

'I am not likely to use it much. I suppose I have heard
it so often from Alfred lately. Please don't think,' she added
rather hastily, 'that I have become a Socialist. Indeed, I dislike the name; I find it implies so many things that I could
never approve of.'

Her way of speaking the last sentence would have amused
a dispassionate critic, it was so distinctively the tone of Puritan
maidenhood. From lips like Adela's it is delicious to hear
such moral babbling. Oh, the gravity of conviction in a white-
souled English girl of eighteen! Do you not hear her say
those words: 'things that I could never approve of'?

As her companion did not immediately reply, she again
raised the field-glass to her eyes and swept the prospect.

'Can you see your brother on the road?' Hubert inquired.

'No, not yet. There is a trap driving this way. Why,
Alfred is sitting in it! Oh, it is Mr. Mutimer's trap I see.
He must have met Alfred at the station and have given him a
ride.'

'Evidently they are great friends,' commented Eldon.

Adela did not reply. After gazing a little longer, she
said—

'He will be home before I can get there.'

She screwed up the glasses and turned as if to take leave.
But Hubert prepared to walk by her side, and together they
reached the lane.

'Now I am going to run down the hill,' Adela said, laughing. 'I can't ask you to join in such childishness, and I
suppose you are not going this way, either?'

'No, I am walking back to the Manor,' the other replied soberly. 'We had better say good-bye. On Monday we shall leave Wanley, my mother and I.'

'On Monday?'

The girl became graver.

'But only to go to Agworth?' she added.

'I shall not remain at Agworth. I am going to London.'

'To—to study?'

'Something or other, I don't quite know what. Good-bye!'

'Won't you come to say good-bye to us—to mother?'

'Shall you be at home to-morrow afternoon, about four o'clock say?'

'Oh, yes; the very time.'

'Then I will come to say good-bye.'

'In that case we needn't say it now, need we? It is only good-afternoon.'

She began to walk down the lane.

'I thought you were going to run,' cried Hubert.

She looked back, and her silver laugh made chorus with the joyous refrain of a yellow-hammer, piping behind the hedge. Till the turn of the road she continued walking, then Hubert had a glimpse of white folds waving in the act of flight, and she was beyond his vision.

CHAPTER VIII.

ADELA reached the house door at the very moment that Mutimer's trap drove up. She had run nearly all the way down the hill, and her soberer pace during the last ten minutes had not quite reduced the flush in her cheeks. Mutimer raised his hat with much *aplomb* before he had pulled up his horse, and his look stayed on her whilst Alfred Waltham was descending and taking leave.

'I was lucky enough to overtake your brother in Agworth,' he said.

'Ah, you have deprived him of what he calls his constitutional,' laughed Adela.

'Have I? Well, it isn't often I'm here over Saturday, so he can generally feel safe.'

G 2

The hat was again aired, and Richard drove away to the Wheatsheaf Inn, where he kept his horse at present.

Brother and sister went together into the parlour, where Mrs. Waltham immediately joined them, having descended from an upper room.

'So Mr. Mutimer drove you home!' she exclaimed, with the interest which provincial ladies, lacking scope for their energies, will display in very small incidents.

'Yes. By the way, I've asked him to come and have dinner with us to-morrow. He hadn't any special reason for going to town, and was uncertain whether to do so or not, so I thought I might as well have him here.'

Mr. Alfred always spoke in a somewhat emphatic first person singular when domestic arrangements were under discussion ; occasionally the habit led to a passing unpleasantness of tone between himself and Mrs. Waltham. In the present instance, however, nothing of the kind was to be feared ; his mother smiled very graciously.

'I'm glad you thought of it,' she said. 'It would have been very lonely for him in his lodgings.'

Neither of the two happened to be regarding Adela, or they would have seen a look of dismay flit across her countenance and pass into one of annoyance. When the talk had gone on for a few minutes Adela interposed a question.

'Will Mr. Mutimer stay for tea also, do you think, Alfred ?'

'Oh, of course ; why shouldn't he ?'

It is the country habit; Adela might have known what answer she would receive. She got out of the difficulty by means of a little disingenuousness.

'He won't want us to talk about Socialism all the time, will he ?'

'Of course not, my dear,' replied Mrs. Waltham. 'Why, it will be Sunday.'

Alfred shouted in mirthful scorn.

'Well, that's one of the finest things I've heard for a long time, mother ! It'll be Sunday, and *therefore* we are not to talk about improving the lot of the human race. Ye gods ! '

Mrs. Waltham was puzzled for an instant, but the Puritan assurance did not fail her.

'Yes, but that is only improvement of their bodies, Alfred —food and clothing. The six days are for that you know.'

'Mother, mother, you will kill me ! You are so uncommonly funny! I wonder your friends haven't long ago found some way of doing without bodies altogether. Now, I pray you, do not talk nonsense. Surely *that* is forbidden on the Sabbath, if only the Jewish one.'

'Mother is quite right, Alfred,' remarked Adela, with quiet affirmativeness, as soon as her voice could be heard. 'Your Socialism is earthly; we have to think of other things besides bodily comforts.'

'Who said we hadn't?' cried her brother. 'But I take leave to inform you that you won't get much spiritual excellence out of a man who lives a harder life than the nigger-slaves. If you women could only put aside your theories and look a little at obstinate facts! You're all of a piece. Which of you was it that talked the other day about getting the vicar to pray for rain? Ho, ho, ho! Just the same kind of thing.'

Alfred's combativeness had grown markedly since his making acquaintance with Mutimer. He had never excelled in the suaver virtues, and now the whole of the time he spent at home was devoted to vociferous railing at capitalists, priests, and women, his mother and sister serving for illustrations of the vices prevalent in the last-mentioned class. In talking he always paced the room, hands in pockets, and at times fairly stammered in his endeavour to hit upon sufficiently trenchant epithets or comparisons. When reasoning failed with his auditors, he had recourse to volleys of contemptuous laughter. At times he lost his temper, muttered words such as ' fools !'— 'idiots!' and flung out into the open air. It looked as if the present evening was to be a stormy one. Adela noted the presage and allowed herself a protest *in limine*.

'Alfred, I do hope you won't go on in this way whilst Letty is here. You mayn't think it, but you pain her very much.'

'Pain her! It's her education. She's had none yet, no more than you have. It's time you both began to learn.'

It being close upon the hour for tea, the young lady of whom there was question was heard to ring the door-bell. We have already had a passing glimpse of her, but since then she has been honoured by becoming Alfred's affianced. Letty Tew fulfilled all the conditions desirable in one called to so trying a destiny. She was a pretty, supple, sweet-mannered girl, and, as is the case with such girls, found it possible to worship a man whom in consistency she must have deemed the most condemnable of heretics. She and Adela were close friends;

Adela, indeed, had no other friend in the nearer sense. The
two were made of very different fibre, but that had not as yet
distinctly shown.

Adela's reproof was not wholly without effect; her brother
got through the evening without proceeding to his extremest
truculence. Still the conversation was entirely of his leading,
consequently not a little argumentative. He had brought
home, as he always did on Saturday, a batch of ultra periodicals, among them the 'Fiery Cross,' and his own eloquence
was supplemented by the reading of excerpts from these lively
columns. It was a combat of three to one, but the majority
did little beyond throwing up hands at anything particularly
outrageous. Adela said much less than usual.

'I tell you what it is, you three!' Alfred cried, at a certain
climax of enthusiasm, addressing the ladies with characteristic
courtesy, 'we'll found a branch of the Union in Wanley; I
mean, in our particular circle of thickheads. Then, as soon as
Mutimer's settlement gets going, we can coalesce. Now you
two girls give next week to going round and soliciting subscrip-
tions for the "Fiery Cross." People have had time to get over
the first scare, and you know they can't refuse such as you.
Quarterly, one-and-eightpence, including postage.'

'But, my dear Alfred,' cried Adela, 'remember that Letty
and I are *not* Socialists!'

'Letty is, because I expect it of her, and you can't refuse
to keep her in countenance.'

The girls laughed merrily at this anticipated lordship; but
Letty said presently—

'I believe father will take the paper if I ask him. One is
better than nothing, isn't it, Alfred?'

'Good. We book Stephen Tew, Esquire.'

'But surely you mustn't call him Esquire?' suggested Adela.

'Oh, he is yet unregenerate; let him keep his baubles.'

'How are the regenerate designated?'

'Comrade, we prefer.'

'Also applied to women?'

'Well, I suppose not. As the word hasn't a feminine, call
yourselves plain Letty Tew and Adela Waltham, without
meaningless prefix.'

'What nonsense you are talking, Alfred!' remarked his
mother. 'As if everybody in Wanley could address young
ladies by their Christian names!'

In this way did Alfred begin the 'propaganda' at home.

Already the village was much occupied with the vague new doctrines represented by the name of Richard Mutimer; the parlour of the Wheatsheaf was loud of evenings with extraordinary debate, and gossips of a higher station had at length found a topic which promised to be inexhaustible. Of course the vicar was eagerly sounded as to his views. Mr. Wyvern preserved an attitude of scrupulous neutrality, contenting himself with correction of palpable absurdities in the stories going about. 'But surely you are not a Socialist, Mr. Wyvern?' cried Mrs. Mewling, after doing her best to pump the reverend gentleman, and discovering nothing. 'I am a Christian, madam,' was the reply, 'and have nothing to do with economic doctrines.' Mrs. Mewling spread the phrase 'economic doctrines,' shaking her head upon the adjective, which was interpreted by her hearers as condemnatory in significance. The half-dozen shop-keepers were disposed to secret jubilation; it was probable that, in consequence of the doings in the valley, trade would look up. Mutimer himself was a centre of interest such as Wanley had never known. When he walked down the street the news that he was visible seemed to spread like wildfire; every house had its gazers. Excepting the case of the Walthams, he had not as yet sought to make personal acquaintances, appearing rather to avoid opportunities. On the whole it seemed likely that he would be popular. The little group of mothers with marriageable daughters waited eagerly for the day when, by establishing himself at the Manor, he would throw off the present semi-incognito, and become the recognised head of Wanley society. He would discover the necessity of having a lady to share his honours and preside at his table. Persistent inquiry seemed to have settled the fact that he was not married already. To be sure, there were awesome rumours that Socialists repudiated laws divine and human in matrimonial affairs, but the more sanguine were inclined to regard this as calumny, their charity finding a support in their personal ambitions. The interest formerly attaching to the Eldons had altogether vanished. Mrs. Eldon and her son were now mere obstacles to be got rid of as quickly as possible. It was the general opinion that Hubert Eldon's illness was purposely protracted, to suit his mother's convenience. Until Mutimer's arrival there had been much talk about Hubert; whether owing to Dr. Mann's indiscretion or through the servants at the Manor, it had become known that the young man was suffering from a bullet-wound, and the story circulated by Mrs.

Mewling led gossips to suppose that he had been murderously assailed in that land of notorious profligacy known to Wanley as 'abroad.' That, however, was now become an old story. Wanley was anxious for the Eldons to go their way, and leave the stage clear.

Everyone of course was aware that Mutimer spent his Sundays in London (a circumstance, it was admitted, not altogether reassuring to the ladies with marriageable daughters), and his unwonted appearance in the village on the evening of the present Saturday excited universal comment. Would he appear at church next morning? There was a general directing of eyes to the Manor pew. This pew had not been occupied since the fateful Sunday when, at the conclusion of the morning service, old Mr. Mutimer was discovered to have breathed his last. It was a notable object in the dim little church, having a wooden canopy supported on four slim oak pillars with vermicular moulding. From pillar to pillar hung dark curtains, so that when these were drawn the interior of the pew was entirely protected from observation. Even on the brightest days its occupants were veiled in gloom. To-day the curtains remained drawn as usual, and Richard Mutimer disappointed the congregation. Wanley had obtained assurance on one point—Socialism involved Atheism.

Then it came to pass that someone saw Mutimer approach the Walthams' house just before dinner time; saw him, moreover, ring and enter. A couple of hours, and the ominous event was everywhere being discussed. Well, well, it was not difficult to see what *that* meant. Trust Mrs. Waltham for shrewd generalship. Adela Waltham had been formerly talked of in connection with young Eldon; but Eldon was now out of the question, and behold his successor, in a double sense! Mrs. Mewling surrendered her Sunday afternoon nap and flew from house to house—of course in time for the dessert wine at each. Her cry was *haro*! Really, this was sharp practice on Mrs. Waltham's part; it was stealing a march before the commencement of the game. Did there not exist a tacit understanding that movements were postponed until Mutimer's occupation of the Manor? Adela was a very nice young girl, to be sure, a very nice girl indeed, but one must confess that she had her eyes open. Would it not be well for united Wanley to let her know its opinion of such doings?

In the meantime Richard was enjoying himself, with as little thought of the Wanley gossips as of—shall we say, the old curtained pew in Wanley Church? He was perfectly aware that the Walthams did not represent the highest gentility, that there was a considerable interval, for example, between Mrs. Waltham and Mrs. Westlake; but the fact remained that he had never yet been on intimate terms with a family so refined. Radical revolutionist though he was, he had none of the grossness or obstinacy which would have denied to the *bourgeois* household any advantage over those of his own class. At dinner he found himself behaving circumspectly. He knew already that the cultivated taste objects to the use of a table-knife save for purposes of cutting; on the whole he saw grounds for the objection. He knew, moreover, that manducation and the absorption of fluids must be performed without audible gusto; the knowledge cost him some self-criticism. But there were numerous minor points of convention on which he was not so clear; it had never occurred to him, for instance, that civilisation demands the breaking of bread, that, in the absence of silver, a fork must suffice for the dissection of fish, that a napkin is a graceful auxiliary in the process of a meal and not rather an embarrassing superfluity of furtive application. Like a wise man, he did not talk much during dinner, devoting his mind to observation. Of one thing he speedily became aware, namely, that Mr. Alfred Waltham was so very much in his own house that it was not wholly safe to regard his demeanour as exemplary. Another point well certified was that if any person in the world could be pointed to as an unassailable pattern of comely behaviour that person was Mr. Alfred Waltham's sister. Richard observed Adela as closely as good manners would allow.

Talking little as yet—the young man at the head of the table gave others every facility for silence—Richard could occupy his thought in many directions. Among other things, he instituted a comparison between the young lady who sat opposite to him and someone—not a young lady, it is true, but of the same sex and about the same age. He tried to imagine Emma Vine seated at this table; the effort resulted in a disagreeable warmth in the lobes of his ears. Yes, but—he attacked himself—not Emma Vine dressed as he was accustomed to see her; suppose her possessed of all Adela Waltham's exterior advantages. As his imagination was working on the hint, Adela herself addressed a question to him. He looked up, he let her voice repeat itself in inward echo. His ears were still more disagreeably warm.

It was a lovely day—warm enough to dine with the windows open. The faintest air seemed to waft sunlight from corner to corner of the room; numberless birds sang on the near boughs and hedges; the flowers on the table were like a careless gift of gold-hearted prodigal summer. Richard transferred himself in spirit to a certain square on the borders of Hoxton and Islington, within scent of the Regent's Canal. The house there was now inhabited by Emma and her sisters; they also would be at dinner. Suppose he had the choice: there or here? Adela addressed to him another question. The square vanished into space.

How often he had spoken scornfully of that word 'lady'! Were not all of the sex women? What need for that hateful distinction? Richard tried another experiment with his imagination. 'I had dinner with some people called Waltham last Sunday. The old woman I didn't much care about; but there was a young woman——' Well, why not? On the other hand, suppose Emma Vine called at his lodgings. 'A young woman called this morning, sir——' Well, why not?

Dessert was on the table. He saw Adela's fingers take an orange, her other hand holding a little fruit-knife. Now, who could have imagined that the simple paring of an orange could be achieved at once with such consummate grace and so naturally? In Richard's country they first bite off a fraction of the skin, then dig away with what of finger-nail may be available. He knew someone who would assuredly proceed in that way.

Metamorphosis! Richard Mutimer speculates on æsthetic problems.

'You, gentlemen, I dare say will be wicked enough to smoke,' remarked Mrs. Waltham, as she rose from the table.

'I tell you what we shall be wicked enough to do, mother,' exclaimed Alfred. 'We shall have two cups of coffee brought out into the garden, and spare your furniture!'

'Very well, my son. Your *two* cups evidently mean that Adela and I are not invited to the garden.'

'Nothing of the kind. But I know you always go to sleep, and Adela doesn't like tobacco smoke.'

'I go to sleep, Alfred! You know very well that I have a very different occupation for my Sunday afternoons.'

'I really don't care anything about smoking,' observed Mutimer, with a glance at Adela.

'Oh, you certainly shall not deprive yourself on my account, Mr. Mutimer,' said the girl, good-naturedly. 'I hope soon to come out into the garden, and I am not at all sure that my objection to tobacco is serious.'

Ah, if Mrs. Mewling could have heard that speech! Mrs. Mewling's age was something less than fifty; probably she had had time to forget how a young girl such as Adela speaks in pure frankness and never looks back to muse over a double meaning.

It was nearly three o'clock. Adela compared her watch with the sitting-room clock, and, the gentlemen having retired, moved about the room with a look of uneasiness. Her mother stood at the window, seemingly regarding the sky, in reality occupying her thoughts with things much nearer. She turned and found Adela looking at her.

'I want just to run over and speak to Letty,' Adela said. 'I shall very soon be back.'

'Very well, dear,' replied her mother, scanning her face absently. 'But don't let them keep you.'

Adela quickly fetched her hat and left the house. It was her habit to walk at a good pace, always with the same airy movement, as though her feet only in appearance pressed the ground. On the way she again consulted her watch, and it caused her to flit still faster. Arrived at the abode of the Tews, she fortunately found Letty in the garden, sitting with two younger sisters, one a child of five years. Miss Tew was reading aloud to them, her book being 'Pilgrim's Progress.' At the sight of Adela the youngest of the three slipped down from her seat and ran to meet her with laughter and shaking of curls.

'Carry me round! carry me round!' cried the little one.

For it was Adela's habit to snatch up the flaxen little maiden, seat her upon her shoulder, and trot merrily round a circular path in the garden. But the sister next in age, whose thirteenth year had developed deep convictions, interposed sharply—

'Eva, don't be naughty! Isn't it Sunday?'

The little one, saved on the very brink of iniquity, turned away in confusion and stood with a finger in her mouth.

'I'll come and carry you round to-morrow, Eva,' said the visitor, stooping to kiss the reluctant face. Then, turning to the admonitress, 'Jessie, will you read a little? I want just to speak to Letty.'

Miss Jessie took the volume, made her countenance yet sterner, and, having drawn Eva to her side, began to read in measured tones, reproducing as well as she could the enunciation of the pulpit. Adela beckoned to her friend, and the two walked apart.

'I'm in such a fix,' she began, speaking hurriedly, 'and there isn't a minute to lose. Mr. Mutimer has been having dinner with us; Alfred invited him. And I expect Mr. Eldon to come about four o'clock. I met him yesterday on the Hill; he came up just as I was looking out for Alfred with the glass, and I asked him if he wouldn't come and say good-bye to mother this afternoon. Of course I'd no idea that Mr. Mutimer would come to dinner; he always goes away for Sunday. Isn't it dreadfully awkward?'

'You think he wouldn't like to meet Mr. Mutimer?' asked Letty, savouring the gravity of the situation.

'I'm sure he wouldn't. He spoke about him yesterday. Of course he didn't say anything against Mr. Mutimer, but I could tell from his way of speaking. And then it's quite natural, isn't it? I'm really afraid. He'll think it so unkind of me. I told him we should be alone, and I shan't be able to explain. Isn't it tiresome?'

'It is, really! But of course Mr. Eldon will understand. To think that it should happen just this day!'

An idea flashed across Miss Tew's mind.

'Couldn't you be at the door when he comes, and just—just say, you know, that you're sorry, that you knew nothing about Mr. Mutimer coming?'

'I've thought of something else,' returned Adela, lowering her voice, as if to impart a project of doubtful propriety. 'Suppose I walk towards the Manor and—and meet him on the way, before he gets very far? Then I could save him the annoyance, couldn't I, dear?'

Letty widened her eyes. The idea was splendid, but—

'You don't think, dear, that it might be a little—that you might find it—— ?'

Adela reddened.

'It is only a piece of kindness. Mr. Eldon will understand, I'm sure. He asked me so particularly if we should be alone. I really feel it a duty. Don't you think I may go? I must decide at once.'

Letty hesitated.

'If you really advise me not to——' pursued Adela. 'But I'm sure I shall be glad when it's done.'

'Then go, dear. Yes, I would go if I were you.'

Adela now faltered.

'You really would go, in my place ?'

'Yes, yes, I'm sure I should. You see, it isn't as if it was Mr. Mutimer you were going to meet.'

'Oh, no, no! That would be impossible.'

'He will be very grateful,' murmured Letty, without looking up.

'If I go, it must be at once.'

'Your mother doesn't know he was coming ?'

'No. I don't know why I haven't told her, really. I suppose we were talking so much of other things last night. And then I only got home just as Alfred did, and he said at once that he had invited Mr. Mutimer. Yes, I will go. Perhaps I'll come and see you again after church.'

Letty went back to 'Pilgrim's Progress.' Her sister Jessie enjoyed the sound of her own voice, and did not offer to surrender the book, so she sat by little Eva's side and resumed her Sunday face.

Adela took the road for the Manor, resisting the impulse to cast glances on either side as she passed the houses at the end of the village. She felt it to be more than likely that eyes were observing her, as it was an unusual time for her to be abroad, and the direction of her walk pointed unmistakably to one destination. But she made no account of secrecy; her errand was perfectly simple and with an object that no one could censure. If people tattled, they alone were to blame. For the first time she experienced a little resentment of the public criticism which was so rife in Wanley, and the experience was useful—one of those inappreciable aids to independence which act by cumulative stress on a character capable of development and softly mould its outlines.

She passed the church, then the vicarage, and entered the hedgeway which by a longe curve led to the Manor. She was slackening her pace, not wishing to approach too near to the house, when she at length saw Hubert Eldon walking towards her. He advanced with a look which was not exactly indifferent yet showed no surprise; the smile only came to his face when he was near enough to speak.

'I have come to meet you,' Adela began, with frankness which cost her a little agitation of breath. 'I am so very sorry to have misled you yesterday. As soon as I reached home, I found that my brother had invited Mr. Mutimer for to-day. I thought it would be best if I came and told you that—that we were not quite alone, as I said we should be.'

As she spoke Adela became distressed by perceiving, or seeming to perceive, that the cause which had led her to this step was quite inadequate. Of course it was the result of her having to forbear mention of the real point at issue; she could not say that she feared it might be disagreeable to her hearer to meet Mutimer. But, put in the other way, her pretext for coming appeared trivial. Only with an extreme effort she preserved her even tone to the end of her speech.

'It is very kind of you,' Hubert replied almost warmly. 'I'm very sorry you have had the trouble.'

As she disclaimed thanks, Eldon's tack discovered the way of safety. Facing her with a quiet openness of look, he said, in a tone of pleasant directness which Adela had often felt to be peculiarly his own—

'I shall best thank you by admitting that I should have found it very unpleasant to meet Mr. Mutimer. You felt that, and hence your kindness. At the same time, no doubt, you pity me for my littleness.'

'I think it perfectly natural that such a meeting should be disagreeable. I believe I understand your feeling. Indeed, you explained it to me yesterday.'

'I explained it?'

'In what you said about the works in the valley.'

'True. Many people would have interpreted me less liberally.'

Adela's eyes brightened a little. But when she raised them, they fell upon something which disturbed her cheerfulness. This was the face of Mrs. Mewling, who had come up from the direction of Wanley and was clearly about to pay a visit at the Manor. The lady smiled and murmured a greeting as she passed by.

'I suppose Mrs. Mewling is going to see my mother,' said Hubert, who also had lost a little of his naturalness

A few more words and they again parted. Nothing further was said of the postponed visit. Adela hastened homewards, dreading lest she had made a great mistake, yet glad that she had ventured to come.

Her mother was just going out into the garden, where Alfred's voice sounded frequently in laughter or denunciation. Adela would have been glad to sit alone for a short time, for Mrs. Waltham seemed to wish for her company. She had only time to glance at herself in her looking-glass and just press a palm against each cheek.

Alfred was puffing clouds from his briar pipe, but Mutimer had ceased smoking. Near the latter was a vacant seat; Adela took it, as there was no other.

'What a good thing the day of rest is!' exclaimed Mrs. Waltham. 'I always feel thankful when I think of the poor men who toil so all through the week in Belwick, and how they must enjoy their Sunday. You surely wouldn't make any change in *that*, Mr. Mutimer?'

'The change I should like to see would be in the other direction,' Richard replied. 'I would have holidays far more frequent. In the towns you can scarcely call Sunday a holiday. There's nothing to do but to walk about the streets. On the whole it does far more harm than good.'

'Do they never go to church?' asked Adela. She was experiencing a sort of irritation against their guest, a feeling traceable to more than one source; Mutimer's frequent glances did not tend to soothe it. She asked the question rather in a spirit of adverse criticism.

'The working people don't,' was the reply, 'except a Dissenting family here and there.'

'Perhaps that is one explanation of the Sundays being useless to them.'

Adela would scarcely have ventured upon such a tone in reference to any secular matter; the subject being religion, she was of course justified in expressing herself freely.

Mutimer smiled and held back his rejoinder for a moment. By that time Alfred had taken his pipe from his lips and was giving utterance to unmeasured scorn.

'But, Mr. Mutimer,' said Mrs. Waltham, waving aside her son's vehemence, 'you don't seriously tell us that the working people have no religion? Surely that would be too shocking!'

'Yes, I say it seriously, Mrs. Waltham. In the ordinary sense of the word, they have no religion. The truth is, they have no time to think of it.'

'Oh, but surely it needs no thought——'

Alfred exploded.

'I mean,' pursued his mother, 'that, however busy we are, there must always be intervals to be spared from the world.'

Mutimer again delayed his reply. A look which he cast at Adela appeared to move her to speech.

'Have they not their evenings free, as well as every Sunday?'

'Happily, Miss Waltham, you can't realise their lives,' Richard began. He was not smiling now; Adela's tone had struck him like a challenge, and he collected himself to meet her. 'The man who lives on wages is never free; he sells himself body and soul to his employer. What sort of freedom does a man enjoy who may any day find himself and his family on the point of starvation just because he has lost his work? All his life long he has before his mind the fear of want—not only of straitened means, mind you, but of destitution and the workhouse. How can such a man put aside his common cares? Religion is a luxury; the working man has no luxuries. Now, you speak of the free evenings; people always do, when they're asking why the working classes don't educate themselves. Do you understand what that free evening means? He gets home, say, at six o'clock, tired out; he has to be up again perhaps at five next morning. What can he do but just lie about half asleep? Why, that's the whole principle of the capitalist system of employment; it's calculated exactly how long a man can be made to work in a day without making him incapable of beginning again on the day following—just as it's calculated exactly how little a man can live upon, in the regulation of wages. If the workman returned home with strength to spare, employers would soon find it out, and workshop legislation would be revised—because of course it's the capitalists that make the laws. The principle is that a man shall have no strength left for himself; it's all paid for, every scrap of it, bought with the wages at each week end. What religion can such men have? Religion, I suppose, means thankfulness for life and its pleasures—at all events, that's a great part of it— and what has a wage-earner to be thankful for?'

'It sounds very shocking,' observed Mrs. Waltham, some-what disturbed by the speaker's growing earnestness. Richard paid no attention and continued to address Adela.

'I dare say you've heard of the early trains—workmen's trains—that they run on the London railways. If only you could travel once by one of those! Between station and station there's scarcely a man or boy in the carriage who can keep awake; there they sit, leaning over against each other, their heads dropping forward, their eyelids that heavy they can't hold them up. I tell you it's one of the most miserable sights to be seen in this world. If you saw it, Miss Waltham, you'd pity them, I'm very sure of that! You only need to know what their life means. People who have never known hardship often speak more cruelly than they think, and of course it always will be so as long as the rich and the poor are two different races, as much apart as if there was an ocean between them.'

Adela's cheeks were warm. It was a novel sensation to be rebuked in this unconventional way. She was feeling a touch of shame as well as the slight resentment which was partly her class-instinct, partly of her sex.

'I feel that I have no right to give any opinion,' she said in an undertone.

'Meaning, Adela,' commented her brother, 'that you have a very strong opinion and stick to it.'

'One thing I dare say you are thinking, Miss Waltham,' Richard pursued, 'if you'll allow me to say it. You think that I myself don't exactly prove what I've been saying—I mean to say, that I at all events have had free time, not only to read and reflect, but to give lectures and so on. Yes, and I'll explain that. It was my good fortune to have a father and mother who were very careful and hard-working and thoughtful people; I and my sister and brother were brought up in an orderly home, and taught from the first that ceaseless labour and strict economy were the things always to be kept in mind. All that was just fortunate chance; I'm not praising myself in saying I've been able to get more into my time than most other working men; it's my father and mother I have to thank for it. Suppose they'd been as ignorant and careless as most of their class are made by the hard lot they have to endure; why, I should have followed them, that's all. We've never had to go without a meal, and why? Just because we've all of us worked like slaves and never allowed ourselves to think of rest or enjoyment. When my father died, of course we had to be more careful than ever; but there were three of us to earn money, fortunately, and we kept up the home. We put our money by for the club every week, what's more.'

'The club?' queried Miss Waltham, to whom the word suggested Pall Mall and vague glories which dwelt in her imagination.

'That's to make provision for times when we're ill or can't get work,' Mutimer explained. 'If a wage-earner falls ill, what has he to look to? The capitalist won't trouble himself to keep him alive; there's plenty to take his place. Well, that's my position, or was a few months ago. I don't suppose any work-

H

ing man has had more advantages. Take it as an example of the most we can hope for, and pray say what it amounts to ! Just on the right side, just keeping afloat, just screwing out an hour here and there to work your brain when you ought to be taking wholesome recreation ! That's nothing very grand, it seems to me. Yet people will point to it and ask what there is to grumble at ! '

Adela sat uneasily under Mutimer's gaze; she kept her eyes down.

' And I'm not sure that I should always have got on as easily,' the speaker continued. ' Only a day or two before I heard of my relative's death, I'd just been dismissed from my employment; that was because they didn't like my opinions. Well, I don't say they hadn't a right to dismiss me, just as I suppose you've a right to kill as many of the enemy as you can in time of war. But suppose I couldn't have got work anywhere. I had nothing but my hands to depend upon; if I couldn't sell my muscles I must starve, that's all.'

Adela looked at him for almost the first time. She had heard this story from her brother, but it came more impressively from Mutimer's own lips. A sort of heroism was involved in it, the championship of a cause regardless of self. She remained thoughtful with troublous colours on her face.

Mrs. Waltham was more obviously uneasy. There are certain things to which in good society one does not refer, first and foremost humiliating antecedents. The present circumstances were exceptional to be sure, but it was to be hoped that Mr. Mutimer would outgrow this habit of advertising his origin. Let him talk of the working-classes if he liked, but always in the third person. The good lady began to reflect whether she might not venture shortly to give him friendly hints on this and similar subjects.

But it was nearly tea-time. Mrs. Waltham shortly rose and went into the house, whither Alfred followed her. Mutimer kept his seat, and Adela could not leave him to himself, though for the moment he seemed unconscious of her presence. When they had been alone together for a little while, Richard broke the silence.

' I hope I didn't speak rudely to you, Miss Waltham. I don't think I need fear to say what I mean, but I know there are always two ways of saying things, and perhaps I chose the roughest.'

Adela was conscious of having said a few hard things mentally, and this apology, delivered in a very honest voice, appealed to her instinct of justice. She did not like Mutimer, and consequently strove against the prejudice which the very sound of his voice aroused in her; it was her nature to aim thus at equity in her personal judgments.

'To describe hard things we must use hard words,' she replied pleasantly, 'but you said nothing that could offend.'

'I fear you haven't much sympathy with my way of looking at the question. I seem to you to be going to work the wrong way.'

'I certainly think you value too little the means of happiness that we all have within our reach, rich and poor alike.'

'Ah, if you could only see into the life of the poor, you would acknowledge that those means are and can be nothing to them. Besides, my way of thinking in such things is the same as your brother's, and I can't expect you to see any good in it.'

Adela shook her head slightly. She had risen and was examining the leaves upon an apple branch which she had drawn down.

'But I'm sure you feel that there is need for doing something,' he urged, quitting his seat. 'You're not indifferent to the hard lives of the people, as most people are who have always lived comfortable lives?'

She let the branch spring up, and spoke more coldly.

'I hope I am not indifferent, but it is not in my power to do anything.'

'Will you let me say that you are mistaken in that?' Mutimer had never before felt himself constrained to qualify and adorn his phrases; the necessity made him awkward. Not only did he aim at polite modes of speech altogether foreign to his lips, but his own voice sounded strange to him in its forced suppression. He did not as yet succeed in regarding himself from the outside and criticising the influences which had got hold upon him; he was only conscious that a young lady—the very type of young lady that a little while ago he would have held up for scorn—was subduing his nature by her mere presence and exacting homage from him to which she was wholly indifferent. 'Everyone can give help in such a cause as this. You can work upon the minds of the people you talk with and get them to throw away their prejudices. The cause of the working classes seems so hopeless just because they're too far away to catch the ears of those who oppress them.

H 2

'I do not oppress them, Mr. Mutimer.'

Adela spoke with a touch of impatience. She wished to bring this conversation to an end, and the man would give her no opportunity of doing so. She was not in reality paying attention to his arguments, as was evident in her echo of his last words.

'Not willingly, but none the less you do so,' he rejoined. 'Everyone who lives at ease and without a thought of changing the present state of society is tyrannising over the people. Every article of clothing you put on means a life worn out somewhere in a factory. What would your existence be without the toil of those men and women who live and die in want of every comfort which seems as natural to you as the air you breathe? Don't you feel that you owe them something? It's a debt that can very easily be forgotten, I know that, and just because the creditors are too weak to claim it. Think of it in that way, and I'm quite sure you won't let it slip from your mind again.'

Alfred came towards them, announcing that tea was ready, and Adela gladly moved away.

'You won't make any impression there,' said Alfred with a shrug of good-natured contempt. 'Argument isn't understood by women. Now, if you were a revivalist preacher——'

Mrs. Waltham and Adela went to church. Mutimer returned to his lodgings, leaving his friend Waltham smoking in the garden.

On the way home after service, Adela had a brief murmured conversation with Letty Tew. Her mother was walking out with Mrs. Mewling.

'It was evidently pre-arranged,' said the latter, after recounting certain details in a tone of confidence. 'I was quite shocked. On *his* part such conduct is nothing less than disgraceful. Adela, of course, cannot be expected to know.'

'I must tell her,' was the reply.

Adela was sitting rather dreamily in her bedroom a couple of hours later when her mother entered.

'Little girls shouldn't tell stories,' Mrs. Waltham began, with playfulness which was not quite natural. 'Who was it that wanted to go and speak a word to Letty this afternoon?'

'It wasn't altogether a story, mother,' pleaded the girl shamed, but with an endeavour to speak independently. 'I did want to speak to Letty.'

'And you put it off, I suppose? Really, Adela, you must remember that a girl of your age has to be mindful of her self-respect. In Wanley you can't escape notice; besides——'

'Let me explain, mother.' Adela's voice was made firm by the suggestion that she had behaved unbecomingly. 'I went to Letty first of all to tell her of a difficulty I was in. Yesterday afternoon I happened to meet Mr. Eldon, and when he was saying good-bye I asked him if he wouldn't come and see you before he left Wanley. He promised to come this afternoon. At the time of course I didn't know that Alfred had invited Mr. Mutimer. It would have been so disagreeable for Mr. Eldon to meet him here, I made up my mind to walk towards the Manor and tell Mr. Eldon what had happened.'

'Why should Mr. Eldon have found the meeting with Mr. Mutimer disagreeable?'

'They don't like each other.'

'I dare say not. Perhaps it was as well Mr. Eldon didn't come. I should most likely have refused to see him.'

'Refused to see him, mother?'

Adela gazed in the utmost astonishment.

'Yes, my dear. I haven't spoken to you about Mr. Eldon, just because I took it for granted that he would never come in your way again. That he should have dared to speak to you is something beyond what I could have imagined. When I went to see Mrs. Eldon on Friday I didn't take you with me, for fear lest that young man should show himself. It was impossible for you to be in the same room with him.'

'With Mr. Hubert Eldon? My dearest mother, what are you saying?'

'Of course it surprises you, Adela. I too was surprised. I thought there might be no need to speak to you of things you ought never to hear mentioned, but now I am afraid I have no choice. The sad truth is that Mr. Eldon has utterly disgraced himself. When he ought to have been here to attend Mr. Mutimer's funeral, he was living at Paris and other such places in the most shocking dissipation. Things are reported of him which I could not breathe to you; he is a bad young man!'

The inclusiveness of that description! Mrs. Waltham's head quivered as she gave utterance to the words, for at least half of the feeling she expressed was genuine. To her hearer the final phrase was like a thunderstroke. In a certain profound work on the history of her country which she had been

in the habit of studying, the author, discussing the character of
Oliver Cromwell, achieved a most impressive climax in the
words, 'He was a bold, bad man.' The adjective 'bad' derived for Adela a dark energy from her recollection of that
passage; it connoted every imaginable phase of moral degradation. 'Dissipation' too; to her pure mind the word had a
terrible sound; it sketched in lurid outlines hideous lurking
places of vice and disease. 'Paris and other such places.'
With the name of Paris she associated a feeling of reprobation;
Paris was the head-quarters of sin—at all events on earth. In
Paris people went to the theatre on Sunday; that fact alone
shed storm-light over the iniquitous capital.

She stood mute with misery, appalled, horrified. It did not
occur to her to doubt the truth of her mother's accusations;
the strange circumstance of Hubert's absence when every sentiment of decency would have summoned him home corroborated
the charge. And she had talked familiarly with this man a
few hours ago! Her head swam.

'Mr. Mutimer knew it,' proceeded her mother, noting with
satisfaction the effect she was producing. 'That was why he
destroyed the will in which he had left everything to Mr.
Eldon; I have no doubt the grief killed him. And one thing
more I may tell you. Mr. Eldon's illness was the result of a
wound he received in some shameful quarrel; it is believed that
he fought a duel.'

The girl sank back upon her chair. She was white and
breathed with difficulty.

'You will understand now, my dear,' Mrs. Waltham continued, more in her ordinary voice, 'why it so shocked me to
hear that you had been seen talking with Mr. Eldon near the
Manor. I feared it was an appointment. Your explanation is
all I wanted : it relieves me. The worst of it is, other people
will hear of it, and of course we can't explain to everyone.'

'Why should people hear?' Adela exclaimed, in a quivering voice. It was not that she feared to have the story known,
but mingled feelings made her almost passionate. 'Mrs.
Mewling has no right to go about talking of me. It is very
ill-bred, to say nothing of the unkindness.'

'Ah, but it is what we have to be prepared for, Adela.
That is the world, my child. You see how very careful one
has to be. But never mind; it is most fortunate that the
Eldons are going. I am so sorry for poor Mrs. Eldon; who
could have thought that her son would turn out so badly! And

to think that he would have dared to come into my house ! At least he had the decency not to show himself at church.'

Adela sat silent. The warring of her heart made outward sounds indistinct.

'After all,' pursued her mother, as if making a great concession, 'I fear it is only too true that those old families become degenerate. One does hear such shocking stories of the aristocracy. But get to bed, dear, and don't let this trouble you. What a very good thing that all that wealth didn't go into such hands, isn't it ? Mr. Mutimer will at all events use it in a decent way ; it won't be scattered in vulgar dissipation. —Now kiss me, dear. I haven't been scolding you, pet ; it was only that I felt I had perhaps made a mistake in not telling you these things before, and I blamed myself rather than you.

Mrs. Waltham returned to her own room, and after a brief turning over of speculations and projects begotten of the new aspect of things, found her reward for conscientiousness in peaceful slumber. But Adela was late in falling asleep. She, too, had many things to revolve, not worldly calculations, but the troubled phantasies of a virgin mind which is experiencing its first shock against the barriers of fate.

CHAPTER IX.

RICHARD MUTIMER had strong domestic affections. The English artisan is not demonstrative in such matters, and throughout his life Richard had probably exchanged no word of endearment with any one of his kin, whereas language of the tempestuous kind was common enough from him to one and all of them ; for all that he clung closely to the hearth, and nothing in truth concerned him so nearly as the well-being of his mother, his sister, and his brother. For them he had rejoiced as much as for himself in the blessing of fortune. Now that the excitement of change had had time to subside, Richard found himself realising the fact that capital creates cares as well as removes them, and just now the centre of his anxieties lay in the house at Highbury to which his family had removed from Wilton Square.

He believed that as yet both the Princess and 'Arry were ignorant of the true state of affairs. It had been represented

to them that he had 'come in for' a handsome legacy **from**
his relative in the Midlands, together with certain business
responsibilities which would keep him much away from home ;
they were given to understand that the change in their own
position and prospects was entirely of their brother's making.
If Alice Maud was allowed to give up her work, to wear more
expensive gowns, even to receive lessons on the pianoforte, she
had to thank Dick for it.   And when 'Arry was told that his
clerkship at the drain-pipe manufactory was about to terminate,
that he might enter upon a career likely to be more fruitful of
distinction, again it was Dick's brotherly kindness.   Mrs.
Mutimer did her best to keep up this deception.

But Richard was well aware that the deception could not be
lasting, and had the Princess alone been concerned he would
probably never have commenced it.   It was about his brother
that he was really anxious.   'Arry might hear the truth any
day, and Richard gravely feared the result of such a discovery.
Had he been destined to future statesmanship, he could not
have gone through a more profitable course of experience and
reasoning than that into which he was led by brotherly solicitude.   For 'Arry represented a very large section of Demos,
alike in his natural characteristics and in the circumstances of
his position; 'Arry, being 'Arry, was on the threshold of
emancipation, and without the smallest likelihood that the
event would change his nature.   Hence the nut to crack :
Given 'Arry, by what rapid process of discipline can he be
prepared for a state in which the 'Arrian characteristics will
surely prove ruinous not only to himself but to all with whom
he has dealings ?

Richard saw reason to deeply regret that the youth had been
put to clerking in the first instance, and not rather trained for
some handicraft, clerkships being about the least hopeful of
positions for a working-class lad of small parts and pronounced
blackguard tendencies.   He came to the conclusion that even
now it was not too late to remedy this error.   'Arry must be
taught what work meant, and, before he came into possession
of his means, he must, if possible, be led to devote his poor
washy brains to some pursuit quite compatible with the standing of a capitalist, to acquire knowledge of a kind which he
could afterwards use for the benefit of his own pocket.   Deficient bodily vigour had had something to do with his eleva-
tion to the office of the drain-pipe factory, but that he appeared
to have outgrown.   Much pondering enabled Richard to hit at

length on what he considered a hopeful scheme; he would apprentice 'Arry to engineering, and send him in the evenings to follow the courses of lectures given to working men at the School of Mines. In this way the lad would be kept constantly occupied, he would learn the meaning of work and study, and when he became of age would be in a position to take up some capitalist enterprise. Thus he might float clear of the shoals of blackguardism and develop into a tolerable member of society, at all events using his wealth in the direct employment of labour.

We have seen Richard engaged in æsthetic speculation; now we behold him busied in the training of a representative capitalist. But the world would be a terrible place if the men of individual energy were at all times consistent. Richard knew well enough that in planning thus for his brother's future he was inconsistency itself; but then the matter at issue concerned someone in whom he had a strong personal interest, and consequently he took counsel of facts. When it was only the world at large that he was bent on benefiting, too shrewd a sifting of arguments was not called for, and might seriously have interfered with his oratorical effects. In regulating private interests one cares singularly little for anything but hard demonstration and the logic of cause and effect.

It was now more than a month since 'Arry had been removed from the drain-pipes and set going on his new course, and Richard was watching the experiment gravely. Connected with it was his exceptional stay at Wanley over the Sunday; he designed to go up to London quite unexpectedly about the middle of the ensuing week, that he might see how things worked in his absence. It is true there had been another inducement to remain in the village, for Richard had troubles of his own in addition to those imposed upon him by his family. The Manor was now at his disposal; as soon as he had furnished it there was no longer a reason for delaying his marriage. In appearance, that is to say; inwardly there had been growing for some weeks reasons manifold. They tormented him. For the first time in his life he had begun to sleep indifferently; when he had resolutely put from his mind thought of Alice and 'Arry, and seemed ready for repose, there crept out of less obvious lurking-places subtle temptations and suggestions which fevered his blood and only allured the more, the more they disquieted him. This Sunday night was the worst he had yet known. When he left the Walthams, he occupied himself for an hour or two in writing letters, resolutely subduing his thoughts to the subjects of his correspondence. Then he ate supper, and after that walked to the top of Stanbury Hill, hoping to tire himself. But he returned as little prepared for sleep as he had set out. Now he endeavoured to think of Emma Vine; by way of help, he sat down and began a letter to her. But composition had never been so difficult; he positively had nothing to say. Still he must think of her. When he went up to town on Tuesday or Wednesday one of his first duties would be to appoint a day for his marriage. And he felt that it would be a duty harder to perform than any he had ever known. She seemed to have drifted so far from him, or he from her. It was difficult even to see her face in imagination; another face always came instead, and indeed needed no summoning.

He rose next morning with a stern determination to marry Emma Vine in less than a month from that date.

On Tuesday he went to London. A hansom put him down before the house in Highbury about six o'clock. It was a semi-detached villa, stuccoed, bow-windowed, of two storeys, standing pleasantly on a wide road skirted by similar dwellings, and with a row of acacias in front. He admitted himself with a latch-key and walked at once into the front room; it was vacant. He went to the dining-room and there found his mother at tea with Alice and 'Arry.

Mrs. Mutimer and her younger son were in appearance very much what they had been in their former state. The mother's dress was of better material, but she was not otherwise outwardly changed. 'Arry was attired nearly as when we saw him in a festive condition on the evening of Easter Sunday; the elegance then reserved for high days and holidays now distinguished him every evening when the guise of the workshop was thrown off. He still wore a waistcoat of pronounced cut, a striking collar, a necktie of remarkable hue. It was not necessary to approach him closely to be aware that his person was sprinkled with perfumes. A recent acquisition was a heavy-looking ring on the little finger of his right hand. Had you been of his intimates, 'Arry would have explained to you the double advantage of this ring; not only did it serve as an adornment, but, as playful demonstration might indicate, it would prove of singular efficacy in pugilistic conflict.

At the sight of his elder brother, 'Arry hastily put his hands beneath the table, drew off the ornament, and consigned it furtively to his waistcoat pocket.

But Alice Maud was by no means what she had been. In all that concerned his sister, Mutimer was weak; he could quarrel with her, and abuse her roundly for frailties, but none the less was it one of his keenest pleasures to see her contented, even in ways that went quite against his conscience. He might rail against the vanity of dress, but if Alice needed a new gown, Richard was the first to notice it. The neat little silver watch she carried was a gift from himself of some years back; with difficulty he had resisted the temptation to replace it with a gold one now that it was in his power to do so. Tolerable taste and handiness with her needle had always kept Alice rather more ladylike in appearance than the girls of her class are wont to be, but such comparative distinction no longer sufficed. After certain struggles with himself, Richard had told his mother that Alice must in future dress ' as a lady '; he authorised her to procure the services of a competent dressmaker, and, within the bounds of moderation, to expend freely. And the result was on the whole satisfactory. A girl of good figure, pretty face, and moderate wit, who has spent some years in a City showroom, does not need much instruction in the art of wearing fashionable attire becomingly. Alice wore this evening a gown which would not have been out of place at five o'clock in a West-end drawing-room; the sleeves were rather short, sufficiently so to exhibit a very shapely lower arm. She had discovered new ways of doing her hair; at present it was braided on either side of the forehead—a style which gave almost a thoughtful air to her face. When her brother entered she was eating a piece of sponge-cake, which she held to her lips with peculiar delicacy, as if rehearsing graces.

' Why, there now ! ' cried Mrs. Mutimer, pleased to see her son. ' If I wasn't saying not five minutes ago as Dick was likely to come some day in the week ! Wasn't I, Alice ? What'll you have for your tea ? There's some chops all ready in the 'ouse, if you'd care for them.'

Richard was not in a cheerful mood. He made no reply immediately, but went and stood before the fireplace, as he had been accustomed to do in the old kitchen.

' Will you have a chop ? ' repeated his mother.

' No; I won't eat just yet. But you can give me a cup of tea.'

Mrs. Mutimer and Alice exchanged a glance, as the former bent over the teapot. Richard was regarding his brother askance, and it resulted in a question, rather sharply put—

'Have you been to work to-day ? '

'Arry would have lied had he dared ; as it was, he made his plate revolve, and murmured, 'No ; he 'adn't.'

'Why not ? '

'I didn't feel well,' replied the youth, struggling for self-confidence and doing his best to put on an air of patient suffering.

Richard tapped his tea-cup and looked the look of one who reserves discussion for a more seasonable time.

'Daniel called last night,' remarked Mrs. Mutimer. 'He says he wants to see you. I think it's something particular ; he seemed disappointed you weren't at the meeting on Sunday.'

'Did he ? I'll see if I can get round to-night. If you like to have something cooked for me about eight o'clock, mother,' he added, consulting his watch, 'I shall be ready for it then.'

He turned to his brother again.

'Is there a class to-night ? No ? Very well, when they've cleared away, get your books out and show me what you've been doing. What are *you* going to do with yourself, Alice ? '

The two addressed, as well as their mother, appeared to have some special cause for embarrassment. Instead of immediately replying, Alice played with crumbs and stole glances on either side.

'Me and 'Arry are going out,' she said at length, with a rather timid smile and a poise of the head in pretty wilfulness.

'Not 'Arry,' Richard observed significantly.

'Why not ? ' came from the younger Mutimer, with access of boldness.

'If you're not well enough to go to work you certainly don't go out at night for your pleasure.'

'But it's a particular occasion,' explained Alice, leaning back with crossed arms, evidently prepared to do battle. 'A friend of 'Arry's is going to call and take us to the theatre.'

'Oh, indeed ! And what friend is that ? '

Mrs. Mutimer, who had been talked over to compliance with a project she felt Richard would not approve—she had no longer the old authority, and spent her days in trying to piece on the present life to the former—found refuge in a habit more suitable to the kitchen than the dining-room ; she had collected all the teaspoons within reach and was pouring hot-water upon them in the slop-basin, the familiar preliminary to washing up.

'A gen'leman as lives near here,' responded 'Arry. 'He writes for the newspapers. His name's Keene.'

'Oh ? And how came you to know him ? '

' Met him,' was the airy reply.

' And you've brought him here ? '

' Well, he's been here once.'

' He said as he wanted to know you, Dick,' put in Mrs. Mutimer. ' He was really a civil-spoken man, and he gave 'Arry a lot of help with his books.'

' When was he here ? '

' Last Friday.'

' And to-night he wants to take you to the theatre ? '

The question was addressed to Alice.

' It won't cost him anything,' she replied. ' He says he can always get free passes.'

' No doubt. Is he coming here to fetch you ? I shall be glad to see him.'

Richard's tone was ambiguous. He put down his cup, and said to Alice—

' Come and let me hear how you get on with your playing.'

Alice followed into the drawing-room. For the furnishing of the new house Richard had not trusted to his own instincts, but had taken counsel with a firm that he knew from advertisements. The result was commonplace, but not intolerable. His front room was regarded as the Princess's peculiar domain ; she alone dared to use it freely—declined, indeed, to sit elsewhere. Her mother only came a few feet within the door now and then ; if obliged by Alice to sit down, she did so on the edge of a chair as near to the door as possible. Most of her time Mrs. Mutimer still spent in the kitchen. She had resolutely refused to keep more than one servant, and everything that servant did she herself performed over again, even to the making of beds. To all Alice's objections she opposed an obstinate silence. What was the poor woman to do ? She had never in her life read more than an occasional paragraph of police news, and could not be expected to take up literature at her age. Though she made no complaint, signs were not wanting that she had begun to suffer in health. She fretted through the nights, and was never really at peace save when she anticipated the servant in rising early, and had an honest scrub at saucepans or fireirons before breakfast. Her main discomfort came of the feeling that she no longer had a house of her own ; nothing about her seemed to be her property with the exception of her old kitchen clock, and one or two articles she could not have borne to part with. From being a rather talkative woman she had become very reticent; she went about uneasily, with a look of suspicion or of fear. Her children she no longer ventured to command; the secret of their wealth weighed upon her, she was in constant dread on their behalf. It is a bad thing for one such as Mrs. Mutimer to be thrown back upon herself in novel circumstances, and practically debarred from the only relief which will avail her—free discussion with her own kind. The result is a species of shock to the system, sure to manifest itself before long in one or other form of debility.

Alice seated herself at the piano, and began a finger exercise, laboriously, imperfectly. For the first week or two it had given her vast satisfaction to be learning the piano; what more certain sign of having achieved ladyhood? It pleased her to assume airs with her teacher—a very deferential lady—to put off a lesson for a fit of languidness; to let it be understood how entirely time was at her command. Now she was growing rather weary of flats and sharps, and much preferred to read of persons to whom the same nomenclature was very applicable in the books she obtained from a circulating library. Her reading had hitherto been confined to the fiction of the penny papers; to procure her pleasure in three gaily-bound volumes was another evidence of rise in the social scale; it was like ordering your wine by the dozen after being accustomed to a poor chance bottle now and then. At present Alice spent the greater part of her day floating on the gentle milky stream of English romance. Her brother was made a little uneasy by this taste; he had not studied the literature in question.

At half past six a loud knock at the front door announced the expected visitor. Alice turned from the piano, and looked at her brother apprehensively. Richard rose, and established himself on the hearthrug, his hands behind him.

'What are you going to say to him, Dick?' Alice asked hurriedly.

'He says he wants to know me. I shall say, "Here I am."'

There were voices outside. 'Arry had opened the door himself, and now he ushered his acquaintance into the drawing-room. Mr. Keene proved to be a man of uncertain age—he might be eight-and-twenty, but was more probably ten years older. He was meagre, and of shrewd visage; he wore a black frock coat—rather shiny at the back—and his collar was obviously of paper. Incipient baldness endowed him in appearance with a noble forehead; he carried eye-glasses.

Whilst 'Arry mumbled a form of introduction, the journalist —so Mr. Keene described himself—stood in a bowing attitude, one hand to his glasses, seeming to inspect Richard with extreme yet respectful interest. When he spoke, it was in a rather mincing way, with interjected murmurs—the involuntary overflow, as it were, of his deep satisfaction.

'There are few persons in England whose acquaintance I desire more than that of Mr. Richard Mutimer; indeed, I may leave the statement unqualified and say at once that there is no one. I have heard you speak in public, Mr. Mutimer. My profession has necessarily led me to hear most of our platform orators, and in one respect you distance them all—in the quality of sincerity. No speaker ever moved me as you did. I had long been interested in your cause; I had long wished for time and opportunity to examine into it thoroughly. Your address—I speak seriously—removed the necessity of further study. I am of your party, Mr. Mutimer. There is nothing I desire so much as to give and take the hand of brotherhood.'

He jerked his hand forward, still preserving his respectful attitude. Richard gave his own hand carelessly, smiling as a man does who cannot but enjoy flattery yet has a strong desire to kick the flatterer out of the room.

'Are you a member of the Union?' he inquired.

'With pride I profess myself a member. Some day—and that at no remote date—I may have it in my power to serve the cause materially.' He smiled meaningly. 'The press—you understand?' He spread his fingers to represent wide dominion. 'An ally to whom the columns of the *bourgeois* press are open—you perceive? It is the task of my life.'

'What papers do you write for?' asked Mutimer bluntly.

'Several, several. Not as yet in a leading capacity. In fact, I am feeling my way. With ends such as I propose to myself it won't do to stand committed to any formal creed in politics. Politics, indeed! Ha, ha!'

He laughed scornfully. Then, turning to Alice—

'You will forgive me, I am sure, Miss Mutimer, that I address myself first to your brother—I had almost said your illustrious brother. To be confessed illustrious some day, depend upon it. I trust you are well?'

'Thanks, I'm very well indeed,' murmured Alice, rather disconcerted by such politeness.

'And Mrs. Mutimer? That is well. By-the-by,' he proceeded to Richard, ' I have a piece of work in hand that will deeply interest you. I am translating the great treatise of Marx, "Das Capital." It occurs to me that a chapter now and then might see the light in the "Fiery Cross." How do you view that suggestion ? '

Richard did not care to hide his suspicion, and even such an announcement as this failed to move him to cordiality.

' You might drop a line about it to Mr. Westlake,' he said.

' Mr. Westlake ? Oh ! but I quite understood that you had practically the conduct of the paper.'

Richard again smiled.

' Mr. Westlake edits it,' he said.

Mr. Keene waved his hand in sign of friendly intelligence. Then he changed the subject.

' I ventured to put at Miss Mutimer's disposal certain tickets I hold—professionally—for the Regent's Theatre to-night—the dress circle. I have five seats in all. May I have the pleasure of your company, Mr. Mutimer ? '

' I'm only in town for a night,' Richard replied; ' and I can't very well spare the time.'

' To be sure, to be sure; I was inconsiderate. Then Miss Mutimer and my friend Harry——'

' I'm sorry they're not at liberty,' was Richard's answer to the murmured interrogation. ' If they had accepted your invitation be so good as to excuse them. I happen to want them particularly this evening.'

' In that case, I have of course not a word to say, save to express my deep regret at losing the pleasure of their company. But another time, I trust. I—I feel presumptuous, but it is my earnest hope to be allowed to stand on the footing not only of a comrade in the cause, but of a neighbour ; I live quite near. Forgive me if I seem a little precipitate. The privilege is so inestimable.'

Richard made no answer, and Mr. Keene forthwith took his leave, suave to the last. When he was gone, Richard went to the dining-room, where his mother was sitting. Mrs. Mutimer would have given much to be allowed to sit in the kitchen ; she had a room of her own upstairs, but there she felt too remote from the centre of domestic operations, and the dining-room was a compromise. Her chair was always placed in a rather dusky corner ; she generally had sewing on her lap, but the consciousness that her needle was not really in demand, and that she might just as well have sat idle, troubled her

habits of mind. She often had the face of one growing prematurely aged.

'I hope you won't let them bring anyone they like,'
Richard said to her. 'I've sent that fellow about his business;
he's here for no good. He mustn't come again.'

'They won't heed me,' replied Mrs. Mutimer, using the
tone of little interest with which she was accustomed to speak of
details of the new order.

'Well, then, they've *got* to heed you, and I'll have that
understood.—Why didn't 'Arry go to work to day?'

'Didn't want to, I s'pose.'

'Has he stayed at home often lately?'

'Not at 'ome, but I expect he doesn't always go to work.'

'Will you go and sit with Alice in the front room? I'll
have a talk with him.'

'Arry came whistling at the summons. There was a nasty
look on his face, the look which in his character corresponded to
Richard's resoluteness. His brother eyed him.

'Look here, 'Arry,' the elder began, 'I want this explaining. What do you mean by shirking your work?'

There was no reply. 'Arry strode to the window and
leaned against the side of it, in the attitude of a Sunday loafer
waiting for the dram-shop to open.

'If this goes on,' Richard pursued, 'you'll find yourself in
your old position again. I've gone to a good deal of trouble to
give you a start, and it seems to me you ought to show a better
spirit. We'd better have an understanding; do you mean to
learn engineering, or don't you?'

'I don't see the use of it,' said the other.

'What do you mean? I suppose you must make your
living somehow?'

'Arry laughed, and in such a way that Richard looked at
him keenly, his brow gathering darkness.

'What are you laughing at?'

'Why, at you. There's no more need for me to work for
a living than there is for you. As if I didn't know that!'

'Who's been putting that into your head?'

No scruple prevented the lad from breaking a promise he
had made to Mr. Keene, the journalist, when the latter explained to him the disposition of the deceased Richard Mutimer's estate; it was only that he preferred to get himself credit
for acuteness.

'Why, you don't think I was to be kept in the dark about

I

a thing like that? It's just like you to want to make a fellow sweat the flesh off his bones when all the time there's a fortune waiting for him. What have I got to work for, I'd like to know? I don't just see the fun of it, and you wouldn't neither, in my case. You've took jolly good care you don't work yourself, trust you! I ain't a-going to work no more, so there it is, plain and flat.'

Richard was not prepared for this; he could not hit at once on a new course of procedure, and probably it was the uncertainty revealed in his countenance that brought 'Arry to a pitch of boldness not altogether premeditated. The lad came from the window, thrust his hands more firmly into his pockets and stood prepared to do battle for his freeman's rights. It is not every day that a youth of his stamp finds himself gloriously capable of renouncing work. There was something like a glow of conscious virtue on his face.

'You're not going to work any more, eh?' said his brother, half to himself. 'And who's going to support you?' he asked, with rather forced indignation.

'There's interest per cent. coming out of my money.'

'Arry must not be credited with conscious accuracy in his use of terms; he merely jumbled together two words which had stuck in his memory.

'Oh? And what are you going to do with your time?'

'That's my business. How do other men spend their time?'

The reply was obvious, but Richard felt the full seriousness of the situation and restrained his scornful impulses.

'Sit down, will you?' he said quietly, pointing to a chair.

His tone availed more than anger would have done.

'You tell me I take good care not to do any work myself? There you're wrong. I'm working hard every day.'

'Oh, we know what kind of work that is!'

'No, I don't think you do. Perhaps it would be as well if you were to see. I think you'd better go to Wanley with me.'

'What for?'

'I dare say I can give you a job for awhile.'

'I tell you I don't want a job.'

Richard's eye wandered rather vacantly. From the first it had been a question with him whether it would not be best to employ 'Arry at Wanley, but on the whole the scheme adopted seemed more fruitful. Had the works been fully established it would have been a different thing. Even now he could keep the lad at work at Wanley, though not exactly in the way he desired. But if it came to a choice between a life of idleness in London and such employment as could be found for him at the works, 'Arry must clearly leave town at once. In a few days the Manor would be furnished; in a few weeks Emma would be there to keep house.

There was the difficulty of leaving his mother and sister alone. It looked as if all would have to quit London. Yet there would be awkwardness in housing the whole family at the Manor; and besides——

What the 'besides' implied Richard did not make formal even in his own thoughts. It stood for a vague objection to having all his relatives dwelling at Wanley. Alice he would not mind; it was not impossible to picture Alice in conversation with Mrs. and Miss Waltham; indeed, he desired that for her. And yet——

Richard was at an awkward pass. Whithersoever he looked he saw stumbling-blocks, the more disagreeable in that they rather loomed in a sort of mist than declared themselves for what they were. He had not the courage to approach and examine them one by one; he had not the audacity to imagine leaps over them; yet somehow they had to be surmounted. At this moment, whilst 'Arry was waiting for the rejoinder to his last reply, Richard found himself wrestling again with the troubles which had kept him wakeful for the last two nights. He had believed them finally thrown and got rid of. Behold, they were more stubborn than ever.

He kept silence so long that his brother spoke.

'What sort of a job is it?'

To his surprise, Richard displayed sudden anger.

'If you weren't such a young fool you'd see what's best for you, and go on as I meant you to! What do you mean by saying you won't work? If you weren't such a thickhead you might go to school and be taught how to behave yourself, and how a man ought to live; but it's no use sending *you* to any such place. Can't you understand that a man with money has to find some sort of position in the world? I suppose you'd like to spend the rest of your life in public-houses and music-halls?'

Richard was well aware that to give way to his temper was worse than useless, and could only defeat every end; but something within him just now gnawed so intolerably that there was nothing for it but an outbreak. The difficulties of life were hedging him in—difficulties he could not have conceived till they became matter of practical experience. And unfortunately a great many of them were not of an honest kind; they would not bear exposing. For a man of decision, Mutimer was getting strangely remote from practical roads.

'I shall live as I like,' observed 'Arry, thrusting out his legs and bending his body forward, a combination of movements which, I know not why, especially suggests dissoluteness.

Richard gave up the contest for the present, and went in silence from the room. As he joined his mother and sister they suddenly ceased talking.

'Don't cook anything for me,' he said, remaining near the door. 'I'm going out.'

'But you must have something to eat,' protested his mother. 'See'—she rose hastily—'I'll get a chop done at once.'

'I couldn't eat it if you did. I dare say you've got some cold meat. Leave it out for me; I don't know what time I shall get back.'

'You're very unkind, Dick,' here remarked Alice, who wore a mutinous look. 'Why couldn't you let us go to the theatre?'

Her brother vouchsafed no reply, but withdrew from the room, and almost immediately left the house. He walked half a mile with his eyes turned to the ground, then noticed a hansom which was passing empty, and had himself driven to Hoxton. He alighted near the Britannia Theatre, and thence made his way by foul streets to a public-house called the 'Warwick Castle.' Only two customers occupied the bar; the landlord stood in his shirt-sleeves, with arms crossed, musing. At the sight of Mutimer he brightened up, and extended his hand.

'How d'you do; how d'you do, sir?' he exclaimed. 'Glad to see you.'

The shake of the hands was a tribute to old times, the 'sir' was a recognition of changed circumstances. Mr. Nicholas Dabbs, the brother of Daniel, was not a man to lose anything by failure to acknowledge social distinctions. A short time ago Daniel had expostulated with his brother on the use of 'sir' to Mutimer, eliciting the profound reply, 'D'you think he'd have 'ad that glass of whisky if I'd called him Dick?'

'Dan home yet?' Mutimer inquired.

'Not been in five minutes. Come round, sir, will you? I know he wants to see you.'

A portion of the counter was raised, and Richard passed into a parlour behind the bar.

'I'll call him,' said the landlord.

Daniel appeared immediately.

'I want a bit of private talk,' ne said to his brother. 'We'll have this door shut, if you don't mind.'

'You may as well bring us a drop of something first, Nick,' put in Richard. 'Give the order, Dan.'

'Wouldn't have 'ad it but for the "sir,"' chuckled Nicholas to himself. 'Never used to when he come here, unless I stood it.'

Daniel drew a chair to the table and stirred his tumbler thoughtfully, his nose over the steam.

'We're going to have trouble with 'Arry,' said Richard, who had seated himself on a sofa in a dispirited way. 'Of course someone's been telling him, and now the young fool says he's going to throw up work. I suppose I shall have to take him down yonder with me.'

'Better do so,' assented Daniel, without much attention to the matter.

'What is it you want to talk about, Dan?'

Mr. Dabbs had a few minutes ago performed the customary evening cleansing of his hands and face, but it had seemed unnecessary to brush his hair, which consequently stood upright upon his forehead, a wiry rampart, just as it had been thrust by the vigorously-applied towel. This, combined with an unwonted lugubriousness of visage, made Daniel's aspect somewhat comical. He kept stirring very deliberately with his sugar-crusher.

'Why, it's this, Dick,' he began at length. 'And understand, to begin with, that I've got no complaint to make of nobody; it's only *things* as are awk'ard. It's this way, my boy. When you fust of all come and told me about what I may call the great transformation scene, you said, "Now it ain't a-goin' to make no difference, Dan," you said. Now wait till I've finished; I ain't complainin' of nobody. Well, and I tried to 'ope as it wouldn't make no difference, though I 'ad my doubts. "Come an' see us all just as usu'l," you said. Well, I tried to do so, and three or four weeks I come reg'lar, lookin' in of a Sunday night. But somehow it wouldn't work; something 'ad got out of gear. So I stopped it off. Then comes 'Arry a-askin' why I made myself scarce, sayin' as th' old lady and the Princess missed me. So I looked in again; but it was wuss than before, I saw I'd done better to stay away. So I've done ever since. Y' understand me, Dick?'

Richard was not entirely at his ease in listening. He tried to smile, but failed to smile naturally.

'I don't see what you found wrong,' he returned, abruptly.

'Why, I'm a-tellin' you, my boy, I didn't find nothing wrong except in myself, as you may say. What's the good o' beatin' about the bush? It's just this 'ere, Dick, my lad. When I come to the Square, you know very well who it was as I come to see. Well, it stands to reason as I can't go to the new 'ouse with the same thoughts as I did to the old. Mind, I can't say as she'd ever a' listened to me; it's more than likely she wouldn't. But now that's all over, and the sooner I forget all about it the better for me. And th' only way to forget is to keep myself to myself,—see, Dick?'

The listener drummed with his fingers on the table, still endeavouring to smile.

'I've thought about all this, Dan,' he said at length, with an air of extreme frankness. 'In fact, I meant to have a talk with you. Of course I can't speak for my sister, and I don't know that I can even speak *to* her about it, but one thing I can say, and that is that she'll never be encouraged by me to think herself better than her old friends.' He gave a laugh. 'Why, that 'ud be a good joke for a man in my position! What am I working for, if not to do away with distinctions between capital and labour? You'll never have my ·advice to keep away, and that you know. Why, who am I going to marry myself? Do you suppose I shall cry off with Emma Vine just because I've got more money than I used to have?'

Daniel's eye was upon him as he said these words, an eye at once reflective and scrutinising. Richard felt it, and laughed yet more scornfully.

'I think we know you better than that,' responded Dabbs. 'But it ain't quite the same thing, you see. There's many a man high up has married a poor girl. I don't know how it is; perhaps because women is softer than men, and takes the polish easier. And then we know very well how it looks when a man as has no money goes after a girl as has a lot. No, no; it won't do, Dick.'

It was said with the voice of a man who emphasises a negative in the hope of eliciting a stronger argument on the other side. But Richard allowed the negative finality in fact, if not in appearance

'Well, it's for your own deciding, Dan. All I have to say is that you don't stay away with my approval. Understand that.'

He left Daniel idly stirring the dregs of his liquor, and went off to pay another visit. This was to the familiar house in Wilton Square. There was a notice in the window that dress-making and millinery were carried on within.

Mrs. Clay (Emma's sister Kate) opened to him. She was better dressed than in former days, but still untidy. Emma was out making purchases, but could not be many minutes. In the kitchen the third sister, Jane, was busy with her needle; at Richard's entrance she rose from her chair with evident feebleness: her illness of the spring had lasted long, and its effects were grave. The poor girl—she closely resembled Emma in gentleness of face, but the lines of her countenance were weaker—now suffered from pronounced heart disease, and the complicated maladies which rheumatic fever so frequently leaves behind it in women. She brightened at sight of the visitor, and her eyes continued to rest on his face with quiet satisfaction.

One of Kate's children was playing on the floor. The mother caught it up irritably, and began lamenting the necessity of washing its dirty little hands and face before packing it off to bed. In a minute or two she went up stairs to discharge these duties. Between her and Richard there was never much exchange of words.

'How are you feeling, Jane?' Mutimer inquired, taking a seat opposite her.

'Better—oh, very much better! The cough hasn't been not near so troublesome these last nights.'

'Mind you don't do too much work. You ought to have put your sewing aside by now.'

'Oh, this is only a bit of my own. I'm sorry to say there isn't very much of the other kind to do yet.'

'Comes in slowly, does it?' Richard asked, without appearance of much interest.

'It'll be better soon, I dare say. People want time, you see, to get to know of us.'

Richard's eyes wandered.

'Have you finished the port wine yet?' he asked, as if to fill a gap.

'What an idea! Why, there's four whole bottles left, and one as I've only had three glasses out of.'

'Emma was dreadfully disappointed when you didn't come as usual,' she said presently.

Richard nodded.

'Have you got into your house?' she asked timidly.

'It isn't quite ready yet; but I've been seeing about the furnishing.'

Jane dreamed upon the word. It was her habit to escape from the suffering weakness of her own life to joy in the lot which awaited her sister.

'And Emma will have a room all to herself?'

Jane had read of ladies' boudoirs; it was her triumph to have won a promise from Richard that Emma should have such a chamber.

'How is it going to be furnished? Do tell me.'

Richard's imagination was not active in the spheres of upholstery.

'Well, I can't yet say,' he replied, as if with an effort to rouse himself. 'How would you like it to be?'

Jane had ever before her mind a vague vision of bright-hued drapery, of glistening tables and chairs, of nobly patterned carpet, setting which her heart deemed fit for that priceless jewel, her dear sister. But to describe it all in words was a task beyond her. And the return of Emma herself saved her from the necessity of trying.

Hearing her enter the house, Richard went up to meet Emma, and they sat together in the sitting-room. This room was just as it had been in Mrs. Mutimer's day, save for a few ornaments from the mantelpiece, which the old lady could not be induced to leave behind her. Here customers were to be received—when they came; a room upstairs was set apart for work.

Emma wore a slightly anxious look; it showed even through her happiness. None the less, the very perceptible change which the last few months had wrought in her was in the direction of cheerful activity; her motions were quicker, her speech had less of self-distrust, she laughed more freely, displayed more of youthful spontaneity in her whole bearing. The joy which possessed her at Richard's coming was never touched with disappointment at his sober modes of exhibiting affection. The root of Emma's character was steadfast faith. She did not allow herself to judge of Richard by the impulses of her own heart; those, she argued, were womanly; a man must be more independent in his strength. Of what a man ought to be she had but one criterion, Richard's self. Her judgment on this point had been formed five or six years ago; she felt that nothing now could ever shake it. All of expressed love that he was pleased to give her she stored in the shrine of her memory; many a light word forgotten by the speaker as soon as it was uttered lived still as a part of the girl's hourly life, but his reticences she accepted with no less devout humility. What need of repetitions? He had spoken to her the decisive word, and it was a column established for ever, a monument of that over which time had no power. Women are too apt to make their fondness a source of infinite fears; in Emma growth of love meant growth of confidence.

'Does all go well at the works?' was her first question. For she had made his interests her own, and was following in ardent imagination the undertaking which stamped her husband with nobility.

Richard talked on the subject for some moments; it was easier to do so than to come at once to the words he had in mind. But he worked round by degrees, fighting the way hard.

'The house is empty at last.'

'Is it? And you have gone to live there?'

'Not yet. I must get some furniture in first.'

Emma kept silence; the shadows of a smile journeyed trembling from her eyes to her lips.

The question voiced itself from Richard:

'When will you be ready to go thither?'

'I'm afraid—I don't think I must leave them just yet—for a little longer.'

He did not look at her. Emma was reading his face; the characters had become all at once a little puzzling; her own fault, of course, but the significance she sought was not readily discoverable.

'Can't they manage without you?' he asked. He believed his tone to express annoyance: in fact, it scarcely did so.

'I think it won't be very long before they can,' Emma replied; 'we have some plain sewing to do for Mrs. Robinson at the "Queen's Head," and she's promised to recommend us. I've just called there, and she really seems anxious to help. If Jane was stronger I shouldn't mind so much, but she mustn't work hard just yet, and Kate has a great deal to do with the children. Besides, Kate can't get out of the slop sewing, and of course that won't do for this kind of work. She'll get the stitch very soon.'

Richard seemed to be musing.

'You see'—she moved nearer to his side,—'it's only just the beginning. I'm so afraid that they wouldn't be able to

look about for work if I left them now. Jane hasn't the
strength to go and see people; and Kate—well, you know,
Richard, she can't quite suit herself to people's fancies. I'm
sure I can do so much in a few weeks; just that'll make all
the difference. The beginning's everything, isn't it ? '

Richard's eye travelled over her face. He was not without
understanding of the nobleness which housed in that plain-clad,
simple-featured woman there before him. It had shot a ray to
the secret places of his heart before now; it breathed a passing
summer along his veins at this present.

' What need is there to bother ? ' he said, of purpose fixing
his eye steadily on hers. ' Work 'll come in time, I dare say.
Let them look after their house.'

Perhaps Emma detected something not wholly sincere in
this suggestion. She let her eyes fall, then raised them more
quickly.

'Oh, but it's far better, Richard ; and we really have made
a beginning. Jane, I'm sure, wouldn't hear of giving it up.
It's wonderful what spirits she has. And she'd be miserable if
she wasn't trying to work—I know so well how it would be.
Just a few weeks longer. She really does get much better, and
she says it's all "the business." It gives her something to
occupy her mind.'

' Well, it's just as you like,' said Richard, rather absently.

' But you do think it best, don't you, dear ? ' she urged.
' It's good to finish things you begin, isn't it ? I should feel
rather dissatisfied with myself if I gave it up, and just when
everything's promising. I believe it's what you really would
wish me to do.'

' All right. I'll get the house furnished. But I can't give
you much longer.'

He continued to talk in a mechanical way for a quarter of
an hour, principally of the works ; then said that he had promised to be home for supper, and took a rather hasty leave.
He called good-night to the sisters from the top of the kitchen
stairs.

Jane's face was full of joyous questioning as soon as her
sister reappeared, but Emma disclosed nothing till they two
were alone in the bed-room. To Emma it was the simplest
thing in the world to put a duty before pleasure ; she had no
hesitation in telling her sister how matters stood. And the
other accepted it as pure love.

' I'm sure it'll only be a week or two before we can

manage for ourselves,' Jane said. 'Of course, people are far readier to give you work than they would be to me or Kate. But it'll be all right when we're once started.'

'I shall be very sorry to leave you, dear,' murmured Emma. 'You'll have to be sure and let me know if you're not feeling well, and I shall come at once.'

'As if you could do that!' laughed the other. 'Besides, it'll be quite enough to keep me well to know you're happy.'

'I do hope Kate won't be trying.'

'Oh, I'm sure she won't. Why, it's quite a long time since she had one of her worst turns. It was only the hard work and the trouble as worried her. And now that's all over. It's you we have to thank for it all, Em.'

'You'll have to come and be with me sometimes, Jane. I know there'll always be something missing as long as you're out of my sight. And you must see to it yourself that the sheets is always aired; Kate's often so careless about that. You will promise me now, won't you? I shall be dreadfully anxious every washing day, I shall indeed. You know that the least thing 'll give you a chill.'

'Yes, I'll be careful,' said the other, half sadly. She was lying in her bed, and Emma sat on a chair by the side. 'But you know it's not much use, love. I don't suppose as I shall live so very long. But I don't care, as soon as I know you're happy.'

'Jane, I should never know happiness if I hadn't my little sister to come and talk to. Don't think like that, don't for my sake, Janey dear?'

They laid their cheeks together upon the pillows.

'He'll be a good husband,' Jane whispered. 'You know that, don't you, Emmy?'

'No better in all this world! Why do you ask so?'

'No—no—I didn't mean anything. He said you mustn't wait much longer, didn't he?'

'Yes, he did. But he'd rather see me doing what's right. I often feel myself such a poor thing by him. I must try and show him that I do my best to follow his example. I'm ashamed almost, sometimes, to think I shall be his wife. It ought to be some one better than me.'

'Where would he find any one better, I'd like to know? Let him come and ask me about that! There's no man good enough for you, sister Emmy.'

Richard was talking with his sister Alice; the others had gone to bed, and the house was quiet.

'I wasn't at all pleased to see that man here to-night,' he said. 'You shouldn't have been so ready to say yes when he asked you to go to the theatre. It was like his impudence!'

'Why, what ever's the harm, Dick? Besides, we must have some friends, and—really he looks a gentleman.'

'I'll tell you a secret,' returned her brother, with a half-smile, half-sneer. 'You don't know a gentleman yet, and you'll have to be very careful till you do.'

'How am I to learn, then?'

'Just wait. You've got enough to do with your music and your reading. Time enough for getting acquainted with gentlemen.'

'Aren't you going to let anybody come and see us, then?'

'You have the old friends,' replied Richard, raising his chin.

'You're thinking of Mr. Dabbs, I suppose. What did he want to see you for, Dick?'

Alice looked at him from the corner of her eye.

'I think I'll tell you. He says he doesn't intend to come here again. You've made him feel uncomfortable.'

The girl laughed.

'I can't help how he feels, can I? At all events, Mr. Dabbs isn't a gentleman, is he, now?'

'He's an honest man, and that's saying a good deal, let me tell you. I rather thought you liked him.'

'Liked him? Oh, in a way, of course. But things are different.'

'How different?'

Alice looked up, put her head on one side, smiled her prettiest, and asked—

'Is it true, what 'Arry says—about the money?'

He had wanted to get at this, and was, on the whole, not sorry to hear it. Richard was studying the derivation of virtue from necessity.

'What if it is?' he asked.

'Well, it makes things more different even than I thought, that's all.'

She sprang to her feet and danced across the room, one hand bent over her head. It was not an ungraceful picture. Her brother smiled.

'Alice, you'd better be guided by me. I know a little of

the world, and I can help you where you'd make mistakes. Just keep to yourself for a little, my girl, and get on with your piano and your books. You can't do better, believe me. Never mind whether you've any one to see you or not; there's time enough. And I'll tell you another secret. Before you can tell a gentleman when you see him, you'll have to teach yourself to be a lady. Perhaps that isn't quite so easy as you think.'

'How am I to learn then?'

'We'll find a way before long. Get on with your playing and reading.'

Presently, as they were about to leave the room, the Princess inquired:

'Dick, how soon are you going to be married?'

'I can't tell you,' was the answer. 'Emma wants to put it off.'

CHAPTER X.

THE declaration of independence so nobly delivered by his brother 'Arry necessitated Richard's stay in town over the following day. The matter was laid before a family council, held after breakfast in the dining-room. Richard opened the discussion with some vehemence, and appealed to his mother and Alice for support. Alice responded heartily; Mrs. Mutimer was slower in coming to utterance, but at length expressed herself in no doubtful terms.

'If he don't go to his work,' she said sternly, 'it's either him or me'll have to leave this house. If he wants to disgrace us all and ruin himself, he shan't do it under my eyes.'

Was there ever a harder case? A high-spirited British youth asserts his intention of living a life of elegant leisure, and is forthwith scouted as a disgrace to the family. 'Arry sat under the gross injustice with an air of doggish defiance.

'I thought you said I was to go to Wanley?' he exclaimed at length, angrily, glaring at his brother.

Richard avoided the look.

'You'll have to learn to behave yourself first,' he replied. 'If you can't be trusted to do your duty here, you're no good to me at Wanley.'

'Arry would give neither yes nor no. The council broke up after formulating an ultimatum.

In the afternoon Richard had another private talk with the lad. This time he addressed himself solely to 'Arry's self-interest, explained to him the opportunities he would lose if he neglected to make himself a practical man. What if there was money waiting for him? The use of money was to breed money, and nowadays no man was rich who didn't constantly increase his capital. As a great ironmaster, he would hold a position impossible for him to attain in any other way; he would employ hundreds, perhaps thousands, of men; society would recognise him. What could he expect to be if he did nothing but loaf about the streets?

This was going the right way to work. Richard found that he was making an impression, and gradually fell into a kinder tone, so that in the end he brought 'Arry to moderately cheerful acquiescence.

'And don't let men like that Keene make a fool of you,' the monitor concluded. 'Can't you see that fellows like him'll hang on and make their profit out of you if you know no better than to let them? You just keep to yourself, and look after your own future.'

A suggestion that cunning was required of him flattered the youth to some purpose. He had begun to reflect that after all it might be more profitable to combine work and pleasure. He agreed to pursue the course planned for him.

So Richard returned to Wanley, carrying with him a small satisfaction and many great anxieties. Nor did he visit London again until four weeks had gone by; it was understood that the pressure of responsibilities grew daily more severe. New Wanley, as the industrial settlement in the valley was to be named, was shaping itself in accordance with the ideas of the committee with which Mutimer took counsel, and the undertaking was no small one.

In spite of Emma's cheerful anticipations, 'the business' meanwhile made little progress. A graver trouble was the state of Jane's health; the sufferer seemed wasting away. Emma devoted herself to her sister. Between her and Mutimer there was no further mention of marriage. In Emma's mind a new term had fixed itself—that of her sister's recovery; but there were dark moments when dread came to her that not Jane's recovery, but something else, would set her free. In the early autumn Richard persuaded her to take the invalid to the sea-side, and to remain with her there for three weeks. Mrs. Clay during that time lived alone, and was very content to receive her future brother-in-law's subsidy, without troubling about the work which would not come in.

Autumn had always been a peaceful and bounteous season at Wanley; then the fruit-trees bent beneath their golden charge, and the air seemed rich with sweet odours. But the autumn of this year was unlike any that had visited the valley hitherto. Blight had fallen upon all produce; the crop of apples and plums was bare beyond precedent. The west wind breathing up between the hill-sides only brought smoke from newly-built chimneys; the face of the fields was already losing its purity, and taking on a dun hue. Where a large orchard had flourished were two streets of small houses, glaring with new brick and slate. The works were extending by degrees, and a little apart rose the walls of a large building which would contain library, reading-rooms, and lecture-hall, for the use of the industrial community. New Wanley was in a fair way to claim for itself a place on the map.

The Manor was long since furnished, and Richard entertained visitors. He had provided himself with a housekeeper, as well as the three or four necessary servants, and kept a saddle-horse as well as that which drew his trap to and fro when he had occasion to go to Agworth station. His establishment was still a modest one; all things considered, it could not be deemed inconsistent with his professions. Of course, stories to the contrary got about; among his old comrades in London, thorough-going Socialists like Messrs. Cowes and Cullen, who perhaps thought themselves a little neglected by the great light of the Union, there passed occasionally nods and winks, which were meant to imply much. There were rumours of banqueting which went on at Wanley; the Manor was spoken of by some who had not seen it as little less than a palace—nay, it was declared by one or two of the shrewder tongued that a man-servant in livery opened the door, a monstrous thing if true. Worse than this was the talk which began to spread among the Hoxton and Islington Unionists of a certain young woman in a poor position to whom Mutimer had in former days engaged himself, and whom he did not now find it convenient to marry. A few staunch friends Richard had, who made it their business stoutly to contradict the calumnies which came within their hearing, Daniel Dabbs the first of them. But even Daniel found himself before long preferring silence to speech on the subject of Emma Vine. He grew uncomfortable about it, and did not know what to think.

The first of Richard's visitors at the Manor were Mr. and
Mrs. Westlake. They came down from London one day, and
stayed over till the next. Other prominent members of the
Union followed, and before the end of the autumn Richard
entertained some dozen of the rank and file, all together, paying
their railway fares and housing them from Saturday to Monday.
These men, be it noted in passing, distinguished themselves
from that day onwards by unsparing detraction whenever the
name of Mutimer came up in private talk, though, of course,
they were the loudest in applause when platform reference to
their leader demanded it. Besides the expressly invited, there
was naturally no lack of visitors who presented themselves
voluntarily. Among the earliest of these was Mr. Keene, the
journalist. He sent in his name one Sunday morning request-
ing an interview on a matter of business, and on being admitted,
produced a copy of the 'Belwick Chronicle,' which contained a
highly eulogistic semi-biographic notice of Mutimer.

'I feel I ought to apologise to you for this liberty,' said
Keene, in his flowing way, 'and that is why I have brought
the paper myself. You will observe that it is one of a series—
notable men of the day. I supply the "Chronicle" with a London
letter, and give them one of these little sketches fortnightly. I
knew your modesty would stand in the way if I consulted you in
advance, so I can only beg pardon *post delictum*, as we say.'

There stood the heading in bold type, 'MEN OF THE DAY,
and beneath it 'XI. Mr. Richard Mutimer.' Mr. Keene had
likewise brought in his pocket the placard of the newspaper,
whereon Richard saw his name prominently displayed. The
journalist stayed for luncheon.

Alfred Waltham was frequently at the Manor. Mutimer
now seldom went up to town for Sunday; if necessity took him
thither, he chose some week-day. On Sunday he always spent
a longer or shorter time with the Walthams, frequently having
dinner at their house. He hesitated at first to invite the ladies
to the Manor; in his uncertainty on social usages he feared
lest there might be impropriety in a bachelor giving such an
invitation. He appealed to Alfred, who naturally laughed the
scruple to scorn, and accordingly Mrs. and Miss Waltham were
begged to honour Mr. Mutimer with their company. Mrs.
Waltham reflected a little, but accepted. Adela would much
rather have remained at home, but she had no choice.

By the end of September this invitation had been repeated,
and the Walthams had lunched a second time at the Manor, no

other guests being present. On the afternoon of the following day Mrs. Waltham and her daughter were talking together in their sitting-room, and the former led the conversation, as of late she almost invariably did when alone with her daughter, to their revolutionary friend.

'I can't help thinking, Adela, that in all essentials I never knew a more gentlemanly man than Mr. Mutimer. There must be something superior in his family; no doubt we were altogether mistaken in speaking of him as a mechanic.'

'But he has told us himself that he was a mechanic,' replied Adela, in the impatient way in which she was wont to speak on this subject.

'Oh, that is his modesty. And not only modesty; his views lead him to pride himself on a poor origin. He was an engineer, and we know that engineers are in reality professional men. Remember old Mr. Mutimer; he was a perfect gentleman. I have no doubt the family is really a very good one. Indeed, I am all but sure that I remember the name in Hampshire; there was a Sir something Mutimer—I'm convinced of it. No one really belonging to the working class ever bore himself as Mr. Mutimer does. Haven't you noticed the shape of his hands, my dear?'

'I've only noticed that they are very large, and just what you would expect in a man who had done much rough work.'

Mrs. Waltham laughed noisily.

'My dear child, how *can* you be so perverse? The shape of the fingers is perfect. Do pray notice them next time.'

'I really cannot promise, mother, to give special attention to Mr. Mutimer's hands.'

Mrs. Waltham glanced at the girl, who had laid down a book she was trying to read, and, with lowered eyes, seemed to be collecting herself for further utterance.

'Why are you so prejudiced, Adela?'

'I am not prejudiced at all. I have no interest of any kind in Mr. Mutimer.'

The words were spoken hurriedly and with a ring almost of hostility. At the same time the girl's cheeks flushed. She felt herself hard beset. A network was being woven about her by hands she could not deem other than loving; it was time to exert herself that the meshes might not be completed, and the necessity cost her a feeling of shame.

'But your brother's friend, my dear. Surely you ought not to say that you have no interest in him at all.'

K

'I do say it, mother, and I wish to say it so plainly that you cannot after this mistake me. Alfred's friends are very far from being necessarily my friends. Not only have I no interest in Mr. Mutimer, I even a little dislike him.'

'I had no idea of that, Adela,' said her mother, rather blankly.

'But it is the truth, and I feel I ought to have tried to make you understand that sooner. I thought you would see that I had no pleasure in speaking of him.'

'But how is it possible to dislike him? I confess that is very hard for me to understand. I am sure his behaviour to you is perfect—so entirely respectful, so gentlemanly.'

'No, mother, that is not quite the word to use. You are mistaken; Mr. Mutimer is *not* a perfect gentleman.'

It was said with much decision, for to Adela's mind this clenched her argument. Granted the absence of certain qualities which she held essential in a gentleman, there seemed to her no reason for another word on the subject.

'Pray, when has he misbehaved himself?' inquired her mother, with a touch of pique.

'I cannot go into details. Mr. Mutimer has no doubt many excellent qualities; no doubt he is really an earnest and a well-meaning man. But if I am asked to say more than that, it must be the truth—as it seems to me. Please, mother dear, don't ask me to talk about him in future. And there is something else I wish to say. I do hope you won't be offended with me, but indeed I—I hope you will not ask me to go to the Manor again. I feel I ought not to go. It is painful; I suffer when I am there.'

'How strange you are to-day, Adela! Really, I think you might allow me to decide what is proper and what is not. My experience is surely the best judge. You are worse than unkind, Adela; it's rude to speak to me like that.'

'Dear mother,' said the girl, with infinite gentleness, 'I am very, very sorry. How could I be unkind or rude to you? I didn't for a moment mean that my judgment was better than yours; it is my feelings that I speak of. You won't ask me to explain—to say more than that? You must understand me?'

'Oh yes, my dear, I understand you too well,' was the stiff reply. 'Of course I am old-fashioned, and I suppose old-fashioned people are a little coarse; *their* feelings are not quite as fine as they might be. We will say no more for the present,

Adela. I will do my best not to lead you into disagreeable situations through my lack of delicacy.'

There were tears in Adela's eyes.

'Mother, now it is you who are unkind. I am so sorry that I spoke. You won't take my words as they were meant. Must I say that I cannot let Mr. Mutimer misunderstand the way in which I regard him? He comes here really so very often, and if we begin to go there too——. People are talking about it, indeed they are; Letty has told me so. How can I help feeling pained?'

Mrs. Waltham drew out her handkerchief and appeared mildly agitated. When Adela bent and kissed her she sighed deeply, then said in an undertone of gentle melancholy:

'I ask your pardon, my dear. I am afraid there has been a little misunderstanding on both sides. But we won't talk any more of it—there, there!'

By which the good lady of course meant that she would renew the subject on the very earliest opportunity, and that, on the whole, she was not discouraged. Mothers are often unaware of their daughters' strong points, but their weaknesses they may be trusted to understand pretty well.

The little scene was just well over, and Adela had taken a seat by the window, when a gentleman who was approaching the front door saw her and raised his hat. She went very pale.

The next moment there was a knock at the front door.

'Mother,' the girl whispered, as if she could not speak louder, 'it is Mr. Eldon.'

'Mr. Eldon?' Mrs. Waltham drew herself up with dignity, then started from her seat. 'The idea of his daring to come here!'

She intercepted the servant who was going to open the door.

'Jane, we are not at home!'

The maid stood in astonishment. She was not used to the polite fictions of society; never before had that welcome mortal, an afternoon visitor, been refused at Mrs. Waltham's.

'What did you say, please, mum?'

'You will say that we are not at home, neither I nor Miss Waltham.'

Even if Hubert Eldon had not seen Adela at the window he must have been dull not to read the meaning of the servant's singular face and tone. He walked away with a quiet 'Thank you.'

Mrs. Waltham cast a side glance at Adela when she heard the outer door close. The girl had reopened her book.

'I'm not sorry that he came. Was there ever such astonishing impudence? If *that* is gentlemanly, then I must confess I—— Really I am not at all sorry he came : it will give him a lesson.'

'Mr. Eldon may have had some special reason for calling,' Adela remarked disinterestedly.

'My dear, I have no business of any kind with Mr. Eldon, and it is impossible that he can have any with me.'

Adela very shortly went from the room.

That evening Richard had for guest at dinner Mr. Willis Rodman ; so that gentleman named himself on his cards, and so he liked to be announced. Mr. Rodman was invaluable as surveyor of the works ; his experience appeared boundless, and had been acquired in many lands. He was now a Socialist of the purest water, and already he enjoyed more of Mutimer's intimacy than anyone else. Richard not seldom envied the easy and, as it seemed to him, polished manner of his subordinate, and wondered at it the more since Rodman declared himself a proletarian by birth, and, in private, was fond of referring to the hardships of his early life. That there may be no needless mystery about Mr. Rodman, I am under the necessity of stating the fact that he was the son of a prosperous railway contractor, that he was born in Canada, and would have succeeded to a fortune on his father's death, but for an unhappy *contretemps* in the shape of a cheque, whereof Mr. Rodman senior (the name was not Rodman, but the true one is of no importance) disclaimed the signature. From that day to the present good and ill luck had alternated in the young man's career. His fortunes in detail do not concern us just now; there will be future occasion for returning to the subject.

'Young Eldon has been in Wanley to-day,' Mr. Rodman remarked as he sat over his wine after dinner.

'Has he?' said Richard, with indifference. 'What's he been after?'

'I saw him going up towards the Walthams'.'

Richard exhibited more interest.

'Is he a particular friend of theirs?' he asked. He had gathered from Alfred Waltham that there had been a certain intimacy between the two families, but desired more detailed information than his disciple had offered.

'Well, he used to be,' replied Rodman, with a significant

smile. 'But I don't suppose Mrs. W. gave him a very affectionate reception to-day. His little doings have rather startled the good people of Wanley, especially since he has lost his standing. It wouldn't have mattered much, I dare say, but for that.'

'But was there anything particular up there?'

Mutimer had a careworn expression as he asked, and he nodded his head as if in the direction of the village with a certain weariness.

'I'm not quite sure. Some say there was, and others deny it, as I gather from general conversation. But I suppose it's at an end now, in any case.'

'Mrs. Waltham would see to that, you mean?' said Mutimer, with a short laugh.

'Probably.'

Rodman made his glass revolve, his fingers on the stem.

'Take another cigar. I suppose they're not too well off, the Walthams?'

'Mrs. Waltham has an annuity of two hundred and fifty pounds, that's all. The girl—Miss Waltham—has nothing.'

'How the deuce do you get to know so much about people, Rodman?'

The other smiled modestly, and made a silent gesture, as if to disclaim any special abilities.

'So he called there to-day? I wonder whether he stayed long?'

'I will let you know to-morrow.'

On the morrow Richard learnt that Hubert Eldon had been refused admittance. The information gave him pleasure. Yet all through the night he had been earnestly hoping that he might hear something quite different, had tried to see in Eldon's visit a possible salvation for himself. For the struggle which occupied him more and more had by this time declared its issues plainly enough; daily the temptation became stronger, the resources of honour more feeble. In the beginning he had only played with dangerous thoughts; to break faith with Emma Vine had appeared an impossibility, and a marriage such as his fancy substituted, the most improbable of things. But in men of Richard's stamp that which allures the fancy will, if circumstances give but a little encouragement, soon take hold upon the planning brain. His acquaintance with the Walthams had ripened to intimacy, and custom nourished his self-confidence; moreover, he could not misunderstand the all but direct encouragement which on one or two recent occasions he had received from Mrs. Waltham. That lady had begun to talk to him, when they were alone together, in almost a motherly way, confiding to him this or that peculiarity in the characters of her children, deploring her inability to give Adela the pleasures suitable to her age, then again pointing out the advantage it was to a girl to have all her thoughts centred in home.

'I can truly say,' remarked Mrs. Waltham in the course of the latest such conversation, ' that Adela has never given me an hour's serious uneasiness. The dear child has, I believe, no will apart from her desire to please me. Her instincts are so beautifully submissive.'

To a man situated like Mutimer this tone is fatal. In truth it seemed to make offer to him of what he supremely desired. No such encouragement had come from Adela herself, but that meant nothing either way; Richard had already perceived that maidenly reserve was a far more complex matter in a girl of gentle breeding, than in those with whom he had formerly associated; for all he knew, increase of distance in manner might represent the very hope that he was seeking. That hope he sought, in all save the hours when conscience lorded over silence, with a reality of desire such as he had never known. Perhaps it was not Adela, and Adela alone, that inspired this passion; it was a new ideal of the feminine addressing itself to his instincts. Adela had the field to herself, and did indeed embody in almost an ideal degree the fine essence of distinctly feminine qualities which appeal most strongly to the masculine mind. Mutimer was not capable of love in the highest sense; he was not, again, endowed with strong appetite; but his nature contained possibilities of refinement which, in a situation like the present, constituted motive force the same in its effects as either form of passion. He was suffering, too, from the *malaise* peculiar to men who suddenly acquire riches; secret impulses drove him to gratifications which would not otherwise have troubled his thoughts. Of late he had been yielding to several such caprices. One morning the idea possessed him that he must have a horse for riding, and he could not rest till the horse was purchased and in his stable. It occurred to him once at dinner time that there were sundry delicacies which he knew by name but had never tasted; forthwith he gave orders that these delicacies should be supplied to him, and so there appeared upon his breakfast table a *pâté de foie gras*. Very similar in kind was his desire to possess Adela Waltham.

And the voice of his conscience lost potency, though it troubled him more than ever, even as a beggar will sometimes become rudely clamorous when he sees that there is no real hope of extracting an alms. Richard was embarked on the practical study of moral philosophy; he learned more in these months of the constitution of his inner being than all his literature of 'free thought' had been able to convey to him. To break with Emma, to cast his faith to the winds, to be branded henceforth in the sight of his intimate friends as a mere traitor, and an especially mean one to boot—that at the first blush was of the things so impossible that one does not trouble to study their bearings. But the wall of habit once breached, the citadel of conscience laid bare, what garrison was revealed? With something like astonishment, Richard came to recognise that the garrison was of the most contemptible and tatterdemalion description. Fear of people's talk—absolutely nothing else stood in his way.

Had he, then, no affection for Emma? Hardly a scrap. He had never even tried to persuade himself that he was in love with her, and the engagement had on his side been an affair of cool reason. His mother had practically brought it about; for years it had been a pet project of hers, and her joy was great in its realisation. Mrs. Vine and she had been lifelong gossips; she knew that to Emma had descended the larger portion of her parent's sterling qualities, and that Emma was the one wife for such a man as Richard. She talked him into approval. In those days Richard had no dream of wedding above his class, and he understood very well that Emma Vine was distinguished in many ways from the crowd of working girls. There was no one else he wished to marry. Emma would feel herself honoured by his choice, and, what he had not himself observed, his mother led him to see that yet deeper feelings were concerned on the girl's side. This flattered him—a form of emotion to which he was ever susceptible—and the match was speedily arranged.

He had never repented. The more he knew of Emma, the more confirmation his favourable judgments received. He even knew at times a stirring of the senses, which is the farthest that many of his kind ever progress in the direction of love. Of the nobler features in Emma's character he of course remained ignorant; they did not enter into his demands upon woman, and he was unable to discern them even when they were brought prominently before him. She would keep his house admirably,

would never contradict him, would mother his children to perfection, and even would go so far as to take an intelligent interest in the Propaganda. What more could a man look for?

So there was no strife between old love and new; so far as
it concerned himself, to put Emma aside would not cost a pang.
The garrison was absolutely mere tongue, mere gossip of public-
house bars, firesides, &c.—more serious, of the Socialist lecture-
rooms. And what of the girl's own feeling? Was there no
sense of compassion in him? Very little. And in saying so I
mean anything but to convey that Mutimer was conspicuously
hard-hearted. The fatal defect in working people is absence of
imagination, the power which may be solely a gift of nature
and irrespective of circumstances, but which in most of us owes
so much to intellectual training. Half the brutal cruelties perpetrated by uneducated men and women are directly traceable
to lack of the imaginative spirit, which comes to mean lack of
kindly sympathy. Mutimer, we know, had got for himself
only the most profitless of educations, and in addition nature
had scanted him on the emotional side. He could not enter
into the position of Emma deserted and hopeless. Want of
money was intelligible to him, so was bitter disappointment at
the loss of a good position, but the former he would not allow
Emma to suffer; and the latter she would, in the nature of
things, soon get over. Her love for him he judged by his own
feeling, making allowance, of course, for the weakness of women
in affairs such as this. He might admit that she would 'fret,'
but the thought of her fretting did not affect him as a reality.
Emma had never been demonstrative, had never sought to
show him all that was in her heart; hence he rated her devotion
lightly.

The opinion of those who knew him ! What of the opinion
of Emma herself? Yes, that went for much; he knew shame
at the thought, perhaps keener shame than in anticipating the
judgment, say, of Daniel Dabbs. No one of his acquaintances
thought of him so highly as Emma did; to see himself de-
throned, the object of her contempt, was a bitter pill to swallow. In all that concerned his own dignity Richard was keenly
appreciative; he felt in advance every pricking of the blood that
was in store for him if he became guilty of this treachery. Yes,
from that point of view he feared Emma Vine.

Considerations of larger scope did not come within the pur-
view of his intellect. It never occurred to him, for instance,
that in forfeiting his honour in this instance he began a process

of undermining which would sooner or later threaten the stability of the purposes on which he most prided himself. A suggestion that domestic perfidy was in the end incompatible with public zeal would have seemed to him ridiculous, and for the simple reason that he recognised no moral sanctions. He could not regard his nature as a whole; he had no understanding for the subtle network of communication between its various parts. Nay, he told himself that the genuineness and value of his life's work would be increased by a marriage with Adela Waltham; he and she would represent the union of classes— of the wage-earning with the *bourgeois*, between which two lay the real gist of the combat. He thought of this frequently, and allowed the thought to inspirit him.

To the question of whether Adela would ever find out what he had done, and, if so, with what result, he gave scarcely a moment. Marriages are not undone by subsequent discovery of moral faults on either side.

This is a tabular exposition of the man's consciousness. Logically, there should result from it a self-possessed state of mind, bordering on cynicism. But logic was not predominant in Mutimer's constitution. So far from contemplating treason with the calm intelligence which demands judgment on other grounds than the common, he was in reality possessed by a spirit of perturbation. Such reason as he could command bade him look up and view with scorn the ragged defenders of the forts; but whence came this hail of missiles which kept him so sore? Clearly there was some element of his nature which eluded grasp and definition, a misty influence making itself felt here and there. To none of the sources upon which I have touched was it clearly traceable; in truth, it arose from them all. The man had never in his life been guilty of offence against his graver conscience; he had the sensation of being about to plunge from firm footing into untried depths. His days were troubled; his appetite was not what it should have been; he could not take the old thorough interest in his work. It was becoming clear to him that the matter must be settled one way or another with brief delay.

One day at the end of September he received a letter addressed by Alice. On opening it he found, with much surprise, that the contents were in his mother's writing. It was so very rarely that Mrs. Mutimer took up that dangerous instrument, the pen, that something unusual must have led to her doing so at present. And, indeed, the letter contained unexpected matter. There were numerous errors of orthography, and the hand was not very legible; but Richard got at the sense quickly enough.

'I write this,' began Mrs. Mutimer, 'because it's a long time since you've been to see us, and because I want to say something that's better written than spoken. I saw Emma last night, and I'm feeling uncomfortable about her. She's getting very low, and that's the truth. Not as she says anything, nor shows it, but she's got a deal on her hands, and more on her mind. You haven't written to her for three weeks. You'll be saying it's no business of mine, but I can't stand by and see Emma putting up with things as there isn't no reason. Jane is in a very bad way, poor girl; I can't think she'll live long. Now, Dick, what I'm aiming at you'll see. I can't understand why you don't get married and done with it. Jane won't never be able to work again, and that Kate 'll never keep up a dressmaking. Why don't you marry Emma, and take poor Jane to live with you, where she could be well looked after? for she won't never part from her sister. And she does so hope and pray to see Emma married before she goes. You can't surely be waiting for her death. Now, there's a good lad of mine, come and marry your wife at once, and don't make delays. That's all, but I hope you'll think of it; and so, from your affectionate old mother,   'S. MUTIMER.'

Richard read the letter several times, and sat at home through the morning in despondency. It had got to the pass that he could not marry Emma; for all his suffering he no longer gave a glance in that direction. Not even if Adela Waltham refused him; to have a 'lady' for his wife was now an essential in his plans for the future, and he knew that the desired possession was purchasable for coin of the realm. No way of retreat any longer; movement must be forward, at whatever cost.

He let a day intervene, then replied to his mother's letter. He represented himself as worked to death and without a moment for his private concerns; it was out of the question for him to marry for a few weeks yet. He would write to Emma, and would send her all the money she could possibly need to supply the sick girl with comforts. She must keep up her courage, and be content to wait a short while longer. He was quite sure she did not complain; it was only his mother's fancy that she was in low spirits, except, of course, on Jane's account.

Another fortnight went by. Skies were lowering towards

winter, and the sides of the valley showed bare patches amid
the rich-hued death of leaves; ere long a night of storm would
leave 'ruined choirs.' Richard was in truth working hard.
He had just opened a course of lectures at a newly established
Socialist branch in Belwick. The extent of his daily correspondence threatened to demand the services of a secretary in
addition to the help already given by Rodman. Moreover, an
event of importance was within view; the New Wanley Public
Hall was completed, and its formal opening must be made an
occasion of ceremony. In that ceremony Richard would be the
central figure. He proposed to gather about him a representative company ; not only would the Socialist leaders attend as a
matter of course, invitations should also be sent to prominent
men in the conventional lines of politics. A speech from a
certain Radical statesman, who could probably be induced to
attend, would command the attention of the press. For the
sake of preliminary trumpetings in even so humble a journal as
the 'Belwick Chronicle,' Mutimer put himself in communication with Mr. Keene. That gentleman was now a recognised
visitor at the house in Highbury ; there was frequent mention
of him in a close correspondence kept up between Richard and
his sister at this time. The letters which Alice received from
Wanley were not imparted to the other members of the family ;
she herself studied them attentively, and with much apparent
satisfaction.

For advice on certain details of the approaching celebration
Richard had recourse to Mrs. Waltham. He found her at home
one rainy morning. Adela, aware of his arrival, retreated to
her little room upstairs. Mrs. Waltham had a slight cold ; it
kept her close by the fireside, and encouraged confidential talk.

'I have decided to invite about twenty people to lunch,'
Richard said. ' Just the members of the committee and a few
others. It'll be better than giving a dinner. Westlake's
lecture will be over by four o'clock, and that allows people to
get away in good time. The workmen's tea will be at half-
past five.'

'You must have refreshments of some kind for casual
comers,' counselled Mrs. Waltham.

'I've thought of that. Rodman suggests that we shall get
the "Wheatsheaf" people to have joints and that kind of thing
in the refreshment-room at the Hall from half-past twelve to
half-past one. We could put up some notice to that effect in
Agworth station.'

'Certainly, and inside the railway carriages.'

Mutimer's private line, which ran from the works to Agworth station, was to convey visitors to New Wanley on this occasion.

'I think I shall have three or four ladies,' Richard pursued. 'Mrs. Westlake 'll be sure to come, and I think Mrs. Eddlestone —the wife of the Trades Union man, you know. And I've been rather calculating on you, Mrs. Waltham; do you think you could——?'

The lady's eyes were turned to the window, watching the sad, steady rain.

'Really, you're making a downright Socialist of me, Mr. Mutimer,' she replied, with a laugh which betrayed a touch of sore throat. 'I'm half afraid to accept such an invitation. Shouldn't I be there on false pretences, don't you think?'

Richard mused; his legs were crossed, and he swayed his foot up and down.

'Well, no, I can't see that. But I tell you what would make it simpler: do you think Mr. Wyvern would come if I asked him?'

'Ah, now, that would be capital! Oh, ask Mr. Wyvern by all means. Then, of course, I should be delighted to accept.'

'But I haven't much hope that he'll come. I rather think he regards me as his enemy. And, you see, I never go to church.'

'What a pity that is, Mr. Mutimer! Ah, if I could only persuade you to think differently about those things! There really are so many texts that read quite like Socialism; I was looking them over with Adela on Sunday. What a sad thing it is that you go so astray! It distresses me more than you think. Indeed, if I may tell you such a thing, I pray for you nightly.'

Mutimer made a movement of discomfort, but laughed off the subject.

'I'll go and see the vicar, at all events,' he said. 'But must your coming depend on his?'

Mrs. Waltham hesitated.

'It really would make things easier.'

'Might I, in that case, hope that Miss Waltham would come?'

Richard seemed to exert himself to ask the question. Mrs. Waltham sank her eyes, smiled feebly, and in the end shook her head.

'On a public occasion, I'm really afraid——'

'I'm sure she would like to know Mrs. Westlake,' urged Richard, without his usual confidence. 'And if you and her brother——'

'If it were not a Socialist gathering.'

Richard uncrossed his legs and sat for a moment looking into the fire. Then he turned suddenly.

'Mrs. Waltham, may I ask her myself?'

She was visibly agitated. There was this time no affectation in the tremulous lips and the troublous, unsteady eyes. Mrs. Waltham was not by nature the scheming mother who is indifferent to the upshot if she can once get her daughter loyally bound to a man of money. Adela's happiness was a very real care to her; she would never have opposed an unobjectionable union on which she found her daughter's heart bent, but circumstances had a second time made offer of brilliant advantages, and she had grown to deem it an ordinance of the higher powers that Adela should marry possessions. She flattered herself that her study of Mutimer's character had been profound; the necessity of making such a study excused, she thought, any little excess of familiarity in which she had indulged, for it had long been clear to her that Mutimer would some day make an offer. He lacked polish, it was true, but really he was more a gentleman than a great many whose right to the name was never contested. And then he had distinctly high aims; such a man could never be brutal in the privacy of his home. There was every chance of his achieving some kind of eminence; already she had suggested to him a Parliamentary career, and the idea had not seemed altogether distasteful. Adela herself was as yet far from regarding Mutimer in the light of a future husband; it was perhaps true that she even disliked him. But then a young girl's likes and dislikes have, as a rule, small bearing on her practical content in the married state; so, at least, Mrs. Waltham's experience led her to believe. Only, it was clear that there must be no precipitancy. Let the ground be thoroughly prepared.

'May I advise you, Mr. Mutimer?' she said, in a lowered voice, bending forward. 'Let me deliver the invitation. I think it would be better, really. We shall see whether you can persuade Mr. Wyvern to be present. I promise you to—in fact, not to interpose any obstacle if Adela thinks she can be present at the lunch.'

'Then I'll leave it so,' said Richard, more cheerfully. Mrs. Waltham could see that his nerves were in a dancing state. Really, he had much fine feeling.

CHAPTER XI.

IT being only midday, Richard directed his steps at once to
the Vicarage, and had the good fortune to find Mr. Wyvern
within.

'Be seated, Mr. Mutimer; I'm glad to see you,' was the
vicar's greeting.

Their mutual intercourse had as yet been limited to an
exchange of courtesies in public, and one or two casual meetings at the Walthams' house. Richard had felt shy of the
vicar, whom he perceived to be a clergyman of other than the
weak-brained type, and the circumstances of the case would
not allow Mr. Wyvern to make advances. The latter proceeded with friendliness of tone, speaking of the progress of
New Wanley.

'That's what I've come to see you about,' said Richard,
trying to put himself at ease by mentally comparing his own
worldly estate with that of his interlocutor, yet failing as often
as he felt the scrutiny of the vicar's dark-gleaming eye. 'We
are going to open the Hall.' He added details. 'I shall have
a number of friends who are interested in our undertaking to
lunch with me on that day. I wish to ask if you will give us
the pleasure of your company.'

Mr. Wyvern reflected for a moment.

'Why, no, sir,' he replied at length, using the Johnsonian
phrase with grave courtesy. 'I'm afraid I cannot acknowledge
your kindness as I should wish to. Personally, I would accept your hospitality with pleasure, but my position here, as I
understand it, forbids me to join you on that particular occasion.'

'Then personally you are not hostile to me, Mr. Wyvern?'

'To you personally, by no means.'

'But you don't like the movement?'

'In so far as it has the good of men in view it interests
me, and I respect its supporters.'

'But you think we go the wrong way to work?'

'That is my opinion, Mr. Mutimer.'

'What would you have us do?'

'To see faults is a much easier thing than to originate a
sound scheme. I am far from prepared with any plan of social
reconstruction.'

Nor could Mr. Wyvern be moved from the negative attitude, though Mutimer pressed him.

'Well, I'm sorry you won't come,' Richard said as he rose to take his leave. 'It didn't strike me that you would feel out of place.'

'Nor should I. But you will understand that my opportunities of being useful in the village depend on the existence of sympathetic feeling in my parishioners. It is my duty to avoid any behaviour which could be misinterpreted.'

'Then you deliberately adapt yourself to the prejudices of unintelligent people?'

'I do so, deliberately,' assented the vicar, with one of his fleeting smiles.

Richard went away feeling sorry that he had courted this rejection. He would never have thought of inviting a 'parson' but for Mrs. Waltham's suggestion. After all, it mattered little whether Adela came to the luncheon or not. He had desired her presence because he wished her to see him as an entertainer of guests such as the Westlakes, whom she would perceive to be people of refinement; it occurred to him, too, that such an occasion might aid his suit by exciting her ambition; for he was anything but confident of immediate success with Adela, especially since recent conversations with Mrs. Waltham. But in any case she would attend the afternoon ceremony, when his glory would be proclaimed.

Mrs. Waltham was anxiously meditative of plans for bringing Adela to regard her Socialist wooer with more favourable eyes. She, too, had hopes that Mutimer's fame in the mouths of men might prove an attraction, yet she suspected a strength of principle in Adela which might well render all such hopes vain. And she thought it only too likely, though observation gave her no actual assurance of this, that the girl still thought of Hubert Eldon in a way to render it doubly hard for any other man to make an impression upon her. It was dangerous, she knew, to express her abhorrence of Hubert too persistently; yet, on the other hand, she was convinced that Adela had been so deeply shocked by the revelations of Hubert's wickedness that her moral nature would be in arms against her lingering inclination. After much mental wear and tear, she decided to adopt the strong course of asking Alfred's assistance. Alfred was sure to view the proposed match with hearty approval, and, though he might not have much influence directly, he could in all probability secure a potent

ally in the person of Letty Tew. This was rather a brilliant
idea; Mrs. Waltham waited impatiently for her son's return
from Belwick on Saturday.

She broached the subject to him with much delicacy.

'I am so convinced, Alfred, that it would be for your sister's
happiness.   There really is no harm whatever in aiding her
inexperience; that is all that I wish to do.   I'm sure you understand me?'

'I understand well enough,' returned the young man; 'but
if you convince Adela against her will you'll do a clever thing.
You've been so remarkably successful in closing her mind against
all arguments of reason——'

'Now, Alfred, do not begin and talk in that way! It has
nothing whatever to do with the matter. This is entirely a
personal question.'

'Nothing of the kind. It's a question of religious prejudice.
She hates Mutimer because he doesn't go to church, there's the
long and short of it.'

'Adela very properly condemns his views, but that's quite a
different thing from hating him.'

'Oh dear, no; they're one and the same thing. Look at
the history of persecution. She would like to see him—and
me too, I dare say—brought to the stake.'

'Well, well, of course if you won't talk sensibly! I had
something to propose.'

'Let me hear it, then.'

'You yourself agree with me that there would be nothing to
repent in urging her.'

'On the contrary, I think she might consider herself precious lucky. It's only that'—he looked dubious for a moment
—' I'm not quite sure whether she's the kind of girl to be content with a husband she found she couldn't convert. I can
imagine her marrying a rake on the hope of bringing him to
regular church-going, but then Mutimer doesn't happen to be
a blackguard, so he isn't very interesting to her.'

'I know what you're thinking of, but I don't think we need
take that into account. And, indeed, we can't afford to take
anything into account but her establishment in a respectable
and happy home. Our choice, as you are aware, is not a wide
one. I am often deeply anxious about the poor girl.'

'I dare say. Well, what was your proposal?'

'Do you think Letty could help us?'

'H'm, can't say. Might or might not. She's as bad as

Adela. Ten to one it'll be a point of conscience with her to fight the project tooth and nail.'

'I don't think so. She has accepted you.'

'So she has, to my amazement. Women are monstrously illogical. She must think of my latter end with mixed feelings.'

'I do wish you were less flippant in dealing with grave subjects, Alfred. I assure you I am very much troubled. I feel that so much is at stake, and yet the responsibility of doing anything is so very great.'

'Shall I talk it over with Letty?'

'If you feel able to. But Adela would be very seriously offended if she guessed that you had done so.'

'Then she mustn't guess, that's all. I'll see what I can do to-night.'

In the home of the Tews there was some difficulty in securing privacy. The house was a small one, and the sacrifice of general convenience when Letty wanted a whole room for herself and Alfred was considerable. To-night it was managed, however ; the front parlour was granted to the pair for one hour.

It could not be said that there was much delicacy in Alfred's way of approaching the subject he wished to speak of. This young man had a scorn of periphrases. If a topic had to be handled, why not be succinct in the handling? Alfred was of opinion that much time was lost by mortals in windy talk.

'Look here, Letty ; what's your idea about Adela marrying Mutimer?'

The girl looked startled.

'She has not accepted him?'

'Not yet. Don't you think it would be a good thing if she did?'

'I really can't say,' Letty replied very gravely, her head aside. 'I don't think any one can judge but Adela herself. Really, Alfred, I don't think we ought to interfere.'

'But suppose I ask you to try and get her to see the affair sensibly?'

'Sensibly? What a word to use!'

'The right word, I think.'

'What a vexatious boy you are! You don't really think so at all. You only speak so because you like to tease me.'

'Well, you certainly do look pretty when you're defending the castles in the air. Give me a kiss.'

'Indeed, I shall not. Tell me seriously what you mean. What does Mrs. Waltham think about it?'

'Give me a kiss, and I'll tell you. If not, I'll go away and leave you to find out everything as best you can.'

'Oh, Alfred, you're a sad tyrant!'

'Of course I am. But it's a benevolent despotism. Well, mother wants Adela to accept him. In fact, she asked me if I didn't think you'd help us. Of course I said you would.'

'Then you were very hasty. I'm not joking now, Alfred. I think of Adela in a way you very likely can't understand. It would be shocking, oh! shocking, to try and make her marry him if she doesn't really wish to.'

'No fear! We shan't manage that.'

'And surely wouldn't wish to?'

'I don't know. Girls often can't see what's best for them. I say, you understand that all this is in confidence?'

'Of course I do. But it's a confidence I had rather not have received. I shall be miserable, I know that.'

'Then you're a little—goose.'

'You were going to call me something far worse.'

'Give me credit, then, for correcting myself. You'll have to help us, Lettycoco.'

The girl kept silence. Then for a time the conversation became graver. It was interrupted precisely at the end of the granted hour.

Letty went to see her friend on Sunday afternoon, and the two shut themselves up in the dainty little chamber. Adela was in low spirits; with her a most unusual state. She sat with her hands crossed on her lap, and the sunny light of her eyes was dimmed. When she had tried for a while to talk of ordinary things, Letty saw a tear glisten upon her cheek.

'What is the matter, love?'

Adela was in sore need of telling her troubles, and Letty was the only one to whom she could do so. In such spirit-gentle words as could express the perplexities of her mind she told what a source of pain her mother's conversation had been to her of late, and how she dreaded what might still be to come.

'It is so dreadful to think, Letty, that mother is encouraging him. She thinks it is for my happiness; she is offended if I try to say what I suffer. Oh, I couldn't! I couldn't!'

She put her palms before her face; her maidenhood shamed to speak of these things even to her bosom friend.

'Can't you show him, darling, that—that he mustn't hope anything?'

'How can I do so? It is impossible to be rude, and everything else it is so easy to misunderstand.'

'But when he really speaks, then it will come to an end.'

'I shall grieve mother so, Letty. I feel as if the best of my life had gone by. Everything seemed so smooth. Oh, why did he fall so, Letty? and I thought he cared for me, dear.'

She whispered it, her face on her friend's shoulder.

'Try to forget, darling; try!'

'Oh, as if I didn't try night and day! I know it is so wrong to give a thought. How could he speak to me as he did that day when I met him on the hill, and again when I went just to save him an annoyance? He was almost the same as before, only I thought him a little sad from his illness. He had no right to talk to me in that way! Oh, I feel wicked, that I can't forget; I hate myself for still—for still——'

There was a word Letty could not hear, only her listening heart divined it.

'Dear Adela! pray for strength, and it will be sure to come to you. How hard it is to know myself so happy when you have so much trouble!'

'I could have borne it better but for this new pain. I don't think I should ever have shown it; even you wouldn't have known all I felt, Letty. I should have hoped for him—I don't mean hoped on my own account, but that he might know how wicked he had been. How—how can a man do things so unworthy of himself, when it's so beautiful to be good and faithful? I think he did care a little for me once, Letty.'

'Don't let us talk of him, pet.'

'You are right; we mustn't. His name ought never to pass my lips, only in my prayers.'

She grew calmer, and they sat hand in hand.

'Try to make your mother understand,' advised Letty. 'Say that it is impossible you should ever accept him.'

'She won't believe that, I'm sure she won't. And to think that, even if I did it only to please her, people would believe I had married him because he is rich!'

Letty spoke with more emphasis than hitherto.

'But you cannot and must not do such a thing to please any one, Adela! It is wrong even to think of it. Nothing, nothing can justify that.'

How strong she was in the purity of her own love, good little Letty! So they talked together, and mingled their tears, and the room was made a sacred place as by the presence of sorrowing angels.

CHAPTER XII.

THE New Wanley Lecture Hall had been publicly dedicated to the service of the New Wanley Commonwealth, and only in one respect did the day's proceedings fall short of Mutimer's expectations. He had hoped to have all the Waltham family at his luncheon party, but in the event Alfred alone felt himself able to accept the invitation. Mutimer had even nourished the hope that something might happen before that day to allow of Adela's appearing not merely in the character of a guest, but, as it were, *ex officio*. By this time he had resolutely forbidden his eyes to stray to the right hand or the left, and kept them directed with hungry, relentless steadiness straight along the path of his desires. He had received no second letter from his mother, nor had Alice anything to report of danger-signals at home; from Emma herself came a letter regularly once a week, a letter of perfect patience, chiefly concerned with her sister's health. He had made up his mind to declare nothing till the irretrievable step was taken, when reproaches only could befall him; to Alice as little as to any one else had he breathed of his purposes. And he could no longer even take into account the uncertainty of his success; to doubt of that would have been insufferable at the point which he had reached in self-abandonment. Yet day after day saw the postponement of the question which would decide his fate. Between him and Mrs. Waltham the language of allusion was at length put aside; he spoke plainly of his wishes, and sought her encouragement. This was not wanting, but the mother begged for time. Let the day of the ceremony come and go.

Richard passed through it in a state of exaltation and anxiety which bordered on fever. Mr. Westlake and his wife came down from London by an early train, and he went over New Wanley with them before luncheon. The luncheon itself did not lack festive vivacity; Richard, in surveying his guests from the head of the board, had feelings not unlike those where-

ın King Polycrates lulled himself of old; there wanted, in
truth, one thing to complete his self-complacence, but an extra
glass or two of wine enrubied his imagination, and he already
saw. Adela's face smiling to him from the table's unoccupied
end.   What was such conquest in comparison with that which
fate had accorded him?

There was a satisfactory gathering to hear Mr. Westlake's
address; Richard did not fail to note the presence of a few
reporters, only it seemed to him that their pencils might have
been more active.   Here, too, was Adela at length; every time
his name was uttered, perforce she heard; every encomium bestowed upon him by the various speakers was to him like a
new bud on the tree of hope.   After all, why should he feel
this humility towards her?   What man of prominence, of
merit, at all like his own would ever seek her hand?   The semblance of chivalry which occasionally stirred within him was,
in fact, quite inconsistent with his reasoned view of things;
the English working class has, on the whole, as little of that
quality as any other people in an elementary stage of civilisation.   He was a man, she a woman.   A lady, to be sure, but
then——

After Mutimer, Alfred Waltham had probably more genuine
satisfaction in the ceremony than any one else present.   Mr.
Westlake he was not quite satisfied with; there was a mildness
and restraint about the style of the address which to Alfred's
taste smacked of feebleness; he was for Cambyses' vein.   Still
it rejoiced him to hear the noble truths of democracy delivered
as it were from the bema.   To a certain order of intellect the
word addressed by the living voice to an attentive assembly is
always vastly impressive; when the word coincides with private
sentiment it excites enthusiasm.   Alfred hated the aristocratic
order of things with a rabid hatred.   In practice he could be
as coarsely overbearing with his social inferiors as that scion of
the nobility—existing of course somewhere—who bears the
bell for feebleness of the pia mater; but that made him none
the less a sound Radical.   In thinking of the upper classes he
always thought of Hubert Eldon, and that name was scarlet to
him.   Never trust the thoroughness of the man who is a revolutionist on abstract principles; personal feeling alone goes to
the root of the matter.

Many were the gentlemen to whom Alfred had the happiness of being introduced in the course of the day.   Among
others was Mr. Keene the journalist.   At the end of a lively

conversation Mr. Keene brought out a copy of the 'Belwick Chronicle,' that day's issue.

'You'll find a few things of mine here,' he said. 'Put it in your pocket, and look at it afterwards. By-the-by, there is a paragraph marked; I meant it for Mutimer. Never mind, give it him when you've done with it.'

Alfred bestowed the paper in the breast pocket of his great-coat, and did not happen to think of it again till late that evening. His discovery of it at length was not the only event of the day which came just too late for the happiness of one with whose fortunes we are concerned.

A little after dark, when the bell was ringing which summoned Mutimer's workpeople to the tea provided for them, Hubert Eldon was approaching the village by the road from Agworth: he was on foot, and had chosen his time in order to enter Wanley unnoticed. His former visit, when he was refused at the Walthams' door, had been paid at an impulse; he had come down from London by an early train, and did not even call to see his mother at her new house in Agworth. Nor did he visit her on his way back; he walked straight to the railway station and took the first train townwards. To-day he came in a more leisurely way. It was certain news contained in a letter from his mother which brought him, and with her he spent some hours before starting to walk towards Wanley.

'I hear,' Mrs. Eldon had written, 'from Wanley something which really surprises me. They say that Adela Waltham is going to marry Mr. Mutimer. The match is surely a very strange one. I am only fearful that it is the making of interested people, and that the poor girl herself has not had much voice in deciding her own fate. Oh, this money! Adela was worthy of better things.'

Mrs. Eldon saw her son with surprise, the more so that she divined the cause of his coming. When they had talked for a while, Hubert frankly admitted what it was that had brought him.

'I must know,' he said, 'whether the news from Wanley is true.

'But can it concern you, Hubert?' his mother asked gently.

He made no direct reply, but expressed his intention of going over to Wanley.

'Whom shall you visit, dear?'

'Mr. Wyvern.'

'The vicar? But you don't know him personally.'

'Yes, I know him pretty well. We write to each other occasionally.'

Mrs. Eldon always practised most reserve when her surprise was greatest—an excellent rule, by-the-by, for general observation. She looked at her son with a half-smile of wonder, but only said 'Indeed?'

'I had made his acquaintance before his coming to Wanley,' Hubert explained.

His mother just bent her head, acquiescent. And with that their conversation on the subject ended. But Hubert received a tender kiss on his cheek when he set forth in the afternoon.

To one entering the valley after nightfall the situation of the much-discussed New Wanley could no longer be a source of doubt. Two blast-furnaces sent up their flare and lit luridly the devastated scene. Having glanced in that direction Hubert did his best to keep his eyes averted during the remainder of the walk. He was surprised to see a short passenger train rush by on the private line connecting the works with Agworth station; it was taking away certain visitors who had lingered in New Wanley after the lecture. Knowing nothing of the circumstances, he supposed that general traffic had been commenced. He avoided the village street, and reached the Vicarage by a path through fields.

He found the vicar at dinner, though it was only half-past six. The welcome he received was, in Mr. Wyvern's manner, almost silent; but when he had taken a place at the table he saw satisfaction on his host's face. The meal was very plain, but the vicar ate with extraordinary appetite; he was one of those men in whom the demands of the stomach seem to be in direct proportion to the activity of the brain. A question Hubert put about the train led to a brief account of what was going on. Mr. Wyvern spoke on the subject with a gravity which was not distinctly ironical, but suggested criticism.

They repaired to the study. A volume of Plato was open on the reading-table.

'Do you remember Socrates' prayer in the "Phædrus"?' said the vicar, bending affectionately over the page. He read a few words of the Greek, then gave a free rendering. 'Beloved Pan, and all ye other gods who haunt this place, give me beauty in the inward soul; and may the outward and inward be at one. May I esteem the wise alone wealthy, and may I have such abundance of wealth as none but the temperate can carry.'

He paused a moment.

'Ah, when I came hither I hoped to find Pan undisturbed. Well, well, after all, Hephæstus was one of the gods.'

'How I envy you your quiet mind?' said Hubert.

'Quiet? Nay, not always so. Just now I am far from at peace. What brings you hither to-day?'

The equivoque was obviated by Mr. Wyvern's tone.

'I have heard stories about Adela Waltham. Is there any truth in them?'

'I fear so; I fear so.'

'That she is really going to marry Mr. Mutimer?'

He tried to speak the name without discourtesy, but his lips writhed after it.

'I fear she is going to marry him,' said the vicar deliberately.

Hubert held his peace.

'It troubles me. It angers me,' said Mr. Wyvern. 'I am angry with more than one.'

'Is there an engagement?'

'I am unable to say. Tattle generally gets ahead of fact.'

'It is monstrous!' burst from the young man. 'They are taking advantage of her innocence. She is a child. Why do they educate girls like that? I should say, how can they leave them so uneducated? In an ideal world it would be all very well, but see what comes of it here? She is walking with her eyes open into horrors and curses, and understands as little of what awaits her as a lamb led to butchery. Do you stand by and say nothing?'

'It surprises me that you are so affected,' remarked the vicar quietly.

'No doubt. I can't reason about it. But I know that my life will be hideous if this goes on to the end.'

'You are late.'

'Yes, I am late. I was in Wanley some weeks ago; I did not tell you of it. I called at their house; they were not at home to me. Yet Adela was sitting at the window. What did that mean? Is her mother so contemptible that my change of fortune leads her to treat me in that way?'

'But does no other reason occur to you?' asked Mr. Wyvern, with grave surprise.

'Other reason! What other?'

'You must remember that gossip is active.'

You mean that they have heard about—— ?'

'Somehow it had become the common talk of the village very shortly after my arrival here.'

Hubert dropped his eyes in bewilderment.

'Then they think me unfit to associate with them ? She—Adela—will look upon me as a vile creature ! But it wasn't so when I saw her immediately after my illness. She talked freely and with just the same friendliness as before.'

'Probably she had heard nothing then.'

'And her mother only began to poison her mind when it was advantageous to do so ?'

Hubert laughed bitterly.

'Well, there is an end of it,' he pursued. 'Yes, I was forgetting all that. Oh, it is quite intelligible; I don't blame them. By all means let her be preserved from contagion ! Pooh ! I don't know my own mind. Old fancies that I used to have somehow got hold of me again. If I ever marry, it must be a woman of the world, a woman with brain and heart to judge human nature. It is gone, as if I had never had such a thought. Poor child, to be sure ; but that's all one can say.'

His tone was as far from petulance as could be. Hubert's emotions were never feebly coloured; his nature ran into extremes, and vehemence of scorn was in him the true voice of injured tenderness. Of humility he knew but little, least of all where his affections were concerned, but there was the ring of noble metal in his self-assertion. He would never consciously act or speak a falsehood, and was intolerant of the lies, petty or great, which conventionality and warped habits of thought encourage in those of weaker personality.

'Let us be just,' remarked Mr. Wyvern, his voice sounding rather sepulchral after the outburst of youthful passion. 'Mrs. Waltham's point of view is not inconceivable. I, as you know, am not altogether a man of formulas, but I am not sure that my behaviour would greatly differ from hers in her position ; I mean as regards yourself.'

'Yes, yes ; I admit the reasonableness of it,' said Hubert more calmly, 'granted that you have to deal with children. But Adela is too old to have no will or understanding. It may be she has both. After all she would scarcely allow herself to be forced into a detestable marriage. Very likely she takes her mother's practical views.'

'There is such a thing as blank indifference in a young girl who has suffered disappointment.'

'I could do nothing,' exclaimed Hubert. 'That she thinks of me at all, or has ever seriously done so, is the merest supposition. There was nothing binding between us. If she is false to herself, experience and suffering must teach her.'

The vicar mused.

'Then you go your way untroubled?' was his next question.

'If I am strong enough to overcome foolishness.'

'And if foolishness persists in asserting itself?'

Hubert kept gloomy silence.

'Thus much I can say to you of my own knowledge,' observed Mr. Wyvern with weight. 'Miss Waltham is not one to speak words lightly. You call her a child, and no doubt her view of the world is childlike; but she is strong in her simplicity. A pledge from her will, or I am much mistaken, bear no two meanings. Her marriage with Mr. Mutimer would be as little pleasing to me as to you, but I cannot see that I have any claim to interpose, or, indeed, power to do so. Is it not the same with yourself?'

'No, not quite the same.'

'Then you have hope that you might still affect her destiny?'

Hubert did not answer.

'Do you measure the responsibility you would incur? I fear not, if you have spoken sincerely. Your experience has not been of a kind to aid you in understanding her, and, I warn you, to make her subject to your caprices would be little short of a crime, whether now—heed me—or hereafter.'

'Perhaps it is too late,' murmured Hubert.

'That may well be, in more senses than one.'

'Can you not discover whether she is really engaged?'

'If that were the case, I think I should have heard of it.'

'If I were allowed to see her! So much at least should be granted me. I should not poison the air she breathes.'

'Do you return to Agworth to-night?' Mr. Wyvern inquired.

'Yes, I shall walk back.'

'Can you come to me again to-morrow evening?'

It was agreed that Hubert should do so. Mr. Wyvern gave no definite promise of aid, but the young man felt that he would do something.

'The night is fine,' said the vicar; 'I will walk half a mile with you.'

They left the Vicarage, and ten yards from the door turned into the path which would enable them to avoid the village street. Not two minutes after their quitting the main road the

spot was passed by Adela herself, who was walking towards
Mr. Wyvern's dwelling. On her inquiring for the vicar, she
learnt from the servant that he had just left home. She hesitated, and seemed about to ask further questions or leave a
message, but at length turned away from the door and retraced
her steps, slowly and with bent head.

She knew not whether to feel glad or sorry that the interview she had come to seek could not immediately take place.
This day had been a hard one for Adela. In the morning her
mother had spoken to her without disguise or affectation, and
had told her of Mutimer's indirect proposal. Mrs. Waltham
went on to assure her that there was no hurry, that Mutimer
had consented to refrain from visits for a short time in order
that she might take counsel with herself, and that—the mother's
voice trembled on the words—absolute freedom was of course
left her to accept or refuse. But Mrs. Waltham could not
pause there, though she tried to. She went on to speak of the
day's proceedings.

'Think what we may, my dear, of Mr. Mutimer's opinions,
no one can deny that he is making a most unselfish use of his
wealth. We shall have an opportunity to-day of hearing how
it is regarded by those who—who understand such questions.'

Adela implored to be allowed to remain at home instead of
attending the lecture, but on this point Mrs. Waltham was in-
flexible. The girl could not offer resolute opposition in a
matter which only involved an hour or two's endurance. She
sat in pale silence. Then her mother broke into tears, bewailed
herself as a luckless being, entreated her daughter's pardon, but
in the end was perfectly ready to accept Adela's self-sacrifice.

On her return from New Wanley, Adela sat alone till tea-
time, and after that meal again went to her room. She was not
one of those girls to whom tears come as a matter of course on
any occasion of annoyance or of grief; her bright eyes had seldom been dimmed since childhood, for the lightsomeness of her
character threw off trifling troubles almost as soon as they were
felt, and of graver afflictions she had hitherto known none since
her father's death. But since the shock she received on that
day when her mother revealed Hubert Eldon's unworthiness,
her emotional life had suffered a slow change. Evil, previously
known but as a dark mystery shadowing far off regions, had
become the constant preoccupation of her thoughts. Drawing
analogies from the story of her faith, she imaged Hubert as the
angel who fell from supreme purity to a terrible lordship of

perdition. Of his sins she had the dimmest conception; she
was told that they were sins of impurity, and her understanding
of such could scarcely have been expressed save in the general
language of her prayers. Guarded jealously at every moment
of her life, the world had made no blur on the fair tablet of her
mind; her Eden had suffered no invasion. She could only
repeat to herself that her heart had gone dreadfully astray
in its fondness, and that, whatsoever it cost her, the old hopes,
the strength of which was only now proved, must be utterly
uprooted. And knowing that, she wept.

Sin was too surely sorrow, though it neared her only in
imagination. In a few weeks she seemed to have almost outgrown girlhood; her steps were measured, her smile was seldom
and lacked mirth. The revelation would have done so much; the
added and growing trouble of Mutimer's attentions threatened
to sink her in melancholy. She would not allow it to be seen
more than she could help; cheerful activity in the life of home
was one of her moral duties, and she strove hard to sustain it.
It was a relief to find herself alone each night, alone with her
sickness of heart.

The repugnance aroused in her by the thought of becoming
Mutimer's wife was rather instinctive than reasoned. From
one point of view, indeed, she deemed it wrong, since it might
be entirely the fruit of the love she was forbidden to cherish.
Striving to read her conscience, which for years had been with
her a daily task and was now become the anguish of every
hour, she found it hard to establish valid reasons for steadfastly
refusing a man who was her mother's choice. She read over the
marriage service frequently. There stood the promise—to love,
to honour, and to obey. Honour and obedience she might render
him, but what of love? The question arose, what did love mean?
Could there be such a thing as love of an unworthy object?
Was she not led astray by the spirit of perverseness which was
her heritage?

Adela could not bring herself to believe that 'to love' in
the sense of the marriage service and to 'be in love' as her
heart understood it were one and the same thing. The Puri-
tanism of her training led her to distrust profoundly those
impulses of mere nature. And the circumstances of her own
unhappy affection tended to confirm her in this way of thinking. Letty Tew certainly thought otherwise, but was not
Letty's own heart too exclusively occupied by worldly considerations?

Yet it said 'love.' Perchance that was something which would come after marriage; the promise, observe, concerned the future. But she was not merely indifferent; she shrank from Mutimer.

She returned home from the lecture to-day full of dread—dread more active than she had yet known. And it drove her to a step she had timidly contemplated for more than a week. She stole from the house, bent on seeing Mr. Wyvern. She could not confess to him, but she could speak of the conflict between her mother's will and her own, and beg his advice; perhaps, if he appeared favourable, ask him to intercede with her mother. She had liked Mr. Wyvern from the first meeting with him, and a sense of trust had been nourished by each succeeding conversation. In her agitation she thought it would not be hard to tell him so much of the circumstances as would enable him to judge and counsel.

Yet it was with relief, on the whole, that she turned homewards with her object unattained. It would be much better to wait and test herself yet further. Why should she not speak with her mother about that vow she was asked to make?

She did not seek solitude again, but joined her mother and Alfred in the sitting-room. Mrs. Waltham made no inquiry about the short absence. Alfred had only just called to mind the newspaper which Mr. Keene had given him, and was unfolding it for perusal. His eye caught a marked paragraph, one of a number under the heading 'Gossip from Town.' As he read it he uttered a 'Hullo!' of surprise.

'Well, here's the latest,' he continued, looking at his companions with an amused eye. 'Something about that fellow Eldon in a Belwick newspaper. What do you think?'

Adela kept still and mute.

'Whatever it is, it cannot interest us, Alfred,' said Mrs. Waltham, with dignity. 'We had rather not hear it.'

'Well, you shall read it for yourself,' replied Alfred on a second thought. 'I think you'd like to know.'

His mother took the paper under protest, and glanced down at the paragraph carelessly. But speedily her attention became closer.

'An item of intelligence,' wrote the London gossiper, 'which I dare say will interest readers in certain parts of —shire. A lady of French extraction who made a name for herself at a leading metropolitan theatre last winter, and who really promises great things in the Thespian art, is back among us from a sojourn on the Continent. She is understood to have spent much labour in the study of a new part, which she is about to introduce to us of the modern Babylon. But Albion, it is whispered, possesses other attractions for her besides appreciative audiences. In brief, though she will of course appear under the old name, she will in reality have changed it for one of another nationality before presenting herself in the radiance of the footlights. The happy man is Mr. Hubert Eldon, late of Wanley Manor. We felicitate Mr. Eldon.'

Mrs. Waltham's hands trembled as she doubled the sheet: there was a gleam of pleasure on her face.

'Give me the paper when you have done with it,' she said.

Alfred laughed, and whistled a tune as he continued the perusal of Mr. Keene's political and social intelligence, on the whole as trustworthy as the style in which it was written was terse and elegant. Adela, finding she could feign indifference no longer, went from the room.

'Where did you get this?' Mrs. Waltham asked with eagerness as soon as the girl was gone.

'From the writer himself,' Alfred replied, visibly proud of his intimacy with a man of letters. 'Fellow called Keene. Had a long talk with him.'

'About this?'

'Oh, no. I've only just come across it. But he said he'd marked something for Mutimer. I'm to pass the paper on to him.'

'I suppose this is the same woman——?'

'No doubt.'

'You think it's true?'

'True? Why, of course it is. A newspaper with a reputation to support can't go printing people's names at haphazard. Keene's very thick with all the London actors. He told me some first-class stories about——'

'Never mind,' interposed his mother. 'Well, to think it should come to this! I'm sure I feel for poor Mrs. Eldon. Really, there is no end to her misfortunes.'

'Just how such families always end up,' observed Alfred complacently. 'No doubt he'll drink himself to death, or something of that kind, and then we shall have the pleasure of seeing a new tablet in the church, inscribed with manifold virtues; or even a stained-glass window: the last of the Eldons deserves something noteworthy.'

'I think it's hardly a subject for joking, Alfred. It is very,

very sad. And to think what a fine handsome boy he used to be ! But he was always dreadfully self-willed.'

'He was always an impertinent puppy ! How he'll play the swell on his wife's earnings ! Oh, our glorious aristocracy !'

Mrs. Waltham went early to her daughter's room. (Adela was sitting with her Bible before her—had sat so since coming upstairs, yet had not read three consecutive verses. Her face showed no effect of tears, for the heat of a consuming suspense had dried the fountains of woe.

'I don't like to occupy your mind with such things, my dear,' began her mother, 'but perhaps as a warning I ought to show you the news Alfred spoke of. It pleases Providence that there should be evil in the world, and for our own safety we must sometimes look it in the face, especially we poor women, Adela. Will you read that ?'

Adela read. She could not criticise the style, but it affected her as something unclean ; Hubert's very name suffered degradation when used in such a way. Prepared for worse things than that which she saw, no shock of feelings was manifest in her. She returned the paper without speaking.

'I wanted you to see that my behaviour to Mr. Eldon was not unjustified,' said her mother. 'You don't blame me any longer, dear ?'

'I have never blamed you, mother.'

'It is a sad, sad end to what might have been a life of usefulness and honour. I have thought so often of the parable of the talents ; only I fear this case is worse. His poor mother ! I wonder if I could write to her ! Yet I hardly know how to.'

'Is this a—a wicked woman, mother ?' Adela asked falteringly.

Mrs. Waltham shook her head and sighed.

'My love, don't you see that she is an actress ?'

'But if all actresses are wicked, how is it that really good people go to the theatre ?'

'I am afraid they oughtn't to. The best of us are tempted into thoughtless pleasure. But now I don't want you to brood over things which it is a sad necessity to have to glance at. Read your chapter, darling, and get to bed.'

To bed—but not to sleep. The child's imagination was aflame. This scarlet woman, this meteor from hell flashing before the delighted eyes of men, she, then, had bound Hubert for ever in her toils ; no release for him now, no ransom to eternity. No instant's doubt of the news came to Adela; in her eyes *imprimatur* was the guarantee of truth. She strove to picture the face which had drawn Hubert to his doom. It must be lovely beyond compare. For the first time in her life she knew the agonies of jealousy.

She could not shed tears, but in her anguish she fell upon prayer, spoke the words above her breath that they might silence that terrible voice within. Poor lost lamb, crying in the darkness, sending forth such pitious utterance as might create a spirit of love to hear and rescue.

Rescue—none. When the fire wasted itself, she tried to find solace in the thought that one source of misery was stopped. Hubert was married, or would be very soon, and if she had sinned in loving him till now, such sin would henceforth be multiplied incalculably; she durst not, as she valued her soul, so much as let his name enter her thoughts. And to guard against it, was there not a means offered her? The doubt as to what love meant was well nigh solved; or at all events she held it proved that the 'love' of the marriage service was something she had never yet felt, something which would follow upon marriage itself. Earthly love had surely led Hubert Eldon to ruin; oh, not that could be demanded of her! What reason had she now to offer against her mother's desire? Letty's arguments were vain; they were but as the undisciplined motions of her own heart. Marriage with a worthy man must often have been salvation to a rudderless life; for was it not the *ceremony* which, after all, constituted the exclusive sanction?

Mutimer, it was true, fell sadly short of her ideal of goodness. He was an unbeliever. But might not this very circumstance involve a duty? As his wife, could she not plead with him and bring him to the truth? Would not that be *loving* him, to make his spiritual good the end of her existence? It was as though a great light shot athwart her darkness. She raised herself in bed, and, as if with her very hands, clung to the inspiration which had been granted her. The light was not abiding, but something of radiance lingered, and that must stead her.

Her brother returned to Belwick next morning after an early breakfast. He was in his wonted high spirits, and talked with much satisfaction of the acquaintances he had made on the previous day, while Adela waited upon him. Mrs. Waltham only appeared as he was setting off.

Adela sat almost in silence whilst her mother breakfasted.

' You don't look well, dear ? ' said the latter, coming to the little room upstairs soon after the meal.

'Yes, I am well, mother. But I want to speak to you.'

Mrs. Waltham seated herself in expectation.

' Will you tell me why you so much wish me to marry Mr. Mutimer ? '

Adela's tone was quite other than she had hitherto used in conversations of this kind. It was submissive, patiently questioning.

' You mustn't misunderstand me,' replied the mother with some nervousness. ' The wish, dear, must of course be yours as well. You know that I—that I really have left you to consult your own——'

The sentence was unfinished.

' But you have tried to persuade me, mother dear, pursued the gentle voice. ' You would not do so if you did not think it for my good.'

Something shot painfully through Mrs. Waltham's heart.

' I am sure I have thought so, Adela ; really I have thought so. I know there are objections, but no marriage is in every way perfect. I feel so sure of his character—I mean of his character in a worldly sense. And you might do so much to— to show him the true way, might you not, darling ? I'm sure his heart is good.'

Mrs. Waltham also was speaking with less confidence than on former occasions. She cast side glances at her daughter's colourless face.

' Mother, may I marry without feeling that—that I love him ?'

The face was flushed now for a moment. Adela had never spoken that word to anyone ; even to Letty she had scarcely murmured it. The effect upon her of hearing it from her own lips was mysterious, awful ; the sound did not die with her voice, but trembled in subtle harmonies along the chords of her being.

Her mother took the shaken form and drew it to her bosom.

' If he is your husband, darling, you will find that love grows. It is always so. Have no fear. On his side there is not only love ; he respects you deeply ; he has told me so.'

' And you encourage me to accept him, mother ? It is your desire ? I am your child, and you can wish nothing that is not for my good. Guide me, mother. It is so hard to judge for myself. You shall decide for me, indeed you shall.'

The mother's heart was wrung. For a moment she strove

to speak the very truth, to utter a word about that love which
Adela was resolutely excluding. But the temptation to accept
this unhoped surrender proved too strong. She sobbed her
answer.

'Yes, I do wish it, Adela. You will find that I—that I
was not wrong.'

'Then if he asks me, I will marry him.'

As those words were spoken Mutimer issued from the Manor
gates, uncertain whether to go his usual way down to the works
or to pay a visit to Mrs. Waltham. The latter purpose prevailed.

The evening before, Mr. Willis Rodman had called at the
Manor shortly after dinner. He found Mutimer smoking, with
coffee at his side, and was speedily making himself comfortable
in the same way. Then he drew a newspaper from his pocket.
' Have you seen the "Belwick Chronicle" of to-day?' he inquired.

'Why the deuce should I read such a paper?' exclaimed
Richard, with good-humoured surprise. He was in excellent
spirits to-night, the excitement of the day having swept his
mind clear of anxieties.

' There's something in it, though, that you ought to see.'

He pointed out the paragraph relating to Eldon.

' Keene's writing, eh?' said Mutimer thoughtfully.

' Yes, he gave me the paper.'

Richard rekindled his cigar with deliberation, and stood for
a few moments with one foot on the fender.

' Who is the woman?' he then asked.

' I don't know her name. Of course it's the same story
continued.'

' And concluded.'

' Well, I don't know about that,' said the other, smiling and
shaking his head.

'This may or may not be true, I suppose,' was Richard's
next remark.

' Oh, I suppose the man hears all that kind of thing. I
don't see any reason to doubt it.'

' May I keep the paper?'

'Oh, yes. Keene told me, by-the-by, that he gave a copy
to young Waltham.'

Mr. Rodman spoke whilst rolling the cigar in his mouth.
Mutimer allowed the subject to lapse.

There was no impossibility, no improbability even, in the
statement made by the newspaper correspondent; yet as Richard

thought it over in the night, he could not but regard it as singular that Mr. Keene should be the man to make public such a piece of information so very opportunely. He was far from having admitted the man to his confidence, but between Keene and Rodman, as he was aware, an intimacy had sprung up. It might be that one or the other had thought it worth while to serve him; why should Keene be particular to put a copy of the paper into Alfred Waltham's hands? Well, he personally knew nothing of the affair. If the news effected anything, so much the better. He hoped it might be trustworthy.

Among his correspondence in the morning was a letter from Emma Vine. He opened it last; anyone observing him would have seen with what reluctance he began to read it.

'My dear Richard,' it ran, 'I write to thank you for the money. I would very much rather have had a letter from you, however short a one. It seems long since you wrote a real letter, and I can't think how long since I have seen you. But I know how full of business you are, dear, and I'm sure you would never come to London without telling me, because if you hadn't time to come here, I should be only too glad to go to Highbury, if only for one word. We have got some mourning dresses to make for the servants of a lady in Islington, so that is good news. But poor Jane is very bad indeed. She suffers a great deal of pain, and most of all at night, so that she scarcely ever gets more than half-an-hour of sleep at a time, if that. What makes it worse, dear Richard, is that she is so very unhappy. Sometimes she cries nearly through the whole night. I try my best to keep her up, but I'm afraid her weakness has much to do with it. But Kate is very well, I am glad to say, and the children are very well too. Bertie is beginning to learn to read. He often says he would like to see you. Thank you, dearest, for the money and all your kindness, and believe that I shall think of you every minute with much love. From yours ever and ever,   'EMMA VINE.'

It would be cruel to reproduce Emma's errors of spelling. Richard had sometimes noted a bad instance with annoyance, but it was not that which made him hurry to the end this morning with lowered brows. When he had finished the letter he crumbled it up and threw it into the fire. It was not heartlessness that made him do so : he dreaded to have these letters brought before his eyes a second time.

He was also throwing the envelope aside, when he discovered that it contained yet another slip of paper. The
writing on this was not Emma's: the letters were cramped and
not easy to decipher.

'Dear Richard, come to London and see me. I want to
speak to you, I must speak to you. I can't have very long to
live, and I *must, must* see you.   'JANE VINE.'

This too he threw into the fire. His lips were hard set,
his eyes wide. And almost immediately he prepared to leave
the house.

It was early, but he felt that he must go to the Walthams'.
He had promised Mrs. Waltham to refrain from visiting the
house for a week, but that promise it was impossible to keep.
Jane's words were ringing in his ears: he seemed to hear her
very voice calling and beseeching. So far from changing his
purpose, it impelled him in the course he had chosen. There
must and should be an end of this suspense.

Mrs. Waltham had just come downstairs from her conversation with Adela, when she saw Mutimer approaching the
door. She admitted him herself. Surely Providence was on
her side; she felt almost young in her satisfaction.

Richard remained in the house about twenty minutes.
Then he walked down to the works as usual.

Shortly after his departure another visitor presented himself. This was Mr. Wyvern. The vicar's walk in Hubert's
company the evening before had extended itself from point to
point, till the two reached Agworth together. Mr. Wyvern
was addicted to night-rambling, and he often covered considerable stretches of country in the hours when other mortals
slept. To-night he was in the mood for such exercise; it
worked off unwholesome accumulations of thought and feeling,
and good counsel often came to him in what the Greeks called
the kindly time. He did not hurry on his way back to Wanley, for just at present he was much in need of calm reflection.

On his arrival at the Vicarage about eleven o'clock the servant informed him of Miss Waltham's having called. Mr.
Wyvern heard this with pleasure. He thought at first of
writing a note to Adela, begging her to come to the Vicarage
again, but by the morning he had decided to be himself the
visitor.

He gathered at once from Mrs. Waltham's face that events

of some agitating kind were in progress. She did not keep him long in uncertainty. Upon his asking if he might speak a few words with Adela, Mrs. Waltham examined him curiously.

'I am afraid,' she said, ' that I must ask you to excuse her this morning, Mr. Wyvern. She is not quite prepared to see anyone at present. In fact,' she lowered her voice and smiled very graciously, ' she has just had an—an agitating interview with Mr. Mutimer—she has consented to be his wife.'

' In that case I cannot of course trouble her,' the vicar replied, with gravity which to Mrs. Waltham appeared excessive, rather adapted to news of a death than of a betrothal. The dark searching eyes, too, made her feel uncomfortable. And he did not utter a syllable of the politeness expected on these occasions.

' What a very shocking thing about Mr. Eldon!' the lady pursued. ' You have heard?'

' Shocking? Pray, what has happened?'

Hubert had left him in some depression the night before, and for a moment Mr. Wyvern dreaded lest some fatality had become known in Wanley.

' Ah, you have not heard? It is in this newspaper.'

The vicar examined the column indicated.

' But,' he exclaimed, with subdued indignation, ' this is the merest falsehood!'

' A falsehood! Are you sure of that Mr. Wyvern?'

' Perfectly sure. There is no foundation for it whatsoever.'

' You don't say so! I am very glad to hear that, for poor Mrs. Eldon's sake.'

' Could you lend me this newspaper for to-day?'

' With pleasure. Really you relieve me, Mr. Wyvern. I had no means of inquiring into the story, of course. But how disgraceful that such a thing should appear in print!'

' I am sorry to say, Mrs. Waltham, that the majority of things which appear in print nowadays are more or less disgraceful. However, this may claim prominence, in its way.'

' And I may safely contradict it? It will be such a happiness to do so.'

' Contradict it by all means, madam. You may cite me as your authority.'

The vicar crushed the sheet into his pocket and strode homewards.

CHAPTER XIII.

In the church of the Insurgents there are many orders. To rise to the supreme passion of revolt, two conditions are indispensable : to possess the heart of a poet, and to be subdued by poverty to the yoke of ignoble labour. But many who fall short of the priesthood have yet a share of the true spirit, bestowed upon them by circumstances of birth and education, developed here and there by the experience of life, yet rigidly limited in the upshot by the control of material ease, the fatal lordship of the comfortable commonplace. Of such was Hubert Eldon. In him, despite his birth and breeding, there came to the surface a rich vein of independence, obscurely traceable, no doubt, in the characters of certain of his ancestors, appearing at length where nineteenth-century influences had thinned the detritus of convention and class prejudice. His nature abounded in contradictions, and as yet self-study—in itself the note of a mind striving for emancipation—had done little for him beyond making clear the manifold difficulties strewn in his path of progress.

You know already that it was no vulgar instinct of sensuality which had made severance between him and the respectable traditions of his family. Observant friends naturally cast him in the category of young men whom the prospect of a fortune seduces to a life of riot; his mother had no means of forming a more accurate judgment. Mr. Wyvern alone had seen beneath the surface, aided by a liberal study of the world, and no doubt also by that personal sympathy which is so important an ally of charity and truth. Mr. Wyvern's early life had not been in smooth waters; in him too revolt was native, tempered also by spiritual influences of the most opposite kind. He felt a deep interest in the young man, and desired to keep him in view. It was the first promise of friendship that had been held out to Hubert, who already suffered from a sense of isolation, and was wondering in what class of society he would have to look for his kith and kin. Since boyhood he had drawn apart to a great extent from the companionships which most readily offered. The turn taken by the circumstances of his family affected the pride which was one of his strongest characteristics; his house had fallen, and it seemed to him that a good deal of pity, if not of contempt, mingled with his reception by the more fortunate of his own standing. He had never overcome a natural hostility to old Mr. Mutimer : the *bourgeois* virtues of the worthy iron-master rather irritated than attracted him, and he suffered intensely in the thought that his mother brought herself to close friendship with one so much her inferior just for the sake of her son's future. In this matter he judged with tolerable accuracy. Mrs. Eldon, finding in the old man a certain unexpected refinement over and above his goodness of heart, consciously or unconsciously encouraged herself in idealising him, that the way of interest might approach as nearly as might be to that of honour. Hubert, with no understanding for the craggy facts of life, inwardly rebelled against the whole situation. He felt that it laid him open to ridicule, the mere suspicion of which always stung him to the quick. When, therefore, he declared to his mother, in the painful interview on his return to Wanley, that it was almost a relief to him to have lost the inheritance, he spoke with perfect truth. Amid the tempest which had fallen on his life there rose in that moment the semblance of a star of hope. The hateful conditions which had weighed upon his future being finally cast off, might he not look forward to some nobler activity than had hitherto seemed possible? Was he not being saved from his meaner self, that part of his nature which tended to conventional ideals, which was subject to empty pride and ignoble apprehensions? Had he gone through the storm without companion, hope might have overcome every weakness, but sympathy with his mother's deep distress troubled his self-control. At her feet he yielded to the emotions of childhood, and his misery increased until bodily suffering brought him the relief of unconsciousness.

To his mother perhaps he owed that strain of idealism which gave his character its significance. In Mrs. Eldon it affected only the inner life ; in Hubert spiritual strivings naturally sought the outlet of action. That his emancipation should declare itself in some exaggerated way was quite to be expected : impatience of futilities and insincerities made common cause with the fiery spirit of youth and spurred him into reckless pursuit of that abiding rapture which is the dream and the despair of the earth's purest souls. The pistol bullet checked his course, happily at the right moment. He had gone far enough for experience and not too far for self-recovery. The wise man in looking back upon his endeavours regrets nothing of which that can be said.

By the side of a passion such as that which had opened
Hubert's intellectual manhood, the mild, progressive attachments sanctioned by society show so colourless as to suggest
illusion.   Thinking of Adela Waltham as he lay recovering
from his illness, he found it difficult to distinguish between
the feelings associated with her name and those which he had
owed to other maidens of the same type. A week or two at
Wanley generally resulted in a conviction that he was in love
with Adela; and had Adela been entirely subject to her
mother's influences, had she fallen but a little short of the
innocence and delicacy which were her own, whether for happiness or the reverse, she would doubtless have been pledged to
Hubert long ere this.   The merest accident had in truth prevented it.   At home for Christmas, the young man had made
up his mind to speak and claim her: he postponed doing so till
he should have returned from a visit to a college friend in the
same county.   His friend had a sister, five or six years older
than Adela, and of a warmer type of beauty, with the finished
graces of the town.   Hubert found himself once more without
guidance, and so left Wanley behind him, journeying to an
unknown land.

Hubert could not remember a time when he had not been
in love.   The objects of his devotion had succeeded each other
rapidly, but each in her turn was the perfect woman.   His
imagination cast a halo about a beautiful head, and hastened to
see in its possessor all the poetry of character which he aspired
to worship.   In his loves, as in every other circumstance of life,
he would have nothing of compromise; for him the world contained nothing but his passion, and existence had no other end.
Between that past and this present more intervened than
Hubert could yet appreciate; but he judged the change in
himself by the light in which that early love appeared to him.
Those were the restless ardours of boyhood: he could not henceforth trifle so with solemn meanings.   The ideal was harder of
discovery than he had thought; perhaps it was not to be found
in the world at all.   But what less perfect could henceforth
touch his heart?

Yet throughout his convalescence he thought often of Adela,
perhaps because she was so near, and because she doubtless often
thought of him.   His unexpected meeting with her on Stanbury
Hill affected him strangely; the world was new to his eyes, and
the girl's face seemed to share in the renewal; it was not quite
the same face that he had held in memory, but had a fresh sig-

rificance. He read in her looks more than formerly he had been able to see. This impression was strengthened by his interview with her on the following day. Had she too grown much older in a few months?

After spending a fortnight with his mother at Agworth, he went to London, and for a time thought as little of Adela as of any other woman. New interests claimed him, interests purely intellectual, the stronger that his mind seemed just aroused from a long sleep. He threw himself into various studies with more zeal than he had hitherto devoted to such interests; not that he had as yet any definite projects, but solely because it was his nature to be in pursuit of some excellence and to scorn mere acquiescence in a life of every-day colour. He lived all but in loneliness, and when the change had had time to work upon him his thoughts began to revert to Adela, to her alone of those who stood on the other side of the gulf. She came before his eyes as a vision of purity; it was soothing to picture her face and to think of her walking in the spring meadows. He thought of her as of a white rose, dew-besprent, and gently swayed by the sweet air of a sunny morning; a white rose newly spread, its heart virgin from the hands of shaping Nature. He could not decide what quality, what absence of thought, made Adela so distinct to him. Was it perhaps the exquisite delicacy apparent in all she did or said? Even the most reverent thought seemed gross in touching her; the mind flitted round about her, kept from contact by a supreme modesty, which she alone could inspire. If her head were painted, it must be against the tenderest eastern sky; all associations with her were of the morning, when heatless rays strike level across the moist earth, of simple devoutness which renders thanks for the blessing of a new day, of mercy robed like the zenith at dawn.

His study just now was of the early Italians, in art and literature. There was more of Adela than he perceived in the impulse which guided him in that direction. When he came to read the 'Vita Nuova,' it was of Adela expressly that he thought. The poet's passion of worship entered his heart; transferring his present feeling to his earlier self, he grew to regard his recent madness as a lapse from the true love of his life. He persuaded himself that he had loved Adela in a far more serious way than any of the others who from time to time had been her rivals, and that the love was now returning to him, strengthened and exalted. He began to write sonnets in Dante's

manner, striving to body forth in words the new piety which
illumined his life. Whereas love had been to him of late a
glorification of the senses, he now cleansed himself from what
he deemed impurity and adored in mere ecstasy of the spirit.
Adela soon became rather a symbol than a living woman; he
identified her with the ends to which his life darkly aspired,
and all but convinced himself that memory and imagination
would henceforth suffice to him.

In the autumn he went down to Agworth, and spent a few
days with his mother. The temptation to walk over to Wanley and call upon the Walthams proved too strong to be resisted.
His rejection at their door was rather a shock than a surprise;
it had never occurred to him that the old friendly relations had
been in any way disturbed; he explained Mrs. Waltham's behaviour by supposing that his silence had offended her, and
perhaps his failure to take leave of her before quitting Wanley.
Possibly she thought he had dealt lightly with Adela. Offence
on purely moral grounds did not even suggest itself.

He returned to London anxious and unhappy. The glimpse
of Adela sitting at the window had brought him back to reality;
after all it was no abstraction that had become the constant
companion of his solitude; his love was far more real for that
moment's vision of the golden head, and had a very real power
of afflicting him with melancholy. He faltered in his studies,
and once again had lost the motive to exertion. Then came the
letter from his mother, telling of Adela's rumoured engagement.
It caused him to set forth almost immediately.

The alternation of moods exhibited in his conversation with
Mr. Wyvern continued to agitate him during the night. Now
it seemed impossible to approach Adela in any way; now he
was prepared to defy every consideration in order to save her
and secure his own happiness. Then, after dwelling for awhile
on the difficulties of his position, he tried to convince himself
that once again he had been led astray after beauty and goodness which existed only in his imagination, that in losing Adela
he only dismissed one more illusion. Such comfort was unsub-
stantial; he was, in truth, consumed in wretchedness at the
thought that she once might easily have been his, and that he
had passed her by. What matter whether we love a reality or
a dream, if the love drive us to frenzy? Yet how could he
renew his relations with her? Even if no actual engagement
bound her, she must be prejudiced against him by stories which
would make it seem an insult if he addressed her. And if the

engagement really existed, what shadow of excuse had he for troubling her with his love ?

When he entered his mother's room in the morning, Mrs. Eldon took a small volume from the table at her side.

'I found this a few weeks ago among the books you left with me,' she said. 'How long have you had it, Hubert ?'

It was a copy of the 'Christian Year,' and writing on the fly-leaf showed that it belonged, or had once belonged, to Adela Waltham.

Hubert regarded it with surprise.

'It was lent to me a year ago,' he said. 'I took it away with me. I had forgotten that I had it.'

The circumstances under which it had been lent to him came back very clearly now. It was after that visit to his friend which had come so unhappily between him and Adela. When he went to bid her good-bye he found her alone, and she was reading this book. She spoke of it, and, in surprise that he had never read it, begged him to take it to Oxford.

'I have another copy,' Adela said. 'You can return that any time.'

The time had only now come. Hubert resolved to take the book to Wanley in the evening ; if no other means offered, Mr. Wyvern would return it to the owner. Might he enclose a note ? Instead of that, he wrote out from memory two of his own sonnets, the best of those he had recently composed under the influence of the 'Vita Nuova,' and shut them between the pages. Then he made the book into a parcel and addressed it.

He started for his walk at the same hour as on the evening before. There was frost in the air, and already the stars were bright. As he drew near to Wanley, the road was deserted ; his footfall was loud on the hard earth. The moon began to show her face over the dark top of Stanbury Hill, and presently he saw by the clear rays that the figure of a woman was a few yards ahead of him ; he was overtaking her. As he drew near to her, she turned her head. He knew her at once, for it was Letty Tew. He had been used to meet Letty often at the Walthams'.

Evidently he was himself recognised ; the girl swerved a little, as if to let him pass, and kept her head bent. He obeyed an impulse and spoke to her.

'I am afraid you have forgotten me, Miss Tew. Yet I don't like to pass you without saying a word.'

'I thought it was—the light makes it difficult——' Letty murmured, sadly embarrassed.

'But the moon is beautiful.'

'Very beautiful.'

They regarded it together. Letty could not help glancing at her companion, and as he did not turn his face she examined him for a moment or two.

'I am going to see my friend Mr. Wyvern,' Hubert proceeded.

A few more remarks of the kind were exchanged, Letty by degrees summoning a cold confidence ; then Hubert said—

'I have here a book which belongs to Miss Waltham. She lent it to me a year ago, and I wish to return it. Dare I ask you to put it into her hands ?'

Letty knew what the book must be. Adela had told her of it at the time, and since had spoken of it once or twice.

'Oh, yes, I will give it her,' she replied, rather nervously again.

'Will you say that I would gladly have thanked her myself, if it had been possible ?'

'Yes, Mr. Eldon, I will say that.'

Something in Hubert's voice seemed to cause Letty to raise her eyes again.

'You wish me to thank her ?' she added, inconsequently perhaps, but with a certain significance.

'If you will be so kind.'

Hubert wanted to say more, but found it difficult to discover the right words. Letty, too, tried to shadow forth something that was in her mind, but with no better success.

'If I remember,' Hubert said, pausing in his walk, 'this stile will be my shortest way across to the Vicarage. Thank you much for your kindness.'

He had raised his hat and was turning, but Letty impulsively put forth her hand. 'Good-bye,' he said, in a friendly voice, as he took the little fingers. 'I wish the old days were back again, and we were going to have tea together as we used to.'

Mr. Wyvern's face gave no promise of cheerful intelligence as he welcomed his visitor.

'What is the origin of this, I wonder ?' he said, handing Hubert the 'Belwick Chronicle.'

The state of the young man's nerves was not well adapted to sustain fresh irritation. He turned pale with anger.

'Is this going the round of Wanley ?'

'Probably. I had it from Mrs. Waltham.'

'Did you contradict it?'

'As emphatically as I could.'

'I will see the man who edits this to-morrow,' cried Hubert hotly. 'But perhaps he is too great a blackguard to talk with.'

'It purports to come, you see, from a London correspondent. But I suppose the source is nearer.'

'You mean—you think that man Mutimer has originated it?'

'I scarcely think that.'

'Yet it is more than likely. I will go to the Manor at once. At least he shall give me yes or no.'

He had started to his feet, but the vicar laid a hand on his shoulder.

'I'm afraid you can't do that.'

'Why not?'

'Consider. You have no kind of right to charge him with such a thing. And there is another reason: he proposed to Miss Waltham this morning, and she accepted him.'

'This morning? And this paper is yesterday's. Why, it makes it more likely than ever. How did they get the paper? Doubtless he sent it them. If she has accepted him this very day——'

The repetition of the words seemed to force their meaning upon him through his anger. His voice failed.

'You tell me that Adela Waltham has engaged herself to that man?'

'Her mother told me, only a few minutes after it occurred.'

'Then it was this that led her to consent.'

'Surely that is presupposing too much, my dear Eldon,' said the vicar gently.

'No, not more than I know to be true. I could not say that to anyone but you; you must understand me. The girl is being cheated into marrying that fellow. Of her own free will she could not do it. This is one of numberless lies. You are right; it's no use to go to him: he wouldn't tell the truth. But *she* must be told. How can I see her?'

'It is more difficult than ever. Her having accepted him makes all the difference. Explain it to yourself as you may, you cannot give her to understand that you doubt her sincerity.'

'But does she know that this story is false?'

'Yes, that she will certainly hear. I have busied myself in contradicting it. If Mrs. Waltham does not tell her, she will hear it from her friend Miss Tew, without question.'

Hubert pondered, then made the inquiry:

'How could I procure a meeting with Miss Tew? I met her just now on the road and spoke to her. I think she might consent to help me.'

Mr. Wyvern looked doubtful.

'You met her? She was coming from Agworth?'

'She seemed to be.'

'Her father and mother are gone to spend to-morrow with friends in Belwick; I suppose she drove into Wanley with them, and walked back.'

The vicar probably meant this for a suggestion; at all events, Hubert received it as one.

'Then I will simply call at the house. She may be alone. I can't weigh niceties.'

Mr. Wyvern made no reply. The announcement that dinner was ready allowed him to quit the subject. Hubert with difficulty sat through the meal, and as soon as it was over took his departure, leaving it uncertain whether he would return that evening. The vicar offered no further remark on the subject of their thoughts, but at parting pressed the young man's hand warmly.

Hubert walked straight to the Tews' dwelling. The course upon which he had decided had disagreeable aspects and involved chances anything but pleasant to face; he had, however, abundance of moral courage, and his habitual scorn of petty obstacles was just now heightened by passionate feeling. He made his presence known at the house-door as though his visit were expected. Letty herself opened to him. It was Saturday night, and she thought the ring was Alfred Waltham's. Indeed she half uttered a few familiar words; then, recognising Hubert, she stood fixed in surprise.

'Will you allow me to speak with you for a few moments, Miss Tew?' Hubert said, with perfect self-possession. 'I ask your pardon for calling at this hour. My business is urgent; I have come without a thought of anything but the need of seeing you.'

'Will you come in, Mr. Eldon?'

She led him into a room where there was no fire, and only one lamp burning low.

'I'm afraid it's very cold here,' she said, with extreme nervousness. 'The other room is occupied—my sister and the children; I hope you——'

A little girl put in her face at the door, asking 'Is it Alfred?' Letty hurried her away, closed the door, and, whilst lighting two candles on the mantelpiece, begged her visitor to seat himself.

'If you will allow me, I will stand,' said Hubert. 'I scarcely know how to begin what I wish to say. It has reference to Miss Waltham. I wish to see her; I must, if she will let me, have an opportunity of speaking with her. But I have no direct means of letting her know my wish; doubtless you understand that. In my helplessness I have thought of you. Perhaps I am asking an impossibility. Will you—can you—repeat my words to Miss Waltham, and beg her to see me?'

Letty listened in sheer bewilderment. The position in which she found herself was so alarmingly novel, it made such a whirlpool in her quiet life, that it was all she could do to struggle with the throbbing of her heart and attempt to gather her thoughts. She did not even reflect that her eyes were fixed on Hubert's in a steady gaze. Only the sound of his voice after silence aided her to some degree of collectedness.

'There is every reason why you should accuse me of worse than impertinence,' Hubert continued, less impulsively. 'I can only ask your forgiveness. Miss Waltham may very likely refuse to see me, but, if you would ask her——'

Letty was borne on a torrent of strange thoughts. How could this man, who spoke with such impressive frankness, with such persuasiveness, be the abandoned creature that she had of late believed him? With Adela's secret warm in her heart she could not but feel an interest in Hubert, and the interest was becoming something like zeal on his behalf. During the past two hours her mind had been occupied with him exclusively; his words when he left her at the stile had sounded so good and tender that she began to question whether there was any truth at all in the evil things said about him. The latest story had just been declared baseless by no less an authority than the vicar, who surely was not a man to maintain friendship with a worthless profligate. What did it all mean? She had heard only half an hour ago of Adela's positive acceptance of Mutimer, and was wretched about it; secure in her own love-match, it was the mystery of mysteries that Adela should consent to marry a man she could scarcely endure. And here a chance of rescue seemed to be offering; was it not her plain duty to give what help she might?

'You have probably not seen her since I gave you the book?' Hubert said, perceiving that Letty was quite at a loss for words.

'No, I haven't seen her at all to-day,' was the reply. 'Do you wish me to go to-night?'

'You consent to do me this great kindness?'

Letty blushed. Was she not committing herself too hastily?

'There cannot be any harm in giving your message,' she said, half interrogatively, her timidity throwing itself upon Hubert's honour.

'Surely no harm in that.'

'But do you know that she—have you heard——?'

'Yes, I know. She has accepted an offer of marriage. It was because I heard of it that I came to you. You are her nearest friend; you can speak to her as others would not venture to. I ask only for five minutes. I entreat her to grant me that.'

To add to her perturbation, Letty was in dread of hearing Alfred's ring at the door; she durst not prolong this interview.

'I will tell her,' she said. 'If I can, I will see her to-night.'

'And how can I hear the result? I am afraid to ask you— if you would write one line to me at Agworth? I am staying at my mother's house.'

He mentioned the address. Letty, who felt herself caught up above the world of common experiences and usages, gave her promise as a matter of course.

'I shall not try to thank you,' Hubert said. 'But you will not doubt that I am grateful?'

Letty said no more, and it was with profound relief that she heard the door close behind her visitor. But even yet the danger was not past; Alfred might at this moment be approaching, so as to meet Hubert near the house. And indeed this all but happened, for Mr. Waltham presented himself very soon. Letty had had time to impose secrecy on her sisters, such an extraordinary proceeding on her part that they were awed, and made faithful promise of discretion.

Letty drew her lover into the fireless room; she had blown out the candles and turned the lamp low again, fearful lest her face should display signs calling for comment.

'I did so want you to come!' she exclaimed. 'Tell me about Adela.'

'I don't know that there's anything to tell,' was Alfred's stolid reply. 'It's settled, that's all. I suppose it's all right.'

'But you speak as if you thought it mightn't be, Alfred?'

'Didn't know that I did.   Well, I haven't seen her since I got home.   She's upstairs.'

'Can't I see her to-night?   I do so want to.'

'I dare say she'd be glad.'

'But what is it, my dear boy?   I'm sure you speak as if you weren't quite satisfied.'

'The mater says it's all right.   I suppose she knows.'

'But you've always been so anxious for it.'

'Anxious?   I haven't been anxious at all.   But I dare say it's the wisest thing she could do.   I like Mutimer well enough.'

'Alfred, I don't think he's the proper husband for Adela.'

'Why not?   There's not much chance that she'll get a better.'

Alfred was manifestly less cheerful than usual.   When Letty continued to tax him with it he grew rather irritable.

'Go and talk to her yourself,' he said at length.   'You'll find it's all right.   I don't pretend to understand her; there's so much religion mixed up with her doings, and I can't stand that.'

Letty shook her head and sighed.

'What a vile smell of candle-smoke there is here!' Alfred cried.   'And the room must be five or six degrees below zero. Let's go to the fire.'

'I think I shall run over to Adela at once,' said Letty, as she followed him into the hall.

'All right.   Don't be vexed if she refuses to let you in.   I'll stay here with the youngsters a bit.'

The truth was that Alfred did feel a little uncomfortable this evening, and was not sorry to be away from the house for a short time.   He was one of those young men who will pursue an end out of mere obstinacy, and who, through default of imaginative power, require an event to declare itself before they can appreciate the ways in which it will affect them.   This marriage of his sister with a man of the working class had possibly, he now felt, other aspects than those which alone he had regarded whilst it was merely a matter for speculation.   He was not seriously uneasy, but wished his mother had been somewhat less precipitate.   Well, Adela could not be such a simpleton as to be driven entirely counter to her inclinations in an affair of so much importance.   Girls were confoundedly hard to understand, in short; probably they existed for the purpose of keeping one mentally active.

Letty found Mrs. Waltham sitting alone, she too seemingly

N

not in the best of spirits.   There was something depressing in
the stillness of the house.   Mrs. Waltham had her volume of
family prayers open before her; her handkerchief lay upon it.

'She is naturally a little—a little fluttered,' she said, speaking of Adela.   'I hoped you would look in.   Try and make her
laugh, my dear; that's all she wants.'

The girl tripped softly upstairs, and softly knocked at
Adela's door.   At her 'May I come in?' the door was opened.
Letty examined her friend with surprise; in Adela's face there
was no indication of trouble, rather the light of some great joy
dwelt in her eyes.   She embraced Letty tenderly.   The two
were as nearly as possible of the same age, but Letty had
always regarded Adela in the light of an elder sister; that feeling was very strong in her just now, as well as a diffidence
greater than she had known before.

'Are you happy, darling?' she asked timidly.

'Yes, dear, I am happy.   I believe, I am sure, I have done
right.   Take your hat off; it's quite early.   I've just been reading the collect for to-morrow.   It's one of those I have never
quite understood, but I think it's clearer to me now.'

They read over the prayer together, and spoke of it for a
few minutes.

'What have you brought me?' Adela asked at length,
noticing a little parcel in the other's hand.

'It's a book I have been asked to give you.   I shall have
to explain.   Do you remember lending—lending someone your
"Christian Year"?'

The smile left Adela's face, and the muscles of her mouth
strung themselves.

'Yes, I remember,' she replied, coldly.

'As I was walking back from Agworth this afternoon, he
overtook me on the road and asked me to return it to you.'

'Thank you, dear.'

Adela took the parcel and laid it aside.   There was an
awkward silence.   Letty could not look up.

'He was going to see Mr. Wyvern,' she continued, as if
anxious to lay stress on this.   'He seems to know Mr. Wyvern
very well.'

'Yes?   You didn't miss Alfred, I hope.   He went out a
very short time ago.'

'No, I saw him.   He stayed with the others.   But I have
something more to tell you, about—about him.'

'About Alfred?'

'About Mr. Eldon.'

Adela looked at her friend with a grave surprise, much as a queen regards a favourite subject who has been over-bold.

'I think we won't talk of him, Letty,' she said from her height.

'Do forgive me, Adela. I have promised to—to say something. There must have been a great many things said that were not true, just like this about his marriage; I am so sure of it.'

Adela endeavoured to let the remark pass without replying to it. But her thought expressed itself involuntarily.

'His marriage? What do you know of it?'

'Mr. Wyvern came to see mother this morning, and showed her a newspaper that your mother gave him. It said that Mr. Eldon was going to marry an actress, and Mr. Wyvern declared there was not a word of truth in it. But of course your mother told you that?'

Adela sat motionless. Mrs. Waltham had not troubled herself to make known the vicar's contradiction. But Adela could not allow herself to admit that. Finding her voice with difficulty, she said:

'It does not at all concern me.'

'But your mother *did* tell you, Adela?' Letty persisted, emboldened by a thought which touched upon indignation.

'Of course she did.'

The falsehood was uttered with cold deliberateness. There was nothing to show that a pang quivered on every nerve of the speaker.

'Who can have sent such a thing to the paper?' Letty exclaimed. 'There must be someone who wishes to do him harm. Adela, I don't believe *anything* that people have said!'

Even in speaking she was frightened at her own boldness. Adela's eyes had never regarded her with such a look as now.

'Adela, my darling! Don't, don't be angry with me!'

She sprang forward and tried to put her arms about her friend, but Adela gently repelled her.

'If you have promised to say something, Letty, you must keep your promise. Will you say it at once, and then let us talk of something else?'

Letty checked a tear. Her trustful and loving friend seemed changed to someone she scarcely knew. She too grew colder, and began her story in a lifeless way, as if it no longer possessed any interest.

'Just when I had had tea and was expecting Alfred to
come, somebody rang the bell. I went to the door myself, and
it was Mr. Eldon. He had come to speak to me of you. He
said he wanted to see you, that he *must* see you, and begged me
to tell you that. That's all, Adela. I couldn't refuse him; I
felt I had no right to; he spoke in such a way. But I am very
sorry to have so displeased you, dear. I didn't think you would
take anything amiss that I did in all sincerity. I am sure there
has been some wretched mistake, something worse than a
mistake, depend upon it. But I won't say any more. And I
think I'll go now, Adela.'

Adela spoke in a tone of measured gravity which was quite
new in her.

'You have not displeased me, Letty. I don't think you
have been to blame in any way; I am sure you had no choice
but to do as he asked you. You have repeated all he said?'

'Yes, all; all the words, that is. There was something
that I can't repeat.'

'And if I consented to see him, how was he to know?'

'I promised to write to him. He is staying at Agworth.'

'You mustn't do that, dear. I will write to him myself,
then I can thank him for returning the book. What is his
address?'

Letty gave it.

'It is, of course, impossible for me to see him,' pursued
Adela, still in the same measured tones. 'If I write myself it
will save you any more trouble. Forget it, if I seemed unkind,
dear.'

'Adela, I can't forget it. You are not like yourself, not at
all. Oh, how I wish this had happened sooner! Why—why
can't you see him, darling? I think you ought to; I do really
think so.'

'I must be the best judge of that, Letty. Please let us
speak of it no more.'

The sweet girl-face was adamant, its expression a proud
virginity; an ascetic sternness moulded the small, delicate lips.
Letty's countenance could never have looked like that.

Left to herself again, Adela took the parcel upon her lap
and sat dreaming. It was long before her face relaxed; when
it did so, the mood that succeeded was profoundly sorrowful.
One would have said that it was no personal grief that absorbed
her, but compassion for the whole world's misery.

When at length she undid the wrapping, her eye was at

once caught by the papers within the volume. She started, and seemed afraid to touch the book, Her first thought was that Eldon had enclosed a letter; but she saw that there was no envelope, only two or three loose slips. At length she examined them and found the sonnets. They had no heading, but at the foot of each was written the date of composition.

She read them. Adela's study of poetry had not gone beyond a school-book of selections, with the works of Mrs. Hemans and of Longfellow, and the ' Christian Year.' Hubert's verses she found difficult to understand; their spirit, the very vocabulary, was strange to her. Only on a second reading did she attain a glimmering of their significance. Then she folded them again and laid them on the table.

Before going to her bedroom she wrote this letter:

'DEAR MR. ELDON,—I am much obliged to you for returning the "Christian Year." Some papers were left in its pages by accident, and I now enclose them.

'Miss Tew also brought me a message from you. I am sorry that I cannot do as you wish. I am unable to ask you to call, and I hope you will understand me when I say that any other kind of meeting is impossible.

'I am, yours truly,
'ADELA WALTHAM.'

It was Adela's first essay in this vein of composition. The writing cost her an hour, and she was far from satisfied with the final form. But she copied it in a firm hand, and made it ready for posting on the morrow.

CHAPTER XIV.

'BETWEEN Richard Mutimer, bachelor, and Adela Marian Waltham, spinster, both of this parish.'

It was the only announcement of the kind that Mr. Wyvern had to make this Sunday. To one of his hearers he seemed to utter the names with excessive emphasis, his deep voice reverberating in the church. The pews were high; Adela almost cowered in her corner, feeling pierced with the eyes, with the thoughts too, of the congregation about her,

She had wondered whether the Manor pew would be occupied to-day, but it was not. When she stood up, her eyes strayed towards it; the red curtains which concealed the interior were old and faded, the wooden canopy crowned it with dreary state. In three weeks that would be her place at service. Sitting there, it would not be hard to keep her thoughts on mortality.

Would it not have been graceful in him to attend church to-day? Would she in future worship under the canopy alone?

No time had been lost. Mr. Wyvern received notice of the proposed marriage less than two hours after Adela had spoken her world-changing monosyllable. She put in no plea for delay, and her mother, though affecting a little consternation at Mutimer's haste, could not seriously object. Wanley, discussing the matter at its Sunday tea-tables, declared with unanimity that such expedition was indecent. By this time the disapproval of the village had attached itself exclusively to Mrs. Waltham; Adela was spoken of as a martyr to her mother's miserable calculations. Mrs. Mewling went about with a story, that only by physical restraint had the unhappy girl been kept from taking flight. The name of Hubert Eldon once more came up in conversation. There was an unauthenticated rumour that he had been seen of late, lurking about Wanley. The more boldly speculative gossips looked with delicious foreboding to the results of a marriage such as this. Given a young man of Eldon's reputation—ah me!

The Walthams all lunched (or dined) at the Manor. Mutimer was in high spirits, or seemed so; there were moments when the cheerful look died on his face, and his thoughts wandered from the conversation; but if his eye fell on Adela he never failed to smile the smile of inner satisfaction. She had not yet responded to his look, and only answered his questions in the briefest words; but her countenance was resolutely bright, and her beauty all that man could ask. Richard did not flatter himself that she held him dear; indeed, he was a good deal in doubt whether affection, as vulgarly understood, was consistent with breeding and education. But that did not concern him; he had gained his end, and was jubilant.

In the course of the meal he mentioned that his sister would come down from London in a day or two. Christmas was only a week off, and he had thought it would be pleasant to have her at the Manor for that season.

Oh, that's very nice !' assented Mrs. Waltham. 'Alice, her name is, didn't you say? Is she dark or fair?'

'Fair, and just about Adela's height, I should think. I hope you'll like her, Adela.'

It was unfortunate that Richard did not pronounce the name of his bride elect quite as it sounds on cultured lips. This may have been partly the result of diffidence; but there was a slurring of the second syllable disagreeably suggestive of vulgarity. It struck on the girl's nerves, and made it more difficult for her to grow accustomed to this form of address from Mutimer.

'I'm sure I shall try to,' she replied to the remark about Alice, this time endeavouring to fix her obstinate eyes for a moment on Richard's face.

'Your brother won't come, then?' Mrs. Waltham asked.

'Not just yet, I'm afraid. He's busy studying.'

'To read and write, I fear,' was the lady's silent comment. On the score of Alice, too, Mrs. Waltham nursed a certain anxiety. The damsels of the working class are, or so she apprehended, somewhat more difficult of acceptance than their fathers and brothers, and for several reasons. An artisan does not necessarily suggest, indeed is very distinct from, the footman or even groom ; but to dissociate an uneducated maiden from the lower regions of the house is really an exertion of the mind. And then, it is to be feared, the moral tone of such young persons leaves for the most part much to be desired. Mrs. Waltham was very womanly in her distrust of her sex.

After luncheon there was an inspection of the house. Adela did not go farther than the drawing-room ; her brother remained with her whilst Mutimer led Mrs. Waltham through the chambers she might care to see. The lady expressed much satisfaction. The furnishing had been performed in a substantial manner, without display ; one might look forward to considerable comfort at the Manor.

'Any change that Adela suggests,' said Richard during this tour, ' shall of course be carried out at once. If she doesn't like the paper in any of the rooms, she's only got to say so and choose a better. Do you think she'd care to look at the stables? I'll get a carriage for her, and a horse to ride, if she likes.'

Richard felt strongly that this was speaking in a generous way. He was not aware that his tone hinted as much, but it unmistakably did. The vulgarity of a man who tries hard not to be vulgar is always particularly distressing.

'Oh, how kind!' murmured Mrs. Waltham. 'Adela has
never ridden; I should think carriage exercise would be enough
for her. We mustn't forget your principles, you know, for I'm
sure they are very admirable.'

'Oh, I don't care anything about luxuries myself, but Adela
shall have everything she wants.'

Alfred Waltham, who knew the house perfectly, led his
mother to inspect the stables, Mutimer remaining with Adela
in the drawing-room.

'You've been very quiet all dinner-time,' he said, taking a
seat near her and bending forward.

'A little, perhaps. I am thinking of so many things.'

'What are they, I wonder?'

'Will you let me have some books about Socialism, and the
other questions in which you are interested?'

'I should think I will! You really mean to study these
things?'

'Yes, I will read and think about them. And I shall be
glad if you will explain to me more about the works. I have
never quite understood all that you wish to do. Perhaps you
will have time when you come to see us some evening.'

'Well, if I haven't time, I'll make it,' said Richard, laughing. 'You can't think how glad I am to hear you say this.'

'When do you expect your sister?'

'On Tuesday; at least, I hope it won't be later. I'm sure
you'll like her, you can't help. She hasn't such looks as you
have, you know, but we've always thought her very fair-looking.
What do you think we often call her? The Princess! That's
part because of her name, Alice Maud, and part from a sort of
way she's always had. Not a flighty way, but a sort of—well,
I can't describe it. I do hope you'll like her.'

It was the first time Adela had heard him speak in a tone
which impressed her as entirely honest, not excepting his talk
of the Propaganda. Here, she felt, was a side of his character
that she had not suspected. His voice was almost tender; the
play of his features betokened genuine feeling.

'I can see she is a great favourite with you,' she replied.
'I have no doubt I shall like her.'

'You'll find a good deal that wants altering, I've no doubt,'
he pursued, now quite forgetful of himself. 'She hasn't had
much education, you know, till just lately. But you'll help
her in that, won't you? She's as good-natured as any girl
living, and whenever you put her right you may be sure she'll

only thank you. I've wanted to have her here before, only I thought I'd wait till I knew whether—you know what I mean.'

As if in a sudden gloom before her eyes Adela saw his face draw nearer. It was a moment's loss of consciousness, in which a ghastly fear flashed upon her soul. Then, with lips that quivered, she began to talk quickly of Socialism, just to dispel the horror.

On the following afternoon Mutimer came, bringing a number of books, pamphlets, and newspapers. Mrs. Waltham had discreetly abandoned the sitting-room.

'I don't want to frighten you,' he said, laying down his bundle. 'You haven't got to read through all these. I was up nearly all last night marking pages that I thought you'd better study first of all. And here's a lot of back numbers of the "Fiery Cross;" I should like you to read all that's signed by Mr. Westlake; he's the editor, you know.'

'Is there anything here of your own writing?' Adela inquired.

'No, I haven't written anything. I've kept to lecturing; it comes easier to me. After Christmas I shall have several lectures to give in London. Perhaps you'll come and hear me?'

'Yes, of course.'

'Then you can get to know Mrs. Westlake, I dare say. She's a lady, you know, like yourself. There's some poetry by her in the paper; it just has her initials, "S. W." She's with us heart and soul, as you'll see by her writing.'

'Is Alice a Socialist?' Adela asked, after glancing fitfully at the papers.

Richard laughed.

'Oh, she's a princess; it would be too much to expect Socialism of her. But I dare say she'll be beginning to think more now. I don't mean she's been thoughtless in the wrong way; it's just a—I can't very well describe it. But I hope you'll see her to-morrow night. May I bring her to you when she comes?'

'I hope you will.'

'I'm glad your brother won't be here. I only mean, you know, I'd rather she got accustomed just to you first of all. I dare say she'll be a bit timid, you won't mind that?'

Adela returned to the graver subject.

'All the people at New Wanley are Socialists?'

'Yes, all of them. They join the Union when they come to work, and we take a good deal of care in choosing our men.'

'And you pay higher wages than other employers?'

'Not much higher, but the rents of the cottages are very low, and all the food sold at the store is cost price. No, we don't pretend to make the men rich. We've had a good lot coming with quite mistaken ideas, and of course they wouldn't suit us. And you mustn't call me the employer. All I have I look upon as the property of the Union; the men own it as much as I do. It's only that I regulate the work, just because somebody must. We're not making any profits to speak of yet, but that'll only come in time; whatever remains as clear profit,—and I don't take anything out of the works myself— goes to the Propaganda fund of the Union.'

'Please forgive my ignorance. I've heard that word "Propaganda" so often, but I don't know exactly what it means.'

Mutimer became patronising, quite without intending it.

'Propaganda? Oh, that's the spreading our ideas, you know; printing paper, giving lectures, hiring places of meeting, and so on. That's what Propaganda means.'

'Thank you,' said Adela musingly. Then she continued,—

'And the workmen only have the advantage, at present, of the low rents and cheap food?'

'Oh, a good deal more. To begin with, they're housed like human beings, and not like animals. Some day you shall see the kind of places the people live in, in London and other big towns. You won't believe your eyes. Then they have shorter hours of work; they're not treated like omnibus horses, calculating just how much can be got out of them without killing them before a reasonable time. Then they're sure of their work as long as they keep honest and don't break any of our rules; that's no slight thing, I can tell you. Why, on the ordinary system a man may find himself and his family without food any week end. Then there's a good school for the children; they pay threepence a week for each child. Then there's the reading-room and library, and the lectures, and the recreation-grounds. You just come over the place with me some day, and talk with the women, and see if they don't think they're well off.'

Adela looked him in the face.

'And it is you they have to thank for all this?'

'Well, I don't want any credit for it,' Mutimer replied, waving his hand. 'What would you think of me if I worked

them like niggers and just enjoyed myself on the profits?
That's what the capitalists do.'

'I think you are doing more than most men would. There
is only one thing.'

She dropped her voice.

'What's that, Adela?'

'I'll speak of it some other time.'

'I know what you mean. You're sorry I've got no religion.
Ay, but I have! There's my religion, down there in New
Wanley. I'm saving men and women and children from
hunger and cold and the lives of brute beasts. I teach them to
live honestly and soberly. There's no public-house in New
Wanley, and there won't be.' (It just flashed across Adela's
mind that Mutimer drank wine himself.) 'There's no bad
language if I can help it. The children 'll be brought up to
respect the human nature that's in them, to honour their
parents, and act justly and kindly to all they have dealings
with. Isn't there a good deal of religion in that, Adela?'

'Yes, but not all. Not the most important part.'

'Well, as you say, we'll talk over that some other time.
And now I'm sorry I can't stay any longer. I've twenty or
thirty letters to get written before post-time.'

Adela rose as he did.

'If there's ever anything I can do to help you,' she said
modestly, 'you will not fail to ask me?'

'That I won't. What I want you to do now is to read
what I've marked in those books. You mustn't tire your eyes,
you know; there's plenty of time.'

'I will read all you wish me to, and think over it as much
as I can.'

'Then you're a right-down good girl, and if I don't think
myself a lucky man, I ought to.'

He left her trembling with a strange new emotion, the
beginning of a self-conscious zeal, an enthusiasm forced into
being like a hothouse flower. It made her cheeks burn; she
could not rest till her study had commenced.

Richard had written to his sister, saying that he wanted
her, that she must come at once. To Alice his thoughts had
been long turning; now that the time for action had arrived,
it was to her that he trusted for aid. Things he would find it
impossible to do himself, Alice might do for him. He did not
doubt his power of persuading her. With Alice principle
would stand second to his advantage. He had hard things to

ask of her, but the case was a desperate one, and she would
endure the unpleasantness for his sake. He blessed her in
anticipation.

Alice received the letter summoning her on Monday morning. Richard himself was expected in Highbury; expected,
too, at a sad little house in Hoxton; for he had constantly
promised to spend Christmas with his friends. The present
letter did not say that he would not come, only that he wanted
his sister immediately. She was to bring her best dress for
wear when she arrived. He told her the train she was to take
on Tuesday morning.

The summons filled Alice with delight. Wanley, whence
had come the marvellous fortune, was in her imagination a
land flowing with milk and honey. Moreover, this would be
her first experience of travel; as yet she had never been farther
out of London than to Epping Forest. The injunction to bring
her best dress excited visions of polite company. All through
Monday she practised ways of walking, of eating, of speaking.

'What can he want you for?' asked Mrs. Mutimer
gloomily. 'I sh'd 'a thought he might 'a taken you with him
after Christmas. It looks as if he wasn't coming.'

The old woman had been habitually gloomy of late. The
reply she had received to her letter was not at all what she
wanted; it increased her impatience; she had read it endless
times, trying to get at the very meaning of it. Christmas must
bring an end to this wretched state of things; at Christmas
Dick would come to London and marry Emma; no doubt he
had that time in view. Fears which she would not consciously
admit were hovering about her night and day. She had begun
to talk to herself aloud, a consequence of over-stress on a brain
never used to anxious thought; she went about the upper
rooms of the house muttering, 'Dick's an honest man.' To
keep moving seemed a necessity to her; the chair in the dim
corner of the dining-room she now scarcely ever occupied, and
the wonted employment of her fingers was in abeyance. She
spent most of her day in the kitchen; already two servants had
left because they could not endure her fidgety supervision.
She was growing suspicious of every one; Alice had to listen
ten times a day to complaints of dishonesty in the domestics or
the tradespeople; the old woman kept as keen a watch over
petty expenditure as if poverty had still to be guarded against.
And she was constantly visiting the Vines; she would rise at
small hours to get her house-work done, so as to be able to

spend the afternoon in Wilton Square. That, in truth, was still her home; the new house could never be to her what the old was; she was a stranger amid the new furniture, and sighed with relief as soon as her eyes rested on the familiar chairs and tables which had been her household gods through a lifetime.

'Arry had given comparatively little trouble of late; beyond an occasional return home an hour or so after midnight, his proceedings seemed to be perfectly regular. He saw a good deal of Mr. Keene, who, as Alice gathered from various remarks in Richard's letters, exercised over him a sort of tutorage. It was singular how completely Richard seemed to have changed in his judgment of Mr. Keene. 'His connection with newspapers makes him very useful,' said one letter. 'Be as friendly with him as you like; I trust to your good sense and understanding of your own interest to draw the line.' When at the house Mr. Keene was profoundly respectful; his position at such times was singular, for as often as not Alice had to entertain him alone. Profound, too, was the journalist's discretion in regard to all doings down at Wanley. Knowing he had several times visited the Manor, Alice often sought information from him about her brother's way of life. Mr. Keene always replied with generalities. He was a man of humour in his way, and Alice came to regard him with amusement. Then his extreme respect flattered her; insensibly she took him for her criterion of gentility in men. He supplied her with 'society' journals, and now and then suggested the new novel that it behoved her to read. Richard had even withdrawn his opposition to the theatre-going; about once in three weeks Mr. Keene presented himself with tickets, and Alice, accompanied by her brother, accepted his invitation.

He called this Monday evening. Mrs. Mutimer, after spending a day of fretful misery, had gone to Wilton Square; 'Arry was away at his classes. Alice was packing certain articles she had purchased in the afternoon, and had just delighted her soul with the inspection of a travelling cloak, also bought to-day. When the visitor was announced, she threw the garment over her shoulders and appeared in it.

'Does this look nice, do you think?' she asked, after shaking hands as joyously as her mood dictated.

'About as nice as a perfect thing always does when it's worn by a perfect woman,' Mr. Keene replied, drawing back and inclining his body at what he deemed a graceful angle.

'Oh, come, that's too much!' laughed Alice.

'Not a bit, Miss Mutimer. I suppose you travel in it to-morrow morning?'

'How did you know that?'

'I have heard from your brother to-day. I thought I might perhaps have the great pleasure of doing you some slight service either to-night or in the morning. You will allow me to attend you to the station?'

'I really don't think there's any need to trouble you,' Alice replied. These respectful phrases always stirred her pleasurably; in listening to them she bore herself with dignity, and endeavoured to make answer in becoming diction.

'Trouble? What other object have I in life but to serve you? I'll put it in another way: you won't refuse me the pleasure of being near you for a few minutes?'

'I'm sure you're very kind. I know very well it's taking you out of your way, but it isn't likely I shall refuse to let you come.'

Mr. Keene bowed low in silence.

'Have you brought me that paper?' Alice asked, seating herself with careful arrangement of her dress. 'The Christmas number with the ghost story you spoke of, you know?'

In the course of a varied life Mr. Keene had for some few months trodden the boards of provincial theatres; an occasional turn of his speech, and still more his favourite gestures, bore evidence to that period of his career. Instead of making direct reply to Alice's question, he stood for a moment as if dazed; then flinging back his body, smote his forehead with a ringing slap, and groaned 'O Heaven!'

'What's the matter?' cried the girl, not quite knowing whether to be amused or alarmed.

But Mr. Keene was rushing from the room, and in an instant the house door sounded loudly behind him. Alice stood disconcerted; then, thinking she understood, laughed gaily and ran upstairs to complete her packing. In a quarter of an hour Mr. Keene's return brought her to the drawing-room again. The journalist was propping himself against the mantelpiece, gasping, his arms hanging limp, his hair disordered. As Alice approached he staggered forward, fell on one knee, and held to her the paper she had mentioned.

'Pardon—forgive!' he panted.

'Why, where ever have you been?' exclaimed Alice.

'No matter! what are time and space? Forgive me, Miss Mutimer! I deserve to be turned out of the house, and never stand in the light of your countenance again.'

'But how foolish! As if it mattered all that. What a state you're in! I'll go and get you a glass of wine.'

She ran to the dining-room, and returned with a decanter and glass on a tray. Mr. Keene had sunk upon a settee, one arm hanging over the back, his eyes closed.

'You have pardoned me?' he murmured, regarding her with weary rapture.

'I don't see what there is to pardon. Do drink a glass of wine! Shall I pour it out for you?'

'Drink and service for the gods!'

'Do you mean the people in the gallery?' Alice asked roguishly, recalling a term in which Mr. Keene had instructed her at their latest visit to the theatre.

'You are as witty as you are beautiful!' he sighed, taking the glass and draining it. Alice turned away to the fire; decidedly Mr. Keene was in a gallant mood this evening; hitherto his compliments had been far more guarded.

They began to converse in a more terrestrial manner. Alice wanted to know whom she was likely to meet at Wanley; and Mr. Keene, in a light way, sketched for her the Waltham family. She became thoughtful whilst he was describing Adela Waltham, and subsequently recurred several times to that young lady. The journalist allowed himself to enter into detail, and Alice almost ceased talking.

It drew on to half-past nine. Mr. Keene never exceeded discretion in the hours of his visits. He looked at his watch and rose.

'I may call at nine?' he said.

'If you really have time. But I can manage quite well by myself, you know.'

'What you *can* do is not the question. If I had my will you should never know a moment's trouble as long as you lived.'

'If I never have worse trouble than going to the railway station, I shall think myself lucky.'

'Miss Mutimer——'

'Yes?'

'You won't drop me altogether from your mind whilst you're away?'

There was a change in his voice. He had abandoned the tone of excessive politeness, and spoke very much like a man who has feeling at the back of his words. Alice regarded him nervously.

'I'm not going to be away more than a day or two,' she said, smoothing a fold in her dress.

'If it was only an hour or two I couldn't bear to think you'd altogether forgotten me.'

'Why, of course I shan't!'

'But—— Miss Mutimer, I'm abusing confidence. Your brother trusts me; he's done me a good many kindnesses. But I can't help it, upon my soul. If you betray me, I'm done for. You won't do that? I put myself in your power, and you're too good to hurt a fly.'

'What do you mean, Mr. Keene?' Alice asked, inwardly pleased, yet feeling uncomfortable.

'I can't go away to-night without saying it, and ten to one it means I shall never see you again. You know what I mean. Well, harm me as you like; I'd rather be harmed by you than done good to by any one else. I've got so far, there's no going back. Do you think some day you could—do you think you *could?*'

Alice dropped her eyes and shook her pretty head slowly.

'I can't give any promise of that kind,' she replied under her breath.

'You hate me? I'm a disagreeable beast to you? I'm a low——'

'Oh dear, don't say such things, Mr. Keene! The idea! I don't dislike you a bit; but of course that's a different thing——'

He held out his hand sadly, dashing the other over his eyes.

'Good-bye, I don't think I can come again. I've abused confidence. When your brother hears of it——. But no matter, I'm only a—a sort of crossing-sweeper in your eyes.'

Alice's laugh rang merrily.

'What things you do call yourself! Now, don't go off like that, Mr. Keene. To begin with, my brother won't hear anything about it——'

'You mean that? You are so noble, so forgiving? Pooh, as if I didn't know you were! Upon my soul, I'd run from here to South Kensington, like the ragamuffins after the cabs with luggage, only just to get a smile from you. Oh, Miss Mutimer——oh!'

'Mr. Keene, I can't say yes, and I don't like to be so unkind to you as to say no. You'll let that do for the present, won't you?'

'Bless your bright eyes, of course I will! If I don't love you for your own sake, I'm the wretchedest turnip-snatcher in London. Good-bye, Princess?'

'Who taught you to call me that?'

'Taught me? It was only a word that came naturally to my lips.'

Curiously, this was quite true. It impressed Alice Maud, and she thought of Mr. Keene for at least five minutes continuously after his departure.

She was extravagantly gay as they drove in a four-wheeled cab to the station next morning. Mr. Keene made no advances. He sat respectfully on the seat opposite her, with a travelling bag on his knees, and sighed occasionally. When she had secured her seat in the railway carriage he brought her sandwiches, buns, and sweetmeats enough for a voyage to New York. Alice waved her hand to him as the train moved away.

She reached Agworth at one o'clock; Richard had been pacing the platform impatiently for twenty minutes. Porters were eager to do his bidding, and his instructions to them were suavely imperative.

'They know me,' he remarked to Alice, with his air of satisfaction. 'I suppose you're half frozen? I've got a foot-warmer in the trap.'

The carriage promised to Adela was a luxury Richard had not ventured to allow himself. Alice mounted to a seat by his side, and he drove off.

'Why on earth did you come second-class?' he asked, after examining her attire with approval.

'Ought it to have been first? It really seemed such a lot of money, Dick, when I came to look at the fares.'

'Yes, it ought to have been first. In London things don't matter, but here I'm known, you see. Did mother go to the station with you?'

'No, Mr. Keene did.'

'Keene, eh?' He bent his brows a moment.

'I hope he behaves himself?'

'I'm sure he's very gentlemanly.'

'Yes, you ought to have come first-class. A princess riding second'll never do. You look well, old girl? Glad to come, eh?'

'Well, guess! And is this your own horse and trap, Dick?'

'Of course it is.'

'Who was that man? He touched his hat to you.'

o

Mutimer glanced back carelessly.

'I'm sure I don't know. Most people touch their hats to
me about here.'

It was an ideal winter day. A feathering of snow had
fallen at dawn, and now the clear, cold sun made it sparkle far
and wide. The horse's tread rang on the frozen highway. A
breeze from the north-west chased the blood to healthsome leaping, and caught the breath like an unexpected kiss. The colour
was high on Alice's fair cheeks; she laughed with delight.

'Oh, Dick, what a thing it is to be rich! And you do look
such a gentleman; it's those gloves, I think.'

'Now we're going into the village,' Mutimer said presently.
'Don't look about you too much, and don't seem to be asking
questions. Everybody 'll be at the windows.'

CHAPTER XV.

BETWEEN the end of the village street and the gates of the
Manor, Mutimer gave his sister hasty directions as to her behaviour before the servants.

'Put on just a bit of the princess,' he said. 'Not too much,
you know, but just enough to show that it isn't the first time
in your life that you've been waited on. Don't always give a
'thank you;' one every now and then'll do. I wouldn't smile
too much or look pleased, whatever you see. Keep that all till
we're alone together. We shall have lunch at once; I'll do
most of the talking whilst the servants are about; you just
answer quietly.'

These instructions were interesting, but not altogether indispensable; Alice Maud had by this time a very pretty notion
of how to conduct herself in the presence of menials. The trying moment was on entering the house; it was very hard indeed
not to utter her astonishment and delight at the dimensions of
the hall and the handsome staircase. This point safely passed,
she resigned herself to splendour, and was conducted to her
room in a sort of romantic vision. The Manor satisfied her
idea of the ancestral mansion so frequently described or alluded
to in the fiction of her earlier years. If her mind had just now
reverted to Mr. Keene, which of course it did not, she would
have smiled very royally indeed.

When she entered the drawing-room, clad in that best gown which her brother had needlessly requested her to bring, and saw that Richard was standing on the hearth-rug quite alone, she could no longer contain herself, but bounded towards him like a young fawn, and threw her arms on his neck.

' Oh, Dick,' she whispered, ' what a thing it is to be rich ! How ever did we live so long in the old way ! If I had to go back to it now I should die of misery.'

' Let's have a look at you,' he returned, holding her at arm's length. ' Yes, I think that'll about do. Now mind you don't let them see that you're excited about it. Sit down here and pretend to be a bit tired. They may come and say lunch is ready any moment.'

' Dick, I never felt so good in my life ! I should like to go about the streets and give sovereigns to everybody I met.'

Richard laughed loudly.

' Well, well, there's better ways than that. I've been giving a good many sovereigns for a long time now. I'm only sorry you weren't here when we opened the Hall.'

' But you haven't told me why you sent for me now.'

' All right, we've got to have a long talk presently. It isn't all as jolly as you think, but I can't help that.'

' Why, what can be wrong Dick ? '

' Never mind; it'll all come out in time.'

Alice came back upon certain reflections which had occupied her earlier in the morning ; they kept her busy through luncheon. Whilst she ate, Richard observed her closely; on the whole he could not perceive a great difference between her manners and Adela's. Difference there was, but in details to which Mutimer was not very sensitive. He kept up talk about the works for the most part, and described certain difficulties concerning rights of way which had of late arisen in the vicinity of the industrial settlement.

' I think you shall come and sit with me in the library,' he said as they rose from table. And he gave orders that coffee should be served to them in that room.

The library did not as yet quite justify its name. There was only one bookcase, and not more than fifty volumes stood on its shelves. But a large writing-table was well covered with papers. There were no pictures on the walls, a lack which was noticeable throughout the house. The effect was a certain severity; there was no air of home in the spacious chambers ; the walls seemed to frown upon their master, the hearths were

cold to him as to an intruding alien. Perhaps Alice felt something of this; on entering the library she shivered a little, and
went to warm her hands at the fire.

'Sit in this deep chair,' said her brother. 'I'll have a cigarette. How's mother?'

'Well, she hasn't been quite herself,' Alice replied, gazing
into the fire. 'She can't get to feel at home, that's the truth
of it. She goes very often to the old house.'

'Goes very often to the old house, does she?'

He repeated the words mechanically, watching smoke that
issued from his lips. 'Suppose she'll get all right in time.'

When the coffee arrived a decanter of cognac accompanied
it. Richard had got into the habit of using the latter rather
freely of late. He needed a stimulant in view of the conversation that was before him. The conversation was difficult to
begin. For a quarter of an hour he strayed over subjects, each
of which, he thought, might bring him to the point. A
question from Alice eventually gave him the requisite impulse.

'What's the bad news you've got to tell me, Dick?' she
asked shyly.

'Bad news? Why, yes, I suppose it is bad, and it's no use
pretending anything else. I've brought you down here just to
tell it you. Somebody must know first, and it had better be
somebody who'll listen patiently, and perhaps help me to get
over it. I don't know quite how you'll take it, Alice. For
anything I can tell you may get up and be off, and have nothing more to do with me.'

'Why, what ever can it be, Dick? Don't talk nonsense.
You're not afraid of *me*, I should think.'

'Yes, I am a bit afraid of you, old girl. It isn't a nice
thing to tell you, and there's the long and short of it. I'm
hanged if I know how to begin.'

He laughed in an irresolute way. Trying to light a new
cigarette from the remnants of the one he had smoked, his
hands shook. Then he had recourse again to cognac.

Alice was drumming with her foot on the floor. She sat
forward, her arms crossed upon her lap. Her eyes were still
on the fire.

'Is it anything about Emma, Dick?' she asked, after a dis-
concerting silence.

'Yes, it is.'

'Hadn't you better tell me at once? It isn't at all nice to
feel like this.'

'Well, I'll tell you. I can't marry Emma; I'm going to marry someone else.'

Alice was prepared, but the plain words caused her a moment's consternation.

'Oh, what ever will they all say, Dick?' she exclaimed in a low voice.

'That's bad enough, to be sure, but I think more about Emma herself. I feel ashamed of myself, and that's the plain truth. Of course I shall always give her and her sisters all the money they want to live upon, but that isn't altogether a way out. If only I could have hinted something to her before now. I've let it go on so long. I'm going to be married in a fortnight.'

He could not look Alice in the face, nor she him. His shame made him angry; he flung the half-smoked cigarette violently into the fire-place, and began to walk about the room. Alice was speaking, but he did not heed her, and continued with impatient loudness.

'Who the devil could imagine what was going to happen? Look here, Alice; if it hadn't been for mother, I shouldn't have engaged myself to Emma. I shouldn't have cared much in the old kind of life; she'd have suited me very well. You can say all the good about her you like, I know it'll be true. It's a cursed shame to treat her in this way, I don't need telling that. But it wouldn't do as things are; why, you can see for yourself—would it now? And that's only half the question: I'm going to marry somebody I do really care for. What's the good of keeping my word to Emma, only to be miserable myself and make her the same? It's the hardest thing ever happened to a man. Of course I shall be blackguarded right and left. Do I deserve it now? Can I help it?'

It was not quite consistent with the tone in which he had begun, but it had the force of a genuine utterance. To this Richard had worked himself in fretting over his position; he was the real sufferer, though decency compelled him to pretend it was not so. He had come to think of Emma almost angrily; she was a clog on him, and all the more irritating because he knew that his brute strength, if only he might exert it, could sweep her into nothingness at a blow. The quietness with which Alice accepted his revelation encouraged him in self-defence. He talked on for several minutes, walking about and swaying his arms, as if in this way he could literally shake himself free of moral obligations. Then, finding his throat dry, he had recourse to cognac, and Alice could at length speak.

'You haven't told me, Dick, who it is you're going to marry.'

'A lady called Miss Waltham—Adela Waltham. She lives here in Wanley.'

'Does she know about Emma?'

The question was simply put, but it seemed to affect Richard very disagreeably.

'No, of course she doesn't. What would be the use?'

He threw himself into a chair, crossed his feet, and kept silence.

'I'm very sorry for Emma,' murmured his sister.

Richard said nothing.

'How shall you tell her, Dick?'

'I can't tell her!' he replied, throwing out an arm. 'How is it likely I can tell her?'

'And Jane's so dreadfully bad,' continued Alice in the undertone. 'She's always saying she cares for nothing but to see Emma married. What *shall* we do? And everything seemed so first-rate. Suppose she summonses you, Dick?'

The noble and dignified legal process whereby maidens right themselves naturally came into Alice's thoughts. Her brother scouted the suggestion.

'Emma's not that kind of girl. Besides, I've told you I shall always send her money. She'll find another husband before long. Lots of men 'ud be only too glad to marry her.'

Alice was not satisfied with her brother. The practical aspects of the rupture she could consider leniently, but the tone he assumed was jarring to her instincts. Though nothing like a warm friendship existed between her and Emma, she sympathised, in a way impossible to Richard, with the sorrows of the abandoned girl. She was conscious of what her judgment would be if another man had acted thus; and though this was not so much a matter of consciousness, she felt that Richard might have spoken in a way more calculated to aid her in taking his side. She wished, in fact, to see only his advantage, and was very much tempted to see everything but that.

'But you can't keep her in the dark any longer,' she urged. 'Why, it's cruel!'

'I can't tell her,' he repeated monotonously.

Alice drew in her feet. It symbolised retiring within her defences. She saw what he was aiming at, and felt not at all disposed to pleasure him. There was a long silence; Alice was determined not to be the first to break it.

'You refuse to help me?' Richard asked at length, between his teeth.

'I think it would be every bit as bad for me as for you,' she replied.

'That you can't think,' he argued. 'She can't blame you; you've only to say I've behaved like a blackguard, and you're out of it.'

'And when do you mean to tell mother?'

'She'll have to hear of it from other people. I can't tell her.'

Richard had a suspicion that he was irretrievably ruining himself in his sister's opinion, and it did not improve his temper. It was a foretaste of the wider obloquy to come upon him, possibly as hard to bear as any condemnation to which he had exposed himself. He shook himself out of the chair.

'Well, that's all I've got to tell you. Perhaps you'd better think over it. I don't want to keep you away from home longer than you care to stay. There's a train at a few minutes after nine in the morning.'

He shuffled for a few moments about the writing-table, then went from the room.

Alice was unhappy. The reaction from her previous high spirits, as soon as it had fully come about, brought her even to tears. She cried silently, and, to do the girl justice, at least half her sorrow was on Emma's account. Presently she rose and began to walk about the room; she went to the window, and looked out on to the white garden. The sky beyond the thin boughs was dusking; the wind, which sang so merrily a few hours ago, had fallen to sobbing.

It was too wretched to remain alone; she resolved to go into the drawing-room; perhaps her brother was there. As she approached the door somebody knocked on the outside, then there entered a dark man of spruce appearance, who drew back a step as soon as he saw her.

'Pray excuse me,' he said, with an air of politeness. 'I supposed I should find Mr. Mutimer here.'

'I think he's in the house,' Alice replied.

Richard appeared as they were speaking.

'What is it, Rodman?' he asked abruptly, passing into the library.

'I'll go to the drawing-room,' Alice said, and left the men together.

In half an hour Richard again joined her. He seemed in a better frame of mind, for he came in humming. Alice, having glanced at him, averted her face again and kept silence. She felt a hand smoothing her hair.   Her brother, leaning over the back of her seat, whispered to her,—

'You'll help me, Princess?'

She did not answer.

'You won't be hard, Alice?   It's a wretched business, and I don't know what I shall do if you throw me over.   I can't do without you, old girl.'

'I can't tell mother, Dick.   You know very well what it'll be.   I daren't do that.'

But even that task Alice at last took upon herself, after another half-hour's discussion.   Alas! she would never again feel towards her brother as before this necessity fell upon her. Her life had undergone that impoverishment which is so dangerous to elementary natures, the loss of an ideal.

'You'll let me stay over to-morrow?' she said.   'There's nothing very pleasant to go back to, and I don't see that a day 'll matter.'

'You can stay if you wish.   I'm going to take you to have tea with Adela now.   If you stay we'll have her to dinner to-morrow.'

'I wonder whether we shall get along?' Alice mused.

'I don't see why not.   You'll get lots of things from her, little notions of all kinds.'

This is always a more or less dangerous form of recommendation, even in talking to one's sister.   To suggest that Adela would benefit by the acquaintance would have been a far more politic procedure.

'What's wrong with me?' Alice inquired, still depressed by the scene she had gone through.

'Oh, there's nothing wrong.   It's only that you'll see differences at first; from the people you've been used to, I mean.   But I think you'll have to go and get your things on; it's nearly five.'

In Alice's rising from her chair there was nothing of the elasticity that had marked her before luncheon.   Before moving away she spoke a thought that was troubling her.

'Suppose mother tries to stop it?'

Richard looked to the ground moodily.

'I meant to tell you,' he said.   'You'd better say that I'm already married.'

'You're giving me a nice job,' was the girl's murmured rejoinder.

'Well, it's as good as true.   And it doesn't make the job any worse.'

As is wont to be the case when two persons come to mutual understanding on a piece of baseness, the tone of brother and sister had suffered in the course of their dialogue. At first meeting they had both kept a certain watch upon their lips, feeling that their position demanded it; a moral limpness was evident in them by this time.

They set forth to walk to the Walthams'. Exercise in the keen air, together with the sense of novelty in her surroundings, restored Alice's good humour before the house was reached. She gazed with astonishment at the infernal glare over New Wanley. Her brother explained the sight to her with gusto.

'It used to be all fields and gardens over there,' he said. 'See what money and energy can do! You shall go over the works in the morning. Perhaps Adela will go with us, then we can take her back to the Manor.'

'Why do they call the house that, Dick?' Alice inquired. 'Is it because people who live there are supposed to have good manners?'

'May be, for anything I know,' was the capitalist's reply. 'Only it's spelt different, you know. I say, Alice, you must be careful about your spelling; there were mistakes in your last letter. Won't do, you know, to make mistakes if you write to Adela.'

Alice gave a little shrug of impatience. Immediately after, they stopped at the threshold sacred to all genteel accomplishments—so Alice would have phrased it if she could have fully expressed her feeling—and they speedily entered the sitting-room, where the table was already laid for tea. Mrs. Waltham and her daughter rose to welcome them.

'We knew of your arrival,' said the former, bestowing on Alice a maternal salute. 'Not many things happen in Wanley that all the village doesn't hear of, do they, Mr. Mutimer? Of course we expected you to tea.'

Adela and her future sister-in-law kissed each other. Adela was silent, but she smiled.

'You'll take your things off, my dear?' Mrs. Waltham continued. 'Will you go upstairs with Miss Mutimer, Adela?'

But for Mrs. Waltham's persistent geniality the hour which followed would have shown many lapses of conversation. Alice appreciated at once those 'differences' at which her brother had hinted, and her present frame of mind was not quite consistent with patient humility. Naturally, she suffered much from self-consciousness; Mrs. Waltham annoyed her by too frequent observation, Adela by seeming indifference. The delicacy of the latter was made perhaps a little excessive by strain of feelings. Alice at once came to the conclusion that Dick's future wife was cold and supercilious. She was not predisposed to like Adela. The circumstances were in a number of ways unfavourable. Even had there not existed the very natural resentment at the painful task which this young lady had indirectly imposed upon her, it was not in Alice's blood and breeding to take kindly at once to a girl of a class above her own. Alice had warm affections; as a lady's maid she might very conceivably have attached herself with much devotion to an indulgent mistress, but in the present case too much was asked of her. Richard was proud of his sister; he saw her at length seated where he had so often imagined her, and in his eyes she bore herself well. He glanced often at Adela, hoping for a return glance of congratulation; when it failed to come, he consoled himself with the reflection that such silent interchange of sentiments at table would be ill manners. In his very heart he believed that of the two maidens his sister was the better featured. Adela and Alice sat over against each other; their contrasted appearances were a chapter of social history. Mark the difference between Adela's gently closed lips, every muscle under control; and Alice's, which could never quite close without forming a saucy pout or a self-conscious primness. Contrast the foreheads; on the one hand that tenderly shadowed curve of brow, on the other the surface which always seemed to catch too much of the light, which moved irregularly with the arches above the eyes. The grave modesty of the one face, the now petulant, now abashed, now vacant expression of the other. Richard in his heart preferred the type he had so long been familiar with; a state of feeling of course in no way inconsistent with the emotions excited in him by continual observation of Adela.

The two returned to the Manor at half-past seven, Alice rising with evident relief when he gave the signal. It was agreed that the latter part of the next morning should be spent in going over the works. Adela was very willing to be of the party.

'They haven't much money, have they?' was Alice's first question as soon as she got away from the door.

'No, they are not rich,' replied her brother. 'You got on very nicely, old girl.'

'Why shouldn't I? You talk as if I didn't know how to behave myself, Dick.'

'No, I don't. I say that you did behave yourself.'

'Yes, and you were surprised at it.'

'I wasn't at all. What do you think of her?'

'She doesn't say much.'

'No, she's always very quiet. It's her way.'

'Yes.'

The monosyllable meant more than Richard gathered from it. They walked on in silence, and were met presently by a gentleman who was coming along the village street at a sharp pace. A lamp discovered Mr. Willis Rodman. Richard stopped.

'Seen to that little business?' he asked, in a cheerful voice.

'Yes,' was Rodman's reply. 'We shall hear from Agworth in the morning.'

'All right.—Alice, this is Mr. Rodman.—My sister, Rodman.'

Richard's right-hand man performed civilities with decidedly more finish than Richard himself had at command.

'I am very happy to meet Miss Mutimer. I hope we shall have the pleasure of showing her New Wanley to-morrow.'

'She and Miss Waltham will walk down in the morning. Good night, Rodman. Cold, eh?'

'Why didn't you introduce him this afternoon?' Alice asked as she walked on.

'I didn't think of it—I was bothered.'

'He seems very gentlemanly.'

'Oh, Rodman's seen a deal of life. He's a useful fellow—gets through work in a wonderful way.'

'But *is* he a gentleman? I mean, was he once?'

Richard laughed.

'I suppose you mean, had he ever money? No, he's made himself what he is.'

Tea having supplied the place of the more substantial evening meal, Richard and his sister had supper about ten o'clock. Alice drank champagne; a few bottles remained from those dedicated to the recent festival, and Mutimer felt the necessity of explaining the presence in his house of a luxury which to his class is more than anything associated with the bloated aristocracy. Alice drank it for the first time in her life, and her spirits grew as light as the foam upon her glass. Brother and sister were quietly confidential as midnight drew near.

'Shall you bring her to London?' Alice inquired, without previous mention of Adela.

'For a week, I think. We shall go to an hotel, of course. She's never seen London since she was a child.'

'She won't come to Highbury?'

'No. I shall avoid that somehow. You'll have to come and see us at the hotel. We'll go to the theatre together one night.'

'What about 'Arry?'

'I don't know. I shall think about it.'

Digesting much at his ease, Richard naturally became dreamful.

'I may have to take a house for a time now and then,' he said.

'In London?'

He nodded.

'I mustn't forget you, you see, Princess. Of course you'll come here sometimes, but that's not much good. In London I dare say I can get you to know some of the right kind of people. I want Adela to be thick with the Westlakes; then your chance 'll come. See, old woman?'

Alice, too, dreamed.

'I wonder you don't want me to marry a Socialist working man,' she said presently, as if twitting him playfully.

'You don't understand. One of the things we aim at is to remove the distinction between classes. I want you to marry one of those they call gentlemen. And you shall too, Alice!'

'Well, but I'm not a working girl now, Dick.'

He laughed, and said it was time to go to bed.

The same evening conversation continued to a late hour between Hubert Eldon and his mother. Hubert was returning to London the next morning.

Yesterday there had come to him two letters from Wanley, both addressed in female hand. He knew Adela's writing from her signature in the 'Christian Year,' and hastily opened the letter which came from her. The sight of the returned sonnets checked the eager flow of his blood; he was prepared for what he afterwards read.

'Then let her meet her fate,'—so ran his thoughts when he had perused the cold note, unassociable with the Adela he imagined in its bald formality. 'Only life can teach her.'

The other letter he suspected to be from Letty Tew, as it was.

'DEAR MR. ELDON,—I cannot help writing a line to you, lest you should think that I did not keep my promise in the way you understood it. I did indeed. You will hear from her; she preferred to write herself, and perhaps it was better; I should only have had painful things to say. I wish to ask you to have no unkind or unjust thoughts; I scarcely think you could have. Please do not trouble to answer this, but believe me, yours sincerely,

'L. TEW.'

'Good little girl!' he said to himself, smiling sadly. 'I feel sure she did her best.'

But his pride was asserting itself, always restive under provocation. To rival with a man like Mutimer! Better that the severance with old days should be complete.

He talked it all over very frankly with his mother, who felt that her son's destiny was not easily foreseen.

'And what do you propose to do, Hubert?' she asked, when they spoke of the future.

'To study, principally art. In a fortnight I go to Rome.'

Mrs. Eldon had gone thither thirty years ago.

'Think of me in my chair sometimes,' she said, touching his hands with her wan fingers.

CHAPTER XVI.

ALICE reached home again on Christmas Eve. It was snowing; she came in chilled and looking miserable. Mrs. Mutimer met her in the hall, passed her, and looked out at the open door, then turned with a few white flecks on her gown.

'Where's Dick?'

'He couldn't come,' replied the girl briefly, and ran up to her room.

'Arry was spending the evening with friends. Since teatime the old woman had never ceased moving from room to room, up and down stairs. She had got out an old pair of Richard's slippers, and had put them before the dining-room fire to warm. She had made a bed for Richard, and had a fire burning in the chamber. She had made arrangements for her eldest son's supper. No word had come from Wanley, but she held to the conviction that this night would see Richard in London.

Alice came down and declared that she was very hungry. Her mother went to the kitchen to order a meal, which in the end she prepared with her own hands. She seemed to have a difficulty in addressing any one. Whilst Alice ate in silence, Mrs. Mutimer kept going in and out of the room ; when the girl rose from the table, she stood before her and asked :

'Why couldn't he come ?'

Alice went to the fireplace, knelt down, and spread her hands to the blaze. Her mother approached her again.

'Won't you give me no answer, Alice ?'

'He couldn't come, mother. Something important is keeping him.'

'Something important ? And why did he want you there ?'

Alice rose to her feet, made one false beginning, then spoke to the point.

'Dick's married, mother.'

The old woman's eyes seemed to grow small in her wrinkled face, as if directing themselves with effort upon something minute. They looked straight into the eyes of her daughter, but had a more distant focus. The fixed gaze continued for nearly a minute.

'What are you talking about, girl ?' she said at length, in a strange, rattling voice. 'Why, I've seen Emma this very morning. Do you think she wouldn't 'a told me if she'd been a wife ?'

Alice was frightened by the look and the voice.

'Mother, it isn't Emma at all. It's someone at Wanley. We can't help it, mother. It's no use taking on. Now sit down and make yourself quiet. It isn't our fault.'

Mrs. Mutimer smiled in a grim way, then laughed—a most unmusical laugh.

'Now what's the good o' joking in that kind o' way ? That's like your father, that is ; he'd often come 'ome an' tell me such things as never was, an' expect me to believe 'em. An' I used to purtend I did, jist to please him. But I'm too old for that kind o' jokin'.—Alice, where's Dick ? How long 'll it be before he's here ? Where did he leave you ?'

'Now do just sit down, mother ; here, in this chair. Just sit quiet for a little, do.'

Mrs. Mutimer pushed aside the girl's hand; her face had become grave again.

'Let me be, child. And I tell you I have seen Emma to-day. Do you think she wouldn't 'a told me if things o' that kind was goin' on?'

'Emma knows nothing about it, mother. He hasn't told any one. He got me to come because he couldn't tell it himself. It was as much a surprise to me as to you, and I think it's very cruel of him. But it's over, and we can't help it. I shall have to tell Emma, I suppose, and a nice thing too!'

The old woman had begun to quiver; her hands shook by her sides, her very features trembled with gathering indignation.

'Dick has gone an' done this?' she stammered. 'He's gone an' broke his given word? He's deceived that girl as trusted to him an' couldn't help herself?'

'Now, mother, don't take on so! You're going to make yourself ill. It can't be helped. He says he shall send Emma money just the same.'

'Money! There you've hit the word; it's money as 'as ruined him, and as 'll be the ruin of us all. Send her money! What does the man think she's made of? Is all his feelings got as hard as money? and does he think the same of every one else? If I know Emma, she'll throw his money in his face. I knew what 'ud come of it, don't tell me I didn't. That very night as he come 'ome an' told me what had 'appened, there was a cold shiver run over me. I told him as it was the worst news ever come into our 'ouse, and now see if I wasn't right! He was angry with me 'cause I said it, an' who's a right to be angry now? It's my belief as money's the curse o' this world; I never knew a trouble yet as didn't somehow come of it, either 'cause there was too little or else too much. And Dick's gone an' done this? And him with all his preachin' about rights and wrongs an' what not! Him as was always a-cryin' down the rich folks 'cause they hadn't no feelin' for the poor! What feeling's *he* had, I'd like to know? It's him as is rich now, an' where's the difference 'tween him and them as he called names? No feelin' for the poor! An' what's Emma Vine? Poor enough by now. There's Jane as can't have not a week more to live, an' she a-nursin' her night an' day. He'll give her money!—has he got the face to say it? Nay, don't talk to me, girl; I'll say what I think, if it's the last I speak in this

world. Don't let him come to me ! Never a word again shall
he have from me as long as I live. He's disgraced himself, an'
me his mother, an' his father in the grave. A poor girl as
couldn't help herself, as trusted him an' wouldn't hear not a
word against him, for all he kep' away from her in her trouble.
I'd a fear o' this, but I wouldn't believe it of Dick ; I wouldn't
believe it of a son o' mine. An' 'Arry 'll go the same way.
It's all the money, an' a curse go with all the money as ever
was made ! An' you too, Alice, wi' your fine dresses, an' your
piannerin', an' your faldedals. But I warn you, my girl.
There 'll no good come of it. I warn you, Alice ! You're
ashamed o' your own mother—oh, I've seen it ! But it's a
mercy if you're not a disgrace to her. I'm thankful as I was
always poor ; I might 'a been tempted i' the same way.'

The dogma of a rude nature full of secret forces found
utterance at length under the scourge of a resentment of very
mingled quality. Let half be put to the various forms of dis-
interested feeling, at least half was due to personal exasperation.
The whole change that her life had perforce undergone was an
outrage upon the stubbornness of uninstructed habit ; the old
woman could see nothing but evil omens in a revolution which
cost her bodily discomfort and the misery of a mind perplexed
amid alien conditions. She was prepared for evil ; for months
she had brooded over every sign which seemed to foretell its
approach ; the egoism of the unconscious had made it plain to
her that the world must suffer in a state of things which so
grievously affected herself. Maternal solicitude kept her rest-
lessly swaying between apprehension for her children and injury
in the thought of their estrangement from her. And now at
length a bitter shame added itself to her torments. She was
shamed in her pride as a mother, shamed before the girl for
whom she nourished a deep affection. Emma's injuries she felt
charged upon herself ; she would never dare to stand before
her again. Her moral code, as much a part of her as the sap
of the plant and as little the result of conscious absorption,
declared itself on the side of all these rushing impulses ; she
was borne blindly on an exhaustless flux of words. After vain
attempts to make herself heard, Alice turned away and sat
sullenly waiting for the outburst to spend itself. Herself
comparatively unaffected by the feelings strongest in her mother,
this ear-afflicting clamour altogether checked her sympathy,
and in a great measure overcame those personal reasons which
had made her annoyed with Richard. She found herself taking

his side, even knew something of his impatience with Emma and her sorrows. When it came to rebukes and charges against herself her impatience grew active. She stood up again and endeavoured to make herself heard.

'What's the good of going on like this, mother? Just because you're angry, that's no reason you should call us all the names. you can turn your tongue to. It's over and done with, and there's an end of it. I don't know what you mean about disgracing you; I think you might wait till the time comes. I don't see what I've done as you can complain of.'

'No, of course you don't,' pursued her mother bitterly. 'It's the money as prevents you from seeing it. Them as was good enough for you before you haven't a word to say to now ; a man as works honestly for his living you make no account of. Well, well, you must go your own way——'

'What is it you want, mother? You don't expect me to look no higher than when I hadn't a penny but what I worked for ? I've no patience with you. You ought to be glad——'

'You haven't no patience, of course you haven't. And I'm to be glad when a son of mine does things as he deserves to be sent to prison for! I don't understand that kind o' gladness. But mind what I say; do what you like with your money, I'll have no more part in it. If I had as much as ten shillings a week of my own, I'd go and live by myself, and leave you to take your own way. But I tell you what I *can* do, and what I will. I'll have no more servants a-waitin' on *me*; I wasn't never used to it, and I'm too old to begin. I go to my own bedroom upstairs, and there I live, and there 'll be nobody go into that room but myself. I'll get my bits o' meals from the kitchen. 'Tain't much as I want, thank goodness, an' it won't be missed. I'll have no more doin's with servants, understand that; an' if I can't be left alone i' my own room, I'll go an' find a room where I can, an' I'll find some way of earnin' what little I want. It's your own house, and you'll do what you like in it. There's the keys, I've done with 'em ; an' here's the money too, I'm glad to be rid of it. An' you'll just tell Dick. I ain't one as says what I don't mean, nor never was, as that you know. You take your way, an' I'll take mine. An' now may be I'll get a night's sleep, the first I've had under this roof.'

As she spoke she took from her pockets the house keys, and from her purse the money she used for current expenses, and threw all together on to the table. Alice had turned to the fire-

place, and she stood so for a long time after her mother had
left the room. Then she took the keys and the money, consulted her watch, and in a few minutes was walking from the
house to a neighbouring cab-stand.

She drove to Wilton Square. Inspecting the front of the
house before knocking at the door, she saw a light in the
kitchen and a dimmer gleam at an upper window. It was
Mrs. Clay who opened to her.

'Is Emma in?' Alice inquired as she shook hands rather
coldly.

'She's sitting with Jane. I'll tell her. There's no fire
except in the kitchen,' Kate added, in a tone which implied
that doubtless her visitor was above taking a seat downstairs.

'I'll go down,' Alice replied, with just a touch of condescension. 'I want to speak a word or two with Emma,
that's all.'

Kate left her to descend the stairs, and went to inform her
sister. Emma was not long in appearing; the hue of her face
was troubled, for she had deceived herself with the belief that
it was Richard who knocked at the door. What more natural
than for him to have come on Christmas Eve? She approached
Alice with a wistful look, not venturing to utter any question,
only hoping that some good news might have been brought her.
Long watching in the sick room had given her own complexion
the tint of ill-health; her eyelids were swollen and heavy; the
brown hair upon her temples seemed to droop in languor. You
would have noticed that her tread was very soft, as if she still
were moving in the room above.

'How's Jane?' Alice began by asking. She could not
quite look the other in the face, and did not know how to begin
her disclosure.

'No better,' Emma gave answer, shaking her head. Her
voice, too, was suppressed; it was weeks since she had spoken
otherwise.

'I am so sorry, Emma. Are you in a hurry to go up
again?'

'No. Kate will sit there a little.'

'You look very poorly yourself. It must be very trying
for you.'

'I don't feel it,' Emma said, with a pale smile. 'She gives
no trouble. It's only her weakness now; the pain has almost
gone.'

'But then she must be getting better.'

Emma shook her head, looking aside. As Alice kept silence, she continued :

' I was glad to hear you'd gone to see Richard. He wouldn't —I was afraid he mightn't have time to get here for Christmas.'

There was a question in the words, a timorously expectant question. Emma had learnt the sad lesson of hope deferred, always to meet discouragement halfway. It is thus one seeks to propitiate the evil powers, to turn the edge of their blows by meekness.

' No, he couldn't come,' said Alice.

She had a muff on her left hand, and was turning it round and round with the other. Emma had not asked her to sit down, merely because of the inward agitation which absorbed her.

' He's quite well ? '

' Oh yes, quite well.'

Again Alice paused. Emma's heart was beating painfully. She knew now that Richard's sister had not come on an ordinary visit ; she felt that the call to Wanley had had some special significance. Alice did not ordinarily behave in this hesitating way.

' Did—did he send me a message ? '

' Yes.'

But even now Alice could not speak. She found a way of leading up to the catastrophe.

' Oh, mother has been going on so, Emma ! What do you think ? She won't have anything to do with the house any longer. She's given me the keys and all the money she had, and she's going to live just in her bedroom. She says she'll get her food from the kitchen herself, and she won't have a thing done for her by any one. I'm sure she means it ; I never saw her in such a state. She says if she'd ever so little money of her own, she'd leave the house altogether. She's been telling me I've no feeling, and that I'm going to the bad, that I shall live to disgrace her, and I can't tell you what. Everything is so miserable ! She says it's all the money, and that she knew from the first how it would be. And I'm afraid some of what she says is true, I am indeed, Emma. But things happen in a way you could never think. I half wish myself the money had never come. It's making us all miserable.'

Emma listened, expecting from phrase to phrase some word which would be to her a terrible enlightenment. But Alice had ceased, and the word still unspoken.

' You say he sent me a message ? '

She did not ask directly the cause of Mrs. Mutimer's anger. Instinct told her that to hear the message would explain all else.

' Emma, I'm afraid to tell you. You'll blame *me*, like mother did.'

' I shan't blame you, Alice. Will you please tell me the message ? '

Emma's lips seemed to speak without her volition. The rest of her face was fixed and cold.

' He's married, Emma.'

' He asked you to tell me ? '

Alice was surprised at the self-restraint proved by so quiet an interrogation.

' Yes, he did. Emma, I'm so, so sorry ! If only you'll believe I'm sorry, Emma ! He *made* me come and tell you. He said if I didn't you'd have to find out by chance, because he couldn't for shame tell you himself. And he couldn't tell mother neither. I've had it all to do. If you knew what I've gone through with mother ! It's very hard that other people should suffer so much just on his account. I am really sorry for you, Emma.'

' Who is it he's married ? ' Emma asked. Probably all the last speech had been but a vague murmur to her ears.

' Some one at Wanley.'

' A lady ? '

' Yes, I suppose she's a lady.'

' You didn't see her, then ? '

' Yes, I saw her. I don't like her.'

Poor Alice meant this to be soothing. Emma knew it, and smiled.

' I don't think she cares much after all,' Alice said to herself.

' But was that the message ? '

' Only to tell you of it, Emma. There was something else,' she added immediately ; ' not exactly a message, but he told me, and I dare say he thought I should let you know. He said that of course you were to have the money still as usual.'

Over the listener's face came a cloud, a deep, turbid red. It was not anger, but shame which rose from the depths of her being. Her head sank ; she turned and walked aside.

' You're not angry with *me*, Emma ? '

'Not angry at all, Alice,' was the reply in a monotone.

'I must say good-bye now. I hope you won't take on much And I hope Jane 'll soon be better.'

'Thank you. I must go up to her; she doesn't like me to be away long.'

Alice went before up the kitchen stairs, the dark, narrow stairs which now seemed to her so poverty-stricken. Emma did not speak, but pressed her hand at the door.

Kate stood above her on the first landing, and, as Emma came up, whispered:

'Has he come?'

'Something has hindered him.' And Emma added, 'He couldn't help it.'

'Well, then, I think he ought to have helped it,' said the other tartly. 'When does he mean to come, I'd like to know?'

'It's uncertain.'

Emma passed into the sick-room. Her sister followed her with eyes of ill-content, then returned to the kitchen.

Jane lay against pillows. Red light from the fire played over her face, which was wasted beyond recognition. She looked a handmaiden of Death.

The atmosphere of the room was warm and sickly. A small green-shaded lamp stood by the looking-glass in front of the window; it cast a disk of light below, and on the ceiling concentric rings of light and shade, which flickered ceaselessly, and were at times all but obliterated in a gleam from the fireplace. A kettle sang on the trivet.

The sick girl's hands lay on the counterpane; one of them moved as Emma came to the bedside, and rested when the warmer fingers clasped it. There was eager inquiry in the sunken eyes; her hand tried to raise itself, but in vain.

'What did Alice say?' she asked, in quick feeble tones. 'Is he coming?'

'Not for Christmas, I'm afraid, dear. He's still very busy.'

'But he sent you a message?'

'Yes. He would have come if he could.'

'Did you tell Alice I wanted to see her? Why didn't she come up? Why did she stay such a short time?'

'She couldn't stay to-night, Jane. Are you easy still, love?'

'Oh, I did so want to see her! Why couldn't she stop, Emma? It wasn't kind of her to go without seeing me. I'd have made time if it had been her as was lying in bed. And

he doesn't even answer what I wrote to him. It was such
work to write—I couldn't now; and he might have answered.'

'He very seldom writes to any one, you know, Jane. He
has so little time.'

'Little time! I have less, Emma, and he must know that.
It's unkind of him. What did Alice tell you? Why did he
want her to go there? Tell me everything.'

Emma felt the sunken eyes burning her with their eager
look. She hesitated, pretended to think of something that had
to be done, and the eyes burned more and more. Jane made
repeated efforts to raise herself, as if to get a fuller view of her
sister's face.

'Shall I move you?' Emma asked. 'Would you like
another pillow?'

'No, no,' was the impatient answer. 'Don't go away from
me; don't take your hand away. I want to know all that
Alice said. You haven't any secrets from me, Emmy. Why
does he stay away so long? It seems years since he came to see
you. It's wrong of him. There's no business ought to keep him
away all this time. Look at me, and tell me what she said.'

'Only that he hadn't time. Dear, you mustn't excite yourself so. Isn't it all right, Jane, as long as I don't mind it?'

'Why do you look away from me? No, it isn't all right.
Oh, I can't rest, I can't lie here! Why haven't I strength to
go and say to him what I want to say? I thought it was him
when the knock came. When Kate told me it wasn't, I felt as
if my heart was sinking down; and I don't seem to have no
tears left to cry It'ud ease me a little if I could. And now
you're beginning to have secrets. Emmy!'

It was a cry of anguish. The mention of tears had brought
them to Emma's eyes, for they lurked very near the surface,
and Jane had seen the firelight touch on a moist cheek. For
an instant she raised herself from the pillows. Emma folded
soft arms about her and pressed her cheek against the heat
which consumed her sister's.

'Emmy, I must know,' wailed the sick girl. 'Is it what
I've been afraid of? No, not that! Is it the worst of all?
You *must* tell me now. You don't love me if you keep away
the truth. I can't have anything between you and me.'

A dry sob choked her she gasped for breath. Emma,
fearful lest the very life was escaping from her embrace, drew
away and looked in anguish. Her involuntary tears had
ceased, but she could no longer practise deception. The cost to

Jane was greater perhaps than if she knew the truth. At least their souls must be united ere it was too late.

'The truth, Emmy!'

'I will tell it you, darling,' she replied, with quiet sadness. 'It's for him that I'm sorry. I never thought anything could tempt him to break his word. Think of it in the same way as I do, dear sister; don't be sorry for me, but for him.'

'He's never coming? He won't marry you?'

'He's already married, Jane. Alice came to tell me.'

Again she would have raised herself, but this time there was no strength. Not even her arms could she lift from the coverlets. But Emma saw the vain effort, raised the thin arms, put them about her neck, and held her sister to her heart as if for eternity.

'Darling, darling, it isn't hard to bear. I care for nothing but your love. Live for my sake, dearest dear; I have forgotten every one and everything but you. It's so much better. I couldn't have changed my life so; I was never meant to be rich. It seems unkind of him, but in a little time we shall see it was best. Only you, Janey; you have my whole heart, and I'm so glad to feel it is so. Live, and I'll give every minute of my life to loving you, poor sufferer.'

Jane could not breathe sound into the words she would have spoken. She lay with her eyes watching the fire-play on the ceiling. Her respiration was quick and feeble.

Mutimer's name was not mentioned by either again that night, by one of them never again. Such silence was his punishment.

Kate entered the room a little before midnight. She saw one of Jane's hands raised to impose silence. Emma, still sitting by the bedside, slept; her head rested on the pillows. The sick had become the watcher.

'She'd better go to bed,' Kate whispered. 'I'll wake her.'

'No, no! You needn't stay, Kate. I don't want anything. Let her sleep as she is.'

The elder sister left the room. Then Jane approached her head to that of the sleeper, softly, softly, and her arm stole across Emma's bosom and rested on her farther shoulder. The fire burned with little whispering tongues of flame; the circles of light and shade quivered above the lamp. Abroad the snow fell and froze upon the ground.

Three days later Alice Mutimer, as she sat at breakfast,

was told that a visitor named Mrs. Clay desired to see her.
It was nearly ten o'clock; Alice had no passion for early
rising, and since her mother's retirement from the common
table she breakfasted alone at any hour which seemed good to
her. 'Arry always—or nearly always—left the house at eight
o'clock.

Mrs. Clay was introduced into the dining-room. Alice
received her with an anxious face, for she was anticipating
trouble from the house in Wilton Square. But the trouble
was other than she had in mind.

'Jane died at four o'clock this morning,' the visitor began,
without agitation, in the quick, unsympathetic voice which she
always used when her equanimity was in any way disturbed.
'Emma hasn't closed her eyes for two days and nights, and now
I shouldn't wonder if she's going to be ill herself. I made her
lie down, and then came out just to ask you to write to your
brother. Surely he'll come now. I don't know what to do
about the burying; we ought to have some one to help us. I
expected your mother would be coming to see us, but she's
kept away all at once. Will you write to Dick?'

Alice was concerned to perceive that Kate was still
unenlightened.

'Did Emma know you were coming?' she asked.

'Yes, I suppose she did. But it's hard to get her to attend
to anything. I've left her alone, 'cause there wasn't any one I
could fetch at once. Will you write to-day?'

'Yes, I'll see to it,' said Alice. 'Have some breakfast,
will you?'

'Well, I don't mind just a cup o' coffee. It's very cold,
and I had to walk a long way before I could get a 'bus.'

Whilst Kate refreshed herself, Alice played nervously with
her tea-spoon, trying to make up her mind what must be done.
The situation was complicated with many miseries, but Alice
had experienced a growth of independence since her return
from Wanley. All she had seen and heard whilst with her
brother had an effect upon her in the afterthought, and her
mother's abrupt surrender into her hands of the household
control gave her, when she had time to realise it, a sense of
increased importance not at all disagreeable. Already she had
hired a capable servant in addition to the scrubby maid-of-all-
work who had sufficed for Mrs. Mutimer, and it was her intention that henceforth domestic arrangements should be established on quite another basis.

'I'll telegraph to Dick,' she said, presently. 'I've no doubt he'll see that everything's done properly.'

'But won't he come himself?'

'We shall see.'

'Is your mother in?'

'She's not very well; I don't think I must disturb her with bad news. Tell Emma I'm very sorry, will you? I do hope she isn't going to be ill. You must see that she gets rest now. Was it sudden?' she added, showing in her face how little disposed she was to dwell on such gloomy subjects as death and burial.

'She was wandering all yesterday. I don't think she knew anything after eight o'clock last night. She went off in a sleep.'

When the visitor had gone, Alice drove to the nearest telegraph office and despatched a message to her brother, giving the news and asking what should be done. By three o'clock in the afternoon no reply had yet arrived; but shortly after Mr. Keene presented himself at the house. Alice had not seen him since her return. He bowed to her with extreme gravity, and spoke in a subdued voice.

'I grieve that I have lost time, Miss Mutimer. Important business had taken me from home, and on my return I found a telegram from Wanley. Your brother directs me to wait upon you at once, on a very sad subject, I fear. He instructs me to purchase a grave in Manor Park Cemetery. No near relative, I trust?'

'No, only a friend,' Alice replied. 'You've heard me speak of a girl called Emma Vine. It's a sister of hers. She died this morning, and they want help about the funeral.'

'Precisely, precisely. You know with what zeal I hasten to perform your'—a slight emphasis on this word—'brother's pleasure, be the business what it may. I'll see about it at once. I was to say to you that your brother would be in town this evening.'

'Oh, very well. But you needn't look so gloomy, you know, Mr. Keene. I'm very sorry, but then she's been ill for a very long time, and it's really almost a relief—to her sisters, I mean.'

'I trust you enjoyed your visit to Wanley, Miss Mutimer?' said Keene, still preserving his very respectful tone and bearing.

'Oh yes, thanks. I dare say I shall go there again before very long. No doubt you'll be glad to hear that.'

'I will try to be, Miss Mutimer. I trust that your pleasure is my first consideration in life.'

Alice was, to speak vulgarly, practising on Mr. Keene. He was her first visitor since she had entered upon rule, and she had a double satisfaction in subduing him with airs and graces. She did not trouble to reflect that under the circumstances he might think her rather heartless, and indeed hypocrisy was not one of her failings. Her *naïveté* constituted such charm as she possessed; in the absence of any deep qualities it might be deemed a virtue, for it was inconsistent with serious deception.

'I suppose you mean you'd really much rather I stayed here?'

Keene eyed her with observation. He himself had slight depth for a man doomed to live by his wits, and he was under the disadvantage of really feeling something of what he said. He was not a rascal by predilection; merely driven that way by the forces which in our social state abundantly make for rascality.

'Miss Mutimer,' he replied, with a stage sigh, 'why do you tempt my weakness? I am on my honour; I am endeavouring to earn your good opinion. Spare me!'

'Oh, I'm sure there's no harm in you, Mr. Keene. I suppose you'd better go and see after your—your business.'

'You are right. I go at once, Princess. I may call you Princess?'

'Well, I don't know about that. Of course only when there's no one else in the room.'

'But I shall think it always.'

'That I can't prevent, you know.'

'Ah, I fear you mean nothing, Miss Mutimer.'

'Nothing at all.'

He took his leave, and Alice enjoyed reflecting upon the dialogue, which certainly had meant nothing for her in any graver sense.

'Now, that's what the books call *flirtation*,' she said to herself. 'I think I can do that.'

And on the whole she could, vastly better than might have been expected of her birth and breeding.

At six o'clock a note was delivered for her. Richard wrote from an hotel in the neighbourhood, asking her to come to him. She found him in a private sitting-room, taking a meal.

'Why didn't you come to the house?' she asked. 'You knew mother never comes down-stairs.'

Richard looked at her with lowered brows.

'You mean to say she's doing that in earnest?'

'That she is! She comes down early in the morning and gets all the food she wants for the day. I heard her cooking something in a frying-pan to-day. She hasn't been out of the house yet.'

'Does she know about Jane?'

'No. I know what it would be if I went and told her.'

He ate in silence. Alice waited.

'You must go and see Emma,' was his next remark. 'Tell her there's a grave in Manor Park Cemetery; her father and mother were buried there, you know. Keene'll look after it all, and he'll come and tell you what to do.'

'Why did you come up?'

'Oh, I couldn't talk about these things in letters. You'll have to tell mother; she might want to go to the funeral.'

'I don't see why I should do all your disagreeable work, Dick!'

'Very well, don't do it,' he replied sullenly, throwing down his knife and fork.

A scene of wrangling followed, without violence, but of the kind which is at once a cause and an effect of demoralisation. The old disagreements between them had been in another tone, at all events on Richard's side, for they had arisen from his earnest disapproval of frivolities and the like. Richard could no longer speak in that way. To lose the power of honest reproof in consequence of a moral lapse is to any man a wide-reaching calamity; to a man of Mutimer's calibre it meant disaster of which the end could not be foreseen.

Of course Alice yielded; her affection and Richard's superior force always made it a foregone result that she should do so.

'And you won't come and see mother?' she asked.

'No. She's behaving foolishly.'

'It's precious dull at home, I can tell you. I can't go on much longer without friends of some kind. I've a good mind to marry Mr. Keene, just for a change.'

Richard started up, with his fist on the table.

'Do you mean to say he's been talking to you in that way?' he cried angrily.

Alice had spoken with thoughtless petulance. She hastened eagerly to correct her error.

'As if I meant it! Don't be stupid, Dick. Of course he

hasn't said a word; I believe he's engaged to somebody; I thought so from something he said a little while ago. The idea of me marrying a man like that!'

He examined her closely, and Alice was not afraid of tell-tale cheeks.

'Well, I can't think you'd be such a fool. If I thought there was any danger of that, I'd soon stop it.'

'Would you, indeed! Why, that would be just the way to make me say I'd have him. You'd have known that if only you read novels.'

'Novels!' he exclaimed, with profound contempt. 'Don't go playing with that kind of thing; it's dangerous. At least you can wait a week or two longer. I've only let him see so much of you because I felt sure you'd got common sense.'

'Of course I have. But what's to happen in a week or two?'

'I should think you might come to Wanley for a little. We shall see. If mother had only 'Arry in the house, she might come back to her senses.'

'Shall I tell her you've been to London?'

'You can if you like,' he replied, with a show of indifference.

Jane Vine was buried on Sunday afternoon, her sisters alone accompanying her to the grave. Alice had with difficulty obtained admission to her mother's room, and it seemed to her that the news she brought was received with little emotion. The old woman had an air of dogged weariness; she did not look her daughter in the face, and spoke only in monosyllables. Her face was yellow, her cheeks like wrinkled parchment.

Manor Park Cemetery lies in the remote East End, and gives sleeping-places to the inhabitants of a vast district. There Jane's parents lay, not in a grave to themselves, but buried amidst the nameless dead, in that part of the ground reserved for those who can purchase no more than a portion in the foss which is filled when its occupants reach statutable distance from the surface. The regions around were then being built upon for the first time; the familiar streets of pale, damp brick were stretching here and there, continuing London, much like the spreading of a disease. Epping Forest is near at hand, and nearer the dreary expanse of Wanstead Flats.

Not grief, but chill desolation makes this cemetery its abode. A country churchyard touches the tenderest memories, and softens the heart with longing for the eternal rest. The cemeteries of wealthy London abound in dear and great associations, or at worst preach homilies which connect themselves with human dignity and pride. Here on the waste limits of that dread East, to wander among tombs is to go hand in hand with the stark and eyeless emblem of mortality; the spirit fails beneath the cold burden of ignoble destiny. Here lie those who were born for toil; who, when toil has worn them to the uttermost, have but to yield their useless breath and pass into oblivion. For them is no day, only the brief twilight of a winter sky between the former and the latter night. For them no aspiration; for them no hope of memory in the dust; their very children are wearied into forgetfulness. Indistinguishable units in the vast throng that labours but to support life, the name of each, father, mother, child, is as a dumb cry for the warmth and love of which Fate so stinted them. The wind wails above their narrow tenements; the sandy soil, soaking in the rain as soon as it has fallen, is a symbol of the great world which absorbs their toil and straightway blots their being.

It being Sunday afternoon the number of funerals was considerable; even to bury their dead the toilers cannot lose a day of the wage week. Around the chapel was a great collection of black vehicles with sham-tailed mortuary horses; several of the families present must have left themselves bare in order to clothe a coffin in the way they deemed seemly. Emma and her sister had made their own funeral garments, and the former, in consenting for the sake of poor Jane to receive the aid which Mutimer offered, had insisted through Alice that there should be no expenditure beyond the strictly needful. The carriage which conveyed her and Kate alone followed the hearse from Hoxton; it rattled along at a merry pace, for the way was lengthy, and a bitter wind urged men and horses to speed. The occupants of the box kept up a jesting colloquy.

Impossible to read the burial service over each of the dead separately; time would not allow it. Emma and Kate found themselves crowded among a number of sobbing women, just in time to seat themselves before the service began. Neither of them had moist eyes; the elder looked about the chapel with blank gaze, often shivering with cold; Emma's face was bent downwards, deadly pale, set in unchanging woe. A world had fallen to pieces about her; she did not feel the ground upon which she trod; there seemed no way from amid the ruins. She had no strong religious faith : a wail in the darkness was all the expression her heart could attain to; in the present anguish she could not turn her thoughts to that far vision of a life hereafter. All day she had striven to realise that a box of wood contained all that was left of her sister. The voice of the clergyman struck her ear with meaningless monotony. Not immortality did she ask for, but one more whisper from the lips that could not speak, one throb of the heart she had striven so despairingly to warm against her own.

Kate was plucking at her arm, for the service was over, and unconsciously she was impeding people who wished to pass from the seats. With difficulty she rose and walked; the cold seemed to have checked the flow of her blood; she noticed the breath rising from her mouth, and wondered that she could have so much whilst those dear lips were breathless. Then she was being led over hard snow, towards a place where men stood, where there was new-turned earth, where a coffin lay upon the ground. She suffered the sound of more words which she could not follow, then heard the dull falling of clods upon hollow wood. A hand seemed to clutch her throat, she struggled convulsively and cried aloud. But the tears would not come.

No memory of the return home dwelt afterwards in her mind. The white earth, the headstones sprinkled with snow, the vast grey sky over which darkness was already creeping, the wind and the clergyman's voice joining in woful chant, these alone remained with her to mark the day. Between it and the days which then commenced lay formless void.

On Tuesday morning Alice Mutimer came to the house. Mrs. Clay chanced to be from home; Emma received the visitor and led her down into the kitchen.

'I am glad you have come,' she said; 'I wanted to see you to-day.'

'Are you feeling better?' Alice asked. She tried in vain to speak with the friendliness of past days; that could never be restored. Her advantages of person and dress were no help against the embarrassment caused in her by the simple dignity of the wronged and sorrowing girl.

Emma replied that she was better, then asked:

'Have you come only to see me, or for something else?'

'I wanted to know how you were; but I've brought you something as well.'

She took an envelope from within her muff. Emma shook her head.

'No, nothing more,' she said, in a tone removed alike from

resentment and from pathos. ' I want you, please, to say that we can't take anything after this.'

' But what are you going to do, Emma ? '

' To leave this house and live as we did before.'

' Oh, but you can't do that ! What does Kate say ? '

' I haven't told her yet ; I'm going to do so to-day.'

' But she'll feel it very hard with the children.'

The children were sitting together in a corner of the kitchen. Emma glanced at them, and saw that Bertie, the elder, was listening with a surprised look.

' Yes, I'm sorry,' she replied simply, ' but we have no choice.'

Alice had an impulse of generosity.

' Then take it from *me*,' she said. ' You won't mind that. You know I have plenty of my own. Live here and let one or two of the rooms, and I'll lend you what you need till the business is doing well. Now you can't have anything to say against that ? '

Emma still shook her head.

' The business will never help us. We must go back to the old work ; we can always live on that. I can't take anything from you, Alice.'

' Well, I think it's very unkind, Emma.'

' Perhaps so, but I can't help it. It's kind of you to offer, I feel that ; but I'd rather work my fingers to the bone than touch one halfpenny now that I haven't earned.'

Alice bridled slightly and urged no more. She left before Kate returned.

In the course of the morning Emma strung herself to the effort of letting her sister know the true state of affairs. It was only what Kate had for a long time suspected, and she freely said as much, expressing her sentiments with fluent indignation.

' Of course I know you won't hear of it,' she said, ' but if I was in your place I'd make him smart. I'd have him up and make him pay, see if I wouldn't. Trust him, he knows you're too soft-hearted, and he takes advantage of you. It's girls like you as encourages men to think they can do as they like. You've no right, you haven't, to let him off. I'd have him in the newspapers and show him up, see if I wouldn't. And he shan't have it quite so easy as he thinks neither ; I'll go about and tell everybody as I know. Only let him come a-lecturin' hereabouts, that's all ! '

' Kate,' broke in the other, ' if you do anything of the kind,

I don't know how I shall speak to you again. It's not you he's harmed; you've no right to spread talk about me. It's my affair, and I must do as I think fit. It's all over, and there's no occasion for neither you nor me to speak of him again. I'm going out this afternoon to find a room for us, and we shall be no worse off than we was before. We've got to work, that's all, and to earn our living like other women do.'

Her sister stared incredulously.

'You mean to say he's stopped sending money?'

'I have refused to take it.'

'You've done *what?* Well, of all the —— !' Comparisons failed her. 'And I've got to take these children back again into a hole like the last? Not me! You do as you like; I suppose you know your own business. But if he doesn't send the money as usual, I'll find some way to make him, see if I don't! You're off your head, I think.'

Emma had anticipated this, and was prepared to bear the brunt of her sister's anger. Kate was not originally blessed with much sweetness of disposition, and an unhappy marriage had made her into a sour, nagging woman. But, in spite of her wretched temper and the low moral tone induced during her years of matrimony, she was not evil-natured, and her chief safeguard was affection for her sister Emma. This seldom declared itself, for she was of those unhappily constituted people who find nothing so hard as to betray the tenderness of which they are capable, and, as often as not, are driven by a miserable perversity to words and actions which seem quite inconsistent with such feeling. For Jane she had cared far less than for Emma, yet her grief at Jane's death was more than could be gathered from her demeanour. It had, in fact, resulted in a state of nervous irritableness; an outbreak of anger came to her as a relief, such as Emma had recently found in the shedding of tears. On her own account she felt strongly, but yet more on Emma's; coarse methods of revenge naturally suggested themselves to her, and to be thwarted drove her to exasperation. When Emma persisted in steady opposition, exerting all the force of her character to subdue her sister's ignoble purposes, Kate worked herself to frenzy. For more than an hour her voice was audible in the street, as she poured forth torrents of furious reproach and menace; all the time Emma stood patient and undaunted, her own anger often making terrible struggle for mastery, but ever finding itself subdued. For she, too, was of a passionate nature, but the treasures of sensibility which her heart enclosed consecrated all her being to noble ends. One invaluable aid she had in a contest such as this—her inability to grow sullen. Righteous anger might gleam in her eyes and quiver upon her lips, but the fire always burnt clear; it is smoulder that poisons the air.

She knew her sister, pitied her, always made for her the gentlest allowances. It would have been easy to stand aside, to disclaim responsibility, and let Kate do as she chose, but the easy course was never the one she chose when endurance promised better results. To resist to the uttermost, even to claim and exert the authority she derived from her suffering, was, she knew, the truest kindness to her sister. And in the end she prevailed. Kate tore her passion to tatters, then succumbed to exhaustion. But she did not fling out of the room, and this Emma knew to be a hopeful sign. The opportunity of strong, placid speech at length presented itself, and Emma used it well. She did not succeed in eliciting a promise, but when she declared her confidence in her sister's better self, Kate made no retort, only sat in stubborn muteness.

In the afternoon Emma went forth to fulfil her intention of finding lodgings. She avoided the neighbourhood in which she had formerly lived, and after long search discovered what she wanted in a woful byway near Old Street. It was one room only, but larger than she had hoped to come upon; fortunately her own furniture had been preserved, and would now suffice.

Kate remained sullen, but proved by her actions that she had surrendered; she began to pack her possessions. Emma wrote to Alice, announcing that the house was tenantless; she took the note to Highbury herself, and left it at the door, together with the house key. The removal was effected after nightfall.

CHAPTER XVII.

MOVEMENTS which appeal to the reason and virtue of humanity, and are consequently doomed to remain long in the speculative stage, prove their vitality by enduring the tests of schism. A Socialistic propaganda in times such as our own, an insistence upon the principles of Christianity in a modern Christian state, the advocacy of peace and good-will in an age when falsehood is the foundation of the social structure, and internecine warfare is presupposed in every compact between man and man, might anticipate that the test would come soon, and be of a stringent nature. Accordingly it did not surprise Mr. Westlake, when he discerned the beginnings of commotion in the Union of which he represented the cultured and leading elements. A comrade named Roodhouse had of late been coming into prominence by addressing himself in fiery eloquence to open-air meetings, and at length had taken upon himself to more than hint that the movement was at a standstill owing to the lukewarmness (in guise of practical moderation) of those to whom its guidance had been entrusted. The reports of Comrade Roodhouse's lectures were of a nature that made it difficult for Mr. Westlake to print them in the 'Fiery Cross; ' one such report arrived at length, that of a meeting held on Clerkenwell Green on the first Sunday of the new year, to which the editor refused admission. The comrade who made it his business to pen notes of the new apostle's glowing words, had represented him as referring to the recognised leader in such very uncompromising terms, that to publish the report in the official columns would have been stultifying. In the lecture in question Roodhouse declared his adherence to the principles of assassination; he pronounced them the sole working principles; to deny to Socialists the right of assassination was to rob them of the very sinews of war. Men who affected to be revolutionists, but were in reality nothing more than rose-water romancers, would of course object to anything which looked like business; they liked to sit in their comfortable studies and pen daintily worded articles, thus earning for themselves a humanitarian reputation at a very cheap rate. That would not do; à bas all such penny-a-liner pretence! Blood and iron! that must be the revolutionists' watchword. Was it not by blood and iron that the present damnable system was maintained? To arms, then —secretly, of course. Let tyrants be made to tremble upon their thrones in more countries than Russia. Let capitalists fear to walk in the daylight. This only was the path of progress.

It was thought by the judicious that Comrade Roodhouse would, if he repeated this oration, find himself the subject of a rather ugly indictment. For the present, however, his words were ignored, save in the Socialist body. To them, of course, he had addressed himself, and doubtless he was willing to run a little risk for the sake of a most practical end, that of splitting the party, and thus establishing a sovereignty for himself; this done, he could in future be more guarded. His reporter purposely sent 'copy' to Mr. Westlake which could not be printed, and the rejection of the report was the signal for secession. Comrade Roodhouse printed at his own expense a considerable number of leaflets, and sowed them broadcast in the Socialist meeting-places. There were not wanting disaffected brethren, who perused these appeals with satisfaction. Schism flourished.

Comrade Roodhouse was of course a man of no means, but he numbered among his followers two extremely serviceable men, one of them a practical printer who carried on a small business in Camden Town; the other an oil merchant, who, because his profits had never exceeded a squalid two thousand a year, whereas another oil merchant of his acquaintance made at least twice as much, was embittered against things in general, and ready to assist any subversionary movement, yea, even with coin of the realm, on the one condition that he should be allowed to insert articles of his own composition in the new organ which it was proposed to establish. There was no difficulty in conceding this trifle, and the 'Tocsin' was the result. The name was a suggestion of the oil merchant himself, and no bad name if Socialists at large could be supposed capable of understanding it; but the oil merchant was too important a man to be thwarted, and the argument by which he supported his choice was incontestable. 'Isn't it our aim to educate the people? Very well, then let them begin by knowing what Tocsin means. I shouldn't know myself if I hadn't come across it in the newspaper and looked it up in the dictionary; so there you are!'

And there was the 'Tocsin,' a weekly paper like the 'Fiery Cross.' The first number appeared in the middle of February, so admirably prepared were the plans of Comrade Roodhouse. It appeared on Friday; the next Sunday promised to be a lively day at Commonwealth Hall and elsewhere. At the original head-quarters of the Union addresses were promised from two leading men, Comrades Westlake and Mutimer. Comrade Roodhouse would in the morning address an assembly on Clerkenwell Green; in the evening his voice would summon adherents to the meeting-place in Hoxton which had been the scene of our friend Richard's earliest triumphs. With few exceptions the Socialists of that region had gone over to the new man and the new paper.

Richard arrived in town on the Saturday, and went to the house in Highbury, whither disagreeable business once more summoned him. Alice, who, owing to her mother's resolute refusal to direct the household, had not as yet been able to spend more than a day or two with Richard and his wife, sent nothing but ill news to Wanley. Mrs. Mutimer seemed to be breaking down in health, and 'Arry was undisguisedly returning to evil ways. For the former, it was suspected—a locked door prevented certainty—that she had of late kept her bed the greater part of the day; a servant who met her downstairs in the early morning reported that she 'looked very bad indeed.' The case of the latter was as hard to deal with. 'Arry had long ceased to attend his classes with any regularity, and he was once more asserting the freeman's right to immunity from day labour. Moreover, he claimed in practice the freeman's right to get drunk four nights out of the seven. No one knew whence he got his money; Richard purposely stinted him, but the provision was useless. Mr. Keene declared with lamentations that his influence over 'Arry was at an end; nay, the youth had so far forgotten gratitude as to frankly announce his intention of 'knockin' Keene's lights out' if he were further interfered with. To the journalist his 'lights' were indispensable; in no sense of the word did he possess too many of them; so it was clear that he must abdicate his tutorial functions. Alice implored her brother to come and 'do something.'

Richard, though a married man of only six weeks' standing, had troubles altogether in excess of his satisfactions. Things were not as they should have been in that earthly paradise called New Wanley. It was not to be expected that the profits of that undertaking would be worth speaking of for some little time to come, but it was extremely desirable that it should pay its own expenses, and it began to be doubtful whether even this moderate success was being achieved. Various members of the directing committee had visited New Wanley recently, and Richard had talked to them in a somewhat discouraging tone; his fortune was not limitless, it had to be remembered; a considerable portion of old Mutimer's money had lain in the vast Belwick concern of which he was senior partner; the surviving members of the firm were under no specified obligation to receive Richard himself as partner, and the product of the realised capital was a very different thing from the share in the profits which the old man had enjoyed. Other capital Richard had at his command, but already he was growing chary of encroachments upon principal

He began to murmur inwardly that the entire fortune did not lie at his disposal; willingly he would have allowed Alice a handsome portion; and as for 'Arry, the inheritance was clearly going to be his ruin. The practical difficulties at New Wanley were proving considerable; the affair was viewed with hostility by ironmasters in general, and the results of such hostility were felt. But Richard was committed to his scheme; all his ambitions based themselves thereupon. And those ambitions grew daily.

These greater troubles must to a certain extent solve themselves, but in Highbury it was evidently time, as Alice said, to 'do something.' His mother's obstinacy stood in the way of almost every scheme that suggested itself. Richard was losing patience with the poor old woman, and suffered the more from his irritation because he would so gladly have behaved to her with filial kindness. One plan there was to which she might possibly agree, and even have pleasure in accepting it, but it was not easy to propose. The house in Wilton Square was still on his hands; upon the departure of Emma and her sister, a certain Mrs. Chattaway, a poor friend of old times, who somehow supported herself and a grandchild, had been put into the house as caretaker, for Richard could not sell all the furniture to which his mother was so attached, and he had waited for her return to reason before ultimately deciding how to act in that matter. Could he now ask the old woman to return to the Square, and, it might be, live there with Mrs. Chattaway? In that case both 'Arry and Alice would have to leave London.

On Saturday afternoon he had a long talk with his sister. To Alice also it had occurred that their mother's return to the old abode might be desirable.

'And you may depend upon it, Dick,' she said, 'she'll never rest again till she does get back. I believe you've only got to speak of it, and she'll go at once.'

'She'll think it unkind,' Richard objected. 'It looks as if we wanted to get her out of the way. Why on earth does she carry on like this? As if we hadn't bother enough!'

'Well, we can't help what she thinks. I believe it'll be for her own good. She'll be comfortable with Mrs. Chattaway, and that's more than she'll ever be here. But what about 'Arry?'

'He'll have to come to Wanley. I shall find him work there—I wish I'd done so months ago.'

There were no longer the objections to 'Arry's appearance

at Wanley that had existed previous to Richard's marriage;
none the less the resolution was courageous, and proved the
depth of Mutimer's anxiety for his brother. Having got the
old woman to Wilton Square, and Alice to the Manor, it would
have been easy enough to bid Mr. Henry Mutimer betake himself—whither his mind directed him. Richard could not adopt
that rough-and-ready way out of his difficulty. Just as he
suffered in the thought that he might be treating his mother
unkindly, so he was constrained to undergo annoyances rather
than abandon the hope of saving 'Arry from ultimate destruction.

'Will he live at the Manor?' Alice asked uneasily.

Richard mused; then a most happy idea struck him.

'I have it! He shall live with Rodman. The very thing!
Rodman's the fellow to look after him. Yes; that's what
we'll do.'

'And I'm to live at the Manor?'

'Of course.'

'You think Adela won't mind?'

'Mind? How the deuce can she mind it?'

As a matter of form Adela would of course be consulted,
but Richard had no notion of submitting practical arrangements in his own household to his wife's decision.

'Now we shall have to see mother,' he said. 'How's that
to be managed?'

'Will you go and speak at her door?'

'That be hanged! Confound it, has she gone crazy? Just
go up and say I want to see her.'

'If I say that, I'm quite sure she won't come.'

Richard waxed in anger.

'But she *shall* come! Go and say I want to see her, and that
if she doesn't come down I'll force the door. There'll have
to be an end to this damned foolery. I've got no time to spend
humbugging. It's four o'clock, and I have letters to write before dinner. Tell her I must see her, and have done with it.'

Alice went upstairs with small hope of success. She
knocked twice before receiving an answer.

'Mother, are you there?'

'What do you want?' came back in a voice of irritation.

'Dick's here, and wants to speak to you. He says he *must*
see you; it's something very important.'

'I've nothing to do with him,' was the reply.

'Will you see him if he comes up here?'

‘ No, I won't.’

Alice went down and repeated this. After a moment's hesitation Mutimer ascended the stairs by threes. He rapped loudly at the bed-room door. No answer was vouchsafed.

‘ Mother, you must either open the door or come downstairs,’ he cried with decision. ‘ This has gone on long enough. Which will you do ? ’

‘ I'll do neither,’ was the angry reply. ‘ What right have you to order me about, I'd like to know ? You mind your business, and I'll mind mine.’

‘ All right. Then I shall send for a man at once, and have the door forced.’

Mrs. Mutimer knew well the tone in which these words were spoken; more than once ere now it had been the preliminary of decided action. Already Richard had reached the head of the stairs, when he heard a key turn, and the bedroom door was thrown open with such violence that the walls shook. He approached the threshold and examined the interior.

There was only one noticeable change in the appearance of the bedroom since he had last seen it. The dressing-table was drawn near to the fire, and on it were a cup and saucer, a few plates, some knives, forks, and spoons, and a folded tablecloth. A kettle and a saucepan stood on the fender. Her bread and butter Mrs. Mutimer kept in a drawer. All the appointments of the chamber were as clean and orderly as could be.

The sight of his mother's face all but stilled Richard's anger; she was yellow and wasted; her hair seemed far more grizzled than he remembered it. She stood as far from him as she could get, in an attitude not devoid of dignity, and looked him straight in the face. He closed the door.

‘ Mother, I've not come here to quarrel with you,’ Mutimer began, his voice much softened. ‘ What's done is done, and there's no helping it. I can understand you being angry at first, but there's no sense in making enemies of us all in this way. It can't go on any longer—neither for your sake nor ours. I want to talk reasonably, and to make some kind of arrangement.’

‘ You want to get me out o' the 'ouse. I'm ready to go, an' glad to go. I've earnt my livin' before now, an' I'm not so old but I can do it again. You always was one for talkin', but the fewest words is best. Them as talks most isn't allus the most straightfor'ard.’

‘ It isn't that kind of talk that'll do any good, mother. I

tell you again, I'm not going to use angry words. You know perfectly well I've never behaved badly to you, and I'm not going to begin now. What I've got to say is that you've no right to go on like this. Whilst you've been shutting yourself up in this room, there's Alice living by herself, which it isn't right she should do; and there's 'Arry going to the bad as fast as he can, and just because you won't help to look after him. If you'll only think of it in the right way, you'll see that's a good deal your doing. If 'Arry turns out a scamp and a black-guard, it's you that 'll be greatly to blame for it. You might have helped to look after him. I always thought you'd more common sense. You may say what you like about me, and I don't care; but when you talk about working for your living, you ought to remember that there's work enough near at hand, if only you'd see to it.'

'I've nothing to do neither with you nor 'Arry nor Alice,' answered the old woman stubbornly. 'If 'Arry disgraces his name, he won't be the first as has done it. I done my best to bring you all up honest, but that was a long time ago, and things has changed. You're old enough to go your own ways, an' your ways isn't mine. I told you how it 'ud be, an' the only mistake I made was comin' to live here at all. Now I can't be left alone, an' I'll go. You've no call to tell me a second time.'

It was a long, miserable wrangle, lasting half an hour, before a possibility of agreement presented itself. Richard at length ceased to recriminate, and allowed his mother to talk herself to satiety. He then said:

'I'm thinking of giving up this house, mother. What I want to know is, whether it would please you to go back to the old place again? I ask you because I can think of no other way for putting you in comfort. You must say and think what you like, only just answer me the one question as I ask it—that is, honestly and good-temperedly. I shall have to take 'Arry away with me; I can't let him go to the dogs without another try to keep him straight. Alice 'll have to go with me too, at all events for a time. Whether we like it or not, she'll have to accustom herself to new ways, and I see my way to helping her. I don't know whether you've been told that Mrs. Chatta-way's been living in the house since the others went away. The furniture's just as you left it; I dare say you'd feel it like going home again.'

'They've gone, have they?' Mrs. Mutimer asked, as if unwilling to show the interest which this proposal had excited in her.

'Yes, they went more than a month ago. We put Mrs. Chattaway in just to keep the place in order. I look on the house as yours. You might let Mrs. Chattaway stay there still, perhaps; but that's just as you please. You oughtn't to live quite alone.'

Mrs. Mutimer did not soften, but, after many words, Richard understood her to agree to what he proposed. She had stood all through the dialogue; now at length she moved to a seat, and sank upon it with trembling limbs. Richard wished to go, but had a difficulty in leaving abruptly. Darkness had fallen whilst they talked; they only saw each other by the light of the fire.

'Am I to come and see you or not, mother, when you get back to the old quarters?'

She did not reply.

'You won't tell me?'

'You must come or stay away, as it suits you,' she said, in a tone of indifference.

'Very well, then I shall come, if it's only to tell you about 'Arry and Alice. And now will you let Alice come up and have some tea with you?'

There was no answer.

'Then I'll tell her she may,' he said kindly, and went from the room.

He found Alice in the drawing-room, and persuaded her to go up.

'Just take it as if there 'd been nothing wrong,' he said to his sister. 'She's had a wretched time of it, I can see that. Take some tea-cakes up with you, and talk about going back to the Square as if she'd proposed it herself. We mustn't be hard with her just because she can't change, poor old soul.'

Socialistic business took him away during the evening. When he returned at eleven o'clock, 'Arry had not yet come in. Shortly before one there were sounds of ineffectual effort at the front-door latch. Mutimer, who happened to be crossing the hall, heard them, and went to open the door. The result was that his brother fell forward at full length upon the mat.

'Get up, drunken beast!' Richard exclaimed angrily.

'Beast yourself,' was the hiccupped reply, repeated several times whilst 'Arry struggled to his feet. Then, propping himself against the door-post, the maligned youth assumed the attitude of pugilism, inviting all and sundry to come on and have their lights extinguished. Richard flung him into the hall and closed the door. 'Arry had again to struggle with gravitation.

'Walk upstairs, if you can!' ordered his brother with contemptuous severity.

After much trouble 'Arry was got to his room, thrust in, and the door slammed behind him.

Richard was not disposed to argue with his brother this time. He waited in the dining-room next morning till the champion of liberty presented himself; then, scarcely looking at him, said with quiet determination :

'Pack your clothes some time to-day. You're going to Wanley to-morrow morning.'

'Not unless I choose,' remarked 'Arry.

'You look here,' exclaimed the elder, with concentrated savageness which did credit to his powers of command. 'What you choose has nothing to do with it, and that you'll please to understand. At half-past nine to-morrow morning you're ready for me in this room; hear that? I'll have an end to this kind of thing, or I'll know the reason why. Speak a word of impudence to me and I'll knock half your teeth out!'

He was capable of doing it. 'Arry got to his morning meal in silence.

In the course of the morning Mr. Keene called. Mutimer received him in the dining-room, and they smoked together. Their talk was of the meetings to be held in the evening.

'There'll be nasty doings up there,' Keene remarked, indicating with his head the gathering place of Comrade Roodhouse's adherents.

'Of what kind?' Mutimer asked with indifference.

'There's disagreeable talk going about. Probably they'll indulge in personalities a good deal.'

'Of course they will,' assented the other after a short pause. 'Westlake, eh?'

'Not only Westlake. There's a more important man.'

Mutimer could not resist a smile, though he was uneasy. Keene understood the smile; it was always an encouragement to him.

'What have they got hold of?'

'I'm afraid there'll be references to the girl.'

'The girl?' Richard hesitated. 'What girl? What do you know about any girl?'

'It's only the gossip I've heard. I thought it would be as well if I went about among them last night just to pick up hints, you know.'

'They're talking about that, are they? Well, let them. It isn't hard to invent lies.'

'Just so,' observed Mr. Keene sympathisingly. 'Of course I know they'd twisted the affair.'

Mutimer glanced at him and smoked in silence.

'I think I'd better be there to-night,' the journalist continued. 'I shall be more useful there than at the hall.'

'As you like,' said Mutimer lightly.

The subject was not pursued.

Though the occasion was of so much importance, Commonwealth Hall contained but a moderate audience when Mr. Westlake rose to deliver his address. The people who occupied the benches were obviously of a different stamp from those wont to assemble at the Hoxton meeting-place. There were perhaps a dozen artisans of intensely sober appearance, and the rest were men and women who certainly had never wrought with their hands. Near Mrs. Westlake sat several ladies, her personal friends. Of the men other than artisans the majority were young, and showed the countenance which bespeaks meritorious intelligence rather than ardour of heart or brain. Of enthusiasts in the true sense none could be discerned. It needed but a glance over this assembly to understand how very theoretical were the convictions that had brought its members together.

Mr. Westlake's address was interesting, very interesting; he had prepared it with much care, and its literary qualities were admired when subsequently it saw the light in one of the leading periodicals. Now and then he touched eloquence; the sincerity animating him was unmistakable, and the ideal he glorified was worthy of a noble mind. Not in anger did he speak of the schism from which the movement was suffering; even his sorrow was dominated by a gospel of hope. Optimism of the most fervid kind glowed through his discourse; he grew almost lyrical in his anticipation of the good time coming. For to-night it seemed to him that encouragement should be the prevailing note; it was always easy to see the dark side of things. Their work, he told his hearers, was but just beginning. They aimed at nothing less than a revolution, and revolutions were not brought about in a day. None of them would in the flesh behold the reign of justice; was that a reason why they should neglect the highest impulses of their nature and sit contented in the shadow of the world's mourning? He spoke with passion of the millions disinherited before their birth, with infinite tenderness of those weak ones whom our social system condemns to a life of torture just because they *are* weak. One loved the man for his great heart and for his gift of moving speech.

His wife sat, as she always did when listening intently, her body bent forward, one hand supporting her chin. Her eyes never quitted his face.

To the second speaker it had fallen to handle in detail the differences of the hour. Mutimer's exordium was not inspiriting after the rich-rolling periods with which Mr. Westlake had come to an end; his hard voice contrasted painfully with the other's cultured tones. Richard was probably conscious of this, for he hesitated more than was his wont, seeking words which did not come naturally to him. However, he warmed to his work, and was soon giving his audience clearly to understand how he, Richard Mutimer, regarded the proceedings of Comrade Roodhouse. Let us be practical—this was the burden of his exhortation. We are Englishmen—and women—not flighty, frothy foreigners. Besides, we have the blessings of free speech, and with the tongue and pen we must be content to fight, other modes of warfare being barbarous. Those who in their inconsiderate zeal had severed the Socialist body, were taking upon themselves a very grave responsibility; not only had they troubled the movement internally, but they would doubtless succeed in giving it a bad name with many who were hitherto merely indifferent, and who might in time have been brought over. Let it be understood that in this hall the true doctrine was preached, and that the 'Fiery Cross' was the true organ of English Socialism as distinguished from foreign crazes. The strength of England had ever been her sobriety; Englishmen did not fly at impossibilities like noisy children. He would not hesitate to say that the revolutionism preached in the newspaper called the 'Tocsin' was dangerous, was immoral. And so on.

Richard was not at his best this evening. You might have seen Mrs. Westlake abandon her attentive position, and lean back rather wearily; you might have seen a covert smile on a few of the more intelligent faces. It was awkward for Mutimer to be praising moderation in a movement directed against capital, and this was not exactly the audience for eulogies of

Great Britain at the expense of other countries. The applause when the orator seated himself was anything but hearty. Richard knew it, and inwardly cursed Mr. Westlake for taking the wind out of his sails.

Very different was the scene in the meeting-room behind the coffee-shop. There, upon Comrade Roodhouse's harangue, followed a debate more stirring than any on the records of the Islington and Hoxton branch. The room was thoroughly full; the roof rang with tempestuous acclamations. Messrs. Cowes and Cullen were in their glory; they roared with delight at each depreciatory epithet applied to Mr. Westlake and his henchmen, and prompted the speakers with words and phrases of a rich vernacular. If anything, Comrade Roodhouse fell a little short of what was expected of him. His friends had come together prepared for gory language, but the murderous instigations of Clerkenwell Green were not repeated with the same crudity. The speaker dealt in negatives; not thus and thus was the social millennium to be brought about, it was open to his hearers to conceive the practical course. For the rest, the heresiarch had a mighty flow of vituperative speech. Aspirates troubled him, so that for the most part he cast them away, and the syntax of his periods was often anacoluthic; but these matters were of no moment.

Questions being called for, Mr. Cowes and Mr. Cullen of course started up simultaneously. The former gentleman got the ear of the meeting. With preliminary swaying of the hand, he looked round as one about to propound a question which would for ever establish his reputation for acumen. In his voice of quiet malice, with his frequent deliberate pauses, with the wonted emphasis on absurd pronunciations, he spoke somewhat thus:—

'In the course of his address—I shall say nothin' about its qualities, the time for discussion will come presently—our Comrade has said not a few 'ard things about certain indivi-dooals who put themselves forward as perractical Socialists——'

'Not 'ard enough!' roared a voice from the back of the room.

Mr. Cowes turned his lank figure deliberately, and gazed for a moment in the quarter whence the interruption had come. Then he resumed.

'I agree with that involuntary exclamation. Certainly, not 'ard enough. And the question I wish to put to our Com rade is this: Is he, or is he not, aweer of certain scandalous doin's on the part of one of these said individooals, I might say actions which, from the Socialist point of view, amount to crimes? If our Comrade is aweer of what I refer to, then it seems to me it was his dooty to distinctly mention it. If he was *not* aweer, then we in this neighbourhood shall be only too glad to enlighten him. I distinctly assert that a certain individooal we all have in our thoughts has proved himself a traitor to the cause of the people. Comrades will understand me. And that's the question I wish to put.'

Mr. Cowes had introduced the subject which a considerable number of those present were bent on publicly discussing. Who it was that had first spread the story of Mutimer's matrimonial concerns probably no one could have determined. It was not Daniel Dabbs, though Daniel, partly from genuine indignation, partly in consequence of slowly growing personal feeling against the Mutimers, had certainly supplied Richard's enemies with corroborative details. Under ordinary circumstances Mutimer's change of fortune would have seemed to his old mates a sufficient explanation of his behaviour to Emma Vine; they certainly would not have gone out of their way to condemn him. But Richard was by this time vastly unpopular with most of those who had once glorified him. Envy had had time to grow, and was assisted by Richard's avoidance of personal contact with his Hoxton friends. When they spoke of him now it was with sneers and sarcasms. Some one had confidently asserted that the so-called Socialistic enterprise at Wanley was a mere pretence, that Mutimer was making money just like any other capitalist, and the leaguers of Hoxton firmly believed this. They encouraged one another to positive hatred of the working man who had suddenly become wealthy; his name stank in their nostrils. This, in a great measure, explained Comrade Roodhouse's success; personal feeling is almost always the spring of public action among the uneducated. In the excitement of the schism a few of the more energetic spirits had determined to drag Richard's domestic concerns into publicity. They suddenly became aware that private morality was at the root of the general good; they urged each other to righteous indignation in a matter for which they did not really care two straws. Thus Mr. Cowes's question was received with vociferous approval. Those present who did not understand the allusion were quickly enlightened by their neighbours. A crowd of Englishmen working itself into a moral rage is as glorious a spectacle as the world can show. Not one of these

men but heartily believed himself justified in reviling the traitor
to his class, the betrayer of confiding innocence. Remember,
too, how it facilitates speech to have a concrete topic on which
to enlarge; in this matter a West End drawing-room and the
Hoxton coffee-shop are akin. Regularity of procedure was at
an end; question grew to debate, and debate was riot. Mr.
Cullen succeeded Mr. Cowes and roared himself hoarse, defying
the feeble protests of the chairman. He abandoned mere allusion, and rejoiced the meeting by declaring names. His
example was followed by those who succeeded him.

Little did Emma think, as she sat working, Sunday though
it was, in her poor room, that her sorrows were being blared
forth to a gross assembly in venomous accusation against the
man who had wronged her. We can imagine that the knowledge would not greatly have soothed her.

Comrade Roodhouse at length obtained a hearing. It was
his policy to deprecate these extreme personalities, and in doing
so he heaped on the enemy greater condemnation. There was
not a little art in the heresiarch's modes of speech; the less
obtuse appreciated him and bade him live for ever. The secretary of the branch busily took notes.

When the meeting had broken up into groups, a number of
the more prominent Socialists surrounded Comrade Roodhouse
on the platform. Their talk was still of Mutimer, of his
shameless hypocrisy, his greed, his infernal arrogance. Near
at hand stood Mr. Keene; a word brought him into conversation with a neighbour. He began by repeating the prevalent
abuse, then, perceiving that his hearer merely gave assent in
general terms, he added :—

'I shouldn't wonder, though, if there was some reason we
haven't heard of—I mean, about the girl, you know.'

'Think so?' said the other.

'Well, I *have* heard it said—but then one doesn't care to
repeat such things.'

'What's that, eh?' put in another man, who had caught
the words.

'Oh, nothing. Only the girl's made herself scarce. Dare
say the fault wasn't altogether on one side.'

And Mr. Keene winked meaningly.

The hint spread among those on the platform. Daniel
Dabbs happened to hear it repeated in a gross form.

'Who's been a-sayin' that?' he roared. 'Where have you
got that from, eh?'

The source was already forgotten, but Daniel would not let the calumny take its way unopposed. He harangued those about him with furious indignation.

'If any man's got a word to say against Emma Vine, let him come an' say it to me, that's all! Now look 'ere, all o' you, I know that girl, and I know that anyone as talks like that about her tells a damned lie.'

'Most like it's Mutimer himself as has set it goin',' observed someone.

In five minutes all who remained in the room were convinced that Mutimer had sent an agent to the meeting for the purpose of assailing Emma Vine's good name. Mr. Keene had already taken his departure, and no suspicious character was discernible; a pity, for the evening might have ended in a picturesque way.

But Daniel Dabbs went home to his brother's public-house, obtained note-paper and an envelope, and forthwith indited a brief epistle which he addressed to the house in Highbury. It had no formal commencement, and ended with 'Yours, &c.' Daniel demanded an assurance that his former friend had not instigated certain vile accusations against Emma, and informed him that whatever answer was received would be read aloud at next Sunday's meeting.

The one not wholly ignoble incident in that evening's transactions.

CHAPTER XVIII.

In the partial reconciliation between Mrs. Mutimer and her children there was no tenderness on either side. The old conditions could not be restored, and the habits of the family did not lend themselves to the polite hypocrisy which lubricates the wheels of the refined world. There was to be a parting, and probably it would be for life. In Richard's household his mother could never have a part, and when Alice married, doubtless the same social difficulty would present itself. It was not the future to which Mrs. Mutimer had looked forward, but, having said her say, she resigned herself and hardened her heart. At least she would die in the familiar home.

Richard had supper with his sister on his return from

Commonwealth Hall, and their plans were discussed in further detail.

'I want you,' he said, 'to go to the Square with mother to-morrow, and to stay there till Wednesday. You won't mind doing that?'

'I think she'd do every bit as well without me,' said Alice.

'Never mind; I should like you to go. I'll take 'Arry down to-morrow morning, then I'll come and fetch you on Wednesday. You'll just see that everything's comfortable in the house, and buy her a few presents, the kind of things she'd like.'

'I don't suppose she'll take anything.'

'Try, at all events. And don't mind her talk; it does no harm.'

In the morning came the letter from Daniel Dabbs. Richard read it without any feeling of surprise, still less with indignation, at the calumny of which it complained. During the night he had wondered uneasily what might have occurred at the Hoxton meeting, and the result was a revival of his ignoble anger against Emma. Had he not anxiety enough that she must bring him new trouble when he believed that all relations between him and her were at an end? Doubtless she was posing as a martyr before all who knew anything of her story; why had she refused his money, if not that her case might seem all the harder? It were difficult to say whether he really believed this; in a nature essentially egoistic, there is often no line to be drawn between genuine convictions and the irresponsible charges of resentment. Mutimer had so persistently trained himself to regard Emma as in the wrong, that it was no wonder if he had lost the power of judging sanely in any matter connected with her. Her refusal to benefit by his generosity had aggravated him; actually, no doubt, because she thus deprived him of a defence against his conscience.

He was not surprised that libellous rumours were afloat, simply because since his yesterday's conversation with Keene the thought of justifying himself in some such way—should it really prove necessary—had several times occurred to him, suggested probably by Keene's own words. That the journalist had found means of doing him this service was very likely indeed. He remembered with satisfaction that no hint of such a thing had escaped his own lips. Still, he was uneasy. Keene might have fallen short of prudence, with the result that Daniel Dabbs might be in a position to trace this calumny to

R

him, Mutimer. It would not be pleasant if the affair, thus
represented, came to the ears of his friends, particularly of
Mr. Westlake.

He had just finished his breakfast, and was glancing over
the newspaper in a dull and irritable mood, when Keene himself arrived. Mutimer expected him. Alice quitted the
dining-room when he was announced, and 'Arry, who at the
same moment came in for breakfast, was bidden go about his
business, and be ready to leave the house in half-an-hour.

'What does this mean?' Richard asked abruptly, handing
the letter to his visitor.

Keene perused the crabbed writing, and uttered sundry
'Ah's' and 'Hum's.'

'Do you know anything about it?' Mutimer continued, in
a tone between mere annoyance and serious indignation.

'I think I had better tell you what took place last night,'
said the journalist, with side glances. He had never altogether
thrown off the deferential manner when conversing with his
patron, and at present he emphasised it. 'Those fellows carry
party feeling too far; the proceedings were scandalous. It
really was enough to make one feel that one mustn't be too
scrupulous in trying to stop their mouths. If I'm not mistaken, an action for defamation of character would lie against
half-a-dozen of them.'

Mutimer was unfortunately deficient in sense of humour.
He continued to scowl, and merely said: 'Go on; what
happened?'

Mr. Keene allowed the evening's proceedings to lose nothing
in his narration. He was successful in exciting his hearer to
wrath, but, to his consternation, it was forthwith turned against
himself.

'And you tried to make things better by going about telling
what several of them would know perfectly well to be lies?'
exclaimed Mutimer, savagely. 'Who the devil gave you
authority to do so?'

'My dear sir,' protested the journalist, 'you have quite
mistaken me. I did not mean to admit that I had told lies.
How could I for a moment suppose that a man of your
character would sanction that kind of thing? Pooh, I hope
I know you better! No, no; I merely in the course of conversation ventured to hint that, as you yourself had explained to
me, there were reasons quite other than the vulgar mind would
conceive for—for the course you had pursued. To my own

apprehension such reasons are abundant, and, I will add, most conclusive. You have not endeavoured to explain them to me in detail; I trust you felt that I was not so dull of understanding as to be incapable of — of appreciating motives when sufficiently indicated. Situations of this kind are *never* to be explained grossly; I mean, of course, in the case of men of intellect. I flatter myself that I have come to know your ruling principles; and I will say that beyond a doubt your behaviour has been most honourable. Of course I was mistaken in trying to convey this to those I talked with last night; they misinterpreted me, and I might have expected it. We cannot give them the moral feelings which they lack. But I am glad that the error has so quickly come to light. A mere word from you, and such a delusion goes no farther. I regret it extremely.'

Mutimer held the letter in his hand, and kept looking from it to the speaker. Keene's subtleties were not very intelligible to him, but, even with a shrewd suspicion that he was being humbugged, he could not resist a sense of pleasure in hearing himself classed with the superior men whose actions are not to be explained by the vulgar. Nay, he asked himself whether the defence was not in fact a just one. After all, was it not possible that his conduct had been praiseworthy? He recovered the argument by which he had formerly tried to silence disagreeable inner voices; a man in his position owed it to society to effect a union of classes, and private feeling must give way before the higher motive. He reflected for a moment when Keene ceased to speak.

'What did you say?' he then asked, still bluntly, but with less anger. 'Just tell me the words, as far as you can remember.'

Keene was at no loss to recall inoffensive phrases; in another long speech, full of cajolery sufficiently artful for the occasion, he represented himself as having merely protested against misrepresentations obviously sharpened by malice.

'It is just possible that I made some reference to her *character*,' he admitted, speaking more slowly, and as if desirous that no word should escape his hearer; 'but it did not occur to me to guard against misunderstandings of the word. I might have remembered that it has such different meanings on the lips of educated and of uneducated men. You, of course, would never have missed my thoughts.'

'If I might suggest,' he added, when Mutimer kept silence, 'I think, if you condescend to notice the letter at all, you should reply only in the most general terms. Who is this man Dabbs, I wonder, who has the impudence to write to you in this way?'

'Oh, one of the Hoxton Socialists, I suppose,' Mutimer answered carelessly. 'I remember the name.'

'A gross impertinence! By no means encourage them in thinking you owe explanations. Your position doesn't allow anything of the kind.'

'All right,' said Richard, his ill-humour gone; 'I'll see to it.'

He was not able, after all, to catch the early train by which he had meant to take his brother to Wanley. He did not like to leave without some kind of good-bye to his mother, and Alice said that the old woman would not be ready to go before eleven o'clock. After half an hour of restlessness he sat down to answer Daniel's letter. Keene's flattery had not been without its fruit. From anger which had in it an element of apprehension he passed to an arrogant self-confidence which character and circumstances were conspiring to make his habitual mood. It *was* a gross impertinence in Daniel to address him thus. What was the use of wealth if it did not exempt one from the petty laws binding on miserable hand-to-mouth toilers! He would have done with Emma Vine; his time was of too much value to the world to be consumed in wranglings about a work-girl. What if here and there someone believed the calumny? Would it do Emma any harm? That was most unlikely. On the whole, the misunderstanding was useful; let it take its course. Men with large aims cannot afford to be scrupulous in small details. Was not New Wanley a sufficient balance against a piece of injustice, which, after all, was only one of words?

He wrote:

'DEAR SIR,—I have received your letter, but it is impossible for me to spend time in refuting idle stories. What's more, I cannot see that my private concerns are a fit subject for discussion at a public meeting, as I understand they have been made. You are at liberty to read this note when and where you please, and in that intention let me add that the cause of Socialism will not be advanced by attacks on the character of those most earnestly devoted to it. I remain, yours truly,   'RICHARD MUTIMER.'

It seemed to Richard that this was the very thing, alike in

tone and phrasing. A week or two previously a certain statesman had written to the same effect in reply to calumnious
statements; and Richard consciously made that letter his model.
The statesman had probably been sounder in his syntax, but
his imitator had, no doubt, the advantage in other points.
Richard perused his composition several times, and sent it to
the post.

At eleven o'clock Mrs. Mutimer descended to the hall,
ready for her journey. She would not enter any room. Her
eldest son came out to meet her, and got rid of the servant
who had fetched a cab.

'Good-bye for the present, mother,' he said, giving his
hand. 'I hope you'll find everything just as you wish it.'

'If I don't, I shan't complain,' was the cold reply.

The old woman had clad herself, since her retreat, in the
garments of former days; and the truth must be told that they
did not add to the dignity of her appearance. Probably no
costume devisable could surpass in ignoble ugliness the attire
of an English working-class widow when she appears in the
streets. The proximity of Alice, always becomingly clad,
drew attention to the poor mother's plebeian guise. Richard,
watching her enter the cab, felt for the first time a distinct
shame. His feelings might have done him more credit but
for the repulse he had suffered.

'Arry contented himself with standing at the front-room
window, his hands in his pockets.

Later in the same day Daniel Dabbs, who had by chance
been following the British workman's practice and devoting
Monday to recreation, entered an omnibus in which Mrs.
Clay was riding. She had a heavy bundle on her lap, shop-
work which she was taking home. Daniel had already received Mutimer's reply, and was nursing a fit of anger. He
seated himself by Kate's side, and conversed with her.

'Heard anything from *him* lately?' he asked, with a motion
of the head which rendered mention of names unnecessary.

'Not we,' Kate replied bitterly, her eyes fixing themselves
in scorn.

'No loss,' remarked Daniel, with an expression of disgust.

'He'll hear from *me* some day,' said the woman, 'and in a
way as he won't like.'

The noise of the vehicle did not favour conversation.
Daniel waited till Kate got out, then he too descended, and
walked along by her side. He did not offer to relieve her of

the bundle—in primitive societies woman is naturally the burden-bearer.

'I wouldn't a' thought it o' Dick,' he said, his head thrust forward, and his eyes turning doggedly from side to side. ' They say as how too much money ain't good for a man, but it's changed *him* past all knowin'.'

'He always had a good deal too much to say for himself,' remarked Mrs. Clay, speaking with difficulty through her quickened breath, the bundle almost more than she could manage.

'I wish just now as he'd say a bit more,' said Daniel. Now, see, here's a letter I've just got from him. I wrote to him last night to let him know of things as was goin' round at the lecture. There's one or two of our men, you know, think he'd ought to be made to smart a bit for the way he's treated Emma, and last night they up an' spoke—you should just a 'eard them. Then someone set it goin' as the fault wasn't Dick's at all. See what I mean ? I don't know who started that. I can't think as he'd try to blacken a girl's name just to excuse himself; that's goin' a bit too far.'

Mrs. Clay came to a standstill.

'He's been saying things of Emma ?' she cried. 'Is that what you mean ?'

'Well, see now. I couldn't believe it, an' I don't rightly believe it yet. I'll read you the answer as he's sent me.'

Daniel gave forth the letter, getting rather lost amid its pretentious periods, with the eccentric pauses and intonation of an uneducated reader. Standing in a busy thoroughfare, he and Kate almost blocked the pavement ; impatient pedestrians pushed against them, and uttered maledictions.

'I suppose that's Dick's new way o' sayin' he hadn't nothin' to do with it,' Daniel commented at the end. 'Money seems always to bring long words with it somehow. It seems to me he'd ought to speak plainer.'

'Who's done it, if he didn't ?' Kate exclaimed, with shrill anger. 'You don't suppose there's another man 'ud go about telling coward lies ? The mean wretch ! Says things about my sister, does he ? I'll be even with that man yet, never you mind.'

'Well, I can't believe it o' Dick,' muttered Dabbs. 'He says 'ere, you see, as he hasn't time to contradict "idle stories." I suppose that means he didn't start 'em.'

'If he tells one lie, won't he tell another ?' cried the woman.

She was obliged to put down her bundle on a doorstep, and used the moment of relief to pour forth vigorous vituperation. Dick listened with an air half of approval, half doggedly doubtful. He was not altogether satisfied with himself.

'Well, I must get off 'ome,' he said at length. 'It's only right as you should know what's goin' on. There's no one believes a word of it, and that you can tell Emma. If I hear it repeated, you may be sure I'll up an' say what I think. It won't go no further if I can stop it. Well, so long! Give my respects to your sister.'

Daniel waved his arm and made off across the street. Kate, clutching her bundle again, panted along by-ways; reaching the house-door she rang a bell twice, and Emma admitted her. They climbed together to an upper room, where Kate flung her burden on to the floor and began at once to relate with vehemence all that Daniel had told her. The calumny lost nothing in her repetition. After listening in surprise for a few moments, Emma turned away and quietly began to cut bread and butter for the children, who were having their tea.

'Haven't you got anything to say?' cried her sister. 'I suppose he'll be telling his foul lies about me next. Oh, he's a good-'earted man, is Mutimer! Perhaps you'll believe me now. Are you going to let him talk what he likes about you?'

Since the abandonment of the house in Wilton Square, Kate had incessantly railed in this way; it was a joy to her to have discovered new matter for invective. Emma's persistent silence maddened her; even now not a word was to be got from the girl.

'Can't you speak?' shrilled Mrs. Clay. 'If you don't do something, I let you know that I shall! I'm not going to stand this kind o' thing, don't think it. If they talk ill of you they'll do the same of me. It's time that devil had something for himself. You might be made o' stone! I only hope I may meet him in the streets, that's all! I'll show him up, see if I don't! I'll let all the people know what he is, the cur! I'll do something to make him give me in charge, and then I'll tell it all out before the magistrates. I don't care what comes, I'll find some way of paying out that beast!'

Emma turned angrily.

'Hold your tongue, Kate! If you go on like this day after day we shall have to part; I can't put up with it, so there now! I've begged and prayed you to stop, and you don't pay the least heed to me; I think you might have more kindness. You'll never make me say a single word about him, do what you will; I've told you that many a time, and I mean what I say. Let him say what he likes and do what he likes. It's nothing to me, and it doesn't concern you. You'll drive me out of the house again, like you did the other night. I can't bear it. Do you understand, Kate?—I can't bear it!'

Her voice shook, and there were tears of uttermost shame and misery in her eyes. The children sitting at the table, though accustomed to scenes of this kind, looked at the disputants with troubled faces, and at length the younger began to cry. Emma at once turned to the little one with smiles of re-assurance. Kate would have preferred to deal slaps, but contented herself with taking a cup of tea to the fireside, and sulking for half an hour.

Emma unrolled the bundle of work, and soon the hum of the sewing-machine began, to continue late into the night.

CHAPTER XIX.

You remember that one side of the valley in which stood New Wanley was clad with trees. Through this wood a public path made transverse ascent to the shoulder of the hill, a way little used save by Wanley ramblers in summer time. The section of the wood above the path was closed against trespassers; among the copses below anyone might freely wander. In places it was scarcely possible to make a way for fern, bramble, and underwood, but elsewhere mossy tracks led one among hazels or under arches of foliage which made of the mid-day sky a cool, golden shimmer. One such track, abruptly turning round a great rock over the face of which drooped the boughs of an ash, came upon a little sloping lawn, which started from a high hazel-covered bank. The bank itself was so shaped as to afford an easy seat, shaded even when the grass in front was all sunshine.

Adela had long known this retreat, and had been accustomed to sit here with Letty, especially when she needed to exchange deep confidences with her friend. Once, just as they were settling themselves upon the bank, they were startled by a movement among the leaves above, followed by the voice of someone addressing them with cheerful friendliness, and making request to be allowed to descend and join them. It was Hubert Eldon, just home for the long vacation. Once or twice subsequently the girls had met Hubert on the same spot; there had been a picnic here, too, in which Mrs. Eldon and Mrs. Waltham took part. But Adela always thought of the place as peculiarly her own. To others it was only a delightfully secluded corner of the wood, fresh and green; for her it had something intimately dear, as the haunt where she had first met her own self face to face and had heard the whispering of secrets as if by another voice to her tremulous heart.

She sat here one morning in July, six months after her marriage. It was more than a year since she had seen the spot, and on reaching it to-day it seemed to her less beautiful than formerly; the leafage was to her eyes thinner and less warm of hue than in earlier years, the grass had a coarser look and did not clothe the soil so completely. An impulse had brought her hither, and her first sense on arriving had been one of disappointment. Was the change in her way of seeing? or had the retreat indeed suffered, perchance from the smoke of New Wanley? The disappointment was like that we experience in revisiting a place kept only in memory since childhood. Adela had not travelled much in the past year, but her growth in experience had put great tracts between her and the days when she came here to listen and wonder. It was indeed a memory of her childhood that led her into the wood.

She had brought with her a German book on Socialism and a little German dictionary. At the advice of Mr. Westlake, given some months ago on the occasion of a visit to the Manor, she had applied herself diligently to this study. But it was not only with a view to using the time that she had selected these books this morning. In visiting a scene which would strongly revive the past, instinct—rather than conscious purpose—had bidden her keep firm hold upon the present. On experiencing her disillusion a sense of trouble had almost led her to retrace her steps at once, but she overcame this, and, seating herself on the familiar bank, began to toil through hard sentences. Such moments of self-discipline were of daily occurrence in her life; she kept watch and ward over her feelings and found in efforts of the mind a short way out of inner conflicts which she durst not suffer to pass beyond the first stage.

Near at hand there grew a silver birch. Hubert Eldon, on one of the occasions when he talked here with Adela and Letty, had by chance let his eyes wander from Adela to the birch tree, and his fancy, just then active among tender images, suggested a likeness between that graceful, gleaming stem with its delicately drooping foliage and the sweet-featured girl who stood before him with her head bowed in unconscious loveliness. As the silver birch among the trees of the wood, so was Adela among the men and women of the world. And to one looking upon her by chance such a comparison might still have occurred. But in face she was no longer what she had then been. Her eyebrows, formerly so smooth and smiling, now constantly drew themselves together as if at a thought of pain or in some mental exertion. Her cheeks had none of their maiden colour. Her lips were closed too firmly, and sometimes trembled like those of old persons who have known much trouble.

In spite of herself her attention flagged from the hard, dull book; the spirit of the place was too strong for her, and, as in summers gone by, she was lost in vision. But not with eyes like these had she been wont to dream on the green branches or on the sward that lay deep in sunlight. On her raised lids sat the heaviness of mourning; she seemed to strain her sight to something very far off, something which withdrew itself from her desire, upon which her soul called and called in vain. Her cheeks showed their thinness, her brow foretold the lines which would mark it when she grew old. It was a sob in her throat which called her back to consciousness, a sob which her lips, well-trained warders, would not allow to pass.

She forced herself to the book again, and for some minutes plied her dictionary with feverish zeal. Then there came over her countenance a strange gleam of joy, as if she triumphed in self-conquest. She smiled as she continued her work, clearly making a happiness of each mastered sentence. And, looking up with the smile still fixed, she found that her solitude was invaded. Letty Tew had just appeared round the rock which sheltered the green haven.

'You here, Adela?' the girl exclaimed. 'How strange!'

'Why strange, Letty?'

'Oh, only because I had a sort of feeling that perhaps I might meet you. Not here, particularly,' she added, as if eager to explain herself, 'but somewhere in the wood. The day is so fine; it tempts one to walk about.'

Letty did not approach her friend as she would have done when formerly they met here. Her manner was constrained, almost timid; it seemed an afterthought when she bent forward for the kiss. Since Adela's marriage the intercourse between them had been comparatively slight. For the first three months they had seen each other only at long intervals, in part owing to circumstances. After the fortnight she spent in London at the time of her marriage, Adela had returned to Wanley in far from her usual state of health; during the first days of February there had been a fear that she might fall gravely ill. Only in advanced spring had she begun to go beyond the grounds of the Manor, and it was still unusual for her to do so except in her carriage. Letty had acquiesced in the altered relations; she suffered, and for various reasons, but did not endeavour to revive an intimacy which Adela seemed no longer to desire. Visits to the Manor were from the first distressing to her; the natural subjects of conversation were those which both avoided, and to talk in the manner of mere acquaintances was scarcely possible. Of course this state of things led to remark. Mrs. Waltham was inclined to suspect some wrong feeling on Letty's side, though of what nature it was hard to determine. Alfred, on the other hand, took his sister's behaviour ill, more especially as he felt a distinct change in her manner to himself. Was the girl going to be spoilt by the possession of wealth? What on earth did she mean by her reserve, her cold dignity? Wasn't Letty good enough for her now that she was lady of the Manor? Letty herself, when the subject was spoken of, pretended to recognise no change beyond what was to be expected. So far from being hurt, her love for Adela grew warmer during these months of seeming estrangement; her only trouble was that she could not go often and sit by her friend's side—sit silently, hand holding hand. That would have been better than speech, which misled, or at best was inadequate. Meantime she supported herself with the hope that love might some day again render her worthy of Adela's confidence. That her friend was far above her she had always gladly confessed; she felt it more than ever now that she tried in vain to read Adela's secret thoughts. The marriage was a mystery to her; to the last moment she had prayed that something might prevent it. Yet, now that Adela was Mrs. Mutimer, she conscientiously put away every thought of discontent, and only wondered what high motive had dictated the choice and—for such she knew it must be—the sacrifice.

'What are you reading?' Letty asked, sitting down on the bank at a little distance.

'It's hardly to be called reading. I have to look out every

other word. It's a book by a man called Schaeffle, on the "Social Question."'

'Oh yes,' said the girl, hazarding a conjecture that the work had something to do with Socialism. 'Of course that interests you.'

'I think I'm going to write a translation of it. My husband doesn't read German, and this book is important.'

'I suppose you are quite a Socialist, Adela?' Letty inquired, in a tone which seemed anxious to presuppose the affirmative answer. She had never yet ventured to touch on the subject.

'Yes, I am a Socialist,' said Adela firmly. 'I am sure anyone will be who thinks about it, and really understands the need for Socialism. Does the word still sound a little dreadful to you? I remember so well when it did to me. It was only because I knew nothing about it.'

'I don't think I have that excuse,' said the other. 'Alfred is constantly explaining. But, Adela——'

She paused, not quite daring to speak her thoughts. Adela smiled an encouragement.

'I was going to say—— I'm sure you won't be offended. But you still go to church?'

'Oh yes, I go to church. You mustn't think that everything Alfred insists upon belongs to Socialism. I believe that all Christians ought to be Socialists; I think it is part of our religion, if only we carry it out faithfully.'

'But does Mr. Wyvern think so?'

'Yes, he does; he does indeed. I talk with Mr. Wyvern frequently, and I never knew, before he showed me, how necessary it is for a Christian to be a Socialist.'

'You surprise me, Adela. Yet he doesn't confess himself a Socialist.'

'Indeed, he does. When did you hear Mr. Wyvern preach a sermon without insisting on justice and unselfishness and love of our neighbour? If we try to be just and unselfish, and to love our neighbour as ourself, we help the cause of Socialism. Mr. Wyvern doesn't deal with politics—it is not necessary he should. That is for men like my husband, who give their lives to the practical work. Mr. Wyvern confines himself to spiritual teaching. He would injure his usefulness if he went beyond that.'

Letty was awed by the exceeding change which showed itself not only in Adela's ways of thought, but in her very voice and manner of speaking. The tone was so authoritative, so free from the diffidence which had formerly kept Adela from asserting strongly even her cherished faiths. She felt, too, that with the maiden hesitancy something else had gone, at all events in a great degree; something that it troubled her to miss; namely, that winning persuasiveness which had been one of the characteristics that made Adela so entirely lovable. At present Mrs. Mutimer scarcely sought to persuade; she uttered her beliefs as indubitable. A competent observer might now and then have surmised that she felt it needful to remind herself of the creed she had accepted.

'You were smiling when I first caught sight of you,' Letty said, after reflecting for a moment. 'Was it something in the book?'

Adela again smiled.

'No, something in myself,' she replied with an air of confidence.

'Because you are happy, Adela?'

'Yes, because I am happy.'

'How glad I am to hear that, dear!' Letty exclaimed, for the first time allowing herself to use the affectionate word. 'You will let me be glad with you?'

Her hands stole a little forward, but Adela did not notice it, for she was gazing straight before her, with an agitated look.

'Yes, I am very happy, I have found something to do in life. I was afraid at first that I shouldn't be able to give my husband any help in his work; I seemed useless. But I am learning, and I hope soon to be of real use, if only in little things. You know that I have begun to give a tea to the children every Wednesday? They're not in need of food and comforts, I'm glad to say; nobody wants in New Wanley; but it's nice to bring them together at the Manor, and teach them to behave gently to each other, and to sit properly at table, and things like that. Will you come and see them to-day?'

'I shall be very pleased.'

'To-day I'm going to begin something new. After tea we shall have a reading. Mr. Wyvern sent me a book this morning—"Andersen's Fairy Tales."'

'Oh, I've read them. Yes, that'll do nicely. Read them "The Ugly Duckling," Adela; it's a beautiful story. I thought perhaps you were going to read something—something instructive, you know.'

Adela laughed. It was Adela's laugh still, but not what it used to be.

'No, I want to amuse them. They get enough instruction in school. I hope soon to give another evening to the older girls. I wonder whether you would like to come and help me then?'

'If only you would let me! There is nothing I should like more than to do something for you.'

'But you mustn't do it for me. It must be for the girls' sake.'

'Yes, for theirs as well, but ever so much more for yours, dear. You can't think how glad I am that you have asked me.'

Again the little hand was put forward, and this time Adela took it. But she did not soften as she once would have done. With eyes still far away, she talked for some minutes of the hopes with which her life was filled. Frequently she made mention of her husband, and always as one to whom it was a privilege to devote herself. Her voice had little failings and uncertainties now and then, but this appeared to come of excessive feeling.

They rose and walked from the wood together.

'Alfred wants us to go to Malvern for a fortnight,' Letty said, when they were near the gates of the Manor. 'We were wondering whether you could come, Adela?'

'No, I can't leave Wanley,' was the reply. 'My husband'—she never referred to Mutimer otherwise than by this name—'spoke of the seaside the other day, but we decided not to go away at all. There is so much to be done.'

When Adela went to the drawing-room just before luncheon, she found Alice Mutimer engaged with a novel. Reading novels had become an absorbing occupation with Alice. She took them to bed with her so as to read late, and lay late in the morning for the same reason. She must have been one of Mr. Mudie's most diligent subscribers. She had no taste for walking in the country, and could only occasionally be persuaded to take a drive. It was not surprising that her face had not quite the healthy colour of a year ago; there was negligence, too, in her dress, and she had grown addicted to recumbent attitudes. Between her and Adela no semblance of friendship had yet arisen, though the latter frequently sought to substitute a nearer relation for superficial friendliness. Alice never exhibited anything short of good-will, but her first impressions were lasting; she suspected her sister-in-law of a desire to patronise, and was determined to allow nothing of the kind. With a more decided character, Alice's prepossessions would certainly have made life at the Manor anything but smooth; as it was, nothing ever occurred to make unpleasantness worth her while. Besides, when not buried in her novels, she gave herself up to absent-mindedness; Adela found conversation with her almost impossible, for Alice would answer a remark with a smiling 'Yes' or 'No,' and at once go off into dreamland, so that one hesitated to disturb her.

'What time is it?' she inquired, when she became aware of Adela moving about the room.

'All but half-past one.'

'Really? I suppose I must go and get ready for lunch. What a pity we can't do without meals!'

'You should go out in the morning and get an appetite. Really, you are getting very pale, Alice. I'm sure you read far too much.'

Adela had it on her lips to say 'too many novels,' but was afraid to administer a direct rebuke.

'Oh, I like reading, and I don't care a bit for going out.'

'What about your practising?' Adela asked, with a playful shake of the head.

'Yes, I know it's very neglectful, but really it is such awful work.'

'And your French?'

'I'll make a beginning to-morrow. At least, I think I will. I don't neglect things wilfully, but it's so awfully hard to really get at it when the time comes.'

The luncheon-bell rang, and Alice, with a cry of dismay, sped to her room. She knew that her brother was to lunch at home to-day, and Richard was terrible in the matter of punctuality.

As soon as the meal was over Alice hastened back to her low chair in the drawing-room. Richard and his wife went together into the garden.

'What do you think Rodman's been advising me this morning?' Mutimer said, speaking with a cigar in his mouth. 'It's a queer idea; I don't quite know what to think of it. You know there'll be a general election some time next year, and he advises me to stand for Belwick.'

He did not look at his wife. Coming to a garden-seat, he put up one foot upon it, and brushed the cigar ash against the

back.   Adela sat down; she had not replied at once, and was
thoughtful.

'As a Socialist candidate?' she asked, when at length he
turned his eyes to her.

'Well, I don't know. Radical rather, I should think. It
would come to the same thing, of course, and there'd be no use
in spoiling the thing for the sake of a name.'

Adela had a Japanese fan in her hand; she put it against
her forehead, and still seemed to consider.

'Do you think you could find time for Parliament?'

'That has to be thought of, of course; but by then I should
think we might arrange it. There's not much that Rodman
can't see to.'

'You are inclined to think of it?'

Adela's tone to her husband was not one of tenderness, but
of studious regard and deference. She very seldom turned her
eyes to his, but there was humility in her bent look. If ever he
and she began to speak at the same time, she checked herself
instantly, and Mutimer had no thought of giving her precedence.
This behaviour in his wife struck him as altogether becoming.

'I almost think I am,' he replied.   'I've a notion I could
give them an idea or two at Westminster. It would be news
to them to hear a man say what he really thinks.'

Adela smiled faintly, but said nothing.

'Would you like me to be in Parliament?' Richard asked,
putting down his foot and leaning back his head a little.

'Certainly, if you feel that it is a step gained.'

'That's just what I think it would be. Well, we must talk
about it again. By-the-by, I've just had to send a fellow about
his business.'

'To discharge a man?' Adela asked, with pain.

'Yes.   It's that man Rendal; I was talking about him the
other day, you remember. He's been getting drunk; I'll
warrant it's not the first time.'

'And you really must send him away? Couldn't you give
him another chance?'

'No. He was impudent to me, and I can't allow that.
He'll have to go.'

Richard spoke with decision. When the fact of impudence
was disclosed Adela felt that it was useless to plead. She
looked at her fan and was sorrowful.

'So you are going to read to the youngsters to-day?'
Mutimer recommenced.

'Yes; Mr. Wyvern has given me a book that will do very well indeed.'

'Oh, has he?' said Richard doubtfully. 'Is it a religious book? That kind of thing won't do, you know.'

'No, it isn't religious at all. Only a book of fairy tales.'

'Fairy tales!' There was scorn in his way of repeating the words. 'Couldn't you find something useful? A history book, you know, or about animals, or something of that kind. We mustn't encourage them in idle reading. And that reminds me of Alice. You really must get her away from those novels. I can't make out what's come to the girl. She seems to be going off her head. Did you notice at lunch?—she didn't seem to understand what I said to her. Do try and persuade her to practise, if nothing else.'

'I am afraid to do more than just advise in a pleasant way,' said Adela.

'Well, I shall lose my temper with her before long.'

'How is Harry doing?' Adela asked, to pass over the difficult subject.

'He's an idle scamp! If some one 'ud give him a good thrashing, that's what *he* wants.'

'Shall I ask him to dinner to-morrow?'

'You can if you like, of course,' Richard replied with hesitation. 'I shouldn't have thought you cared much about having him.'

'Oh, I am always very glad to have him. I have meant to ask you to let him dine with us oftener. I am so afraid he should think we neglect him, and that would be sure to have a bad effect.'

Mutimer looked at her with satisfaction, and assented to her reasoning.

'But about the fairy tales,' Adela said presently, when Richard had finished his cigar and was about to return to the works. 'Do you seriously object to them? Of course I could find another book.'

'What do *you* think? I am rather surprised that Wyvern suggested reading of that kind; he generally has good ideas.'

'I fancy he wished to give the children a better kind of amusement,' said Adela, with hesitation.

'A better kind, eh? Well, do as you like. I dare say it's no great harm.'

'But if you really——'

'No, no; read the tales. I dare say they wouldn't listen to
a better book.'

It was not very encouraging, but Adela ventured to abide
by the vicar's choice. She went to her own sitting-room and
sought the story that Letty had spoken of. From 'The Ugly
Duckling' she was led on to the story of the mermaid, from
that to the enchanted swans. The book had never been in her
hands before, and the delight she received from it was of a kind
quite new to her. She had to make an effort to close it and
turn to her specified occupations. For Adela had so systema-
tised her day that no minute's margin was left for self-indul-
gence. Her reading was serious study. If ever she was
tempted to throw open one of the volumes which Alice left
about, a glance at the pages was enough to make her push it
away as if it were impure. She had read very few stories of
any kind, and of late had felt a strong inclination towards such
literature; the spectacle of Alice's day-long absorption was
enough to excite her curiosity, even if there had not existed
other reasons. But these longings for a world of romance she
crushed down as unworthy of a woman to whom life had
revealed its dread significances : and, though she but conjectured
the matter and tone of the fiction Alice delighted in, instinctive fear would alone have restrained her from it. For pleasure
in the ordinary sense she did not admit into her scheme of
existence; the season for that had gone by. Henceforth she
must think, and work, and pray. Therefore she had set herself
gladly to learn German; it was a definite task to which such
and such hours could be devoted, and the labour would
strengthen her mind. Her ignorance she represented as a great
marsh which by toil had to be filled up and converted into solid
ground. She had gone through the library catalogue and made
a list of books which seemed needful to be read; and Mr.
Wyvern had been of service in guiding her, as well as in lending volumes from his own shelves. The vicar, indeed, had surprised her by the zealous kindness with which he entered into
all her plans; at first she had talked to him with apprehension,
remembering that chance alone had prevented her from appeal-
ing to him to save her from this marriage. But Mr. Wyvern,
with whose philosophy we have some acquaintance, exerted
himself to make the best of the irremediable, and Adela already
owed him much for his unobtrusive moral support. Even
Mutimer was putting aside his suspicions and beginning to
believe that the clergyman would have openly encouraged

Socialism had his position allowed him to do so. He was glad to see his wife immersed in grave historical and scientific reading; he said to himself that in this way she would be delivered from her religious prejudices, and some day attain to 'free thought.' Adela as yet had no such end in view, but already she understood that her education, in the serious sense, was only now beginning. As a girl, her fate had been that of girls in general; when she could write without orthographical errors, and could play by rote a few pieces of pianoforte music, her education had been pronounced completed. In the profound moral revolution which her nature had recently undergone her intellect also shared; when the first numbing shock had spent itself, she felt the growth of an intellectual appetite formerly unknown. Resolutely setting herself to exalt her husband, she magnified his acquirements, and, as a duty, directed her mind to the things he deemed of importance. One of her impulses took the form of a hope which would have vastly amused Richard had he divined it. Adela secretly trusted that some day her knowledge might be sufficient to allow her to cope with her husband's religious scepticism. It was significant that she could face in this way the great difficulty of her life; the stage at which it seemed sufficient to iterate creeds was already behind her. Probably Mr. Wyvern's conversation was not without its effect in aiding her to these larger views, but she never spoke to him on the subject directly. Her native dignity developed itself with her womanhood, and one of the characteristics of the new Adela was a reserve which at times seemed to indicate coldness or even spiritual pride.

The weather made it possible to spread the children's tea in the open air. At four o'clock Letty came, and was quietly happy in being allowed to superintend one of the tables. Adela was already on affectionate terms with many of the little ones, though others regarded her with awe rather than warmth of confidence. This was strange, when we remember how childlike she had formerly been with children. But herein, too, there was a change; she could not now have caught up Letty's little sister and trotted with her about the garden as she was used to do. She could no longer smile in the old simple, endearing way; it took some time before a child got accustomed to her eyes and lips. Her movements, though graceful as ever, were subdued to matronly gravity; never again would Adela turn and run down the hill, as after that meeting with Hubert Eldon. But her sweetness was in the end irresistible to all

who came within the circle of its magic. You saw its influence
in Letty, whose eyes seemed never at rest save when they were
watching Adela, who sprang to her side with delight if the
faintest sign did but summon her. You saw its influence,
moreover, when, the tea over, the children ranged themselves
on the lawn to hear her read. After the first few sentences,
everywhere was profoundest attention; the music of her
sweetly modulated voice, the art which she learnt only from
nature, so allied themselves with the beauty of the pages she
read that from beginning to end not a movement interrupted
her.

Whilst she was reading a visitor presented himself at the
Manor, and asked if Mrs. Mutimer was at home. The servant
explained how and where Mrs. Mutimer was engaged, for the
party was held in a quarter of the garden hidden from the
approach to the front door.

'Is Miss Mutimer within?' was the visitor's next inquiry.

Receiving an affirmative reply, he begged that Miss
Mutimer might be informed of Mr. Keene's desire to see her.
And Mr. Keene was led to the drawing-room.

Alice was reposing on a couch; she did not trouble herself to rise when the visitor entered, but held a hand to
him, at the same time scarcely suppressing a yawn. Novel
reading has a tendency to produce this expression of weariness. Then she smiled, as one does in greeting an old acquaintance.

'Who ever would have expected to see you!' she began,
drawing away her hand when it seemed to her that Mr.
Keene had detained it quite long enough. 'Does Dick expect
you?'

'Your brother does not expect me, Miss Mutimer,' Keene
replied. He invariably began conversation with her in a
severely formal and respectful tone, and to-day there was melancholy in his voice.

'You've just come on your own—because you thought you
would?'

'I have come because I could not help it, Miss Mutimer.
It is more than a month since I had the happiness of seeing
you.'

He stood by the couch, his body bent in deference, his eyes
regarding her with melancholy homage.

'Mrs. Mutimer has a tea-party of children from New

Wanley,' said Alice with a provoking smile. 'Won't you go
and join them? She's reading to them, I believe; no doubt
it's something that would do you good.'

'Of course I will go if you send me. I would go anywhere
at your command.'

'Then please do. Turn to the right when you get out into
the garden.'

Keene stood for an instant with his eyes on the ground,
then sighed deeply—groaned, in fact—smote his breast, and
marched towards the door like a soldier at drill. As soon as
he had turned his back Alice gathered herself from the couch,
and, as soon as she stood upright, called to him ·

'Mr. Keene!'

He halted and faced round.

'You needn't go unless you like, you know.'

He almost ran towards her.

'Just ring the bell, will you? I want some tea, and I'll
give you a cup if you care for it.'

She took a seat, and indicated with a finger the place where
he might repose. It was at a three yards' distance. Then
they talked as they were wont to, with much coquetry on Alice's
side, and on Keene's always humble submissiveness tempered
with glances and sighs. They drank tea, and Keene used the
opportunity of putting down his cup to take a nearer seat.

'Miss Mutimer——'

'Yes?'

'Is there any hope for me? You remember you said I was
to wait a month, and I've waited longer.'

'Yes, you have been very good,' said Alice, smiling
loftily.

'Is there any hope for me?' he repeated, with an air of
encouragement.

'Less than ever,' was the girl's reply, lightly given, indeed,
but not to be mistaken for a jest.

'You mean that? Come, now, you don't really mean
that? There must be, at all events, as much hope as before.'

'There isn't. There never was so little hope. There's no
hope at all, *not a scrap!*'

She pressed her lips and looked at him with a grave face.
He too became grave, and in a changed way.

'I am not to take this seriously?' he asked with bated
breath,

'You are. There's not one scrap of hope, and it's better you should know it.'

'Then—there—there must be somebody else?' he groaned, his distress no longer humorous.

Alice continued to look him in the face for a moment, and at length nodded twice.

'There *is* somebody else?'

She nodded three times.

'Then I'll go. Good-bye, Miss Mutimer. Yes, I'll go.'

He did not offer to shake hands, but bowed and moved away dejectedly.

'But you're not going back to London?' Alice asked.

'Yes.'

'You'd better not do that. They'll know you've called. You'd far better stay and see Dick; don't you think so?'

He shook his head and still moved towards the door.

'Mr. Keene!' Alice raised her voice. 'Please do as I tell you. It isn't my fault, and I don't see why you should pay no heed to me all at once. Will you attend to me, Mr. Keene?'

'What do you wish me to do?' he asked, only half turning.

'To go and see Mrs. Mutimer in the garden, and accept her invitation to dinner.'

'I haven't got a dress-suit,' he groaned.

'No matter. If you go away I'll never speak to you again, and you know you wouldn't like that.'

He gazed at her miserably—his face was one which lent itself to a miserable expression, and the venerable appearance of his frockcoat and light trousers filled in the picture of mishap.

'Have you been joking with me?'

'No, I've been telling you the truth. But that's no reason why you should break loose all at once. Please do as I tell you; go to the garden now and stop to dinner. I am not accustomed to ask a thing twice.'

She was almost serious. Keene smiled in a sickly way, bowed, and went to do her bidding.

CHAPTER XX.

AMONG the little girls who had received invitations to the tea-party were two named Rendal, the children of the man whose dismissal from New Wanley had been announced by Mutimer. Adela was rather surprised to see them in the garden. They were eight and nine years old respectively, and she noticed that both had a troubled countenance, the elder showing signs of recent tears. She sought them out particularly for kind words during tea-time. After the reading she noticed them standing apart, talking to each other earnestly; she saw also that they frequently glanced at her. It occurred to her that they might wish to say something and had a difficulty in approaching. She went to them, and a question or two soon led the elder girl to disclose that she was indeed desirous of speaking in private. Giving a hand to each, she drew them a little apart. Then both children began to cry, and the elder sobbed out a pitiful story. Their mother was wretchedly ill and had sent them to implore Mrs. Mutimer's good word that the father might be allowed another chance. It was true he had got drunk—the words sounded terrible to Adela from the young lips—but he vowed that henceforth he would touch no liquor. It was ruin to the family to be sent away; Rendal might not find work for long enough; there would be nothing for it but to go to a Belwick slum as long as their money lasted, and thence to the workhouse. For it was well understood that no man who had worked at New Wanley need apply to the ordinary employers; they would have nothing to do with him. The mother would have come herself, but could not walk the distance.

Adela was pierced with compassion.

'I will do my best,' she said, as soon as she could trust her voice. 'I promise you I will do my best.'

She could not say more, and the children evidently hoped she would have been able to grant their father's pardon forthwith. They had to be content with Adela's promise, which did not sound very cheerful, but meant more than they could understand.

She could not do more than give such a promise, and even as she spoke there was a coldness about her heart. The coldness became a fear when she met her husband on his return from the works. Richard was not in the same good temper as at mid-day. He was annoyed to find Keene in the house—of late he had grown to dislike the journalist very cordially—and he had heard that the Rendal children had been to the party, which enraged him. You remember he accused the man of impudence in addition to the offence of drunkenness. Rendal, foolishly joking in his cups, had urged as extenuation of his own weakness the well-known fact that 'Arry Mutimer had been seen one evening unmistakably intoxicated in the street of Wanley village. Someone reported these words to Richard, and from that moment it was all over with the Rendals.

Adela, in her eagerness to plead, quite forgot (or perhaps she had never known) that with a certain order of men it is never wise to prefer a request immediately before dinner. She was eager, too, to speak at once; a fear, which she would not allow to become definite, drove her upon the undertaking without delay. Meeting Richard on the stairs she begged him to come to her room.

' What is it ?' he asked with small ceremony, as soon as the door closed behind him.

She mastered her voice, and spoke with a sweet clearness of advocacy which should have moved his heart to proud and noble obeisance. Mutimer was not very accessible to such emotions.

' It's like the fellow's impertinence,' he said, ' to send his children to you. I'm rather surprised you let them stay after what I had told you. Certainly I shall not overlook it. The thing's finished ! it's no good talking about it.'

The fear had passed, but the coldness about her heart was more deadly. For a moment it seemed as if she could not bring herself to utter another word; she drew apart, she could not raise her face, which was beautiful in marble pain. But there came a rush of such hot anguish as compelled her to speak again. Something more than the fate of that poor family was at stake. Is not the quality of mercy indispensable to true nobleness? Had she voiced her very thought, Adela would have implored him to exalt himself in her eyes, to do a good deed which cost him some little effort over himself. For she divined with cruel certainty that it was not the principle that made him unyielding.

' Richard, are you sure that the man has offended before ?'

' Oh, of course he has. I've no doubt of it. I remember feeling uncertain when I admitted him first of all. I didn't like his look.'

'But you have not really had to complain of him before. Your suspicions *may* be groundless. And he has a good wife, I feel sure of that. The children are very clean and nicely dressed. She will help him to avoid drink in future. It is impossible for him to fall again, now that he knows how dreadful the results will be to his wife and his little girls.'

'Pooh! What does he care about them? If I begin letting men off in that way, I shall be laughed at. There's an end of my authority. Don't bother your head about them. I must go and get ready for dinner.'

An end of *my* authority. Yes, was it not the intelligence of her maiden heart returning to her? She had no pang from the mere refusal of a request of hers; Richard had never affected tenderness—not what she understood as tenderness—and she did not expect it of him. The union between them had another basis. But the understanding of his motives was so terribly distinct in her! It had come all at once; it was like the exposure of something dreadful by the sudden raising of a veil. And had she not known what the veil covered? Yet for the poor people's sake, for his own sake, she must try the woman's argument.

'Do you refuse me, Richard? I will be guarantee for him. I promise you he shall not offend again. He shall apologise humbly to you for his—his words. You won't really refuse me?'

'What nonsense! How can you promise for him, Adela? Ask for something reasonable, and you may be sure I shan't refuse you. The fellow has to go as a warning. It mustn't be thought we're only playing at making rules. I can't talk any more; I shall keep dinner waiting.'

Pride helped her to show a smooth face through the evening, and in the night she conquered herself anew. She expelled those crying children from her mind; she hardened her heart against their coming misery. It was wrong to judge her husband so summarily; nay, she had not judged him, but had given way to a wicked impulse, without leaving herself a moment to view the case. Did he not understand better than she what measures were necessary to the success of his most difficult undertaking? And then was it certain that expulsion meant ruin to the Rendals? Richard would insist on the letter of the regulations, just, as he said, for the example's sake; but of course he would see that the man was put in the way of getting new employment and did not suffer in the meantime. In the morning she made atonement to her husband.

'I was wrong in annoying you yesterday,' she said as she walked with him from the house to the garden gate. 'In such things you are far better able to judge. You won't let it trouble you?'

It was a form of asceticism; Adela had a joy in humbling herself and crushing her rebel instincts. She even raised her eyes to interrogate him. On Richard's face was an uneasy smile, a look of puzzled reflection. It gratified him intensely to hear such words, yet he could not hear them without the suspicions of a vulgar nature brought in contact with nobleness.

'Well, yes,' he replied, 'I think you were a bit too hasty: you're not practical, you see. It wants a practical man to manage those kind of things.'

The reply was not such as completes the blessedness of pure submission. Adela averted her eyes. Another woman would perchance have sought to assure herself that she was right in crediting him with private benevolence to the family he was compelled to visit so severely. Such a question Adela could not ask. It would have been to betray doubt; she imagined a replying glance which would shame her. To love, to honour, to obey :—many times daily she repeated to herself that three-fold vow, and hitherto the first article had most occupied her striving heart. But she must not neglect the second; perhaps it came first in natural order.

At the gate Richard nodded to her kindly.

'Good-bye. Be a good girl.'

What was it that caused a painful flutter at her heart as ne spoke so? She did not answer, but watched him for a few moments as he walked away.

Did *he* love *her*? The question which she had not asked herself for a long time came of that heart-tremor. She had been living so unnatural a life for a newly wedded woman, a life in which the intellect and the moral faculties held morbid predominance. 'Be a good girl.' How was it that the simple phrase touched her to emotion quite different in kind from anything she had known since her marriage, more deeply than any enthusiasm, as with a comfort more sacred than any she had known in prayer? As she turned to go back to the house a dizziness affected her eyes; she had to stand still for a moment. Involuntarily she clasped her hands upon her bosom and looked away into the blue summer sky. Did he love her? She had never asked him that, and all at once she felt a longing to hasten after him and utter the question. Would he know what she meant?

Was it the instantaneous reward for having conscientiously striven to honour him? That there should be love on his side had not hitherto seemed of so much importance; probably she had taken it for granted; she had been so preoccupied with her own duties. Yet now it had all at once become of moment that she should know. 'Be a good girl.' She repeated the words over and over again, and made much of them. Perhaps she had given him no opportunity, no encouragement, to say all he felt; she knew him to be reserved in many things.

As she entered the house the dizziness again troubled her. But it passed as before.

Mr. Keene, who had stayed over-night, was waiting to take leave of her; the trap which would carry him to Agworth station had just driven up. Adela surprised the poor journalist by the warmth with which she shook his hand, and the kindness of her farewell. She was not deceived as to the motive of his visit, and just now she allowed herself to feel sympathy for him, though in truth she did not like the man.

This morning she could not settle to her work. The dreaming mood was upon her, and she appeared rather to encourage it, seeking a quiet corner of the garden and watching for a whole hour the sun-dappled trunk of a great elm. At times her face seemed itself to be a source of light, so vivid were the thoughts that transformed it. Her eyes were moist once or twice, and then no dream of artist-soul ever embodied such passionate loveliness, such holy awe, as came to view upon her countenance. At lunch she was almost silent, but Alice, happening to glance at her, experienced a surprise; she had never seen Adela so beautiful and so calmly bright.

After lunch she attired herself for walking, and went to the village to see her mother. Lest Mrs. Waltham should be lonely, it had been arranged that Alfred should come home every evening, instead of once a week. Even thus, Adela had frequently reproached herself for neglecting her mother. Mrs. Waltham, however, enjoyed much content. The material comforts of her life were considerably increased, and she had many things in anticipation. Adela's unsatisfactory health rendered it advisable that the present year should pass in quietness, but Mrs. Waltham had made up her mind that before long there should be a house in London, with the delights appertaining thereto. She did not feel herself at all too old to enjoy the outside view of a London season; more than that it would probably be difficult to obtain just yet. To-day she was in excellent spirits, and welcomed her daughter exuberantly.

'You haven't seen Letty yet?' she asked. 'To-day, I mean.'

'No. Has she some news for me?'

'Alfred has an excellent chance of promotion. That old Wilkinson is dead, and he thinks there's no doubt he'll get the place. It would be two hundred and fifty a year.'

'That's good news, indeed.'

Of course it would mean Letty's immediate marriage. Mrs. Waltham discussed the prospect in detail. No doubt the best and simplest arrangement would be for the pair to live on in the same house. For the present, of course. Alfred was now firm on the commercial ladder, and in a few years his income would doubtless be considerable; then a dwelling of a very different kind could be found. With the wedding, too, she was occupying her thoughts.

'Yours was not quite what it ought to have been, Adela. I felt it at the time, but then things were done in such a hurry. Of course the church must be decorated. The breakfast you will no doubt arrange to have at the Manor. Letty ought to have a nice, a really nice *trousseau*; I know you will be kind to her, my dear.'

As Alice had done, Mrs. Waltham noticed before long that Adela was far brighter than usual. She remarked upon it.

'You begin to look really well, my love. It makes me happy to see you. How much we have to be thankful for! I've had a letter this morning from poor Lizzie Henbane; I must show it you. They're in such misery as never was. Her husband's business is all gone to nothing, and he is cruelly unkind to her. How thankful we ought to be!'

'Surely not for poor Lizzie's unhappiness!' said Adela, with a return of her maiden archness.

'On our own account, my dear. We have had so much to contend against. At one time, just after your poor father's death, things looked very cheerless: I used to fret dreadfully on your account. But everything, you see, was for the best.'

Adela had something to say and could not find the fitting moment. She first drew her chair a little nearer to her mother.

'Yes, mother, I am happy,' she murmured.

'Silly child! As if I didn't know best. It's always the same, but *you* had the good sense to trust to my experience.'

Adela slipped from her seat and put her arms about her mother.

' What is it, dear?'

The reply was whispered. Adela's embrace grew closer; her face was hidden, and all at once she began to sob.

' Love me, mother! Love me, dear mother!'

Mrs. Waltham beamed with real tenderness. For half an hour they talked as mother and child alone can. Then Adela walked back to the Manor, still dreaming. She did not feel able to call and see Letty.

There was an afternoon postal delivery at Wanley, and the postman had just left the Manor as Adela returned. Alice, who for a wonder had been walking in the garden, saw the man going away, and, thinking it possible there might be a letter for her, entered the house to look. Three letters lay on the hall table : two were for Richard, the other was addressed to Mrs. Mutimer. This envelope Alice examined curiously. Whose writing could that be? She certainly knew it; it was a singular hand, stiff, awkward, untrained. Why, it was the writing of Emma's sister Kate, Mrs. Clay. Not a doubt of it. Alice had received a note from Mrs. Clay at the time of Jane Vine's death, and remembered comparing the hand with her own and blessing herself that at all events she wrote with an elegant slope, and not in that hideous upright scrawl. The post-mark? Yes, it was London, E.C. But if Kate addressed a letter to Mrs. Mutimer it must be with sinister design, a design not at all difficult to imagine. Alice had a temptation. To take this letter and either open it herself or give it secretly to her brother? But the servant might somehow make it known that such a letter had arrived.

' Anything for me, Alice?'

It was Adela's voice. She had approached unheard; Alice was so intent upon her thoughts.

' Yes, one letter.'

There was no help for it. Alice glanced at her sister-in-law, and strolled away again into the garden.

Adela examined the envelope. She could not conjecture from whom the letter came; certainly from some illiterate person. Was it for her husband? Was not the ' Mrs.' a mistake for ' Mr.' or perhaps mere ill-writing that deceived the eye? No, the prefix was so very distinct. She opened the envelope where she stood.

' Mrs. Mutimer, I dare say you don't know me nor my

name, but I write to you because I think it only right as you
should know the truth about your husband, and because me
and my sister can't go on any longer as we are. My sister's
name is Emma Vine. She was engaged to be married to
Richard M. two years before he knew you, and to the last he
put her off with make-believe and promises, though it was easy
to see what was meant. And when our sister Jane was on her
very death-bed, which she died not a week after he married you,
and I know well as it was grief as killed her. And now we
haven't got enough to eat for Emma and me and my two little
children, for I am a widow myself. But that isn't all. Because
he found that his friends in Hoxton was crying shame on him,
he got it said as Emma had misbehaved herself, which was a
cowardly lie, and all to protect himself. And now Emma is
that ill she can't work; it's come upon her all at once, and
what's going to happen God knows. And his own mother
cried shame on him, and wouldn't live no longer in the big
house in Highbury. He offered us money—I will say so much
—but Emma was too proud, and wouldn't hear of it. And
then he went giving her a bad name. What do you think of
your husband now, Mrs. Mutimer? I don't expect nothing,
but it's only right you should know. Emma wouldn't take
anything, not if she was dying of starvation, but I've got my
children to think of. So that's all I have to say, and I'm glad
I've said it.—Yours truly, KATE CLAY.'

Adela remained standing for a few moments when she had
finished the letter, then went slowly to her room.

Alice returned from the garden in a short time. In passing
through the hall she looked again at the two letters which remained. Neither of them had a sinister appearance; being
addressed to the Manor they probably came from personal
friends. She went to the drawing-room and glanced around
for Adela, but the room was empty. Richard would not be
home for an hour yet; she took up a novel and tried to pass
the time so, but she had a difficulty in fixing her attention. In
the end she once more left the house, and, after a turn or two
on the lawn, strolled out of the gate.

She met her brother a hundred yards along the road. The
sight of her astonished him.

'What's up now, Princess?' he exclaimed. 'House on
fire? Novels run short?'

'Something that I expect you won't care to hear. Who do
you think's been writing to Adela? Someone in London.'

Richard stayed his foot, and looked at his sister with the eyes which suggested disagreeable possibilities.

'Who do you mean?' he asked briefly. 'Not mother?'

The change in him was very sudden. He had been merry and smiling.

'No; worse than that. She's got a letter from Kate.'

'From Kate? Emma's sister?' he asked in a low voice of surprise which would have been dismay had he not governed himself.

'I saw it on the hall table; I remember her writing well enough. Just as I was looking at it Adela came in.'

'Have you seen her since?'

Alice shook her head. She had this way of saving words. Richard walked on. His first movement of alarm had passed, and now he affected to take the matter with indifference. During the week immediately following his marriage he had been prepared for this very incident; the possibility had been one of the things he faced with a certain recklessness. But impunity had set his mind at ease, and the news in the first instant struck him with a trepidation which a few minutes' thought greatly allayed. By a mental process familiar enough he at first saw the occurrence as he had seen it in the earlier days of his temptation, when his sense of honour yet gave him frequent trouble; he had to exert himself to recover his present standpoint. At length he smiled.

'Just like that woman,' he said, turning half an eye on Alice.

'If she means trouble, you'll have it,' returned the girl sententiously.

'Well, it's no doubt over by this time.'

'Over? Beginning, I should say,' remarked Alice, swinging her parasol at a butterfly.

They finished their walk to the house in silence, and Richard went at once to his dressing-room. Here he sat down. After all, his mental disquiet was not readily to be dismissed; it even grew as he speculated and viewed likelihoods from all sides. Probably Kate had made a complete disclosure. How would it affect Adela?

You must not suppose that his behaviour in the case of the man Rendal had argued disregard for Adela's opinion of him. Richard was incapable of understanding how it struck his wife, that was all. If he reflected on the matter, no doubt he was very satisfied with himself, feeling that he had displayed a manly resolution and consistency. But the present difficulty was grave. Whatever Adela might say, there could be no doubt as to her thought; she would henceforth—yes, despise him. That cut his thick skin to the quick; his nature was capable of smarting when thus assailed. For he had by no means lost his early reverence for Adela; nay, in a sense it had increased. His primitive ideas on woman had undergone a change since his marriage. Previously he had considered a wife in the light of property; intellectual or moral independence he could not attribute to her. But he had learnt that Adela was by no means his chattel. He still knew diffidence when he was inclined to throw a joke at her, and could not take her hand without involuntary respect—a sensation which occasionally irritated him. A dim inkling of what was meant by woman's strength and purity had crept into his mind; he knew—in his heart he knew—that he was unworthy to touch her garment. And, to face the whole truth, he all but loved her; that was the meaning of his mingled sentiments with regard to her. A danger of losing her in the material sense would have taught him that better than he as yet knew it; the fear of losing her respect was not attributable solely to his restless egoism. He had wedded her in quite another frame of mind than that in which he now found himself when he thought of her. He cared much for the high opinion of people in general; Adela was all but indispensable to him. When he said, ' My wife,' he must have been half-conscious that the word bore a significance different from that he had contemplated. On the lips of those among whom he had grown up the word is desecrated, or for the most part so; it has contemptible, and ridiculous, and vile associations, scarcely ever its true meaning. Formerly he would have laughed at the thought of standing in awe of his wife; nay, he could not have conceived the possibility of such a thing; it would have appeared unnatural, incompatible with the facts of wedded life. Yet he sat here and almost dreaded to enter her presence.

A man of more culture might have thought: A woman cannot in her heart be revolted because another has been cast off for her. Mutimer could not reason so far. It would have been reasoning inapplicable to Adela, but from a certain point of view it might have served as a resource. Richard could only accept his instincts.

But it was useless to postpone the interview; come of it what would, he must have it over and done with. He could not decide how to speak until he knew what the contents of Kate's letter were. He was nervously anxious to know.

Adela sat in her boudoir, with a book open on her lap. After the first glance on his entering she kept her eyes down. He sauntered up and stood before her in an easy attitude.

'Who has been writing to you from London?' he at once asked, abruptly in consequence of the effort to speak without constraint.

Adela was not prepared for such a question. She remembered all at once that Alice had seen the letter as it lay on the table. Why had Alice spoken to her brother about it? There could be only one explanation of that, and of his coming thus directly. She raised her eyes for a moment, and a slight shock seemed to affect her.

She was unconscious how long she delayed her reply.

'Can't you tell me?' Richard said, with more roughness than he intended. He was suffering, and suffering affected his temper.

Adela drew the letter from her pocket and in silence handed it to him. He read it quickly, and, before the end was reached, had promptly chosen his course.

'What do you think of this?' was his question, as he folded the letter and rolled it in his hand. He was smiling, and enjoyed complete self-command.

'I cannot think,' fell from Adela's lips. 'I am waiting for your words.'

He noticed at length, now he was able to inspect her calmly, that she looked faint, pain-stricken.

'Alice told me who had written to you,' Richard pursued, in his frankest tones. 'It was well she saw the letter; you might have said nothing.'

'That would have been very unjust to you,' said Adela in a low regular voice. 'I could only have done that if—if I had believed it.'

'You don't altogether believe it, then?'

She looked at him with full eyes and made answer:

'You are my husband.'

It echoed in his ears; not to many men does it fall to hear those words so spoken. Another would have flung himself at her feet and prayed to her. Mutimer only felt a vast relief, mingled with gratitude. The man all but flattered himself that she had done him justice.

'Well, you are quite right,' he spoke. 'It isn't true, and if

T

you knew this woman you would understand the whole affair. I dare say you can gather a good deal from the way she writes. It's true enough that I was engaged to her sister, but it was broken off before I knew you, and for the reasons she says here. I'm not going to talk to you about things of that kind; I dare say you wouldn't care to hear them. Of course she says I made it all up. Do you think I'm the kind of man to do that?'

Perhaps she did not know that she was gazing at him. The question interrupted her in a train of thought which was going on in her mind even while she listened. She was asking herself why, when they were in London, he had objected to a meeting between her and his mother. He had said his mother was a crotchety old woman who could not make up her mind to the changed circumstances, and was intensely prejudiced against women above her own class. Was that a very convincing description? She had accepted it at the time, but now, after reading this letter——? But could any man speak with that voice and that look, and lie? Her agitation grew intolerable. Answer she must; could she, could she say 'No' with truth? Answer she must, for he waited. In the agony of striving for voice there came upon her once more that dizziness of the morning, but in a more severe form. She struggled, felt her breath failing, tried to rise, and fell back unconscious.

At the same time Alice was sitting in the drawing-room, in conversation with Mr. Willis Rodman. 'Arry having been invited for this evening, Rodman was asked with him, as had been the case before. 'Arry was at present amusing himself in the stables, exchanging sentiments with the groom. Rodman sat near Alice, or rather he knelt upon a chair, so that at any moment he could assume a standing attitude before her. He talked in a low voice.

'You'll come out to-night?'

'No, not to-night. You must speak to him to-night.'

Rodman mused.

'Why shouldn't you?' resumed the girl eagerly, in a tone as unlike that she used to Mr. Keene as well could be. She was in earnest; her eyes never moved from her companion's face; her lips trembled. 'Why should you put it off? I can't see why we keep it a secret. Dick can't have a word to say against it; you know he can't. Tell him to-night after dinner. Do! do!'

Rodman frowned in thought.

'He wont' like it.'

'But why not? I believe he will. He will, he shall, he must! I'm not to depend on him, surely?'

'A day or two more, Alice.'

'I can't keep up the shamming!' she exclaimed. 'Adela suspects, I feel sure. Whenever you come in I feel that hot and red.' She laughed and blushed. 'If you won't do as I tell you, I'll give you up, I will indeed!'

Rodman stroked his moustache, smiling.

'You will, will you?'

'See if I don't. To-night! It must be to-night! Shall I call you a pretty name? It's only because I couldn't bear to be found out before you tell him.'

He still stroked his moustache. His handsome face was half amused, half troubled. At last he said:

'Very well; to-night.'

Shortly after, Mutimer came into the room.

'Adela isn't up to the mark,' he said to Alice. 'She'd better have dinner by herself, I think; but she'll join us afterwards.'

Brother and sister exchanged looks.

'Oh, it's only a headache or something of the kind,' he continued. 'It'll be all right soon.'

And he began to talk with Rodman cheerfully, so that Alice felt it must really be all right. She drew aside and looked into a novel.

Adela did appear after dinner, very pale and silent, but with a smile on her face. There had been no further conversation between her and her husband. She talked a little with 'Arry, in her usual gentle way, then asked to be allowed to say good-night. 'Arry at the same time took his leave, having been privately bidden to do so by his sister. He was glad enough to get away; in the drawing-room his limbs soon began to ache, from inability to sit at his ease.

Then Alice withdrew, and the men were left alone.

Adela did not go to bed. She suffered from the closeness of the evening and sat by her open windows, trying to read a chapter in the New Testament. About eleven o'clock she had a great desire to walk upon the garden grass for a few minutes before undressing; perhaps it might help her to the sleep she so longed for yet feared she would not obtain. The desire became so strong that she yielded to it, passed quietly downstairs, and out into the still night. She directed her steps to her favourite remote corner. There was but little moonlight, and scarcely a star was visible. When she neared the laburnums behind which she often sat or walked, her ear caught the sound of voices. They came nearer, on the other side of the trees. The first word which she heard distinctly bound her to the spot and forced her to listen.

'No, I shan't put it off.' It was Alice speaking. 'I know what comes of that kind of thing. I am old enough to be my own mistress.'

'You are not twenty-one,' replied Richard in an annoyed voice. 'I shall do everything I can to put it off till you are of age. Rodman is a good enough fellow in his place; but it isn't hard to see why he's talked you over in this way.'

'He hasn't talked me over!' cried Alice, passionately. 'I needn't have listened if I hadn't liked.'

'You're a foolish girl, and you want someone to look after you. If you'll only wait you can make a good marriage. This would be a bad one, in every sense.'

'I shall marry him.'

'And I shall prevent it. It's for your own sake, Alice.'

'If you try to prevent it—I'll tell Adela everything about Emma! I'll tell her the whole plain truth, and I'll prove it to her. So hinder me if you dare!'

Alice hastened away.

CHAPTER XXI.

IN the month of September Mr. Wyvern was called upon to unite in holy matrimony two pairs in whom we are interested. Alice Mutimer became Mrs. Willis Rodman, and Alfred Waltham took home a bride who suited him exactly, seeing that she was never so happy as when submitting herself to a stronger will. Alfred and Letty ran away and hid themselves in South Wales. Mr. and Mrs. Rodman fled to the Continent.

Half Alice's fortune was settled upon herself, her brother and Alfred Waltham being trustees. This was all Mutimer could do. He disliked the marriage intensely, and not only because he had set his heart on a far better match for Alice; he had no real confidence in Rodman. Though the latter's extreme usefulness and personal tact had from the first led Richard to admit him to terms of intimacy, time did not favour the friendship. Mutimer, growing daily more ambitious and more punctilious in his intercourse with all whom, notwithstanding his principles, he deemed inferiors from the social point of view, often regretted keenly that he had allowed any relation between himself and Rodman more than that of master and man. Experience taught him how easily he might have made the most of Rodman without granting him a single favour. The first suggestion of the marriage enraged him; in the conversation with Rodman, which took place, moreover, at an unfavourable moment, he lost his temper and flung out very broad hints indeed as to the suitor's motives. Rodman was calm; life had instructed him in the advantages of a curbed tongue; but there was heightened colour on his face, and his demeanour much resembled that of a proud man who cares little to justify himself, but will assuredly never forget an insult. It was one of the peculiarities of this gentleman that his exterior was most impressive when the inner man was most busy with ignoble or venomous thoughts.

But for Alice's sake Mutimer could not persist in his hostility. Alice had a weapon which he durst not defy, and, the marriage being inevitable, he strove hard to see it in a more agreeable light, even tried to convince himself that his prejudice against Rodman was groundless. He loved his sister, and for her alone would put up with things otherwise intolerable. It was a new exasperation when he discovered that Rodman could not be persuaded to continue his work at New Wanley. All inducements proved vain. Richard had hoped that at least one advantage might come of the marriage, that Rodman would devote capital to the works; but Rodman's Socialism cooled strangely from the day when his ends were secured. He purposed living in London, and Alice was delighted to encourage him. The girl had visions of a life such as the heroines of certain novels rejoice in. For a wonder, her husband was indispensable to the brightness of that future. Rodman had inspired her with an infatuation. Their relations once declared, she grudged him every moment he spent away from her. It was strangely like true passion, the difference only marked by an extravagant selfishness. She thought of no one, cared for no one, but herself, Rodman having become part of that self. With him she was imperiously slavish; her tenderness was a kind of greed; she did not pretend to forgive her brother for his threatened opposition, and, having got hold of the idea that Adela took part against Rodman, she hated her and would not be alone in her company for a moment. On her marriage day she refused Adela's offered kiss and did her best to let everyone see how delighted she was to leave them behind.

The autumn was a time of physical suffering for Adela. Formerly she had sought to escape her mother's attentions, now she accepted them with thankfulness. Mrs. Waltham had grave fears for her daughter; doctors suspected some organic disease, one summoned from London going so far as to hint at a weakness of the chest. Early in November it was decided to go south for the winter, and Exmouth was chosen, chiefly because Mrs. Westlake was spending a month there. Mr. Westlake, whose interest in Adela had grown with each visit he paid to the Manor, himself suggested the plan. Mrs. Waltham and Adela left Wanley together; Mutimer promised visits as often as he could manage to get away. Since Rodman's departure Richard found himself overwhelmed with work. None the less he resolutely pursued the idea of canvassing Belwick at the coming general election. Opposition, from whomsoever it came, aggravated him. He was more than ever troubled about the prospects of New Wanley; there even loomed before his mind a possible abandonment of the undertaking. He had never contemplated the sacrifice of his fortune, and though anything of that kind was still very far off, it was daily more difficult for him to face with equanimity even moderate losses. Money had fostered ambition, and ambition full grown had more need than ever of its nurse. New Wanley was no longer an end in itself, but a stepping-stone. You must come to your own conclusions in judging the value of Mutimer's social zeal; the facts of his life up to this time are before you, and you will not forget how complex a matter is the mind of a strong man with whom circumstances have dealt so strangely. His was assuredly not the vulgar self-seeking of the gilded *bourgeois* who covets an after-dinner sleep on Parliamentary benches. His ignorance of the machinery of government was profound; though he spoke scornfully of Parliament and its members, he had no conception of those powers of dulness and respectability which seize upon the best men if folly lures them within the precincts of St. Stephen's. He thought, poor fellow! that he could rise in his place and thunder forth his indignant eloquence as he did in Commonwealth Hall and elsewhere; he imagined a conscience-stricken House, he dreamed of passionate debates on a Bill which really had the good of the people for its sole object. Such Bill would of course bear *his* name; shall we condemn him for that?

Adela was at Exmouth, drinking the mild air, wondering whether there was in truth a life to come, and, if so, whether it was a life wherein Love and Duty were at one. A year ago such thoughts could not have entered her mind. But she had spent several weeks in close companionship with Stella Westlake, and Stella's influence was subtle. Mrs. Westlake had come here to regain strength after a confinement; the fact drew her near to Adela, whose time for giving birth to a child was not far off.

Adela at first regarded this friend with much the same feeling of awe as mingled with Letty's affection for Adela herself. Stella Westlake was not only possessed of intellectual riches which Adela had had no opportunity of gaining; her character was so full of imaginative force, of dreamy splendours, that it addressed itself to a mind like Adela's with magic irresistible and permanent. No rules of the polite world applied to Stella; she spoke and acted with an independence so spontaneous that it did not suggest conscious opposition to the received ways of thought to which ordinary women are confined, but rather a complete ignorance of them. Adela felt herself startled, but never shocked, even when the originality went most counter to her own prejudices; it was as though she had drunk a draught of most unexpected flavour, the effect of which was to set her nerves delightfully trembling, and make her long to taste it again. It was not an occasional effect, the result of an effort on Stella's part to surprise or charm; the commonest words had novel meanings when uttered in her voice; a profound sincerity seemed to inspire every lightest question or remark. Her presence was agitating; she had but to enter the room and sit in silence, and Adela forthwith was raised from the depression of her broodings to a vividness of being, an imaginative energy, such as she had never known. Adela doubted for some time whether Stella regarded her with affection; the little demonstrations in which women are wont to indulge were incompatible with that grave dreaminess, and Stella seemed to avoid even the common phrases of friendship. But one day, when Adela had not been well enough to rise, and as she lay on the borderland of sleeping and waking, she half dreamt, half knew, that a face bent over her, and that lips were pressed against her own; and such a thrill struck through her that, though now fully conscious, she had not power to stir, but lay as in the moment of some rapturous death. For when the presence entered into her dream, when the warmth melted upon her lips, she imagined it the kiss which might once have come to her but now was lost for ever. It was pain to open her eyes, but when she did so, and met Stella's silent gaze, she knew that love was offered her, a love of which it was needless to speak.

Mrs. Waltham was rather afraid of Stella; privately she doubted whether the poor thing was altogether in her perfect mind. When the visitor came the mother generally found occupation or amusement elsewhere, conversation with Stella was so extremely difficult. Mr. Westlake was also at Exmouth, but much engaged in literary work. There was, too, an artist and his family, with whom the Westlakes were acquainted, their name Boscobel. Mrs. Boscobel was a woman of the world, five-and-thirty, charming, intelligent; she read little, but was full of interest in literary and artistic matters, and talked as only a woman can who has long associated with men of brains. To her Adela was interesting, personally and still more as an illustration of a social experiment.

'How young she is!' was her remark to Mr. Westlake shortly after making Adela's acquaintance. 'It will amuse you, the thought I had; I really must tell it you. She realises my idea of a virgin mother. Haven't you felt anything of the kind?'

Mr. Westlake smiled.

'Yes, I understand. Stella said something evidently traceable to the same impression; her voice, she said, is full of forgiveness.'

'Excellent! And has she much to forgive, do you think?'

'I hope not.'

'Yet she is not exactly happy, I imagine?'

Mr. Westlake did not care to discuss the subject. The lady had recourse to Stella for some account of Mr. Mutimer.

'He is a strong man,' Stella said in a tone which betrayed the Socialist's enthusiasm. 'He stands for earth-subduing energy. I imagine him at a forge, beating fire out of iron.'

'H'm! That's not quite the same thing as imagining him that beautiful child's husband. No education, I suppose?'

'Sufficient. With more, he would no longer fill the place he does. He can speak eloquently; he is the true voice of the millions who cannot speak their own thoughts. If he were more intellectual he would become commonplace; I hope he will never see further than he does now. Isn't a perfect type more precious than a man who is neither one thing nor another?'

'Artistically speaking, by all means.'

'In his case I don't mean it artistically. He is doing a great work.'

'A friend of mine—you don't know Hubert Eldon, I think?—tells me he has ruined one of the loveliest valleys in England.'

'Yes, I dare say he has done that. It is an essential part of his protest against social wrong. The earth renews itself, but a dead man or woman who has lived without joy can never be recompensed.'

'She, of course, is strongly of the same opinion?'

'Adela is a Socialist.'

Mrs. Boscobel laughed rather satirically.

'I doubt it!'

Stella, when she went to sit with Adela, either at home or by the sea-shore, often carried a book in her hand, and at Adela's request she read aloud. In this way Adela first came to know what was meant by literature, as distinguished from works of learning. The verse of Shelley and the prose of Landor fell upon her ears; it was as though she had hitherto lived in deafness. Sometimes she had to beg the reader to pause for that day; her heart and mind seemed overfull; she could not even speak of these new things, but felt the need of lying back in twilight to marvel and repeat melodies.

Mrs. Boscobel happened to approach them once whilst this reading was going on.

'You are educating her?' she said to Stella afterwards.

'Perhaps—a little,' Stella replied absently.

'Isn't it just a trifle dangerous?' suggested the understanding lady.

'Dangerous? How?'

'The wife of the man who makes sparks fly out of iron? The man who is on no account to learn anything?'

Stella shook her head, saying, 'You don't know her.'

'I should much like to,' was Mrs. Boscobel's smiling rejoinder.

In Stella's company it did not seem very likely that Adela would lose her social enthusiasm, yet danger there was, and that precisely on account of Mrs. Westlake's idealist tendencies. When she spoke of the toiling multitude, she saw them in a kind of exalted vision; she beheld them glorious in their woe, ennobled by the tyranny under which they groaned. She had seen little if anything of the representative proletarian, and perchance even if she had the momentary impression would have faded in the light of her burning soul. Now Adela was in the very best position for understanding those faults of the working class which are ineradicable in any one generation. She knew her husband, knew him better than ever now that she regarded him from a distance; she knew 'Arry Mutimer; and now she was getting to appreciate with a thoroughness impossible hitherto, the monstrous gulf between men of that kind and cultured human beings. She had, too, studied the children and the women of New Wanley, and the results of such study were arranging themselves in her mind. All unconsciously, Stella Westlake was cooling Adela's zeal with every fervid word she uttered; Adela at times with difficulty restrained herself from crying, 'But it is a mistake! They have not these feelings you attribute to them. Such suffering as you picture them enduring comes only of the poetry-fed soul at issue with fate.' She could not as yet have so expressed herself, but the knowledge was growing within her. For Adela was not by nature a social enthusiast. When her heart leapt at Stella's chant, it was not in truth through contagion of sympathy, but in admiration and love of the noble woman who could thus think and speak. Adela—and who will not be thankful for it?—was, before all things, feminine; her true enthusiasms were personal. It was a necessity of her nature to love a human being, this or that one, not a crowd. She had been starving, killing the self which was her value. This home on the Devon coast received her like an earthly paradise; looking back on New Wanley, she saw it murky and lurid; it was hard to believe that the sun ever shone there. But for the most part, she tried to keep it altogether from her mind, tried to dissociate her husband from his public tasks, and to remember him as the man with whom her life was irrevocably bound up. When delight in Stella's poetry was followed by fear, she strengthened herself by thought of the child she bore beneath her heart; for that child's sake she would accept the beautiful things offered to her, some day to bring them as rich gifts to the young life. Her own lot was fixed; she might not muse upon it, she durst not consider it too deeply. There were things in the past which she had determined, if by any means it were possible, utterly to forget. For the future, there was her child.

Mutimer came to Exmouth when she had been there three weeks, and he stayed four days. Mrs. Boscobel had an opportunity of making his acquaintance.

' Who contrived that marriage ?' she asked of Mr. Westlake subsequently. ' Our lady mother, presumably.'

'I have no reason to think it was not well done,' replied Mr. Westlake with reserve.

' Most skilfully done, no doubt,' rejoined the lady.

But at the end of the year, the Westlakes returned to London, the Boscobels shortly after. Mrs. Waltham and her daughter had made no other close connections, and Adela's health alone allowed of her leaving the house for a short drive on sunny days. At the end of February the child was born prematurely; it entered the world only to leave it again. For a week they believed that Adela would die. Scarcely was she pronounced out of danger by the end of March. But after that she recovered strength.

May saw her at Wanley once more. She had become impatient to return. The Parliamentary elections were very near at hand, and Mutimer almost lived in Belwick ; it seemed to Adela that duty required her to be near him, as well as to supply his absence from New Wanley as much as was possible. She was still only the ghost of her former self, but disease no longer threatened her, and activity alone could completely restore her health. She was anxious to recommence her studies, to resume her readings to the children ; and she desired to see Mr. Wyvern. She understood by this time why he had chosen Andersen's Tales for her readings ; of many other things which he had said, causing her doubt, the meaning was now clear enough to her. She had so much to talk of with the vicar, so many questions to put to him, not a few of a kind that would —she thought— surprise and trouble him. None the less, they must be asked and answered. Part of her desire to see him again was merely the result of her longing for the society of well-read and thoughtful people. She knew that he would appear to her in a different light from formerly ; she would be far better able to understand him.

She began by seeking his opinion of her husband's chances in Belwick. Mr. Wyvern shook his head and said frankly that he thought there was no chance at all. Mutimer was looked upon in the borough as a mischievous interloper, who came to make disunion in the Radical party. The son of a lord and an ironmaster of great influence were the serious candidates. Had he seen fit, Mr. Wyvern could have mentioned not a few lively incidents in the course of the political warfare ; such, for instance, as the appearance of a neat little pamphlet which pur-

ported to give a full and complete account of Mutimer's life.
In this pamphlet nothing untrue was set down, nor did it contain
anything likely to render its publisher amenable to the law of
libel; but the writer, a gentleman closely connected with Comrade
Roodhouse, most skilfully managed to convey the worst possible
impression throughout. Nor did the vicar hesitate to express
his regret that Mutimer should be seeking election at all.
Adela felt with him.

She found Richard in a strange state of chronic excitement.
On whatever subject he spoke it was with the same nervous
irritation, and the slightest annoyance set him fuming. To
her he paid very little attention, and for the most part seemed
disinclined to converse with her; Adela found it necessary to
keep silence on political matters; once or twice he replied to
her questions with a rough impatience which kept her miserable
throughout the day, so much had it revealed of the working
man. As the election day approached she suffered from a sinking of the heart, almost a bodily fear; a fear the same in kind as
that of the wretched woman who anticipates the return of a
brute-husband late on Saturday night. The same in kind; no
reasoning would overcome it. She worked hard all day long,
that at night she might fall on deep sleep. Again she had
taken up her hard German books, and was also busy with
French histories of revolution, which did indeed fascinate her,
though, as she half perceived, solely by the dramatic quality of
the stories they told. And at length the morning of her fear
had come.

When he left home Mutimer bade her not expect him till
the following day. She spent the hours in loneliness and misery.
Mr. Wyvern called, but even him she begged through a servant
to excuse her; her mother likewise came, and her she talked
with for a few minutes, then pleaded headache. At nine o'clock
in the evening she went to her bedroom. She had a soporific
at hand, remaining from the time of her illness, and in dread of
a sleepless night she had recourse to it.

It seemed to her that she had slept a very long time when
a great and persistent noise awoke her. It was someone knocking at her door, even, as she at length became aware, turning
the handle and shaking it. Being alone, she had locked herself
in. She sprang from bed, put on her dressing-gown, and went
to the door. Then came her husband's voice, impatiently calling
her name. She admitted him.

Through the white blind the morning twilight just made

objects visible in the room; Adela afterwards remembered noticing the drowsy pipe of a bird near the window. Mutimer
came in, and, without closing the door, began to demand angrily
why she had locked him out. Only now she quite shook off
her sleep, and could perceive that there was something unusual
in his manner. He smelt strongly of tobacco, and, as she
fancied, of spirits; but it was his staggering as he moved to
draw up the blind that made her aware of his condition. She
found afterwards that he had driven all the way from Belwick,
and the marvel was that he had accomplished such a feat; probably his horse deserved most of the credit. When he had
pulled the blind up, he turned, propped himself against the
dressing-table, and gazed at her with terribly lack-lustre eyes.
Then she saw the expression of his face change; there came
upon it a smile such as she had never seen or imagined, a
hideous smile that made her blood cold. Without speaking, he
threw himself forward and came towards her. For an instant
she was powerless, paralysed with terror; but happily she found
utterance for a cry, and that released her limbs. Before he
could reach her, she had darted out of the room, and fled to
another chamber, that which Alice had formerly occupied, where
she locked herself against him. To her surprise he did not discover her retreat; she heard him moving about the passages,
stumbling here and there, then he seemed to return to his
bedroom. She wrapped herself in a counterpane, and sat in a
chair till it was full morning.

He was absent for a week after that. Of course his polling
at the election had been ridiculously small compared with that
of the other candidates. When he returned he went about his
ordinary occupations; he was seemingly not in his usual health,
but the constant irritableness had left him. Adela tried to
bear herself as though nothing unwonted had come to pass, but
Mutimer scarcely spoke when at home; if he addressed her
it was in a quick, off-hand way, and without looking at her.
Adela again lived almost alone. Her mother and Letty understood that she preferred this. Letty had many occupations;
before long she hoped to welcome her first child. The children
of New Wanley still came once a week to the Manor; Adela
endeavoured to amuse them, to make them thoughtful, but it
had become a hard, hard task. Only with Mr. Wyvern did she
occasionally speak without constraint, though not of course
without reserve; speech of *that* kind she feared would never
again be possible to her. Still she felt that the vicar saw far

into her life. On some topics she was more open than she had
hitherto ventured to be; a boldness, almost a carelessness, for
which she herself could not account, possessed her at such times.

Late in June she received from Stella Westlake a pressing
invitation to come and spend a fortnight in London. It was
like sunshine to her heart; almost without hesitation she resolved to accept it. Her husband offered no objection, seemed to
treat the proposal with indifference. Later in the day he said:

'If you have time, you might perhaps give Alice a call.'

'I shall do that as soon as ever I can.'

He had something else to say.

'Perhaps Mrs. Westlake might ask her to come, whilst you
are there.'

'Very likely, I think,' Adela replied, with an attempt at
confidence.

It was only her second visit to London: the first had been
in winter time, and under conditions which had not allowed
her to attend to anything she saw. But for Stella's presence
there she would have feared London; her memory of it was like
that of an ill dream long past; her mind only reverted to it in
darkest hours, and then she shuddered. But now she thought
only of Stella; Stella was light and joy, a fountain of magic
waters. Her arrival at the house in Avenue Road was one of
the most blissful moments she had ever known. The servant
led her upstairs to a small room, where the veiled sun made
warmth on rich hangings, on beautiful furniture, on books and
pictures, on ferns and flowers. The goddess of this sanctuary
was alone; as the door opened the notes of a zither trembled
into silence, and Adela saw a light-robed loveliness rise and
stand before her. Stella took both her hands very gently, then
looked into her face with eyes which seemed to be new from
some high vision, then drew her within the paradise of an
embrace. The kiss was once more like that first touch of lips
which had come to Adela on the verge of sleep; she quivered
through her frame.

Mr. Westlake shortly joined them, and spoke with an extreme kindness which completed Adela's sense of being at home.
No one disturbed them through the evening; Adela went to
bed early and slept without a dream.

Stella and her husband talked of her in the night. Mr.
Westlake had, at the time of the election, heard for the first
time the story of Mutimer and the obscure work-girl in Hoxton,
and had taken some trouble to investigate it. It had not

reached his ears when the Hoxton Socialists made it a subject of public discussion; Comrade Roodhouse had inserted only a very general report of the proceedings in his paper the 'Tocsin,' and even this Mr. Westlake had not seen. But a copy of the pamphlet which circulated in Belwick came into his hands, and when he began to talk on the subject with an intimate friend, who, without being a Socialist, amused himself with following the movement closely, he heard more than he liked. To Stella he said nothing of all this. His own ultimate judgment was that you cannot expect men to be perfect, and that great causes have often been served by very indifferent characters.

'She looks shockingly ill,' he began to-night when alone with Stella. 'Wasn't there something said about consumption when she was at Exmouth? Has she any cough?'

'No, I don't think it is that,' Stella answered.

'She seems glad to be with you.'

'Very glad, I think.'

'Did the loss of her child affect her deeply?'

'I cannot say. She has never spoken of it.'

'Poor child!'

Stella made no reply to the exclamation.

The next day Adela went to call on Mrs. Rodman. It was a house in Bayswater, not large, but richly furnished. Adela chose a morning hour, hoping to find her sister-in-law alone, but in this she was disappointed. Four visitors were in the drawing-room, three ladies and a man of horsey appearance, who talked loudly as he leaned back with his legs crossed, a walking-stick held over his knee, his hat on the ground before him. The ladies were all apparently middle-aged; one of them had a great quantity of astonishingly yellow hair, and the others made up for deficiency in that respect with toilets in very striking taste. The subject under discussion was a recent murder. The gentleman had the happiness of being personally acquainted with the murderer, at all events had frequently met him at certain resorts of the male population. When Mrs. Rodman had briefly welcomed Adela, the discussion continued. Its tone was vulgar, but perhaps not more so than the average tone among middle-class people who are on familiar terms with each other. The gentleman, still leading the conversation, kept his eyes fixed on Adela, greatly to her discomfort.

In less than half an hour these four took their departure.

'So Dick came a cropper!' was Alice's first remark, when alone with her sister-in-law.

Adela tried in vain to understand.

'At the election, you know. I don't see what he wanted to go making himself so ridiculous. Is he much cut up?'

'I don't think it troubles him much,' Adela said; 'he really had no expectation of being elected. It was just to draw attention to Socialism.'

'Of course he'll put it in that way. But I'd no idea you were in London. Where are you living?'

Alice had suffered, had suffered distinctly, in her manners, and probably in her character. It was not only that she affected a fastness of tone, and betrayed an ill-bred pleasure in receiving Adela in her fine drawing-room; her face no longer expressed the idle good-nature which used to make it pleasant to contemplate, it was thinner, less wholesome in colour, rather acid about the lips. Her manner was hurried, she seemed to be living in a whirl of frivolous excitements. Her taste in dress had deteriorated; she wore a lot of jewellery of a common kind, and her headgear was fantastic.

'We have a few friends to-morrow night,' she said when the conversation had with difficulty dragged itself over ten minutes. 'Will you come to dinner? I'm sure Willis will be very glad to see you.'

Adela heard the invitation with distress. Fortunately it was given in a way which all but presupposed refusal.

'I am afraid I cannot,' she answered. 'My health is not good; I never see people. Thank you very much.'

'Oh, of course I wouldn't put you out,' said Alice, inspecting her relative's face curiously. And she added, rather more in her old voice, 'I'm sorry you lost your baby. I believe you're fond of children? I don't care anything about them myself; I hope I shan't have any.'

Adela could not make any reply; she shook hands with Alice and took her leave, only breathing freely when once more in the street. All the way back to St. John's Wood she was afflicted by the thought that it would be impossible to advise a meeting between Stella and Mrs. Rodman. Yet she had promised Richard to do so. Once more she found herself sundered from him in sympathies. Affection between Alice and her there could be none, yet Alice was the one person in the world whom Richard held greatly dear.

The enchanted life of those first weeks at Exmouth was now resumed. The golden mornings passed with poetry and music; in the afternoon visits were paid to museums and galleries, or to the studios of artists who were Mrs. Westlake's friends, and who, as Adela was pleased to see, always received Stella with reverential homage. The evening, save when a concert called them forth, was generally a time of peaceful reading and talking, the presence of friends making no difference in the simple arrangements of the home. If a man came to dine at this house, it was greatly preferred that he should not present himself in the costume of a waiter, and only those came who were sufficiently intimate with the Westlakes to know their habits. One evening weekly saw a purely Socialist gathering; three or four artisans were always among the guests. On that occasion Adela was sorely tempted to plead a headache, but for several reasons she resisted. It was a trial to her, for she was naturally expected to talk a good deal with the visitors, several of whom she herself had entertained at Wanley. Watching Stella, she had a feeling which she could not quite explain or justify; she was pained to see her goddess in this company, and felt indignant with some of the men who seemed to make themselves too much at their ease. There was no talk of poetry.

Among the studios to which Stella took her was that of Mr. Boscobel. Mrs. Boscobel made much of them, and insisted on Adela's coming to dine with her. An evening was appointed. Adela felt reproofs of conscience, remembering the excuse she had offered to Alice, but in this case it was impossible to decline. Stella assured her that the party would be small, and would be sure to comprise none but really interesting people. It was so, in fact. Two men whom, on arriving, they found in the drawing-room Adela knew by fame, and the next to enter was a lady whose singing she had heard with rapture at a concert on the evening before. She was talking with this lady when a new announcement fell upon her ear, a name which caused her to start and gaze towards the door. Impossible for her to guard against this display of emotion; the name she heard so distinctly seemed an unreal utterance, a fancy of her brain, or else it belonged to another than the one she knew. But there was no such illusion; he whom she saw enter was assuredly Hubert Eldon.

A few hot seconds only seemed to intervene before she was called upon to acknowledge him, for Mrs. Boscobel was presenting him to her.

' I have had the pleasure of meeting Mrs. Mutimer before,' Hubert said as soon as he saw that Adela in voice and look recognised their acquaintance.

Mrs. Boscobel was evidently surprised. She herself had met Hubert at the house of an artist in Rome more than a year ago, but the details of his life were unknown to her. Subsequently, in London, she happened once to get on the subject of Socialism with him, and told him, as an interesting story, what she heard from the Westlakes about Richard Mutimer. Hubert admitted knowledge of the facts, and made the remark about the valley of Wanley which Mrs. Boscobel repeated at Exmouth, but he revealed nothing more. Having no marriageable daughter, Mrs. Boscobel was under no necessity of searching into his antecedents. He was one of ten or a dozen young men of possible future whom she liked to have about her.

Hubert seated himself by Adela, and there was a moment of inevitable silence.

'I saw you as soon as I got into the room,' he said, in the desperate necessity for speech of some kind. 'I thought I must have been mistaken; I was so unprepared to meet you here.'

Adela replied that she was staying with Mrs. Westlake.

'I don't know her,' said Hubert, 'and am very anxious to. Boscobel's portrait of her—I saw it in the studio just before it went away—was a wonderful thing.'

This was necessarily said in a low tone; it seemed to establish confidence between them.

Adela experienced a sudden and strange calm; in a world so entirely new to her, was it not to be expected that things would happen of which she had never dreamt? The tremor with which she had faced this her first evening in general society had allayed itself almost as soon as she entered the room, giving place to a kind of pleasure for which she was not at all prepared, a pleasure inconsistent with the mood which governed her life. Perhaps, had she been brought into this world in those sunny days before her marriage, just such pleasure as this, only in a more pronounced degree, would have awoke in her and have been fearlessly indulged. The first shock of the meeting with Hubert having passed, she was surprised at her self-control, at the ease with which she found she could converse. Hubert took her down to dinner; on the stairs he twice turned to look at her face, yet she felt sure that her hand had betrayed no agitation as it lay on his arm. At table he talked freely; did he know—she asked herself—that this would relieve her? And his conversation was altogether unlike what it had been two years and a half ago—so long it was since she had talked with him under ordinary conditions. There

was still animation, and the note of intellectual impatience was
touched occasionally, but the world had ripened him, his judgments were based on sounder knowledge, he was more polished,
more considerate—'gentler,' Adela afterwards said to herself.
And decidedly he had gained in personal appearance; a good
deal of the bright, eager boy had remained with him in his days
of storm and stress, but now his features had the repose of
maturity and their refinement had fixed itself in lines of strength.

He talked solely of the present, discussed with her the
season's pictures, the books, the idle business of the town. At
length she found herself able to meet his glance without fear,
even to try and read its character. She thought of the day
when her mother told her of his wickedness. Since then she had
made acquaintance with wickedness in various forms, and now
she marvelled at the way in which she had regarded him. 'I
was a child, a child,' she repeated to herself. Thinking thus,
she lost none of his words. He spoke of the things which
interested her most deeply; how much he could teach her, were
such teaching possible !

At last she ventured upon a personal question.

'How is Mrs. Eldon ?'

She thought he looked at her gratefully; certainly there was
a deep kindness in his eyes, a look which was one of the new
things she noted in him.

'Very much as when you knew her,' he replied. 'Weaker,
I fear. I have just spent a few days at Agworth.'

Doubtless he had often been at Agworth; perchance he was
there, so close by, in some of the worst hours of her misery.

When the ladies withdrew Mrs. Boscobel seated herself by
Adela for a moment.

'So you really knew Mr. Eldon ?'

'Yes, but it is some time since I saw him,' Adela replied
simply, smiling in the joy of being so entirely mistress of herself.

'You were talking pictures, I heard. You can trust him
there; his criticism is admirable. You know he did the Gros-
venor for the—— ?'

She mentioned a weekly paper.

'There are so many things I don't know,' Adela replied
laughingly, 'and that is one of them.'

Hubert shortly after had his wish in being presented to
Mrs. Westlake. Adela observed them as they talked together.
Gladness she could hardly bear possessed her when she saw on

Stella's face the expression of interest which not everyone could call forth. She did not ask why she was so glad; for this one evening it might be allowed her to rest and forget and enjoy.

There was singing, and the sweetest of the songs went home with her and lived in her heart all through a night which was too voiceful for sleep. Might she think of him henceforth as a friend? Would she meet him again before her return to —to the darkness of that ravaged valley? Her mood was a strange one; conscience gave her no trouble, appeared suspended. And why should conscience have interfered with her? Her happiness was as apart from past and future as if by some magic she had been granted an intermezzo of life wholly distinct from her real one. These people with whom she found living so pleasant did not really enter her existence; it was as though she played parts to give her pleasure; she merely looked on for the permitted hour.

But Stella was real, real as that glorious star whose name she knew not, the brightest she could see from her chamber window. To Stella her soul clung with passion and worship. Stella's kiss had power to make her all but faint with ecstasy; it was the kiss which woke her from her dream, the kiss which would for ever be to her a terror and a mystery.

CHAPTER XXII.

HER waking after a short morning sleep was dark and troubled. The taste of last night's happiness was like ashes on her tongue; fearing to face the daylight, she lay with lids heavily closed on a brain which ached in its endeavour to resume the sensations of a few hours ago. The images of those with whom she had talked so cheerfully either eluded her memory, or flitted before her unexpectedly, mopping and mowing, so that her heart was revolted. It is in wakings such as these that Time finds his opportunity to harry youth; every such unwinds from about us one of the veils of illusion, bringing our eyes so much nearer to the horrid truth of things. Adela shrank from the need of rising; she would have abandoned herself to voiceless desolation, have lain still and dark whilst the current of misery swept over her, deeper and deeper. When she viewed her

face, its ring-eyed pallor fascinated her with incredulity.   Had
she looked at all like that whilst Hubert Eldon and the others
were talking to her?   What did they secretly think of her?
The others might attribute to her many more years than she
had really seen ; but Hubert knew her age.   Perhaps that was
why he glanced at her twice or thrice on the stairs.

For the first time she wished not to be alone with Stella,
fearing lest the conversation should turn on Hubert.   Yet,
when they had sat together for nearly an hour, and Stella had
not named him, she began to suffer from a besieging desire to
speak of him, a recurrent impulse to allude to him, however
distantly, so that her companion might be led to the subject.
The impulse grew to a torment, more intolerable each time
she resisted it.   And at last she found herself uttering the
name involuntarily, overcome by something stronger than her
dread.

'I was surprised to meet Mr. Eldon.'

'Did you know him?' Stella asked simply.

'He used to live at Wanley Manor.'

Stella seemed to revive memories.

'Oh, that was how I knew the name.   Mr. Westlake told
me of him, at the time when the Manor passed to Mr. Mutimer.'

Her husband was from home, so had not been at the Boscobels' last evening.

Adela could rest now that she had spoken.   She was searching for a means of leading the conversation into another channel,
when Stella continued,—

'You knew him formerly?'

'Yes, when he still lived at Wanley.   I have not met him
since he went away.'

Stella mused.

'I suppose he came to live in London?'

'I understood so.'

At length Adela succeeded in speaking of something else.
Mental excitement had set her blood flowing more quickly, as
though an obstruction were removed.   Before long the unreasoning lightness of heart began to take possession of her again.
It was strangely painful.   To one whom suffering has driven
upon self-study the predominance of a mere mood is always
more or less a troublesome mystery; in Adela's case it was becoming a source of fear.   She seemed to be losing self-control ;
in looking back on last evening she doubted whether her own
will had been at all operative in the state of calm enjoyment

to which she had attained. Was it physical weakness which put her thus at the mercy of the moment's influences ?

There came a letter from Mutimer to-day ; in it he mentioned Alice and reminded Adela of her promise. This revived a trouble which had fallen out of activity for a day or two. She could not come to any decision. When at Alice's house she had not even suggested a return visit; at the moment it had seemed so out of the question for Alice to meet Mrs. Westlake. In any case, was it worth while exposing Stella to the difficulties of such a meeting when it could not possibly lead to anything further ? One reason against it Adela was ashamed to dwell upon, yet it weighed strongly with her : she was so jealous of her friend's love, so fearful of losing anything in Stella's estimation, that she shrank from the danger of becoming associated with Mrs. Rodman in Stella's mind. Could she speak freely of Alice ? Mutimer's affectionate solicitude was honourable to him, and might veil much that was disagreeable in Alice. But the intimacy between Adela and Mrs. Westlake was not yet of the kind which permits a free disclosure of troubles to which, rightly or wrongly, there attaches a sense of shame. Such troubles are always the last to be spoken of between friends ; friendship must be indeed far-reaching before it includes them within its scope. They were still but learning to know each other, and that more from silent observation, from the sympathy of looks, from touchings of hands and lips, than by means of direct examination or avowal. The more she strove with her difficulty, the less able Adela felt herself to ask Mrs. Rodman to come or to mention her to Stella. The trouble spoilt her enjoyment of a concert that evening, and kept her restless in the night; for, though seemingly a small matter, it had vital connection with the core of her life's problem ; it forced her relentlessly to a consciousness of many things from which she had taught herself to avert her eyes.

Another thing there was which caused her anxious debate —a project which had been in her mind for nearly a year. You will not imagine that Adela had forgotten the letter from Mrs. Clay. The knowledge it brought her made the turning-point of her life. No word on the subject passed between her and Mutimer after the conversation which ended in her fainting-fit. The letter he retained, and the course he had chosen made it advisable that he should pay no heed to its request for assistance. Adela remembered the address of the writer, and made a note of it, but it was impossible to reply. Her state of mind after overhearing the conversation between Richard and his sister was such that she durst not even take the step of privately sending money, lest her husband should hear of it and it should lead to further question. She felt that, hard as it was to live with that secret, to hear Mutimer repeat his calumnies would involve her in yet worse anguish, leading perhaps to terrible things; for, on her return to the house that night, she suffered a revelation of herself which held her almost mute for the following days. In her heart there fought passions of which she had not known herself capable ; above all a scorn so fierce, that had she but opened her lips it must have uttered itself. That she lived down by the aid of many strange expedients ; but she formed a purpose, which seemed indeed nothing less than a duty, to use the opportunity of her first visit to London to seek for means of helping Emma Vine and her sister. Her long illness had not weakened this resolve; but now that she was in London the difficulties of carrying it out proved insuperable. She had always imagined herself procuring the services of some agent, but what agent was at hand? She might go herself to the address she had noted, but it was to incur a danger too great even for the end in view. If Mutimer heard of such a visit— and she had no means of assuring herself that communication between him and those people did not still exist—how would it affect him?

Adela's position would not suffer the risk of ever so slight a difference between herself and her husband. She had come to fear him, and now there was growing in her a yet graver fear of herself.

The condition of her health favoured remissness and postponement. An hour of mental agitation left her with headache and a sense of bodily feebleness. Emma Vine she felt in the end obliged to dismiss from her thoughts; the difficulty concerning Alice she put off from day to day.

The second week of her visit was just ending, and the return to Wanley was in view, when, on entering the drawing-room in the afternoon, she found Hubert Eldon sitting there with Mrs. Westlake. If it had been possible to draw back her foot and escape unnoticed! But she was observed; Hubert had already risen. Adela fancied that Stella was closely observing her ; it was not so in reality, but the persuasion wrung her heart to courage. Hubert, who did make narrow observance of her face, was struck with the cold dignity of her smile. In speaking to him she was much less friendly than at the Boscobers'. He thought he understood, and was in a measure right. A casual meeting in the world was one thing; a visit which might be supposed half intended to herself called for another demeanour. He addressed a few remarks to her, then pursued his conversation with Mrs. Westlake. Adela had time to consider his way of speaking; it was entirely natural, that of a polished man who has the habit of society, and takes pleasure in it. With utter inconsistency she felt pain that he could be so at his ease in her presence. In all likelihood he had come with no other end save that of continuing his acquaintance with Mrs. Westlake. As she listened to his voice, once more an inexplicable and uncontrollable mood possessed her—a mood of petulance, of impatience with him and with herself; with him for almost ignoring her presence, with herself for the distant way in which she had met him. An insensate rebellion against circumstances encouraged her to feel hurt; by a mystery of the mind intervening time was cancelled, and it seemed unnatural, hard to bear, that Hubert should by preference address another than herself. An impulse similar to that which had forced her to speak his name in conversation with Stella now constrained her to break silence, to say something which would require a reply. Her feeling became a sort of self-pity; he regarded her as beneath his notice, he wished her to see that his indifference was absolute; why should he treat her so cruelly?

She added a few words to a remark Mrs. Westlake made, and, the moment she had spoken, was sensible that her tone had been strangely impulsive. Stella glanced at her. Hubert, too, turned his eyes, smiled, and made some reply; she had no understanding of what he said. Had not force failed her she would have risen and left the room. Her heart sank in yet crueller humiliation; she believed there were tears in her eyes, yet had no power to check them. He was still addressing Mrs. Westlake; herself he deemed incapable of appreciating what he said. Perhaps he even—the thought made clanging in her ears, like a rude bell—perhaps he even regarded her as a social inferior since her marriage. It was almost hysteria, to such a pitch of unreason was she wrought. Her second self looked on, anguished, helpless. The voices in the room grew distant and confused.

Then the door was opened and the servant announced—

'Mr. Mutimer.'

It saved her. She saw her husband enter, and an ice-cold breath made frigid her throbbing veins. She fixed her eyes upon him, and could not remove them ; they followed him from the door to where Stella stood to receive him. She saw that he almost paused on recognising Eldon, that his brows contracted, that involuntarily he looked at *her.*

'You know Mr. Eldon,' Stella said, perhaps in not quite her ordinary voice, for the meeting could in no case be a very happy one.

'Oh yes,' replied Mutimer, scarcely looking at Hubert, and making an idle effort at a bow.

Hubert did not reseat himself. He took leave of Stella cordially ; to Adela he inclined himself at respectful distance.

Mrs. Westlake supplied conversation. Adela, leaving her former chair, took a seat by her friend's side, but could not as yet trust her voice. Presently her husband addressed her ; it was for the first time ; he had not even given his hand.

'Alice is very anxious that you should dine with her before you go home. Do you think Mrs. Westlake could spare you this evening ? '

And, on Stella's looking an inquiry, he added :

'My sister, Mrs. Rodman. I don't think you know her ? '

Adela had no choice but to procure her hostess's assent to this arrangement.

'I'll call for you at seven o'clock,' Mutimer said.

Adela knew that he was commanding himself; his tone was not quite discourteous, but he had none of the genial satisfaction which he ordinarily showed in the company of refined people. She attributed his displeasure to her neglect of Alice. But it did not affect her as it had been wont to ; she was disposed to resent it.

The time between his departure and seven o'clock she spent by herself, unoccupied, sitting as if tired. She put off the necessary changing of garments till there was scarcely time for it. When at length she was summoned she went down with flushed face.

'I feel as if I were going to have a fever,' she said to Stella in the drawing-room. She could not help uttering the words, but laughed immediately.

'Your hand is really very hot,' Stella replied.

Mutimer had a cab at the door, and was waiting in the hall.

'You're a long time,' was his greeting, with more impatience than he had ever used to her.

When they were together in the hansom :

'Why did you refuse Alice's invitation before?' he asked, with displeasure.

'I didn't think she really wished me to accept it.'

She spoke without misgiving, still resenting his manner.

'Didn't think? Why, what do you mean?'

She made no reply.

'You didn't ask her to call, either?'

'I ought to have done so. I am very sorry to have neglected it.'

He looked at her with surprise which was very like a sneer, and kept silence till they reached the house.

One of the ladies whom Adela had already met, and a gentleman styled Captain something, were guests at dinner. Alice received her sister-in-law with evident pleasure, though not perhaps that of pure hospitableness.

'I do hope it won't be too much for you,' she said. 'Pray leave as soon as you feel you ought to. I should never forgive myself if you took a cold or anything of the kind.'

Really, Alice had supplied herself with most becoming phrases. The novels had done much; and then she had been living in society. At dinner she laughed rather too loud, it might be, and was too much given to addressing her husband as 'Willis;' but her undeniable prettiness in low-necked evening dress condoned what was amiss in manner. Mr. Rodman looked too gentlemanly; he reminded one of a hero of polite melodrama on the English-French stage. The Captain talked stock-exchange, and was continually inquiring about some one or other, 'Did he drop much?'

Mutimer was staying at the house over-night. After dinner he spoke aside with Adela.

'I suppose you go back to-morrow?'

'Yes, I meant to.'

'We may as well go together, then. I'll call for you at two o'clock.'

He considered, and changed the hour.

'No, I'll come at ten. I want you to go with me to buy some things. Then we'll have lunch here.'

'And go back for my luggage?'

'We'll take it away at ten o'clock and leave it at the station. I suppose you can be ready?'

'Yes, I can be ready,' Adela answered mechanically.

He drove back with her to Avenue Road in the Rodmans' carriage, and left her at the door.

Mr. Westlake was expected home to-night, but had telegraphed to say that he would return in the morning. Stella had spent the evening alone; Adela found her in the boudoir, with a single lamp, reading.

'Are you still feverish?' Stella asked, putting to her cheek the ungloved hand.

'I think not—I can't say.'

Stella waited to hear something about the evening, but Adela broke the silence to say:

'I must leave at ten in the morning. My husband will call for me.'

'So early?'

'Yes.'

There was silence again.

'Will you come and see me before long, Stella?'

'I will,' was the gentle reply.

'Thank you. I shall look forward to it very much.'

Then Adela said good night, speaking more cheerfully.

In her bedroom she sat as before dinner. The fever had subsided during the past two hours, but now it crept into her blood again, insidious, tingling. And with it came so black a phantom of despair that Adela closed her eyes shudderingly, lay back as one lifeless, and wished that it were possible by the will alone to yield the breath and cease. The night pulsed about her, beat regularly like a great clock, and its pulsing smote upon her brain.

To-morrow she must follow her husband, who would come to lead her home. Home? what home had she? What home would she ever have but a grave in the grassy churchyard of Wanley? Why did death spare her when it took the life which panted but for a moment on her bosom?

She must leave Stella and go back to her duties at the Manor; must teach the children of New Wanley; must love, honour, obey her husband. Returning from Exmouth, she was glad to see her house again; now she had rather a thousand times die than go back. Horror shook her like a palsy; all that she had borne for eighteen months seemed accumulated upon her now, waited for her there at Wanley to be endured again. Oh! where was the maiden whiteness of her soul? What malignant fate had robbed her for ever of innocence and peace?

Was this fever or madness? She rose and flung her arms against a hideous form which was about to seize her. It would not vanish, it pressed upon her. She cried, fled to the door, escaped, and called Stella's name aloud.

A door near her own opened, and Stella appeared. Adela clung to her, and was drawn into the room. Those eyes of infinite pity gazing into her own availed to calm her.

'Shall I send for some one?' Stella asked anxiously, but with no weak bewilderment.

'No; it is not illness. But I dread to be alone; I am nervous.'

'Will you stay with me, dear?'

'Oh, Stella, let me, let me! I want to be near to you whilst I may!'

Stella's child slept peacefully in a crib; the voices were too low to wake it. Almost like another child, Adela allowed herself to be undressed.

'Shall I leave a light?' Stella asked.

'No; I can sleep. Only let me feel your arms.'

They lay in unbroken silence till both slept.

CHAPTER XXIII.

In a character such as Mutimer's there will almost certainly be found a disposition to cruelty, for strong instincts of domination, even of the nobler kind, only wait for circumstances to develop crude tyranny—the cruder, of course, in proportion to the lack of native or acquired refinement which distinguishes the man. We had a hint of such things in Mutimer's progressive feeling with regard to Emma Vine. The possibility of his becoming a tyrannous husband could not be doubted by any one who viewed him closely.

There needed only the occasion, and this at length presented itself in the form of jealousy. Of all possible incentives it was the one most calamitous, for it came just when a slow and secret growth of passion was making demand for room and air. Mutimer had for some time been at a loss to understand his own sensations; he knew that his wife was becoming more and more a necessity to him, and that too when the progress of time would have led him to expect the very opposite. He knew it during her absence at Exmouth, more still now that she was away in London. It was with reluctance that he let her leave home, only his satisfaction in her intimacy with the Westlakes and his hopes for Alice induced him to acquiesce in her departure. Yet he could show nothing of this. A lack of self-confidence, a strange shyness, embarrassed him as often as he would give play to his feelings. They were intensified by suppression, and goaded him to constant restlessness. When at most a day or two remained before Adela's return, he could no longer resist the desire to surprise her in London.

Not only did he find her in the company of the man whom he had formerly feared as a rival, but her behaviour seemed to him distinctly to betray consternation at his arrival. She was colourless, agitated, could not speak. From that moment his love was of the quality which in its manifestations is often indistinguishable from hatred. He resolved to keep her under his eye, to enforce to the uttermost his marital authority, to make her pay bitterly for the freedom she had stolen. His exasperated egoism flew at once to the extreme of suspicion; he was ready to accuse her of completed perfidy. Mrs. Westlake became his enemy; the profound distrust of culture, which was inseparable from his mental narrowness, however ambition might lead him to disguise it, seized upon the occasion to declare itself; that woman was capable of conniving at his dishonour, even of plotting it. He would not allow Adela to remain in the house a minute longer than he could help. Even the casual absence of Mr. Westlake became a suspicious circumstance; Eldon of course chose the time for his visit.

Adela was once more safe in the Manor, under lock and key, as it were. He had not spoken of Eldon, though several times on the point of doing so. It was obvious that the return home cost her suffering, that it was making her ill. He could not get her to converse; he saw that she did not study. It was impossible to keep watch on her at all moments of the day; yet how otherwise discover what letters she wrote or received? He pondered the practicability of bribing her maid to act as a spy upon her, but feared to attempt it. He found opportunities of secretly examining the blotter on her writing-desk, and it convinced him that she had written to Mrs. Westlake. It maddened him that he had not the courage to take a single open step, to forbid, for instance, all future correspondence with London. To do so would be to declare his suspicions. He wished to declare them; it would have gratified him intensely to vomit impeachments, to terrify her with coarseness and violence; but, on the other hand, by keeping quiet he might surprise positive evidence, and if only he did!

She was ill; he had a distinct pleasure in observing it. She longed for quiet and retirement; he neglected his business to force his company upon her, to laugh and talk loudly. She with difficulty read a page; he made her read aloud to him by the hour, or write translations for him from French and German. The pale anguish of her face was his joy; it fascinated him, fired his senses, made him a demon of vicious cruelty. Yet he durst not as much as touch her hand when she sat before him. Her purity, which was her safeguard, stirred his venom; he worshipped it, and would have smothered it in foulness.

'Hadn't you better have the doctor to see you?' he began one morning when he had followed her from the dining-room to her boudoir.

'The doctor? Why?'

'You don't seem up to the mark,' he replied, avoiding her look.

Adela kept silence.

'You were well enough in London, I suppose?'

'I am never very strong.'

'I think you might be a bit more cheerful.'

'I will try to be.'

This submission always aggravated his disease—by what other name to call it? He would have had her resist him, that he might know the pleasure of crushing her will.

He walked about the room, then suddenly:

'What is that man Eldon doing?'

Adela looked at him with surprise. It had never entered her thoughts that the meeting with Eldon would cost him more than a passing annoyance—she knew he disliked him—and least of all that such annoyance would in any way be connected with herself. It was possible, of course, that some idle tongue had gossiped of her former friendship with Hubert, but there was no one save Letty who knew what her feelings really had been, and was not the fact of her marriage enough to remove any suspicion that Mutimer might formerly have entertained? But the manner of his question was so singular, the introduction of Eldon's name so abrupt, that she could not but discern in a measure what was in his mind.

She made reply:

'I don't understand. Do you mean how is he engaged?'

'How comes he to know Mrs. Westlake?'

'Through common friends—some people named Boscobel. Mr. Boscobel is an artist, and Mr. Eldon appears to be studying art.'

Her voice was quite steady through this explanation. The surprise seemed to have enabled her to regard him unmoved, almost with curiosity.

'I suppose he's constantly there—at the Westlakes'?'

'That was his first visit. We met him a few evenings before at the Boscobels', at dinner. It was then he made Mrs. Westlake's acquaintance.'

Mutimer moved his head as if to signify indifference. But Adela had found an unexpected relief in speaking thus openly; she was tempted to go further.

'I believe he writes about pictures. Mrs. Boscobel told me that he had been some time in Italy.'

'Well and good; I don't care to hear about his affairs. So you dined with these Boscobel people?'

'Yes.'

He smiled disagreeably.

'I thought you were rather particular about telling the truth. You told Alice you never dined out.'

'I don't think I said that,' Adela replied quietly.

He paused; then :

'What fault have you to find with Alice, eh?'

Adela was not in the mood for evasions; she answered in much the same tone as she had used in speaking of Hubert.

'I don't think she likes me. If she did, I should be able to be more friendly with her. Her world is very different from ours.'

'Different? You mean you don't like Rodman?'

'I was not thinking of Mr. Rodman. I mean that her friends are not the same as ours.'

Mutimer forgot for a moment his preoccupation in thought of Alice.

'Was there anything wrong with the people you met there?'

She was silent.

'Just tell me what you think. I want to know. What did you object to?'

'I don't think they were the best kind of people.'

'The best kind? I suppose they are what you call ladies and gentlemen?'

'You must have felt that they were not quite the same as the Westlakes, for instance.'

'The Westlakes!'

He named them sneeringly, to Adela's astonishment. And ne added as he walked towards the door:

'There isn't much to be said for some of the people you meet there.'

A new complexity was introduced into her life. Viewed by this recent light, Mutimer's behaviour since the return from London was not so difficult to understand; but the problem of how to bear with it became the harder. There were hours when Adela's soul was like a bird of the woods cage-pent: it dashed itself against the bars of fate, and in anguish conceived the most desperate attempts for freedom. She could always die, but was it not hard to perish in her youth and with the world's cup of bliss untasted? Flight? Ah! whither could she flee? The thought of the misery she would leave behind her, the disgrace that would fall upon her mother—this would alone make flight impossible. Yet could she conceive life such as this prolonging itself into the hopeless years, renunciation her strength and her reward, duty a grinning skeleton at her bed-side? It grew harder daily. More than a year ago she thought that the worst was over, and since then had known the solace of self-forgetful idealisms, of ascetic striving. It was all illusion, the spinning of a desolate heart. There was no help now, for she knew herself and the world. Foolish, foolish child, who with her own hand had flung away the jewel of existence like a thing of no price! Her lot appeared single in its haplessness. She thought of Stella, of Letty, even of Alice; *they* had not been doomed to learn in suffering. To her, alone of all women, knowledge had come with a curse.

A month passed. Since Rodman's departure from Wanley, 'Arry Mutimer was living at the Manor. Her husband and 'Arry were Adela's sole companions; the former she dreaded, the approach of the latter always caused her insuperable disgust. To Letty there was born a son; Adela could not bend to the little one with a whole heart; her own desolate motherhood wailed the more bitterly.

Once more a change was coming. Alice and her husband were going to spend August at a French watering-place, and Mutimer proposed to join them for a fortnight; Adela of course would be of the party. The invitation came from Rodman, who had reasons for wishing to get his brother-in-law aside for a little quiet talk. Rodman had large views, was at present pondering a financial scheme in which he needed a partner—one with capital of course. He knew that New Wanley was proving anything but a prosperous concern, commercially speaking; he divined, moreover, that Mutimer was not wholly satisfied with the state of affairs. By judicious management the Socialist might even be induced to abandon the non-paying enterprise, and, though not perhaps ostensibly, embark in one that promised very different results—at all events to Mr. Rodman. The scheme was not of mushroom growth; it dated from a time but little posterior to Mr. Rodman's first meeting with Alice Mutimer. 'Arry had been granted appetising sniffs at the cookery in progress, though the youth was naturally left without precise information as to the ingredients. The result was a surprising self-restraint on 'Arry's part. The influence which poor Keene had so bunglingly tried to obtain over him, the more astute Mr. Rodman had compassed without difficulty; beginning with the loan of small sums, to be repaid when 'Arry attained his majority, he little by little made the prospective man of capital the creature of his directions; in something less than two more years Rodman looked to find ample recompense for his expenditure and trouble. But that was a mere parergon; to secure Richard Mutimer was the great end steadily held in view.

Rodman and his wife came to Wanley to spend three days before all together set out for the Continent. Adela accepted the course of things, and abandoned herself to the stream. For a week her husband had been milder; we know the instinct that draws the cat's paws from the flagging mouse.

Alice, no longer much interested in novels, must needs talk with some one; she honoured Adela with much of her confidence, seeming to forget and forgive, in reality delighted to recount her London experiences to her poor tame sister-in-law. Alice, too, had been at moments introduced to her husband's kitchen; she threw out vague hints of a wonderful repast in preparation.

'Willis is going to buy me a house in Brighton,' she said, among other things. 'I shall run down whenever I feel it would do me good. You've no idea how kind he is.'

There was, in fact, an 'advancement clause' in Alice's deed of settlement. If Mr. Rodman showed himself particularly anxious to cultivate the friendship of Mr. Alfred Waltham, possibly one might look for the explanation to the terms of that same document.

There came a Sunday morning. Preparations for departure

X

on the morrow were practically completed. The weather was delightful. Adela finished breakfast in time to wander a little about the garden before it was the hour for church; her husband and Rodman breakfasted with her, and went to smoke in the library. Alice and 'Arry did not present themselves till the church bells had ceased.

Adela was glad to be alone in the dusky pew. She was the first of the congregation to arrive, and she sat, as always, with the curtains enclosing her save in front. The bells ringing above the roof had a soothing effect upon her, and gave strange turns to her thought. So had their summoning rung out to generation after generation; so would it ring long after she was buried and at rest. Where would her grave be? She was going for the first time to a foreign country; perhaps death might come to her there. Then she would lie for ever among strangers, and her place be forgotten. Would it not be the fitting end of so sad and short a life?

In the front of the pew was a cupboard; the upper portion, which contained the service books, was closed with a long, narrow door, opening downwards on horizontal hinges; the shelf on which the books lay went back into darkness, being, perhaps, two feet broad. Below this shelf was the door of the lower and much larger receptacle; it slid longitudinally, and revealed a couple of buffets, kept here to supplement the number in the pew when necessary. Adela had only once opened the sliding door, and then merely to glance into the dark hollows and close it again. Probably the buffets had lain undisturbed for years.

On entering the pew this morning she had as usual dropped the upper door, and had laid her large church service open on the shelf, where she could reach it as soon as Mr. Wyvern began to read. Then began her reverie. From thoughts of the grave she passed to memories of her wedding day. How often the scene of that morning had re-enacted itself in her mind! Often she dreamed it all over, and woke as from a nightmare. She wished it had not taken place in this church; it troubled the sacred recollections of her maiden peace. She began to think it over once more, attracted by the pain it caused her, and, on coming to the bestowal of the ring, an odd caprice led her to draw the circlet itself from her finger. When she had done it she trembled. The hand looked so strange. Oh, her hand, her hand! Once ringless indeed, once her own to give, to stretch forth in pledge of the heart's imperishable faith! Now a prisoner for ever; but, thus ringless, so like a maiden hand once more. There came a foolish sense of ease. She would keep her finger free yet a little, perhaps through the service. She bent forward and laid the ring on the open book.

More dreams, quite other than before; then the organ began its prelude, a tremor passing through the church before the sound broke forth. Adela sank deeper in reverie. At length Mr. Wyvern's voice roused her; she stood up and reached her book; but she had wholly forgotten that the ring lay upon it, and was only reminded by a glimpse of it rolling away on the shelf, rolling to the back of the cupboard. But it did not stop there; surely it was the ring that she heard fall down below, behind the large sliding door. She had a sudden fright lest it should be lost, and stooped at once to search for it.

She drew back the door, pushed aside the buffets, then groped in the darkness. She touched the ring. But something else lay there; it seemed a long piece of thick paper, folded. This too she brought forth, and, having slipped the ring on her finger, looked to see what she had found.

It was parchment. She unfolded it, and saw that it was covered with writing in a clerkly hand. How strange!

'This is the last will and testament of me, RICHARD MUTIMER——'

Her hand shook. She felt as if the sides of the pew were circling about her, as if she stood amid falling and changing things.

She looked to the foot of the sheet.

'In witness whereof I, the said Richard Mutimer, have hereunto set my hand this seventeenth day of October, 187–.'

The date was some six months prior to old Richard Mutimer's death. This could be nothing but the will which every one believed him to have destroyed.

Adela sank upon the seat. Her ring! Had she picked it up? Yes; it was again upon her finger. How had it chanced to fall down below? She rose again and examined the cupboard; there was a gap of four or five inches at the back of the upper shelf.

Had the will fallen in the same way? Adela conjectured that thus it had been lost, though when or under what circumstances she could not imagine. We, who are calmer, may conceive the old man to have taken his will to church with him on the morning of his death, he being then greatly troubled about the changes he had in view. Perhaps he laid the folded parchment on the shelf and rested one of the large books in front of it. He breathed his last. Then the old woman, whose duty it was to put the pews in order, hurriedly throwing the books into the cupboard as soon as the dead man was removed, perchance pushed the document so far back that it slipped through the gap and down behind the buffets.

At all events, no one has ever hit upon a likelier explanation.

CHAPTER XXIV.

SHE could not sit through the service, yet to leave the church she would have to walk the whole length of the aisle. What did it matter? It would very soon be known why she had gone away, and to face for a moment the wonder of Sunday-clad villagers is not a grave trial. Adela opened the pew door and quitted the church, the parchment held beneath her mantle.

As she issued from the porch the sun smote warm upon her face; it encouraged a feeling of gladness which had followed her astonishment. She had discovered the tenor of the will; it affected her with a sudden joy, undisturbed at first by any reflection. The thought of self was slow in coming, and had not power to trouble her greatly even when she faced it. Befall herself what might, she held against her heart a power which was the utmost limit of that heart's desire. So vast, so undreamt, so mysteriously given to her, that it seemed preternatural. Her weakness was become strength ; with a single word she could work changes such as it had seemed no human agency could bring about.

To her, to her it had been given! What was all her suffering, crowned with power like this?

She durst not take the will from beneath her mantle, though burning to reassure herself of its contents. Not till she was locked in her room. If any one met her as she entered the house, her excuse would be that she did not feel well.

But as she hurried toward the Manor, she all at once found herself face to face with her brother. Alfred was having a ramble, rather glad to get out of hearing of the baby this Sunday morning.

Hollo, what's up?' was his exclamation.

Adela feared lest her face had betrayed her. She was conscious that her look could not be that of illness.

'I am obliged to go home,' she said, 'I have forgotten something.'

'I should have thought you'd rather have let the house burn down than scutter away in this profane fashion. All right, I won't stop you.'

She hesitated, tempted to give some hint. But before she could speak, Alfred continued :

'So Mutimer's going to throw it up.'

'What?' she asked in surprise.

He nodded towards New Wanley.

'Throw it up?'

'So I understand. Don't mention that I said anything; I supposed you knew.'

'I knew nothing. You mean that he is going to abandon the works?'

'Something of the kind, I fancy. I don't know that it's decided, but that fellow Rodman—well, time enough to talk about it. It's a pity, that's all I can say. Still, if he's really losing——'

'Losing? But he never expected to make money.'

'No, but I fancy he's beginning to see things in a different light. I tell you what it is, Adela; I can't stand that fellow Rodman. I've got an idea he's up to something. Don't let him lead Mutimer by the nose, that's all. But this isn't Sunday talk. Youngster rather obstreperous this morning.'

Adela had no desire to question further : she let her brother pass on, and continued her own walk at a more moderate pace.

Alfred's words put her in mind of considerations to which in her excitement she had given no thought. New Wanley was no longer her husband's property, and the great Socialist undertaking must come to an end. In spite of her personal feeling, she could not view with indifference the failure of an attempt which she had trained herself to regard as nobly planned, and full of importance to the world at large. Though she no longer saw Mutimer's character in the same light as when first she bent her nature to his direction, she still would have attributed to him a higher grief than the merely self-regarding ; she had never suspected him of insincerity in his public zeal. Mutimer had been scrupulous to avoid any utterance which might betray half-heartedness ; in his sullen fits of late he had even made it a reproach against her that she cared little for his own deepest interests. To his wife last of all he would have confessed a failing in his enthusiasm : jealousy had made him discourteous, had lowered the tone of his intercourse with her; but to figure as a hero in her eyes was no less, nay more, than ever a leading motive in his life. But if what Alfred said was true, Adela saw that in this also she had deceived herself : the man whose very heart was in a great cause would sacrifice everything, and fight on to the uttermost verge of hope. There was no longer room for regret on his account.

On reaching the Manor gates she feared to walk straight up to the house; she felt that, if she met her husband, she could not command her face, and her tongue would falter. She took a path which led round to the gardens in the rear. She had remembered a little summer-house which stood beyond the kitchen-garden, in a spot sure to be solitary at this hour. There she could read the will attentively, and fix her resolution before entering the house.

Trees and bushes screened her. She neared the summer-house, and was at the very door before she perceived that it was occupied. There sat 'Arry and a kitchenmaid, very close to each other, chatting confidentially. 'Arry looked up, and something as near a blush as he was capable of came to his face. The kitchen damsel followed the direction of his eyes, and was terror-stricken.

Adela hastened away. An unspeakable loathing turned her heart. She scarcely wondered, but pressed the parchment closer, and joyed in the thought that she would so soon be free of this tainted air.

She no longer hesitated to enter, and was fortunate enough to reach her room without meeting any one. She locked the door, then unfolded the will and began to peruse it with care.

The testator devised the whole of his real estate to Hubert Eldon; to Hubert also he bequeathed his personal property, subject to certain charges. These were—first, the payment of a legacy of one thousand pounds to Mrs. Eldon; secondly, of a legacy of five hundred pounds to Mr. Yottle, the solicitor; thirdly, of an annuity of one hundred and seven pounds to the testator's great-nephew, Richard Mutimer, such sum being the yearly product of a specified investment. The annuity was to extend to the life of Richard's widow, should he leave one; but power was given to the trustee to make over to Richard Mutimer, or to his widow, any part or the whole of the invested capital, if he felt satisfied that to do so would be for the annuitant's benefit. 'It is not my wish'—these words followed the directions—' to put the said Richard Mutimer above the need of supporting himself by honest work, but only to aid him to make use of the abilities which I understand he possesses, and to become a credit to the class to which he belongs.'

The executors were Hubert Eldon himself and the lawyer Mr. Yottle.

A man of the world brought face to face with startling revelations of this kind naturally turns at once to thought of technicalities, evasions, compromises. Adela's simpler mind fixed itself upon the plain sense of the will; that meant restitution to the uttermost farthing. For more than two years Hubert Eldon had been kept out of his possessions; others had been using them, and lavishly. Would it be possible for her husband to restore? He must have expended great sums, and of his own he had not a penny.

Thought for herself came last. Mutimer must abandon Wanley, and whither he went, thither must she go also. Their income would be a hundred and seven pounds. Her husband became once more a working man. Doubtless he would return to London; their home would be a poor one, like that of ordinary working folk.

How would he bear it? How would he take this from *her*?

Fear crept insidiously about her heart, though she fought to banish it. It was a fear of the instinct, clinging to trifles in the memory, feeding upon tones, glances, the impressions of forgotten moments. She was conscious that here at length was the crucial test of her husband's nature, and in spite of every generous impulse she dreaded the issue. To that dread she durst not abandon herself; to let it grow even for an instant cost her a sensation of faintness, a desire to flee for cover to those who would naturally protect her. To give up all—and to Hubert Eldon! She recalled his voice when the other day he spoke of Hubert. He had not since recurred to the subject, but his manner still bore the significance with which that conversation had invested it. No dream of suspicions on his part had come to her, but it was enough that something had happened to intensify his dislike of Hubert. Of her many fears, here was one which couched dark and shapeless in the background.

A feeble woman would have chosen anyone—her mother, her brother—rather than Mutimer himself for the first participant in such a discovery. Adela was not feeble, and the very danger, though it might chill her senses, nerved her soul. Was she not making him too ignoble? Was she not herself responsible for much of the strangeness in his behaviour of late? The question she had once asked herself, whether he loved her, she could not answer doubtfully; was it not his love that had set her icily against him? If she could not render him love in return, that was the wrong she did him, the sin she had committed in becoming his wife. Adela by this time knew too well that, in her threefold vows, love had of right the foremost place; honour and obedience could not exist without love. Her wrong was involuntary, none the less she owed him such reparation as was possible; she must keep her mind open to his better qualities. A man might fall, yet not be irredeemably base. Oh, that she had never known of that poor girl in London! Base, doubly and trebly base, had been his behaviour there, for one ill deed had drawn others after it. But his repentance, his humiliation, must have been deep, and of the kind which strengthens against ill-doing in the future.

It had to be done, and had better be done quickly. Adela went to her boudoir and rang the bell. The servant who came told her that Mutimer was in the house. She summoned him.

It was five minutes before he appeared. He was preoccupied, though not gloomily so.

'I thought you were at church,' he said, regarding her absently.

'I came away—because I found something—this!'

She had hoped to speak with calmness, but the interval of waiting had agitated her, and the fear which no effort could allay struck her heart as he entered. She held the parchment to him.

'What is it?' he asked, his attention gradually awakened by surprise. He did not move forward to meet her extended hand.

'You will see—it is the will that we thought was destroyed —old Mr. Mutimer's will.'

She rose and brought it to him. He looked at her with a sceptical smile, which was involuntary, and lingered on his face even after he had begun to read the document.

Adela seated herself again; she had scarcely power to stand. There was a long silence.

'Where did you find this?' Mutimer inquired at length. His tone astonished her; it was almost indifferent. But he did not raise his eyes.

She explained. It was needless, she thought, to give a reason for her search in the lower cupboard; but the first thing that occurred to Mutimer was to demand such reason.

A moment's hesitation; then:

'A piece of money rolled down behind the shelf on which the books are; there is a gap at the back. I suppose that is how the will fell down.'

His eye was now steadily fixed upon her, coldly scrutinising, as one regards a suspected stranger. Adela was made wretched by the inevitable falsehood. She felt herself reddening under his gaze.

He seemed to fall into absent-mindedness, then re-read the document. Then he took out his watch.

'The people are out of church. Come and show me where it was.'

With a deep sense of relief she went away to put on her bonnet. To escape for a moment was what she needed, and the self-command of his voice seemed to assure her against her worst fears. She felt grateful to him for preserving his dignity. The future lost one of its terrors if only she could respect him.

They walked side by side to the church in silence: Mutimer had put the will into his pocket. At the wicket he paused.

'Will Wyvern be in there?'

The question was answered by the appearance of the vicar himself, who just then came forth from the front doorway. He approached them, with a hope that Adela had not been obliged to leave through indisposition.

'A little faintness,' Mutimer was quick to reply. 'We are going to look for something she dropped in the pew.'

Mr. Wyvern passed on. Only the pew-opener was moving about the aisles. She looked with surprise at the pair as they entered.

'Tell her the same,' Mutimer commanded, under his breath.

The old woman was of course ready with offers of assistance, but a word from Richard sufficed to keep her away.

The examination was quickly made, and they returned as they had come, without exchanging a word on the way. They went upstairs again to the boudoir.

'Sit down,' Mutimer said briefly.

He himself continued to stand, again examining the will.

'I should think,' he began slowly, 'it's as likely as not that this is a forgery.'

'A forgery? But who could have——'

Her voice failed.

'He's not likely to have run the risk himself, I suppose,' Mutimer pursued, with a quiet sneer, 'but no doubt there are people who would benefit by it.'

Adela had an impulse of indignation. It showed itself in her cold, steady reply.

'The will was thick with dust. It has been lying there a long time.'

'Of course. They wouldn't bungle over an important thing like this.'

He was once more scrutinising her. The suspicion was a genuine one, and involved even more than Adela could imagine. If there had been a plot, such plot assuredly included the discoverer of the document. Could he in his heart charge Adela with that? There were two voices at his ear, and of equal persuasiveness. Even to look into her face did not silence the calumnious whispering. Her beauty was fuel to his jealousy, and his jealousy alone made the supposition of her guilt for a moment tenable. It was on his lips to accuse her, to ease himself with savage innuendoes, those 'easy things to understand' which come naturally from such a man in such a situation. But to do that would be to break with her for ever, and the voice that urged her innocence would not let him incur such risk. The loss of his possessions was a calamity so great that as yet he could not realise its possibility; the loss of his wife impressed his imagination more immediately, and was in this moment the more active fear.

He was in the strange position of a man who finds all at once that he *dare* not believe that which he has been trying his best to believe. If Adela were guilty of plotting with Eldon, it meant that he himself was the object of her utter hatred, a hideous thought to entertain. It threw him back upon her innocence. Egoism had to do the work of the finer moral perceptions.

'Isn't it rather strange,' he said, not this time sneeringly, but seeking for support against his intolerable suspicions, 'that you never moved those buffets before?'

'I never had need of them.'

'And that hole has never been cleaned out?'

'Never; clearly never.'

She had risen to her feet, impelled by a glimmering of the thought in which he examined her. What she next said came

from her without premeditation. Her tongue seemed to speak
independently of her will.

'One thing I have said that was not true. It was not
money that slipped down, but my ring. I had taken it off and
laid it on the Prayer-book.'

'Your ring?' he repeated, with cold surprise. 'Do you
always take your ring off in church, then?'

As soon as the words were spoken she had gone deadly
pale. Was it well to say that? Must there follow yet more
explanation? She with difficulty overcame an impulse to speak
on and disclose all her mind, the same kind of impulse she had
known several times of late. Sheer dread this time prevailed.
The eyes that were upon her concealed fire; what madness
tempted her to provoke its outburst?

'I have never done so before,' she replied confusedly.

'Why to-day, then?'

She did not answer.

'And why did you tell—why did you say it was money?'

'I can't explain that,' she answered, her head bowed. 'I
took off the ring thoughtlessly; it is rather loose; my finger is
thinner than it used to be.'

On the track of cunning Mutimer's mind was keen enough;
only amid the complexities of such motives as sway a pure
heart in trouble was he quite at a loss. This confession of
untruthfulness might on the face of it have spoken in Adela's
favour; but his very understanding of that made him seek for
subtle treachery. She saw he suspected her; was it not good
policy to seem perfectly frank, even if such frankness for the
moment gave a strengthening to suspicion? What devilish
ingenuity might after all be concealed in this woman, whom he
had taken for simplicity itself.

The first bell for luncheon disturbed his reflections.

'Please sit down,' he said, pointing to the chair. 'We can't
end our talk just yet.'

She obeyed him, glad again to rest her trembling limbs.

'If you suspect it to be a forgery,' she said, when she had
waited in vain for him to speak further, 'the best way of deciding is to go at once to Mr. Yottle. He will remember; it was
he drew up the will.'

He flashed a glance at her.

'I'm perfectly aware of that. If this is forged, the lawyer
has of course given his help. He would be glad to see me.'

Again the suspicion was genuine. Mutimer felt himself

hedged in; every avenue of escape to which his thoughts turned was closed in advance. There was no one he would not now have suspected. The full meaning of his position was growing upon him; it made a ferment in his mind.

'Mr. Yottle!' Adela exclaimed in astonishment. 'You think it possible that he—— Oh, that is folly!'

Yes, it was folly; her voice assured him of it, proclaiming at the same time the folly of his whole doubt. It was falling to pieces, and, as it fell, disclosing the image of his fate, inexorable, inconceivable.

He stood for more than five minutes in silence. Then he drew a little nearer to her, and asked in an unsteady voice:

'Are you glad of this?'

'Glad of it?' she repeated under her breath.

'Yes; shall you be glad to see me lose everything?'

'You cannot wish to keep what belongs to others. In that sense I think we ought to be glad that the will is found.'

She spoke so coldly that he drew away from her again. The second bell rang.

'They had better have lunch without us,' he said.

He rang and bade the servant ask Mr. and Mrs. Rodman to lunch alone. Then he returned to an earlier point of the discussion.

'You say it was thick with dust?'

'It was. I believe the lower cupboard has never been open since Mr. Mutimer's death.'

'Why should he take a will to church with him?'

Adela shook her head.

'If he did,' Mutimer pursued, 'I suppose it was to think over the new one he was going to make. You know, of course, that he never intended *this* to be his will?'

'We do not know what his last thoughts may have been,' Adela replied, in a low voice but firmly.

'Yes, I think we do. I mean to say, we are quite sure he meant to alter *this*. Yottle was expecting the new will.'

'Death took him before he could make it. He left this.'

Her quiet opposition was breath to the fire of his jealousy. He could no longer maintain his voice of argument.

'It just means this: you won't hear anything against the will, and you're glad of it.'

'Your loss is mine.'

He looked at her and again drew nearer.

'It's not very likely that you'll stay to share it,'

' Stay ?' She watched his movements with apprehension.
'How can I separate my future from yours ?'

He desired to touch her, to give some sign of his mastery,
whether tenderly or with rude force mattered little.

' It's easy to say that, but we know it doesn't mean much.'

His tongue stammered. As Adela rose and tried to move
apart, he caught her arm roughly, then her waist, and kissed
her several times about the face. Released, she sank back
upon the chair, pale, terrified, her breath caught with voiceless
sobs. Mutimer turned away and leaned his arms upon the
mantelpiece. His body trembled.

Neither could count the minutes that followed. An inexplicable shame kept Mutimer silent and motionless. Adela,
when the shock of repugnance had passed over, almost forgot
the subject of their conversation in vain endeavours to understand this man in whose power she was. His passion was
mysterious, revolting—impossible for her to reconcile with his
usual bearing, with his character as she understood it. It was
more than a year since he had mingled his talk to her with any
such sign of affection, and her feeling was one of outrage.
What protection had she ? The caresses had followed upon
an insult, and were themselves brutal, degrading. It was a
realisation of one of those half-formed fears which had so long
haunted her in his presence.

What would life be with him, away from the protections of
a wealthy home, when circumstances would have made him
once more the London artisan, and in doing so would have
added harshness to his natural temper; when he would no
longer find it worth while to preserve the semblance of gentle
breeding ? Was there strength in her to endure that ?

Presently he turned, and she heard him speak her name.
She raised her eyes with a half-smile of abashment. He approached and took her hand.

' Have you thought what this means to me ?' he asked, in a
much softer voice.

' I know it must be very hard.'

' I don't mean in that way. I'm not thinking of the change
back to poverty. It's my work in New Wanley, my splendid
opportunity of helping on Socialism. Think, just when everything is fairly started ! You can't feel it as I do, I suppose.
You haven't the same interest in the work. I hoped once you
would have had.'

Adela remembered what her brother had said, but she could

not allude to it.   To question was useless.   She thought of
a previous occasion on which he had justified himself when
accused.

He still held her hand.

'Which would do the most good with this money, he or I ?'

'We cannot ask that question.'

'Yes, we can.   We ought to.   At all events, *I* ought to.
Think what it means.   In my hands the money is used for the
good of a suffering class, for the good of the whole country in the
end.   He would just spend it on himself, like other rich men.   It
isn't every day that a man of my principles gets the means of
putting them into practice.   Eldon is well enough off; long ago
he's made up his mind to the loss of Wanley.   It's like robbing
poor people just to give money where it isn't wanted.'

She withdrew her hand, saying coldly :

'I can understand your looking at it in this way.   But we
can't help it.'

'Why can't we ?'   His voice grew disagreeable in its effort
to be insinuating.   'It seems to me that we can and ought to
help it.   It would be quite different if you and I had just been
enjoying ourselves and thinking of no one else.'   He thought
it a skilful stroke to unite their names thus.   'We haven't
done anything of the kind; we've denied ourselves all sorts of
things just to be able to spend more on New Wanley.   You
know what I've always said, that I hold the money in trust for
the Union.   Isn't it true?   I don't feel justified in giving it up.
The end is too important.   The good of thousands, of hundreds
of thousands, is at stake.'

Adela looked him in the face searchingly.

'But how can we help it ?   There is the will.'

Mutimer met her eyes.

'No one knows of it but ourselves, Adela.'

It was not indignation that her look expressed, but at first
a kind of shocked surprise and then profound trouble.   It was
with difficulty that she found words.

'You are not speaking in earnest ?'

'I am !' he exclaimed, almost hopefully.   'In downright
earnest.   There's nothing to be ashamed of.'   He said it because he felt that her gaze was breeding shame in him.   'It
isn't for myself, it's for the cause, for the good of my fellow-
men.   Don't say anything till you've thought.   Look, Adela,
you're not hard-hearted, and you know how it used to pain you
to read of the poor wretches who can't earn enough to keep

themselves alive. It's for their sake. If they could be here
and know of this, they'd go down on their knees to you. You
can't rob them of a chance! It's like snatching a bit of bread
out of their mouths when they're dying of hunger.'

The fervour with which he pleaded went far to convince
himself; for the moment he lost sight of everything but the
necessity of persuading Adela, and his zeal could scarcely have
been greater had he been actuated by the purest unselfishness.
He was speaking as Adela had never heard him speak, with
modulations of the voice which were almost sentimental, like
one pleading for love. In his heart he despaired of removing
her scruples, but he overcame this with vehement entreaty. A
true instinct forbade him to touch on her own interests; he
had not lived so long with Adela without attaining some perception of the nobler ways of thought. But as often as he
raised his eyes to hers he saw the futility of all his words. Her
direct gaze at length brought him to unwilling silence.

'Would you then,' Adela asked gravely, 'destroy this
will?'

'Yes.'

The monosyllable was all he cared to reply.

'I can scarcely believe you. Such a thing is impossible.
You could not do it.'

'It's my duty to do it.'

'This is unworthy of you. It is a crime, in law and in
conscience. How can you so deceive yourself? After such an
act as that, whatever you did would be worthless, vain.'

'Why?'

'Because no one can do great work of the kind you aim at
unless he is himself guided by the strictest honour. Every
word you spoke would be a falsehood. Oh, can't you see that,
as plainly as the light of day? The results of your work!
Why, nothing you could possibly do with all this money would
be one-half as good as to let everyone know that you honourably gave it up when it was in your power dishonestly to keep
it! Oh, surely *that* is the kind of example that the world
needs! What causes all the misery but dishonesty and selfishness? If you do away with that, you gain all you are working
for. The example! You should prize the opportunity. You
are deceiving yourself; it is a temptation that you are yielding
to. Think a moment; you will see that I am right. You
cannot do a thing so unworthy of yourself.'

He stood for a moment doggedly, then replied :

'I can and I shall do it.'

'Never!' Adela rose and faced him. 'You shall listen to me till you understand. You, who pride yourself on your high motives! For your own sake scorn this temptation. Let me take the will away. I will put it somewhere till to-morrow. You will see clearly by then. I know how dreadful this loss seems to you, but you must be stronger.'

He stood between her and the table on which the parchment lay, and waved her back as she approached. Adela's voice trembled, but there was not a note in it that he could resent.

'You wrong yourself, and you are cruel to me. How could I live with you if you did such a thing? How could I remain in this house when it was no longer yours? It is impossible, a thousand times impossible. You *cannot* mean it! If you do this in spite of everything I can say, you are more cruel than if you raised your hand and struck me. You make my life a shame; you dishonour and degrade me.'

'That's all nonsense,' he replied sullenly, the jealous motive possessing him again at the sight of her gleaming eyes. 'It's you who don't understand, and just because you have no sympathy with my work. Any one would think you cared for nothing but to take the money from me, just to—— '

Even in his access of spiteful anger he checked himself, and dropped to another tone.

'I take all the responsibility. You have nothing to do with it. What seems right to me, I shall do. I am your husband, and you've no voice in a thing like this.'

'No voice? Have I no right to save you from ruin? Must a wife stand by and see her husband commit a crime? Have you no duty to me? What becomes of our married life if you rob me of all respect for you?'

'I tell you I am doing it with a good motive. If you were a thorough Socialist, you would respect me all the more. This money was made out of overworked—— '

He was laying his hand on the will; she sprang forward and grasped his arm.

'Richard, give it to me!'

'No, I shall not.'

He had satisfied himself that if the will was actually destroyed she would acquiesce in silence; the shame she spoke of would constrain her. He pushed her away without violence, and moved towards the door. But her muteness caused him to turn and regard her. She was leaning forward, her lips parted, her eyes fixed in despair.

'Richard!'

'Well?'

'Are you trying me?'

'What do you mean?'

'Do you believe that I should let you do that and help you to hide it?'

'You will come to see that I was right, and be glad that I paid no heed to you.'

'Then you don't know me. Though you are my husband I would make public what you had done. Nothing should silence me. Do you drive me to that?'

The absence of passion in her voice impressed him far more than violence could have done. Her countenance had changed from pleading to scorn.

He stood uncertain.

'Now indeed,' Adela continued, 'I am doing what no woman should have to do.' Her voice became bitter. 'I have not a man's strength; I can only threaten you with shame which will fall more heavily on myself.'

'Your word against mine,' he muttered, trying to smile.

'You could defend yourself by declaring me infamous?'

Did he know the meaning of that flash across her face? Only when the words were uttered did their full significance strike Adela herself.

'You could defend yourself by saying that I lied against you?'

He regarded her from beneath his eyebrows as she repeated the question. In the silence which followed he seated himself on the chair nearest to him. Adela too sat down.

For more than a quarter of an hour they remained thus, no word exchanged. Then Adela rose and approached her husband.

'If I order the carriage,' she said softly, 'will you come with me at once to Belwick?'

He gave no answer. He was sitting with his legs crossed, the will held over his knee.

'I am sorry you have this trial,' she continued, 'deeply sorry. But you have won, I know you have won!'

He turned his eyes in a direction away from her, hesitated, rose.

'Get your things on.'

He was going to the door.

' Richard ! '

She held her hand for the parchment.

' You can't trust me to the bottom of the stairs ? ' he asked bitterly.

She all but laughed with glad confidence.

' Oh, I will trust you ! '

CHAPTER XXV.

ADELA and her husband did not return from Belwick till eight o'clock in the evening. In the first place, Mr. Yottle had to be sent for from a friend's house in the country, where he was spending Sunday ; then there was long waiting for a train back to Agworth. The Rodmans, much puzzled to account for the disorder, postponed dinner. Adela, however, dined alone, and but slightly, though she had not eaten since breakfast. Then fatigue overcame her. She slept an unbroken sleep till sunrise.

On going down next morning she found 'Arry alone in the dining-room ; he was standing at the window with hands in pocket, and, after a glance round, averted his face again, a low growl his only answer to her morning salutation. Mr. Rodman was the next to appear. He shook hands as usual. In his ' I hope you are well ? ' there was an accent of respectful sympathy. Personally, he seemed in his ordinary spirits. He proceeded to talk of trifles, but in such a tone as he might have used had there been grave sickness in the house. And presently, with yet lower voice and a smile of good-humoured resignation, he said—

' Our journey, I fear, must be postponed.'

Adela smiled, not quite in the same way, and briefly assented.

' Alice is not very well,' Rodman then remarked. ' I advised her to have breakfast upstairs. I trust you excuse her ? '

Mutimer made his appearance. He just nodded round, and asked, as he seated himself at table—

' Who's been letting Freeman loose ? He's running about the garden.'

The dog furnished a topic for a few minutes' conversation, then there was all but unbroken silence to the end of the meal. Richard's face expressed nothing in particular, unless it were a bad night. Rodman kept up his smile, and, eating little himself, devoted himself to polite waiting upon Adela. When he rose from the table, Richard said to his brother—

'You'll go down as usual. I shall be at the office in half-an-hour.'

Adela presently went to the drawing-room. She was surprised to find Alice sitting there. Mrs. Rodman had clearly not enjoyed the unbroken rest which gave Adela her appearance of freshness and calm; her eyes were swollen and red, her lips hung like those of a fretful child that has tired itself with sobbing, her hair was carelessly rolled up, her attire slatternly. She sat in sullen disorder. Seeing Adela, she dropped her eyes, and her lips drew themselves together. Adela hesitated to approach her, but was moved to do so by sheer pity.

'I'm afraid you've had a bad night,' she said kindly.

'Yes, I suppose I have,' was the ungracious reply.

Adela stood before her for a moment, but could find nothing else to say. She was turning when Alice looked up, her red eyes almost glaring, her breast shaken with uncontrollable passion.

'I think you might have had some consideration,' she exclaimed. 'If you didn't care to speak a word for yourself, you might have thought about others. What are we to do, I should like to know?'

Adela was struck with consternation. She had been prepared for petulant bewailing, but a vehement outburst of this kind was the last thing she could have foreseen, above all to have it directed against herself.

'What do you mean, Alice?' she said with pained surprise.

'Why, it's all your doing, I suppose,' the other pursued, in the same voice. 'What right had you to let him go off in that way without saying a word to us? If the truth was known, I expect you were at the bottom of it; he wouldn't have been such a fool, whatever he says. What right had you, I'd like to know?'

Adela calmed herself as she listened. Her surprise at the attack was modified and turned into another channel by Alice's words.

'Has Richard told you what passed between us?' she inquired. It cost her nothing to speak with unmoved utterance; the difficulty was not to seem too indifferent.

'He's told us as much as he thought fit. His duty! I like that! As if you couldn't have stopped him, if you'd chosen! You might have thought of other people.'

'Did he tell you that I tried to stop him?' Adela asked, with the same quietness of interrogation.

'Why, did you?' cried Alice, looking up scornfully.

'No.'

'Of course not! Talk about duty! I should think that was plain enough duty. I only wish he'd come to me with his talk about duty. It's a duty to rob people, I suppose? Oh, I understand *him* well enough. It's an easy way of getting out of his difficulties; as well lose his money this way as any other. He always thinks of himself first, trust him! He'll go down to New Wanley and make a speech, no doubt, and show off—. with his duty and all the rest of it! What's going to become of me? You'd no right to let him go before telling us.'

'You would have advised him to say nothing about the will?'

'Advised him!' she laughed angrily. 'I'd have seen if I couldn't do something more than advise.'

'I fear you wouldn't have succeeded in making your brother act dishonourably,' Adela replied.

It was the first sarcasm that had ever passed her lips, and as soon as it was spoken she turned to leave the room, fearful lest she might say things which would afterwards degrade her in her own eyes. Her body quivered. As she reached the door Rodman opened it and entered. He bowed to let her pass, searching her face the while.

When she was gone he approached to Alice, whom he had at once observed.

'What have you been up to?' he asked sternly.

Her head was bent before him, and she gave no answer.

'Can't you speak? What's made her look like that? Have you been quarrelling with her?'

'Quarrelling?'

'You know what I mean well enough. Just tell me what you said. I thought I told you to stay upstairs? What's been going on?'

'I told her she ought to have let us know,' replied Alice, timorous, but affecting the look and voice of a spoilt child.

'Then you've made a fool of yourself!' he exclaimed with subdued violence. 'You've got to learn that when I tell you to do a thing you do it—or I'll know the reason why! You'd no business to come out of your room. Now you'll just find her and apologise. You understand? You'll go and beg her pardon at once.'

Alice raised her eyes in wretched bewilderment.

'Beg her pardon?' she faltered. 'Oh, how can I? Why, what harm have I done, Willis? I'm sure I shan't beg her pardon.'

'You won't? If you talk to me in that way you shall go down on your knees before her. You won't?'

His voice had such concentrated savagery in its suppression that Alice shrank back in terror.

'Willis! How can you speak so! What have I done?'

'You've made a confounded fool of yourself, and most likely spoilt the last chance you had, if you want to know. In future, when I say a thing understand that I mean it; I don't give orders for nothing. Go and find her and beg her pardon. I'll wait here till you've done it.'

'But I *can't*! Willis, you won't force me to do that? I'd rather die than humble myself to her.'

'Do you hear me?'

She stood up, almost driven to bay. Her eyes were wet, her poor, crumpled prettiness made a deplorable spectacle.

'I can't, I can't! Why are you so unkind to me? I have only said what any one would. I hate her! My lips won't speak the words. You've no right to ask me to do such a thing.'

Her wrist was caught in a clutch that seemed to crush the muscles, and she was flung back on to the chair. Terror would not let the scream pass her lips: she lay with open mouth and staring eyes.

Rodman looked at her for an instant, then seemed to master his fury and laughed.

'That doesn't improve your beauty. Now, no crying out before you're hurt. There's no harm done. Only you've to learn that I mean what I say, that's all. Now I haven't hurt you, so don't pretend.'

'Oh, you *have* hurt me!' she sobbed wretchedly, with her fingers round her injured wrist. 'I never thought you could be so cruel. Oh, my hand! What harm have I done? And you used to say you'd never be unkind to me, never! Oh, how miserable I am! Is this how you're going to treat me? As if I could help it! Willis, you won't begin to be cruel? Oh, my hand!'

'Let me look at it. Pooh, what's amiss?' He spoke all at once in his usual good-natured voice. 'Now go and find Adela, whilst I wait here.'

'You're going to force me to do that?'

'You're going to do it. Now don't make me angry again.'

She rose, frightened again by his look. She took a step or two, then turned back to him.

'If I do this, will you be kind to me, the same as before?'

'Of course I will. You don't take me for a brute?'

She held her bruised wrist to him.

'Will you—will you kiss it well again?'

The way in which she said it was as nearly pathetic as anything from poor Alice could be. Her misery was so profound, and this childish forgiveness of an outrage was so true a demonstration of womanly tenderness which her character would not allow to be noble. Her husband laughed rather uneasily, and did her bidding with an ill grace. But yet she could not go.

'You'll promise never to speak——'

'Yes, yes, of course I promise. Come back to me. Mind, I shall know how you did it.'

'But why? What is she to us?'

'I'll tell you afterwards.'

There was a dawning of jealousy in her eyes.

'I don't think you ought to make your wife lower herself——'

His brow darkened.

'Will you do as I tell you?'

She moved towards the door, stopped to dry her wet cheeks, half looked round. What she saw sped her on her way.

Adela was just descending the stairs, dressed to go out. Alice let her go past without speaking, but followed her through the hall and into the garden. Adela turned, saying gently—

'Do you wish to speak to me?'

'I'm sorry I said those things. I didn't mean it. I don't think it was your fault.'

The other smiled; then in that voice which Stella had spoken of as full of forgiveness—

'No, it is not my fault, Alice. It couldn't be otherwise. Don't think of it another moment.'

Alice would gladly have retreated, but durst not omit what seemed to her the essential because the bitterest words.

'I beg your pardon.'

'No, no!' exclaimed Adela quickly. 'Go and lie down a little: you look so tired. Try not to be unhappy; your husband will not let harm come to you.'

Alice returned to the house, hating her sister-in-law with a perfect hatred.

The hated one took her way into Wanley. She had no pleasant mission—that of letting her mother and Letty know what had happened. The latter she found in the garden behind the house dancing her baby-boy up and down in the sunlight. Letty did not look very matronly, it must be confessed; but what she lacked in mature dignity was made up in blue-eyed and warm-cheeked happiness. At the sight of Adela she gave a cry of joy.

'Why, mother's just getting ready to go and say good-bye to you. As soon as she comes down and takes this little rogue I shall just slip my own things on. We didn't think you'd come here.'

'We're not going to-day,' Adela replied, playing with the baby's face.

'Not going?'

'Business prevents Richard.'

'How you frightened us by leaving church yesterday! I was on my way to ask about you, but Mr. Wyvern met me and said there was nothing the matter. And you went to Agworth, didn't you?'

'To Belwick. We had to see Mr. Yottle, the solicitor.'

Mrs. Waltham issued from the house, and explanations were again demanded.

'Could you give baby to the nurse for a few minutes?' Adela asked Letty. 'I should like to speak to you and mother quietly.'

The arrangement was effected and all three went into the sitting-room. There Adela explained in simple words all that had come to pass; emotionless herself, but the cause of utter dismay in her hearers. When she ceased there was blank silence.

Mrs. Waltham was the first to find her voice.

'But surely Mr. Eldon won't take everything from you? I don't think he has the power to—it wouldn't be just; there must be surely some kind of provision in the law for such a thing. What did Mr. Yottle say?'

'Only that Mr. Eldon could recover the whole estate.'

'The estate!' exclaimed Mrs. Waltham eagerly. 'But not the money?'

Adela smiled.

'The estate includes the money, mother. It means every-thing.'

'Oh, Adela!' sighed Letty, who sat with her hands on her lap, bewildered.

'But surely not Mrs. Rodman's settlement?' cried the elder lady, who was rapidly surveying the whole situation.

'Everything,' affirmed Adela.

'But what an extraordinary, what an unheard-of thing! Such injustice I never knew! Oh, but Mr. Eldon is a gentle-man—he can never exact his legal rights to the full extent. He has too much delicacy of feeling for that.'

Adela glanced at her mother with a curious openness of look—the expression which by apparent negation of feeling reveals feeling of special significance. Mrs. Waltham caught the glance and checked her flow of speech.

'Oh, he could never do that!' she murmured the next moment, in a lower key, clasping her hands together upon her knees. I am sure he wouldn't.'

'You must remember, mother,' remarked Adela with re-serve, 'that Mr. Eldon's disposition cannot affect us.'

'My dear child, what I meant was this: it is impossible for him to go to law with your husband to recover the uttermost farthing. How are you to restore money that is long since spent? and it isn't as if it had been spent in the ordinary way —it has been devoted to public purposes. Mr. Eldon will of course take all these things into consideration. And really one must say that it is very strange for a wealthy man to leave his property entirely to strangers.'

'Not entirely,' put in Adela rather absently.

'A hundred and seven pounds a year!' exclaimed her mother protestingly. 'My dear love, what *can* be done with such a paltry sum as that!'

'We must do a good deal with it, dear mother. It will be all we have to depend upon until Richard finds—finds some position.'

'But you are not going to leave the Manor at once?'

'As soon as ever we can. I don't know what arrange-ment my husband is making. We shall see Mr. Yottle again to-morrow.'

'Adela, this is positively shocking! It seems incredible; I never thought such things could happen. No wonder you looked white when you went out of church. How little I imagined ! But you know you can come here at any moment. You can sleep with me, or we'll have another bed put up in the room. Oh, dear ; oh, dear ! 'It will take me a long time to understand it. Your husband could not possibly object to your living here till he found you a suitable home. What *will* Alfred say ? Oh, you must certainly come here. I shan't have a moment's rest if you go away somewhere whilst things are in this dreadful state.'

'I don't think that will be necessary,' Adela replied with a reassuring smile. 'It might very well have happened that we had nothing at all, not even the hundred pounds ; but a wife can't run away for reasons of that kind—can she, Letty ? '

Letty gazed with her eyes of loving pity, and sighed, 'I suppose not, dear.'

Adela sat with them for only a few minutes more. She did not feel able to chat at length on a crisis such as this, and the tone of her mother's sympathy was not soothing to her. Mrs. Waltham had begun to put a handkerchief to her eyes.

'You mustn't take it to heart,' Adela said as she bent and kissed her cheek. You can't think how little it troubles me—on my own account. Letty, I look to you to keep mother cheerful. Only think what numbers of poor creatures would dance for joy if they had a hundred a year left them ! We must be philosophers, you see. I couldn't shed a tear if I tried ever so hard. Good-bye, dear mother ! '

Mrs. Waltham did not rise, but Letty followed her friend into the hall. She had been very silent and undemonstrative ; now she embraced Adela tenderly. There was still something of the old diffidence in her manner, but the effect of her motherhood was discernible. Adela was childless—a circumstance in itself provocative of a gentle sense of protection in Letty's heart.

'You'll let us see you every day, darling ? '

'As often as I can, Letty. Don't let mother get low-spirited. There's nothing to grieve about.'

Letty returned to the sitting-room ; Mrs. Waltham was still pressing the handkerchief on this cheek and that alternately.

'How wonderful she is ! ' Letty exclaimed. 'I feel as if I could never again fret over little troubles.'

'Adela has a strong character.' assented the mother with mournful pride.

Letty, unable to sit long without her baby, fetched it from the nurse's arms. The infant's luncheon-hour had arrived, and the nourishment was still of Letty's own providing. It was strange to see on her face the slow triumph of this ineffable bliss over the grief occasioned by the recent conversation. Mrs. Waltham had floated into a stream of talk.

'Now, what a strange thing it is!' she observed, after many other reflections, and when the sound of her own voice had had time to soothe. 'On the very morning of the wedding I had the most singular misgiving, a feeling I couldn't explain. One would almost think I had foreseen this very thing. And you know very well, my dear, that the marriage troubled me in many ways. It was not *the* match for Adela, but then——. Adela, as you say, has a strong character; she is not very easy to reason with. I tried to make both sides of the question clear to her. But then her prejudice against Mr. Eldon was very strong, and how naturally, poor child! Young people don't like to trust to time; they think everything must be done quickly. If she had been one to marry for reasons of interest it might look like a punishment; but then it was so far other-wise. How much better it would have been to wait a few years! One really never knows what is going to happen. Young people really ought to trust others' experience.'

Letty was only lending half an ear. The general character of her mother-in-law's monologues did not encourage much attention. She was conscious of a little surprise, even now and then of a mild indignation; but the baby sucking at her breast lulled her into a sweet maternal apathy. She could only sigh from time to time and wonder whether it was a good thing or the contrary that Adela had no baby in her trials,

---

CHAPTER XXVI.

MUTIMER did not come to the Manor for luncheon. Rodman, who had been spending an hour at the works, brought word that business pressed; a host of things had to be unexpectedly finished off and put in order. He, Alice, and Adela made pre-tence of a midday meal; then he went into the library to smoke a cigar and meditate. The main subject of his meditation was an interview with Adela which he purposed seeking in the course of the afternoon. But he had also half-a-dozen letters of the first importance to despatch to town by the evening post, and these it was well to get off hand. He had finished them by half-past three. Then he went to the drawing-room, but found it vacant. He sought his wife's chamber. Alice was endeavouring to read a novel, but there was recent tear-shedding about her eyes, which had not come of the author's pathos.

'You'll be a pretty picture soon if that goes on,' Rodman remarked, with a frankness which was sufficiently brutal in spite of his jesting tone.

'I can't think how you take it so lightly,' Alice replied with utter despondency, flinging the book aside.

'What's the good of taking it any other way? Where's Adela?'

'Adela?' She looked at him as closely as her eyes would let her. 'Why do you want her?'

'I asked you where she was. Please to get into the habit of answering my questions at once. It'll save time in future.'

She seemed about to resent his harshness, but the effort cost her too much. She let her head fall forward almost upon her knees and sobbed unrestrainedly.

Rodman touched her shoulder and shook her, but not roughly.

'Do not be such an eternal fool!' he grumbled. 'Do you know where Adela is or not?'

'No, I don't,' came the smothered reply. Then, raising her head, 'Why do you think so much about Adela?'

He leaned against the dressing-table and laughed mockingly.

'That's the matter, eh? You think I'm after her! Don't be such a goose.'

'I'd rather you call me a goose than a fool, Willis.'

'Why, there's not much difference. Now if you'll sit up and behave sensibly, I'll tell you why I want her.'

'Really? Will you give me a kiss first?'

'Poor blubbery princess! Pah! your lips are like a baby's. Now just listen, and mind you hold your tongue about what I say. You know there used to be something between Adela and Eldon. I've a notion it went farther than we know of. Well, I don't see why we shouldn't get her to talk him over into letting you keep your money, or a good part of it. So you see it's you I'm thinking about after all, little stupid.'

'Oh, you really mean that! Kiss me again—look, I've wiped my lips. You really think you can do that, Willis?'

'No, I don't think I can, but it's worth having a try.
Eldon has a soft side, I know. The thing is to find *her* soft
side. I'm going to have a try to talk her over. Now, where
is she likely to be?—out in the garden?'

'Perhaps she's at her mother's.'

'Confound it! Well, I'll go and look about; I can't lose
time.'

'You'll never get her to do anything for *me*, Willis.'

'Very likely not. But the things that you succeed in are
always the most unlikely, as you'd understand if you'd lived my
life.'

'At all events, I shan't have to give up my dresses?'

'Hang your dresses——on the wardrobe pegs!'

He went downstairs again and out into the garden, thence
to the entrance gate. Adela had passed it but a few minutes
before, and he saw her a little distance off. She was going in
the direction away from Wanley, seemingly on a mere walk.
He decided to follow her and only join her when she had gone
some way. She walked with her head bent, walked slowly and
with no looking about her. Presently it was plain that she
meant to enter the wood. This was opportune. But he lost
sight of her as soon as she passed among the trees. He quickened his pace; saw her turning off the main path among the
copses. In his pursuit he got astray; he must have missed her
track. Suddenly he was checked by the sound of voices, which
seemed to come from a lower level just in front of him.
Cautiously he stepped forward, till he could see through hazel
bushes that there was a steep descent before him. Below, two
persons were engaged in conversation, and he could hear every
word.

The two were Adela and Hubert Eldon. Adela had come
to sit for the last time in the green retreat which was painfully
dear to her. Her husband's absence gave her freedom; she
used it to avoid the Rodmans and to talk with herself. She
was, as we may conjecture, far from looking cheerfully into the
future. Nor was she content with herself, with her behaviour
in the drama of these two days. In thinking over the scene
with her husband she experienced a shame before her conscience
which could not at first be readily accounted for, for of a truth
she had felt no kind of shame in steadfastly resisting Mutimer's
dishonourable impulse. But she saw now that in the judgment
of one who could read all her heart she would not come off with
unmingled praise. Had there not been another motive at

work in her besides zeal for honour? Suppose the man benefiting by the will had been another than Hubert Eldon? Surely
that would not have affected her behaviour? Not in practice,
doubtless; but here was a question of feeling, a scrutiny of the
soul's hidden velleities. No difference in action, be sure; that
must ever be upright. But what of the heroism in this particular case? The difference declared itself; here there had
been no heroism whatever. To strip herself and her husband
when a moment's winking would have kept them well clad?
Yes, but on whose behalf? Had there not been a positive
pleasure in making herself poor that Hubert might be rich?
There was the fatal element in the situation. She came out of
the church palpitating with joy; the first assurance of her husband's ignominious yielding to temptation filled her with, not
mere scorn, but with dread. Had she not been guilty of mock
nobleness in her voice, her bearing? At the time she did not
feel it, for the thought of Hubert was kept altogether in the
background. Yes, but she saw now how it had shed light and
warmth upon her; the fact was not to be denied, because her
consciousness had not then included it. She was shamed.

A pity, is it not? It were so good to have seen her purely
noble, indignant with unmixed righteousness. But, knowing
our Adela's heart, is it not even sweeter to bear with her?
You will go far before you find virtue in which there is no dear
sustaining comfort of self. For my part, Adela is more to me
for the imperfection, infinitely more to me for the confession of
it in her own mind. How can a woman be lovelier than when
most womanly, or more precious than when she reflects her own
weakness in clarity of soul?

As she made her way through the wood her trouble of conscience was lost in deeper suffering. The scent of undergrowths,
which always brought back to her the glad days of maidenhood,
filled her with the hopelessness of the future. There was no
return on the path of life; every step made those memories of
happiness more distant and thickened the gloom about her.
She could be strong when it was needful, could face the world
as well as any woman who makes a veil of pride for her bleeding
heart; but here, amid the sweet wood-perfumes, in silence and
secrecy, self-pity caressed her into feebleness. The light was
dimmed by her tears; she rather felt than saw her way. And
thus, with moist eyelashes, she came to her wonted resting-
place. But she found her seat occupied, and by the man whom
in this moment she could least bear to meet.

Hubert sat there, bareheaded, lost in thought. Her light footfall did not touch his ear. He looked up to find her standing before him, and he saw that she had been shedding tears. For an instant she was powerless to direct herself; then sheer panic possessed her and she turned to escape.

Hubert started to his feet.

'Mrs. Mutimer! Adela!'

The first name would not have stayed her, for her flight was as unreasoning as that of a fawn. The second, her own name, uttered with almost desperate appeal, robbed her of the power of movement. She turned to bay, as though an obstacle had risen in her path, and there was terror in her white face.

Hubert drew a little nearer and spoke hurriedly.

'Forgive me! I could not let you go. You seem to have come in answer to my thought; I was wishing to see you. Do forgive me!'

She knew that he was examining her moist eyes; a rush of blood passed over her features.

'Not unless you are willing,' Hubert pursued, his voice at its gentlest and most courteous. 'But if I might speak to you for a few minutes——?'

'You have heard from Mr. Yottle?' Adela asked, without raising her eyes, trying her utmost to speak in a merely natural way.

'Yes. I happened to be at my mother's house. He came last night to obtain my address.'

The truth was, that a generous impulse, partly of his nature, and in part such as any man might know in a moment of unanticipated good fortune, had bade him put aside his prejudices and meet Mutimer at once on a footing of mutual respect. Incapable of ignoble exultation, it seemed to him that true delicacy dictated a personal interview with the man who, judging from Yottle's report, had so cheerfully acquitted himself of the hard task imposed by honour. But as he walked over from Agsworth this zeal cooled. Could he trust Mutimer to appreciate his motive? Such a man was capable of acting honourably, but the power of understanding delicacies of behaviour was not so likely to be his. Hubert's prejudices were insuperable; to his mind class differences necessarily argued a difference in the grain. And it was not only this consideration that grew weightier as he walked. In the great joy of recovering his ancestral home, in the sight of his mother's profound happiness, he all but forgot the thoughts that had besieged him since his meetings with Adela in London. As he drew near to Wanley his imagination busied itself almost exclusively with her; distrust and jealousy of Mutimer became fear for Adela's future. Such a change as this would certainly have a dire effect upon her life. He thought of her frail appearance; he remembered the glimpse of her face that he had caught when her husband entered Mrs. Westlake's drawing-room, the startled movement she could not suppress. It was impossible to meet Mutimer with any show of good-feeling; he wondered how he could have set forth with such an object. Instead of going to the Manor he turned his steps to the Vicarage, and joined Mr. Wyvern at luncheon. The vicar had of course heard nothing of the discovery as yet. In the afternoon Hubert started to walk back to Agworth, but instead of taking the direct road he strayed into the wood. He was loth to leave the neighbourhood of the Manor; intense anxiety to know what Adela was doing made him linger near the place where she was. Was she already suffering from brutal treatment? What wretchedness might she not be undergoing within those walls!

He said she seemed to have sprung up in answer to his desire. In truth, her sudden appearance overcame him; her tearful face turned to irresistible passion that yearning which, consciously or unconsciously, was at all times present in his life. Her grief could have but one meaning; his heart went out to her with pity as intense as its longing. Other women had drawn his eyes, had captured him with the love of a day; but the deep still affection which is independent of moods and impressions flowed ever towards Adela. As easily could he have become indifferent to his mother as to Adela. As a married woman she was infinitely more to him than she had been as a girl; from her conversation, her countenance, he knew how richly she had developed, how her intelligence had ripened, how her character had established itself in maturity. In that utterance of her name the secret escaped him before he could think how impossible it was to address her so familiarly. It was the perpetual key-word of his thoughts; only when he had heard it from his own lips did he realise what he had done.

When he had given the brief answer to her question he could find no more words. But Adela spoke.

'What do you wish to say to me, Mr. Eldon?'

Whether or no he interpreted her voice by his own feelings, she seemed to plead with him to be manly and respect her womanhood.

'Only to say the common things which anyone must say in my position, but to say them so that you will believe they are not only a form. The circumstances are so strange. I want to ask you for your help; my position is perhaps harder than yours and Mr. Mutimer's. We must remember that there is justice to be considered. If you will give me your aid in doing justice as far as I am able——'

In fault of any other possible reply he had involved himself in a subject which he knew it was far better to leave untouched. He could not complete his sentence, but stood before her with his head bent.

Adela scarcely knew what he said; in anguish she sought for a means of quitting him, of fleeing and hiding herself among the trees. His accent told her that she was the object of his compassion, and she had invited it by letting him see her tears. Of necessity he must think that she was sorrowing on her own account. That was true, indeed, but how impossible for him to interpret her grief rightly? The shame of being misjudged by him all but drove her to speak, and tell him that she cared less than nothing for the loss that had befallen her. Yet she could not trust herself to speak such words. Her heart was beating insufferably; all the woman in her rushed towards hysteria and self-abandonment. It was well that Hubert's love was of quality to stand the test of these terrible moments. Something he must say, and the most insignificant phrase was the best.

'Will you sit—rest after your walk?'

She did so; scarcely could she have stood longer. And with the physical ease there seemed to come a sudden mental relief. A thought sprang up, opening upon her like a haven of refuge.

'There is one thing I should like to ask of you,' she began, forcing herself to regard him directly. 'It is a great thing, I am afraid; it may be impossible.'

'Will you tell me what it is?' he said, quietly filling the pause that followed.

'I am thinking of New Wanley.'

She saw a change in his face, slight, but still a change. She spoke more quickly.

'Will you let the works remain as they are, on the same plan? Will you allow the workpeople to live under the same rules? I have been among them constantly, and I am sure that nothing but good results have come of—of what my husband has done. There is no need to ask you to deal kindly with them, I know that. But if you could maintain the purpose——? It will be such a grief to my husband if all his work comes to nothing. There cannot be anything against your principles in what I ask. It is so simply for the good of men and women whose lives are so hard. Let New Wanley remain as an example. Can you do this?'

Hubert, as he listened, joined his hands behind his back, and turned his eyes to the upper branches of the silver birch, which once in his thoughts he had likened to Adela. What he heard from her surprised him, and upon surprise followed mortification. He knew that she had in appearance adopted Mutimer's principles, but his talk with her in London at Mrs. Boscobel's had convinced him that her heart was in far other things than economic problems and schemes of revolution. She had listened so eagerly to his conversation on art and kindred topics; it was so evident that she was enjoying a temporary release from a mode of life which chilled all her warmer instincts. Yet she now made it her entreaty that he would continue Mutimer's work. Beginning timidly, she grew to an earnestness which it was impossible to think feigned. He was unprepared for anything of the kind; his emotions resented it. Though consciously harbouring no single unworthy desire, he could not endure to find Adela zealous on her husband's behalf.

Had he misled himself? Was the grief that he had witnessed really that of a wife for her husband's misfortune? For whatever reason she had married Mutimer—and that *could* not be love—married life might have engendered affection. He knew Adela to be deeply conscientious; how far was it in a woman's power to subdue herself to love at the bidding of duty?

He allowed several moments to pass before replying to her. Then he said, courteously but coldly:

'I am very sorry that you have asked the one thing I cannot do.'

Adela's heart sank. In putting a distance between him and herself she had obeyed an instinct of self-preservation; now that it was effected, the change in his voice was almost more than she could bear.

'Why do you refuse?' she asked, trying, though in vain, to look up at him.

'Because it is impossible for me to pretend sympathy with

Mr. Mutimer's views.   In the moment that I heard of the will
my action with regard to New Wanley was determined.   What
I purpose doing is so inevitably the result of my strongest convictions that nothing could change me.'

'Will you tell me what you are going to do?' Adela
asked, in a tone more like his own.

'It will pain you.'

'Yet I should like to know.'

'I shall sweep away every trace of the mines and the works
and the houses, and do my utmost to restore the valley to its
former state.'

He paused, but Adela said nothing.   Her fingers played
with the leaves which grew beside her.

'Your associations with Wanley of course cannot be as strong
as my own.   I was born here, and every dearest memory of my
life connects itself with the valley as it used to be.   It was one
of the loveliest spots to be found in England.   You can have
no idea of the feelings with which I saw this change fall upon
it, this desolation and defilement—I must use the words which
come to me.   I might have overcome that grief if I had sympathised with the ends.   But, as it is, I should act in the same
way even if I had no such memories.   I know all that you
will urge.   It may be inevitable that the green and beautiful
spots of the world shall give place to furnaces and mechanics'
dwellings.   For my own part, in this little corner, at all events,
the ruin shall be delayed.   In this matter I will give my instincts free play.   Of New Wanley not one brick shall remain
on another.   I will close the mines, and grass shall again grow
over them; I will replant the orchards and mark out the
fields as they were before.'

He paused again.

'You see why I cannot do what you ask.'

It was said in a gentler voice, for insensibly his tone had
become almost vehement.

He found a strange pleasure in emphasising his opposition
to her.   Perhaps he secretly knew that Adela hung upon his
words, and in spite of herself was drawn into the current of his
enthusiasm.   But he did not look into her face.   Had he done
so he would have seen it fixed and pale.

'Then you think grass and trees of more importance than
human lives?'

She spoke in a voice which sounded coldly ironical in its
attempt to be merely calm.

'I had rather say that I see no value in human lives in a world from which grass and trees have vanished. But, in truth, I care little to make my position logically sound. The ruling motive in my life is the love of beautiful things; I fight against ugliness because it's the only work in which I can engage with all my heart. I have nothing of the enthusiasm of humanity. In the course of centuries the world may perhaps put itself right again; I am only concerned with the present, and I see that everywhere the tendency is towards the rule of mean interests, ignoble ideals.'

'Do you call it ignoble,' broke in Adela, 'to aim at raising men from hopeless and degrading toil to a life worthy of human beings?'

'The end which *you* have in mind cannot be ignoble. But it is not to be reached by means such as these.' He pointed down to the valley. 'That may be the only way of raising the standard of comfort among people who work with their hands; I take the standpoint of the wholly unpractical man, and say that such efforts do not concern me. From my point of view no movement can be tolerated which begins with devastating the earth's surface. You will clothe your workpeople better, you will give them better food and more leisure; in doing so you injure the class that has finer sensibilities, and give power to the class which not only postpones everything to material wellbeing, but more and more regards intellectual refinement as an obstacle in the way of progress. Progress—the word is sufficient; you have only to think what it has come to mean. It will be good to have an example of reaction.'

'When reaction means misery to men and women and little children?'

'Yes, even if it meant that. As far as I am concerned, I trust it will have no such results. You must distinguish between humanity and humanitarianism. I hope I am not lacking in the former; the latter seems to me to threaten everything that is most precious in the world.'

'Then you are content that the majority of mankind should be fed and clothed and kept to labour?'

'Personally, quite content; for I think it very unlikely that the majority will ever be fit for anything else. I *know* that at present they desire nothing else.'

'Then they must be taught to desire more.'

Hubert again paused. When he resumed it was with a smile which strove to be good-humoured.

'We had better not argue of these things. If I said all that I think you would accuse me of brutality. In logic you will overcome me. Put me down as one of those who represent reaction and class-prejudice. I am all prejudice.'

Adela rose.

'We have talked a long time,' she said, trying to speak lightly. 'We have such different views. I wish there were less class-prejudice.'

Hubert scarcely noticed her words. She was quitting him, and he clung to the last moment of her presence.

'Shall you go—eventually go to London?' he asked.

'I can't say. My husband has not yet been able to make plans.'

The word irritated him. He half averted his face.

'Good-bye, Mr. Eldon.'

She did not offer her hand—durst not do so. Hubert bowed without speaking.

When she was near the Manor gates she heard footsteps behind her. She turned and saw her husband. Her cheeks flushed, for she had been walking in deep thought. It seemed to her for an instant as if the subject of her preoccupation could be read upon her face.

'Where have you been?' Mutimer asked, indifferently.

'For a walk. Into the wood.'

He was examining her, for the disquiet of her countenance could not escape his notice.

'Why did you go alone? It would have done Alice good to get her out a little.'

'I'm afraid she wouldn't have come.'

He hesitated.

'Has she been saying anything to you?'

'Only that she is troubled and anxious.'

They walked on together in silence, Mutimer with bowed head and knitted brows.

CHAPTER XXVI.

THE making a virtue of necessity, though it argues lack of ingenuousness, is perhaps preferable to the wholly honest demonstration of snarling over one's misfortunes. It may result in good even to the hypocrite, who occasionally surprises himself with the pleasure he finds in wearing a front of nobility, and is thereby induced to consider the advantages of upright behaviour adopted for its own sake. Something of this kind happened in the case of Richard Mutimer. Seeing that there was no choice but to surrender his fortune, he set to work to make the most of abdication, and with the result that the three weeks occupied in settling his affairs at New Wanley and withdrawing from the Manor were full of cheerful activity. He did not meet Hubert Eldon, all business being transacted through Mr. Yottle. When he heard from the latter that it was Eldon's intention to make a clean sweep of mines, works, and settlements, though for a moment chagrined, he speedily saw that such action, by giving dramatic completeness to his career at Wanley and investing its close with something of tragic pathos, was in truth what he should most have desired. It enabled him to take his departure with an air of profounder sadness; henceforth no gross facts would stand in the way of his rhetoric when he should enlarge on the possibilities thus nipped in the bud. He was more than ever a victim of cruel circumstances; he could speak with noble bitterness of his life's work having been swept into oblivion.

He was supported by a considerable amount of epistolary sympathy. The local papers made an interesting story of what had happened in the old church at Wanley, and a few of the London journals reported the circumstances; in this way Mutimer became known to a wider public than had hitherto observed him. Not only did his fellow-Unionists write to encourage and moralise, but a number of those people who are ever ready to indite letters to people of any prominence, the honestly admiring and the windily egoistic, addressed communications either to Wanley Manor or to the editor of the 'Fiery Cross.' Mutimer read eagerly every word of each most insignificant scribbler; his eyes gleamed and his cheeks grew warm. All such letters he brought to Adela, and made her read them aloud; he stood with his hands behind his back, his face slightly elevated and at a listening angle. At the end he regarded her, and his look said: 'Behold the man who is your husband!'

But at length there came one letter distinct from all the rest; it had the seal of a Government office. With eyes which scarcely credited what they saw Mutimer read some twenty or thirty words from a Minister of the Crown, a gentleman of vigorously Radical opinions, who had 'heard with much regret that the undertaking conceived and pursued with such single-hearted zeal' had come to an untimely end. Mutimer rushed to Adela like a schoolboy who has a holiday to announce.

'Read that now! What do you think of that? Now there's some hope of a statesman like that!'

Adela gave forth the letter in a voice which was all too steady. But she said:

'I am very glad. It must gratify you. He writes very kindly.'

'You'll have to help me to make an answer.'

Adela smiled, but said nothing.

The ceremonious opening of the hall at New Wanley had been a great day; Mutimer tried his best to make the closing yet more effective. Mr. Westlake was persuaded to take the chair, but this time the oration was by the founder himself. There was a numerous assembly. Mutimer spoke for an hour and a quarter, reviewing what he had done, and enlarging on all that he might and would have done. There was as much applause as even he could desire. The proceedings closed with the reading of an address which was signed by all the people of the works, a eulogium and an expression of gratitude, not without one or two sentences of fiery Socialism. The spokesman was a fine fellow of six feet two, a man named Redgrave, the ideal of a revolutionist workman. He was one of the few men at the works whom Adela, from observation of their domestic life, had learnt sincerely to respect. Before reading the document he made a little speech of his own, and said in conclusion:

'Here's an example of how the law does justice in a capitalist society. The man who makes a grand use of money has it all taken away from him by the man who makes no use of it at all, except to satisfy his own malice and his own selfishness. If we don't one and all swear to do our utmost to change such a state of things as that, all I can say is we're a poor lot, and deserve to be worse treated than the animals, that haven't the sense to use their strength!'

In his reply to the address Richard surpassed himself. He rose in excitement; the words that rushed to his lips could scarcely find articulate flow. After the due thanks:

'To-morrow I go to London; I go as poor as the poorest of you, a mechanical engineer in search of work. Whether I shall find it or not there's no saying. If they turned me out because of my opinions three years ago, it's not very likely that they've grown fonder of me by this time. As poor as the poorest of you, I say. Most of you probably know that a small legacy is left to me under the will which gives this property into other hands. That money will be used, every penny of it, for the furtherance of our cause!'

It was a magnificent thought, one of those inspirations which reveal latent genius. The hall echoed with shouts of glorification. Adela, who sat with her mother and Letty (Mrs. Westlake had not accompanied her husband), kept her eyes fixed on the ground; the uproar made her head throb.

All seemed to be over and dispersal was beginning, when a gentleman stood up in the middle of the hall and made signs that he wished to be heard for a moment. Mutimer aided him in gaining attention. It was Mr. Yottle, a grizzle-headed, ruddy-cheeked veteran of the law.

'I merely desire to use this opportunity of reminding those who have been employed at the works that Mr. Eldon will be glad to meet them in this hall at half-past ten o'clock to-morrow morning. It will perhaps be better if the men alone attend, as the meeting will be strictly for business purposes.'

Adela was among the last to leave the room. As she was moving between the rows of benches Mr. Westlake approached her. He had only arrived in time to take his place on the platform, and he was on the point of returning to London.

'I have a note for you from Stella,' he said. 'She has been ailing for a fortnight; it wasn't safe for her to come. But she will soon see you, I hope.'

'I hope so,' Adela replied mechanically, as she took the letter.

Mr. Westlake only added his 'good-bye,' and went to take leave of Mutimer, who was standing at a little distance.

Among those who remained to talk with the hero of the day was our old friend Keene. Keene had risen in the world, being at present sub-editor of a Belwick journal. His appearance had considerably improved, and his manner was more ornate than ever. He took Mutimer by the arm and led him aside.

'A suggestion—something that occurred to me whilst you were speaking. You must write the history of New Wanley. Not too long; a thing that could be printed in pamphlet form and sold at a penny or twopence. Speak to Westlake; see if the Union won't publish. Some simple title : " My Work in New Wanley," for instance. I'll see that it's well noticed in our rag.'

'Not a bad idea !' Mutimer exclaimed, throwing back his head.

'Trust me, not half bad. Be of use in the Propaganda. Just think it over, and, if you care to, allow me to read it in manuscript. There's a kind of art—eh ? you know what I mean ; it's only to be got by journalistic practice. Yes, " My Work in New Wanley " ; I think that would do.'

'I'm going to lecture at Commonwealth Hall next Sunday,' Mutimer observed. 'I'll take that for my title.'

'By-the-bye, how—what was I going to say ? Oh yes, how is Mrs. Rodman ?'

'Tolerable, I believe.'

'In London, presumably ?'

'Yes.'

'Not much—not taking it to heart much, I hope ?'

'Not particularly, I think.'

'I should be glad to be remembered—a word when you see her. Thanks, Mutimer, thanks. I must be off.'

Adela was making haste to reach the Manor, that she might read Stella's letter. She and her husband were to dine this evening with the Walthams—a farewell meal. With difficulty she escaped from her mother and Letty ; Stella's letter demanded a quarter of an hour of solitude.

She reached her room, and broke the envelope. Stella never wrote at much length, but to-day there were only a few lines.

' My love to you, heart's darling. I am not well enough to come, and I think it likely you had rather I did not. But in a few hours you will be near me. Come as soon as ever you can. I wait for you like the earth for spring.   ' STELLA.'

She kissed the paper and put it in the bosom of her dress. It was already time to go to her mother's.

She found her mother and Letty with grave faces; something seemed to have disturbed them. Letty tried to smile and appear at ease, but Mrs. Waltham was at no pains to hide the source of her dissatisfaction.

'Did you know of that, Adela ?' she asked, with vexation. ' About the annuity, I mean. Had Richard spoken to you of his intention ?'

Adela replied with a simple negative. She had not given the matter a thought.

'Then he certainly should have done. It was his duty, I consider, to tell *me*. It is in express contradiction of all he has led me to understand. What are you going to live on, I should like to know? It's very unlikely that he will find a position immediately. He is absolutely reckless, wickedly thoughtless! My dear, it is not too late even now. I insist on your staying with us until your husband has found an assured income. The idea of your going to live in lodgings in an obscure part of London is more than I can bear, and *now* it really appals me. Adela, my child, it's impossible for you to go under these circumstances. The commonest decency will oblige him to assent to this arrangement.'

'My dear mother,' Adela replied seriously, 'pray do not reopen that. It surely ought to be needless for me to repeat that it is my duty to go to London.'

'But, Adela darling,' began Letty, very timorously, 'wouldn't it be relieving your husband? How much freer he would be to look about, knowing you are here safe and in comfort. I really—I do really think mother is right.'

Before Adela could make any reply there sounded a knock at the front door; Richard came in. He cast a glance round at the three. The others might have escaped his notice, but Mrs. Waltham was too plainly perturbed.

'Has anything happened?' he asked in an offhand way.

'I am distressed, more than I can tell you,' began his mother-in-law. 'Surely you did not mean what you said about the money——'

'Mother!' came from Adela's lips, but she checked herself.

Mutimer thrust his hands into his pockets and stood smiling.

'Yes, I meant it.'

'But, pray, what are you and Adela going to live upon?'

'I don't think we shall have any difficulty.'

'But surely one must more than *think* in a matter such as this. You mustn't mind me speaking plainly, Richard. Adela is my only daughter, and the thought of her undergoing needless hardships is so dreadful to me that I really must speak. I have a plan, and I am sure you will see that it is the very best for all of us. Allow Adela to remain with me for a little while, just till you have—have made things straight. It certainly would ease your mind. She is so very welcome to a share of ʋur home. You would feel less hampered. I am sure you will consent to this.'

Mutimer's smile died away. He avoided Mrs. Waltham's face, and let his eyes pass in a cold gaze from Letty, who almost shrank, to Adela, who stood with an air of patience.

'What do you say to this?' he asked of his wife, in a tone civil indeed, but very far from cordial.

'I have been trying to show mother that I cannot do as she wishes. It is very kind of her, but, unless you think it would be better for me to stay, I shall of course accompany you.'

'You can stay if you like.'

Adela understood too well what that permission concealed.

'I have no wish to stay.'

Mutimer turned his look on Mrs. Waltham, without saying anything.

'Then I can say no more,' Mrs. Waltham replied. 'But you must understand that I take leave of my daughter with the deepest concern. I hope you will remember that her health for a long time has been anything but good, and that she was never accustomed to do hard and coarse work.'

'We won't talk any more of this, mother,' Adela interposed firmly. 'I am sure you need have no fear that I shall be tried beyond my strength. You must remember that I go with my husband.'

The high-hearted one! She would have died rather than let her mother perceive that her marriage was less than happy. To the end she would speak that word 'my husband,' when it was necessary to speak it at all, with the confidence of a woman who knows no other safeguard against the ills of life. To the end she would shield the man with her own dignity, and protect him as far as possible even against himself.

Mutimer smiled again, this time with satisfaction.

'I certainly think we can take care of ourselves,' he remarked briefly.

In a few minutes they were joined by Alfred, who had only just returned from Belwick, and dinner was served. It was not a cheerful evening. At Adela's request it had been decided in advance that the final leave-taking should be to-night; she and Mutimer would drive to Agworth station together with Alfred the first thing in the morning. At ten o'clock the parting came. Letty could not speak for sobbing; she just kissed Adela and hurried from the room. Mrs. Waltham preserved a rather frigid stateliness.

'Good-bye, my dear,' she said, when released from her daughter's embrace. 'I hope I may have good news from you.'

With Mutimer she shook hands.

It was a starry and cold night. The two walked side by side without speaking. When they were fifty yards on their way, a figure came out of a corner of the road, and Adela heard Letty call her name.

'I will overtake you,' she said to her husband.

'Adela, my sweet, I *couldn't* say good-bye to you in the house!'

Letty hung about her dear one's neck. Adela choked; she could only press her cheek against that moist one.

'Write to me often—oh, write often,' Letty sobbed. 'And tell me the truth, darling, will you?'

'It will be all well, dear sister,' Adela whispered.

'Oh, that is a dear name! Always call me that. I can't say good-bye, darling. You will come to see us as soon as ever you can?'

'As soon as I can, Letty.'

Adela found her husband awaiting her.

'What did she want?' he asked, with genuine surprise.

'Only to say good-bye.'

'Why, she'd said it once.'

The interior of the Manor was not yet disturbed, but all the furniture was sold, and would be taken away on the morrow. They went to the drawing-room. After some insignificant remarks Mutimer asked:

'What letter was that Westlake gave you?'

'It was from Stella—from Mrs. Westlake.'

He paused. Then:

'Will you let me see it?'

'Certainly, if you wish.'

She felt for it in her bosom and handed it to him. It shook in her fingers.

'Why does she think you'd rather she didn't come?'

'I suppose because the occasion seems to her painful.'

'I don't see that it was painful at all. What did you think of my speech?'

'The first one or the second?'

'Both, if you like. I meant the first.'

'You told the story very well.'

'You'll never spoil me by over-praise.'

Adela was silent.

'About this,' he resumed, tapping the note which he still held. 'I don't think you need go there very often. It seems to me you don't get much good from them.'

She looked at him inquiringly.

'Theirs isn't the kind of Socialism I care much about,' he continued, with the air of giving a solid reason. 'It seems to me that Westlake's going off on a road of his own, and one that leads nowhere. All that twaddle to-day about the development of society! I don't think he spoke of me as he might have done. You'll see there won't be half a report in the "Fiery Cross."'

Adela was still silent.

'I don't mean to say you're not to see Mrs. Westlake at all, if you want to,' he pursued. 'I shouldn't have thought she was the kind of woman to suit you. If the truth was known, I don't think she's a Socialist at all. But then, no more are you, eh?'

'There is no one with a more passionate faith in the people than Mrs. Westlake,' Adela returned.

'Faith! That won't do much good.'

He was silent a little, then went to another subject.

'Rodman writes that he's no intention of giving up the money. I knew it would come to that.'

'But the law will compel him,' Adela exclaimed.

'It's a roundabout business. Eldon's only way of recovering it is to bring an action against me. Then I shall have to go to law with Rodman.'

'But how can he refuse? It is——'

She checked herself, remembering that words were two-edged.

'Oh, he writes in quite a friendly way—makes a sort of joke of it. We've to get what we can of him, he says. But he doesn't get off if I can help it. I must see Yottle on our way to-morrow.

'Keene wants me to write a book about New Wanley,' he said presently.

'A book?'

'Well, a small one. It could be called, "My Work at New Wanley." It might do good.'

'Yes, it might,' Adela assented absently.

'You look tired. Get off to bed; you'll have to be up early in the morning, and it'll be a hard day.'

Adela went, hopeful of oblivion till the 'hard day' should dawn.

The next morning they were in Belwick by half-past nine. Alfred took leave of them and went off to business. He promised to 'look them up' in London before very long, probably at Christmas. Between him and Mutimer there was make-believe of cordiality at parting; they had long ceased to feel any real interest in each other.

Adela had to spend the time in the railway waiting-room whilst her husband went to see Yottle. It was a great bare place; when she entered, she found a woman in mourning, with a little boy, sitting alone. The child was eating a bun, his mother was silently shedding tears. Adela seated herself as far from them as possible, out of delicacy, but she saw the woman look frequently towards her, and at last rise as if to come and speak. She was a feeble, helpless-looking being of about thirty; evidently the need of sympathy overcame her, for she had no other excuse for addressing Adela save to tell that her luggage had gone astray, and that she was waiting in the hope that something might be heard of it. Finding a gentle listener, she talked on and on, detailing the wretched circumstances under which she had recently been widowed, and her miserable prospects in a strange town whither she was going. Adela made an effort to speak in words of comfort, but her own voice sounded hopeless in her ears. In the station was a constant roaring and hissing, bell-ringing and the shriek of whistles, the heavy trundling of barrows, the slamming of carriage-doors; everywhere a smell of smoke. It impressed her as though all the world had become homeless, and had nothing to do but journey hither and thither in vain search of a resting-place. And her waiting lasted more than an hour. But for the effort to dry another's tears it would have been hard to restrain her own.

The morning had threatened rain; when at length the journey to London began, the black skies yielded a steady downpour. Mutimer was anything but cheerful; establishing himself in a corner of the third-class carriage, he for a time employed himself with a newspaper; then, throwing it on to Adela's lap, closed his eyes as if he hoped to sleep. Adela glanced up and down the barren fields of type, but there was nothing that could hold her attention, and, by chance looking at her husband's face, she continued to examine it. Perhaps he was asleep, perhaps only absorbed in thought. His lips were sullenly loose beneath the thick reddish moustache; his eyebrows had drawn themselves together, scowling. She could not avert her gaze; it seemed to her that she was really scrutinising his face for the first time, and it was as that of a stranger. Not one detail had the stamp of familiarity: the whole repelled her. What was the meaning now first revealed to her in that countenance? The features had a massive regularity; there was nothing grotesque, nothing on the surface repulsive; yet, beholding the face as if it were that of a man unknown to her, she felt that a whole world of natural antipathies was between it and her.

It was the face of a man by birth and breeding altogether beneath her.

Never had she understood that as now; never had she conceived so forcibly the reason which made him and her husband and wife only in name. Suppose that apparent sleep of his to be the sleep of death; he would pass from her consciousness like a shadow from the field, leaving no trace behind. Their life of union was a mockery; their married intimacy was an unnatural horror. He was not of her class, not of her world; only by violent wrenching of the laws of nature had they come together. She had spent years in trying to convince herself that there were no such distinctions, that only an unworthy prejudice parted class from class. One moment of true insight was worth more than all her theorising on abstract principles. To be her equal this man must be born again, of other parents, in other conditions of life. ' I go back to London a mechanical engineer in search of employment.' They were the truest words he had ever uttered; they characterised him, classed him.

She had no claims to aristocratic descent, but her parents were gentlefolk; that is to say, they were both born in a position which encouraged personal refinement rather than the contrary, which expected of them a certain education in excess of life's barest need, which authorised them to use the service of ruder men and women in order to secure to themselves a margin of life for life's sake. Perhaps for three generations her ancestors could claim so much gentility; it was more than enough to put a vast gulf between her and the Mutimers. Favourable circumstances of upbringing had endowed her with delicacy of heart and mind not inferior to that of any woman living; mated with an equal husband, the children born of her might hope to take their place among the most beautiful and the most intelligent. And her husband was a man incapable of understanding her idlest thought.

He opened his eyes, looked at her blankly for a moment, stirred his limbs to make his position easier.

Pouring rain in London streets. The cab drove eastward, but for no great distance. Adela found herself alighting at a lodging-house not far from the reservoir at the top of Pentonville Hill. Mutimer had taken these rooms a week ago.

A servant fresh from the blackleading of a grate opened the door to them, grinning with recognition at the sight of Mutimer. The latter had to help the cabman to deposit the trunks in the passage. Then Adela was shown to her bedroom.

It was on the second floor, the ordinary bedroom of cheap furnished lodgings, with scant space between the foot of the bed and the fireplace, with a dirty wall-paper and a strong musty odour. The window looked upon a backyard.

She passed from the bedroom to the sitting-room; here was the same vulgar order, the same musty smell. The table was laid for dinner.

Mutimer read his wife's countenance furtively. He could not discover how the abode impressed her, and he put no question. When he returned from the bedroom she was sitting before the fire, pensive.

' You're hungry, I expect ? ' he said.

Her appetite was far from keen, but in order not to appear discontented she replied that she would be glad of dinner.

The servant, her hands and face half washed, presently appeared with a tray on which were some mutton-chops, potatoes, and a cabbage. Adela did her best to eat, but the chops were ill-cooked, the vegetables poor in quality. There followed a rice-pudding; it was nearly cold; coagulated masses of rice appeared beneath yellowish water. Mutimer made no remark about the food till the table was cleared. Then he said:

' They'll have to do better than that. The first day, of course —— You'll have a talk with the landlady whilst I'm out to-night. Just let her see that you won't be content with *anything*; you have to talk plainly to these people.'

' Yes, I'll speak about it,' Adela replied.

' They made a trouble at first about waiting on us,' Mutimer pursued. ' But I didn't see how we could get our own meals very well. You can't cook, can you ? '

He smiled, and seemed half ashamed to ask the question.

'Oh yes; I can cook ordinary things,' Adela said. 'But— we haven't a kitchen, have we?'

'Well, no. If we did anything of that kind, it would have to be on this fire. She charges us four shillings a week more for cooking the dinner.'

He added this information in a tone of assumed carelessness.

'I think we might save that,' Adela said. 'If I had the necessary things—— I should like to try, if you will let me.'

'Just as you please. I don't suppose the stuff they send us up will ever be very eatable. But it's too bad to ask you to do work of that kind.'

'Oh, I shan't mind it in the least! It will be far better, better in every way.'

Mutimer brightened up.

'In that case we'll only get them to do the housemaid work. You can explain that to the woman; her name is Mrs. Gulliman.'

He paused.

'Think you can make yourself at home, here?'

'Yes, certainly.'

'That's all right. I shall go out now for an hour or so. You can unpack your boxes and get things in order a bit.'

Adela had her interview with Mrs. Gulliman in the course of the evening, and fresh arrangements were made, not perhaps to the landlady's satisfaction, though she made a show of absorbing interest and vast approval. She was ready to lend her pots and pans till Adela should have made purchase of those articles.

Adela had the satisfaction of saving four shillings a week.

Two days later Mutimer sought eagerly in the 'Fiery Cross' for a report of the proceedings at New Wanley. Only half a column was given to the subject, the speeches being summarised. He had fully expected that the week's 'leader' would be concerned with his affairs, but there was no mention of him.

He bought the 'Tocsin.' Foremost stood an article headed, 'The Bursting of a Soap Bubble.' It was a satirical review of the history of New Wanley, signed by Comrade Roodhouse. He read in one place: 'Undertakings of this kind, even if pursued with genuine enthusiasm, are worse than useless; they are positively pernicious. They are half measures, and can only result in delaying the Revolution. It is assumed that working men can be kept in a good temper with a little better housing and a little more money. That is to aid the capitalists, to smooth over huge wrongs with petty concessions, to cry peace where there is no peace. We know this kind of thing of old. It is the whole system of wage-earning that must be overthrown —the ideas which rule the relations of employers and employed. Away with these palliatives; let us rejoice when we see working men starving and ill-clad, for in that way their eyes will be opened. The brute who gets the uttermost farthing out of the toil of his wage-slaves is more a friend to us and our cause than any namby-pamby Socialist, such as the late Dukeling of New Wanley. Socialist indeed! But enough. We have probably heard the last of this *parvenu* and his loudly trumpeted schemes. No true friend of the Revolution can be grieved.'

Mutimer bit his lip.

'Heard the last of me, have they? Don't be too hasty, Roodhouse.'

CHAPTER XXVII.

A WEEK later; the scene, the familiar kitchen in Wilton Square. Mrs. Mutimer, upon whom time has laid unkind hands since last we saw her, is pouring tea for Alice Rodman, who has just come all the way from the West End to visit her. Alice, too, has suffered from recent vicissitudes; her freshness is to seek, her bearing is no longer buoyant, she is careless in attire. To judge from the corners of her mouth, she is confirmed in querulous habits; her voice evidences the same.

She was talking of certain events of the night before.

'It was about half-past twelve—I'd just got into bed— when the servant knocks at my door. "Please, mum," she says, "there's a policeman wants to see master." You may think if I wasn't frightened out of my life! I don't think it was two minutes before I got downstairs, and there the policeman stood in the hall. I told him I was Mrs. Rodman, and then he said a young man called Henry Mutimer had got locked up for making a disturbance outside a music hall, and he'd sent to my husband to bail him out. Well, just as we were talking in comes Willis. Rare and astonished he was to see me with all my things huddled on and a policeman in the house. We did so laugh afterwards; he said he thought I'd been committing a robbery. But he wouldn't bail 'Arry, and I couldn't blame

him. And now he says 'Arry 'll have to do as best he can.
He won't get him another place.'

'He's lost his place too?' asked the mother gloomily.

'He was dismissed yesterday. He says that's why he
went drinking too much. Out of ten days that he's been in
the place he's missed two and hasn't been punctual once. I
think you might have seen he got off at the proper time in the
morning, mother.'

'What's the good o' blamin' me?' exclaimed the old woman
fretfully. 'A deal o' use it is for me to talk. If I'm to be
held 'countable he doesn't live here no longer; I know that
much.'

'Dick was a fool to pay his fine. I'd have let him go to
prison for seven days; it would have given him a lesson.'

Mrs. Mutimer sighed deeply, and lost herself in despondent
thought. Alice sipped her tea and went on with her voluble
talk.

'I suppose he'll show up some time to-night unless Dick
keeps him. But he can't do that, neither, unless he makes him
sleep on the sofa in their sitting-room. A nice come-down for
my lady, to be living in two furnished rooms! But it's my
belief they're not so badly off as they pretend to be. It's all
very well for Dick to put on his airs and go about saying he's
given up every farthing; he doesn't get me to believe that.
He wouldn't go paying away his pounds so readily. And they
have attendance from the landlady; Mrs. Adela doesn't soil
her fine fingers, trust her. You may depend upon it, they've
plenty. She wouldn't speak a word for us; if she cared to, she
could have persuaded Mr. Eldon to let me keep my money, and
then there wouldn't have been all this law bother.'

'What bother's that?'

'Why, Dick says he'll go to law with my husband to
recover the money he paid him when we were married. It
seems he has to answer for it, because he's what they call the
administrator, and Mr. Eldon can compel him to make it all
good again.'

'But I thought you said you'd given it all up?'

'That's my own money, what was settled on me. I don't
see what good it was to me; I never had a penny of it to
handle. Now they want to get all the rest out of us. How
are we to pay back the money that's spent and gone, I'd like
to know? Willis says they'll just have to get it if they can.
And here's Dick going on at me because we don't go into

lodgings! I don't leave the house before I'm obliged, I know that much. We may as well be comfortable as long as we can.

'The mean thing, that Adela!' she pursued after a pause. 'She was to have married Mr. Eldon, and broke it off when she found he wasn't going to be as rich as she thought; then she caught hold of Dick. I should like to have seen her face when she found that will!—I wish it had been me!'

Alice laughed unpleasantly. Her mother regarded her with an air of curious inquiry, then murmured:

'Dick and she did the honest thing. I'll say so much for them.'

'I'll be even with Mrs. Adela yet,' pursued Alice, disregarding the remark. 'She wouldn't speak for me, but she's spoken for herself, no fear. She and her airs!'

There was silence; then Mrs. Mutimer said:

'I've let the top bedroom for four-and-six.'

''Arry's room? What's he going to do then?'

'He'll have to sleep on the chair-bedstead, here in the kitchen. That is, if I have him in the 'ouse at all. And I don't know yet as I shall.'

'Have you got enough money to go on with?' Alice asked.

'Dick sent me a pound this morning. I didn't want it.'

'Has he been to see you yet, mother?'

The old woman shook her head.

'Do you want him to come, or don't you?'

There was silence. Alice looked at her mother askance. The leathern mask of a face was working with some secret emotion.

'He'll come if he likes, I s'pose,' was her abrupt answer.

In the renewed silence they heard some one enter the house and descend the kitchen stairs. 'Arry presented himself. He threw his hat upon a chair, and came forward with a swagger to seat himself at the tea-table.

His mother did not look at him.

'Anything to eat?' he asked, more loudly than was necessary, as if he found the silence oppressive.

'There's bread and butter,' replied Alice, with lofty scorn.

'Hullo! Is it you?' exclaimed the young man, affecting to recognise his sister. 'I thought you was above coming here! Have they turned you out of your house?'

'That's what'll happen to you, I shouldn't wonder.'

'Arry cast a glance towards his mother. Seeing that her

eyes were fixed in another direction, he began pantomimic interrogation of Alice. The latter disregarded him.

'Arry presented an appearance less than engaging. He still bore the traces of last night's debauch and of his sojourn in the police-cell. There was dry mud on the back of his coat, his shirt-cuffs and collar were of a slaty hue, his hands and face filthy. He began to eat bread and butter, washing down each morsel with a gulp of tea. The spoon remained in the cup whilst he drank. To 'Arry it was a vast relief to be free from the conventionalities of Adela's table.

'That lawyer fellow Yottle's been to see them to-day,' he remarked presently.

Alice looked at him eagerly.

' What about?'

' There was talk about you and Rodman.'

' What did they say?'

'Couldn't hear. I was in the other room. But I heard Yottle speaking your name.'

He had, in fact, heard a few words through the keyhole, but not enough to gather the sense of the conversation, which had been carried on in discreet tones.

'There you are!' Alice exclaimed, addressing her mother. 'They're plotting against us, you see.'

'I don't think it 'ud be Dick's wish to do you harm,' said Mrs. Mutimer absently.

' Dick 'll do whatever she tells him.'

' Adela, eh?' observed 'Arry. ' She's a cat.'

' You mind your own business!' returned his sister.

' So it is my business. She looked at me as if I wasn't good enough to come near her 'igh-and-mightiness. I'm glad to see *her* brought down a peg, chance it!'

Alice would not condescend to join her reprobate brother, even in abuse of Adela. She very shortly took leave of her mother, who went up to the door with her.

' Are you going to see Dick?' Mrs. Mutimer said, in the passage.

' I shan't see him till he comes to my house,' replied Alice sharply.

The old woman stood on the doorstep till her daughter was out of sight, then sighed and returned to her kitchen.

Alice returned to her more fashionable quarter by omnibus. Though Rodman had declined to make any change in their establishment, he practised economy in the matter of his wife's pin-money. Gone were the delights of shopping, gone the little lunches in confectioners' shops to which Alice, who ate sweet things like a child, had been much addicted. Even the carriage she could seldom make use of, for Rodman had constant need of it—to save cab-fares, he said. It was chiefly employed in taking him to and from the City, where he appeared to have much business at present.

On reaching home Alice found a telegram from her husband.

'Shall bring three friends to dinner. Be ready for us at half-past seven.'

Yet he had assured her that he would dine quietly alone with her at eight o'clock. Alice, who was weary of the kind of men her husband constantly brought, felt it as a bitter disappointment. Besides, it was already after six, and there were no provisions in the house. But for her life she durst not cause Rodman annoyance by offering a late or insufficient dinner. She thanked her stars that her return had been even thus early.

The men when they presented themselves were just of the kind she expected—loud-talking—their interests divided between horse-racing and the money-market; she was a cipher at her own table, scarcely a remark being addressed to her. The conversation was meaningless to her; it seemed, indeed, to be made purposely mysterious; terms of the stock-exchange were eked out with nods and winks. Rodman was in far better spirits than of late, whence Alice gathered that some promising rascality was under consideration.

The dinner over, she was left to amuse herself as she could in the drawing-room. Rodman and his friends continued their talk round the table, and did not break up till close upon midnight. Then she heard the men take their departure. Rodman presently came up to her and threw himself into a chair. His face was very red, a sign with which Alice was familiar; but excessive potations apparently had not produced the usual effect, for he was still in the best of tempers.

'Seen that young blackguard?' he began by asking.

'I went to see mother, and he came while I was there.'

'He'll have to look after himself in future. You don't catch me helping him again.'

'He says Mr. Yottle came to see them to-day.'

'To see who?'

'Dick and his wife. He heard them talking about us.'

Rodman laughed.

'Let 'em go ahead! I wish them luck.'

'But can't they ruin us if they like?'

'It's all in a life. It wouldn't be the first time I've been ruined, old girl. Let's enjoy ourselves whilst we can. There's nothing like plenty of excitement.'

'It's all very well for you, Willis. But if you had to sit at home all day doing nothing, you wouldn't find it so pleasant.'

'Get some novels.'

'I'm tired of novels,' she replied, sighing.

'So Yottle was with them?' Rodman said musingly, a smile still on his face. 'I wish I knew what terms they've come to with Eldon.'

'I wish I could do something to pay out that woman!' exclaimed Alice bitterly. 'She's at the bottom of it all. She hates both of us. Dick 'ud never have gone against you but for her.'

Rodman, extended in the low chair at full length, fixed an amused look on her.

'You'd like to pay her out, eh?'

'Wouldn't I just!'

'Ha! ha! what a vicious little puss you are! It's a good thing I don't tell you everything, or you might do damage.'

Alice turned to him with eagerness.

'What do you mean?'

He let his head fall back, and laughed with a drunken man's hilarity. Alice persisted with her question.

'Come and sit here,' Rodman said, patting his knee.

Alice obeyed him.

'What is it, Willis? What have you found out? Do tell me, there's a dear!'

'I'll tell you one thing, old girl: you're losing your good looks. Nothing like what you were when I married you.'

She flushed and looked miserable.

'I can't help my looks. I don't believe you care how I look.'

'Oh, don't I, though! Why, do you think I'd have stuck to you like this if I didn't? What was to prevent me from realising all the cash I could and clearing off, eh? 'Twouldn't have been the first——'

'The first what?' Alice asked sharply.

'Never mind. You see I didn't do it. Too bad to leave the Princess in the lurch, wouldn't it be?'

Alice seemed to have forgotten the other secret. She searched his face for a moment, deeply troubled, then asked:

'Willis, I want to know who Clara is?'

He moved his eyes slowly, and regarded her with a puzzled look.

'Clara? What Clara?'

'Somebody you know of. You've got a habit of talking in your sleep lately. You were calling out 'Clara!' last night, and that's the second time I've heard you.'

He was absent for a few seconds, then laughed and shook his head.

'I don't know anybody called Clara. It's your mistake.'

'I'm quite sure it isn't,' Alice murmured discontentedly.

'Well, then, we'll say it is,' he rejoined in a firmer voice. 'If I talk in my sleep, perhaps it'll be better for you to pay no attention. I might find it inconvenient to live with you.'

Alice looked frightened at the threat.

'You've got a great many secrets from me,' she said despondently.

'Of course I have. It is for your good. I was going to tell you one just now, only you don't seem to care to hear it.'

'Yes, yes, I do!' Alice exclaimed, recollecting. 'Is it something about Adela?'

He nodded.

'Wouldn't it delight you to go and get her into a terrible row with Dick?'

'Oh, do tell me! What's she been doing?'

'I can't quite promise you the fun,' he replied, laughing. 'It may miss fire. What do you think of her meeting Eldon alone in the wood that Monday afternoon, the day after she found the will, you know?'

'You mean that?'

'I saw them together.'

'But she—you don't mean she—— ?'

Even Alice, with all her venom against her brother's wife, had a difficulty in attributing this kind of evil to Adela. In spite of herself she was incredulous.

'Think what you like,' said Rodman. 'It looks queer, that's all.'

It was an extraordinary instance of malice perpetrated out of sheer good-humour. Had he not been assured by what he heard in the wood of the perfectly innocent relations between Adela and Eldon, he would naturally have made some profit-

able use of his knowledge before this. As long as there was **a**
possibility of advantage in keeping on good terms with Adela,
he spoke to no one of that meeting which he had witnessed.
Even now he did not know but that Adela had freely disclosed
the affair to her husband. But his humour was genially
mischievous. If he could gratify Alice and at the same time
do the Mutimers an ill turn, why not amuse himself?

' I'll tell Dick the very first thing in the morning!' Alice
declared, aglow with spiteful anticipation.

Rodman approved the purpose, and went off to bed laughing uproariously.

CHAPTER XXVIII.

ADELA allowed a week to pass before speaking of her desire
to visit Mrs. Westlake. In Mutimer a fit of sullenness had
followed upon his settlement in lodgings. He was away from
home a good deal, but his hours of return were always uncertain, and Adela could not help thinking that he presented
himself at unlikely times, merely for the sake of surprising her
and discovering her occupation. Once or twice she had no
knowledge of his approach until he opened the door of the
room; when he remarked on his having ascended the stairs so
quietly, he professed not to understand her. On one of those
occasions she was engaged on a letter to her mother; he
inquired to whom she was writing, and for reply she merely
held out the sheet for his perusal. He glanced at the super-
scription, and handed it back. Breathing this atmosphere of
suspicion, she shrank from irritating him by a mention of
Stella, and to go without his express permission was impossible. Stella did not write; Adela began to fear lest her illness
had become more serious. When she spoke at length, it was
in one of the moments of indignation, almost of revolt, which
at intervals came to her, she knew not at what impulse. At
Wanley her resource at such times had been to quit the house,
and pace her chosen walk in the garden till she was weary.
In London she had no refuge, and the result of her loss of
fresh air had speedily shown itself in moods of impatience
which she found it very difficult to conquer. Her husband
came home one afternoon about five o'clock, and, refusing to

have any tea, sat for several hours in complete silence; occasionally he pretended to look at a pamphlet which he had brought in with him, but for the most part he sat, with his legs crossed, frowning at vacancy. Adela grew feverish beneath the oppression of this brooding ill-temper; her endeavour to read was vain; the silence was a constraint upon her moving, her breathing. She spoke before she was conscious of an intention to do so.

'I think I must go and see Mrs. Westlake to-morrow morning.'

Mutimer vouchsafed no answer, gave no sign of having heard. She repeated the words.

'If you must, you must.'

'I wish to,' Adela said with an emphasis she could not help. 'Do you object to my going?'

He was surprised at her tone.

'I don't object. I've told you I think you get no good there. But go if you like.'

She said after a silence:

'I have no other friend in London; and if it were only on account of her kindness to me, I owe her a visit.'

'All right, don't talk about it any more; I'm thinking of something.'

The evening wore on. At ten o'clock the servant brought up a jug of beer, which she fetched for Mutimer every night; he said he could not sleep without this sedative. It was always the sign for Adela to go to bed.

She visited Stella in the morning, and found her still suffering. They talked for an hour, then it was time for Adela to hasten homewards, in order to have dinner ready by half-past one. From Stella she had no secret, save the one which she did her best to make a secret even to herself; she spoke freely of her mode of life, though without comment. Stella made no comments in her replies.

'And you cannot have lunch with me?' she asked when her friend rose.

'I cannot, dear.'

'May I write to you?' Stella said with a meaning look.

'Yes, to tell me how you are.'

Adela had not got far from the house when she saw her husband walking towards her. She looked at him steadily.

'I happened to be near,' he explained, 'and thought I might as well go home with you.'

'I might have been gone.'

'Oh, I shouldn't have waited long.'

The form of his reply discovered that he had no intention of calling at the house; Adela understood that he had been in Avenue Road for some time, probably had reached it very soon after her.

The next morning there arrived for Mutimer a letter from Alice. She desired to see him; her husband would be from home all day, and she would be found at any hour; her business was of importance—underlined.

Mutimer went shortly after breakfast, and Alice received him very much as she would have done in the days before the catastrophe. She had arrayed herself with special care; he found her leaning on cushions, her feet on a stool, the eternal novel on her lap. Her brother had to stifle anger at seeing her thus in appearance unaffected by the storm which had swept away his own happiness and luxuries.

'What is it you want?' he asked at once, without preliminary greeting.

'You are not very polite,' Alice returned. 'Perhaps you'll take a chair.'

'I haven't much time, so please don't waste what I can afford.'

'Are you so busy? Have you found something to do?'

'I'm likely to have enough to do with people who keep what doesn't belong to them.'

'It isn't my doing, Dick,' she said more seriously.

'I don't suppose it is.'

'Then you oughtn't to be angry with me.'

'I'm not angry. What do you want?'

'I went to see mother yesterday. I think she wants you to go; it looked like it.'

'I'll go some day.'

'It's too bad that she should have to keep 'Arry in idleness.'

'She hasn't to keep him. I send her money'

'But how are you to afford that?'

'That's not your business.'

Alice looked indignant.

'I think you might speak more politely to me in my own house.'

'It isn't your own house.'

'It is as long as I live in it. I suppose you'd like to see

me go back to a workroom. It's all very well for you; if you live in lodgings, that doesn't say you've got no money. We have to do the best we can for ourselves; we haven't got your chances of making a good bargain.'

It was said with much intention; Alice half closed her eyes and curled her lips in a disdainful smile.

' What chances? What do you mean?'

'Perhaps if *I*'d been a particular friend of Mr. Eldon's— never mind.'

He flashed a look at her.

' What are you talking about? Just speak plainly, will you? What do you mean by " particular friend?" I'm no more a friend of Eldon's than you are, and I've made no bargain with him.'

' I didn't say *you*.'

' Who then?' he exclaimed sternly.

' Don't you know? Some one is so very proper, and such a fine lady, I shouldn't have thought she'd have done things without your knowing.'

He turned pale, and seemed to crush the floor with his foot, that he might stand firm.

' You're talking of Adela?'

Alice nodded.

' What about her? Say at once what you've got to say.'

Inwardly she was a little frightened, perhaps half wished that she had not begun. Yet it was sweet to foresee the thunderbolt that would fall on her enemy's head. That her brother would suffer torments did not affect her imagination; she had never credited him with strong feeling for his wife; and it was too late to draw back.

' You know that she met Mr. Eldon in the wood at Wanley on the day after she found the will?'

Mutimer knitted his brows to regard her. But in speaking he was more self-governed than before.

' Who told you that?'

' My husband. He saw them together.'

' And heard them talking?'

' Yes.'

Rodman had only implied this. Alice's subsequent interrogation had failed to elicit more from him than dark hints.

Mutimer drew a quick breath.

' He must be good at spying. Next time I hope he'll find out something worth talking about.'

Alice was surprised.

'You know about it?'

'Just as much as Rodman, do you understand that!'

'You don't believe?'

She herself had doubts.

'It's nothing to you whether I believe it or not. Just be good enough in future to mind your own business; you'll have plenty of it before long. I suppose that's what you brought me here for?'

She made no answer; she was vexed and puzzled.

'Have you anything else to say?'

Alice maintained a stubborn silence.

'Alice, have you anything more to tell me about Adela?'

'No, I haven't.'

'Then you might have spared me the trouble. Tell Rodman with my compliments that it would be as well for him to keep out of my way.'

He left her.

On quitting the house he walked at a great pace for a quarter of a mile before he remembered the necessity of taking either train or omnibus. The latter was at hand, but when he had ridden for ten minutes the constant stoppages so irritated him that he jumped out and sought a hansom. Even thus he did not travel fast enough; it seemed an endless time before the ascent of Pentonville Hill began. He descended a little distance from his lodgings.

As he was paying the driver another hansom went by; he by chance saw the occupant, and it was Hubert Eldon. At least he felt convinced of it, and he was in no mind to balance the possibilities of mistake. The hansom had come from the street which Mutimer was just entering.

He found Adela engaged in cooking the dinner; she wore an apron, and the sleeves of her dress were pushed up. As he came into the room she looked at him with her patient smile; finding that he was in one of his worst tempers, she said nothing and went on with her work. A coarse cloth was thrown over the table; on it lay a bowl of vegetables which she was preparing for the saucepan.

Perhaps it was the sight of her occupation, of the cheerful simplicity with which she addressed herself to work so unworthy of her; he could not speak at once as he had meant to. He examined her with eyes of angry, half-foiled suspicion.

She had occasion to pass him ; he caught her arm and stayed her before him.

'What has Eldon been doing here ? '

She paused and shrank a little.

'Mr. Eldon has not been here.'

He thought her face betrayed a guilty agitation.

'I happen to have met him going away. I think you'd better tell me the truth.'

'I have told you the truth. If Mr. Eldon has been to the house, I was not aware of it.'

He looked at her in silence for a moment, then asked :

'Are you the greatest hypocrite living ? '

Adela drew farther away. She kept her eyes down. Long ago she had suspected what was in Mutimer's mind, but she had only been apprehensive of the results of jealousy on his temper and on their relations to each other ; it had not entered her thought that she might have to defend herself against an accusation. This violent question affected her strangely. For a moment she referred it entirely to the secrets of her heart, and it seemed impossible to deny what was imputed to her, impossible even to resent his way of speaking. Was she not a hypocrite ? Had she not many, many times concealed with look and voice an inward state which was equivalent to infidelity ? Was not her whole life a pretence, an affectation of wifely virtues ? But the hypocrisy was involuntary ; her nature had no power to extirpate its causes and put in their place the perfect dignity of uprightness.

'Why do you ask me that ? ' she said at length, raising her eyes for an instant.

'Because it seems to me I've good cause. I don't know whether to believe a word you say.'

'I can't remember to have told you falsehoods.' Her cheeks flushed. 'Yes, one ; that I confessed to you.'

It brought to his mind the story of the wedding ring.

'There's such a thing as lying when you tell the truth. Do you remember that I met you coming back to the Manor that Monday afternoon, a month ago, and asked you where you'd been ? '

Her heart stood still.

'Answer me, will you ? '

'I remember it.'

'You told me you'd been for a walk in the wood. You forgot to say who it was you went to meet.'

How did he know of this? But that thought came to her only to pass. She understood at length the whole extent of his suspicion. It was not only her secret feelings that he called in question, he accused her of actual dishonour as it is defined by the world—that clumsy world with its topsy-turvydom of moral judgments. To have this certainty flashed upon her was, as soon as she had recovered from the shock, a sensible assuagement of her misery. In face of this she could stand her ground. Her womanhood was in arms; she faced him scornfully.

'Will you please to make plain your charge against me?'

'I think it's plain enough. If a married woman makes appointments in quiet places with a man she has no business to see anywhere, what's that called? I fancy I've seen something of that kind before now in cases before the Divorce Court.'

It angered him that she was not overwhelmed. He saw that she did not mean to deny having met Eldon, and to have Alice's story thus confirmed inflamed his jealousy beyond endurance.

'You must believe of me what you like,' Adela replied in a slow, subdued voice. 'My word would be vain against that of my accuser, whoever it is.'

'Your accuser, as you say, happened not only to see you, but to hear you talking.'

He waited for her surrender before this evidence. Instead of that Adela smiled.

'If my words were reported to you, what fault have you to find with me?'

Her confidence, together with his actual ignorance of what Rodman had heard, troubled him with doubt.

'Answer this question,' he said. 'Did you make an appointment with that man?'

'I did not.'

'You did not? Yet you met him?'

'Unexpectedly.'

'But you talked with him?'

'How can you ask? You know that I did.'

He collected his thoughts.

'Repeat to me what you talked about.'

'That I refuse to do.'

'Of course you do!' he cried, driven to frenzy. 'And you think I shall let this rest where it is? Have you forgotten that I came to the Westlakes and found Eldon there with you?

And what was he doing in this street this morning if he hadn't come to see you? I begin to understand why you were so precious eager about giving up the will. That was your fine sense of honesty, of course! You are full of fine senses, but your mistake is to think I've no sense at all. What do you take me for?'

The thin crust of refinement was shattered; the very man came to light, coarse, violent, whipped into fury by his passions, of which injured self-love was not the least. Whether he believed his wife guilty or not he could not have said; enough that she had kept things secret from him, and that he could not overawe her. Whensoever he had shown anger in conversation with her, she had made him sensible of her superiority; at length he fell back upon his brute force and resolved to bring her to his feet, if need be by outrage. Even his accent deteriorated as he flung out his passionate words; he spoke like any London mechanic, with defect and excess of aspirates, with neglect of g's at the end of words, and so on. Adela could not bear it; she moved to the door. But he caught her and thrust her back; it was all but a blow. Her face half recalled him to his senses.

'Where are you going?' he stammered.

'Anywhere, anywhere, away from this house and from you!' Adela replied. Effort to command herself was vain; his heavy hand had completed the effect of his language, and she, too, spoke as nature impelled her. 'Let me pass! I would rather die than remain here!'

'All the same, you'll stay where you are!'

'Yes, your strength is greater than mine. You can hold me by force. But you have insulted me beyond forgiveness, and we are as much strangers as if we had never met. You have broken every bond that bound me to you. You can make me your prisoner, but like a prisoner my one thought will be of escape. I will touch no food whilst I remain here. I have no duties to you, and you no claim upon me!'

'All the same, you stay!'

Before her sobbing vehemence he had grown calm. These words were so unimaginable on her lips that he could make no reply save stubborn repetition of his refusal. And having uttered that he went from the room, changing the key to the outside and locking her in. Fear lest he might be unable to withhold himself from laying hands upon her was the cause of his retreat. The lust of cruelty was boiling in him, as once or

twice before. Her beauty in revolt made a savage of him. He
went into the bedroom and there waited.

Adela sat alone, sobbing still, but tearless. Her high-
spirited nature once thoroughly aroused, it was some time before
she could reason on what had come to pass. The possibility of
such an end to her miseries had never presented itself even in
her darkest hours; endurance was all she could ever look forward to. As her blood fell into calmer flow she found it hard
to believe that she had not dreamt this scene of agony. She
looked about the room. There on the table were the vegetables
she had been preparing; her hands bore the traces of the work
she had done this morning. It seemed as though she had only
to rise and go on with her duties as usual.

Her arm was painful, just below the shoulder. Yes, that
was where he had seized her with his hard hand to push her away
from the door.

What had she said in her distraction? She had broken
away from him, and repudiated her wifehood. Was it not well
done? If he believed her unfaithful to him——

At an earlier period of her married life such a charge would
have held her mute with horror. Its effect now was not quite
the same; she could face the thought, interrogate herself as to
its meaning, with a shudder, indeed, but a shudder which came
of fear as well as loathing. Life was no longer an untried
country, its difficulties and perils to be met with the sole aid of
a few instincts and a few maxims; she had sounded the depths
of misery and was invested with the woeful knowledge of what
we poor mortals call the facts of existence. And sitting here,
as on the desert bed of a river whose water had of a sudden
ceased to flow, she could regard her own relation to truths,
however desolating, with the mind which had rather brave all
than any longer seek to deceive itself.

Of that which he imputed to her she was incapable; that
such suspicion of her could enter his mind branded him with
baseness. But his jealousy was justified; howsoever it had
awakened in him, it was sustained by truth. Was it her duty
to tell him that, and so to render it impossible for him to seek
to detain her?

But would the confession have any such result? Did he not
already believe her criminal, and yet forbid her to leave him?
On what terms did she stand with a man whose thought was
devoid of delicacy, who had again and again proved himself
without understanding of the principles of honour? And could

she indeed make an admission which would compel her at the same time to guard against revolting misconceptions?

The question of how he had obtained this knowledge recurred to her. It was evident that the spy had intentionally calumniated her, professing to have heard her speak incriminating words. She thought of Rodman. He had troubled her by his private request that she would appeal to Eldon on Alice's behalf, a request which was almost an insult. Could he have been led to make it in consequence of his being aware of that meeting in the wood? That might well be; she distrusted him and believed him capable even of a dastardly revenge.

What was the troublesome thought that hung darkly in her mind and would not come to consciousness? She held it at last; Mutimer had said that he met Hubert in the street below. How to explain that? Hubert so near to her, perhaps still in the neighbourhood?

Again she shrank with fear. What might it mean, if he had really come in hope of seeing her? That was unworthy of him. Had she betrayed herself in her conversation with him? Then he was worse than cruel to her.

It seemed to her that hours passed. From time to time she heard a movement in the next room; Mutimer was still there. There sounded at the house door a loud postman's knock, and in a few minutes someone came up the stairs, doubtless to bring a letter. The bedroom door opened; she heard her husband thank the servant and again shut himself in.

The fire which she had been about to use for cooking was all but dead. She rose and put fresh coals on. There was a small oblong mirror over the mantelpiece; it showed her so ghastly a face that she turned quickly away.

If she succeeded in escaping from her prison, whither should she go? Her mother would receive her, but it was impossible to go to Wanley, to live near the Manor. Impossible, too, to take refuge with Stella. If she fled and hid herself in some other part of London, how was life to be supported? But there were graver obstacles. Openly to flee from her husband was to subject herself to injurious suspicions—it might be, considering Mutimer's character, to involve Hubert in some intolerable public shame. Or, if that worst extremity were avoided, would it not be said that she had deserted her husband because he had suddenly become poor?

That last thought brought the blood to her cheeks.

But to live with him after this, to smear over a deadly

wound and pretend it was healed, to read hourly in his face the
cowardly triumph over her weakness, to submit herself—Oh,
what rescue from this hideous degradation! She went to the
window, as if it had been possible to escape by that way; she
turned again and stood moaning, with her hands about her
head. When was the worst to come in this life so long since
bereft of hope, so forsaken of support from man or God? The
thought of death came to her; she subdued the tumult of her
agony to weigh it well. Whom would she wrong by killing
herself? Herself, it might be; perchance not even death would
be sacred against outrage.

She heard a neighbouring clock strike five, and shortly after
her husband entered the room. Had she looked at him she
would have seen an inexplicable animation in his face. He
paced the floor once or twice in silence, then asked in a hard
voice, though the tone was quite other than before:

'Will you tell me what it was you talked of that day in
the wood?'

She did not reply.

'I suppose by refusing to speak you confess that you dare
not let me know?'

Physical torture could not have wrung a word from her.
She felt her heart surge with hatred.

He went to the cupboard in which food was kept, took out
a loaf of bread, and cut a slice. He ate it, standing before
the window. Then he cleared the table and sat down to write
a letter; it occupied him for half an hour. When it was
finished, he put it in his pocket and began again to pace the
room.

'Are you going to sit like that all night?' he asked suddenly.

She drew a deep sigh and rose from her seat. He saw that
she no longer thought of escaping him. She began to make
preparations for tea. As helpless in his hands as though he
had purchased her in a slave-market, of what avail to sit like
a perverse child? The force of her hatred warned her to keep
watch lest she brought herself to his level. Without defence
against indignities which were bitter as death, by law his
chattel, as likely as not to feel the weight of his hand if she
again roused his anger, what remained but to surrender all
outward things to unthinking habit, and to keep her soul apart,
nourishing in silence the fire of its revolt? It was the most
pity-moving of all tragedies, a noble nature overcome by sordid

circumstances. She was deficient in the strength of character which will subdue all circumstances; her strength was of the kind that supports endurance rather than breaks a way to freedom. Every day, every hour, is some such tragedy played through; it is the inevitable result of our social state. Adela could have wept tears of blood; her shame was like a branding iron upon her flesh.

She was on the second floor of a lodging-house in Pentonville, making tea for her husband.

That husband appeared to have undergone a change since he quitted her a few hours ago. He was still venomous towards her, but his countenance no longer lowered dangerously. Something distinct from his domestic troubles seemed to be occupying him, something of a pleasant nature. He all but smiled now and then; the glances he cast at Adela were not wholly occupied with her. He plainly wished to speak, but could not bring himself to do so.

He ate and drank of what she put before him. Adela took a cup of tea, but had no appetite for food. When he had satisfied himself, she removed the things.

Another half-hour passed. Mutimer was pretending to read. Adela at length broke the silence.

'I think,' she said, 'I was wrong in refusing to tell you what passed between Mr. Eldon and myself when I by chance met him. Someone seems to have misled you. He began by hoping that we should not think ourselves bound to leave the Manor until we had had full time to make the necessary arrangements. I thanked him for his kindness, and then asked something further. It was that, if he could by any means do so, he would continue the works at New Wanley without any change, maintaining the principles on which they had been begun. He said that was impossible, and explained to me what his intentions were, and why he had formed them. That was our conversation.'

Mutimer observed her with a smile which affected incredulity.

'Will you take your oath that that is true?' he asked.

'No. I have told you because I now see that the explanation was owing, since you have been deceived. If you disbelieve me, it is no concern of mine.'

She had taken up some sewing, and, having spoken, went on with it. Mutimer kept his eyes fixed upon her. His suspicions never resisted a direct word from Adela's lips, though other feelings might exasperate him. What he had just heard he believed the more readily because it so surprised him; it was one of those revelations of his wife's superiority which abashed him without causing evil feeling. They always had the result of restoring to him for a moment something of the reverence with which he had approached her in the early days of their acquaintance. Even now he could not escape the impression.

'What was Eldon doing about here to-day?' he asked after a pause.

'I have told you that I did not even know he had been near.'

'Perhaps not. Now, will you just tell me this: Have you written to Eldon, or had any letter from him since our marriage?'

Her fingers would not continue their work. A deadening sensation of disgust made her close her eyes as if to shut out the meaning of his question. Her silence revived his distrust.

'You had rather not answer?' he said significantly.

'Cannot you see that it degrades me to answer such a question? What is your opinion of me? Have I behaved so as to lead you to think that I am an abandoned woman?'

After hesitating he muttered: 'You don't give a plain yes or no.'

'You must not expect it. If you think I use arts to deceive you—if you have no faith whatever in my purity—it was your duty to let me go from you when I would have done so. It is horrible for us to live together from the moment that there is such a doubt on either side. It makes me something lower than your servant—something that has no name!'

She shuddered. Had not that been true of her from the very morrow of their marriage? Her life was cast away upon shoals of debasement; no sanctity of womanhood remained in her. Was not her indignation half a mockery? She could not even defend her honesty, her honour in the vulgarest sense of the word, without involving herself in a kind of falsehood, which was desolation to her spirit. It had begun in her advocacy of uprightness after her discovery of the will; it was imbuing her whole nature, making her to her own conscience that which he had called her—a very hypocrite.

He spoke more conciliatingly.

'Well, there's one thing, at all events, that you can't refuse to explain. Why didn't you tell me that you had met Eldon, and what he meant to do?'

She had not prepared herself for the question, and it went to the root of her thoughts; none the less she replied instantly, careless how he understood the truth.

'I kept silence because the meeting had given me pain, because it distressed me to have to speak with Mr. Eldon at that place and at that time, because I *knew* how you regard him, and was afraid to mention him to you.'

Mutimer was at a loss. If Adela had calculated her reply with the deepest art she could not have chosen words better fitted to silence him.

'And you have told me every word that passed between you?' he asked.

'That would be impossible. I have told you the substance of the conversation.'

'Why did you ask him to keep the works going on my plan?'

'I can tell you no more.'

Her strength was spent. She put aside her sewing and moved towards the door.

'Where are you going?'

'I don't feel well. I must rest.'

'Just stop a minute. I've something here I want to show you.'

She turned wearily. Mutimer took a letter from his pocket.

'Will you read that?'

She took it. It was written in a very clear, delicate hand, and ran thus:—

'DEAR SIR,—I who address you have lain for two years on a bed from which I shall never move till I am carried to my grave. My age is three-and-twenty; an accident which happened to me a few days after my twenty-first birthday left me without the use of my limbs; it often seems to me that it would have been better if I had died, but there is no arguing with fate, and the wise thing is to accept cheerfully whatever befalls us. I hoped at one time to take an active part in life, and my interest in the world's progress is as strong as ever, especially in everything that concerns social reform. I have for some time known your name, and have constantly sought information about your grand work at New Wanley. Now I venture to write (by the hand of a dear friend), to express my admiration for your high endeavour, and my grief at the circumstances which have made you powerless to continue it.

'I am possessed of means, and, as you see, can spend but little on myself. I ask you, with much earnestness, to let me be of some small use to the cause of social justice, by putting in your hands the sum of five hundred pounds, to be employed as may seem good to you. I need not affect to be ignorant of your position, and it is my great fear lest you should be unable to work for Socialism with your undivided energies. Will you accept this money, and continue by means of public lecturing to spread the gospel of emancipation? That I am convinced is your first desire. If you will do me this great kindness, I shall ask your permission to arrange that the same sum be paid to you annually, for the next ten years, whether I still live or not. To be helping in this indirect way would cheer me more than you can think. I enclose a draft on Messrs. ——.

'As I do not know your private address, I send this to the office of the " Fiery Cross." Pardon me for desiring to remain anonymous; many reasons necessitate it. If you grant me this favour, will you advertise the word " Accepted " in the " Times " newspaper within ten days?

'With heartfelt sympathy and admiration,

'I sign myself,

'A FRIEND.'

Adela was unmoved; she returned the letter as if it had no interest for her.

'What do you think of that?' said Mutimer, forgetting their differences in his exultation.

'I am glad you can continue your work,' Adela replied absently.

She was moving away when he again stopped her.

'Look here, Adela.' He hesitated. 'Are you still angry with me?'

She was silent.

'I am sorry I lost my temper. I didn't mean all I said to you. Will you try and forget it?'

Her lips spoke for her.

'I will try.'

'You needn't go on doing housework now,' he said assuringly. 'Are you going? Come and say good-night.'

He approached her and laid his hand upon her shoulder. Adela shrank from his touch, and for an instant gazed at him with wide eyes of fear.

He dropped his hands and let her go.

CHAPTER XXIX

THE valley rested. On the morning of Mutimer's departure
from Wanley there was no wonted clank of machinery, no
smoke from the chimneys, no roar of iron-melting furnaces;
the men and women of the colony stood idly before their
houses, discussing prospects, asking each other whether it was
seriously Mr. Eldon's intention to raze New Wanley, many of
them grumbling or giving vent to revolutionary threats. They
had continued in work thus long since the property in fact
changed hands, and to most of them it seemed unlikely, in
spite of everything, that they would have to go in search of
new employments. This morning they would hear finally.

The valley rested. For several days there had been constant rain; though summer was scarcely over, it had turned
cold and the sky was cheerless. Over Stanbury Hill there
were always heavy, dripping clouds, and the leaves of Adela's
favourite wood were already falling. At the Manor there was
once more disorder; before Mutimer and his wife took their
departure the removal of furniture had commenced. Over the
whole scene brooded a spirit of melancholy. It needed faith in
human energy to imagine the pollutions swept away, and the
seasons peacefully gliding as of old between the hillsides and
amid meadows and garden closes.

Hubert Eldon drove over from Agworth, and was in the
Public Hall at the appointed time. His business with the
men was simple and brief. He had to inform them that their
employment here was at an end, but that each one would
receive a month's wages and permission to inhabit their present
abodes for yet a fortnight. After that they had no longer
right of tenancy. He added that if any man considered himself specially aggrieved by this arrangement, he was prepared
to hear and judge the individual case.

There was a murmur of discontent through the room, but
no one took upon himself to rise and become spokesman of the
community. Disregarding the manifestation, Hubert described
in a few words how and when this final business would be
transacted; then he left the hall by the door which led from the
platform.

Then followed a busy week. Claims of all kinds were

addressed to him, some reasonable, most of them not to be entertained. Mr. Yottle was constantly at the Manor; there he and Hubert held a kind of court. Hubert was not well fitted for business of this nature; he easily became impatient, and, in spite of humane intentions, often suffered from a tumult of his blood, when opposed by some dogged mechanic.

'I can't help it!' he exclaimed to Mr. Wyvern one night, after a day of peculiar annoyance. 'We are all men, it is true; but for the brotherhood—feel it who can! I am illiberal, if you like, but in the presence of those fellows I feel that I am facing enemies. It seems to me that I have nothing in common with them but the animal functions. Absurd? Yes, of course, it is absurd; but I speak of how intercourse with them affects me. They are our enemies, yours as well as mine; they are the enemies of every man who speaks the pure English tongue and does not earn a living with his hands. When they face me I understand what revolution means; some of them look at me as they would if they had muskets in their hands.'

'You are not conciliating,' remarked the vicar.

'I am not, and cannot be. They stir the worst feelings in me; I grow arrogant, autocratic. As long as I have no private dealings with them I can consider their hardships and judge their characters dispassionately; but I must not come to close quarters.'

'You have special causes of prejudice.'

'True. If I were a philosopher I should overcome all that. However, my prejudice is good in one way; it enables me thoroughly to understand the detestation with which they regard me and the like of me. If I had been born one of them I should be the most savage anarchist. The moral is, that I must hold apart. Perhaps I shall grow cooler in time.'

The special causes of prejudice were quite as strong on the side of the workmen; Hubert might have been far less aristocratic in bearing, they would have disliked him as cordially. Most of them took it as a wanton outrage that they should be driven from the homes in which they had believed themselves settled for life. The man Redgrave—he of the six feet two who had presented the address to Mutimer—was a powerful agent of ill-feeling; during the first few days he was constantly gathering impromptu meetings in New Wanley and haranguing them violently on the principles of Socialism. But in less than a week he had taken his departure, and the main trouble seemed at an end.

Mrs. Eldon was so impatient to return to the Manor that a room was prepared for her as soon as possible, and she came from her house at Agworth before Mutimer had been gone a week. Through the summer her strength had failed rapidly; it was her own conviction that she could live but a short time longer. The extreme agitation caused by the discovery of the will had visibly enfeebled her; it was her one desire to find herself once more in her old home, and there to breathe her last. The journey from Agworth cost her extreme suffering; she was prostrate, almost lifeless, for three days after it. But her son's society revived her. Knowing him established in his family possessions, she only cared to taste for a little while this unhoped-for joy. Lying on a couch in her familiar chamber, she delighted to have flowers brought to her from the garden, even leaves from the dear old trees, every one of which she knew as a friend. But she had constant thought for those upon whose disaster her own happiness was founded; of Adela she spoke often.

'What will become of that poor child?' she asked one evening, when Hubert had been speaking of Rodman's impracticable attitude, and of the proceedings Mutimer was about to take. 'Do you know anything of her life, Hubert?'

'I met her in the wood here a few weeks ago,' he replied, mentioning the incident for the first time. 'She wanted to make a Socialist of me.'

'Was that after the will came to light?'

'The day after. She pleaded for New Wanley—hoped I should keep it up.'

'Then she has really accepted her husband's views?'

'It seems so. I am afraid she thought me an obstinate tyrant.'

He spoke carelessly.

'But she must not suffer, dear. How can they be helped?'

'They can't fall into absolute want. And I suppose his Socialist friends will do something for him. I have been as considerate as it was possible to be. I dare say he will make me a commonplace in his lectures henceforth, a type of the brutal capitalist.'

He laughed when he had said it, and led the conversation to another subject.

About the workmen, too, Mrs. Eldon was kindly thoughtful. Hubert spared her his prejudices and merely described what he was doing. She urged him to be rather too easy than too

exacting with them. It was the same in everything; the blessing which had fallen upon her made her full of gentleness and
sweet charity.

The fortnight's grace was at an end, and it was announced
to Hubert that the last family had left New Wanley. The
rain still continued; as evening set in Hubert returned from
an inspection of the deserted colony, his spirits weighed upon
by the scene of desolation. After dinner he sat as usual with
his mother for a couple of hours, then went to his own room
and read till eleven o'clock. Just as he had thrown aside his
book the silence of the night was riven by a terrific yell, a
savage cry of many voices, which came from the garden in the
front of the house, and at the same instant there sounded a
great crashing of glass. The windows behind his back were
broken and a couple of heavy missiles thundered near him
upon the floor—stones they proved to be. He rushed from the
room. All the lights in the house except his own and that in
Mrs. Eldon's room were extinguished. He reached his mother's
door. Before he could open it the yell and the shower of stones
were repeated, again with ruin of windows, this time on the
east side of the Manor. In a moment he was by his mother's
bed; he saw her sitting up in terror; she was speechless and
unable even to stretch her arms towards him. An inner door
opened and the woman who was always in attendance rushed
in half dressed. At the same time there were sounds of movement in other parts of the house. Once more the furious voices
and the stone-volley; Hubert put his arm about his mother
and tried to calm her.

'Don't be frightened; it's those cowardly roughs. They
have had their three shots, now they'll take to their heels.
Mrs. Winter is here, mother; she will stay with you whilst I
go down and see what has to be done. I'll be back directly if
there is no more danger.'

He hastened away. The servants had collected upon the
front staircase, with lamps and candles, in fright and disorder
unutterable. Hubert repeated to them what he had said to
his mother, and it seemed to be the truth, for the silence outside was unbroken.

'I shouldn't wonder,' he cried, 'if they've made an attempt
to set the house on fire. We must go about and examine.'

The door-bell was rung loudly. The servants rushed back
up the stairs; Hubert went into the dining-room, carrying no
light, and called through the shattered windows asking who

had rung. It was the vicar; the shouts had brought him
forth.

'They are gone,' he said, in his strong, deep voice, in itself
reassuring. 'I think there were only some ten or a dozen;
they've made off up the hill. Is anybody hurt?'

'No, they have only broken all the windows,' Hubert re
plied. 'But I am terribly afraid for the effect upon my mother.
We must have the doctor round at once.'

The vicar was admitted to the house, and a messenger
forthwith despatched for the medical man, who resided half-
way between Wanley and Agworth. On returning to his
mother's room Hubert found his fears only too well justified;
Mrs. Eldon lay motionless, her eyes open, but seemingly without intelligence. At intervals of five minutes a sigh was
audible, else she could scarcely be perceived to breathe. The
attendant said that she had not spoken.

It was some time before the doctor arrived. After a brief
examination, he came out with Hubert; his opinion was that
the sufferer would not see daybreak.

She lived, however, for some twelve hours, if that could be
called life which was only distinguishable from the last silence
by the closest scrutiny. Hubert did not move from the bedside, and from time to time Mr. Wyvern came and sat with
him. Neither of them spoke. Hubert had no thought of food
or rest; the shadow of a loss, of which he only understood the
meaning now that it was at hand, darkened him and all the
world. Behind his voiceless misery was immeasurable hatred
of those who had struck him this blow; at moments a revengeful fury all but maddened him. He held his mother's hand; if
he could but feel one pressure of the slight fingers before they
were impotent for ever! And this much was granted him.
Shortly before midday the open eyes trembled to consciousness,
the lips moved in endeavour to speak. To Hubert it seemed
that his intense gaze had worked a miracle, effecting that which
his will demanded. She saw him and understood.

'Mother, can you speak? Do you know me, dear?'

She smiled, and her lips tried to shape words. He bent
over her, close, close. At first the faint whisper was unintelligible, then he heard:

'They did not know what they were doing.'

Something followed, but he could not understand it. The
whisper ended in a sigh, the smiling features quivered. He
held her, but was alone. . . .

A hand was laid gently upon his shoulder. Through blinding tears he discerned Mr. Wyvern's solemn countenance. He resisted the efforts to draw him away, but was at length persuaded.

Early in the evening he fell asleep, lying dressed upon his bed, and the sleep lasted till midnight. Then he left his room, and descended the stairs, for the lower part of the house was still lighted. In the hall Mr. Wyvern met him.

'Let us go into the library,' he said to the clergyman. 'I want to talk to you.'

He had resumed his ordinary manner. Without mention of his mother, he began at once to speak of the rioters.

'They were led by that man Redgrave; there can be no doubt of that. I shall go to Agworth at once and set the police at work.'

'I have already done that,' replied the vicar. 'Three fellows have been arrested in Agworth.'

'New Wanley men?'

'Yes; but Redgrave is not one of them.'

'He shall be caught, though!'

Hubert appeared to have forgotten everything but his desire of revenge. It supported him through the wretched days that followed—even at the funeral his face was hard-set and his eyes dry. But in spite of every effort it was impossible to adduce evidence against any but the three men who had loitered drinking in Agworth. Redgrave came forward voluntarily and proved an alibi; he was vastly indignant at the charge brought against him, declared that window-breaking was not his business, and that had he been on the spot he should have used all his influence to prevent such contemptible doings. He held a meeting in Belwick of all the New Wanleyers he could gather together: those who came repudiated the outrage as useless and unworthy. On the whole, it seemed probable that only a handful of good-for-nothings had been concerned in the affair, probably men who had been loafing in the Belwick public-houses, indisposed to look for work. The 'Fiery Cross' and the 'Tocsin' commented on the event in their respective ways. The latter organ thought that an occasional demonstration of this kind was not amiss; it was a pity that apparently innocent individuals should suffer (an allusion to the death of Mrs. Eldon); but, after all, what member of the moneyed classes was in reality innocent? An article on the subject in the 'Fiery Cross' was signed 'Richard Mutimer.' It breathed

righteous indignation and called upon all true Socialists to
make it known that they pursued their ends in far other ways
than by the gratification of petty malice. A copy of this paper
reached Wanley Manor. Hubert glanced over it.

It lay by him when he received a visit from Mr. Wyvern
the same evening.

' How is it to be explained,' he asked ; ' a man like Westlake
mixing himself up with this crew ? '

' Do you know him personally ? ' the vicar inquired.

' I have met him. But I have seen more of Mrs. Westlake.
She is a tenth muse, the muse of lyrical Socialism. From
which of them the impulse came I have no means of knowing,
but surely it must have been from her. In her case I can
understand it; she lives in an æsthetic reverie; she idealises
everything. Naturally she knows nothing whatever of real life.
She is one of the most interesting women I ever met, but I
should say that her influence on Westlake has been deplorable.'

' Mrs. Mutimer is greatly her friend, I believe,' said the
vicar.

' I believe so. But let us speak of this paper. I want, if
possible, to understand Westlake's position. Have you ever
read the thing ? '

' Frequently.'

' Now here is an article signed by Westlake. You know
his books ? How has he fallen to this ? His very style has
abandoned him, his English smacks of the street corners, of
Radical clubs. The man is ruined; it is next to impossible
that he should ever again do good work, such as we used to
have from him. The man who wrote "Daphne" ! Oh, it is
monstrous ! '

' It is something of a problem to me,' Mr. Wyvern admitted.
' Had he been a younger man, or if his writing had been of a
different kind. Yet his sincerity is beyond doubt.'

' I doubt it,' Hubert broke in. ' Not his sincerity in the
beginning ; but he must long since have ached to free himself.
It is such a common thing for a man to commit himself to some
pronounced position in public life and for very shame shrink
from withdrawing. He would not realise what it meant. Now
in the revolutionary societies of the Continent there is something that appeals to the imagination. A Nihilist, with Siberia
or death before him, fighting against a damnable tyranny—the
best might sacrifice everything for that. But English Socialism ! It is infused with the spirit of shopkeeping ; it appeals

to the vulgarest minds; it keeps one eye on personal safety, the other on the capitalist's strong-box; it is stamped commonplace, like everything originating with the English lower classes. How does it differ from Radicalism, the most contemptible claptrap of politics, except in wanting to hurry a little the rule of the mob? Well, I am too subjective. Help me, if you can, to understand Westlake.'

Hubert was pale and sorrow-stricken; his movements were heavy with weariness, but he had all at once begun to speak with the old fire, the old scorn. He rested his chin upon his hand and waited for his companion's reply.

'At your age,' said Mr. Wyvern, smiling half sadly, 'I, too, had a habit of vehement speaking, but it was on the other side. I was a badly paid curate working in a wretched parish. I lived among the vilest and poorest of the people, and my imagination was constantly at boiling-point. I can only suppose that Westlake has been led to look below the surface of society and has been affected as I was then. He has the mind of a poet; probably he was struck with horror to find over what a pit he had been living in careless enjoyment. He is tender-hearted; of a sudden he felt himself criminal, to be playing with beautiful toys whilst a whole world lived only to sweat and starve. The appeal of the miserable seemed to be to him personally. It is what certain sects call conversion in religion, a truth addressing itself with unwonted and invincible force to the individual soul.'

'And you, too, were a Socialist?'

'At that age and under those conditions it was right and good. I should have been void of feeling and imagination otherwise. Such convictions are among relative truths. To be a social enthusiast is in itself neither right nor wrong, neither praiseworthy nor the opposite; it is a state to be judged in relation to the other facts of a man's life. You will never know that state; if you affected it you would be purely contemptible. And I myself have outgrown it.'

'But you must not think that I am inhuman,' said Hubert. 'The sight of distress touches me deeply. To the individual poor man or woman I would give my last penny. It is when they rise against me as a class that I become pitiless.'

'I understand you perfectly, though I have not the same prejudices. My old zeal lingers with me in the form of tolerance. I can enter into the mind of a furious proletarian as easily as into the feeling which you represent.'

'But how did your zeal come to an end?'

'In this way. I worked under the conditions I have described to you till I was nearly thirty. Then I broke down physically. At the same time it happened that I inherited a small competency. I went abroad, lived in Italy for a couple of years. I left England with the firm intention of getting my health and then returning to work harder than ever. But during those two years I educated myself. When I reached England again I found that it was impossible to enter again on the old path; I should have had to force myself; it would have been an instance of the kind of thing you suggest in explanation of Westlake's persistence. Fortunately I yielded to my better sense and altogether shunned the life of towns. I was no longer of those who seek to change the world, but of those who are content that it should in substance remain as it is.'

'But how can you be content, if you are convinced that the majority of men live only to suffer?'

'It is you who attribute the conviction to me,' said the vicar, smiling good-naturedly. 'My conviction is the very opposite. One of the pet theories I have developed for myself in recent years is, that happiness is very evenly distributed among all classes and conditions. It is the result of sober reflection on my experience of life. Think of it a moment. The bulk of men are neither rich nor poor, taking into consideration their habits and needs; they live in much content, despite social imperfections and injustices, despite the ills of nature. Above and below are classes of extreme characterisation ; I believe the happiness assignable to those who are the lowest stratum of civilisation is, relatively speaking, no whit less than that we may attribute to the thin stratum of the surface, using the surface to mean the excessively rich. It is a paradox, but anyone capable of thinking may be assured of its truth. The life of the very poorest is a struggle to support their bodies ; the richest, relieved of that one anxiety, are overwhelmed with such a mass of artificial troubles that their few moments of genuine repose do not exceed those vouchsafed to their antipodes. You would urge the sufferings of the criminal class under punishment? I balance against it the misery of the rich under the scourge of their own excesses. It is a mistake due to mere thoughtlessness, or ignorance, to imagine the labouring, or even the destitute, population as ceaselessly groaning beneath the burden of their existence. Go along the poorest street in the East End

of London, and you will hear as much laughter, witness as
much gaiety, as in any thoroughfare of the West. Laughter
and gaiety of a miserable kind? I speak of it as relative to
the habits and capabilities of the people. A being of superior
intelligence regarding humanity with an eye of perfect understanding would discover that life was enjoyed every bit as much
in the slum as in the palace.'

'You would consider it fair to balance excessive suffering of
the body in one class against excessive mental suffering in
another?'

'Undoubtedly. It is a fair application of my theory. But
let me preach a little longer. It is my belief that, though this
equality of distribution remains a fact, the sum total of happiness in nations is seriously diminishing. Not only on account
of the growth of population; the poor have more to suffer, the
rich less of true enjoyment, the mass of comfortable people fall
into an ever-increasing anxiety. A Radical will tell you that
this is a transitional state. Possibly, if we accept the Radical
theories of progress. I held them once in a very light-
hearted way; I am now far less disposed to accept them as even
imaginably true. Those who are enthusiastic for the spirit of
the age proceed on the principle of countenancing evil that
good may some day come of it. Such a position astonishes me.
Is the happiness of a man now alive of less account than that
of the man who shall live two hundred years hence? Altruism
is doubtless good, but only so when it gives pure enjoyment;
that is to say, when it is embraced instinctively. Shall I frown
on a man because he *cannot* find his bliss in altruism and bid
him perish to make room for a being more perfect? What
right have we to live thus in the far-off future? Thinking in
this way, I have a profound dislike and distrust of this same
progress. Take one feature of it—universal education. That,
I believe, works most patently for the growing misery I speak
of. Its results affect all classes, and all for the worse. I said
that I used to have a very bleeding of the heart for the half-
clothed and quarter-fed hangers-on to civilisation; I think far
less of them now than of another class in appearance much
better off. It is a class created by the mania of education, and
it consists of those unhappy men and women whom unspeakable cruelty endows with intellectual needs whilst refusing
them the sustenance they are taught to crave. Another generation, and this class will be terribly extended, its existence
blighting the whole social state. Every one of these poor

creatures has a right to curse the work of those who clamour progress, and pose as benefactors of their race.'

'All that strikes me as very good and true,' remarked Hubert; 'but can it be helped? Or do you refuse to believe in the modern conception of laws ruling social development?'

'I wish I could do so. No; when I spoke of the right to curse, I should have said, from their point of view. In truth, I fear we must accept progress. But I cannot rejoice in it; I will even do what little I can in my own corner to support the old order of things. You may be aware that I was on very friendly terms with the Mutimers, that I even seemed to encourage them in their Socialism. Yes, and because I felt that in that way I could best discharge my duty. What I really encouraged was sympathy and humanity. When Mutimer came asking me to be present at his meetings I plainly refused. To have held apart from him and his wife would have been as wrong in me as to publicly countenance their politics.'

Mr. Wyvern was on the point of referring to his private reasons for befriending Adela, but checked himself.

'What I made no secret of approving was their substitution of human relations between employer and employed for the detestable "nexus of cash payment," as Carlyle calls it. That is only a return to the good old order, and it seems to me that it becomes more impossible every day. Thus far I am with the Socialists, in that I denounce the commercial class, the *bourgeois*, the capitalists—call them what you will—as the supremely maleficent. They hold us at their mercy, and their mercy is nought. Monstrously hypocritical, they cry for progress when they mean increased opportunities of swelling their own purses at the expense of those they employ, and of those they serve; vulgar to the core, they exalt a gross ideal of well-being, and stink in their prosperity. The very poor and the uncommercial wealthy alike suffer from them; the intellect of the country is poisoned by their influence. They it is who indeed are oppressors; they grow rich on the toil of poor girls in London garrets and of men who perish prematurely to support their children. I won't talk of these people; I should lose my calm views of things and use language too much like this of the "Fiery Cross."'

Hubert was thoughtful.

'What is before us?' he murmured.

'Evil; of that I am but too firmly assured. Progress will have its way, and its path will be a path of bitterness. A pillar of dark cloud leads it by day, and of terrible fire by night. I do not say that the promised land may not lie ahead of its guiding, but woe is me for the desert first to be traversed! Two vices are growing among us to dread proportions—indifference and hatred: the one will let poverty anguish at its door, the other will hound on the vassal against his lord. Papers like the "Fiery Cross," even though such a man as Westlake edit them, serve the cause of hatred; they preach, by implication at all events, the childish theory of the equality of men, and seek to make discontented a whole class which only needs regular employment on the old conditions to be perfectly satisfied.'

'Westlake says here that they have no *right* to be satisfied.'

'I know. It is one of the huge fallacies of the time; it comes of the worship of progress. I am content with the fact that, even in our bad day, as a class they *are* satisfied. No, these reforms address themselves to the wrong people; they begin at the wrong end. Let us raise our voices, if we feel impelled to do so at all, for the old simple Christian rules, and do our best to get the educated by the ears. I have my opinion about the clergy; I will leave you to guess it.'

'Have you any belief in the possibility of this revolution they threaten?'

'None whatever. Changes will come about, but not of these men's making or devising. And for the simple reason that they are not sincere. I put aside an educated enthusiast such as Westlake. The proletarian Socialists do not believe what they say, and therefore they are so violent in saying it. They are not themselves of pure and exalted character; they cannot ennoble others. If the movement continue we shall see miserable examples of weakness led astray by popularity, of despicable qualities aping greatness.'

He paused somewhat abruptly, for he was thinking of Mutimer, and did not wish to make the application too obvious. Hubert restrained a smile.

They parted shortly after, but not till Hubert had put one more question.

'Do you, or do you not, approve of what I am doing down in the valley?'

Mr. Wyvern thought a moment, and replied gravely:

'You being yourself, I approve it heartily. It will gladden my eyes to see the grass growing when spring comes round.'

He shook Hubert's hand affectionately and left him.

CHAPTER XXX.

WE must concern ourselves for a little with the affairs of our old acquaintance, Daniel Dabbs.

Daniel's disillusionment with regard to Richard Mutimer did not affect his regularity of attendance at the Socialist lectures. In most things a typical English mechanic, he was especially so in his relation to the extreme politics of which he declared himself a supporter. He became a Socialist because his friend Dick was one; when that was no longer a reason, he numbered himself among the followers of Comrade Roodhouse —first as a sort of angry protest against Mutimer's private treachery, then again because he had got into the habit of listening to inflammatory discourses every Sunday night, and on the whole found it a pleasant way of passing the evening. He enjoyed the oratory of Messrs. Cowes and Cullen; he liked to shout 'Hear, hear!' and to stamp when there was general applause; it affected him with an agreeable sensation, much like that which follows upon a good meal, to hear himself pitied as a hard-working, ill-used fellow, and the frequent allusion to his noble qualities sweetly flattered him. When he went home to the public-house after a lively debate, and described the proceedings to his brother Nicholas, he always ended by declaring that it was 'as good as a play.'

He read the 'Tocsin,' that is to say, he glanced his eye up and down the columns and paused wherever he caught words such as 'villains,' 'titled scoundrels,' 'vampires,' and so on. The expositions of doctrine he passed over; anything in the nature of reasoning muddled him. From hearing them incessantly repeated he knew the root theories of Socialism, and could himself hold forth on such texts as 'the community of the means of production' with considerable fluency and vehemence; but in very fact he concerned himself as little with economic reforms as with the principles of high art, and had as little genuine belief in the promised revolution as in the immortality of his own soul. Had he been called upon to suffer in any way for the 'cause of the people,' it would speedily have been demonstrated of what metal his enthusiasm was made.

But there came a different kind of test. In the winter which followed upon Mutimer's downfall, Nicholas Dabbs fell ill and died. He was married but had no children, and his wife had been separated from him for several years. His brother Daniel found himself in flourishing circumstances, with a public-house which brought in profits of forty pounds a week. It goes without saying that Daniel forthwith abandoned his daily labour and installed himself behind the bar. The position suited him admirably ; with a barmaid and a potman at his orders (he paid them no penny more than the market rate), he stood about in his shirt sleeves and gossiped from morn to midnight with such of his friends as had leisure (and money) to spend in the temple of Bacchus. From the day that saw him a licensed victualler he ceased to attend the Socialist meetings ; it was, of course, a sufficient explanation to point to the fact that he could not be in two places at the same time, for Sunday evening is a season of brisk business in the liquor trade. At first he was reticent on the subject of his old convictions, but by degrees he found it possible to achieve the true innkeeper's art, and speak freely in a way which could offend none of his customers. And he believed himself every bit as downright and sincere as he had ever been.

Comfortably established on a capitalist basis, his future assured because it depended upon the signal vice of his class, it one day occurred to Daniel that he ought to take to himself a helpmeet, a partner of his joys and sorrows. He had thought of it from time to time during the past year, but only in a vague way ; he had even directed his eyes to the woman who might perchance be the one most suitable, though with anything but assurance of his success if he seriously endeavoured to obtain her. Long ago he had ceased to trouble himself about his first love ; with characteristic acceptance of the accomplished fact, he never really imagined that Alice Mutimer, after she became an heiress, could listen to his wooing, and, to do him justice, he appreciated the delicacy of his position, if he should continue to press his suit. It cost him not a little suffering altogether to abandon his hopes, for the Princess had captivated him, and if he could have made her his wife he would—for at least twelve months—have been a proud and exultant man. But all that was over ; Daniel was heart-free, when he again began to occupy himself with womankind ; it was a very different person towards whom he found himself attracted. This was Emma Vine.

After that chance meeting with Mrs. Clay in the omnibus he lost sight of the sisters for a while, but one day Kate came to the public-house and desired to see him. She was in great misery. Emma had fallen ill, gravely ill, and Kate had no money to pay a doctor. The people in the house where she lodged were urging her to send for the parish doctor, but that was an extremity to be avoided as long as a single hope remained. She had come to borrow a few shillings in order that she might take Emma in a cab to the hospital; perhaps they would receive her as an in-patient. Daniel put his hand in his pocket. He did more; though on the point of returning from breakfast to his work, he sacrificed the morning to accompany Mrs. Clay and help her to get the sick girl to the hospital. Fortunately it was found possible to give her a bed; Emma remained in the hospital for seven weeks.

Daniel was not hasty in forming attachments. During the seven weeks he called three or four times to inquire of Mrs. Clay what progress her sister was making, but when Emma came home again, and resumed her usual work, he seemed to have no further interest in her. At length Kate came to the public-house one Saturday night and wished to pay back half the loan. Daniel shook his head. ' All right, Mrs. Clay; don't you hurt yourself. Let it wait till you're a bit better off.' Nicholas was behind the bar, and when Kate had gone he asked his brother if he hadn't observed something curious in Mrs. Clay's behaviour. Daniel certainly had; the brothers agreed that she must have been drinking rather more than was good for her.

' I shouldn't wonder,' said Daniel, ' if she started with the whole o' the money.'

Which, indeed, was a true conjecture.

Time went on, and Daniel had been six months a licensed victualler. It was summer once more, and thirsty weather. Daniel stood behind the bar in his shirt sleeves, collarless for personal ease, with a white waistcoat, and trousers of light tweed. Across his stomach, which already was more portly than in his engineering days, swayed a heavy gold chain; on one of his fingers was a demonstrative ring. His face and neck were very red; his hair, cropped extremely short, gleamed with odorous oils. You could see that he prided himself on the spotlessness of his linen; his cuffs were turned up to avoid alcoholic soilure; their vast links hung loose for better observance by customers. Daniel was a smiling and a happy man.

It was early on Sunday evening; Hoxton had shaken itself from the afternoon slumber, had taken a moderate tea, and was

in no two minds about the entirely agreeable way of getting
through the hours till bedtime. Daniel beamed on the good
thirsty souls who sought refuge under his roof from the still
warm rays of the sun. Whilst seeing that no customer lacked
due attention, he conversed genially with a group of his special
friends. One of these had been present at a meeting held on
Clerkenwell Green that morning, a meeting assembled to hear
Richard Mutimer. Richard, a year having passed since his
temporary eclipse, was once more prominent as a popular leader.
He was addressing himself to the East End especially, and had
a scheme to propound which, whatever might be its success or
the opposite, kept him well before the eyes of men.

'What's all this 'ere about?' cried one of the group in an
impatiently contemptuous tone. 'I can't see nothin' in it
myself.'

'I can see as he wants money,' observed another, laughing.
'There's a good many ways o' gettin' money without earnin' it,
particular if you've got a tongue as goes like a steam engine.'

'I don't think so bad of him as all that,' said the man who
had attended the meeting. ' 'Tain't for himself as he wants the
money. What do *you* think o' this 'ere job, Dan?'

'I'll tell you more about that in a year's time,' replied
Dabbs, thrusting his fingers into his waistcoat pockets. ' 'Cord-
ing to Mike, we're all goin' to be rich before we know it. Let's
hope it'll come true.'

He put his tongue in his cheek and let his eye circle round
the group.

'Seems to me,' said the contemptuous man, 'he'd better
look after his own people first. Charity begins at 'ome, eh,
mates?'

'What do you mean by that?' inquired a voice.

'Why, isn't his brother — what's his name? Bill—
Jack——'

''Arry,' corrected Daniel.

'To be sure, 'Arry; I don't know him myself, but I 'eard
talk of him. It's him as is doin' his three months' 'ard
labour.'

'That ain't no fault o' Dick Mutimer's,' asserted the apolo-
gist. 'He always was a bad 'un, that 'Arry. Why, you can
say so much, Dan? No, no, I don't 'old with a man's bein'
cried down 'cause he's got a brother as disgraces himself. It
was Dick as got him his place, an' a good place it was. It
wasn't Dick as put him up to thievin', I suppose?'

'No, no, that's right enough,' said Dabbs. 'Let a man be judged by his own sayin's and doin's. There's queer stories about Dick Mutimer himself, but—was it Scotch or Irish, Mike?'

Mike had planted his glass on the counter in a manner suggesting replenishment.

'Now that's what I call a cruel question!' cried Mike humorously. 'The man as doesn't stick to his country, I don't think much of him.'

The humour was not remarkable, but it caused a roar of laughter to go up.

'Now what I want to know,' exclaimed one, returning to the main subject, 'is where Mutimer gets his money to live on. He does no work, we know that much.'

'He told us all about that this mornin',' replied the authority. 'He has friends as keeps him goin', that's all. As far as I can make out it's a sort o' subscription.'

'Now, there you are!' put in Daniel with half a sneer. 'I don't call that Socialism. Let a man support himself by his own work, then he's got a right to say what he likes. No, no, *we* know what Socialism means, eh, Tom?'

The man appealed to answered with a laugh.

'Well, blest if I do, Dan! There's so many kinds o' Socialism nowadays. Which lot does he pretend to belong to? There's the "Fiery Cross," and there's Roodhouse with his "Tocsin," and now I s'pose Dick'll be startin' another paper of his own.'

'No, no,' replied Mutimer's supporter. 'He holds by the "Fiery Cross," still, so he said this mornin'. I've no opinion o' Roodhouse myself. He makes a deal o' noise, but I can't see as he *does* anything.'

'You won't catch Dick Mutimer sidin' with Roodhouse,' remarked Daniel with a wink. 'That's an old story, eh, Tom?'

Thus the talk went on, and the sale of beverages kept pace with it. About eight o'clock the barmaid informed Daniel that Mrs. Clay wished to see him. Kate had entered the house by the private door, and was sitting in the bar-parlour. Daniel went to her at once.

She was more slovenly in appearance than ever, and showed all the signs of extreme poverty. Her face was not merely harsh and sour, it indicated a process of degradation. The smile with which she greeted Daniel was disagreeable through excessive anxiety to be ingratiating. Her eyes were restless and shrewd. Daniel sat down opposite to her, and rested his elbows on the table.

'Well, how's all at 'ome?' he began, avoiding her look as he spoke.

'Nothing much to boast of,' Kate replied with an unpleasant giggle. 'We keep alive.'

'Emma all right?'

'She's all right, except for her bad 'ead-aches. She's had another of 'em this week. But I think it's a bit better to-day.'

'She'll have a rest to-morrow.'

The following day was the August bank-holiday.

'No, she'll have no rest. She's going to do some cleaning in Goswell Road.'

Daniel drummed with his fingers on the table.

'She isn't fit to do it, that's quite certain,' Mrs. Clay continued. 'I wish I could get her out for an hour or two. She wants fresh air, that's what it is. I s'pose you're going somewhere to-morrow?'

It was asked insinuatingly, and at the same time with an air of weary resignation.

'Well, I did think o' gettin' as far as Epping Forest. D'you think you could persuade Emma to come? you and the children as well, you know. I'll have the mare out if she will.'

'I can ask her and see. It 'ud be a rare treat for us. I feel myself as if I couldn't hold up much longer, it's that hot!'

She threw a glance towards the bar.

'Will you have a bottle o' lemonade?' Daniel asked.

'It's very kind of you. I've a sort o' fainty feeling. If you'd just put ever such a little drop in it, Mr. Dabbs.'

Daniel betrayed a slight annoyance. But he went to the door and gave the order.

'Still at the same place?' he asked on resuming his seat.

'Emma, you mean? Yes, but it's only been half a week's work, this last. And I've as good as nothing to do. There's the children runnin' about with no soles to their feet.'

The lemonade—with a dash in it—was brought to her, and she refreshed herself with a deep draught. Perhaps the dash was not perceptible enough; she did not seem entirely satisfied, though pretending to be so.

'Suppose I come round to-night and ask her myself?' Daniel said, as the result of a short reflection.

' It 'ud be kind of you if you would, Mr. Dabbs. I'm afraid
..e'll tell me she can't afford to lose the day.'

He consulted his watch, then again reflected, still drumming
on the table.

' All right, we'll go,' he said, rising from his chair.

His coat was hanging on a peg behind the door. He drew
it on, and went to tell the barmaid that he should be absent
exactly twenty minutes. It was Daniel's policy to lead his
underlings to expect that he might return at any moment,
though he would probably be away a couple of hours.

The sisters were now living in a street crossing the angle
between Goswell Road and the City Road. Daniel was not, as
a rule, lavish in his expenditure, but he did not care to walk
any distance, and there was no line of omnibuses available.
He took a hansom.

It generally fell to Emma's share to put her sister's children
to bed, for Mrs. Clay was seldom at home in the evening. But
for Emma, indeed, the little ones would have been sadly off for
motherly care. Kate had now and then a fit of maternal zeal,
but it usually ended in impatience and slappings; for the most
part she regarded her offspring as encumbrance, and only drew
attention to them when she wished to impress people with the
hardships of her lot. The natural result was that the boy and
girl only knew her as mother by name; they feared her, and
would shrink to Emma's side when Kate began to speak crossly.

All dwelt together in one room, for life was harder than
ever. Emma's illness had been the beginning of a dark and
miserable time. Whilst she was in the hospital her sister took
the first steps on the path which leads to destruction; with
scanty employment, much time to kill, never a sufficiency of
food, companions only too like herself in their distaste for
home duties and in the misery of their existence, poor Kate
got into the habit of straying aimlessly about the streets, and,
the inevitable consequence, of seeking warmth and company in
the public-house. Her children lived as the children of such
mothers do : they played on the stairs or on the pavements, had
accidents, were always dirty, cried themselves to sleep in
hunger and pain. When Emma returned, still only fit for a
convalescent home, she had to walk about day after day in
search of work, conciliating the employers whom Mrs. Clay had
neglected or disgusted, undertaking jobs to which her strength
was inadequate, and, not least, striving her hardest to restore
order in the wretched home. It was agreed that Kate should

use the machine at home, whilst Emma got regular employment in a workroom.

Emma never heard of that letter which her sister wrote to Mutimer's wife. Kate had no expectation that help would come of it; she hoped that it had done Mutimer harm, and the hope had to satisfy her. She durst not let Emma suspect that she had done such a thing.

Emma heard, however, of the loan from Daniel Dabbs, and afterwards thanked him for his kindness, but she resolutely set her face against the repetition of such favours, though Daniel would have willingly helped when she came out of the hospital. Kate, of course, was for accepting anything that was offered; she lost her temper, and accused Emma of wishing to starve the children. But she was still greatly under her sister's influence, and when Emma declared that there must be a parting between them if she discovered that anything was secretly accepted from Mr. Dabbs, Kate sullenly yielded the point.

Daniel was aware of all this, and it made an impression upon him.

To-night Emma was as usual left alone with the children. After tea, when Kate left the house, she sat down to the machine and worked for a couple of hours; for her there was small difference between Sunday and week day. Whilst working she told the children stories; it was a way of beguiling them from their desire to go and play in the street. They were strange stories, half recollected from a childhood which had promised better things than a maidenhood of garret misery, half Emma's own invention. They had a grace, a spontaneity, occasionally an imaginative brightness, which would have made them, if they had been taken down from the lips, models of tale-telling for children. Emma had two classes of story: the one concerned itself with rich children, the other with poor; the one highly fanciful, the other full of a touching actuality, the very essence of a life such as that led by the listeners themselves. Unlike the novel which commends itself to the world's grown children, these narratives had by no means necessarily a happy ending; for one thing Emma saw too deeply into the facts of life, and was herself too sad, to cease her music on a merry chord; and, moreover, it was half a matter of principle with her to make the little ones thoughtful and sympathetic; she believed that they would grow up kinder and more self-reliant if they were in the habit of thinking that we are ever dependent on each other for solace and strengthening under the burden of life. The most elaborate of her stories, one wholly of her own invention, was called 'Blanche and Janey.' It was a double biography. Blanche and Janey were born on the same day, they lived ten years, and then died on the same day. But Blanche was the child of wealthy parents ; Janey was born in a garret. Their lives were recounted in parallel, almost year by year, and there was sadness in the contrast. Emma had chosen the name of the poor child in memory of her own sister, her ever dear Jane, whose life had been a life of sorrow.

The story ended thus :

' Yes, they died on the same day, and they were buried on the same day. But not in the same cemetery, oh no ! Blanche's grave is far away over there '—she pointed to the west— ' among tombstones covered with flowers, and her father and mother go every Sunday to read her name, and think and talk of her. Janey was buried far away over yonder '—she pointed to the east—' but there is no stone on her grave, and no one knows the exact place where she lies, and no one, no one ever goes to think and talk of her.'

The sweetness of the story lay in the fact that the children were both good, and both deserved to be happy; it never occurred to Emma to teach her hearers to hate little Blanche just because hers was the easier lot.

Whatever might be her secret suffering, with the little ones Emma was invariably patient and tender. However dirty they had made themselves during the day, however much they cried when hunger made them irritable, they went to their aunt's side with the assurance of finding gentleness in reproof and sympathy with their troubles. Yet once she was really angry. Bertie told her a deliberate untruth, and she at once discovered it. She stood silent for a few moments, looking as Bertie had never seen her look. Then she said :

' Do you know, Bertie, that it is wrong to try and deceive ?'

Then she tried to make him understand why falsehood was evil, and as she spoke to the child her voice quivered, her breast heaved. When the little fellow was overcome, and began to sob, Emma checked herself, recollecting that she had lost sight of the offender's age, and was using expressions which he could not understand. But the lesson was effectual. If ever the brother and sister were tempted to hide anything by a false-hood they remembered 'Aunt Emma's' face, and durst not incur the danger of her severity.

So she told her stories to the humming of the machine, and

when it was nearly the children's bedtime she broke off to ask
them if they would like some bread and butter. Among all
the results of her poverty the bitterest to Emma was when she
found herself *hoping that the children would not eat much.* If
their appetite was poor it made her anxious about their health,
yet it happened sometimes that she feared to ask them if they
were hungry lest the supply of bread should fail. It was so
to-night. The week's earnings had been three shillings; the
rent itself was four. But the children were as ready to eat as
if they had had no tea. It went to her heart to give them each
but one half-slice and tell them that they could have no more.
Gladly she would have robbed herself of breakfast next morning
on their account, but that she durst not do, for she had under-
taken to scrub out an office in Goswell Road, and she knew
that her strength would fail if she went from home fasting.

She put them to bed—they slept together on a small bed-
stead, which was a chair during the day—and then sat down
to do some patching at a dress of Kate's. Her face when she
communed with her own thoughts was profoundly sad, but far
from the weakness of self-pity. Indeed she did her best not to
think of herself; she knew that to do so cost her struggles with
feelings she held to be evil, resentment and woe of passion and
despair. She tried to occupy herself solely with her sister and
the children, planning how to make Kate more home-loving
and how to find the little ones more food.

She had no companions. The girls whom she came to know
in the workroom for the most past took life very easily; she
could not share in their genuine merriment; she was often
revolted by their way of thinking and speaking. They thought
her dull, and paid no attention to her. She was glad to be
relieved of the necessity of talking.

Her sister thought her hard. Kate believed that she was
for ever brooding over her injury. This was not true, but a
certain hardness in her character there certainly was. For her
life, both of soul and body, was ascetic; she taught herself to
expect, to hope for, nothing. When she was hungry she had a
sort of pleasure in enduring; when weary she worked on as if
by effort she could overcome the feeling. But Kate's chief
complaint against her was her determination to receive no help
save in the way of opportunity to earn money. This was something more than ordinary pride. Emma suffered intensely in
the recollection that she had lived at Mutimer's expense during
the very months when he was seeking the love of another

woman, and casting about for means of abandoning herself. When she thought of Alice coming with the proposal that she and her sister should still occupy the house in Wilton Square, and still receive money, the heat of shame and anger never failed to rise to her cheeks. She could never accept from any-one again a penny which she had not earned. She believed that Daniel Dabbs had been repaid, otherwise she could not have rested a moment.

It was her terrible misfortune to have feelings too refined for the position in which fate had placed her. Had she only been like those other girls in the workroom! But we are interesting in proportion to our capacity for suffering, and dignity comes of misery nobly borne.

As she sat working on Kate's dress, she was surprised to hear a heavy step approaching. There came a knock at the door; she answered, admitting Daniel.

He looked about the room, partly from curiosity, partly through embarrassment. Dusk was falling.

'Young 'uns in bed?' he said, lowering his voice.

'Yes, they are asleep,' Emma replied.

'You don't mind me coming up?'

'Oh no!'

He went to the window and looked at the houses opposite, then at the flushed sky.

'Bank holiday to-morrow. I thought I'd like to ask you whether you and Mrs. Clay and the children 'ud come with me to Epping Forest. If it's a day like this, it'll be a nice drive—do you good. You look as if you wanted a breath of fresh air, if you don't mind me sayin' it.'

'It's very kind of you, Mr. Dabbs,' Emma replied. 'I am very sorry I can't come myself, but my sister and the children perhaps——'

She could not refuse for them likewise, yet she was troubled to accept so far.

'But why can't *you* come?' he asked good-naturedly, slapping his hat against his leg.

'I have some work that'll take me nearly all day.'

'But you've no business to work on a bank holiday. I'm not sure as it ain't breakin' the law.'

He laughed, and Emma did her best to show a smile. But she said nothing.

'But you *will* come, now? You can lose just the one day! It'll do you a power o' good. You'll work all the better on

Tuesday, now see if you don't.   Why, it ain't worth livin', never to get a holiday.'

'I'm very sorry.   It was very kind indeed of you to think of it, Mr. Dabbs.   I really can't come.'

He went again to the window, and thence to the children's bedside.   He bent a little and watched them breathing.

'Bertie's growin' a fine little lad.'

'Yes, indeed, he is.'

'He'll have to go to school soon, I s'pose—I'm afraid he gives you a good deal of trouble, that is, I mean—you know how I mean it.'

'Oh, he is very good,' Emma said, looking at the sleeping face affectionately.

'Yes, yes.'

Daniel had meant something different; he saw that Emma would not understand him.

'We see changes in life,' he resumed, musingly.   'Now who'd a' thought I should end up with having more money than I know how to use?   The 'ouse has done well for eight years now, an' it's likely to do well for a good many years yet, as far as I can see.'

'I am glad to hear that,' Emma replied constrainedly.

'Miss Vine, I wanted you to come to Epping Forest to-morrow because I thought I should have a chance of a little talk.   I don't mean that was the only reason; it's too bad you never get a holiday, and I should like it to a' done you good. But I thought I might a' found a chance o' sayin' something, something I've thought of a long time, and that's the honest truth.   I want to help you and your sister and the young 'uns, but *you* most of all.   I don't like to see you livin' such a hard life, 'cause you deserve something better, if ever anyone did. Now will you let me help you?   There's only one way, and it's the way I'd like best of any.   The long an' the short of it is, I want to ask you if you'll come an' live at the 'ouse, come and bring Mrs. Clay an' the children?'

Emma looked at him in surprise and felt uncertain of his meaning, though his speech had painfully prepared her with an answer.

'I'd do my right down best to make you a good 'usband, that I would, Emma!'   Daniel hurried on, getting flustered. 'Perhaps I've been a bit too sudden?   Suppose we leave it till you've had time to think over?   It's no good talking to you about money an' that kind o' thing; you'd marry a poor man as soon as a rich, if only you cared in the right way for him I won't sing my own praises, but I don't think you'd find much to complain of in me. I'd never ask you to go into the bar, 'cause I know you ain't suited for that, and, what's more, I'd rather you didn't. Will you give it a thought?'

It was modest enough, and from her knowledge of the man Emma felt that he was to be trusted for more than his word. But he asked an impossible thing. She could not imagine herself consenting to marry any man, but the reasons why she could not marry Daniel Dabbs were manifold. She felt them all, but it was only needful to think of one.

Yet it was a temptation, and the hour of it might have been chosen. With a scarcity of food for the morrow, with dark fears for her sister, suffering incessantly on the children's account, Emma might have been pardoned if she had taken the helping hand. But the temptation, though it unsteadied her brain for a moment, could never have overcome her. She would have deemed it far less a crime to go out and steal a loaf from the baker's shop than to marry Daniel because he offered rescue from destitution.

She refused him, as gently as she could, but with firmness which left him no room for misunderstanding her. Daniel was awed by her quiet sincerity.

'But I can wait,' he stammered; 'if you'd take time to think it over?'

Useless; the answer could at no time be other.

'Well, I've no call to grumble,' he said. 'You say straight out what you mean. No woman can do fairer than that.'

His thought recurred for a moment to Alice, whose fault had been that she was ever ambiguous.

'It's hard to bear. I don't think I shall ever care to marry any other woman. But you're doin' the right thing and the honest thing; I wish all women was like you.'

At the door he turned.

'There'd be no harm if I take Mrs. Clay and the children, would there?'

'I am sure they will thank you, Mr. Dabbs.'

It did not matter now that there was a clear understanding.

At a little distance from the house door Daniel found Mrs. Clay waiting.

'No good,' he said cheerlessly.

'She won't go?'

'No. But I'll take you and the children, if you'll come.'

Kate did not immediately reply. A grave disappointment showed itself in her face.

'Can't be helped,' Daniel replied to her look. 'I did my best.'

Kate accepted his invitation, and they arranged the hour of meeting. As she approached the house to enter, now looking ill-tempered, a woman of her acquaintance met her. After a few minutes' conversation they walked away together.

Emma sat up till twelve o'clock. The thought on which she was brooding was not one to make the time go lightly; it was—how much and how various evil can be wrought by a single act of treachery. And the instance in her mind was more fruitful than her knowledge allowed her to perceive.

Kate appeared shortly after midnight. She had very red cheeks and very bright eyes, and her mood was quarrelsome. She sat down on the bed and began to talk of Daniel Dabbs, as she had often done already, in a maundering way. Emma kept silence; she was beginning to undress.

'There's a man with money,' said Kate, her voice getting louder; 'money, I tell you, and you've only to say a word. And you won't even be civil to him. You've got no feeling; you don't care for nobody but yourself. I'll take the children and leave you to go your own way, that's what I'll do!'

It was hard to make no reply, but Emma succeeded in commanding herself. The maundering talk went on for more than an hour. Then came the wretched silence of night.

Emma did not sleep. She was too wobegone to find a tear. Life stood before her in the darkness like a hideous spectre.

In the morning she told her sister that Daniel had asked her to marry him and that she had refused. It was best to have that understood. Kate heard with black brows. But even yet she knew something of shame when she remembered her return home the night before; it kept her from giving utterance to her anger.

There followed a scene such as had occurred two or three times during the past six months. Emma threw aside all her coldness, and with passionate entreaty besought her sister to draw back from the gulf's edge whilst there was yet time. For her own sake, for the sake of Bertie and the little girl, by the memory of that dear dead one who lay in the waste cemetery!

'Pity me, too! Think a little of me, Kate dear! You are driving me to despair.'

Kate was moved, she had not else been human. The

children were looking up with frightened, wondering eyes.
She hid her face and muttered promises of amendment.

Emma kissed her, and strove hard to hope.

CHAPTER XXXI.

WITH his five hundred pounds lodged in the bank, Mutimer
felt ill at ease in the lodgings in Pentonville. He began to
look about for an abode more suitable to the dignity of his
position, and shortly discovered a house in Holloway, the rent
twenty-eight pounds, the situation convenient for his purposes.
By way of making some amends to Adela for his less than civil
behaviour, he took the house and had it modestly furnished (at
the cost of one hundred and ten pounds) before saying anything
to her of his plans. Then, on the pretext of going to search
for pleasanter lodgings, he one day took her to Holloway and
led her into her own dwelling. Adela was startled, but did her
best to seem grateful.

They returned to Pentonville, settled their accounts, packed
their belongings, and by evening were able to sit down to a
dinner cooked by their own servant—under Adela's supervision.
Mutimer purchased a couple of bottles of claret on the way
home, that the first evening might be wholly cheerful. Of a
sudden he had become a new man; the sullenness had passed,
and he walked from room to room with much the same air of
lofty satisfaction as when he first surveyed the interior of
Wanley Manor. He made a show of reading in the hour
before dinner, but could not keep still for more than a few
minutes at a time; he wanted to handle the furniture, to
survey the prospect from the windows, to walk out into the
road and take a general view of the house. When their meal
had begun, and the servant, instructed to wait at table, chanced
to be out of the room, he remarked :

'We'll begin, of course, to dine at the proper time again.
It's far better, don't you think so ?'

'Yes, I think so.'

'And, by-the-by, you'll see that Mary has a cap.'

Adela smiled.

'Yes, I'll see she has.'

Mary herself entered. Some impulse she did not quite

understand led Adela to look at the girl in her yet capless condition. She said something which would require Mary to answer, and found herself wondering at the submissive tone, the repeated 'Mum.'

'Yes,' she mused with herself, 'she is our creature. We pay her and she must attire herself to suit our ideas of propriety. She must remember her station.'

'What is it?' Mutimer asked, noticing that she had again smiled.

'Nothing.'

His pipe lit, his limbs reposing in the easy-chair, Mutimer became expansive. He requested Adela's attention whilst he rendered a full account of all the moneys he had laid out, and made a computation of the cost of living on this basis.

'The start once made,' he said, 'you see it isn't a bit dearer than the lodgings. And the fact is, I couldn't have done much in that hole. Now here, I feel able to go to work. It isn't in reality spending money on ourselves, though it may look like it. You see I must have a place where people can call to see me; we'd no room before.'

He mused.

'You'll write and tell your mother?'

'Yes.'

Don't say anything about the money. You haven't done yet, I suppose?'

'No.'

'Better not. That's our own business. You can just say you're more comfortable. Of course,' he added, 'there's no secret. I shall let people understand in time that I am carrying out the wishes of a Socialist friend. That's simple enough. But there's no need to talk about it just yet. I must get fairly going first.'

His face gathered light as he proceeded.

'Ah, *now* I'll do something! see if I don't. You see, the fact of the matter is, there are some men who are cut out for leading in a movement, and I have the kind of feeling—well, for one thing, I'm readier at public speaking than most. You think so, don't you?'

Adela was sewing together some chintzes. She kept her eyes closely on the work.

'Yes, I think so.'

'Now the first thing I shall get done,' her husband pursued, a little disappointed that she gave no warmer assent, 'is that book, " My Work at New Wanley." The Union 'll publish it. It ought to have a good sale in Belwick and round about there. You see I must get my name well known; that's everything. When I've got that off hand, then I shall begin on the East End. I mean to máke the East End my own ground. I'll see if something can't be done to stir 'em up. I haven't quite thought it out yet. There must be some way of getting them to take an interest in Socialism. Now we'll see what can be done in twelve months. What'll you bet me that I don't add a thousand members to the Union in this next year?'

' I dare say you can.'

' There's no " dare say " about it. I mean to ! I begin to think I've special good luck; things always turn out right in the end. When I lost my work because I was a Socialist, then came Wanley. Now I've lost Wanley, and here comes five hundred a year for ten years ! I wonder who that poor fellow may be? I suppose he'll die soon, and then no doubt we shall hear his name. I only wish there were a few more like him.'

' The East End !' he resumed presently. ' That's my ground. I'll make the East End know me as well as they know any man in England. What we want is personal influence. It's no use asking them to get excited about a *movement*; they must have a *man*. Just the same in *bourgeois* politics. It isn't Liberalism they care for; it's Gladstone. Wait and see !'

He talked for three hours, at times as if he were already on the platform before a crowd of East Enders who were shouting, ' Mutimer for ever !' Adela fell into physical weariness; at length she with difficulty kept her eyes open. His language was a mere buzzing in her ears ; her thoughts were far away.

' My Work at New Wanley ' was written and published; Keene had the glory of revising the manuscript. It made a pamphlet of thirty-two pages, and was in reality an autobiography. It presented the ideal working man; the author stood as a type for ever of the noble possibilities inherent in his class. Written of course in the first person, it contained passages of monumental self-satisfaction. Adela, too, was mentioned; to her horror she found a glowing description of the work she had done among the women and children. After reading that page she threw the pamphlet aside and hid her face in her hands. She longed for the earth to cover her.

But the publication had no sale worth speaking of. A hundred copies were got rid of at the Socialist centres, and a

couple of hundred more when the price was reduced from twopence to a penny. This would not satisfy Mutimer. He took
the remaining three hundred off the hands of the Union and
sowed them broadcast over the East End, where already
he was actively at work. Then he had a thousand more
struck off, and at every meeting which he held gave away
numerous copies. Keene wrote to suggest that in a new
edition there should be a woodcut portrait of the author on
the front. Mutimer was delighted with the idea, and at once
had it carried out.

Through this winter and the spring that followed he worked
hard. It had become a necessity of his existence to hear his
name on the lips of men, to be perpetually in evidence. Adela
saw that day by day his personal vanity grew more absorbing.
When he returned from a meeting he would occupy her for
hours with a recitation of the speeches he had made, with a
minute account of what others had said of him. He succeeded
in forming a new branch of the Union in Clerkenwell, and by
contributing half the rent obtained a room for meetings. In
this branch he was King Mutimer.

In the meantime the suit against Rodman was carried
through; it could have of course but one result. Rodman was
sold up, but the profit accruing to Hubert Eldon was trifling,
for the costs were paid out of the estate, and it appeared that
Rodman, making hay whilst the sun shone, had spent all but
the whole of his means. There remained the question whether
he was making fraudulent concealments. Mutimer was
morally convinced that this was the case, and would vastly have
enjoyed laying his former friend by the heels for the statutable
six weeks, but satisfactory proofs were not to be obtained.
Through Mr. Yottle, Eldon expressed the desire that, as far as
he was concerned, the matter might rest. But it was by no
means with pure zeal for justice that Mutimer had proceeded
thus far. He began the suit in anger, and, as is wont to be
the case with litigants, grew more bitter as it went on. The
selling up of Rodman's house was an occasion of joy to him;
he went about singing and whistling.

Adela marvelled that he could so entirely forget the sufferings of his sister; she had had so many proofs of his affection
for Alice. In fact he was far from forgetting her, but he made
strange distinction between her and her husband, and had a
feeling that in doing his utmost to injure Rodman he was in a
manner avenging Alice. His love for Alice was in no degree

weakened, but—if the state can be understood—he was jealous
of the completeness with which she had abandoned him to
espouse the cause of her husband. Alice had renounced her
brother; she never saw him, and declared that she never would
speak to him again. And Mutimer had no fear lest she should
suffer want. Rodman had a position of some kind in the City;
he and his wife lived for a while in lodgings, then took a house
at Wimbledon.

One of Mutimer's greatest anxieties had been lest he should
have a difficulty henceforth in supporting his mother in the
old house. The economical plan would have been for Adela
and himself to go and live with the old woman, but he felt that
to be impossible. His mother would never become reconciled
to Adela, and, if the truth must be told, he was ashamed to
make known to Adela his mother's excessive homeliness.
Then again he was still estranged from the old woman.
Though he often thought of what Alice had said to him on that
point, month after month went by and he could not make up
his mind to go to Wilton Square. Having let the greater part
of her house, Mrs. Mutimer needed little pecuniary aid; once
she returned money which he had sent to her. 'Arry still
lived with her, and 'Arry was a never-ending difficulty. After
his appearance in the police court, he retired for a week or two
into private life; that is to say, he contented himself with
loafing about the streets of Hoxton and the City, and was at
home by eleven o'clock nightly, perfectly sober. The character
of this young man was that of a distinct class, comprising the
sons of mechanics who are ruined morally by being taught to
consider themselves above manual labour. Had he from the
first been put to a craft, he would in all likelihood have been
no worse than the ordinary English artisan—probably drinking too much and loafing on Mondays, but not sinking below
the level of his fellows in the workshop. His positive fault
was that shared by his brother and sister—personal vanity. It
was encouraged from the beginning by immunity from the only
kind of work for which he was fitted, and the undreamt-of revolution in his prospects gave fatal momentum to all his worst
tendencies. Keene and Rodman successively did their best,
though unintentionally, to ruin him. He was now incapable
of earning his living by any continuous work. Since his return
to London he had greatly extended his circle of acquaintances,
which consisted of idle fellows of the same type, youths who
hang about the lowest fringe of clerkdom till they definitely

class themselves either with the criminal community or with those who make a living by unrecognised pursuits which at any time may chance to bring them within the clutches of the law. To use a coarse but expressive word, he was a hopeless blackguard.

Let us be just; 'Arry had, like every other man, his better moments. He knew that he had made himself contemptible to his mother, to Richard, and to Alice, and the knowledge was so far from agreeable that it often drove him to recklessness. That was his way of doing homage to the better life; he had no power of will to resist temptation, but he could go to meet it doggedly out of sheer dissatisfaction with himself. Our social state ensures destruction to such natures; it has no help for them, no patient encouragement. Naturally he hardened himself in vicious habits. Despised by his own people, he soothed his injured vanity by winning a certain predominance among the contemptible. The fact that he had been on the point of inheriting a fortune in itself gave him standing; he told his story in public-houses and elsewhere, and relished the distinction of having such a story to tell. Even as his brother Richard could not rest unless he was prominent as an agitator, so it became a necessity to 'Arry to lead in the gin-palace and the music-hall. He made himself the aristocrat of rowdyism.

But it was impossible to live without ready money, and his mother, though supplying him with board and lodging, refused to give him a penny. He made efforts on his own account to obtain employment, but without result. At last there was nothing for it but to humble himself before Richard.

He did it with an ill-enough grace. Early one morning he presented himself at the house in Holloway. Richard was talking with his wife in the sitting-room, breakfast being still on the table. On the visitor's name being brought to him, he sent Adela away and allowed the scapegrace to be admitted.

'Arry shuffled to a seat and sat leaning forward, holding his hat between his knees.

'Well, what do you want?' Richard asked severely. He was glad that 'Arry had at length come, and he enjoyed assuming the magisterial attitude.

'I want to find a place,' 'Arry replied, without looking up, and in a dogged voice. 'I've been trying to get one, and I can't. I think you might help a feller.'

'What's the good of helping you? You'll be turned out of any place in a week or two.'

' No, I shan't ! '

' What sort of a place do you want ? '

' A clerk's, of course.'

He pronounced the word ' clerk ' as it is spelt; it made him seem yet more ignoble.

' Have you given up drink ? '

No answer.

' Before I try to help you,' said Mutimer, ' you'll have to take the pledge.'

' All right,' 'Arry muttered.

Then a thought occurred to Richard. Bidding his brother stay where he was, he went in search of Adela and found her in an upper room.

' He's come to ask me to help him to get a place,' he said. ' I don't know very well how to set about it, but I suppose I must do something. He promises to take the pledge.'

' That will be a good thing,' Adela replied.

' Good if he keeps it. But I can't talk to him; I'm sick of doing so. And I don't think he even listens to me.' He hesitated. ' Do you think you—would you mind speaking to him ? I believe you might do him good.'

Adela did not at once reply.

' I know it's a nasty job,' he pursued. ' I wouldn't ask you if I didn't really think you might do some good. I don't see why he should go to the dogs. He used to be a good enough fellow when he was a little lad.'

It was one of the most humane speeches Adela had ever heard from her husband. She replied with cheerfulness :

' If you really think he won't take it amiss, I shall be very glad to do my best.'

'That's right; thank you.'

Adela went down and was alone with 'Arry for half-an-hour. She was young to undertake such an office, but suffering had endowed her with gravity and understanding beyond her years, and her native sweetness was such that she could altogether forget herself in pleading with another for a good end. No human being, however perverse, could have taken ill the words that were dictated by so pure a mind, and uttered in so musical and gentle a voice. She led 'Arry to speak frankly.

' It seems to me a precious hard thing,' he said, ' that they've let Dick keep enough money to live on comfortable, and won't give me a penny. My right was as good as his.'

'Perhaps it was,' Adela replied kindly. 'But you must remember that money was left to your brother by the will.'

'But you don't go telling me that he lives on two pounds a week? Everybody knows he doesn't. Where does the rest come from?'

'I don't think I must talk about that. I think very likely your brother will explain if you ask him seriously. But is it really such a hard thing after all, Harry? I feel so sure that you will only know real happiness when you are earning a livelihood by steady and honourable work. You remember how I used to go and see the people in New Wanley? I shall never forget how happy the best of them were, those who worked their hardest all day and at night came home to rest with their families and friends. And you yourself, how contented you used to be when your time was thoroughly occupied! But I'm sure you feel the truth of this. You have been disappointed; it has made you a little careless. Now work hard for a year and then come and tell me if I wasn't right about that being the way to happiness. Will you?'

She rose and held her hand to him, the hand to which he should have knelt. But he said nothing; there was an obstacle in his throat. Adela understood his silence and left him.

Richard went to work among his friends, and in a fortnight had found his brother employment of a new kind. It was a place in an ironmonger's shop in Hoxton; 'Arry was to serve at the counter and learn the business. For three months he was on trial and would receive no salary.

Two of the three months passed, and all seemed to be going well. Then one day there came to Mutimer a telegram from 'Arry's employer; it requested that he would go to the shop as soon as possible. Foreseeing some catastrophe, he hastened to Hoxton. His brother was in custody for stealing money from the till.

The ironmonger was inexorable. 'Arry passed through the judicial routine and was sentenced to three months of hard labour.

It was in connection with this wretched affair that Richard once more met his mother. He went from the shop to tell her what had happened.

He found her in the kitchen, occupied as he had seen her many, many times, ironing newly washed linen. One of the lodgers happened to come out from the house as he ascended the steps, so he was able to go down without announcing himself. The old woman had a nervous start; the iron stopped in its smooth backward and forward motion; the hand with which she held it trembled. She kept her eyes on Richard's face, which foretold evil.

'Mother, I have brought you bad news.'

She pushed the iron aside and stood waiting. Her hard lips grew harder; her deep-set eyes had a stern light. Not much ill could come to pass for which she was not prepared.

He tried to break the news. His mother interrupted him.

'What's he been a-doin'? You've no need to go round about. I like straightforwardness.'

Richard told her. It did not seem to affect her strongly; she turned to the table and resumed her work. But she could no longer guide the iron. She pushed it aside and faced her son with such a look as one may see in the eyes of a weak animal cruelly assailed. Her tongue found its freedom and bore her whither it would.

'What did I tell you? What was it I said that night you come in and told me you was all rich? Didn't I warn you that there'd no good come of it. Didn't I say you'd remember my words? You laughed at me; you got sharp-tempered with me an' as good as called me a fool. An' what *has* come of it? What's come of it to me? I had a 'ome once an' children about me, an' now I've neither the one nor the other. You call it a 'ome with strangers takin' up well nigh all the 'ouse? Not such a 'ome as I thought to end my days in. It fair scrapes on my heart every time I hear their feet going up an' down the stairs. An' where are my children gone? Two of 'em as 'ud never think to come near me if it wasn't to bring ill news, an' one in prison. How 'ud that sound in your father's ears, think you? I may have been a fool, but I knew what 'ud come of a workin' man's children goin' to live in big 'ouses, with their servants an' their carriages. What better are you? It's come an' it's gone, an' there's shame an' misery left be'ind it!'

Richard listened without irritation; he was heavy-hearted, the shock of his brother's disgrace had disposed him to see his life on its dark side. And he pitied his poor old mother. She had never been tender in her words, could not be tender; but he saw in her countenance the suffering through which she had gone, and read grievous things in the eyes that could no longer weep. For once he yielded to rebuke. Her complaint that he had not come to see her touched him, for he had desired to come, but could not subdue his pride. Her voice was feebler than when he last heard it raised in reproach; it reminded him that there would come a day when he might long to hear even words of upbraiding, but the voice would be mute for ever. It needed a moment such as this to stir his sluggish imagination.

'What you say is true, mother, but we couldn't help it. It's turned out badly because we live in bad times. It's the state of society that's to blame.'

He was sincere in saying it; that is to say, he used the phrase so constantly that it had become his natural utterance in difficulty; it may be that in his heart he believed it. Who, indeed, shall say that he was wrong? But what made such an excuse so disagreeable in his case was that he had not—intellectually speaking—the right to avail himself of it. The difference between truth and cant often lies only in the lips that give forth the words.

'Yes, that's what you always said,' replied Mrs. Mutimer impatiently. 'It's always someone else as is to blame, an' never yourself. The world's a good enough world if folk 'ud only make it so. Was it the bad times as made you leave a good, honest girl when you'd promised to marry her? No, you must have a fine lady for your wife; a plain girl as earnt her own bread, an' often had hard work to get it, wasn't good enough for you. Don't talk to me about bad times. There's some men as does right an' some as does wrong; it always was so, an' the world's no worse nor no better, an' not likely to be.'

The poor woman could not be generous. A concession only led her on to speak the thoughts it naturally suggested to her. And her very bitterness was an outcome of her affection; it soothed her to rail at her son after so long a silence. He had injured her by his holding aloof; she was urged on by this feeling quite as much as by anger with his faults. And still Mutimer showed no resentment. In him, too, there was a pleasure which came of memories revived. Let her say to him what she liked, he loved his mother and was glad to be once more in her presence.

'I wish I could have pleased you better, mother,' he said. 'What's done can't be helped. We've trouble to bear together, and it won't be lighter for angry words.'

The old woman muttered something inaudible and, after feeling her iron and discovering that it was cold, she put it down before the fire. Her tongue had eased itself, and she fell again into silent grief.

Mutimer sat listening to the tick of the familiar clock.

That and the smell of the fresh linen made his old life very present to him; there arose in his heart a longing for the past, it seemed peaceful and fuller of genuine interests than the life he now led. He remembered how he used to sit before the kitchen fire reading the books and papers which stirred his thought to criticism of the order of things; nothing now absorbed him in the same way. Coming across a sentence that delighted him, he used to read it aloud to his mother, who perchance was ironing as now, or sewing, or preparing a meal, and she would find something to say against it; so that there ensued a vigorous debate between her old-fashioned ideas and the brand-new theories of the age of education. Then Alice would come in and make the dispute a subject for sprightly mockery. Alice was the Princess in those days. He quarrelled with her often, but only to resume the tone of affectionate banter an hour after. Alice was now Mrs. Rodman, and had declared that she hated him, that in her life she would never speak to him again. Would it not have been better if things had gone the natural course? Alice would no doubt have married Daniel Dabbs, and would have made him a good wife, if a rather wilful one. 'Arry would have given trouble, but surely could not have come to hopeless shame. He, Richard, would have had Emma Vine for his wife, a true wife, loving him with all her heart, thinking him the best and cleverest of working men. Adela did not love him; what she thought of his qualities it was not easy to say. Yes, the old and natural way was better. He would have had difficulties enough, because of his opinions, but at least he would have continued truly to represent his class. He knew very well that he did not represent it now; he belonged to no class at all; he was a professional agitator, and must remain so through his life—or till the Revolution came. The Revolution? . . .

His mother was speaking to him, asking what he meant to do about 'Arry. He raised his eyes, and for a moment looked at her sadly.

'There's nothing to be done. I can pay a lawyer, but it'll be no good.'

He remained with his mother for yet an hour; they talked intermittently, without in appearance coming nearer to each other, though in fact the barrier was removed. She made tea for him, and herself made pretence of taking some. When he went away he kissed her as he had used to. He left her happier than she had been for years, in spite of the news he had brought.

Thenceforward Mutimer went to Wilton Square regularly once a week. He let Adela know of this, saying casually one morning that he could not do something that day because his mother would expect him in the afternoon as usual. He half hoped that she might put some question which would lead to talk on the subject, for the reconciliation with his mother had brought about a change in his feelings, and it would now have been rather agreeable to him to exhibit his beautiful and gentle-mannered wife. But Adela merely accepted the remark.

He threw himself into the work of agitation with more energy than ever. By this time he had elaborated a scheme which was original enough to ensure him notoriety if only he could advertise it sufficiently throughout the East End. He hit upon it one evening when he was smoking his pipe after dinner. Adela was in the room with him reading. He took her into his confidence at once.

' I've got it at last! I want something that'll attract their attention. It isn't enough to preach theories to them; they won't wake up; there's no getting them to feel in earnest about Socialism. I've been racking my brain for something to set them talking, it didn't much matter what, but better of course if it was useful in itself at the same time. Now I think I've got it. It's a plan for giving them a personal interest, a money interest, in me and my ideas. I'll go and say to them, " How is it you men never save any money even when you could? I'll tell you: it's because the savings would be so little that they don't seem worth while; you think you might as well go and enjoy yourselves in the public-house while you can. What's the use of laying up a few shillings? The money comes and goes, and it's all in a life." Very well, then, I'll put my plan before them. " Now look here," I'll say, " instead of spending so much on beer and spirits, come to me and *let me keep your money for you!*" They'll burst out laughing at me, and say, " Catch us doing that!" Yes, but I'll persuade them, see if I don't. And in this way. " Suppose," I'll say, " there's five hundred men bring me threepence each every week. Now what man of you doesn't spend threepence a week in drink, get the coppers how he may? Do you know how much that comes to, five hundred threepenny bits? Why, it's six pounds five shillings. And do you know what that comes to in a year? Why, no less than three hundred and twenty-five pounds! Now just listen to that, and think about it. Those threepenny bits are no use to you; you *can't* save them, and you spend them in a way that does you no good, and it may be harm. Now what do you think I'll do with that money? Why, I'll use it as the capitalists do. I'll put it out to interest; I'll get three per cent. for it, and perhaps more. But let's say three per cent. What's the result? Why, this: in one year your three hundred and twenty-five pounds has become three hundred and thirty-four pounds fifteen; I owe each of you thirteen shillings and fourpence halfpenny, and a fraction more." '

He had already jotted down calculations, and read from them, looking up between times at Adela with the air of conviction which he would address to his audience of East Enders.

' " Now if you'd only saved the thirteen shillings—which you wouldn't and couldn't have done by yourselves—it would be well worth the while; but you've got the interest as well, and the point I want you to understand is that you can only get that increase by clubbing together and investing the savings as a whole. You may say fourpence halfpenny isn't worth having. Perhaps not, but those of you who've learnt arithmetic—be thankful if our social state allowed you to learn anything—will remember that there's such a thing as compound interest. It's a trick the capitalists found out. Interest was a good discovery, but compound interest a good deal better. Leave your money with me a second year, and it'll grow more still, I'll see to that. You're all able, I've no doubt, to make the calculation for yourselves." '

He paused to see what Adela would say.

' No doubt it will be a very good thing if you can persuade them to save in that way,' she remarked.

' Good, yes; but I'm not thinking so much of the money. Don't you see that it'll give me a hold over them? Every man who wants to save on my plan must join the Union. They'll come together regularly; I can get at them and make them listen to me. Why, it's a magnificent idea! It's fighting the capitalists with their own weapons! You'll see what the "Tocsin" 'll say. Of course they'll make out that I'm going against Socialist principles. So I am, but it's for the sake of Socialism for all that. If I make Socialists, it doesn't much matter how I do it.'

Adela could have contested that point, but did not care to do so. She said:

' Are you sure you can persuade the men to trust you with their money?'

' That's the difficulty, I know; but see if I don't get over it. I'll have a committee, holding themselves responsible for all sums paid to us. I'll publish weekly accounts—just a leaflet, you know. And do you know what? I'll promise that as soon as they've trusted me with a hundred pounds, I'll add another hundred of my own. See if that won't fetch them!'

As usual when he saw a prospect of noisy success he became excited beyond measure, and talked incessantly till midnight.

'Other men don't have these ideas!' he exclaimed at one moment. 'That's what I meant when I told you I was born to be a leader. And I've the secret of getting people's confidence. They'll trust me, see if they don't!'

In spite of Adela's unbroken reserve, he had seldom been other than cordial in his behaviour to her since the recommencement of his prosperity. His active life gave him no time to brood over suspicions, though his mind was not altogether free from them. He still occasionally came home at hours when he could not be expected, but Adela was always occupied either with housework or reading, and received him with the cold self-possession which came of her understanding his motives. Her life was lonely; since a visit they had received from Alfred at the past Christmas she had seen no friend. One day in spring Mutimer asked her if she did not wish to see Mrs. Westlake; she replied that she had no desire to, and he said nothing more. Stella did not write; she had ceased to do so since receiving a certain lengthy letter from Adela, in which the latter begged that their friendship might feed on silence for a while. When the summer came there were pressing invitations from Wanley, but Adela declined them. Alfred and his wife were going again to South Wales; was it impossible for Adela to join them? Letty wrote a letter full of affectionate pleading, but it was useless.

In August, Mutimer proposed to take his wife for a week to the Sussex coast. He wanted a brief rest himself, and he saw that Adela was yet more in need of change. She never complained of ill-health, but was weak and pale. With no inducement to leave the house, it was much if she had an hour's open-air exercise in the week; often the mere exertion of rising and beginning the day was followed by a sick languor which compelled her to lie all the afternoon on the couch. She studied much, reading English and foreign books which required mental exertion. They were not works relating to the 'Social Question'—far other. The volumes she used to study were a burden and a loathing to her as often as her eyes fell upon them.

In her letters from Wanley there was never a word of what was going on in the valley. Week after week she looked eagerly for some hint, yet was relieved when she found none. For it had become her habit to hand over to Mutimer every letter she received. He read them.

Shortly after their return from the seaside, 'Arry's term of imprisonment came to an end. He went to his mother's house, and Richard first saw him there. Punishment had had its usual effect; 'Arry was obstinately taciturn, conscious of his degradation, inwardly at war with all his kind.

'There's only one thing I can do for you now,' his brother said to him. 'I'll pay your passage to Australia. Then you must shift for yourself.'

'Arry refused the offer.

'Give me the money instead,' was his reply.

Argument was vain; Richard and the old woman passed to entreaty, but with as little result.

'Give me ten pounds and let me go about my business,' 'Arry exclaimed irritably. 'I want no more from you, and you won't get any good out o' me by jawin'.'

The money was of course refused, in the hope that a week or two would change the poor fellow's mind. But two days after he went out and did not return. Nothing was heard of him. Mrs. Mutimer sat late every night, listening for a knock at the door. Sometimes she went and stood on the steps, looking hither and thither in the darkness. But 'Arry came no more to Wilton Square.

Mutimer had been pressing on his scheme for five months. Every night he addressed a meeting somewhere or other in the East End; every Sunday he lectured morning and evening at his head-quarters in Clerkenwell. Ostensibly he was working on behalf of the Union, but in reality he was forming a party of his own, and would have started a paper could he have commanded the means. The 'Tocsin' was savagely hostile, the 'Fiery Cross' grew more and more academical, till it was practically an organ of what is called in Germany *Katheder-Sozialismus*. Those who wrote for it were quite distinct from the agitators of the street and of the Socialist halls; men—and women—with a turn for 'advanced' speculation, with anxiety for style. At length the name of the paper was changed, and it appeared as the 'Beacon,' adorned with a headpiece by the well-known artist, Mr. Boscobel. Mutimer glanced through the pages and flung it aside in scornful disgust.

' I knew what this was coming to,' he said to Adela. ' A deal of good *they*'ll do! You don't find Socialism in drawing-rooms. I wonder that fellow Westlake has the impudence to call himself a Socialist at all, living in the way he does. Perhaps he thinks he'll be on the safe side when the Revolution comes. Ha, ha! We shall see.'

The Revolution .... In the meantime the cry was ' Democratic Capitalism.' That was the name Mutimer gave to his scheme! The 'Fiery Cross' had only noticed his work in a brief paragraph, a few words of faint and vague praise. ' Our comrade's noteworthy exertions in the East End. . . . The gain to temperance and self-respecting habits which must surely result. . . .' The ' Beacon,' however, dealt with the movement more fully, and on the whole in a friendly spirit.

' Damn their patronage! ' cried Mutimer.

You should have seen him addressing a crowd collected by chance in Hackney or Poplar. The slightest encouragement, even one name to inscribe in the book which he carried about with him, was enough to fire his eloquence; nay, it was enough to find himself standing on his chair above the heads of the gathering. His voice had gained in timbre; he grew more and more perfect in his delivery, like a conscientious actor who plays night after night in a part that he enjoys. And it was well that he had this inner support, this *brio* of the born demagogue, for often enough he spoke under circumstances which would have damped the zeal of any other man. The listeners stood with their hands in their pockets, doubting whether to hear him to the end or to take their wonted way to the public-house. One moment their eyes would be fixed upon him, filmy, unintelligent, then they would look at one another with a leer of cunning, or at best a doubtful grin. Socialism, forsooth! They were as ready for translation to supernal spheres. Yet some of them were attracted : 'percentage,' 'interest,' 'compound interest,' after all, there might be something in this! And perhaps they gave their names and their threepenny bits, engaging to make the deposit regularly on the day and at the place arranged for in Mutimer's elaborate scheme. What is there a man cannot get if he asks for it boldly and persistently enough ? . . .

The year had come full circle; it was time that Mutimer received another remittance from his anonymous supporter.

He needed it, for he had been laying out money without regard to the future. Not only did he need it for his own support; already he and his committee held sixty pounds of trust money, and before long he might be called upon to fulfil his engagement and contribute a hundred pounds—the promised hundred which had elicited more threepences than all the rest of his eloquence. A week, a month, six weeks, and he had heard nothing. Then there came one day a communication couched in legal terms, signed by a solicitor. It was to the effect that his benefactor—name and address given in full—had just died. The decease was sudden, and though the draft of a will had been discovered, it had no signature, and was consequently inoperative. But—pursued the lawyer—it having been the intention of the deceased to bequeath to Mutimer an annuity of five hundred pounds for nine years, the administrators were unwilling altogether to neglect their friend's wish, and begged to make an offer of the one year's payment which it seemed was already due. For more than that they could not hold themselves responsible.

Before speaking to Adela, Mutimer made searching inquiries. He went to the Midland town where his benefactor had lived, and was only too well satisfied of the truth of what had been told him. He came back with his final five hundred pounds.

Then he informed his wife of what had befallen. He was not cheerful, but with five hundred pounds in his pocket he could not be altogether depressed. What might not happen in a year? He was becoming prominent; there had been mention of him lately in London journals. Pooh! as if he would ever really want!

'The great thing,' he exclaimed, 'is that I can lay down the hundred pounds! If I'd failed in that it would have been all up. Come, now, why can't you give me a bit of encouragement, Adela? I tell you what it is. There's no place where I'm thought so little of as in my own home, and that's a fact.'

She did not worship him, she made no pretence of it. Her cold, pale beauty had not so much power over him as formerly, but it still chagrined him keenly as often as he was reminded that he had no high place in his wife's judgment. He knew well enough that it was impossible for her to admire him; he was conscious of the thousand degrading things he had said and done, every one of them stored in her memory. Perhaps not once since that terrible day in the Pentonville lodgings had he looked her straight in the eyes. Yes, her beauty appealed to him less than even a year ago; Adela knew it, and it was the one solace in her living death. Perhaps occasion could again have stung him into jealousy, but Adela was no longer a vital interest in his existence. He lived in external things, his natural life. Passion had been an irregularity in his development. Yet he would gladly have had his wife's sympathy. He neither loved nor hated her, but she was for ever above him, and, however unconsciously, he longed for her regard. Irreproachable, reticent, it might be dying, Adela would no longer affect interests she did not feel. To these present words of his she replied only with a grave, not unkind, look; a look he could not understand, yet which humbled rather than irritated him.

The servant opened the door and announced a visitor— 'Mr. Hilary.'

Mutimer seemed struck with a thought as he heard the name.

'The very man!' he exclaimed below his breath, with a glance at Adela. 'Just run off and let us have this room. My luck won't desert me, see if it does!'

CHAPTER XXXII.

MR. WILLIS RODMAN scarcely relished the process which deprived him of his town house and of the greater part of his means, but his exasperation happily did not seek vent for itself in cruelty to his wife. It might very well have done so, would all but certainly, had not Alice appealed to his sense of humour by her zeal in espousing his cause against her brother. That he could turn her round his finger was an old experience, but to see her spring so actively to arms on his behalf, when he was conscious that she had every excuse for detesting him, and even abandoning him, struck him as a highly comical instance of his power over women, a power on which he had always prided himself. He could not even explain it as self-interest in her; numberless things proved the contrary. Alice was still his slave, though he had not given himself the slightest trouble to preserve even her respect. He had shown himself

to her freely as he was, jocosely cynical on everything that
women prize, brutal when he chose to give way to his temper,
faithless on principle, selfish to the core; perhaps the secret of
the fascination he exercised over her was his very ingenuousness, his boldness in defying fortune, his clever grasp of circumstances. She said to him one day, when he had been telling
her that as likely as not she might have to take in washing or
set up a sewing-machine:

'I am not afraid. You can always get money. There's
nothing you can't do.'

He laughed.

'That may be true. But how if I disappear some day and
leave you to take care of yourself?'

He had often threatened this in his genial way, and it never
failed to blanch her cheeks.

'If you do that,' she said, 'I shall kill myself.'

At which he laughed yet more loudly.

In her house at Wimbledon she perished of *ennui,* for she
was as lonely as Adela in Holloway. Much lonelier; she had
no resources in herself. Rodman was away all day in London,
and very often he did not return at night; when the latter
was the case, Alice cried miserably in her bed for hours, so that
the next morning her face was like that of a wax doll that has
suffered ill-usage. She had an endless supply of novels, and
day after day bent over them till her head ached. Poor
Princess! She had had her own romance, in its way brilliant
and strange enough, but only the rags of it were left. She
clung to them, she hoped against hope that they would yet
recover their gloss and shimmer. If only he would not so
neglect her! All else affected her but little now that she really
knew what it meant to see her husband utterly careless, not to
be held by any pettings or entreaties. She heard through him
of her brother 'Arry's disgrace; it scarcely touched her. Her
brother Richard she was never tired of railing against, railed
so much, indeed, that it showed she by no means hated him as
much as she declared. But nothing would have mattered if
only her husband had cared for her.

She had once said to Adela that she disliked children and
hoped never to have any. It was now her despair that she
remained childless. Perhaps that was why he had lost all
affection?

In the summer Rodman once quitted her for nearly three
weeks, during which she only heard from him once. He was

in Ireland, and, he asserted, on business. The famous 'Irish Dairy Company,' soon to occupy a share of public attention, was getting itself on foot. It was Rodman who promoted the company and who became its secretary, though the name of that functionary in all printed matter appeared as 'Robert Delancey.' However, I only mention it for the present to explain our friend's absence in Ireland. Alice often worked herself up to a pitch of terror lest her husband had fulfilled his threat and really deserted her. He returned when it suited him to do so, and tortured her with a story of a wealthy Irish widow who had fallen desperately in love with him.

'And I've a good mind to marry her,' he added with an air of serious reflection. 'Of course I didn't let her know my real name. I could manage it very nicely, and you would never know anything about it; I should remit you all the money you wanted, you needn't be afraid.'

Alice tried to assume a face of stony indignation, but as usual she ended by breaking down and shedding tears. Then he told her that she was getting plainer than ever, and that it all came of her perpetual ' water-works.'

Alice hit upon a brilliant idea. What if she endeavoured to make him jealous? In spite of her entreaties, he never would take her to town, though he saw that she was perishing for lack of amusement. Suppose she made him believe that she had gone on her own account, and at the invitation of someone whose name she would not divulge? I believe she found the trick in one of her novels. The poor child went to work most conscientiously. One morning when he came down to breakfast she pretended to have been reading a letter, crushed an old envelope into her pocket on his entering the room, and affected confusion. He observed her.

'Had a letter?' he asked.

'Yes—no. Nothing of any importance.'

He smiled and applied himself to the ham, then left her in his ordinary way, without a word of courtesy, and went to town. She had asked him particularly when he should be back that night. He named the train, which reached Wimbledon a little after ten.

They had only one servant. Alice took the girl into her confidence, said she was going to play a trick, and it must not be spoilt. By ten o'clock at night she was dressed for going out, and when she heard her husband's latch-key at the front door she slipped out at the back. It was her plan to walk about the roads for half an hour, then to enter and—make the best of the situation.

Rodman, unable to find his wife, summoned the servant.

'Where is your mistress ?'

'Out, sir.'

He examined the girl shrewdly, with his eyes and with words. It was perfectly true that women—of a kind—could not resist him. In the end he discovered exactly what had happened. He laughed his wonted laugh of cynical merriment.

'Go to bed,' he said to the servant. 'And if you hear anyone at the door, pay no attention.'

Then he locked up the house, front and back, and, having extinguished all lights except a small lantern by which he could read in the sitting-room without danger of its being discerned from outside, sat down with a sense of amusement. Presently there came a ring at the bell ; it was repeated again and again. The month was October, the night decidedly cool. Rodman chuckled to himself ; he had a steaming glass of whisky before him and sipped it delicately. The ringing continued for a quarter of an hour, then five minutes passed, and no sound came. Rodman stepped lightly to the front door, listened, heard nothing, unlocked and opened. Alice was standing in the middle of the road, her hands crossed over her breast and holding her shoulders as though she suffered from the cold. She came forward and entered the house without speaking.

In the sitting-room she found the lantern and looked at her husband in surprise. His face was stern.

'What's all this ?' he asked sharply.

'I've been to London,' she answered, her teeth chattering with cold and her voice uncertain from fear.

'Been to London? And what business had you to go without telling me ?'

He spoke savagely. Alice was sinking with dread, but even yet had sufficient resolve to keep up the comedy.

'I had an invitation. I don't see why I shouldn't go. I don't ask you who you go about with.'

The table was laid for supper. Rodman darted to it, seized a carving-knife, and in an instant was holding it to her throat. She shrieked and fell upon her knees, her face ghastly with mortal terror. Then Rodman burst out laughing and showed that his anger had been feigned.

She had barely strength to rise, but at length stood before

him trembling and sobbing, unable to believe that he had not been in earnest.

'You needn't explain the trick,' he said, with the appearance of great good-humour, 'but just tell me why you played it. Did you think I should believe you were up to something queer, eh?'

'You must think what you like,' she sobbed, utterly humiliated.

He roared with laughter.

'What a splendid idea! The Princess getting tired of propriety and making appointments in London! Little fool! do you think I should care one straw? Why shouldn't you amuse yourself?'

Alice looked at him with eyes of wondering misery.

'Do you mean that you don't care enough for me to—to——'

'Don't care one farthing's worth! And to think you went and walked about in the mud and the east wind! Well, if that isn't the best joke I ever heard! I'll have a rare laugh over this story with some men I know to-morrow.'

She crept away to her bedroom. He had gone far towards killing the love that had known no rival in her heart.

He bantered her ceaselessly through breakfast next morning, and for the first time she could find no word to reply to him. Her head drooped; she touched nothing on the table. Before going off he asked her what the appointment was for to-day, and advised her not to forget her latch-key. Alice scarcely heard him, she was shame-stricken and wobegone.

Rodman, on the other hand, had never been in better spirits. The 'Irish Dairy Company' was attracting purchasers of shares. It was the kind of scheme which easily recommended itself to a host of the foolish people who are ever ready to risk their money, also to some not quite so foolish. The prospectus could show some respectable names: one or two Irish lords, a member of Parliament, some known capitalists. The profits could not but be considerable, and think of the good to 'the unhappy sister country'—as the circular said. Butter, cheese, eggs of unassailable genuineness, to be sold in England at absurdly low prices, yet still putting the producers on a footing of comfort and proud independence. One of the best ideas that had yet occurred to Mr. Robert Delancey.

He—the said Mr. Delancey, *alias* Mr. Willis Rodman, *alias* certain other names—spent much of his time just now in the society of a Mr. Hilary, a gentleman who, like himself, had seen men and manners in various quarters of the globe, and was at present making a tolerable income by the profession of philanthropy. Mr. Hilary's name appeared among the directors of the company; it gave confidence to many who were familiar with it in connection with not a few enterprises started for the benefit of this or that depressed nationality, this or the other exploited class. He wrote frequently to the newspapers on the most various subjects; he was known to members of Parliament through his persistent endeavours to obtain legislation with regard to certain manufactures proved to be gravely deleterious to the health of those employed in them. To-day Mr. Delancey and Mr. Hilary passed some hours together in the latter's chambers. Their talk was of the company.

'So you saw Mutimer about it?' Rodman asked, turning to a detail in which he was specially interested.

'Yes. He is anxious to have shares.'

Mr. Hilary was a man of past middle age, long-bearded, somewhat cadaverous of hue. His head was venerable.

'You were careful not to mention me?'

'I kept your caution in mind.'

Their tone to each other was one of perfect gravity. Mr. Hilary even went out of his way to choose becoming phrases.

'He won't have anything to do with it if he gets to know who R. Delancey is.'

'I was prudent, believe me. I laid before him the aspects of the undertaking which would especially interest him. I made it clear to him that our enterprise is no less one of social than of commercial importance; he entered into our views very heartily. The first time I saw him, I merely invited him to glance over our prospectus; yesterday he was more than willing to join our association—and share our profits.'

'Did he tell you how much he'd got out of those poor devils over there?'

'A matter of sixty pounds, I gathered. I am not a little astonished at his success.'

'Oh, he'd talk the devil himself into subscribing to a mission if it suited him to try.'

'He is clearly very anxious to get the highest interest possible for his money. His ideas on business seemed, I confess, rather vague. I did my best to help him with suggestions.'

'Of course.'

'He talked of taking some five hundred pounds' worth of shares on his own account.'

The men regarded each other. Rodman's lips curled; Mr. Hilary was as grave as ever.

'You didn't balk him?'

'I commended his discretion.'

Rodman could not check a laugh.

'I am serious,' said Mr. Hilary. 'It may take a little time, but——'

'Just so. Did he question you at all about what we were doing?'

'A good deal. He said he should go and look over the Stores in the Strand.'

'By all means. He's a clever man if he distinguishes between Irish butter and English butterine—I'm sure I couldn't. And things really are looking up at the Stores?'

'Oh, distinctly.'

'By-the-by, I had rather a nasty letter from Lord Mountorry yesterday. He's beginning to ask questions : wants to know when we're going to conclude our contract with that tenant of his—I've forgotten the fellow's name.'

'Well, that must be looked into. There's perhaps no reason why the contract should not be concluded. Little by little we may come to justify our name ; who knows? In the meantime, we at all events do a *bonâ fide* business.'

'Strictly so.'

Rodman had a good deal of business on hand besides that which arose from his connection with Irish dairies. If Alice imagined him strolling at his ease about the fashionable lounges of the town, she was much mistaken. He worked hard and enjoyed his work, on the sole condition that he was engaged in overreaching someone. This flattered his humour.

He could not find leisure to dine till nearly nine o'clock. He had made up his mind not to return to Wimbledon, but to make use of a certain *pied à-terre* which he had in Pimlico. His day's work ended in Westminster, he dined at a restaurant with a friend. Afterwards billiards were proposed. They entered a house which Rodman did not know, and were passing before the bar to go to the billiard-room, when a man who stood there taking refreshment called out, 'Hollo, Rodman!' To announce a man's name in this way is a decided breach of etiquette in the world to which Rodman belonged. He looked annoyed, and would have passed on, but his acquaintance, who had perhaps exceeded the limits of modest refreshment, called him again and obliged him to approach the bar. As he did so Rodman happened to glance at the woman who stood ready to fulfil the expected order. The glance was followed by a short but close scrutiny, after which he turned his back and endeavoured by a sign to draw his two acquaintances away. But at the same moment the barmaid addressed him.

'What is yours, Mr. Rodman?'

He shrugged his shoulders, muttered a strong expression, and turned round again. The woman met his look steadily. She was perhaps thirty, rather tall, with features more refined than her position would have led one to expect. Her figure was good but meagre; her cheeks were very thin, and the expression of her face, not quite amiable at any time, was at present almost fierce. She seemed about to say something further, but restrained herself.

Rodman recovered his good temper.

'How do, Clara?' he said, keeping his eye fixed on hers. 'I'll have a drop of absinthe, if you please.'

Then he pursued his conversation with the two men. The woman, having served them, disappeared. Rodman kept looking for her. In a few minutes he pretended to recollect an engagement and succeeded in going off alone. As he issued on to the pavement he found himself confronted by the barmaid, who now wore a hat and cloak.

'Well?' he said, carelessly.

'Rodman's your name, is it?' was the reply.

'To my particular friends. Let's walk on; we can't chat here very well.'

'What is to prevent me from calling that policeman and giving you in charge?' she asked, looking into his face with a strange mixture of curiosity and anger.

'Nothing, except that you have no charge to make against me. The law isn't so obliging as all that. Come, we'll take a walk.'

She moved along by his side.

'You coward!' she exclaimed, passionately but with none of the shrieking virulence of women who like to make a scene in the street. 'You mean, contemptible, cold-blooded man! I suppose you hoped I was starved to death by this time, or in the workhouse, or—what did *you* care where I was! I knew I should find you some day.'

'I rather supposed you would stay on the other side of the

water,' Rodman remarked, glancing at her. 'You're changed a good deal. Now it's a most extraordinary thing. Not so very long ago I was dreaming about you, and you were serving at a bar—queer thing, wasn't it?'

They were walking towards Whitehall. When they came at length into an ill-lighted and quiet spot, the woman stopped.

'Where do you live?' she asked.

'Live? Oh, just out here in Pimlico. Like to see my rooms?'

'What do you mean by talking to me like that? Do you make a joke of deserting your wife and child for seven years, leaving them without a penny, going about enjoying yourself, when, for anything you knew, they were begging their bread? You always were heartless—it was the blackest day of my life that I met you; and you ask me if I'd like to see your rooms! What thanks to you that I'm not as vile a creature as there is in London? How was I to support myself and the child? What was I to do when they turned me into the streets of New York because I couldn't pay what you owed them nor the rent of a room to sleep in? You took good care *you* never went hungry. I'd only one thing to hold me up: I was an honest woman, and I made up my mind I'd keep honest, though I had such a man as you for my husband. I've hungered and worked, and I've made a living for myself and my child as best I could. I'm not like you: I've done nothing to disgrace myself. Now I will slave no more. You won't run away from me this time. Leave me for a single night, and I go to the nearest police-station and tell all I know about you. If I wasn't a fool I'd do it now. But I've hungered and worked for seven years, and now it's time *my husband* did something for me.'

'You always had a head for argument, Clara,' he replied coolly. 'But I can't get over that dream of mine. Really a queer thing, wasn't it? Who'd have thought of you turning barmaid? With your education, I should have thought you could have done something in the teaching line. Never mind. The queerest thing of all is that I'm really half glad to see you. How's Jack?'

The extraordinary conversation went on as they walked towards the street where Clara lived. It was in a poor part of Westminster. Reaching the house, Clara opened the door with a latchkey.

Two women were standing in the passage.

'This is my husband, Mrs. Rook,' Clara said to one of them. 'He's just got back from abroad.'

'Glad to see you, Mr. Williamson,' said the landlady, scrutinising him with unmistakable suspicion.

The pair ascended the stairs, and Mrs. Williamson—she had always used the name she received in marriage—opened a door which disclosed a dark bedroom. A voice came from within— the voice of a little lad of eight years old.

'That you, mother? Why, I've only just put myself to bed. What time is it?'

'Then you ought to have gone to bed long ago,' replied his mother whilst she was striking a light.

It was a very small room, but decent. The boy was discovered sitting up in bed—a brightfaced little fellow with black hair. Clara closed the door, then turned and looked at her husband. The light made a glistening appearance on her eyes; she had become silent, allowing facts to speak for themselves.

The child stared at the stranger in astonishment.

' Who are you ? ' he asked at length.

Rodman laughed as heartily as if there had been nothing disagreeable in the situation.

' I have the honour to be your father, sir,' he replied. ' You're a fine boy, Jack—a deuced fine boy.'

The child was speechless. Rodman turned to the mother. Her hands held the rail at the foot of the bed, and as the boy looked up at her for explanation she let her face fall upon them and sobbed.

'If you're father come back,' exclaimed Jack indignantly, ' why do you make mother cry?'

Rodman was still mirthful.

' I like you, Jack,' he said. ' You'll make a man some day. Do you mind if I smoke a cigar, Clara?'

To his astonishment, he felt a weakness which had to be resisted ; tobacco suggested itself as a resource. When he had struck a light, his wife forced back her tears and seated herself with an unforgiving countenance.

Rodman began to chat pleasantly as he smoked.

Decidedly it was a *contretemps*. It introduced a number of difficulties into his life. If he remained away for a night, he had little doubt that his wife would denounce him ; she knew of several little matters which he on the whole preferred to be reticent about. She was not a woman like Alice, to be turned round his finger. It behoved him to be exceedingly cautious.

He had three personalities. As Mr. Willis Rodman his

task was comparatively a light one, at all events for the present. He merely informed Alice by letter that he was kept in town by business and would see her in the course of a week. It was very convenient that Alice had no intercourse with her relatives. Secondly, as Mr. Williamson his position was somewhat more difficult. Not only had he to present himself every night at the rooms he had taken in Brixton, but it was necessary to take precautions lest his abode should be discovered by those who might make awkward use of the knowledge. He had, moreover, to keep Clara in the dark as to his real occupations and prevent her from knowing his resorts in town. Lastly, as Mr. Robert Delancey he had to deal with matters of a very delicate nature indeed, in themselves quite enough to occupy a man's mental energy. But our friend was no ordinary man. If you are not as yet satisfied of that, it will ere long be made abundantly clear to you.

His spirits were as high as ever. When he said—with an ingenious brutality all his own—that he was more than half glad to see his wife, he, for a wonder, told the truth. But perhaps it was little Jack who gave him most pleasure, and did most to reconcile him to the difficulties of his situation. In a day or two he conquered the child's affections so completely that Jack seemed to care little for his mother in comparison; Jack could not know the hardships she had endured for his sake. Rodman—so we will continue to call him for convenience' sake—already began to talk of what he would make the lad, who certainly gave promise of parts. The result of this was that for a week or two our friend became an exemplary family man. His wife almost dared to believe that her miseries were over. Yet she watched him with lynx eyes.

The 'Irish Dairy Company' flourished. Rodman rubbed his hands with a sinister satisfaction when he inscribed among the shareholders the name of Richard Mutimer, who invested all the money he had collected from the East-Enders, and three hundred pounds of his own—not five hundred, as he had at first thought of doing. Mutimer had the consent of his committee, whom he persuaded without much difficulty—the money was not theirs—that by this means he would increase his capital beyond all expectation. He told Adela what he had done.

'There's not the least risk. They've got the names of several lords! And it isn't a mere commercial undertaking: the first object is to benefit the Irish; so that there can be nothing against my principles in it. They promise a dividend of thirty per cent. What a glorious day it will be when I tell the people what I have made of their money! Now confess that it isn't everyone could have hit on this idea.'

Of course he made no public announcement of his speculation : that would have been to spoil the surprise. But he could not refrain from talking a good deal about the Company to his friends. He explained with zeal the merit of the scheme; it was dealing directly with the producers, the poor small-farmers who could never get fair treatment. He saw a great deal of Mr. Hilary, who was vastly interested in his East-End work. A severe winter had begun. Threepenny bits came in now but slowly, and Mutimer exerted himself earnestly to relieve the growing want in what he called his 'parishes.' He began in truth to do some really good work, moving heaven and earth to find employment for those long out of it, and even bestowing money of his own. At night he would return to Holloway worn out, and distress Adela with descriptions of the misery he had witnessed.

'I'm not sorry for it,' he once exclaimed. 'I cannot be sorry. Let things get worse and worse; the mending'll be all the nearer. Why don't they march in a body to the West End? I don't mean march in a violent sense, though that'll have to come, I expect. But why don't they make a huge procession and go about the streets in an orderly way—just to let it be seen what their numbers are—just to give the West End a hint? I'll propose that one of these days. It'll be a risky business, but we can't think of that when thousands are half starving. I could lead them, I feel sure I could! It wants someone with authority over them, and I think I've got that. There's no telling what I may do yet. I say, Adela, how would it sound—" Richard Mutimer, First President of the English Republic?"'

And in the meantime Alice sat in her house at Wimbledon, abandoned. The solitude seemed to be driving her mad. Rodman came down very occasionally for a few hours in the daytime, but never passed a night with her. He told her he had a great affair on hand, a very great affair, which was to make their fortunes ten times over. She must be patient; women couldn't understand business. If she resisted his coaxing and grumbled, he always had his threat ready. He would realise his profits and make off, leaving her in the lurch. Weeks became months. In pique at the betrayal of her famous stratagem, Alice had wanted to dismiss her servant, but Rodman

objected to this. She was driven by desperation to swallow her
pride and make a companion of the girl. But she did not complain to her of her husband—partly out of self-respect, partly
because she was afraid to. Indeed it was a terrible time for the
poor Princess. She spent the greater part of every day in a
state of apathy; for the rest she wept. Many a time she was
on the point of writing to Richard, but could not quite bring
herself to that. She could not leave the house, for it rained or
snowed day after day; the sun seemed to have deserted the
heavens as completely as joy her life. She grew feeble-minded,
tried to amuse herself with childish games, played 'Beggar My
Neighbour' with the servant for hours at night. She had fits
of hysteria, and terrified her sole companion with senseless
laughter, or with alarming screams. Reading she was no longer
equal to; after a few pages she lost her understanding of a
story. And her glass—as well as her husband—told her that
she suffered daily in her appearance. Her hair was falling; she
one day told the servant that she would soon have to buy a
wig. Poor Alice! And she had not even the resource of railing against the social state. What a pity she had never studied
that subject!

So the time went on till February of the new year. Alice's
release was at hand.

CHAPTER XXXIII.

'ARRY MUTIMER, not long after he left his mother's house for
good, by chance met Rodman in the City. Presuming on old
acquaintance, he accosted the man of business with some familiarity; it was a chance of getting much-needed assistance once
more. But Rodman was not disposed to renew the association.
He looked into 'Arry's face with a blank stare, asked contemptuously, 'Who are you?' and pursued his walk.

'Arry hoped that he might some day have a chance of being
even with Mr. Rodman.

As indeed he had. One evening towards the end of February, 'Arry was loafing about Brixton. He knew a certain
licensed victualler in those parts, a man who had ere now given
him casual employment, and after a day of fasting he trudged
southwards to see if his friend would not at all events be good

for a glass of beer and a hunch of bread and cheese. Perhaps he might also supply the coppers to pay for a bed in the New Cut. To his great disappointment, the worthy victualler was away from home; the victualler's wife had no charitable tendencies. 'Arry whined to her, but only got for an answer that times was as 'ard with her as with anyone else. The representative of unemployed labour went his way despondently, hands thrust deep in pockets, head slouching forwards, shoulders high up against the night blast.

He was passing a chemist's shop, when a customer came out. He recognised Rodman. After a moment's uncertainty he made up his mind to follow him, wondering how Rodman came to be in this part of London. Keeping at a cautious distance, he saw him stop at a small house and enter it by aid of a latchkey.

' Why, he lives there!' 'Arry exclaimed to himself. ' What's the meanin' o' this go?'

Rodman, after all, had seriously come down in the world, then. It occurred to 'Arry that he might do worse than pay his sister a visit; Alice could not be hard-hearted enough to refuse him a few coppers. But the call must be made at an hour when Rodman was away. Presumably that would be some time after eight in the morning.

Our unconventional friend walked many miles that night. It was one way of keeping warm, and there was always a possibility of aid from one or other of the acquaintances whom he sought. The net result of the night's campaign was half-a-pint of 'four-half.' The front of a draper's shop in Kennington tempted him sorely; he passed it many times, eyeing the rolls of calico and flannel exposed just outside the doorway. But either courage failed him or there was no really good opportunity. Midnight found him still without means of retiring to that familiar lodging in the New Cut. At half-past twelve sleet began to fall. He discovered a very dark corner of a very dark slum, curled himself against the wall, and slept for a few hours in defiance of wind and weather.

'Arry was used to this kind of thing. On the whole he deemed it preferable to the life he would have led at his mother's.

By eight o'clock next morning he was back in Brixton, standing just where he could see the house which Rodman had entered, without himself attracting attention. Every rag on his back was soaked; he had not eaten a mouthful for thirty

hours.   After such a run of bad luck perhaps something was
about to turn up.

But it was ten o'clock before Rodman left home.   'Arry
had no feeling left in any particle of his body.   Still here at
length was the opportunity of seeing Alice.   He waited till
Rodman was out of sight, then went to the door and
knocked.

It was Clara who opened the door.   Seeing 'Arry, she took
him for a beggar, shook her head, and was closing the door
against him, when she heard—

'Is Mrs. Rodman in, mum ?'

'Mrs. —— who ?'

'Mrs. Rodman.'

Clara's eyes flashed as they searched his face.

'What do you want with Mrs. Rodman ?'

'Want to see her, mum.'

'Do you know her when you see her ?'

'Sh' think I do,' replied 'Arry with a grin.   But he thought
it prudent to refrain from explanation.

'How do you know she lives here ?'

''Cause I just see her 'usband go out.'

Clara hesitated a moment, then bade him enter.   She introduced him to a parlour on the ground floor.   He stood looking
uneasily about him.   The habits of his life made him at all
times suspicious.

'Mrs. Rodman doesn't live here,' Clara began, lowering her
voice and making a great effort to steady it.

'Oh, she don't ?' replied 'Arry, beginning to discern that
something was wrong.

'Can you tell me what you want with her ?'

He looked her in the eyes and again grinned.

'Dare say I could if it was made worth my while.'

She took a purse from her pocket and laid half-a-crown on
the table.   Her hand shook.

'I can't afford more than that.   You shall have it if you
tell me the truth.'

'Arry took counsel with himself for an instant.   Probably
there was no more to be got, and he saw from the woman's
agitation that he had come upon some mystery.   The chance of
injuring Rodman was more to him than several half-crowns.

'I won't ask more,' he said, 'if you'll tell me who *you* are.
That's fair on both sides, eh ?'

'My name is Mrs. Williamson.'

'Oh? And might it 'appen that Mr. Rodman calls himself Mr. Williamson when it suits him?'

'I don't know what you mean,' she replied hurriedly. 'Tell me who it is you call Mrs. Rodman.'

'I don't *call* her so. That's her married name. She's my sister.'

The door opened. Both turned their heads and saw Rod-man. He had come back for a letter he had forgotten to take with him to post. At a glance he saw everything, including the half-crown on the table, which 'Arry instantly seized. He walked forward, throwing a murderous look at Clara as he passed her. Then he said to 'Arry, in a perfectly calm voice—

'There's the door.'

'I see there is,' the other replied, grinning. 'Good-mornin', Mr. Rodman Williamson.'

Husband and wife faced each other as soon as the front door slammed. Clara was a tigress; she could not be terrified as Alice might have been by scowls and savage threats. Rodman knew it, and knew, moreover, that his position was more peril-ous than any he had been in for a long time.

'What do you know?' he asked quietly.

'Enough to send you to prison, Mr. Rodman. You can't do *quite* what you like! If there's law in this country I'll see you punished!'

He let her rave for a minute or two, and by that time had laid his plans.

'Will you let me speak? Now I give you a choice. Either you can do as you say, or you can be out of this country, with me and Jack, before to-morrow morning. In a couple of hours I can get more money than you ever set eyes on; I'll be back here with it'—he looked at his watch—'by one o'clock. No, that wouldn't be safe either—that fellow might send some-one here by then. I'll meet you on Westminster Bridge, the north end, at one. Now you've a minute to choose; he may have gone straight away to the police station. Punish me if you like—I don't care a curse. But it seems to me the other thing's got more common sense in it. I haven't seen that woman for a month, and never care to see her again. I don't care over much for you either; but I do care for Jack, and for his sake I'll take you with me, and do my best for you. It's no good looking at me like a wild beast. You've sense enough to make a choice.'

She clasped her hands together and moaned, so dreadful

F F

was the struggle in her between passions and temptations and fears. The mother's heart bade her trust him; yet *could* she trust him to go and return?

'You have the cunning of a devil,' she groaned, 'and as little heart! Let you go, when you only want the chance of deserting me again!'

'You'll have to be quick,' he replied, holding his watch in his hand, and smiling at the compliment in spite of his very real anxiety. There may be no choice in a minute or two.'

'I'll go with you now; I'll follow you where you go to get the money!'

'No, you won't. Either you trust me or you refuse. You've a free choice, Clara. I tell you plainly I want little Jack, and I'm not going to lose him if I can help it.'

'Have you any other children?'

'No—never had.'

At least he had not been deceiving her in the matter of Jack. She knew that he had constantly come home at early hours only for the sake of playing with the boy.

'I'll go with you. No one shall see that I'm following you.'

'It's impossible. I shall have to go post haste in a cab. I've half-a-dozen places to go to. Meet me on Westminster Bridge at one. I may be a few minutes later, but certainly not more than half-an-hour.'

He went to the window and looked uneasily up and down the street. Clara pressed her hands upon her head and stared at him like one distracted.

'Where is she?' came from her involuntarily.

'Don't be a fool, woman!' he replied, walking to the door. She sprang to hold him. Instead of repulsing her, he folded his arm about her waist and kissed her lips two or three times.

'I can get thousands of pounds,' he whispered. 'We'll be off before they have a trace. It's for Jack's sake, and I'll be kind to you as well, old woman.'

She had suffered him to go; the kisses made her powerless, reminding her of a long-past dream. A moment after she rushed to the house door, but only to see him turning the corner of the street. Then she flew to the bedroom. Jack was ill of a cold—she was nursing him in bed. But now she dressed him hurriedly, as if there were scarcely time to get to Westminster by the appointed hour. All was ready before eleven o'clock, but it was now raining, and she durst not wait with the child in the open air for longer than was necessary. But all at once the fear possessed her lest the police might come to the house and she be detained. Ignorant of the law, and convinced from her husband's words that the stranger in rags had some sinister aim, she no sooner conceived the dread than she bundled into a hand-bag such few articles as it would hold and led the child hastily from the house. They walked to a tramway-line and had soon reached Westminster Bridge. But it was not half-past eleven, and the rain descended heavily. She sought a small eating-house not far from the Abbey, and by paying for some coffee and bread-and-butter, which neither she nor Jack could touch, obtained leave to sit in shelter till one o'clock.

At five minutes to the hour she rose and hurried to the north end of the bridge, and stood there, aside from the traffic, shielding little Jack as much as she could with her umbrella, careless that her own clothing was getting wet through. Big Ben boomed its one stroke. Minute after minute passed, and her body seemed still to quiver from the sound. She was at once feverishly hot and so deadly chill that her teeth clattered together; her eyes throbbed with the intensity of their gaze into the distance. The quarter-past was chimed. Jack kept talking to her, but she could hear nothing. The rain drenched her; the wind was so high that she with difficulty held the umbrella above the child. Half-past, and no sign of her husband. . . .

She durst not go away from this spot. Her eyes were blind with tears. A policeman spoke to her; she could only chatter meaningless sounds between her palsied lips. Jack coughed incessantly, begged to be taken home. 'I'm so cold, mother, so cold!' 'Only a few minutes more,' she said. He began to cry, though a brave little soul. . . .

Four o'clock struck. . . .

From Brixton our unconventional friend betook himself straight to Holloway. Having, as he felt sure, the means of making things decidedly uncomfortable for Mr. Rodman Williamson, it struck him that the eftest way would be to declare at once to his brother Richard all he knew and expected; Dick would not be slow in bestirring himself to make Rodman smart. 'Arry was without false shame; he had no hesitation in facing his brother. But Mr. Mutimer, he was told, was not at home. Then he would see Mrs. Mutimer. But the servant was indisposed to admit him, or even to trouble her mistress. 'Arry had to request her to say that ' Mr. 'Enery Mutimer ' desired to see the lady of the house. He chuckled to see the astonishment produced by his words. Thus he got admittance to Adela.

She was shocked at the sight of him, could find no words, yet gave him her hand. He told her he wished to see his brother on very particular business. But Richard would not be back before eight o'clock in the evening, and it was impossible to say where he could be found. 'Arry would not tell Adela what brought him, only assured her that it had nothing to do with his own affairs. He would call again in the evening. Adela felt inhuman in allowing him to go out into the rain, but she could not risk giving displeasure to her husband by inviting 'Arry to stay.

He came again at half-past eight. Mutimer had been home nearly an hour and was expecting him. 'Arry lost no time in coming to the point.

' He's married that other woman, I could see that much. Go and see for yourself. She give me 'alf-a-crown to tell all about him. I'm only afraid he's got off by this time.'

' Why didn't you go and give information to the police at once ?' Mutimer cried, in exasperation.

'Arry might have replied that he had a delicacy in waiting upon those gentlemen. But his brother did not stay for an answer. Rushing from the room, he equipped himself instantly with hat, coat, and umbrella.

' Show me the way to that house. Come along, there's no time to lose. Adela ! ' he called, ' I have to go out; can't say when I shall be back. Don't sit up if I'm late.'

A hansom bore the brothers southwards as fast as hansom could go.

They found Clara in the house, a haggard, frenzied woman. Already she had been to the police, but they were not inclined to hurry matters; she had no satisfactory evidence to give them. To Mutimer, when he had explained his position, she told everything—of her marriage in London nine years ago, her going with her husband to America, his desertion of her. Richard took her at once to the police-station. They would have to attend at the court next morning to swear an information.

By ten o'clock Mutimer was at Waterloo, taking train for Wimbledon. At Rodman's house he found darkness, but a little ringing brought Alice herself to the door. She thought it was her husband, and, on recognising Richard, all but dropped with fear; only some ill news could explain his coming thus. With difficulty he induced her to go into a room out of the hall. She was in her dressing-gown, her long beautiful hair in disorder, her pretty face white and distorted.

'What is it, Dick? what is it, Dick?' she kept repeating mechanically, with inarticulate moanings between. She had forgotten her enmity against her brother and spoke to him as in the old days. He, too, was all kindness.

'Try and keep quiet a little, Alice. I want to talk to you. Yes, it's about your husband, my poor girl; but there's nothing to be frightened at. He's gone away, that's all. I want you to come to London with me.'

She had no more control over herself than a terrified child; her words and cries were so incoherent that Mutimer feared lest she had lost her senses. She was, in truth, on the borders of idiocy. It was more than half-an-hour before, with the servant's assistance, he could allay her hysterical anguish. Then she altogether refused to accompany him. If she did so she would miss her husband; he would not go without coming to see her. Richard was reminded by the servant that it was too late to go by train. He decided to remain in the house through the night.

He had not ventured to tell her all the truth, nor did her state encourage him to do so in the morning. But he then succeeded in persuading her to come with him; Rodman, he assured her, must already be out of England, for he had committed a criminal offence and knew that the police were after him. Alice was got to the station more dead than alive; they were at home in Holloway by half past ten. Richard then left her in Adela's hands and sped once more to Brixton.

He got home again at two. As he entered Adela came down the stairs to meet him.

'How is she?' he asked anxiously.

'The same. The doctor was here an hour ago. We must keep her as quiet as possible. But she can't rest for a moment.' She added—

'Three gentlemen have called to see you. They would leave no name, and, to tell the truth, were rather rude. They seemed to doubt my word when I said you were not in.'

At his request she attempted to describe these callers, Mutimer recognised them as members of his committee,

'Rude to you? You must have mistaken. What did they come here for? I shall in any case see them to-night.'

They returned to the subject of Alice's illness.

'I've half a mind to tell her the truth,' Mutimer said. 'Surely she'd put the blackguard out of her head after that.'

'No, no; you mustn't tell her!' Adela interposed. 'I am sure it would be very unwise.'

Alice was growing worse; in an hour or two delirium began to declare itself. She had resisted all efforts to put her to bed; at most she would lie on a couch. Whilst Richard and his wife were debating what should be done, it was announced to them that the three gentlemen had called again. Mutimer went off angrily to see them.

He was engaged for half-an-hour. Then Adela heard the visitors depart; one of them was speaking loudly and with irritation. She waited for a moment at the head of the stairs, expecting that Mutimer would come out to her. As he did not, she went into the sitting-room.

Mutimer stood before the fireplace, his eyes on the ground, his face discoloured with vehement emotion.

'What has happened?' she asked.

He looked up and beckoned to her to approach.

CHAPTER XXXIV.

ADELA had never seen him so smitten with grave trouble. She knew him in brutal anger and in surly ill-temper; but his present mood had nothing of either. He seemed to stagger beneath a blow which had all but crushed him and left him full of dread. He began to address her in a voice very unlike his own—thick, uncertain; he used short sentences, often incomplete.

'Those men are on the committee. One of them got a letter this morning—anonymous. It said they were to be on their guard against me. Said the Company's a swindle—that I knew it—that I've got money out of the people on false pretences. And Hilary's gone—gone off—taking all he could lay hands on. The letter says so—I don't know. It says I'm thick with the secretary—a man I never even saw. That he's a well-known swindler—Delancey his name is. And these fellows believe it—demand that I shall prove I'm innocent. What proof can I give? They think I kept out of the way on purpose this morning.'

He ceased speaking, and Adela stood mute, looking him in the face. She was appalled on his account. She did not love him; too often his presence caused her loathing. But of late she had been surprised into thinking more highly of some of his qualities than it had hitherto been possible for her to do. She could never forget that he toiled first and foremost for his own advancement to a very cheap reputation; he would not allow her to lose sight of it had she wished. But during the present winter she had discerned in him a genuine zeal to help the suffering, a fervour in kindly works of which she had not believed him capable. Very slowly the conviction had come to her, but in the end she could not resist it. One evening, in telling her of the hideous misery he had been amongst, his voice failed and she saw moisture in his eyes. Was his character changing? Had she wronged him in attaching too much importance to a fault which was merely on the surface? Oh, but there were too many indisputable charges against him. Yet a man's moral nature may sometimes be strengthened by experience of the evil he has wrought. All this rushed through her mind as she now stood gazing at him.

'But how can they credit an anonymous letter?' she said. 'How can they believe the worst of you before making inquiries?'

'They have been to the office of the Company. Everything is upside down. They say Hilary isn't to be found.'

'Who can have written such a letter?'

'How do I know? I have enemies enough, no doubt. Who hasn't that makes himself a leader?'

There was the wrong note again. It discouraged her; she was silent.

'Look here, Adela,' he said, 'do you believe this?'

'Believe it!'

'Do you think I'm capable of doing a thing like that—scraping together by pennies the money of the poorest of the poor just to use it for my own purposes—could I do that?'

'You know I do not believe it.'

'But you don't speak as if you were certain. There's something —— But how am I to prove I'm innocent? How can I make people believe I wasn't in the plot? They've only my word—who'll think that enough? Anyone can tell a lie and stick to it, if there's no positive proof against him. How am I to make *you* believe that I was taken in?'

'But I tell you that a doubt of your innocence does not enter my mind. If it were necessary, I would stand up in public before all who accused you and declare that they were wrong. I do not need your assurance. I recognise that it would be impossible for you to commit such a crime.'

'Well, it does me good to hear you say that,' he replied, with light of hope in his eyes. 'I wanted to feel sure of that. You might have thought that'—he sank his voice—'that because I could think of destroying that will ——'

'Don't speak of that!' she interrupted, with a gesture of pain. 'I say that I believe you. It is enough. Don't speak about me any more. Think of what has to be done.'

'I have promised to be in Clerkenwell at eight o'clock. There'll be a meeting. I shall do my best to show that I am innocent. You'll look after Alice? It's awful to have to leave her whilst she's like that.'

'Trust me. I will not leave her side for a moment. The doctor will be here again to-night.'

A thought struck him.

'Send out the girl for an evening paper. There may be something in it.'

The paper was obtained. One of the first headings his eye fell upon was: 'Rumoured Collapse of a Public Company: Disappearance of the Secretary.' He showed it to Adela, and they read together. She saw that the finger with which he followed the lines quivered like a leaf. It was announced in a brief paragraph that the Secretary of the Irish Dairy Company was missing; that he seemed to have gone off with considerable sums. Moreover, that there were rumours in the City of a startling kind, relative to the character of the Company itself. The name of the secretary was Mr. Robert Delancey, but that was now believed to be a mere *alias*. The police were actively at work.

'It'll be the ruin of me!' Mutimer gasped. 'I can never prove that I knew nothing. You see, nothing's said about Hilary. It's that fellow Delancey who has run.'

'You must find Mr. Hilary,' said Adela urgently. 'Where does he live?'

'I have no idea. I only had the office address. Perhaps it isn't even his real name. It'll be my ruin.'

Adela was astonished to see him so broken down. He let himself sink upon a chair; his head and hands fell.

'But I can't understand why you should despair so !' she exclaimed. 'You will speak to the meeting to-night. If the money is lost you will restore it. If you have been imprudent, that is no crime.'

'It is—it is—when I had money of that kind entrusted to me ! They won't hear me. They have condemned me already. What use is it to talk to them ? They'll say everything comes to smash in my hands.'

She spoke to him with such words of strengthening as one of his comrades might have used. She did not feel the tenderness of a wife, and had no power to assume it. But her voice was brave and true. She had made his interest, his reputation, her own. By degrees he recovered from the blow, and let her words give him heart.

'You're right,' he said, 'I'm behaving like a fool; I couldn't go on different if I was really guilty. Who wrote that letter ? I never saw the letter before, as far as I know. I wanted to keep it, but they wouldn't let me—trust them ! What blackguards they are! They're jealous of me. They know they can't speak like I do, that they haven't the same influence I have. So they're ready to believe the first lie that's brought against me. Let them look to themselves to-night ! I'll give them a piece of my mind—see if I don't! What's to day ? Friday. On Sunday I'll have the biggest meeting ever gathered in the East End. If they shout out against me, I'll tell them to their faces that they're mean-spirited curs. They haven't the courage to rise and get by force what they'll never have by asking for it, and when a man does his best to help them they throw mud at him !'

'But they won't do so,' Adela urged. 'Don't be unjust. Wait and see. They will shout *for*, not *against* you.'

'Why didn't you keep 'Arry here ?' he asked suddenly.

'He refused to stay. I gave him money.'

'You should have forced him to stay ! How can I have a brother of my own living a life like that ? You did wrong to give him money. He'll only use it to make a beast of himself. I must find him again; I can't let him go to ruin.'

'Arry had come back to Holloway the previous night to inform Adela that her husband might not return till morning. As she said, it had been impossible to detain him. He was too far gone in unconventionality to spend a night under a decent roof. Home-sickness for the gutter possessed him.

In the meantime Alice had become quieter. It was half-past six; Mutimer had to be at the meeting-place in Clerkenwell by eight. Adela sat by Alice whilst the servant hurriedly prepared a meal; then the girl took her place, and she went down to her husband. They were in the middle of their meal when they heard the front-door slam. Mutimer started up.

'Who's that? Who's gone out?'

Adela ran to the foot of the stairs and called the servant's name softly. It was a minute before the girl appeared.

'Who hast just gone out, Mary?'

'Gone out? No one, mum!'

'Is Mrs. Rodman lying still?'

The girl went to see. She had left Alice for a few moments previously. She appeared again at the head of the stairs with a face of alarm.

'Mrs. Rodman isn't there, mum!'

Mutimer flew up the staircase. Alice was nowhere to be found. It could not be doubted that she had fled in a delirious state. Richard rushed into the street, but it was very dark, and rain was falling. There was no trace of the fugitive. He came back to the door, where Adela stood; he put out his hand and held her arm as if she needed support.

'Give me my hat! She'll die in the street, in the rain! I'll go one way; the girl must go the other. My hat!'

'I will go one way myself,' said Adela hurriedly. 'You must take an umbrella: it pours. Mary! my waterproof!'

They ran in opposite directions. It was a quiet by-street, with no shops to cast light upon the pavement. Adela encountered a constable before she had gone very far, and begged for his assistance. He promised to be on the look-out, but advised her to go on a short distance to the police-station and leave a description of the missing woman. She did so; then, finding the search hopeless in this quarter, turned homewards. Mutimer was still absent, but he appeared in five minutes, as unsuccessful as herself. She told him of her visit to the station.

'I must keep going about,' he said. 'She can't be far off; her strength, surely, wouldn't take her far.'

Adela felt for him profoundly; for once he had not a thought of himself, his distress was absorbing. He was on the point of leaving the house again, when she remembered the meeting at which he was expected. She spoke of it.

'What do I care?' he replied, waving his arm. 'Let them think what they like. I must find Alice.'

Adela saw in a moment all that his absence would involve. He could of course explain subsequently, but in the meantime vast harm would have been done. It was impossible to neglect the meeting altogether. She ran after him and stopped him on the pavement.

'I will go to this meeting for you,' she said. 'A cab will take me there and bring me back. I will let them know what keeps you away.'

He looked at her with astonishment.

'You! How can you go? Among those men?'

'Surely I have nothing to fear from them? Have you lost all your faith suddenly? You cannot go, but someone must. I will speak to them so that they cannot but believe me. You continue the search; I will go.'

They stood together in the pouring rain. Mutimer caught her hand.

'I never knew what a wife could be till now,' he exclaimed hoarsely. 'And I never knew *you*!'

'Find me a cab and give the man the address. I will be ready in an instant.'

Her cheeks were on fire; her nerves quivered with excitement. She had made the proposal almost involuntarily; only his thanks gave her some understanding of what she was about to do. But she did not shrink; a man's—better still, a woman's—noblest courage throbbed in her. If need were, she too could stand forward in a worthy cause and speak the truth undauntedly.

The cab was bearing her away. She looked at her watch in the moment of passing a street lamp and just saw that it was eight o'clock. The meeting would be full by this; they would already be drawing ill conclusions from Mutimer's absence. Faster, faster! Every moment lost increased the force of prejudice against him. She could scarcely have felt more zeal on behalf of the man whom her soul loved. In the fever of her brain she was conscious of a wish that even now that love could be her husband's. Ah no, no! But serve him she could, and loyally. The lights flew by in the streets of Islington; the driver was making the utmost speed he durst. A check among thronging vehicles anguished her. But it was past, and here at length came the pause.

A crowd of perhaps a hundred men was gathered about the

ill-lighted entrance to what had formerly been a low-class
dancing-saloon. Adela saw them come thronging about the cab,
heard their cries of discontent and of surprise when she showed
herself.

'Wait for me!' she called to the driver, and straightway
walked to the door. The men made way for her. On the
threshold she turned.

'I wish to see some member of the committee. I am Mrs.
Mutimer.'

There was a coarse laugh from some fellows, but others
cried, 'Shut up! she's a lady.' One stepped forward and
announced himself as a committee-man. He followed her into
the passage.

'My husband cannot come,' she said. 'Will you please
show me where I can speak to the meeting and tell them the
reason of his absence?'

Much amazed, the committee-man led her into the hall. It
was whitewashed, furnished with plain benches, lit with a few
gas-jets. There was scarcely room to move for the crowd.
Every man seemed to be talking at the pitch of his voice. The
effect was an angry roar. Adela's guide with difficulty made a
passage for her to the platform, for it took some time before the
crowd realised what was going on. At length she stood in a
place whence she could survey the assembly. On the wall
behind her hung a great sheet of paper on which were inscribed
the names of all who had deposited money with Mutimer.
Adela glanced at it and understood. Instead of being agitated
she possessed an extraordinary lucidity of mind, a calmness of
nerve which she afterwards remembered as something mira-
culous.

The committee-man roared for silence, then in a few words
explained Mrs. Mutimer's wish to make 'a speech.' To Adela's
ears there seemed something of malice in this expression; she
did not like, either, the laugh which it elicited. But quiet was
speedily restored by a few men of sturdy lungs. She stepped
to the front of the platform.

The scene was a singular one. Adela had thrown off her
waterproof in the cab; she stood in her lady-like costume of
home, her hat only showing that she had come from a distance.
For years her cheeks had been very pale; in this moment her
whole face was white as marble. Her delicate beauty made
strange contrast with the faces on each side and in front of her
—faces of rude intelligence, faces of fathomless stupidity, faces

degraded into something less than human. But all were listening, all straining towards her. There were a few whispers
of honest admiration, a few of vile jest. She began to speak.

'I have come here because my husband cannot come. It
is most unfortunate that he cannot, for he tells me that someone has been throwing doubt upon his honesty. He would be
here, but that a terrible misfortune has befallen him. His
sister was lying ill in our house. A little more than an hour
ago she was by chance left alone and, being delirious—out of
her mind—escaped from the house. My husband is now searching for her everywhere; she may be dying somewhere in the
streets. That is the explanation I have come to give you. But
I will say a word more. I do not know who has spoken ill of
my husband; I do not know his reasons for doing so. This,
however, I know, that Richard Mutimer has done you no
wrong, and that he is incapable of the horrible thing of which
he is accused. You must believe it; you wrong yourselves if you
refuse to. To-morrow, no doubt, he will come and speak for
himself. Till then I beg you to take the worthy part and credit
good rather than evil.'

She ceased, and, turning to the committee-man, who still
stood near her, requested him to guide her from the room. As
she moved down from the platform the crowd recovered itself from the spell of her voice. The majority cheered, but there
were not a few dissentient howls. Adela had ears for nothing ;
a path opened before her, and she walked along it with bowed
head. Her heart was now beating violently ; she felt that she
must walk quickly or perchance her strength would fail her
before she reached the door. As she disappeared there again
arose the mingled uproar of cheers and groans ; it came to her
like the bellow of a pursuing monster as she fled along the
passage. And in truth Demos was on her track. A few kept
up with her; the rest jammed themselves in the door-way,
hustled each other, fought. The dozen who came out to the
pavement altogether helped her into the cab, then gave a hearty
cheer as she drove away.

The voice of Demos, not malevolent at the last, but to
Adela none the less something to be fled from, something which
excited thoughts of horrible possibilities, in its very good-
humour and its praise of her a sound of fear.

CHAPTER XXXV.

His search being vain, Mutimer hastened from one police-station to another, leaving descriptions of his sister at each. When he came home again Adela had just arrived. She was suffering too much from the reaction which followed upon her excitement to give him more than the briefest account of what she had heard and said; but Mutimer cared little for details. He drew an easy-chair near to the fire and begged her to rest. As she lay back for a moment with closed eyes, he took her faint hand and put it to his lips. He had never done so before; when she glanced at him he averted his face in embarrassment.

He would have persuaded her to go to bed, but she declared that sleep was impossible; she had much rather sit up with him till news came of Alice, as it surely must do in course of the night. For Mutimer there was no resting; he circled continually about the neighbouring streets, returning to the house every quarter of an hour, always to find Adela in the same position. Her heart would not fall to its normal beat, and the vision of those harsh faces would not pass from her mind.

At two o'clock they heard that Alice was found. She had been discovered several miles from home, lying unconscious in the street, and was now in a hospital. Mutimer set off at once; he returned with the report that she was between life and death. It was impossible to remove her.

Adela slept a little between six and eight; her husband took even shorter rest. When she came down to the sitting-room, he was reading the morning paper. As she entered he uttered a cry of astonishment and rage.

'Look here!' he exclaimed to her. 'Read that!'

'He pointed to an account of the Irish Dairy Company frauds, in which it was stated that the secretary, known as Delancey, appeared also to have borne the name of Rodman.

They gazed at each other.

'Then it was Rodman wrote that letter!' Mutimer cried. 'I'll swear to it. He did it to injure me at the last moment. Why haven't they got him yet? The police are useless. But they've got Hilary, I see—yes, they've got Hilary. He was caught at Dover. Ha, ha! He denies everything—says he didn't even know of the secretary's decamping. The lying

scoundrel! Says he was going to Paris on private business.
But they've got him! And see here again : " The same Rodman is at present wanted by the police on a charge of bigamy."
Wanted! If they weren't incompetent fools they'd have had
him already. Ten to one he's out of England.'

It was a day of tumult for Mutimer. At the hospital he
found no encouragement, but he could only leave Alice in the
hands of the doctors. From the hospital he went to his mother's
house ; he had not yet had time to let her know of anything.
But his main business lay in Clerkenwell and in various parts
of the East End, wherever he could see his fellow-agitators. In
hot haste he wrote an announcement of a meeting on Clerkenwell Green for Sunday afternoon, and had thousands of copies
printed on slips ; by evening these were scattered throughout
his 'parishes.' He found that the calumny affecting him was
already widely known ; several members of his committee met
him with black looks. Here and there an ironical question
was put to him about his sister's health. With the knowledge
that Alice might be dying or dead, he could scarcely find words
of reply. His mood changed from fear and indignation to a
grim fury ; within a few hours he made many resolute enemies
by his reckless vehemence and vituperation.

The evening papers brought him a piece of intelligence
which would have rejoiced him but for something with which
it was coupled. Delancey, *alias* Rodman, *alias* Williamson,
was arrested ; he had been caught in Hamburg. The telegram
added that he talked freely and had implicated a number of
persons—among them a certain Socialist agitator, name not
given. As Mutimer read this he fell for a moment into blank
despair. He returned at once to Holloway, all but resolved to
throw up the game—to abandon the effort to defend himself,
and wait for what might result from the judicial investigations.
Adela resisted this to the uttermost. She understood that such
appearance of fear would be fatal to him. With a knowledge
of Demos which owed much to her last night's experience, she
urged to him that behind his back calumny would thrive un-
checked, would grow in a day to proportions altogether irresistible. She succeeded in restoring his courage, though at the
same time there revived in Mutimer the savage spirit which
could only result in harm to himself.

' This is how they repay a man who works for them!' he
cried repeatedly. ' The ungrateful brutes! Let me once clear
myself, and I'll throw it up, bid them find someone else to fight

their battles for them. It's always been the same: history shows it. What have I got for myself out of it all, I'd like to know? Haven't I given them every penny I had? Let them do their worst! Let them bark and bray till they are hoarse!'

He would have kept away from Clerkenwell that evening, but even this Adela would not let him do. She insisted that he must be seen and heard, that the force of innocence would prevail even with his enemies. The couple of hours he passed with her were spent in ceaseless encouragement on her side, in violent tirades on his. He paced the room like a caged lion, at one moment execrating Rodman, the next railing against the mob to whose interests he had devoted himself. Now and then his voice softened, and he spoke of Alice.

'The scoundrel set even her against me! If she lives, perhaps she'll believe I'm guilty; how can my word stand against her husband's? Why, he isn't her husband at all! It's a good thing if she dies—the best thing that could happen. What will become of her? What are we to call her? She's neither married nor single. Can we keep it from her, do you think? No, that won't do; she must be free to marry an honest man. You'll try and make friends with her, Adela—if ever you've the chance? She'll have to live with us, of course; unless she'd rather live with mother. We mustn't tell her for a long time, till she's strong enough to bear it.'

He with difficulty ate a few mouthfuls and went off to Clerkenwell. In the erstwhile dancing-saloon it was a night of tempest. Mutimer had never before addressed an unfriendly audience. After the first few interruptions he lost his temper, and with it his cause, as far as these present hearers were concerned. When he left them, it was amid the mutterings of a storm which was not quite—only not quite—ready to burst in fury.

'Who knows you won't take yer 'ook before to-morrow?' cried a voice as he neared the door.

'Wait and see!' Mutimer shouted in reply, with a savage laugh. 'I've a word or two to say yet to blackguards like you.'

He could count on some twenty pairs of fists in the room, if it came to that point; but he was allowed to depart unmolested.

On the way home he called at the hospital. There was no change in Alice's condition.

The next day he remained at home till it was time to start for Clerkenwell Green. He was all but worn out, and there was nothing of any use to be done before the meeting assembled. Adela went for him to the hospital and brought back still the same report. He ate fairly well of his midday dinner, seeming somewhat calmer. Adela, foreseeing his main danger, begged him to address the people without anger, assured him that a dignified self-possession would go much farther than any amount of blustering. He was induced to promise that he would follow her advice.

He purposed walking to the Green; the exercise would perhaps keep his nerves in order. When it was time to start, he took Adela's hand, and for a second time kissed it. She made an effort over herself and held her lips to him. The 'good-bye' was exchanged, with a word of strengthening from Adela; but still he did not go. He was endeavouring to speak.

'I don't think I've thanked you half enough,' he said at length, 'for what you did on Friday night.'

'Yes, more than enough,' was the reply.

'You make little of it, but it's a thing very few women would have done. And it was hard for you, because you're a lady.'

'No less a woman,' murmured Adela, her head bowed.

'And a good woman—I believe with all my heart. I want to ask you to forgive me—for things I once said to you. I was a brute. Perhaps if I had been brought up in the same kind of way that you were—that's the difference between us, you see. But try if you can to forget it. I'll never think anything but good of you as long as I live.'

She could not reply, for a great sob was choking her. She pressed his hand; the tears broke from her eyes as she turned away.

It being Sunday afternoon, visitors were admitted to the hospital in which Alice lay. Mutimer had allowed himself time to pass five minutes by his sister's bedside on the way to Clerkenwell. Alice was still unconscious; she lay motionless, but her lips muttered unintelligible words. He bent over her and spoke, but she did not regard him. It was perhaps the keenest pain Mutimer had ever known to look into those eyes and meet no answering intelligence. By close listening he believed he heard her utter the name of her husband. It was useless to stay; he kissed her and left the ward.

On his arrival at Clerkenwell Green—a large triangular space which merits the name of Green as much as the Strand —

he found a considerable gathering already assembled about the cart from which he was to speak. The inner circle consisted of his friends—some fifty who remained staunch in their faith. Prominent among them was the man Redgrave, he who had presented the address when Mutimer took leave of his New Wanley workpeople. He had come to London at the same time as his leader, and had done much to recommend Mutimer's scheme in the East End. His muscular height made those about him look puny. He was red in the face with the excitement of abusing Mutimer's enemies, and looked as if nothing would please him better than to second words with arguments more cogent. He and those about him hailed the agitator's appearance with three ringing cheers. A little later came a supporter whom Richard had not expected to see—Mr. Westlake. Only this morning intelligence of what was going on had reached his ears. At once he had scouted the accusations as incredible; he deemed it a duty to present himself on Mutimer's side. Outside this small cluster was an indefinable mob, a portion of it bitterly hostile, a part indifferent; among the latter a large element of mere drifting blackguardism, the raff of a city, anticipating with pleasure an uproar which would give them unwonted opportunities of violence and pillage. These gentlemen would with equal zeal declare for Mutimer or his opponents, as the fortune of the day directed them.

The core of the hostile party consisted of those who followed the banner of Comrade Roodhouse, the ralliers to the 'Tocsin.' For them it was a great occasion. The previous evening had seen a clamorous assembly in the room behind the Hoxton coffee-shop. Comrade Roodhouse professed to have full details of the scandal which had just come to light. According to him, there was no doubt whatever that Mutimer had known from the first the character of the bogus Company, and had wittingly used the money of the East-Enders to aid in floating a concern which would benefit himself and a few others. Roodhouse disclosed the identity of Mr. Robert Delancey, and explained the relations existing between Rodman and Mutimer, ignoring the fact that a lawsuit had of late turned their friendship to mutual animosity. It was an opportunity not to be missed for paying back the hard things Mutimer had constantly said of the 'Tocsin' party. Comrade Roodhouse was busy in the crowd, sowing calumnies and fermenting wrath. In the crowd were our old acquaintances Messrs. Cowes and Cullen, each haranguing as many as could be got to form a circle and listen, indulging themselves in measureless vituperation, crying shame on traitors to the noble cause. Here, too, was Daniel Dabbs, mainly interested in the occasion as an admirable provocative of thirst. He was much disposed to believe Mutimer guilty, but understood that it was none of his business to openly take part with either side. He stood well on the limits of the throng; it was not impossible that the debate might end in the cracking of crowns, in which case Mr. Dabbs, as a respectable licensed victualler whose weekly profits had long since made him smile at the follies of his youth, would certainly incur no needless risk to his own valuable scalp.

The throng thickened; it was impossible that the speakers should be audible to the whole assembly. Hastily it was decided to arrange two centres. Whilst Mutimer was speaking at the lower end of the Green, Redgrave would lift up his voice in the opposite part, and make it understood that Mutimer would repeat his address there as soon as he had satisfied the hearers below. The meeting was announced for three o'clock, but it was half an hour later before Mutimer stood up on the cart and extended his hand in appeal for silence. It at first seemed as if he could not succeed in making his voice heard at all. A cluster of Roodhouse's followers, under the pretence of demanding quiet, made incessant tumult. But ultimately the majority, those who were merely curious, and such of the angry East-Enders as really wanted to hear what Mutimer had to say for himself, imposed silence. Richard began his speech.

He had kept Adela's warning in mind, and determined to be calmly dignified in his refutal of the charges brought against him. For five minutes he impressed his hearers. He had never spoken better. In the beginning he briefly referred to the facts of his life, spoke of the use he had made of wealth when he possessed it, demanded if it was likely that he should join with swindlers to rob the very class to which he himself was proud to belong, and for which he had toiled unceasingly. He spoke of Rodman, and denied that he had ever known of this man's connection with the Company—a man who was his worst enemy. He it was, this Rodman, who doubtless had written the letter which first directed suspicion in the wrong quarter; it was an act such as Rodman would be capable of, for the sake of gratifying his enmity. And how had that enmity arisen? He told the story of the lawsuit; showed how, in that matter, he had stood up for common honesty, though at the time Rodman was his friend. Then he passed to the subject

G G 2

of his stewardship. Why had he put that trust money into a concern without sufficient investigation? He could make but one straightforward answer : he had believed that the Company was sound, and he bought shares because the dividends promised to be large, and it was his first desire to do the very best he could for those who had laid their hard-earned savings in his hands.

For some minutes he had had increasing difficulty in holding his voice above the noise of interruptions, hostile or friendly. It now became impossible for him to proceed. A man who was lifted on to the shoulders of two others began to make a counter-speech, roaring so that those around could not but attend to him. He declared himself one of those whom Mutimer had robbed ; all his savings for seven months were gone ; he was now out of work, and his family would soon be starving. Richard's blood boiled as he heard these words.

'You lie !' he bellowed in return ; 'I know you. You are the fellow who said last night that I should run away, and never come at all to this meeting. I called you a blackguard then, and I call you a liar now. You have put in my hand six threepences, and no more. The money you might have saved you constantly got drunk upon. Your money is waiting for you : you have only to come and apply for it. And I say the same to all the rest. I am ready to pay all the money back, and pay it too with interest.'

'Of course you are !' vociferated the other. 'You can't steal it, so you offer to give it back. We know that game.'

It was the commencement of utter confusion. A hundred voices were trying to make themselves heard. The great crowd swayed this way and that. Mutimer looked on a tempest of savage faces—a sight which might have daunted any man in his position. Fists were shaken at him, curses were roared at him from every direction. It was clear that the feeling of the mob was hopelessly against him ; his explanations were ridiculed. A second man was reared on others' shoulders ; but instead of speaking from the place where he was, he demanded to be borne forward and helped to a standing on the cart. This was effected after a brief struggle with Mutimer's supporters. Then all at once there was a cessation of the hubbub that the new speaker might be heard.

'Look at this man !' he cried, pointing at Mutimer, who had drawn as far aside as the cart would let him. 'He's been a-tellin' you what he did when somebody died an' left him a fortune. There's just one thing he's forgot, an' shall I tell you what that is? When he was a workin' man like ourselves, mates, he was a-goin' to marry a pore girl, a workin' girl. When he gets his money, what does he do? Why, he pitches her over, if you please, an' marries a fine lady, as took him because he was rich—that's the way *ladies* always chooses their husbands, y'understand.'

He was interrupted by a terrific yell, but by dint of vigorous pantomime secured a hearing again.

'But wait a bit, maties; I haven't done yet. He pitches over the pore girl, but he does worse afterwards. He sets a tale a-goin' as she'd disgraced herself, as she wasn't fit to be a honest man's wife. An' it was all a damned lie, as lots of us knows. Now what d'ye think o' that! This is a friend o' the People, this is! This is the man as 'as your interests at 'art, mates! If he'll do a thing like that, won't he rob you of your savin's?'

As soon as he knew what the man was about to speak of, Mutimer felt the blood rush back upon his heart. It was as when a criminal hears delivered against him a damning item of evidence. He knew that he was pale, that every feature declared his consciousness of guilt. In vain he tried to face the mob and smile contemptuously. His eyes fell; he stood without the power of speech.

The yell was repeated, and prolonged, owing to another cause than the accusation just heard. When the accuser was borne forwards to the cart, a rumour spread among those more remote that an attack was being made on Mutimer and his friends. The rumour reached that part of the Green where Redgrave was then haranguing. At once the listeners faced about in the direction of the supposed conflict. Redgrave himself leaped down, and called upon all supporters of Mutimer to follow him. It was the crash between two crowds which led to the prolonging of the yell.

The meeting was over, the riot had begun.

Picture them, the indignant champions of honesty, the avengers of virtue defamed! Demos was roused, was tired of listening to mere articulate speech; it was time for a good wild-beast roar, for a taste of bloodshed. Scarcely a face in all the mob but distorted itself to express as much savagery as can be got out of the human countenance. Mutimer, seeing what had come, sprang down from the cart. He was at once carried yards away in an irresistible rush. Impossible for him and his friends to endeavour to hold their ground : they were too vastly outnumbered ; the most they could do was to hold together and use every opportunity of retreat, standing in the meanwhile on the defensive. There was no adequate body of police on the Green ; the riot would take its course unimpeded by the hired servants of the capitalist State. Redgrave little by little fought his way to within sight of Mutimer ; he brought with him a small but determined contingent. On all sides was the thud of blows, the indignant shouting of the few who desired to preserve order mingled with the clamour of those who combated. Demos was having his way ; civilisation was blotted out, and club law proclaimed.

Mutimer lost his hat in jumping from the cart ; in five minutes his waistcoat and shirt were rent open, whether by friends in guarding him, or by foes in assailing, it was impossible to say. But his bodyguard held together with wonderful firmness, only now and then an enemy got near enough to dash a fist in his face. If he fell into the hands of the mob he was done for ; Mutimer knew that, and was ready to fight for his life. But the direction taken by the main current of the crowd favoured him. In about twenty minutes he was swept away from the Green, and into a street. There were now fewer foes about him ; he saw an opportunity, and together with Redgrave burst away. There was no shame in taking to flight where the odds against him were so overwhelming. But pursuers were close behind him ; their cry gave a lead to the chase. He looked for some by-way as he rushed along the pavement. But an unexpected refuge offered itself. He was passing a little group of women, when a voice from among them cried loudly—'In here ! In here !' He saw that a house-door was open, saw a hand beckon wildly, and at once sprang for the retreat. A woman entered immediately behind him and slammed the door, but he did not see that a stick which the foremost of his pursuers had flung at him came with a terrible blow full upon his preserver's face.

For a moment he could only lean against the wall of the passage, recovering his breath. Where he stood it was almost dark, for the evening was drawing in. The woman who had rescued him was standing near, but he could not distinguish her face. He heard the mob assembling in the narrow street, their shouts, their trampling, and speedily there began a great noise at the door. A beating with sticks and fists, a thundering at the knocker.

'Are you the landlady?' Mutimer asked, turning to his silent companion.

'No,' was the reply. 'She is outside, I must put up the chain. They might get her latchkey from her.'

At the first syllable he started; the voice was so familiar to him. The words were spoken with an entire absence of womanish consternation; the voice trembled a little, but for all that there was calm courage in its sound. When she had made the door secure and turned again towards him, he looked into her face as closely as he could.

'Is it Emma?'

'Yes.'

Both were silent. Mutimer forgot all about his danger; that at this moment he should meet Emma Vine, that it should be she who saved him, impressed him with awe which was stronger than all the multitude of sensations just now battling within him. For it was her name that had roused the rabble finally against him. For his wrong to her he knew that he would have suffered justly; yet her hand it was that barred the door against his brutal pursuers. A sudden weakness shook his limbs; he had again to lean upon the wall for support, and, scarcely conscious of what he did, he sobbed three or four times.

'Are you hurt?' Emma asked.

'No, I'm not hurt, no.'

Two children had come down the stairs, and were clinging to Emma, crying with fright. For the noise at the door was growing terrific.

'Who is there in the house?' Mutimer asked.

'No one, I think. The landlady and two other women who live here are outside. My sister is away somewhere.'

'Can I get off by the back?'

'No. There's a little yard, but the walls are far too high.'

'They'll break the door through. If they do, the devils are as likely to kill you as me. I must go upstairs to a window and speak to them. I may do something yet. Sooner than put you in danger I'll go out and let them do their worst. Listen to them! That's the People, that is! I deserve killing, fool that I am, if only for the lying good I've said of them. Let me go up into your room, if it has a window in the front.'

He led up the stairs, and Emma showed him the door of her room—the same in which she had received the visit of

Daniel Dabbs. He looked about it, saw the poverty of it.
Then he looked at Emma.

'Good God! Who has hit you?'

There was a great cut on her cheek, the blood was running
down upon her dress.

'Somebody threw a stick,' she answered, trying to smile.
'I don't feel it; I'll tie a handkerchief on it.'

Again a fit of sobbing seized him; he felt as weak as a
child.

'The cowardly roughs! Give me the handkerchief—I'll
tie it. Emma!'

'Think of your own safety,' she replied hurriedly. 'I tell
you I don't feel any pain. Do you think you can get them to
listen to you?'

'I'll try. There's nothing else for it. You stand at the
back of the room; they may throw something at me.'

'Oh, then, don't open the window! They can't break the
door. Some help will come.'

'They *will* break the door. You'd be as safe among wild
beasts as among those fellows if they get into the house.'

He threw up the sash, though Emma would not go from
his side. In the street below was a multitude which made
but one ravening monster; all its eyes were directed to the
upper storeys of this house. Mutimer looked to the right and
to the left. In the latter quarter he saw the signs of a struggle.
Straining his eyes through the dusk, he perceived a mounted
police-officer forcing his way through the throng; on either
side were visible the helmets of constables. He drew a deep
sigh of relief, for the efforts of the mob against the house door
could scarcely succeed unless they used more formidable weapons
for assault, and that would now be all but impossible.

He drew his head back into the room and looked at Emma
with a laugh of satisfaction.

'The police are making way! There's nothing to fear
now.'

'Come away from the window, then,' Emma urged. 'It is
useless to show yourself.'

'Let them see me, the blackguards! They're so tight
packed they haven't a hand among them to aim anything.'

As he spoke, he again leaned forward from the window-sill,
and stretched his arms towards the approaching rescuers. That
same instant a heavy fragment of stone, hurled with deadly
force and precision, struck him upon the temple. The violence

of the blow flung him back into the room; he dropped to his knees, threw out a hand as if to save himself, then sank face foremost upon the floor. Not a sound had escaped his lips.

Emma, with a low cry of horror, bent to him and put her arm about his body. Raising his head, she saw that, though his eyes were staring, they had no power of sight; on his lips were flecks of blood. She laid her cheeks to his lips, but could discern no breath; she tore apart the clothing from his breast, but her hand could not find his heart. Then she rushed for a pillow, placed it beneath his head, and began to bathe his face. Not all the great love which leaped like flame in her bosom could call the dead to life.

The yells which had greeted Mutimer's appearance at the window were followed by a steady roar, mingled with scornful laughter at his speedy retreat; only a few saw or suspected that he had been gravely hit by the missile. Then the tumult began to change its character; attention was drawn from the house to the advancing police, behind whom came a band of Mutimer's adherents, led by Redgrave. The latter were cheering; the hostile rabble met their cheers with defiant challenges. The police had now almost more than they could do to prevent a furious collision between the two bodies; but their numbers kept increasing, as detachments arrived one after another, and at length the house itself was firmly guarded, whilst the rioters on both sides were being put to flight. It was not a long street; the police cleared it completely and allowed no one to enter at either end.

It was all but dark when at length the door of Emma's room was opened and six or seven women appeared, searching for Mutimer. The landlady was foremost : she carried a lamp. It showed the dead man at full length on the floor, and Emma kneeling beside him, holding his hand. Near her were the two children, crying miserably. Emma appeared to have lost her voice; when the light flashed upon her eyes she covered them with one hand, with the other pointed downwards. The women broke into cries of fright and lamentation. They clustered around the prostrate form, examined it, demanded explanations. One at length sped down to the street and shortly returned with two policemen. A messenger was despatched for a doctor.

Emma did not move; she was not weeping, but paid no attention to any words addressed to her. The room was thronged with curious neighbours, there was a hubbub of talk.

When at length the medical man arrived, he cleared the chamber of all except Emma. After a brief examination of the body he said to her :

' You are his wife ? '

She, still kneeling, looked up into his face with pained astonishment.

' His wife ? Oh no ! I am a stranger.'

The doctor showed surprise.

' He was killed in your presence ? '

' He is dead—really dead ? ' she asked under her breath. And, as she spoke, she laid her hand upon his arm.

' He must have been killed instantaneously. Did the stone fall in the room ? Was it a stone ? '

No one had searched for the missile. The doctor discovered it not far away. Whilst he was weighing it in his hand there came a knock at the door. It was Mr. Westlake who entered. He came and looked at the dead man, then, introducing himself, spoke a few words with the doctor. Assured that there was no shadow of hope, he withdrew, having looked closely at Emma, who now stood a little apart, her hands held together before her.

The doctor departed a few moments later. He had examined the wound on the girl's face, and found that it was not serious. As he was going, Emma said to him :

' Will you tell them to keep away—all the people in the house ? '

' This is your own room ? '

' I live here with my sister.'

' I will ask them to respect your wish. The body must stay here for the present, though.'

' Oh yes, yes, I know.'

' Is your sister at home ? '

' She will be soon. Please tell them not to come here.'

She was alone again with the dead. It cost her great efforts of mind to convince herself that Mutimer really had breathed his last; it seemed to her but a moment since she heard him speak, heard him laugh ; was not a trace of the laugh even now discernible on his countenance ? How was it possible for life to vanish in this way ? She constantly touched him, spoke to him. It was incredible that he should not be able to hear her.

Her love for him was immeasurable. Bitterness she had long since overcome, and she had thought that love, too, was gone with it. She had deceived herself. Her heart, incredible as it may seem, had even known a kind of hope—how else could she have borne the life which fate laid upon her?—the hope that is one with love, that asks nothing of the reason, nor yields to reason's contumely? He had been smitten dead at the moment that she loved him dearest.

Her sister Kate came in. She had been spending the day with friends in another part of London. When just within the door she stopped and looked at the body nervously.

'Emma!' she said. 'Why don't you come downstairs? Mrs. Lake'll let us have her back room, and tea's waiting for you. I wonder how you *can* stay here.'

'I can't come. I want to be alone, Kate. Tell them not to come up.'

'But you can't stay here all night, child!'

'I can't talk. I wan't to be alone. Perhaps I'll come down before long.'

Kate withdrew and went to gossip with the people who were incessantly coming and going in the lower part of the house. The opening and shutting of the front door, the sound of voices, the hurrying feet upon the staircase, were audible enough to Emma. She heard, too, the crowds that kept passing along the street, their shouts, their laughter, the voices of the policemen bidding them move on. It was all a nightmare, from which she strove to awake.

At length she was able to weep. Gazing constantly at the dead face, she linked it at last with some far-off memory of tenderness, and that brought her tears. She held the cold hand against her heart and eased herself with passionate sobbing, with low wails, with loving utterance of his name. Thus it happened that she did not hear when someone knocked lightly at the door and entered. A shadow across the still features told her of another's presence. Starting back, she saw a lady from whose pale, beautiful face a veil had just been raised. The stranger, who was regarding her with tenderly compassionate eyes, said :

'I am Mrs. Mutimer.'

Emma rose to her feet and drew a little apart. Her face fell.

'They told me downstairs,' Adela pursued, 'that I should find Miss Vine in the room. Is your name Emma Vine?'

Emma asked herself whether this lady, his wife, could know anything of her story. It seemed so, from the tone of the question. She only replied :

'Yes, it is.'

Then she again ventured to look up at the woman whose beauty had made her life barren. There were no signs of tears on Adela's face; to Emma she seemed cold, though so grave and gentle. Adela gazed for a while at the dead man. She, too, felt as though it were all a dream. The spectacle of Emma's passionate grief had kept her emotion within her heart, perhaps had weakened it.

'You have yourself been hurt,' she said, turning again to the other.

Emma only shook her head. She suffered terribly from Adela's presence.

'I will go,' she said in a whisper.

'This is your room, I think?'

Yes.'

'May I stay here?'

'Of course—you must.'

Emma was moving towards the door.

'You wish to go?' Adela said, uttering the words involuntarily.

'Yes, I must.'

Adela, left alone, stood gazing at the dead face. She did not kneel by her husband, as Emma had done, but a terrible anguish came upon her as she gazed; she buried her face in her hands. Her feeling was more of horror at the crime that had been committed than of individual grief. Yet grief she knew. The last words her husband had spoken to her were good and worthy; in her memory they overcame all else. That parting when he left home had seemed to her like the beginning of a new life for him. Could not his faults be atoned for otherwise than by this ghastly end? She had no need to direct her thoughts to the good that was in him. Even as she had taken his part against his traducers, so she now was stirred in spirit against his murderers. She felt a solemn gladness in remembering that she had stood before that meeting in the Clerkenwell room and served him as far as it was in a woman's power to do. All her long sufferings were forgotten; this supreme calamity of death outweighed them all. His enemies had murdered him; would they not continue to assail his name? She resolved that his memory should be her care. That had nothing to do with love; simple justice demanded it. Justice and gratitude for the last words he had spoken to her.

She had as yet scarcely noticed the room in which she was.

At length she surveyed it; its poverty brought tears to her eyes. There had been a fire, but the last spark was dead. She began to feel cold.

Soon there was the sound of someone ascending the stairs, and Emma, after knocking, again entered. She carried a tray with tea-things, which she placed upon the table. Then, having glanced at the fireplace, she took from a cupboard wood and paper and was beginning to make a fire when Adela stopped her, saying:

'You must not do that for me. I will light the fire myself, if you will let me.'

Emma looked up in surprise.

'It is kind of you to bring me the tea,' Adela continued. 'But let me do the rest.'

'If you wish to—yes,' the other replied, without understanding the thought which prompted Adela. She carefully held herself from glancing towards the dead man, and moved away.

Adela approached her.

'Have you a room for the night?'

'Yes, thank you.'

'Will you—will you take my hand before you leave me?'

She held it forth; Emma, with eyes turned to the ground, gave her own.

'Look at me,' Adela said, under her breath.

Their eyes met, and at last Emma understood. In that grave, noble gaze was far more than sympathy and tenderness; it was a look that besought pardon.

'May I come to you in the night to see if you need anything?' Emma asked.

'I shall need nothing. Come only if you can't sleep.'

Adela lit the fire and began her night's watching.

CHAPTER XXXVI.

A DEEP breath of country air. It is springtime, and the valley of Wanley is bursting into green and flowery life, peacefully glad as if the foot of Demos had never come that way. Incredible that the fume of furnaces ever desecrated that fleece-sown sky of tenderest blue, that hammers clanged and engines roared

where now the thrush utters his song so joyously. Hubert
Eldon has been as good as his word. In all the valley no
trace is left of what was called New Wanley. Once more we
can climb to the top of Stanbury Hill and enjoy the sense of
remoteness and security when we see that dark patch on the
horizon, the cloud that hangs over Belwick.

Hubert and the vicar of Wanley stood there together one
morning in late April, more than a year after the death of
Richard Mutimer. Generally there was a strong breeze on this
point, but to-day the west was breathing its gentlest, warm
upon the cheek.

'Well, it has gone,' Hubert said. 'May will have free
playing-ground.'

'In one sense,' replied the vicar, 'I fear it will never be
gone. Its influence on the life of the people in Wanley and in
some of the farms about has been graver than you imagine.
I find discontent where it was formerly unknown. The
typical case is that lad of Bolton's. They wanted him sadly
at home; by this time he would have been helping his unfortunate father. Instead of that he's the revolutionary oracle of
Belwick pothouses, and appears on an average once a fortnight
before the magistrates for being drunk and disorderly.'

'Yes, the march of progress has been hastened a little,
doubtless,' said Hubert. 'I have to content myself with the
grass and the trees. Well, I have done all I could, now other
people must enjoy the results. Ah, look! there is a van of
the Edgeworth's furniture coming to the Manor. They are
happy people! Something like an ideal married couple, and
with nothing to do but to wander about the valley and enjoy
themselves.'

'I am rather surprised you gave them so long a lease,'
remarked Mr. Wyvern.

'Why not? I shall never live here again. As long as I
had work to do it was all right; but to continue to live in that
house was impossible. And in twenty years it would be no
less impossible. I should fall into a monomania, and one of a
very loathsome kind.'

Mr. Wyvern pondered. They walked on a few paces before
Hubert again spoke.

'There was a letter from her in the "Belwick Chronicle"
yesterday morning. Something on the placard in Agworth
station caused me to buy a copy. The Tory paper, it seems,
had a leader a day or two ago on Socialism, and took occasion

to sneer at Mutimer, not by name, but in an unmistakable way—the old scandal of course. She wrote a letter to the editor, and he courteously paid no attention to it. So she wrote to the 'Chronicle.' They print her in large type, and devote a leader to the subject—party capital, of course.'

He ceased on a bitter tone, then, before his companion could reply, added violently:

'It is hideous to see her name in such places!'

'Let us speak freely of this,' returned Mr. Wyvern. 'You seem to me to be very unjust. Your personal feeling makes you less acute in judging than I should have expected. Surely her behaviour is very admirable.'

'Oh, I am not unjust in that sense. I have never refused to believe in his innocence technically.'

'Excuse me, that has nothing to do with the matter. All we have to look at is this. She is herself convinced of his innocence, and therefore makes it her supreme duty to defend his memory. It appears to me that she acts altogether nobly. In spite of all the evidence that was brought on his side, the dastardly spirit of politics has persisted in making Mutimer a sort of historical character, a type of the hypocritical demagogue, to be cited whenever occasion offers. Would it be possible to attach a more evil significance to a man's name than that which Mutimer bears, and will continue to bear, among certain sections of writing and speechifying vermin? It is a miserable destiny. If every man who achieves notoriety paid for his faults in this way, what sort of reputations would history consist of? I won't say that it isn't a good thing, speaking generally, but in the individual case it is terribly hard. Would you have his widow keep silence? That would be the easier thing to do, be sure of it—for *her*, a thousand times the easier. I regard her as the one entirely noble woman it has been my lot to know. And if you thought calmly you could not speak of her with such impatience.'

Hubert kept silence for a moment.

'It is all true. Of course it only means that I am savagely jealous. But I cannot—upon my life I cannot—understand her having given her love to such a man as that!'

Mr. Wyvern seemed to regard the landscape. There was a sad smile on his countenance.

'Let there be an end of it,' Hubert resumed. 'I didn't mean to say anything to you about the letter. Now, we'll talk of other things. Well, I am going to have a summer among

the German galleries; perhaps I shall find peace there. You
have let your son know that I am coming?'

The vicar nodded. They continued their walk along the
top of the hill. Presently Mr. Wyvern stopped and faced his
companion.

'Are you serious in what you said just now? I mean
about her love for Mutimer?'

'Serious? Of course I am. Why should you ask such a
question?'

'Because I find it difficult to distinguish between the things
a young man says in jealous pique and the real belief he enter-
tains when he is not throwing savage words about. You have
convinced yourself that she loved her husband in the true
sense of the word?'

'The conviction was forced upon me. Why did she marry
him at all? What led her to give herself, heart and soul, to
Socialism, she who under ordinary circumstances would have
shrunk from that and all other *isms?* Why should she make
it a special entreaty to me to pursue her husband's work?
The zeal for his memory is nothing unanticipated; it issues
naturally from her former state of mind.'

'Your vehemence,' replied the vicar, smiling, 'is sufficient
proof that you don't think it impossible for all these questions
to be answered in another sense. I can't pretend to have read
the facts of her life infallibly, but suppose I venture a hint or
two, just to give you matter for thought. Why she married
him I cannot wholly explain to myself, but remember that she
took that step very shortly after being brought to believe that
you, my good friend, were utterly unworthy of any true
woman's devotion. Remember, too, her brother's influence,
and—well, her mother's. Now, on the evening before she
accepted Mutimer, she called at the Vicarage alone. Unfortunately I was away—was walking with you, in fact. What
she desired to say to me I can only conjecture; but it is not
impossible that she was driven by the common impulse which
sends young girls to their pastor when they are in grievous
trouble and without other friends.'

'Why did you never tell me of that?' cried Hubert.

'Because it would have been useless, and, to tell you the
truth, I felt I was in an awkward position, not far from acting
indiscreetly. I did go to see her the next morning, but only
saw her mother, and heard of the engagement. Adela never
spoke to me of her visit.'

'But she may have come for quite other reasons. Her subsequent behaviour remains.'

'Certainly. Here again I may be altogether wrong, but it seems to me that to a woman of her character there was only one course open. Having become his wife, it behoved her to be loyal, and especially—remember this—it behoved her to put her position beyond doubt in the eyes of others, in the eyes of one, it may be, beyond all. Does that throw no light on your meeting with her in the wood, of which you make so much?'

Hubert's countenance shone, but only for an instant.

'Ingenious,' he replied, good-humouredly.

'Possibly no more,' Mr. Wyvern rejoined. 'Take it as a fanciful sketch of how a woman's life *might* be ordered. Such a life would not lack its dignity.'

Neither spoke for a while.

'You will call on Mrs. Westlake as you pass through London?' Mr. Wyvern next inquired.

'Mrs. Westlake?' the other repeated absently. 'Yes, I dare say I shall see her.'

'Do, by all means.'

They began to descend the hill.

The Walthams no longer lived in Wanley. A year ago the necessities of Alfred Waltham's affairs had led to a change; he and his wife and their two children, together with Mrs. Waltham the dowager, removed to what the auctioneers call a commodious residence on the outskirts of Belwick. Alfred remarked that it was as well not to be so far from civilisation; he pointed out, too, that it was time for him to have an eye to civic dignities, if only a place on the Board of Guardians to begin with. Our friend was not quite so uncompromising in his political and social opinions as formerly. His wife observed that he ceased to subscribe to Socialist papers, and took in a daily of orthodox Liberal tendencies—that is to say, an organ of capitalism. Letty rejoiced at the change, but knew her husband far too well to make any remark upon it.

To their house, about three months after her husband's death, came Adela. The intermediate time she had passed with Stella. All were very glad to have her at Belwick—Letty, in particular, who, though a matron with two bouncing boys, still sat at Adela's feet and deemed her the model of womanhood. Adela was not so sad as they had feared to find her. She kept a great deal to her own room, but was always engaged in study, and seemed to find peace in that way. She

H H

was silent in her habits, scarcely ever joining in general conversation ; but when Letty could steal an hour from household
duties and go to Adela's room she was always sure of hearing
wise and tender words in which her heart delighted. Her
pride in Adela was boundless. On the day when the latter
first attired herself in modified mourning, Letty, walking with
her in the garden, could not refrain from saying how Adela's
dress became her.

' You are more beautiful every day, dear,' she added, in
spite of a tremor which almost checked her in uttering a compliment which her sister might think too frivolous.

But Adela blushed, one would have thought it was with
pleasure. Sadness, however, followed, and Letty wondered
whether the beautiful face was destined to wear its pallor
always.

On this same spring morning, when Hubert Eldon was
taking leave of Wanley, Mrs. Waltham and Letty were talking of a visit Adela was about to pay to Stella in London.
They spoke also of a visitor of their own, or, perhaps, rather of
Adela's, who had been in the house for a fortnight and would
return to London on the morrow. This was Alice Mutimer—
no longer to be called Mrs. Rodman. Alice had lived with
her mother in Wilton Square since her recovery from the
illness which for a long time had kept her in ignorance of the
double calamity fallen upon her. It was Adela who at length
told her that she had no husband, and that her brother
Richard was dead. Neither disclosure affected her gravely.
The months of mental desolation followed by physical collapse
seemed to have exhausted her powers of suffering. For several
days she kept to herself and cried a good deal, but she exhibited no bitter grief. It soon became evident that she
thought but little of the man who had so grossly wronged her ;
he was quite gone from her heart. Even when she was summoned to give evidence against him in court, she did it without
much reluctance, yet also without revengeful feeling ; her state
was one of enfeebled vitality, she was like a child in all the
concerns of life. Rodman went into penal servitude, but it
did not distress her, and she never again uttered his name.

Adela thought it would be a kindness to invite her to
Belwick, and Alice at once accepted the invitation. Yet she
was not at her ease in the house. She appeared to have for-
given Adela, overcome by the latter's goodness, but her nature
was not of the kind to grow in liberal feeling. Mrs. Waltham

the elder she avoided as much as possible. Perhaps Letty best succeeded in conciliating her, for Letty was homely and had the children to help her.

'I wish I had a child,' Alice said one day when she sat alone with Letty, and assisted in nursery duties. But at once her cheeks coloured. 'I suppose you're ashamed of me for saying that. I'm not even a married woman.'

Letty replied, as she well knew how to, very gently and with comfort.

'I wonder where she goes to when she sets off by herself,' said Mrs. Waltham this morning. 'She seems to object to walk with any of us.'

'She always comes back in better spirits,' said Letty. 'I think the change is doing her good.'

'But she won't be sorry to leave us, my dear, I can see that. To be sure it was like Adela to think of having her here, but I scarcely think it would be advisable for the visit to be repeated. She is not at home with us. And how can it be expected? It's in her blood, of course; she belongs so distinctly to an inferior class.'

'I am so very sorry for her,' Letty replied. 'What dreadful things she has gone through!'

'Dreadful, indeed, my dear; but after all such things don't happen to ladies. We must remember that. It isn't as if you or Adela had suffered in that way. That, of course, would be shocking beyond all words. I can't think that persons of her class have quite the same feelings.'

'Oh, mother!' Letty protested. And she added, less seriously, 'You mustn't let Alfred hear you say such a thing as that.'

'I'm glad to say,' replied Mrs. Waltham, 'that Alfred has grown much more sensible in his views of late.'

Adela entered the room. Letty was not wrong in saying that she grew more beautiful. Life had few joys for her, save intellectual, but you saw on her countenance the light of freedom. In her manner there was an unconscious dignity which made her position in the house one of recognised superiority; even her mother seldom ventured to chat without reserve in her presence. Alfred drew up in the midst of a tirade if she but seemed about to speak. Yet it was happiness to live with her; where she moved there breathed an air of purity and sweetness.

She asked if Alice had returned from her walk. Receiving a reply in the negative, she went out into the garden,

'Adela looks happy to-day,' said Letty. 'That article in the paper has pleased her very much.'

'I really hope she won't do such a thing again,' remarked Mrs. Waltham, with dignified disapproval. 'It seems very unlady-like to write letters to the newspapers.'

'But it was brave of her.'

'To be sure, we must not judge her as we should ordinary people. Still, I am not sure that she is always right. I shall never allow that she did right in paying back that money to those wretches in London. I am sure she wanted it far more than they did. The bloodthirsty creatures!'

Letty shuddered, but would not abandon defence of Adela.

'Still it was very honourable of her, mother. She understands those things better than we can.'

'Perhaps so, my dear,' said Mrs. Waltham, meaning that her own opinion was not likely to be inferior in justice to that of anyone else.

Adela had been in the garden for a few minutes when she saw Alice coming towards her. The poor Princess had a bright look, as if some joyful news had just come to her. Adela met her with a friendly smile.

'There is someone you used to know,' Alice said, speaking with embarrassment, and pointing towards the road. 'You remember Mr. Keene? I met him. He says he wrote that in the "Chronicle." He would like to speak to you if you'll let him.'

'I shall be glad to,' Adela replied, with a look of curiosity.

They walked to the garden gate. Mr. Keene was just outside; Alice beckoned to him to enter. His appearance was a great improvement on the old days; he had grown a beard, and in his eye you saw the responsible editor. Altogether he seemed to have gained in moral solidity. None the less, his manner of approaching Adela, hat in hand, awoke reminiscences of the footlights.

'It is a great pleasure to me to see you, Mrs. Mutimer. I trust that my few comments on your admirable letter were of a nature to afford you satisfaction.'

'Thank you very much, Mr. Keene,' Adela replied. 'You wrote very kindly.'

'I am amply rewarded,' he said, bowing low. 'And now that I have had my desire, permit me to hasten away. My duty calls me into the town.'

He again bowed low to Adela, smiled a farewell to Alice, and departed.

The two walked together in the garden. Adela turned to her companion.

'I think you knew Mr. Keene a long time ago?'

'Yes, a long time. He once asked me to marry him.'

Adela replied only with a look.

'And he's asked me again this morning,' Alice pursued, breaking off a leaf from an elder bush.

'And you——?'

'I didn't refuse him this time,' Alice replied with confidence.

'I am very glad, very glad. He has been faithful to you so long that I am sure he will make you happy.'

Alice no longer concealed her joy. It was almost exultation. Natural enough under the circumstances, poor, disinherited Princess! Once more she felt able to face people; once more she would have a name. She began to talk eagerly.

'Of course I shall just go back to tell mother, but we are going to be married in three weeks. He has already decided upon a house; we went to see it this morning. I didn't like to tell you, but I met him for the first time a week ago—quite by chance.'

'I'm afraid your mother will be lonely,' Adela said.

'Not she! She'd far rather live alone than go anywhere else. And now I shall be able to send her money. It isn't fair for you to have to find everything.'

'I have wanted to ask you,' Adela said presently, 'do you ever hear of Harry?'

Alice shook her head.

'The less we hear the better,' she replied. 'He's gone to the bad, and there's no help for it.'

It was true; unfortunate victim of prosperity.

Next morning Adela and Alice travelled to town together. The former did not go to Wilton Square. On the occasion of Richard's death she had met Mrs. Mutimer, but the interview had been an extremely difficult one, in spite of the old woman's endeavour to be courteous. Adela felt herself to be an object of insuperable prejudice. Once again she was bidden sound the depth of the gulf which lies between the educated and the uneducated. The old woman would not give her hand, but made an old-fashioned curtsey, which Adela felt to be half ironical. In speaking of her son she was hard. Pride would not allow her to exhibit the least symptom of the anguish which wrung her heart. She refused to accept any share of the income which was continued to her son's widow under the Wanley will. Alice, however, had felt no scruple in taking the half which Adela offered her, and by paying her mother for board and lodgings she supplemented the income derived from letting as much of the house as possible.

Once more under the roof of her dearest friend, Adela was less preoccupied with the sad past which afflicted her mind with the stress of a duty ever harder to perform. After an hour passed with Stella she could breathe freely the atmosphere of beauty and love. Elsewhere she too often suffered from a sense of self-reproach; between her and the book in which she tried to lose herself there would come importunate visions of woe, of starved faces, of fierce eyes. The comfort she enjoyed, the affection and respect with which she was surrounded, were often burdensome to her conscience. In Stella's presence all that vanished; listening to Stella's voice she could lay firm hold on the truth that there is a work in the cause of humanity other than that which goes on so clamorously in lecture-halls and at street corners, other than that which is silently performed by faithful hearts and hands in dens of misery and amid the horrors of the lazar-house; the work of those whose soul is taken captive of loveliness, who pursue the spiritual ideal apart from the world's tumult, and, ever ready to minister in gentle offices, know that they serve best when nearest home. She was far from spiritual arrogance; her natural mood was a profound humility; she deemed herself rather below than above the active toilers, whose sweat was sacred; but life had declared that such toil was not for her, and from Stella she derived the support which enabled her to pursue her path in peace—a path not one with Stella's. Before that high-throned poet-soul Adela bent in humble reverence. Between Stella and those toilers, however noble and devoted, there could be no question of comparison. She was of those elect whose part it is to inspire faith and hope, of those highest but for whom the world would fall into apathy or lose itself among subordinate motives. Stella never spoke of herself; Adela could not know whether she had ever stood at the severance of ways and made deliberate choice. Probably not, for on her brow was visible to all eyes the seal of election; how could she ever have doubted the leading of that spirit that used her lips for utterance?

On the morning after her arrival in London Adela took a long journey by herself to the far East End. Going by omnibus it seemed to her that she was never to reach that street off Bow Road which she had occasion to visit. But at last the conductor bade her descend, and gave her a brief direction. The thoroughfare she sought was poor but not squalid; she saw with pleasure that the house of which she had the number in mind was, if anything, cleaner and more homelike in appearance than its neighbours. A woman replied to her knock.'

She asked if Miss Vine was at home.

'Yes, mum; she's at 'ome. Shall I tell her, or will you go up?'

'I will go up, thank you. Which room is it?'

'Second floor front you'll find her.'

Adela ascended. Standing at the door she heard the hum of a sewing-machine. It made her heart sink, so clearly did it speak of incessant monotonous labour.

She knocked loudly. The machine did not stop, but she was bidden to enter.

Emma was at work, one of her sister's children sitting by her, writing on a slate. She had expected the appearance of the landlady; seeing who the visitor was, she let her hands fall abruptly; an expression of pain passed over her features.

Adela went up to her and kissed her forehead, then exchanged a few words with the child. Emma placed a chair for her, but without speaking. The room was much like the other in which the sisters had lived, save that it had a brighter outlook. There were the two beds and the table covered with work.

'Do you find it better here?' Adela began by asking.

'Yes, it is better,' Emma replied quietly. 'We manage to get a good deal of work, and it isn't badly paid.'

The voice was not uncheerful; it had that serenity which comes of duties honestly performed and a life tolerably free from sordid anxiety. More than that could not be said of Emma's existence. But, such as it was, it depended entirely upon her own effort. Adela, on the evening when she first met her in the room where Mutimer lay dead, had read clearly Emma's character; she knew that, though it was one of her strongest desires to lighten the burden of this so sorely tried woman, direct aid was not to be dreamt of. She had taken counsel with Stella, Stella with her husband. After much vain seeking they discovered an opportunity of work in this part of the East End. Mr. Westlake made it known to Emma; she acknowledged that it would be better than the over-swarmed neighbourhood in which she was living, and took the advice gratefully. She had hopes, too, that Kate might be got away from her evil companions. And indeed the change had not been without its effect on Mrs. Clay; she worked more steadily, and gave more attention to her children.

'She's just gone with the eldest to the hospital,' Emma replied to a question of Adela's. 'He's got something the matter with his eyes. And this one isn't at all well. He ought to be at school, only he's had such a dreadful cough we're afraid to send him out just yet. They're neither of them strong, I'm afraid.'

'And you—isn't your health better since you have lived here?' Adela asked.

'I think so. But I never ail much as long as I have plenty of work to do.'

'I am staying with a friend in London,' Adela said after a pause. 'I thought I might come to see you. I hoped you would still be in the same house.'

'Yes, we are very comfortable, very,' Emma replied. 'I hope we shan't need to move for a long time; I'm sure we couldn't do better.'

She added, without raising her eyes:

'Thank you for coming.'

Adela knew that constraint between them was inevitable; it was enough that Emma spoke with good-will.

'If ever you should have to move,' she said, 'will you let me know where you go? I have written on this paper the address of my mother's house; I live with her. Will you show me so much friendship?'

Emma glanced at her, and saw a look which recalled to her something she had seen in those eyes before.

'I will write and tell you if we do move,' she said.

Adela went away with a heart not altogether sad; it was rather as though she had been hearing solemn music, which stirred her soul even while it touched upon the source of tears.

It was only on certain days that Stella sat to receive during visitors' hours. To-day was not one of them; consequently when Hubert Eldon called, about half-past four, the servant came up to the drawing-room to ask if Mrs. Westlake would be at home to him. Adela was in the room; at the mention of the name she rose.

'I must write a letter before dinner,' she said. 'I will go and get it done whilst you are engaged.'

'Won't you stay? Do stay!'

'I had much rather not. I don't feel able to talk with anyone just now.'

She left the room without meeting Stella's look. The latter said she would receive Mr. Eldon.

Adela went to the exquisitely furnished little boudoir, which was now always called *her* room, and sat down with the resolve to write to her mother on the subjects she had in mind. But her strength of will proved unequal to the task; after writing a word or two with shaking hand she laid down her pen and rested her face upon her hands. A minute or two ago she had been untroubled by a thought which concerned herself; now her blood was hot, and all her being moved at the impulse of a passionate desire. She had never known such a rebellion of her life. In her ears there rang the word 'Free! free!' She was free, and the man whom she loved with the love of years, with the first love of maidenhood and the confirmed love of maturity, was but a few yards from her—it might be, had even come here on purpose to meet her.

Oh, why was he not poor! Had he but been some struggling artist, scarce able to support the woman of his choice, how would she have stood before him and let him read the tenderness on her face! Hubert's wealth was doubly hateful.

She started from her chair, with difficulty suppressing a cry. Someone had knocked at her door. Perhaps he was already gone; she could not say how long she had sat here. It was Stella.

'Mr. Eldon wishes to speak to you, dear.'

She caught her friend's hand and almost crushed it between her own.

'I can't see him! Stella, I dare not see him!'

'But he says it is purely a matter of business he wishes to speak of,' said Stella with a pained voice.

Adela sank her head in anguish of shame. Stella put an arm about her, fearing she would fall. But in an instant pride had sprung up; Adela freed herself, now deadly pale.

'I will go.'

She moved mechanically, spoke mechanically the conventional words when she found that somehow she was in his presence.

'I hope I do not disturb you,' Hubert said with equal self-control. 'I was about to address a letter to you before I left England. I did not know that you were here. It is better, perhaps, to do my business by word of mouth, if you will allow me.'

He was very courteous, but she could not distinguish a note in his voice that meant more than courtesy. She prayed him to be seated, and herself took a place on an ottoman. She was able very calmly to regard his face. He leaned forward with his hands together and spoke with his eyes on her.

'It is with regard to the legacy which is due to you under Mr. Mutimer's will. You will remember that, as trustee, I have it in my power to make over to you the capital sum which produces the annuity, if there should be reason for doing so. I am about to leave England, perhaps for some few years; I have let the Manor to some friends of mine on a twenty years' lease. I think I should like to transfer the money to you before I go. It is simpler, better. Will you let me do that, Mrs. Mutimer?'

His words chilled her. His voice seemed harder as he proceeded; it had the ring of metal, of hard cash counted down.

What was his object? He wished to have done with her, to utterly abolish all relations between them. It might well be that he was about to marry, and someone abroad, someone who would not care to live in an English country house. Why otherwise should he have let the Manor for so long a period? She felt as she had done long ago, when she heard of that other foreign woman. Cold as ice; not a spark of love in all her being.

She replied:

'Thank you. If you are willing to make that change, perhaps it will be best.'

Hubert, his eyes still on her, imagined he saw pleasure in her face. She might have a project for the use of the money, some Socialist scheme, something perhaps to preserve the memory of her husband. He rose.

'In that case I will have a deed prepared at once, and you shall be informed when it is ready for signature.'

He said to himself that she could not forgive his refusal of her request that day in the wood.

They shook hands, Adela saying:

'You are still busy with art?'

'In my dilettante way,' he replied smiling.

Adela returned to her room, and there remained till the

hour of dinner. At the meal she was her ordinary self. Afterwards Mr. Westlake asked her to read in proof an article about to appear in the 'Beacon'; she did so, and commented upon it with a clear mind. In the course of the evening she told her friends of the arrangement between Mr. Eldon and herself.

Two days later she had to call at the solicitor's office to sign the deed of release. Incidentally she learnt that Hubert was leaving England the same evening.

Had she been at home, these days would have been spent in solitude. For the first time she suffered in Stella's company. All allusion to Hubert was avoided between them. Sometimes she could hardly play her part; sickness of the soul wasted her.

It was morning; he was now on the Continent, perhaps already talking with someone he loved.

She was shamed to have so deceived herself; she had feared him, because she believed he loved her, and that by sympathy he might see into her heart. Had it been so, he could not have gone from her in this way. Forgetting her own pride, her own power of dissimulation, she did not believe it possible for him so to disguise tenderness. She would listen to no argument of hope, but crushed her heart with perverse cruelty.

The annual payment of money had been a link between him and her; when she signed the deed releasing him, the cold sweat stood on her forehead.

She would reason. Of what excellence was he possessed that her life should so abandon itself at his feet? In what had he proved himself generous or capable of the virtues that subdue? Such reasoning led to self-mockery. She was no longer the girl who questioned her heart as to the significance of the vows required in the marriage service; in looking back upon those struggles she could have wept for pity. Love would submit to no analysis; it was of her life; as easy to account for the power of thought. Her soul was bare to her and all its needs. There was no refuge in ascetic resolve, in the self-deceit of spiritual enthusiasm. She could say to herself: You are free to love him; then love and be satisfied. Could she, when a-hungered, look on food, and bid her hunger be appeased by the act of sight?

Thus long she had held up, but despair was closing in upon her, and an anguish worse than death. She must leave this house and go where she might surrender herself to misery. There was no friend whose comfort could be other than torment and bitter vanity; such woe as hers only time and weariness could aid.

She was rising with the firm purpose of taking leave of Stella when a servant came to her door, announcing that Mr. Eldon desired to see her.

She was incredulous, required the servant to repeat the name. Mr. Eldon was in the drawing-room and desired to see her.

There must have been some error, some oversight in the legal business. Oh, it was inhuman to torture her in this way! Careless of what her countenance might indicate, she hastened to the drawing-room. She could feign no longer. Let him think what he would, so that he spoke briefly and released her.

But as soon as she entered the room she knew that he had not come to talk of business. He was pale and agitated. As he did not speak at once she said:

'I thought you were gone. I thought you left England last night.'

'I meant to do so, but found it impossible. I could not go till I had seen you once more.'

'What more have you to say to me?'

She knew that she was speaking recklessly, without a thought for dignity. Her question sounded as if it had been extorted from her by pain.

'That if I go away from you now and finally, I go without a hope to support my life. You are everything to me. You are offended; you shrink from me. It is what I expected. Years ago, when I loved you without knowing what my love really meant, I flung away every chance in a moment of boyish madness. When I should have consecrated every thought to the hope of winning you, I made myself contemptible in your eyes—worse, I made you loathe me. When it was too late I understood what I had done. Then I loved you as a man loves the one woman whom he supremely reverences, as I love you, and, I believe, shall always love you. I could not go without saying this to you. I am happier in speaking the words than I ever remember to have been in my life before.'

Adela's bosom heaved, but excess of joy seemed to give her power to deal lightly with the gift that was offered her.

'Why did you not say this the last time?' she asked. One would have said, from her tone, that it was a question of the merest curiosity. She did not realise the words that passed her lips.

'Because the distance between us seemed too great. I began to speak of that money in the thought that it might lead me on. It had the opposite effect. You showed me how cold you could be. It is natural enough. Perhaps your sympathies are too entirely remote; and yet not long ago you talked with me as if your interests could be much the same as mine. I can understand that you suppress that side of your nature. You think me useless in the world. And indeed my life has but one purpose, which is a vain one. I can do nothing but feed my love for you. You have convictions and purposes; you feel that they are opposed to mine. All that is of the intellect; I only live in my passion. We are different and apart.'

'Why do you say that, as if you were glad of it?'

'Glad? I speak the words that come to my tongue. I say aloud to you what I have been repeating again and again to myself. It is mere despair.'

She drew one step nearer to him.

'You disregard those differences which you say are only of the intellect, and still love me. Can I not do the same? There *was* a distance between us, and my ends were other than yours. That is the past; the present is mine to make myself what you would have me. I have no law but your desire—so much I love you.'

How easily said after all! And when he searched her face with eyes on fire with their joy, when he drew her to his heart in passionate triumph, the untruth of years fell from her like a veil, and she had achieved her womanhood.

THE END.

PRINTED BY
SPOTTISWOODE AND CO., NEW-STREET SQUARE
LONDON

Notes to the Text

1. p. 12, l.24.
A man's a man. From Robert Burns, *For a' that and a' that.*

2. p. 17, l.4.
Nisi dominus, or *Nisi dominus frustra*: Except the Lord keep the city the watchman waketh but in vain. *Psalms*, CXXVII. I (Vulgate) abridged. Motto of the City of Edinburgh.

3. p. 25, ch. III, l.4.
Gissing had lived not far from Wilton Square, at 5 Hanover Street, Islington, from late 1879 to February 1881. His windows looked over the Regent's Canal.

4. p. 25, ch. III, l.14.
Maladetta e sventurata fossa: accursed and ill-fated ditch. From Dante's *Divine Comedy,* Purgatory, Canto XIV, 1.51.

5. p. 27.
Gissing makes here a clever and historically accurate use of Chartism (1837–1848) as a background. His own father, as a young man, had responded sympathetically to it.

6. p. 42, l.22.
The names mentioned here (Malthus, Owen, de Volney, Paine and Voltaire) are interesting in so far as they are symbolical of various political, social and economic issues which informed radical thought in the early nineteenth century. Gissing had Owen's New Lanark in mind when describing New Wanley.

7. p. 42, l.40.
The death of Tennyson gave Gissing an opportunity to express at some length his candid opinion on poetry and the people. See his letter to Edmund Gosse on this subject in Gosse's *Questions at Issue* (1893), pp. 325–31.

8. p. 57, l.29.
Commonwealth Hall was a meeting place of Socialists in London. In its review of *Demos*, the Conservative *Scottish Review* remarked significantly after praising the book: 'We only hope the writer may

never find himself recognized in "Commonwealth Hall", or any other seminary for the diffusion of the doctrine of universal brotherhood.' (April 1886, pp. 328–30).

9. p. 61, 1.1
'By the waters of Babylon we sat down and wept: when we remembered thee, O Sion.' *Psalms*, CXXXVII. I. 'Get thee up into the top of Pisgah, and lift up thine eyes westward.' *Deuteronomy*, III, 27.

10. p. 62, 1.24.
I must speak in passion, and I will do it in King Cambyses' vein.' *Henry IV*, Part I, II, iv, 430.

11. p. 62, 1.25.
The pamper'd jades of Asia. From *Henry IV*, Part II, II, iv, 177 or *Tamburlaine*, Part II, 1.3980.

12. p. 65, 1.15.
Aposiopesis: sudden breaking-off in speech. Gissing also alludes humorously to this device in *The Town Traveller*, ch. III: 'It was a habit of hers to imply a weighty opinion by suddenly breaking off; a form of speech known to the grammarians by a name which would have astonished Mrs. Clover.'

13. p. 68, 1.3.
Infinite ugliness in a little space. Doubtless an echo from 'infinite riches in a little room' (Marlowe, *The Jew of Malta*, 1.72), which Gissing noted down in his *Commonplace Book* (1962) p. 28.

14. p. 79, 1.12.
The day must perish. An echo from *Job*, iii, 3. 'Let the day perish wherein I was born.'

15. p. 91, 1.25.
On Bunyan's *Pilgrim's Progress* (1678), see Gissing's *Commonplace Book*, p. 52.

16. p. 97, 1.35.
Burial Clubs were one of the main forms of self-help among the working classes. They are mentioned in *The Nether World* (ch. XXI), in which Gissing describes an incident of all too common occurrence in actual life, the mismanagement of funds and the defection of the secretary with the money. Mutimer's own disastrous venture in the latter part of *Demos* offers another variation on the same theme.

17. p. 100, 1.23.
Revivalism had its roots in eighteenth-century pietism, with its emphasis upon Christianity as an inner experience and way of life. Gissing made fun of revivalists in Ch. V of *Denzil Quarrier*.

18. p. 102, 1.3.
He was a bold, bad man. From *Henry VIII,* II, ii, 44 or Spenser, *The Faerie Queene,* Book I, Canto I, xxxvii.

19. p. 105, 1.4.
The Royal School of Mines was founded by the Prince Consort in 1851.

20. p. 110, 1.20.
See *Mudie's Circulating Library and The Victorian Novel* by Guinevere L. Griest (Illinois and Newton Abbot, 1971).

21. p. 112, 1.3.
Karl Marx, died in 1883, three years before the publication of *Demos.*

22. p. 139, 1.3.
Ruined choirs is from Shakespeare's *Sonnets,* 73.

23. p. 142, 1.23.
Samuel Johnson (1709—84) was very fond of retorting in this way. For instance, 'Why, Sir, most schemes of political improvement are very laughable things,' or, 'No, Sir, when a man is tired of London, he is tired of life.' Gissing quotes a retort of this kind in *The Private Papers of Henry Ryecroft,* Spring V.

24. p. 149, 1.1.
Polycrates was a tyrant of Samos, celebrated for his good luck, who acquired great riches by his piratical enterprises.

25. p. 151, 1.38.
Phaedrus: one of Plato's Dialogues in which Socrates conducts the discussion.

26. p. 159, 1.26.
The parable of the talents. Matthew, XXV, 14—30.

27. p. 159, 1.41.
Scarlet woman. 'And the woman was arrayed in purple and scarlet colour.' *Revelation,* XVII, 4.

28. p. 169, 1.36.
Vita Nuova by Dante Alighieri (1265—1321), relates his love for Beatrice, who died in 1290. Allusions to Dante occur in all Gissing's novels up to *New Grub Street* (1891) (except *Isabel Clarendon* and *The Nether World*), as well as in *The Crown of Life* and *Henry Ryecroft.*

29. p. 171, 1.7.
The Christian Year, a collection of sacred poems by Keble (1792—1866), published in 1827.

30. p. 181, 1.9.
Mrs. Felicia Dorothea Hemans (1793—1835), once a highly popular

writer, author of 'Casabianca', 'The Landing of the Pilgrim Fathers', 'England's Dead' and 'The Better Land.' Her fame was comparable to that of Longfellow (1807—82).

31. p. 205, 1.21.
Hubert Eldon's plan to study art in Rome is a striking anticipation of the development of Gissing's life in 1888—89. See his correspondence with his family and his friend Eduard Bertz.

32. p. 211, 1.6.
'Hope deferred maketh the heart sick.' *Proverbs*, XIII, 12.

33. p. 226, 1.30.
Blood and iron (Blut und Eisen). A quotation from Bismarck's speech in the Prussian House of Deputies, on 28 January 1886: 'Place in the hands of the King of Prussia the strongest possible military power, then he will be able to carry out the policy you wish; this policy cannot succeed through speeches, and shooting-matches, and songs; it can only be carried out through blood and iron.' It is interesting to notice that Gissing inserted this phrase when revising his manuscript, as is testified by his letters. On 17 January 1886 he wrote to his sister Ellen that he was 'near the end of the first quarter of the second volume', which was to have twelve chapters. When Bismarck delivered his speech, Gissing was definitely well ahead of the first manuscript page of Ch. V of Volume II in which the quotation appears, and on 31 January he predicted he would reach the end of Volume II in three days. The manuscript, however, bears no trace of alteration of this passage. Gissing would frequently rewrite whole pages that the printers might work more comfortably.

34. p. 238, 11. 41—43.
Perhaps an echo from Macaulay's essay on Moore's *Life of Lord Byron* (June 1830): 'We know no spectacle so ridiculous as the British public in one of its periodical fits of morality.'

35. p. 252, 1.1.
Albrecht Schaeffle (1831—1904), a professor of political economy at Tubingen in 1860 and at the University of Vienna in 1868; published a famous and widely translated pamphlet, *Die Quintessenz des Sozialismus* (1875), casually mentioned here.

36. p. 254, 1.35.
Charles Edward Mudie (1818—90), founder of the principal (morally-censorious) circulating library, whose heyday coincided with that of the three-volume novel.

37. p. 264, 11. 23—13.
In *New Grub Street,* Ch. VII, Gissing also touches on this question: 'Even the average man of a certain age is an alarming creature when dinner delays itself; the literary man in such a moment goes beyond all parallel.'

38. p. 381.
More than anywhere before, Gissing had William Morris in mind when describing Westlake's falling off in power and dignity. See Introduction.

39. p. 383, 1.8.
When I reached England again I found that it was impossible to enter again on the old path. Gissing predicted here the effect upon himself of his first stay in Italy in 1888—89. With *The Emancipated* (1890), which he wrote on his return, his work took an altogether new direction. Except in a few short stories he showed no more interest in the working classes as subject-matter.

40. p. 385, 1.22.
'In epochs when cash payment has become the sole nexus of man to man.' *Chartism*, Ch. VI. 'Cash-payment is not the sole nexus of man with man.' *Past and Present*, Book iii, Ch. IX.

41. p. 385, 1.43.
A pillar of dark cloud. . . An allusion to *Exodus*, XIII, 21: 'And the Lord went before them by day in a pillar of cloud, to lead them the way; and by night in a pillar of fire, to give them light; to go by day and night,'

42. p. 403, 1.24.
W. E. Gladstone (1809—1898) formed his third cabinet in February 1886 as Gissing was completing *Demos*.

43. p. 415, 11. 9—12.
These lines on imprisonment clearly have some autobiographical interest.

44. p. 415, 1.38.
Katheder-Sozialismus: lecture-room socialism.

45. p. 423, 1.1.
A gentleman who, like himself, had seen men and manners in various quarters of the globe. Perhaps an allusion to the *Odyssey*, Book I, 3: 'He saw the cities of many men, and knew their mind.'

Bibliographical Note

Demos was first published in London by Smith, Elder & Co. in three volumes late in March 1886, priced at 31s.6d. It was Gissing's third published but his seventh completed full-length novel, since an unnamed story was written before *Workers in the Dawn* (1880), the now lost *Mrs. Grundy's Enemies* came between *Workers* and *The Unclassed* (1884), and both *Isabel Clarendon* (1886) and *A Life's Morning* (1888) were finished in 1885.

Of the original anonymously published three-volume edition, in dark-brown cloth, 750 copies were printed in 1886. A one-volume edition consisting of 1,000 copies, also anonymous, appeared in November of the same year. This was followed in May and October 1888 by reprints of 2,000 and 1,000 copies respectively, nearly all of which were issued as popular yellow-backs. Further reprints of 1,000 copies were called for in 1890 and 1892, and other reprints were issued in 1897, 1908, 1915, 1928 and 1936. The novel has not been reprinted since.

In America *Demos* was brought out in wrappers by Harper in their Franklin Square Library (No. 522) at the very low price of twenty-five cents, and by Dutton in 1928. Tauchnitz published a continental edition in 1886, (two vols.). There have been French, German and Russian translations.

The original handwriten manuscript was sold late in 1912 for eleven guineas by Algernon Gissing, the author's brother and literary executor, to Redway, the Wimbledon bookseller. Algernon's receipt is dated 3rd January 1913. The manuscript, the first page of which is reproduced in Jacob Korg, *George Gissing, a Critical Biography* (Seattle, 1963; London, 1965), is 361 pages in length, numbered 120 + 121 + 120, and bears Harry Glemby's bookplate. It is now held by the Berg Collection of the New York Public Library.

NOTE ON THE MANUSCRIPT

The textual interest of Gissing's manuscripts when compared
with printed versions varies considerably, and the manuscript
of *Demos* certainly ranks among the least interesting. It bears
few corrections and their density tends to decrease as the
narrative progresses. Many handwritten pages show no
difference whatever with the text of the three-volume edition
and that of the many impressions of the one-volume edition
which Gissing was never given any opportunity to revise. (He
corrected the proofs of the first edition but, as he had sold the
copyright for a lump sum of £100 the publishers henceforth
considered the book as their property in the strictest sense of
the word).

The variations between the manuscript and the book
resulted from alterations at three different stages in the early
history of the novel. First, when Gissing was actually writing
and re-reading his story—the changes here being either in the
line or above it. An example of a change made in the run of
the pen occurs on p. 112 of the MS, p. 154, last line, when
after 'the village street', he began a sentence with 'By doing
this they just', which he deleted immediately. Secondly, some
changes took place between the author's delivery of his manuscript and the typesetting. Several hands were obviously at
work, that of the manuscript reader, James Payn, and
probably that of the compositor setting up the passage
concerned. To Payn was certainly due the change from 'that
cloaca maxima of small talk' to 'her small talk' in an early
passage where Alfred Waltham refers to Mrs. Mewling (p. 11,
1. 27, MS p. 8). (See Anne Pilgrim, 'A Censored Metaphor in
Demos', *Gissing Newsletter*, January 1971, pp. 9–11). More
likely the compositors were responsible for the correction of
such slips as 'He look[ed] at her with compassion' (p. 24, 1.
21) or 'town' for 'time' (p. 14, 1. 12). Conversely Gissing
overlooked at least one mistake made by the printers, who
misread 'rose' for 'roared' (p. 37, 1. 42). Thirdly, some modi-
fications occurred at proof stage. For instance, on p. 2, 1. 23,
where we now have 'Fortunately . . . owner', the manuscript
reads: 'Fate intervened; the Manor stands to this day in its
wonted calm, still the home of an Eldon.' Also, this same

paragraph was somewhat longer originally: '... mentioned to them; thereby, in their memories, hangs a tale of an opportunity lost, of strange vicissitudes of fortune, of a popular Hero who promised great things, but, before he could achieve them, passed from the eyes of men in storm-black cloud.

Of this futile endeavour I have it in mind to tell the story ...'

The changes made by Gissing on the manuscript testify to a number of intentions which it would be easier to determine in some cases if he had not rendered the original word or words extremely difficult to decipher. As a rule the longer the correction the less legible the first phrasing. Sometimes a word was substituted for another in order to avoid an unfelicitous repetition ('somewhat aggressive' became 'rather aggressive', p. 9, 1. 10), or to improve the accuracy of the vocabulary (the 'New Wanley League' was changed to the 'New Wanley Union' throughout at proof stage), or to improve the grammar ('speaking like/as one wearied with suffering', p. 22, 1. 16; 'he might be trusted to vary from/in his variance from the wonted modes', p. 6, 1. 4). Occasionally a superfluous adjective ('this dainty little home', p. 10, 1. 24) or adverb ('very strangely', p. 4, 1. 37) was removed or, far more seldom, a fragment of dialogue was replaced by an apparently more appropriate one ('So, it is understood, though he does not seem to have chosen any profession yet'/'Yes. He is quite a youth—only two-and-twenty', p. 8, 1. 21). Some hesitation in the numbering of Ch. III and IV of Vol. III (i.e. the *second* chapter XXVI and Ch. XXVII of the present one-volume critical edition) points to a temporary uncertainty in the chronology of events when Gissing reached this late stage of his narrative. The order of the chapters was at first reversed. Pages 16 and 17 of the final MS version of the third volume (beginning of Ch. III in the book) were originally pp. 22–3 (beginning of Ch. IV) while Ch. IV as we know it was at first numbered III (pp. 16–21 eventually became pp. 26–31). The sequence of events as planned originally was an odd one, perhaps implying a flashback, as it showed Alice visiting her mother in London after her vacating the Manor at New Wanley, the scene taking place before the Socialistic community was liquidated. The manuscript reveals that Gissing decided to rearrange his narrative shortly after setting out to describe the closing down of New Wanley. Two further remodellings must be recorded. The end of Ch. XVIII, showing the two Vine sisters at work, was as follows:

Emma unrolled the bundle of work and set it in order. When the calm in the room was becoming oppressive, she said:

'I'll just get this second shirt done for downstairs. Will you sew a button on the other, Kate? Then I can take them down.'

The garments in question belonged to a lodger who occupied the kitchen; they had been given to the sisters for mending. They were finished in a short time, and Emma wrapped [afterwards: folded] them up together.

'What shall we charge?' she asked.

More important, a close examination of five deleted sections of the manuscript reveals that Gissing had contemplated having four children in the Mutimer household. The additional member of the family was Joseph, whose personality is only vaguely sketched in the dozen lines or so devoted to him.

(i) p. 29, 1. 38. After the words describing Richard's occupation, Gissing pursued: 'His brother Joseph, younger by two years, earned his living as a mechanical draughtsman. The third child was a girl . . .'

(ii) p. 34. The dialogue continued after the last line: '. . . a thirsty night of it.–Jo,' he added, turning waggishly to the ascetic, 'come an' have 'arf a pint on the quiet! Trust me, my boy, *I* won't round on you!'

Joseph's reaction, described in half a dozen words is heavily scored.

(iii) p. 35, 1. 35. The following passage came after 'per'aps'.

'Hullo, Jo!' was Dan's next exclamation, as he leaned back in his chair, knife and fork held erect. 'No supper? Something amiss with your inside?'

'O, leave him alone,' interposed the mother. 'Jo has queer fancies at times. He'll come round when he grows up.'

Joseph, thus facetiously alluded to as a child, had shoved his seat so as to have a full view of the table; his martyrdom was at its height. The smile which he kept up had become terribly sour; anger was shrivelling up the side of his mouth, his eyes glared upon the viands. Poor Joseph! he once more took out the hymn-book from his pocket, and resumed [?] his learning by heart.

(iv) p. 41, Ch. V, 1. 8. After 'another hour', a short illegible sentence reflected Joseph's attitude: 'Joseph confessed that . . .'

(v) p. 46, 1. 18. Joseph spoke for the first time, but his short remark is also illegible.

A sixth undeleted remark on the same manuscript page was overlooked by Gissing when reading over his manuscript: 'With Joseph she still maintained something of maternal authority, though it mostly took the form of banter or primitive irony.' In going through the proofs he found this substitute of about the same length: 'In practice she still maintained something of maternal authority, often gaining her point by merely seeming offended.' What part Joseph the ascetic was to play in the story is impossible to say. He was sharply contrasted with his brothers and sister, and Daniel Dabbs, the future publican, made fun of his abstemiousness, but Gissing had not yet suggested his likely development when he chose to dispense with a character who was not strictly necessary. I like to imagine that Joseph, the inheritor of the better qualities of his ancestors, might have kept apart and resisted the corrupting influence of money, thus offering a contrast with Richard, Alice and 'Arry, and developing into a sort of working-class Wyvern.

Bibliography

1. *Articles and reviews dealing with the first edition* (all published in 1886)

The Daily News, 1 April, p. 3.
Public Opinion, 2 April, p. 422.
Vanity Fair, 3 April, p. 196.
The Times, 3 April, p. 5.
The Bookseller, 6 April, p. 321.
The Whitehall Review, 8 April, p. 18.
The Athenaeum, 10 April, p. 485.
The Spectator, 10 April, pp. 486–87.
The Daily Telegraph, 13 April, p. 2.
The Guardian, 14 April, p. 544.
St. Stephen's Review, 17 April, p. 34.
John Bull, 17 April, pp. 255–56.
The Court Journal, 17 April, p. 443.
The Echo, 21 April, p. 1.
The Morning Post, 22 April, p. 3.
The Weekly Dispatch, 25 April, p. 6.
The World, 28 April, p. 19.
The Scotish Review, April, pp. 328–30.
The Graphic, 1 May, p. 482.
The New York Daily Tribune, 9 May, p. 10.
The Daily Chronicle, 22 May, p. 6.
The Literary World (London), 28 May, pp. 507–08.
The Scotsman, 29 May, p. 12.
The Literary News (New York), June, p. 174.
The Nation (New York), 1 July, p. 14.
The Manchester Guardian, 29 July, p. 8.
The Queen, 31 July, p. 143.
The Westminster Review, July, p. 291.

The Saturday Review, 21 August, p. 261.

The Contemporary Review, August, pp. 295–96 (by Julia Wedgwood).

2. Books on Gissing containing material on Demos

Coustillas, P. (ed.). *Collected Articles on George Gissing.* London, and New York, 1968.

Coustillas, P. *George Gissing. Essays and Fiction.* Baltimore & London, 1970.

Coustillas, P. and Partridge, C. *Gissing: The Critical Heritage.* London & Boston, 1972. Contains reviews of *Demos* and a number of articles discussing the novel.

Davis, Oswald H. *George Gissing. A Study in Literary Leanings.* London, 1966.

Donnelly, Mabel Collins. *George Gissing, Grave Comedian.* Cambridge, Mass. 1954.

Gissing, Algernon and Ellen (ed.). *Letters of George Gissing to Members of His Family.* London, 1927.

Gordan, John D. *George Gissing 1857–1903. An Exhibition from the Berg Collection.* New York, 1954.

Haydock, James J. 'The Woman Question in the Novels of George Gissing', Unpublished Dissertation, North Carolina, 1965; abstract in *Dissertation Abstracts,* January 1966, XXVI, no 7, p. 3923.

Korg, Jacob. *George Gissing, a Critical Biography.* Seattle, 1963; London, 1965.

McKay, Ruth Capers. *George Gissing and his Critic Frank Swinnerton.* Philadelphia, 1933.

Roberts, Morley. *The Private Life of Henry Maitland.* London and New York, 1912. New editions 1923 and 1958.

Roberts, Morley. Introduction to *Demos*. London, 1928.

Rogers, James A., 'The Art and Challenge of George Gissing', Unpublished Dissertation, New York University, 1968; abstract in *Dissertation Abstracts,* June 1969, XXIX, no 12, p. 4501 A.

Seccombe, Thomas. Introduction to Gissing's *The House of Cobwebs.* London and New York, 1906.

Spiers, J. and Coustillas, P. *The Rediscovery of George Gissing.* London, 1971.

Swinnerton, Frank. *George Gissing, a Critical Study.* London, 1912. New editions, 1923 and 1966.

Weber, Anton. *George Gissing und die soziale Frage.* Leipzig, 1932; new impression, New York, 1967.

3. Articles containing material on Demos

Anon., 'George Gissing as a Novelist', *Pall Mall Gazette,* 28 June, 1887, p. 3. Reprinted in *Gissing: The Critical Heritage.*

Anon., 'The Novel of Misery', *Quarterly Review,* October 1902, pp. 391–414. Reprinted in *Gissing: The Critical Heritage.*

Bennett, E. A., 'Mr. George Gissing—an Inquiry', *Academy,* 16 December, 1899, pp. 724–26. Reprinted in Bennett's *Fame and Fiction* (1901) and in *Gissing: The Critical Heritage.*

Goode, John, 'Gissing, Morris and English Socialism', *Victorian Studies,* December 1968, pp. 201–26.

Goode, John, and Lelchuk, Alan. 'Gissing's *Demos*: A Controversy', *Victorian Studies,* June 1969, pp. 431–40.

Jump, John D., 'Victorian Studies', *Notes and Queries,* January 1970, pp. 4–5. Comment on the Goode-Lelchuk controversy over *Demos.*

Kejzlarova, Inge, 'Gissinguv roman *Demos* a anglicky socialismus [Gissing's novel *Demos* and English socialism]', *Casopis pro moderni filologii,* XL, 1958, pp. 136–43.

Kocmanova, Jessie, 'The Revolt of the Workers in the Novels of Gissing, James, Conrad', *Brno Studies in English,* I, 1959, pp. 119–135.

Lelchuk, Alan, '*Demos*: The Ordeal of the Two Gissings', *Victorian Studies,* March 1969, pp. 357–74.

Orwell, George, 'Not Enough Money, A Sketch of George Gissing' *Tribune,* 2 April, 1943, p. 15; reprinted, *Gissing Newsletter,* July 1969, pp. 1–4.

Orwell, George, 'George Gissing', *London Magazine,* June 1960, pp. 36–43. Reprinted in Vol. IV of *Collected Essays, Journalism and Letters of George Orwell,* ed. Sonia Orwell and Ian Angus (1968) and in *Collected Articles on George Gissing.*

Pilgrim, Anne, 'A Censored Metaphor in *Demos*', *Gissing Newsletter,* January 1971, pp. 9–11.

Sichel, Edith, 'Two Philanthropic Novelists: Mr. Walter Besant and Mr. George Gissing', *Murray's Magazine,* April 1888, pp. 506–18. Reprinted in *Gissing: The Critical Heritage.*

Sporn, Paul, 'Gissing's *Demos*: Late-Victorian Values and the Displacement of Conjugal Love', *Studies in the Novel,* Fall, 1969, pp. 334–46.

4. *Other related material*

Allen, Walter. *The English Novel,* London, 1954.

Baker, Ernest A. *The History of the English Novel,* Vol. IX, London, 1936.

Brewster, Dorothy, and Burrell, Angus. *Adventure and Experience,* New York, 1930.

Cazamian, Madeleine L. *Le Roman et les Idées en Angleterre. Vol. I. L'Influence de la Science,* Strasbourg and Paris, 1923.

Coustillas, P. (ed.), *Isabel Clarendon,* by George Gissing, edited with introduction and notes, Brighton, The Harvester Press, 'Society & The Victorians' no. 1, 1969.

Ford, Boris (ed.). *From Dickens to Hardy,* Harmondsworth, 1958.

Frierson, William C. *L'Influence du Naturalisme francais sur les romanciers anglais de 1885 à 1900,* Paris, 1925.

Gissing, George. *Notes on Social Democracy.* With an Introduction by Jacob Korg, London, 1968.

Howard, D., Lucas, J., and Goode, John. *Tradition and Tolerance in Nineteenth Century Fiction,* London, 1966.

Keating, P. J. *The Working Classes in Victorian Fiction,* London, 1971.

Korg, Jacob (ed.), *George Gissing's Commonplace Book,* A manuscript in the collection of the New York Public Library, edited with introduction by Jacob Korg, New York, 1962.

Lucas, John, *Literature and Politics in the Nineteenth Century,* London, 1971.

Pollard, Arthur (ed.), *The Victorians,* London, 1970.

Thompson, E. P. *William Morris, Romantic to Revolutionary,* London, 1955.

Williams, Raymond. *Culture and Society 1780–1950,* London, 1958.

Young, W. T. *Cambridge History of English Literature,* Vol. XIII, Ch. XIV, Cambridge, 1916.

m₁